The Lincoln Lords

The
Lincoln
Lords

a novel by

CAMERON HAWLEY

Little, Brown and Company
Boston   *Toronto*

PS
3558
A824 L5
L5

Published simultaneously in Canada
by Little, Brown & Company (Canada) Limited

PRINTED IN THE UNITED STATES OF AMERICA

Again, as always,
for
Elaine

The Lincoln Lords

I

LINCOLN LORD turned off Fifth Avenue and entered the Greenbank Club at exactly high noon, the hands precisely overlapped on the
clock above the iron-strapped door. He was aware that he was early —
members of stature rarely came in before twelve-thirty — but the forenoon had been a torture that demanded ending.

Inside the lobby, he accepted the instantaneous recognition of William, the ancient guardian of the club's portals, and stopped to ask the
old man about his granddaughter. She had been stricken with a mild
attack of polio some years before and, although she had long since
made a complete recovery, her health remained a staple topic of inquiry, repeatable every day of the week with no apparent diminution
of its ability to incite old William's gratitude.

Across the lobby, he left his coat and hat with Frank, another club
retainer of the same vintage as old William, to whom he addressed a
no less effective question about a son who was an attorney in some
small town in New Jersey.

"He'll be proud to know you were asking about him, Mr. Lord,"
Frank beamed. "I'll tell him the next time I see him."

"You do that," Lincoln Lord said earnestly, his tone and manner as
freshly sincere as if this were not the third time in five days that he
had made the same response to the same statement, varied now only
by adding, "He must be a fine boy."

"They all say he's the best lawyer in the county," Frank responded,
giving special attention to selecting a hanger for Mr. Lincoln Lord's
custom-tailored topcoat.

3

"I'm sure it's true," he agreed, his hand extended in the standard pretense of expecting a brass check.

Frank shook his head. "No need for a check, Mr. Lord. Not likely I'd be forgetting you, sir."

And this, too, was a routine now firmly established. There was nothing unusual about it — Lincoln Lord was accustomed to being recognized and remembered — yet it was rather pleasant and, these days, carried the extra significance that there had been no deterioration in the regard with which he was held by the club employees. They were always the first to demote a member who had lost stature.

Tall and straight, his shoulders squared, his handsome head held high, he walked boldly to the bulletin board. Although his attention was seemingly centered upon the results of last month's progressive bridge tournament, his true interest was revealed by a guarded glance to the left, where there was a posting of the names of members whose bar and restaurant bills were unpaid. The list was the same one that had been there for five weeks, originally thirteen names, seven of which were now obliterated with heavy penciling. Apparently there was nothing too unusual about a busy member temporarily overlooking the payment of a bill. The Greenbank was, above all else, a gentleman's club.

Relief warmed his mind, arousing again the retrospective realization that joining the Greenbank Club had been the wisest move that he had made in the past six years. He could not, however, credit himself with foresight. Actually, his acceptance of membership had been no more than a fortunate happenstance. He had been president of the Frazer Glass Company at the time and, when Fred Foyle had asked the privilege of proposing his name, he had felt it undiplomatic to refuse, Foyle being the president of the New York bank from which Frazer Glass secured most of its short-term loans. Although even the nonresident dues were rather high, they had been a deductible item on his personal tax return and, in the bracket where his income had then placed him, the net cost had been negligible. Now, with no income, the expense was totally his own, a burden only temporarily offset by the possibility of charging his luncheon checks. Eventually there would be a day of reckoning but, if worse came to worst, there was still the possibility of borrowing on his life insurance.

Now, again routinely, he turned right and took the three long strides that brought him to the brass-grilled wicket in front of the telephone switchboard. "Good morning, Katherine," he said, not calling her Katie

4

as some of the members did, speaking in the tone that he had learned to use when addressing wealthy widows in stockholders' meetings.

The tone of her response was, as always, incongruous with her appearance. The enforcedly sedentary means by which she earned her livelihood, coupled with an insatiable appetite for pastry leftovers spirited in from the kitchen, had turned her into a fat woman of sideshow proportions, her body grown so huge that she had abandoned the standard operator's stool and now tended the switchboard while seated in an oversized chair appropriated from the lobby. Her full-moon face led one to expect a gurgling wheeze. Instead, she spoke in the clear treble of a small girl perpetually on the verge of giggling laughter.

"If there are any calls for me, Katherine, I'll be in the reading room for a few minutes."

"And then you'll be in the grill, won't you, Mr. Lord?" she asked, a rush of words that made her sound like a child supplying the last line of a well-remembered fairy story.

"Right," he said, smiling. "And if it wouldn't be too much trouble, Katherine, I wonder if you'd mind ringing my wife?"

" 'Course not, Mr. Lord," she said, gaily disregarding the new club rule that all outgoing calls were to be made through the pay telephone recently installed in the corridor outside the billiard room.

"Eldorado 5-3000," he supplied, giving her the number of the Waldorf-Astoria Hotel, reducing the risk that she might, out of habit, call the number of the Waldorf Towers and thus discover that he and Maggie were no longer living in a Tower suite, but had now moved to one room in the transient section of the hotel.

"She doesn't answer, Mr. Lord," Katherine finally piped. "I guess she must have run away and left you."

"Wouldn't blame her if she did," he said, an easy laugh barely covering a betrayal of the chill that went through him.

Moving with the grace of complete composure, he walked through the shielded entrance to the washroom. The dead stillness reminded him again of his too-early arrival. In a half-hour this would be the gathering place of some of the biggest men in New York. With the bars of dignity and restraint momentarily dropped, formality made ridiculous by circumstances, a camaraderie would be achieved that could never be quite matched in any of the outer rooms. It was here, five years ago, that he had first met K. C. Wright. Less than three weeks later, Wright had offered him the presidency of the Luxor Pharmacal Corporation.

Today, the washroom was deserted except for a single prior arrival, a man whom he knew only as Carpenter, a lower-rung member with no business or professional connections of any kind, his dues and bar bills reputedly paid by a wife with independent means and a desire to rid herself of the burden of an unfortunate marriage. Carpenter stood now at the long line of marble-topped and brass-spigoted lavatories, critically examining his bloodshot eyes in the mirror, an inspection self-consciously abandoned as he suddenly realized that he was no longer alone.

"How are you, Mr. Carpenter?" Lincoln Lord asked in a tone that gave that hackneyed question a quality of genuine concern.

"Well, not too bad," Carpenter responded, blinking his gratified surprise that anyone could be so interested in the state of his health. "And you, Mr. Lord?"

"Good enough," he said, businesslike, taking off his coat, unlinking his shirt cuffs, rolling up his sleeves, vigorously scrubbing his hands and forearms, washing away the invisible grime of the morning that now lay behind him.

Carpenter waited, pathetically hungry for any bit of attention tossed his way, anxiously suggesting a drink together at the bar. With a refusal so adroitly managed that the man could not possibly take offense, Lincoln Lord side-stepped the invitation and took the elevator to the second floor reading room. Only one lamp was lighted. As usual, old Colonel Tebbetts was in his self-assigned lair under the spreading rack of the moosehead over the fireplace. His bald dome came up over the back of the chair, a turtle head emerging from its brown shell. "Linc!" he barked, more the field commander now than he had ever been during his World War I service in the Quartermaster Corps.

"Good morning, sir," Lincoln Lord snapped back, his voice automatically taking on a military ring.

"Saw your picture in the *Times*."

"Oh," he said, troubled as always by the narrow line that separated courteous acknowledgment from immodesty. "Just one of those things, you know. I suppose the publicity people thought they had to build it up as much as possible."

"Good for you!" the colonel said explosively, abruptly turtling back into his shell again, the nature of his approval undisclosed.

Lincoln Lord crossed the room, resolutely resisting the temptation to take the *Times* from the newspaper rack, walking to the table where the magazines were laid out, picking up the January issue of *Fortune*.

Selecting the nearest chair, he sat down without turning on the reading light, settling into the soft leather cushions, relishing this first chance of the morning for a few minutes of cloistered rest. Wearily, he reached out and hooked the footstool with the toe of his left shoe, pulling it into a position where he could rest his tired feet. He closed his eyes purposefully, hoping that his brain, too, might be induced to relax, an end that might have been achievable if only old Tebbetts had not reminded him of the story in the *Times*. That was where his day had started, when that false omen of good fortune had deluded him into thinking that he was at last emerging from the eclipsing shadow that six months ago had so mysteriously fallen upon him.

This morning, a few minutes after eight o'clock, escaping the grating spectacle of Maggie preparing a makeshift breakfast by heating coffee water over a can of Sterno on the window sill, he had gone down to the lobby for a morning paper. Leafing through the financial pages, searching for some scrap of news that might give him a clue to an opening for a high-level corporation executive, he had been abruptly startled to find himself staring at his own picture, even more surprised when he discovered that the *Times* had picked up two long paragraphs from the talk he had made last night to the Manhattan chapter of the Chesapeake College Alumni Association. Brooke Potter, whose fundraising agency had arranged last night's dinner meeting, had told him that advance copies of his speech had been sent to all of the metropolitan papers, but he had never imagined, even for a moment, that it would be reported in the most important newspaper in the country.

Lincoln Lord was not an inordinately vain man, nor was he unaccustomed to publicity — in April, when he had received a White House appointment to the Far East Trade Mission, his picture had been on the front page of dozens of newspapers — but against the background of these last six months, this unexpected reappearance in the public eye had given him an enormous lift of spirit, last night's effort suddenly seen in an entirely new light. Returning to the hotel after the meeting, he had felt himself badly defeated. There had, of course, been a fleeting pleasure in the standing ovation that the crowd had given him and some sensing of accomplishment in the announcement that the pledges signed afterward had totaled more than had ever before been contributed on a single evening to the Chesapeake College Endowment Fund; yet he had completely failed in his real purpose. He had accepted the invitation to speak because G. T. Ransing was on the dinner committee, a fact pertinently linked to his certain knowledge that Ransing was looking for a new president to head one of the subsidiary companies controlled by Ransing Enterprises. The Chesapeake dinner had seemingly offered a chance to get next to Ransing, literally as well as figuratively, and he had gone through some diplomatically difficult juggling of place cards at the speakers' table in order to make sure that Ransing would be seated next to him. The effort had proved a total waste. The seat had gone unoccupied. Ransing had not put in an appearance until the dinner was half over, arriving then with a stranger from whom he refused to be separated, the two of them slipping into empty seats at one of the overflow tables in the back of the room.

Even then something might have been salvaged if Maggie had only been quick enough to intercept Ransing and delay his departure after the end of the meeting. It would have been easy enough for her to do it — she had been seated at the next table — had she not been so anxious to talk to old Anderson Phelps about what was happening to Brick Mitchell's new public relations agency, a preoccupation revealed by the remark that he had overheard her make when, finally shaking off the congratulatory crowd that had gathered around the speakers' table, he had gone back to where she was still sitting with Phelps. Afterwards, in the taxi on the way back to the hotel, she had excused herself by insisting that he had never told her that he wanted to talk to Ransing and, in all fairness, he had been forced to admit that he had not done so, a lapse secretly explained by his reluctance to raise any new hope that, unfulfilled, would give her another reason to think that there was something beyond bad luck in his mysteriously persistent inability to find a new connection. He had not criticized her, yet a strain had come between them and a chill fear had hung over him as he had lain awake in the night, knowing from the sound of Maggie's tossing movements in the other bed that she, too, was finding it difficult to go to sleep.

He had finally succumbed to fatigue, but sleep had accomplished little. He had awakened with a mind still tortured by night fears, persistent and unshakable until the instant he had caught sight of his picture in the *Times*. The news story was almost unbelievably fortunate, a personal advertisement beyond valuation, perfectly written to serve his purpose, not only identifying him as the former president of both the Luxor Pharmacal Corporation and the Frazer Glass Company, but also noting that he had recently completed a term of public service as chairman of the so-called "Lord Committee" investigating trade and economic relations with the Far East. About all the *Times* writer had failed to say was that he was now available for another top-level assignment, but even that was so plainly written between the lines that it could hardly be missed. Read and reread, first standing there in the lobby and then as he had gone up in the elevator, it had seemed an exciting certainty that among all of the hundreds of thousands of *Times* readers there would surely be one powerfully influential man who, learning that Lincoln Lord was available, would jump at the opportunity to employ him to head some major enterprise.

That first flush of new hope had been broadly expanded in the next few minutes. He had opened the door of their room to find Maggie holding a telephone call for him, whispering the explanation as she handed him the instrument that the man on the other end of the line was Dean Whittaker, the acting head of Chesapeake College, who had stayed overnight in New York after making a special trip up from Brighton to attend last night's meeting. In the first minute or two Whittaker's call had seemed no more than a reiteration of appreciation for last night's talk and another round of congratulations on the record-breaking pledge total that had resulted from it. Then suddenly he became aware that Whittaker had called with a far more important purpose. Although the dean's cautious ambiguity made it difficult to know exactly what he had on his mind, it eventually became clear enough to be accepted as a certainty that Whittaker was leading up to some kind of offer. What he had actually said was characteristically inconclusive, yet it had been pointed enough to spark a flaring consciousness that major changes would shortly have to be made in the upper echelon at Chesapeake College. Dr. Radcliff, the old president, had suffered a paralytic stroke in October and Dean Whittaker's temporary status as acting head of the institution presented a situation that the board of regents could hardly allow to go on much longer. Whittaker would undoubtedly be given the presidency, but a new high-level officer would surely be needed to handle the college's financial affairs.

There had been a moment of disappointment when Dean Whittaker had explained that he himself, unfortunately, had to return immediately to Brighton, asking him then if he would be willing to have a preliminary discussion with Brooke Potter, explaining that he had just finished breakfasting with Potter, that Potter was thoroughly familiar with his thinking and would be calling him any minute now for an appointment. Would he be willing to talk to him?

Hesitating only long enough to observe the propriety of careful con-

9

sideration, he had agreed to listen to Potter's proposal, knowing from prior experience that it was quite normal to employ a go-between in negotiations of this sort. Admittedly, Potter was almost perfectly qualified for that role, close enough to the board of regents so that he could speak with an intimate knowledge of college affairs, yet not an officer of the college who might be embarrassed by his inability to side-step commitment.

Hanging up after the call from Dean Whittaker, he had no more than touched the receiver to the cradle when the telephone rang again. It was Potter asking him to come to his office for a nine-thirty meeting. Under more normal circumstances, he would have forced Potter to come to see him but, since he was no longer living in a Tower suite, he had agreed to go to Potter's office, contenting himself with the minor face-saving of changing the time to ten o'clock.

He had left the hotel at nine-thirty, giving himself far more time than was necessary to walk the half-dozen blocks, yet afraid that if he waited any longer Maggie would surely guess that he was expecting far more than he had admitted when he told her that he imagined all that Dean Whittaker had in mind was inducing him to make another speech or two at some other Chesapeake alumni meetings. In order to delay his arrival, he had walked up to Fifty-seventh Street and, still too early, had circled the block twice.

At ten-five, he had walked into Potter's office. Twelve minutes later he was out on Madison Avenue again. In retrospect it was possible to believe that he had, perhaps, too favorably interpreted some of Dean Whittaker's ambiguities, yet he had surely been led to expect something more than an offer to join the roadshow crew that Potter was organizing to send out around the country to stage money-raising rallies for Chesapeake College. Potter could hardly have been more purposely demeaning if he had tried to hire him as a spieler for a carnival side show, an impression made all the more vivid by the recollection that only a year ago young Potter had come to him, hat in hand and groveling, begging him to make a pace-setting corporate contribution to last year's drive — but then, of course, he had been president of the Chemical Service Corporation.

Blindly he had walked down the avenue, striding along without purpose or destination, two empty hours ahead of him before he could go to the Greenbank Club, unable to return to the hotel after having told Maggie that his meeting with Potter would probably take the entire forenoon, a prediction that he had confidently expected would be fulfilled. Furthermore, since they had moved out of the Tower suite, he had become acutely conscious of the dangers of too close confinement. Cooped up in one room, it was impossible to escape the feeling, true or not, that Maggie was always wondering why he was not out looking for a job. And so, in these last few weeks, he had spent almost all of his mornings walking the streets.

Three months ago he might have gone to the government-leased loft building on Thirty-eighth Street where as chairman of the Far East Trade Mission he had been given the use of a small office. Although it had been only a windowless cubicle, sparsely furnished with a battered table-desk and two straight-backed chairs, his tenancy reluctantly granted by the more permanently constituted Federal agency that controlled the building, it had nevertheless provided him with a refuge from the streets. Now, with the final report completed, the last draft unanimously approved by the full task force and sent along to Washington, that one haven was no longer open to him. Unbelievable as it seemed, there was now not a single place in all of this enormous city where, on a cold January morning, he could settle down in reasonable comfort and privacy to outwait the slow crawl of the minute hand around the face of his watch.

Experimentally, he had tried for several days to use the reading room of the New York Public Library, a trial abandoned after he had overheard a seedy-looking old character tell his chair-side neighbor that he had once been the president of the largest sheet-metal stamping company in Manhattan. After that disturbing incident, all libraries seemed to be principally patronized by shaggy-haired old bums who could too easily be imagined as having once been successful corporation executives.

Art exhibits, when first discovered as a possible outlet for the wasting of time, had helped him through several days. They had proved to be, however, largely filled with repetitively duplicated nonsense for which he found it difficult to arouse the required show of interest, and since inspection demanded that he remain on his feet, the galleries offered little advantage over the streets. The art auction rooms did not have that disadvantage — an usher always found a seat for him, even if an extra chair had to be brought in — but his trial experiences had revealed that, with the current interest in the purchase of paintings as tax-dodge investments, there was the constant danger of an encounter with some old acquaintance who would insist upon asking him what he was now doing.

He had always thought of New York as a city filled with endless places to spend time — he and Maggie had often talked, in years gone by, of taking a full week just to do some of the things that there had never been time enough to do before — but now that getting through the endless hours of empty days had become an objective in itself, he had discovered that the metropolis offered much less by way of free diversion than he had imagined. All too often what seemed an opportunity to ease the passage of time turned out to be hedged with an admission charge and a demanded hat-check tip, unpleasant reminders that, for the first time since he had gotten out of college twenty-five years ago, what happened to the odd coins in his pocket was a matter of serious concern. By the process of elimination, Lincoln Lord had discovered that there was little left for him to do but walk.

Habitually he walked Fifth, Park, Madison and Lexington. This morning a cold north wind was sweeping the length of the avenues, now and then driving a stinging spit of sleetlike snow; and by the time he had exhausted the mind-blanking anger that Brooke Potter had aroused, he was chilled through. Forced to seek warmth, he had slipped into an automobile showroom, a diversion that he had recently denied himself. Earlier experimentation had proved that it was futile. Other men were allowed to walk in and spend an unmolested ten minutes, but for some reason, the moment he stepped inside he was invariably pounced upon by a salesman who refused to believe that he was not a hot prospect. He had found some comfort in knowing that he was still unbranded by visible evidences of his unemployment, yet that minor assurance had never outweighed the discomfiture of pretense that he had any legitimate reason to consider the purchase of anything, let alone a high-priced automobile. This morning, quite without realization until he was inside, he had found himself in a showroom that he had visited before, the scene of an embarrassingly intense solicitation when he had been subjected to the high-pressure tactics of a British-accented salesman who had tried to sell him an Italian-made Pantheon. The moment he had gotten inside the door today, the same salesman had stridden toward him. Then, three steps away, recognizing him, he had turned without a word and walked back to the rear of the showroom.

Out on the street again, unmindful now of the wind and cold, Lincoln Lord had resumed his blind walking, unaware of making a right turn at Fifth Avenue, consciousness of location regained only when he found himself at the entrance of the building where Sellcox & Lloyd had its offices. Conceivably, this was less accidental than it seemed, perhaps explained by a subconscious urge to talk to Otis Sellcox, repressed for the last month by the fear that appearing at his office might be judged an inexcusable intrusion. The last time he had gone up to see Sellcox, his simple question as to whether or not there had been any new developments had produced nothing but a sharply negative response and an acid warning that he was expecting entirely too much if he thought that Sellcox & Lloyd could place him in another corporation presidency overnight.

The point was, of course, that it had not been overnight. More than eight months had passed since he had gone to Sellcox, who, reputedly, had found jobs for more fifty-thousand-dollar men than any executive placement specialist in New York. Judging by results in his own case, he was beginning to think Sellcox an overrated fraud, fulfilling expectations only in his disagreeable personality. The man who had told Lincoln Lord the most about Sellcox had said, "You'll hate the cocky little bastard, but if you can get him to take you on, one way or another he'll get you on someone's payroll." After all these months, Sellcox had not even gotten him an interview. It was true, of course, that he had been away for two months on the Japan trip, but Sellcox had approved his going, agreeing that accepting appointment to the Far East Trade Mission might add to his prestige, characteristically saying, "You never can tell what will sucker somebody into giving a man a job."

Back from Japan, it had taken him almost a month to catch Otis Sellcox in his office, the suspicion growing that he was avoiding him. He had finally gotten in to see him, only to have Sellcox lash out, "You might as well face it, Linc — you're a hard guy to place. When a company's going outside its own organization to find a new president, what they're looking for is new blood." And when he had tried to argue the case for experience and maturity, Sellcox had snapped back, "All right, how old were you when you got the presidency of Union Packing — thirty-eight! And you were only forty-one when you went into Frazer Glass. You're no boy wonder any more, Linc. You're only a year or so away from being fifty. I'm doing the best I can for you, Linc, but there's one thing I can't do — change your birth date."

This morning, going up in the elevator to Sellcox's fortieth floor suite of luxurious offices, the *New York Times* story had seemed, if not something worth talking about, at least a chance to prove that he was keeping his name before prospective employers — and that, judging by results, was far more than Otis Sellcox was doing for him.

In what had first seemed a stroke of good fortune, he had caught

Sellcox in the reception foyer, his coat still on, apparently just arriving for the day, the *New York Times* in his hand. "Yes, I saw it," he said, twisting his thin lips. "Too bad you got yourself fouled up with that liberal arts pitch. What businessmen want is more engineers and scientists." And with that he had disappeared, his office door slammed with the sound of a thrown lock.

Outside on the street again, he had flipped the *Times* into a wastepaper hamper, the final deflation of this morning's delusion, an act that he hoped would help him to face the future realistically. Anger tempted him to drop Sellcox & Lloyd and place himself with some other agency, yet hope had been so completely drained that he could not bring himself to believe that it would do any good.

He had walked on then, heading downtown, trying to fill the time that still remained before he could go to the Greenbank Club. He had gone all the way down to Fourteenth Street before he turned back, dead-tired then by the fast pace that he felt it necessary to maintain, consciously because of the cold, subconsciously because of his fear that if he slowed down to a wandering gait someone who knew him would see him as a purposeless man with no place to go. And that was not a pointless concern. He was always being recognized by someone who remembered him as president of Luxor Pharmacal — or Frazer Glass — or Union Packing — or even as executive vice-president of Rabson Foods. Only a few days ago he had run into someone who remembered him from the days when he had been Chicago sales manager for Quincy Canning.

Now, having finally gained the warmth and shelter of the club, he found himself disconcertingly unable to stop the flow of wildly errant thought that streamed through his mind. Instead of finding relief, everything that had happened since he had stepped inside the door reminded him of fears that could not be put down, senseless yet insistent. Had there been a knowing needle in old Tebbett's voice when he reminded him of the *New York Times* . . . had Katherine suspected something . . . that crack about Maggie running away and leaving him . . . ?

No, now he *was* being a fool! He could count on Maggie . . . she'd always stuck by him, she always would . . . nothing strange about her not being at the hotel . . . no, not at all . . . someone had probably invited her out to lunch . . . but who?

He turned on the reading lamp. But the blaze of light did not reach back far enough into the shadowy recesses of his mind to erase the dark fears that gnawed at his consciousness . . . had Maggie left the hotel be-

14

cause she couldn't face another confession of failure? No, that couldn't be true ... she hadn't known what he'd been expecting ... at least he'd been wise enough not to tell her. But even if he had ... no, she'd never run out on him. She knew that something would turn up one of these days ... it always had, it would again. All a man had to do was keep his chin up ... keep fighting ... never let down ... play for the break. There might have been one last night if Maggie had only stopped Ransing ...

Uncontrollably, letting it slip past his weakened guard, Lincoln Lord heard his wife's voice repeat the joyful exclamation that he had overheard as he walked up to the table where she had been sitting with Anderson Phelps ... *Oh, I'm so happy that Brick is doing so well!* ... yes, that's what she had said ... he couldn't possibly have been mistaken. And then, afterwards, going home in the taxi, so pointedly refusing to talk about Brick ... always changing the subject ... trying to soft-soap him by telling him how wonderful his speech had been. Why couldn't she be more honest with him ... come right out and say it? Why not? He was willing to admit it ... he *had* admitted it ... Chemical Service had been a bad move and Brick had been smart when he had refused to come along with him ... yes, smarter than he'd been. All right, Brick had gone off and started his own public relations firm ... and he was making a success of it. Was that something that couldn't be talked about? Why not? Didn't he know that Brick Mitchell was a good man? Would he have kept him on all those years if he hadn't been ... taking him from one company to another ... promotions ... raises ... assistant to the president? Why shouldn't Brick make a success of a little public relations outfit ... all of the experience that he'd given him?

Maybe that's what he ought to do, too ... start his own company ... *Lincoln Lord Associates — Management Consultants.* Why not? He had the background, didn't he? Where was there another man who had as wide a range of management experience in as many different types of business? Every one of the big fields ... food ... drugs ... cosmetics ... chemicals ... *Specializing in the Marketing of Packaged Products* ...

The forward rush of free thought carried him beyond the solid ground of reason. Abruptly recognizing what had happened, he beat a hasty retreat. It would take money ... a lot of it ... rent, salaries ... everything going out and nothing coming in ... probably be a year before he could get it on a paying basis. Everything would be different, of course, if he only had enough capital to . . .

15

His guard was down and the stylus of his mind slipped into a groove deeply cut by repetition, compelling him to yield again to the fascination of what had lately become an obsessive riddle. Uncounted times, walking the streets, he had added up all of the money he had made during the last twelve years. Despite the difficulty of doing mental arithmetic while walking, he always came to the same total — four hundred thousand dollars!

But that was not the answer to the riddle. It was easy enough to add up his earnings. What he couldn't figure out was what in the world had happened to all of that money! Of course, there'd been income tax ... yes, that had taken a lot of it ... but still there had been thousands and thousands of dollars that simply couldn't be accounted for ... yes, the trip to Japan ... Maggie's mink ... Cadillacs ... Nassau ... but what else could he have done? When you were the president of a corporation, you had a position to maintain. That was why they paid you a big salary ... contributions ... entertaining ... living at the Waldorf Towers ... sending your son to Forgehill ... yes, one of these days he'd have to do something about Kip's tuition for the second quarter ...

Had he been wrong in turning down Brooke Potter? He had said something about an honorarium ... even a few hundred dollars right now would ... *no!* A man didn't dare let himself slip. He had to keep up his standards ... hang on. If you lost faith in yourself, other people would lose faith too. You had to keep your chin up ... let the world know that you weren't licked ... keep fighting ...

He closed his eyes against the glare of the reading lamp. A moment later, *Fortune* slipped from his relaxing fingers. Lincoln Lord was asleep.

2

Maggie Lord stood on the steps of Old Main, looking out across the campus of Forgehill Academy, warned by the campanile chimes that it was too early to cross to the cottage where Kip lived. She had told her son when she had called him yesterday that she would surely not arrive at Hawthorne Cottage earlier than twelve-thirty, a prediction turned into a promise by the memory of how Kip, even as a young child, had always shown a flare of angry resistance when, unthinkingly, she would enter his bedroom without a warning knock.

The ten minutes that now had to be wasted were the result of miscalculation. She had expected that it would take at least an hour to convince Dr. Summerfield that Kip be allowed to remain at Forgehill even though his tuition remained temporarily unpaid, an anticipation based upon her recollection of the long and difficult fifty minutes that it had taken last spring to convince the headmaster that her son be permitted to enter Forgehill for the last quarter, a touch-and-go battle finally won, not by any argument that she had advanced but rather by the headmaster's being suddenly and unaccountably impressed by the irrelevant fact that Kip's father was Lincoln Lord, the president of the Chemical Service Corporation.

She had been prepared for trouble this morning, so fearful of failure that she had not told her husband what she was attempting. On the train coming up from New York, she had rehearsed every argument that she could invent, every possible rebuttal of the objections that Dr. Summerfield could logically be expected to raise. Her worry and concern had proved pointless. All that was needed had been supplied by fortunate coincidence. Dr. Summerfield had already seen this morning's *New York Times,* the newspaper on his desk as she had entered his office, the headmaster saying soon afterward, "Oh, it does mean so much to us, you know, to be entrusted with the education of the sons of famous men like Mr. Lord." Afterwards, more cunningly, he had asked, "Do you suppose that your handsome husband might possibly be induced to honor us by addressing *our* old grads — the kickoff of our endowment fund campaign, you know?" Her only promise had been that she would relay the invitation. That was all that had been needed to make the headmaster gush, "Oh, how really kind of you, my dear Mrs. Lord — and do tell your husband that the tuition may be paid whenever it's most convenient."

She had accomplished what she had set out to do, yet it had brought her no feeling of victory. Starting down the steps, surveying the campus, she wondered again if it might not have been better for her son's sake if she had failed. She could not believe that Forgehill Academy, under Dr. Summerfield's direction, could possibly be as good a school as it was supposed to be. Tangibly there was no justification for its reputation. The buildings were old and in a bad state of repair, the facilities inadequate for its enrollment, the educational standards plainly set low enough to save distinguished parents the embarrassment of having a son fail scholastically. Forgehill's only distinction was that it somehow got away with charging the highest tuition rate of any boys' school in the country, a fact baldly stated in the elaborate brochure with which Forgehill solicited the parents of prospective students, explained with the statement that "our program is geared to meet the special requirements of the sons of men of big affairs." There were, apparently, enough fathers who were willing to pay a ridiculously high price to be admitted to that select coterie, accepting entrance as a favor supposedly awarded as a social distinction but which, confusingly, was granted only at an exorbitant cost.

In the beginning Lincoln Lord had brushed aside the high cost of putting his son in Forgehill, charging it off as one of those things that the president of a big corporation had to do, one of the reasons he was paid fifty thousand dollars a year. By September, when the new school year had started, he had long since been out of a job; but she had been no more able to argue that Kip should not be sent back to Forgehill than to maintain that it was silly for them to go on living in a Tower suite. By then, in a peculiar perversion of cause and purpose, continuing to live at the Waldorf-Astoria and sending his son to Forgehill had been evidence of stature which she had dared not force her husband to abandon. To have done so would have destroyed the last vestiges of his self-esteem, the source of the strange courage that kept him believing that by some miracle he would get back on top again. Small as that hope had been then, it was even smaller now. Yet somehow it had to be kept alive. There was no other.

Furthermore, there was no alternative to keeping Kip at Forgehill. She remembered only too well what she had gone through when he had been abruptly dismissed from Island Point. It had happened during those last awful days at Chemical Service when Lincoln Lord had been so frantically engaged in the wild maneuvering that had finally made it possible for him to announce that he was resigning in order to accept appointment to the Far East Trade Mission. Trying to shield him from even more trouble, she had stepped in and assumed the burden of finding some school that would take Kip. Forgehill had been her husband's first choice — he had made that plain enough by continually quoting someone at the Greenbank Club whose son, paralleling Kip's experience, had been in all sorts of school difficulties until, happily, they had gotten him into Forgehill — but she had put it last rather than first on a list of five possibilities. The other four, however, had quickly scratched themselves off, three with the excuse that they were filled, the fourth with the blunt explanation that they were not interested in enrolling a boy who had been dismissed from two other

18

schools. Forgehill had thus become a last chance and, desperate, she had finally embraced it.

Her husband's gratitude on that day when she had returned to the hotel with the news that everything was all set for Kip at Forgehill had been so great that it had overwhelmed her attempt to tell him what had really happened. He had said then, "Maggie, it's so wonderful to be married to someone who can handle things the way you do." Afterward he had often said as an offset to despair, "Well, at least — thanks to you — we've done our best for Kip," a repeated compliment that had dimmed, until today, her original unfavorable impression of Forgehill Academy. Now, crossing the campus, she was more certain than ever that this was the wrong place for Kip. But again there was no alternative. It was highly questionable if any better school would take him in the middle of the year — surely not without an advance payment of tuition.

Pacing herself with the campanile clock, she started down Cottage Row looking for a HAWTHORNE porch sign on one of the old houses that, in the Forgehill brochure, were described as "homelike small cottages, each with its own housemaster, a wellborn and cultured man whose warmly personal supervision means so much in the molding of character." On her hurried inspection last spring, she had been shown what Dr. Summerfield had described as a typical cottage and met a young housemaster introduced in similar terms. Today, finally locating Hawthorne Cottage, she saw that it was a far cry from the supposedly representative sample. It was the last house on Cottage Row, barracks-like, three stories high, painted an allover mustard unrelieved even by a color accent. The depressing drabness carried over into the room in which she found herself after she had stepped through the front door, admitted by an elderly woman in a filthy house dress, a gray rag tied around her hair, who introduced herself as Mrs. Grandon.

"Yeah, I know," the old woman cut off her explanation that she was there to see her son, shouting in the general direction of the staircase, "Kip! Your mom's here." Turning back, her hands clenched on the handle of the dustmop, she said, "He'll be down in a minute or two. Unless he's up there sulking again. You got a problem with that boy, Mrs. Lord. But I guess you know that, huh? If you didn't you wouldn't have sent him up here."

Maggie Lord's throat went dry with anger. Fortunately the need for response was canceled by the sound of footsteps on the stairs. She watched her son come down, first the seemingly endless expanse of gangling legs and arms, then finally his face, big-eyed, that odd blankness of expression that he always had in these moments of first meeting, invariably giving her the feeling that he was guarding himself against any show of emotion.

"Hello, Kip," she greeted him, self-consciously aware of Mrs. Grandon's surveillance.

"Hi," Kip replied, tight-lipped.

"I hope I didn't —" she began.

Mrs. Grandon broke in without excusing the interruption. "I guess you won't be staying here, will you?"

"No," she said, sharply positive, and then as an unmistakable dismissal, "Thank you, Mrs. Grandon."

The woman stood her ground, her eyes on Kip. "You better be telling her what I was talking to you about."

Kip gave her a loose-shouldered shrug.

Mrs. Grandon sniffed and left the room.

"What was that all about, Kip?"

"Nothing. It's a shakedown, that's all. She wants me to tip her."

"Tip her?"

"She says we're supposed to. The other guys give her a dollar a week to take care of their rooms. I don't."

"But, Kip, the school is supposed —"

"I take care of my own room. I don't want her messing around my things."

"Have you talked to your housemaster about it?"

"We haven't got one now."

"But what —"

"Old Lucing? He was a queer. They caught him with —"

"Can we go somewhere for lunch?" she cut in, a quick bid for escape. "You haven't eaten, have you?"

"I can get something afterwards."

"But I want to talk to you, Kip."

"I guess we could go down to the Inn," he said uncertainly. "Only it's kind of expensive."

"We'll go somewhere," she said, a decision made against her better judgment, knowing that it was the wrong approach to an attempt to convince Kip that he had to save every cent that he possibly could.

He got his coat and they walked down Cottage Row, Kip so obviously uncomfortable when they met other boys that she tried her best to distract him by talking rapidly. His responses, mumbled and noncomittal, only increased her consciousness that this boy walking beside her was a half head taller now than she was, no longer a child but a man — a man annoyed by a woman who talked too much.

They walked on in a silence too easily accepted, sustained by experience. Kip had always been a strangely self-contained child. Even as a very young boy he had seemed happiest when alone, disturbingly self-sufficient, always withdrawing from companionship, often giving the impression of a heart that lacked the capacity for love. Yet, at other times, unexpectedly, he would respond to affection as if his need for it was a secret hunger that she, embarrassingly, had somehow failed to satisfy, largely because she had never been able to know when it was wanted.

They came to the edge of the campus and she asked, "How far is it?"

"The Inn?"

"If there's any place that's less expensive —" she began in an attempted recovery of position.

"I don't know," he said. "I haven't been eating around much. I guess I figured I hadn't ought to spend the money."

"Thanks, Kip," she said.

"For what?"

She hesitated and then said, not mother to son, but woman to man, adult to adult, "For making it unnecessary to deliver my little speech about not spending any more money than you have to."

He stood looking at her as if weighing a solemn decision. "I guess we could go to Sammy's."

"Where's that?"

"You might not like it."

"Would you?"

"There'd probably be a lot of the guys around."

"Would that matter?"

"Sometimes they got the jukebox going pretty loud."

"Let's go," she said, sensing that it was the right thing to do, sure of it when she saw the shadow of doubt leave his face. Crossing the street, his hand took her arm, not protectively but possessively, a feeling that persisted even after his hand had dropped.

They walked down a narrow street, hardly more than an alleyway between the old houses that crowded the campus, and then turned right into the town's business section. Sammy's was in a semibasement, four steps down from the sidewalk and, as Kip had predicted, the air was heavy with the odor of onions and hot cooking fat, vibrant with the

21

speaker-rattling blare of a jukebox playing at full volume. He took her arm again, guiding her through the crowded tables, and now she saw that he was responding more easily to the greetings of the boys who spoke to him, showing none of the self-conscious embarrassment that had been so evident when they had been walking down Cottage Row.

There was a vacant booth in the back of the room and they slipped in, Kip clearing the dirty dishes by pushing them to the front of the table.

"I told you it wasn't much of a place," he apologized.

"It's fine," she said. "But all of these boys — they're from school, aren't they?"

"Sure."

"Then why are they eating here?"

"The food's pretty crummy over there — especially at lunch — soup and tapioca, stuff like that." He was looking at her with a purposeful intentness. "The whole place is pretty crummy."

She stared back at him, tempted to acceptance. But frightened of the consequences, she quickly chose evasion. "Kip, this won't make you miss a class, will it?"

"It doesn't matter," he said. "It's just French. I'm flunking that anyway."

Full self-control was needed to hold back the expression of alarmed disapproval that Kip was plainly expecting, his offhand manner of announcement notwithstanding.

"How are your other grades?" she asked calmly.

"All right, I guess," he said, rewarding her with the same expression of relieved apprehension that she had seen when she had agreed to come here to Sammy's. "It doesn't make any difference now, anyway."

"Of course it makes a difference."

"Not now."

"Why do you say that?"

"Isn't that what you're going to tell me?" He paused, nervously meeting her look of inquiry, then blurting out, "Look, it's all right with me. You don't have to worry about what I'll think. Like I said — well, that's it, isn't it?"

"What's it?" she asked, adding a smile that she wished could have been withdrawn when she saw that it had no effect on his intently earnest expression.

"You're taking me out of here, aren't you?"

"No."

22

His lips twisted and then went slack. "I thought — I guess I thought that's what you wanted to tell me."

"No."

"Dad's got another job — is that it?" he asked, strangely as if it were the acceptance of catastrophe. "That's what I've been afraid was going to happen — he'd get another job and then I'd have to stay."

Her natural reaction was the humorless laughter of denial, but she quelled it and said simply, "No, he doesn't have another job yet, Kip."

"Then why are you leaving me here?" he appealed. "It's crazy expensive and the place is a dump, honest it is. And I'm not saying that just because I'm flunking French. It's true. All the guys say so. You know Mike — the guy I wrote you about? His folks took him out. Mike's mother came up and, man did she tell off old Summerfield."

The waitress saved her from the need to reply, clearing the dirty dishes and asking for their orders.

"What shall I have, Kip?"

"I guess maybe you could get a salad or something," he said uncertainly.

"What are you having?"

"Hamburger and a chocolate malt."

"Fine. I'll have the same."

There was a welcome repetition of Kip's hinted approval but it did not stop him from stubbornly returning to the subject that she was hoping the interruption had closed. "Look, it doesn't make sense — keeping me here when it costs so much money."

"We'll manage, Kip."

"But why?" he demanded. "For what it costs here — holy creeps, it's just crazy. I mean — well, a lot of things — like you moving out of your suite at the hotel and just having one room. If it wasn't costing so much to keep me here, you could —"

"We're comfortable enough," she said, catching herself before she fell into the trap of implying that the suite had been willingly given up in order that their son's education might be financed.

The table seemed to widen now, Kip farther away from her, the closeness that there had been between them suddenly lost. She tried to think of something to say that would close the gap. Everything that suggested itself sounded like a self-righteous mother talking to a small child or, even worse, was a too obvious pretense of according him an adulthood that he would be sure to label as insincere. Driven by the need to break her son's sullen silence, she finally said, "I think it would

23

be a mistake, Kip, for you to leave here without finishing out the year."

"Why?" he demanded, not looking up at her.

"Well, for one thing, it would be hard to get in anywhere else in the middle of the year," she said, a sparse sampling of all that was in her mind.

"Isn't it because of Dad?" he demanded, oddly tense, almost as if there was anger behind the question. "Hasn't he got an idea that there's something hot-shot about having his son at Forgehill?"

"Kip!" she snapped, an uncontainable reaction.

"Okay," he mumbled, again with the loose-jointed shrug with which he rejected Mrs. Grandon.

Desperately Maggie Lord tried to fight off the feeling that it was now or never, that unless she broke down and talked to her son as she had never talked to him before, this would be her last chance ... but how could she talk to him with the honesty and integrity that their relationship now demanded without making admissions that would raise even higher the barrier that there had always been between her husband and her son?

Nothing in all her married life had troubled Maggie Lord more than the unexplainable fact that her husband, despite his ability to make almost everyone else like him, had failed so completely with his son. She could never be certain whether or not Linc fully appreciated how great his failure as a father had been. She strongly suspected at times that he had closed his mind to it, as he so often closed his mind to other unpleasant truths, and Kip had made that easy to do, never openly exhibiting antagonism, always retiring into a silence that was too easy to misinterpret as filial respect. When she and Kip were alone, however, he had occasionally broken that silence, never before with so open a deprecation of his father as he had just made, never before forcing her to fight back against his criticism, yet often edging close to it, seemingly nudging her toward an admission of his father's shortcomings. Before, there had always been the chance to ignore it. Now she sensed that the easy way out was no longer open to her. She was torn between two loyalties, neither one of which could be violated — between two loves that made demands that were in terrifying conflict.

Silence was no solution. "I don't think you really understand your father, Kip," she said, cautiously precise. "I don't think you ever have."

His forefinger was doodling a design in the greasy film on the plastic table top. "Maybe not," he mumbled.

"And perhaps he doesn't understand you as well as he might," she went on, hoping that Kip would accept it as an offset to criticism of himself. "Maybe I don't understand you either."

"You're all right," he said, unmistakably a gruff man-voiced expression of affection.

She was frightened by the tear-mist that came to her eyes. "And your father is all right, too, Kip. More than all right." She paused, repeating then what she had said as they had walked down Cottage Row, fairly certain now that Kip had not been listening to her then. "I wish you could have heard him last night at the Chesapeake dinner. He made a wonderful talk. Dean Whittaker told me afterward that it was the most successful meeting they'd ever had."

Kip's eyes raised to challenge her. "Who wrote his speech for him — you?"

For an instant she was stunned, never having imagined that her son's perception could be so deeply probing. Recovery was as quick as she could manage, her voice crisp. "No, I didn't write his speech."

"What was it then — one of the old ones that Uncle Brick wrote?"

He had doubly tricked her, not only exposing a half truth — the speech had been an adaptation of one that Brick Mitchell had written — but also, by calling him "Uncle Brick," a name that he used as a young boy, Kip made himself seem a child again. To add to her confusion, his perception had unknowingly probed the uncomfortable truth that she herself had been thinking far too much about Brick Mitchell in the last twelve hours. Mr. Phelps had brought up Brick's name at the dinner, telling her how well he was doing with his new public relations firm, and then Linc had insisted on talking about him all the way back to the hotel. Unavoidably, on the train this morning, thoughts of Brick Mitchell had kept edging their way into her resistant mind.

"It was, wasn't it?" Kip asked.

"There's nothing wrong with using a speech that someone else wrote," she said. "Almost all speakers do it."

"Sure."

The waitress brought their hamburgers and then, with a side trip to the soda fountain, their malted milks. The interruption offered a chance to change the subject. Maggie Lord sipped from the upthrust straws and said, "You can't imagine how long it's been since I've had one of these."

Kip's fleeting smile was poor pay for the rush of memories that the taste in her mouth brought back...that first year in Brighton... drinking a malted milk at the Sugar Bowl with Linc and Brick...

Kip's voice crashed in on her. "You seen him lately?"

"Who?" she asked, knowing only too well.

"Uncle Brick."

"Not since we got back from Japan," she said, true enough as far as it went, yet not revealing that it had been even longer than that. "But I heard quite a lot about him last night," she said, feeling a peculiar boldness. "I happened to be sitting next to a Mr. Phelps at the dinner. He's been using Brick's new public relations firm. Apparently, he's doing very well with it."

"He's a good guy," Kip said, making it something more than simple approval. "What I mean is —"

She watched his face, features twisting as if he were physically attempting to wring from his mind some unreleasable expression. Sympathetically, she said, "I think I know what you mean."

Kip shook his head vigorously. "No, you don't. What I mean is —" This time he gulped himself past the block. "Uncle Brick never does anything just to make somebody like him."

She inspected her sandwich, weathering the first shock, wondering if what Kip had voiced as praise of Brick was intentionally an inverted criticism of his father. There was the possibility that it might have been unwitting and, slim though that chance was, it offered a loophole. "That isn't really true, Kip. Brick's done lots of things in his life that have made people like him. You for one. Don't you remember the time he brought you a fishing rod and took you — ?"

"That's different," Kip objected. "He didn't do it because he thought he was going to get something for himself out of it. He did it because — well, he didn't do it because Dad was his boss, did he?"

"No, of course not."

"That's what I mean." He doused his hamburger with catsup. "Anyway, he's a swell guy." The bottle top was methodically replaced. "You know what I been thinking?"

"No."

"I thought — but I guess it's out now if I have to stay here." He punctuated with a bite from the sandwich, swallowed before he went on. "Maybe next summer. Anyway, I thought maybe I'd get a job working for him."

"Doing what, Kip?"

"You know, just help him — office boy or something like that."

"I doubt if he'd need an office boy," she said, fearing Kip's ultimate disappointment as much as the danger of discouraging him now. "It isn't a very large organization. From what Mr. Phelps told me, it's only Brick and a girl."

"You wouldn't want me to do it, huh?" he asked, chomping down on his sandwich.

"Why would you think that? You can ask him if you want to."

"What about Dad? Would he let me?"

"Why not?"

"They had a fight, didn't they?"

"Of course not. Whatever in the world made you think that?"

He shrugged. "I don't know. I just thought it, I guess. You don't ever see him any more."

"But we've invited him," she said, reaching back in her memory almost two years to make it true. "We just haven't been able to get together, that's all. We were away — Japan — and then Brick's been busy, too."

Kip cocked his head. "You mean Uncle Brick and Dad didn't — you know, have a fight or something?"

"No indeed."

"Then why didn't Uncle Brick go with him to Chemical Service?"

"Your father offered him a chance but —"

"He did?"

"Of course. But by then, Brick had started his own firm."

"Oh."

"I am right, Kip," she said gently. "You do misunderstand your father. Here you were imagining that there was some trouble between him and Brick — and there isn't."

There was no reply, his head bent as he sipped the malted milk.

"And Kip, right now he needs understanding — from both of us. This is a very difficult time for him. It's not easy, you know — he's always been so busy and so active, so many important things to do, and now there's this awful business of waiting until something develops."

He looked up, raising his eyes without a head movement. "You think he's ever going to get another job?"

"Kip! What a thing to say. Of course he will."

"He's getting pretty old."

She laughed. "Now you are being silly. Your father is only forty-eight. I know that seems ancient to you, but — well, it just isn't, that's all. Men don't retire until they're sixty-five. That's still" — she made the quick calculation, surprising herself, "— seventeen years. That's as many years as you are old."

Kip's acknowledgment was lost as she was struck with the never before recognized fact that the years until Linc reached retirement age were exactly matched by the years that stretched back to that week after Kip had been born ... Linc bending over her hospital bed, so handsome in his lieutenant-commander's uniform, telling her the news that he had been selected for Admiral Rabson's staff ... "This little guy is going to be proud of his old man, Maggie." And she had said ...

"I guess maybe it is kind of tough on him," Kip was saying, an admission reluctantly forced. "What do you want me to do?"

"Do?" It took her a moment to get her bearings again. "Well, the thing for both of us to do, Kip, is to make it as easy for him as we can. He has enough worries right now. I know that everything here at school isn't what it's supposed to be, but — will you try to make the best of it, Kip?"

"Sure."

And this time there was no shrug. He reached out for the check.

She protested but he took it. "I got money," he said. "I been saving some."

Following her son as he strode toward the cashier at the front of the restaurant, she hoped that he wouldn't turn back, afraid that if he did he might see the tears in her eyes, knowing that they would make her seem too much like a sentimental mother.

3

Outside the exit of the Wall Street subway station, Brick Mitchell decided that walking would be faster than taking a taxicab. The streets were jammed with noontime traffic, and the offices of Weeks, Phelps & Harrison were only a few blocks away. He walked rapidly, shouldering a passage through the sidewalk crowds, checking his watch against a jeweler's clock, reassuring himself that he would not be late. There was too much at stake today to take a chance on arousing Anderson Phelps's displeasure with a tardy arrival.

To his annoyance he passed the entrance of the Ashaway Building without recognizing it, discovering only after he had retraced his steps that the exterior had been remodeled during the three months that had elapsed since the last time he had been called down to see Anderson Phelps. There had, however, been no change on the twelfth floor. The atmosphere of Victorian mustiness was as carefully preserved as ever, obviously with purpose and point. The financial community had a high regard for solvent antiquity, and Weeks, Phelps & Harrison had every right to display that desirable status. Three family fortunes had been built in these quarters, and Anderson Phelps, now the third-generation head of the firm, was not a man to tamper with the attributes of success. He was, in fact, rigidly devoted to the preservation of his inheritance.

There was not the slightest concession to modernity in the entrance foyer of the suite of offices. The walls were paneled in time-blackened mahogany, the furniture clearly a hold-over from the long-ago past, the receptionist a gray-haired woman in a choker-collared black dress, whose name had always struck Brick Mitchell as a little too perfectly matched to the setting, almost as if she had been christened by the founders of the firm, those three stern-visaged and bewhiskered gentlemen whose portraits glowered their perpetual guardianship of propriety.

"Hi, Miss Peabody," he said, tossing out the greeting as he hurriedly stripped off his well-worn trench coat.

Her acknowledgment was a stiffly formal, "Mr. Mitchell," plainly a criticism of his too brash manner.

"How've you been?" he asked, dumping his coat on the settee — an act less casually performed than he made it seem, the coat purposefully wadded to conceal a torn sleeve lining.

Miss Peabody was standing now, stiff-backed and tight-lipped. "I'll tell Mr. Phelps that you're here," she said finally, the dignity of her exit maintained by the precision with which she opened and closed the door behind her.

Alone, shrugging his thick-set shoulders, he attempted to shake off his awareness that his old brown tweed suit was hardly appropriate for a luncheon with Anderson Phelps. Unfortunately the call had come so late that there had been no chance to change. Neither had there been time for a haircut. He fumbled for a comb, found that he did not have one, and contented himself with a quick finger raking of his wiry thatch, once a brickish red but now well-shot with gray.

Preoccupation with his personal appearance was abnormal enough to make him conscious of it and, introspectively alert, he excused himself with the explanation that his only concern was that Anderson Phelps might suspect how badly he needed a thousand-dollar fee. He was coming precariously close to the end of the stake of savings that, two years ago, he had decided to gamble on the establishment of his own business. He had gone into it with his eyes open, knowing that he was playing a long shot. New York was full of little one-man-and-a-girl public relations outfits, most of them doomed to fail — the hopeless struggle of some has-been from one of the big advertising agencies who had been squeezed off the payroll with an expensive farewell luncheon, the best wishes of the management in whatever new connection he might make, and a mimeographed office bulletin containing the rubber-stamped statement that the victim's future plans would be announced at a later date. In his own case there had been no farewell luncheon, no speeches, no bulletin — except, of course, the press release that Lincoln Lord had resigned as president of the Luxor Pharmacal Corporation. No one had asked Brick Mitchell to leave the company. There had, in fact, been a cautiously veiled suggestion that there might be a continuing place for him in the organization. He had, however, come in under Lincoln Lord's banner, and there had been, somehow, the feeling that there was no alternative to leaving in the same way. He had written a curt note of resignation, cleaned out his desk and, within twenty-four hours, had rented a two-room office suite on Madison Avenue.

Although the actual establishment of Mitchell Associates, Inc., was a precipitate move, the decision was solidly grounded. It was precisely and exactly what he had planned to do for the past ten years, having sworn to himself on a hundred sleepless nights that he would break away from Lincoln Lord. Once, right after Frazer Glass, he had even gone so far as to look around for an office . . . had his letterhead all designed . . . and, damn it, he'd have gone through with it if it hadn't been for his one mistake . . . one slip . . . like an alcoholic taking just one little drink . . . one last dinner with Linc and Maggie Lord. That's all it had taken . . . one misstep and he'd been right back on the Lincoln Lord merry-go-round again, a new job every two or three years . . . Lincoln Lord's waterboy . . . "Assistant to the President" . . . writing his speeches, feeding him ideas, keeping the straw stuffed in his shirt. He'd have been ten years ahead if he'd made the break when he should have made it, right after he'd gotten out of the Navy . . . Mike Buchanan all ready to go in with him . . . and Mike's old man would have been good for at least two big accounts. That's what tore a man's guts out, knowing that you'd been right, that you'd had it made, and then throwing it all away ... again and again ... always giving Lincoln Lord one more chance.

But fifty wasn't too old ... and damn it, he was getting by! At least MITCHELL ASSOCIATES was still on the office door. The janitor hadn't come up yet with a sharp razor blade to scrape him out of existence because the rent wasn't paid. January and February were the worst months ... things would get rolling again in March ... most companies starting on new budgets ... another boost from Anderson Phelps would carry him over the hump ... cover the overhead for a couple of months, the rent and the telephone bill ... and Tommy's salary. Yes, he had to do something about her ... if he let it run on the way it was going, he'd be in over his head before he knew it ...

Miss Peabody returned, composing herself at her desk before she said, "Mr. Phelps will see you directly."

He thanked her and walked to the window, snapping a light to a cigarette, trying to banish the premonition that Anderson Phelps had something less remunerative on his mind today than a job for one of the firms for which Weeks, Phelps & Harrison supplied financing. This was the way it had always started before, Anderson Phelps calling him down for a conference ... except that today Phelps had invited him to lunch. But why shouldn't he? Perfectly normal thing to do ... right now, all over town, men were doing business over luncheon tables ... no, Phelps *must* have another job for him ...

The door behind Miss Peabody's desk clicked open and Brick turned quickly, prepared to face Anderson Phelps. He saw instead a man starting toward the corridor door, putting on his coat, a face that was undeniably familiar but not instantly recognizable.

"Brick!" the man exclaimed. "Well, this is a pleasant surprise!"

It was the sound of his voice that clinched recognition ... Dewey Franklin, treasurer of Frazer Glass during the three years that Lincoln Lord had headed the corporation ... wasn't he executive vice-president now?

"Good to see you, Dewey," he said, shaking hands.

"Been a long time," Franklin replied heartily. "Don't believe I've seen you since you left the company. Where are you now?"

"In business for myself."

"You don't say. Well, that's fine, Brick. Advertising?"

"Public relations."

"Oh, good! Big field — public relations. How is the old boy, anyway?"

Brick hesitated.

"Lincoln Lord," Franklin explained.

"I really don't know," Brick said, making a conscious effort to keep his voice from cooling too noticeably.

"Oh, I see," Franklin said, clearing his throat. "Sorry. Took it for granted that you were still tied up with him. Well — good to see you, Brick."

They shook hands again, a forced formality now, and Franklin's quick exit without a backward glance was an accusation of a situation badly handled.

He stumped out his cigarette, angrily self-critical, telling himself that at least he should have given Dewey Franklin his business card . . . but that damned Lincoln Lord business again! Why did everyone insist on reminding him of what a fool he had been . . . all those years wasted.

He lit another cigarette, grimly determined not to let his mind go off on another Lincoln Lord binge . . . had to stop thinking about Linc . . . and Maggie, too. That was all in the past now, over and done with. He'd made the break . . . no, not burning up the world but still not doing too badly either . . . at least proving that he could get by on his own . . . took time . . . couldn't expect to build up a business overnight. All he needed was a good bread-and-butter account to cover his overhead. This job that Anderson Phelps was going to give him today might turn out to be just that . . . something more than another one-shot . . .

"Ah, Mr. Mitchell, there you are." Unnoticed, Anderson Phelps had slipped into the room.

"Good to see you, Mr. Phelps," Brick said, cringing at the syrupy sound of his voice, feeling that he had already betrayed his anxiety.

Anderson Phelps seemed not to notice. "I do hope you'll pardon me for keeping you waiting," he said, his voice reflecting the same high polish that he always managed to give his appearance, the Edwardian elegance with which he kept himself from being too anachronistically misplaced in these turn-of-the-century offices.

"Do come along, please," Phelps said, guiding him through the inner door, according him the status of an honored guest.

Cautiously, Brick refused to accept the encouragement of deference. Acting the perfect host was, he knew, no indication of what the financier had on his mind. Anderson Phelps was always, under every circumstance, the perfect gentleman.

They walked through the general office, deserted now during the noon hour except for one elderly man who, suggesting a theatrical fitting of character to scene, was actually wearing a green eye shade. A half-dozen golden oak desks were heavily laden with papers stacked as if there was a general distrust of such modern innovations as filing cabinets. One side of the room was largely taken up with an enormous safe, its black-enameled doors ornamented with a landscape much varnished and yellowed with age. Above the painting, the firm name was lettered in a gold-leaf rendition of Spencerian script. Below, there was the single word, *Investments*.

Despite curiosity and inquiry, Brick Mitchell had only a vague idea of the exact nature of the firm's activities. He knew that there was no longer either a Weeks or a Harrison, that Anderson Phelps shared his control with no partners, and that he must be a rich man. He suspected, although without definite confirmation, that most of the firm's business involved the investment of Mr. Phelps's own money, and that he was an active but silent partner in those companies in which he had taken a financial interest. Although holding no offices other than directorships, he plainly exercised a wide-ranging influence on their management. He was, however, no quick-buck operator, engaging neither in the buying and selling of companies, nor in any major speculations in their securities. In all instances of which Brick Mitchell was aware, the Phelps investments were of long standing, many of them going back to his father's time.

Anderson Phelps's unflinching goal, freely admitted, was to make as much money as he could, a materialism which he excused with the explanation that every cent of the firm's profit now went into the Phelps Foundation. It was a justification, Brick suspected, that delighted the old man. Without it he might have felt himself prevented from exercising a talent for the accumulation of wealth that, otherwise, would have made him seem a misplaced holdover from an earlier era, a too-perfect denizen of these gaslight era offices. As it was, he had found a happy blending of talent and purpose — a robber baron acquisitiveness applied to an end currently applauded by society. He had every reason to be a satisfied man.

Until the crossing of the threshold of Anderson Phelps's private office, there was no feeling of an atmosphere purposefully created. The rest of the suite seemed no more than an achievement in preservation. His own office aroused, however, the speculation that here he might be exercising a private sense of humor — at least with the roll-

33

top desk and the never-used brass spittoon — a suspicion that would have been easier for Brick Mitchell to accept if he had been certain that a sense of humor was something that Anderson Phelps positively possessed. On the occasion of their first meeting, aware of a faintly visible smile of suppressed amusement, he had thought that he did. Later he had discovered that Phelps's expression was a more or less standardized mask worn by all rich men whose grandfathers had taught them that a frozen smile was an effective shield against Johnny-come-latelies who might have the idea that a solidly successful life was something that could be achieved without genetic benefit.

Brick Mitchell had never been greatly impressed by the blue bloods, yet he had never seen Anderson Phelps, as he was seeing him now, without recalling — simply as a memory, colored neither by envy nor regret — that his own father had been a laborer in the Homestead Gold mines, that his two years of college had been at the South Dakota School of Mines, and that his sole inheritance had been his father's pearl stickpin and, later, the Bible on whose flyleaf his mother had inscribed, as the hopeful beginning of a family record, the single entry that recorded the date of his own birth. He had, however, never felt himself handicapped by any lack of inheritance, nor had he ever been consciously aware of being misplaced in any of the worlds, so different from that of his childhood, through which he had moved during his adult life. He might have felt somewhat differently had he not been, temperamentally, so much more the observer than the participant. Now, watching Anderson Phelps cross his office and open a door in the side wall, he saw him less as a man to be respected for wealth and social position than as another example of the perpetually puzzling variety of mankind.

"You've not seen my private dining room before?" Phelps asked.

Brick stepped to the open doorway and looked into a tiny windowless room whose principal use was plainly the storage of old records and stationery supplies. The walls, floor to ceiling, were covered with rough shelving, the space between shelves solidly packed with the exposed bulges of wrapped bundles, the ends of crayon-marked cardboard containers, and the red leather spines of old account books. In the center of the room there was a folding card table and, on top of it, a wicker lunch basket.

"Do you mind sharing potluck?" Phelps asked, courteously waiting for an inconceivable rejection before he flipped back the lid of the hamper. "There's sure to be enough. Elizabeth always packs extra in case I have a guest. Not wasted though. Anything that's left goes home to the dogs."

With a token tuck at his coat sleeves, momentarily exposing a band of starched shirt cuffs and the glitter of diamond-studded links, Anderson Phelps reached into the hamper and lifted out a linen cloth that he spread over the table with solemnity and practiced grace, a ritual that suggested to Brick, incongruously until he remembered the source, a brook bank and a willow tree, tandem bicycles standing against a rail fence, a picnic with two girls wearing veiled straw boaters and groundsweeping dresses . . . yes, the illustration that he'd had Henri Pierre do for the Luxor advertisement that Lincoln Lord had liked so much that . . . *damn . . . why couldn't he forget Lincoln Lord!*

"How have you been, Mr. Mitchell? Busy? How are things?"

"Not bad, sir, not bad at all," he said, perhaps again a too quick response. Yet, weighed, it seemed a successful straddle, neither an obviously anxious grab for a fee-paying job nor a denial that he was free enough to give adequate attention to any assignment that Phelps might have in mind.

"Delighted that you were free to join me," Phelps said after they were seated.

"Glad to have the chance, sir."

Phelps delicately lifted the tissue wrapping of a sandwich. "Chicken?"

"Fine."

The financier poured a steaming amber liquid from a vacuum bottle. "Hope you don't mind tea? Elizabeth always insists on giving me the stuff — knows I dislike it, you see — all a part of her wifely duty to keep me in a constant state of mild annoyance."

Brick took a chance on responding with a smile.

"Oh, but she's quite right!" Phelps protested, as if surprised that his point had been missed. "At sixty, you know, a man has a quite alarming tendency toward self-satisfaction. Being forced to drink tea when you don't like it jars you out of the rut. Keeps you from going stale."

"I'd say there wasn't much danger of that," Brick said, again debating whether or not Phelps had a sense of humor as he saw him now, with obvious relish, swallow a swig of tea.

"You're not married, are you, Mr. Mitchell?" Phelps asked unexpectedly.

35

"No — no, I'm not," he said, the admission oddly forced over an unexplainable barrier.

Anderson Phelps sat regarding him for a thoughtful moment, his enigmatic smile now a look of inquiry. But the expected demand for an explanation of bachelorhood was not forthcoming and they ate in a silence that Brick felt no inclination to break, his sandwich consumed before Phelps finally said, "I dare say you suspected that there was some motive behind my asking you down here today."

"Well, I thought you probably had something on your mind."

"Quite right," Phelps said crisply, refilling his tea cup. "I do. I need your help."

"Be happy to do anything I can, sir."

"Mr. Mitchell —" The financier's voice hung strangely suspended, a sudden alerting to danger. "— I want you to tell me everything you know about Lincoln Lord."

Shock struck hard, creating the momentary illusion that he had again lost control of his mind... Lincoln Lord... *Lincoln Lord*... what in god's name was happening...?

Dry-mouthed, he managed to say, "That's a big order."

"Are you pressed for time?" Phelps asked, blandly innocent.

"No, but —" He waited for the recovery of poise. "I've known him for a good many years."

"And his wife?"

"Yes, Maggie, too."

"So I understand," the financier said, as if clinching an important point. "I'm sure you're the man to tell me what I want to know." He waited, immobilely expectant, then suddenly nodded as if he had heard an unasked question. "Quite so — you do have a right to know why I am questioning you. Does the name Coastal Foods Company mean anything to you?"

"Well, it does sound vaguely familiar, but I don't seem to be able to tie it up. What do they pack?"

"Precisely the difficulty, Mr. Mitchell. You've put your finger right on the problem. Up to now, they've gotten almost all of their business from one of the supermarket chains — Gellman Stores. Now, as you may be aware, Gellman has merged with another chain."

"Yes, I know — Silver Crescent," Brick said, grateful for the memory of a news item that Tommy had clipped for him.

"Exactly," Phelps said, the brightness of his response pleasant evidence that he had been favorably impressed. "As you may also know,

Mr. Mitchell, Silver Crescent brought a cannery into the merger. Naturally, that cannery will pack Gellman's private brands."

"So Coastal Foods has lost the business?"

"Quite so. And the problem, of course, is to replace that volume. To do so by taking on another supermarket chain, even if that were possible, would only be asking for a repetition of the same thing. Therefore, the decision has been made — wisely, I'm sure, even though belatedly, perhaps — to rebuild their business with a line of food products packed under their own label. Yes, quite so, Mr. Mitchell — a difficult task, I'll grant you that, but hardly an impossible one, would you say?"

"Of course not," he said hurriedly.

"And there are some strong plus factors in Coastal Foods' favor. They have an excellent plant, absolutely modern in every way, and a top-notch production organization. So it's by no means a case of starting from scratch. Furthermore, there's adequate financing, either in hand or available, to do whatever needs to be done."

"Sounds good," he said, a guarded sampling of rising hope...this could be *it*...that backbone account...food...right down his alley...

"On the other hand," Phelps went on, "Coastal Foods has a weakness that must be overcome. There's no sales or promotional organization. Under its past policy — selling to Gellman on an annual contract basis — naturally, there was no need for anything of that sort. Now, of course, that side of the organization must be developed. The answer — as always, I might say — lies in finding the right man. Whether or not Mr. Lord is the man —"

The financier's voice cut off and Brick Mitchell knew why. He had let his face betray the shock of sudden reorientation. Distracted by self-interest, caught up by the fascination that merchandising problems always held for him, he had momentarily forgotten why Phelps had undertaken to explain the Coastal Foods situation.

"You seem surprised," Phelps said, sharply concerned.

He shook his head...no, not surprised...why should he be? It had happened so many times before...always Lincoln Lord...why, why, why? How could a smart man like Anderson Phelps think that Lincoln Lord was...

"You don't think Lord would be the man for it?" Phelps demanded.

"No, I — no, I don't mean that, sir."

37

"He does know the food business?"

"It's been a long time since I — well, I haven't seen them for quite a while now." Inescapably, there was the flinching retreat from error ... damn it, why had he said *them* ... dragging Maggie into it ... just a slip of the tongue ... maybe Phelps wouldn't notice it.

"So she said," Phelps said, a destruction of hope. "Very attractive person, isn't she?"

He knew that he had been caught blank-faced, staring.

"I had the good fortune of having dinner with Mrs. Lord last evening."

He felt his head snap back, an uncontrollable reflex.

"We were at the same table," the financier explained. "We've been making some grants to Chesapeake College — the Phelps Foundation, that is — and so they've put me on the board of regents. Doesn't mean a thing, never go to their meetings, but last night they did dragoon me into attending their annual dinner for the New York alumni. Mr. Lord was the principal speaker. No doubt you saw an account of it in the *Times* this morning?"

He nodded affirmatively ... yes, this was the way it always happened ... just when you thought Linc was all washed up, someone heard him make a speech ...

"Quite a speaker, isn't he?" Phelps probed.

He mumbled agreement, an admission superimposed on the silent question of who was writing Linc's speeches for him now ... there had to be someone to put the words in his mouth ... probably Maggie ... still sticking by him. Wasn't she ever going to realize ... ?

Phelps's voice faded into his consciousness again, "— as much as the way he said it. I've been to a good many fund-raising affairs and I must say I've never seen anything like it. Had that crowd right in the palm of his hand. Over a hundred thousand dollars pledged in a half-hour. Even nicked me for an extra contribution! And my own money, mind you, not the Foundation's."

"He must have been in good form."

"He was," Phelps came back, his attempt at a rueful expression not altogether successful, a failure that he recognized with an abrupt change of subject. "I've spent the morning checking Lord's record. Talked to a number of people who've had some contact with him over the years. The last one was Franklin of Frazer Glass. You may have met him outside as he left?"

38

"Yes," he said, the pieces falling into place now, a nightmare hardening into validity.

"There seems to be a rather wide range of opinion about Mr. Lord."

"Yes, I suppose there is."

"Tell me the truth, Mr. Mitchell — is he or isn't he?"

"Is he or isn't he what?" he repeated, not only an honest request for clarification but a feinting delay to give himself the chance that he needed to decide on a general course of action.

"A two-year man," Phelps snapped back. "That's what someone called him this morning. Not a bad name, you know, for a certain type of man — these razzle-dazzle boys who get by on front and nothing else. That's about as long as they usually last — two years — one year to catch up with them, another year to get rid of them."

"No, it's not a bad name," Brick said, relieved in this vindication of his earlier judgment that Anderson Phelps was no fool.

"So you agree that that's what he is?" Phelps demanded.

"No, I didn't mean — I don't know, Mr. Phelps."

"I see." The financier's tone was noticeably cooler. "I had not anticipated that your loyalty to Lord would keep you from talking frankly to me."

"It's not that," he said . . . no, not loyalty . . . why should it be? He owed Lincoln Lord nothing . . . all those years wasted . . .

"He fits the pattern, doesn't he — five jobs in ten years — more or less."

"Yes, but — well, I'd look a little foolish criticizing any man for that. I've done some job-jumping myself."

"But only because you'd tied your wagon to the Lincoln Lord star," Phelps amended. "When he changed jobs, you went along. Isn't that true?"

"It was partly that," he granted, an admission made only because it was inescapable.

"Frankly that's why I was particularly anxious to talk to you," Phelps pressed. "Obviously the man must have something or you wouldn't have stayed with him as long as you did, following him from one job to another."

He attempted to squirm away from the feeling that it was he, not Lincoln Lord, who was on trial in Anderson Phelps's eyes . . . but what difference did it make now? There was nothing for him in any company that hired Lincoln Lord as its president . . . no, he wouldn't

39

take the account even if it were offered . . . no matter how badly he needed the money . . . even if he had to close the office! Never again . . . no more Lincoln Lord . . . he'd made the break . . .

Anderson Phelps knifed in with, "Am I to assume that you would prefer not to discuss Mr. Lord?"

The knife was sharp, cutting through the truth . . . no, he didn't want to talk about Lincoln Lord . . . nor think about him either . . . but he dared not admit it. "No, it's not that, Mr. Phelps."

"Then tell me what you think of him."

It was a shock for Brick Mitchell to face the belated realization that, despite the persistent impression that he had spent most of his adult life thinking about Lincoln Lord, his thoughts had never crystallized into an appraisal sharply enough defined to permit translation into words.

"No, Mr. Phelps, I don't mind talking about him. It's just that — well, I don't know. Maybe he is what you called him — a two-year man. Maybe he is, maybe he isn't. That's never been an easy thing for me to do — judge any man and come up with an answer that you can put in one pat phrase."

"Well said," Phelps replied. "And you're quite right, of course. We do have a tendency — all of us, I dare say — to simplify our human relationships by trying to fit everyone we know into convenient little pigeonholes. Too frequently, I'm sure, such judgments are based upon quite inadequate evidence. Lord, for example — such a handsome fellow, such an extraordinarily convincing manner, not at all difficult to understand why he makes such a good first impression. When you see him in action, as I saw him last night, it's easy to imagine him a superman, capable of doing anything."

"He's not that," he muttered into his teacup.

"Of course not. But isn't it true that when he took some of the jobs that he's held he was expected to live up to that fantastically good first impression? Hasn't that been the basis of some of his difficulty?"

"Perhaps."

"Let me ask you this, Mr. Mitchell — is that first impression calculated? Does Lord consciously oversell himself?"

"Well, I suppose every man tries to make as good an impression as he can."

"Of course," Phelps agreed. "And you can't blame him for that?"

"No."

The financier's expression reflected the dominance of amazement

40

over doubt. "And the man does have ability, you can't deny that. Any-one who can do what he did last night — it was really fantastic! He had that whole crowd on its feet, waving pledge cards like a bunch of fools who'd suddenly decided that the only way to salvation was a bank-busting donation to Chesapeake College." He paused, a retro-spectively puzzled expression on his face. "The astounding thing is that you can't figure out how he does it. At least I can't. He just stands up there and talks — no oratory, no histrionics, no emotional-ism — amazing! I suppose the secret is that he gives the impression of being so absolutely and totally sincere."

"I know."

"Is he?"

"I beg your pardon?"

"That quality that Lord has — call it *sincerity* or whatever you will — is it genuine?"

"Well, I —"

"Quite so," Phelps conceded. "An unfair question. But that is the secret of his success, isn't it?"

"I suppose so," Brick said, less an acknowledgment of what he was actually thinking than a convenient chance for agreement.

Anderson Phelps redirected his attack. "Suppose we go back to the beginning, Mr. Mitchell. Where did you first know him? At this can-ning company down in Maryland? I gathered from what Mrs. Lord said last night that the three of you were down there together."

"Yes, Quincy Canning."

"That was where you first met them?"

"That's where I first met Linc."

"Oh. You'd known Mrs. Lord before?"

"Yes. Here in New York. We were both working for one of the magazines — *Hearthside*. It's out of business now, folded up in the depression. I left first — went down to Quincy Canning — so when Maggie lost her job — well, Mr. Quincy had authorized hiring a home economist so naturally I thought of her."

"Naturally," Phelps repeated, clearing his throat. "And Lord was there too — at the Quincy Canning Company?"

"Yes, he — well, he came in afterwards — that fall."

"Under what circumstances? How did he get his job? Why did Mr. Quincy hire him?"

"Because of a speech he made," he said, unaware until the words had slipped out that Anderson Phelps might think him guilty of an

41

attempt at sardonic humor by citing such an obvious parallel to the circumstances that had aroused his own interest in Lincoln Lord.

"Really?" Phelps asked, flatly expressionless.

He felt the need to rush past danger. "It was 1936 — I don't know whether you remember or not, but those were the NRA days."

"Very well."

"And then there was the AAA. That was a setup where the government collected processing taxes from food manufacturers and used the money for agricultural relief."

"Yes, I recall that."

"Well, all of those Washington schemes were red flags to Mr. Quincy — he hated Roosevelt as if he were the devil himself — and so he fought anything and everything that came along."

"A rugged individualist, I take it."

"As rugged as they came. Well, Washington was on his neck all the time, of course — one law suit after another — and naturally he was a wide-open target for all the agitators that the New Dealers sent out to stir up trouble against the capitalistic manufacturers. I don't know how much of that sort of thing really went on — maybe not as much as Mr. Quincy suspected — but at least all the professors at the college were pretty New Dealish in those days and they weren't missing any bets to keep the town stirred up against the Quincy Canning Company. It finally came to a boil — not the people in the plant as much as the college boys. They started dumping truck-loads of tomatoes in the main street of town. Actually I guess you'd call it more of a riot than a strike. Anyway, right in the middle of it, Linc climbed up to the second story of the bank building, stuck his head out of the window and started talking to the crowd."

"I can anticipate the end of the story," Phelps said with an appreciative chuckle. "Apparently Mr. Lord's gifted tongue is no recent acquisition?"

He nodded agreement, by-passing the temptation to add that Linc had not said a single word that afternoon that had not been a repetition of what, the night before, had been said by someone else in Mr. Quincy's library. "Well, you asked about his start with the Quincy Canning Company — the next day Mr. Quincy called in Linc and gave him a job."

"Then he hadn't been working for Quincy before?"

"Only temporarily — a vacation job during the tomato season. His regular job was up at the college. He'd graduated a couple of years before. I'm not certain what year — '33 or '34. Anyway, it was the bottom of the depression. The missionary society hadn't been able to scrape together enough money to send him overseas, so he'd stayed on around the campus, running the YMCA, handling some of the student activities —"

Phelps stopped him. "Are you telling me that Lincoln Lord was planning to be a missionary?"

"Of course. He'd graduated from the seminary and —"

"I'll be damned!" Phelps exploded, the first complete break of composure that Brick had witnessed. It was, however, almost instantly remedied. "Still and all, it's really not out of character. Evangelism is a form of selling, I suppose — sales promotion — whatever you want to call it."

Brick responded to the nudge of conscience-clearing honesty. "I don't think that missionary work was anything that Linc ever — well, I'm sure he'd never felt any great call to preach the gospel or anything like that. You see, his father had been a minister, and back in those days Chesapeake was a church college. Linc had gotten his seminary scholarship as a minister's son and — well, he didn't hesitate very long about taking the job that Mr. Quincy offered him."

"What did he do? What was his job?"

"He started out working on sales promotion mostly — putting on meetings for wholesale grocers. Then Mr. Quincy sent him out to Chicago to open a sales office. He left him there for a year or so and then he brought him back to Brighton as sort of — well, general sales manager."

"And that lasted how long?"

"Until he went into the service."

"He was in the Navy, I believe she told me."

"Yes."

"Why did he go into the service? Surely he could have secured a deferment because of his job's being essential."

"I'm sorry, Mr. Phelps, but I don't know anything about that," he said, resolutely by-passing the long-held suspicion that Lincoln Lord's fast grab of a commission in the Navy had been a strategic escape from Mr. Quincy's disillusionment with the fair-haired boy to whom he had entrusted so much of the company's management.

"I was simply exploring his relationship with the Quincy family,"

Phelps explained. "Apparently it must have been on a very good basis. Mrs. Lord, I understand, lived there on the Quincy estate all during the war."

"Yes, that's right," Brick acknowledged, admitting a minor point against his theory.

"But after the war Lord didn't come back to Quincy Canning?"

"No."

"What happened?"

"Well, he'd met this admiral in the Navy — Admiral Rabson."

"Rabson? Wasn't that the name of —?" Phelps glanced at the small notebook he now held in his hand.

"Yes, the admiral's family owned Rabson Foods."

"I assume that they must have offered Lord an opportunity that he didn't feel he had with Mr. Quincy."

"I imagine so."

"There must have been some rather substantial inducement," the financier pressed. "After all, it was Mr. Quincy who had given Lord his chance, brought him along in his company, taken care of his wife and child during the war — a bit strange that Lord should have walked out on him, wouldn't you say?"

"Mr. Phelps, I'm in no position to criticize him. I did the same thing. I went along with him."

"But under quite different circumstances," the financier objected. "There's a point to all of this, Mr. Mitchell. These are not idle questions. As far as I'm concerned, the key factor in any man's character is the way he responds to the demands of loyalty. If I felt for one minute that Lincoln Lord was a man who couldn't be counted upon to remain loyal to something beyond his own personal interests, I'd scratch him off right now. There are too many of those fellows around these days — job-jumpers — men who have hop-skipped their way up the ladder simply because of their ability to put up a front. If that's all Lord is —" He shrugged his dismissal.

"It must be a hard decision to have to make," Brick said, pushing back from the table, hoping that it would be a hint that would lead to the granting of Anderson Phelps's permission to leave.

Phelps followed his move, rising from the table, but he quickly made it plain that he had no intention of releasing him. "We'll carry on in my office," he decreed. "More comfortable there."

4

Dr. Arthur Bell Whittaker, Dean of Chesapeake College — and, since Dr. Radcliff's stroke, the acting head of the institution — arrived back in Brighton, Maryland, a few minutes before one o'clock, completing the overnight round trip that he had made to New York in order to attend the alumni meeting. By the time he had maneuvered his car into the parking space reserved for him in the lot behind the Administration Building, he was already late for a meeting of the Budget Committee. Important as that meeting was, however, he judged it even more important to get a report from Brooke Potter on what had happened in New York this morning, a call that it would be unwise to make on any telephone less private than the one in his own office.

Luckily the call went through immediately. Less fortunately, the news was not good. "It's no go, Dean," he heard Potter say, a cryptically cocky response that the dean found unpleasantly grating, again raising the question of whether another fund-raising agency — perhaps a bit less New Yorkerish — might better serve Chesapeake College's interests.

"Am I to take it that Mr. Lord rejected your proposal?" Whittaker asked, pressing for a clear-cut and positive statement, something that he so often found it difficult to get from Brooke Potter.

"Dean, you know what I told you yesterday — you just can't expect to interest a man like Lincoln Lord."

"That's very disappointing."

"Look, Dean — sure, Lord did a good job last night. I'm not questioning that for one minute. But don't get the idea that we can't get along without him. We'll put over those other meetings. Don't worry about that."

"I wish that it were possible for me to share your confidence," Whittaker said, bluntly frank.

"Honestly, Dean, I don't know what's worrying you," Potter said, making no effort to hide his annoyance. "Why don't you just relax and let us take care of things? We've been in business a long time and we've handled a lot of campaigns that were bigger than this one. If we weren't delivering the goods, we'd have closed our doors a long time ago."

"I'm not questioning your competence," Whittaker said courteously. "But I do wish that it were possible for us to bring in Mr. Lord in some capacity or other."

45

"So do I, Dean, so do I — like nothing better. But after all we do have to be realistic, don't we?"

"You did, of course, offer to compensate Mr. Lord for —"

"Look, Dean, expense money doesn't mean anything to a man like that. Do you have any idea of how much he's worth? I don't either — exactly — but you can bet it's plenty! I don't know how big a slice he got when they cut up that Chemical Service melon, but I do happen to know one of the other men who was in on it and he came out with — well, this is confidential, Dean, but it was more than a million. And all capital gains. Lord must have done at least that well, maybe better. Take this Japanese junket he's just been on. A man doesn't go in for that kind of thing if he's got any worries about where his next meal is coming from. You know that, Dean."

"Yes, I appreciate all that, Mr. Potter," Whittaker said patiently. "What I was hoping, of course, was that the same motivation of public service that had induced Mr. Lord to undertake that mission for the government might lead to some continuing association with Chesapeake College."

"Continuing association?" Potter questioned coldly. "What do you mean by that, Dean?"

"In some capacity or other," Whittaker said, purposefully vague, regretting that he had revealed even this much of the plan that had been in the back of his mind when he had suggested to Brooke Potter that Lincoln Lord be engaged to head the Chesapeake drive. He had not told Potter, nor did he intend to do so now, that his real objective had been to maneuver Lincoln Lord into a position that would be a logical steppingstone to a high administrative post in Chesapeake College.

"You're not thinking of taking on Lord yourself, are you?" Potter asked, undoubtedly a guess but an uncomfortably close one.

"Anything of that sort would have to be decided by the board of regents," Whittaker said stiffly.

"Just let me give you this little piece of advice, Dean — don't ever stick out your own neck and suggest it."

"Why do you say that?"

"Just let well enough alone, Dean, just let well enough alone."

"I see," he said, his voice chilled. "Well, thank you, Mr. Potter."

"Look, Dean, we'll be in touch with you in a few days about the program for the Philadelphia meeting. If you want —"

"Good-by, sir," the dean said, hanging up, positive now that Potter's resistance to Lincoln Lord was grounded in a suspicion that, if Lord came in, the fund-raising agency would rather quickly find itself out in the cold ... no more such windfalls as they'd snapped up last night ... almost five thousand dollars in two hours! And what had they done to earn it? Absolutely nothing. It was Lincoln Lord who had gotten those pledges.

Dean Whittaker sat with his hand still on the telephone instrument, debating the possibility of placing a call for Lincoln Lord in New York. It was now plain that he had made a mistake in plotting an indirect approach. Unquestionably, the thing to do was to talk to Lord himself. But could that be done without ...?

Reluctantly he decided that a delay would be necessary. Despite the favorable discussion at the last meeting of the board, the general idea unopposed by a single regent, there had been no formal action that authorized him to ask anyone if he would be willing to have his name considered for a new high-ranking post — *Executive Director* had been suggested as a suitable and attractive title — an office that would make the man who filled it completely responsible for the administration of all business and financial affairs of Chesapeake College, everything except the academic program.

He had not, of course, mentioned Lincoln Lord's name in the board meeting — he had not been certain until last night that Lord was the man he wanted — but the possibility was one that he had kept tucked away in his mind ever since the time he had heard him make a speech before a meeting of the American Society of Economics. Even then he had been looking ahead to the day when he would become president of Chesapeake College and, foresightedly, had started marking men who might be drawn in to supply qualities that he had long recognized as being deficient in himself. He simply could not, no matter how hard he tried, be the hail and hearty speechmaker that the financial welfare of the college demanded. A team of two top executives was clearly the answer, each doing the job for which he was best fitted by temperament and ability. He had no doubt about himself in his own field and now, after last night, there was no longer any question that Lincoln Lord was the man he wanted beside him.

Looking at his watch, he saw how late he was for the Budget Committee meeting, again proving how badly he needed to be relieved of nonacademic responsibilities. Reaching for a pencil, he wrote *Lincoln Lord* on his desk pad, an unnecessary reminder to put the subject high on the agenda for the next meeting of the board of regents. At-

47

tempting to bring in Lord by working through Potter's agency had been a mistake, precisely the sort of mistake that he would continue to make if he kept on doing things that were outside of his own field. Obviously, with a man of Mr. Lord's caliber, the proper course was to secure board authorization and then have someone make a direct approach.

5

Anderson Phelps was proving himself an indefatigable inquisitor and Brick Mitchell had resigned himself to making the best of a situation from which there was no immediate escape. He had no desire to talk about Lincoln Lord, even less to inflict upon himself the memories that were being aroused, but Phelps was almost his only hope of keeping Mitchell Associates alive and offending him by walking out would be the height of folly. Lighting a cigarette, he let himself be mildly intrigued by the intensity with which, during the morning, Phelps must have carried on his investigation of Lincoln Lord's background. If it were true, as the financier claimed, that his interest in him had only been aroused at the Chesapeake College dinner last night, he had done a remarkable job of gathering information in the few intervening hours.

Phelps turned another page in his notebook. "Under those circumstances, Mr. Mitchell, how could you blame Lord for severing his connection with Rabson Foods?"

"I'm not blaming him for anything," he said as positively as he dared, wishing that there was some way to make at least that one point stick in Phelps's mind.

"In any event," Phelps continued, "Lord left Rabson and went on to Union Packing as president of the company?"

"That's right."

"The owner of the business — this Mr. Kassleman — retired?"

"Yes — after six months or so."

"He must have been satisfied with the job Lord was doing or he wouldn't have retired and left him in charge?"

"There was no reason why he shouldn't have been satisfied," he said, caught up by a vivid memory of those early months at Union Packing . . . the first big-time advertising copy he had ever written . . . his first page in the *Post* . . .

"Was Kassleman a Jew?"

He blinked. "A Jew? No, I don't think so. No, I'm certain that he wasn't."

Phelps sat for a moment, preoccupied, studying his notebook. Then, without looking up, he asked, "Tell me this, Mr. Mitchell — was Lord actually running the show himself? Or was it still Kassleman pulling the strings from behind the scenes?"

"No, I'd say the old man was pretty much out of it — well, at least for the first year."

The financier's eyes came up, sharply inquiring. "And then Kassleman began to reassume executive control?"

"That's right."

"Was that because Lord wasn't doing a job? Or was it because Kassleman had become bored with retirement and wanted to get back into harness again?"

"That may have been a part of it," he said, finding himself trapped in a situation where any other response would have been a criticism of himself . . . if it were true that a job hadn't been done at Union Packing, it would have been his fault more than Linc's . . . every idea had been his . . .

"Then you wouldn't say that it was too black a mark on Lord's record — his deciding to get out after Kassleman broke his word and began to take back some of the authority that he had given him?"

He forced a smile. "Well, at least Linc came out on top — president of Frazer Glass — ten thousand a year more than he'd been making."

"Yes, Frazer Glass," Phelps acknowledged, turning back to his roll-top desk, picking up a sheet of notes. "How did that come about, Mr. Mitchell? What was the beginning?"

Anderson Phelps's challenging expression warned him against saying again that he didn't know . . . and yet it was true . . . he didn't. There'd been those rumors around the office that Kassleman had put the heat on Linc to quit, but no real evidence that Linc had ever known that he was on the spot.

"As I get the story," Phelps prompted, "Lord was hired by Mr. T. J. Coates, who at that time was chairman of the board of Frazer Glass."

"That's right."

"I suppose he heard Lord make a speech," Phelps commented drily.

He hesitated, uncertain whether or not the financier's needling thrust called for a smile, quickly deciding against it. "They met at a convention in Florida. As far as I know, Linc didn't make any speeches. But he was on a discussion panel. I'm quite certain that's how he came to meet Mr. Coates. It was a panel on glass packaging — we'd been doing some experimenting with glass food containers at Union Packing — and Mr. Coates, of course, was very much interested. He had a plantation in South Carolina and he invited Linc to stop off on his way north."

"And Coates offered Lord the presidency of Frazer Glass?"

He nodded.

"Right then — while they were together on Mr. Coates's plantation?"

"Yes, sir. Anyway, he came home with the offer."

"And he resigned from Union Packing and went to Frazer Glass?"

"Yes."

"And you went with him?"

"Yes."

"As advertising manager?"

"No, I — well, my title was Assistant to the President."

"Just what all did that involve, Mr. Mitchell?"

For an instant he felt himself driven to retort that it was Lincoln Lord, not himself, who was being scrutinized, a danger by-passed by Phelps's perceptive interruption.

"My only interest is in trying to get a line on Lord," the financier explained. "The kind of work that an assistant does is usually a good indication of the capabilities of the man who is being assisted."

"I know," he acknowledged, immediately realizing that if he detailed the load that he had carried at Frazer Glass he would make himself sound like the worst kind of a braggart. "Well, there was a lot to do," he began cautiously, aiming for an unnoticed evasion. "You see — well, up to that point, Frazer Glass had more or less limited its business to the Jersey food canneries. I've forgotten the exact figure, but something over three-quarters of the volume was in catsup and chili sauce bottles."

"Very competitive and a low-profit margin," Phelps commented knowingly.

"That's right. So we started out to convert some of that volume to private mold business — special designs of glassware that could be sold at a little better price. That meant getting over into the drug and cosmetic field — customers that we'd never served before. We had to set up a whole new sales and promotional operation, offer package

50

designing service, everything that —" Out of nowhere, a memory flashed. When Phelps had first mentioned Coastal Foods, the name had seemed vaguely familiar, recognition now completed by the recollection that one of the first special design jobs at Frazer Glass had been a jar for Coastal Foods . . . there'd been some trouble about labeling it . . .

Phelps snatched him back with an insistent question. "This new policy that was put into effect at Frazer Glass — was it Lord's idea?"

He paused, blocked by modesty from claiming credit for himself. "It was the obvious way to turn."

The financier made a note. "And what happened? How much progress did you make? Were you able to get some of that new business?"

"Yes, we — well, actually the trouble was that we got too much of it. Too much, I mean, for the kind of plant we had. You see, the factory wasn't really geared up to make what we were selling. They'd been turning out standard bottles in long runs — just put on the molds and let the machines go. When we tried to swing over to these special designs, we couldn't get out the production. The plant just wasn't set up to turn out that kind of ware. For one thing, the tanks were too big. There's no use going into a lot of detail but —"

"No, no, go ahead," Phelps demanded. "This is interesting."

"It's quite a while ago — I don't know that I can recall all the detail," he said, an evasion denied by the vivid memory of how old MacIntosh, the plant superintendent, had double-crossed him by withholding, until it was too late, a warning that should have been volunteered when the program had been first discussed. But that had been Linc's fault . . . talking to MacIntosh without calling him in . . .

"You say the tanks were too large?" Phelps prodded.

Brick snuffed out his cigarette. "You see, Mr. Phelps, in order to use a glass furnace economically you have to draw out the molten glass at a certain rate. With a given number of bottle machines hooked to it, the amount of glass you pull depends upon how big a bottle you're making. For instance, when we started out to make nail polish bottles, we were drawing less than a tenth as much glass as when those same machines were used to make catsup bottles."

"But wouldn't it have been possible to add more machines?"

"Well, there was a problem there," he said, his tone unavoidably colored by the recollection of how foolish MacIntosh had made him look in front of Linc when he had made that same suggestion. "The way the plant was laid out, there wasn't enough room to crowd in more machines. The only solution was to rebuild a whole section of the plant."

"And you went ahead on that basis?"

"Yes, eventually. But it was quite a battle."

"A battle? With whom?"

"Well, there were two factions in the company — two families that owned most of the stock — the Coateses and the Stacks. Mr. Coates was sold on the new plant. He was chairman of the board so he finally jammed it through but —"

"One moment," Phelps interrupted. "You say that Mr. Coates was sold on the new plant?"

"Yes."

"Who sold him — Lord?"

He canceled hesitation and said, "Yes," a truth demanded by the memory of that night he and Maggie had waited for Linc to get back from old man Coates's house . . . Maggie . . .

"What was the basis of the opposition?"

He paused, listening to the faraway echo of his own voice, the words that were re-forming in his mind, paraphrasing what he had tried at the time to make Lincoln Lord realize. "The Stacks crowd — at least old Harvey Stacks himself — was more interested in milking cash out of the company than he was in building for the future. The company had piled up a fair-sized cash surplus during the war and Stacks wanted to get his hands on it. At least the Stacks crowd didn't want to see it get tied up in fixed assets."

"They represented the opposition to Lincoln Lord?"

"Yes."

Anderson Phelps glanced at his notebook. "This gentleman to whom I just talked — Mr. Franklin — he was in the group that was opposed?"

"Naturally. He'd married one of Harvey Stacks's daughters."

"And he was against the plant expansion?"

"Of course."

"How strong would you say that opposition was — as far as Franklin himself was concerned?"

He felt himself blinded by the unrevealed point of the financier's questioning, yet the truth pointed a clear path. "Well, Dewey was treasurer of the company at the time and that put him in a pretty strong position."

"And that position was anti-Lord?"

"Yes."

A faintly amused smirk came to the financier's face. "Mr. Franklin seems to have changed his attitude."

"How's that, sir?"

"When I talked to him this morning he was most complimentary about the job that Lincoln Lord did for the Frazer Glass Company," Phelps said, his dry smile taunting. "He says that most of their growth in the last few years is a direct result of the policies that Lord initiated while he was president of their company. Franklin says — I believe these are more or less his words — that it was Lord who kicked them out of the rut that they'd been in."

"Yes, that is a change of attitude," he said, momentarily stunned by Dewey Franklin's about-face, then rescued by a strong surge of self-justification . . . hadn't he argued with Linc, night after night during that last month, trying to make him see that if they fought their way through, the opposition would eventually cave in? But no, Linc had lost his guts . . . given up . . . quit the fight and taken another job . . . president of Luxor Pharmacal . . .

"Perhaps hindsight has given Mr. Franklin a more balanced judgment," Phelps said drily.

"Apparently."

"It is true, you know, that Frazer Glass has shown quite remarkable progress over the past two or three years."

"I haven't followed it too closely."

"At least it seems reasonably clear that Lord did the company no harm."

He lighted a cigarette, silent as he watched Phelps turn back to his desk and pick up still another sheet of notes.

"And that brings us up to Luxor Pharmacal," the financier said. "I know the circumstances under which he was employed. K. C. Wright happens to be an acquaintance of mine and I talked to him this morning. He says that Lord did an excellent job in building up their sales organization."

A nod was enough of a response . . . the less he said, the better . . . the sooner this would be over . . .

"As a matter of fact, he gave Lord a clean record all the way through — no real black marks against him anywhere."

He nodded again, acknowledgment more than agreement . . . but why shouldn't he agree? It was true . . . Linc had let no black marks be chalked up against him at Luxor . . . no, indeed! He'd run the com-

53

pany as if it were a personal popularity contest . . . never crossing swords with anyone, always backing away from trouble, letting committees make his decisions for him, soft-soaping the heart out of any opposition that threatened to develop. No, there'd been no black marks at Luxor . . . but there'd been no gold stars for accomplishment either. What had put Linc on the spot at Luxor wasn't what he *had* done . . . it was what he *hadn't* done! There was no reason why sales should have gone off so badly that last year . . . except that Linc had let the board cut the advertising budget . . . afraid to take the plunge into television . . .

Phelps was regarding him with an unblinking stare. "Mr. Mitchell, why did Lord leave Luxor? I'm positive it wasn't because he'd had a better offer from Chemical Service. What really happened?"

Again it would have been an honest answer to say that he didn't know, but Phelps's narrowed eyes were even more demanding than they had been before. "Well, the company had a bad year. Sales were off and the profit dropped from something over a million the year before to less than a hundred thousand."

"Why?"

"Frankly, I — well, I may be prejudiced because it was in my own department —"

"You mean the cut in the advertising budget?"

He nodded, surprised again that Anderson Phelps had picked up as much detail as he had.

"Wright mentioned that — said that the board hadn't backed up Lord when he wanted to go into an expanded advertising program. A situation like that puts the president of a company in an almost impossible position. You can hardly blame any president for resigning if his board won't stand behind him."

He couldn't believe his ears . . . didn't Phelps realize that the budget *could* have been sold? Linc could sell anything if he only put his heart in it. What was Phelps trying to do . . . whitewash him?

The financier went on with a shocking confirmation. "Strange, isn't it, how different a man's record looks when you dig in and get the facts behind it. On the face of it, you'd say that Lincoln Lord was a job-jumper — a two-year man — yet in every case where he's changed jobs there's been a sound reason behind it. Yes, I know — Chemical Service was a mistake, something he should never have gotten into in the first place — but, outside of that, it's not a bad record, not bad at all. I must say that he seems very much like the sort of man who might do a job for Coastal Foods."

He was struck speechless, grateful that Phelps had not asked him a direct question. But at least it was over. Somehow he had managed to get through without cutting his throat. He stood up. "I'm sorry I haven't been able to be more helpful —"

The financier was startled. "Here, here, Mr. Mitchell. I've not told you yet where you fit into this picture. Surely you've not been thinking that I'd take up this much of your time without having a little plum on the tree for you."

Words suddenly rushed to Brick Mitchell's lips, unbacked by decision, forced out by the flash reaction that Anderson Phelps was buying him off with a handout. "I think you'd better count me out, Mr. Phelps."

"Count you out?" Phelps demanded. "What do you mean?"

"I'm sorry, sir. It's just that — well, it isn't that I don't want to work for you, Mr. Phelps. I do. I appreciate the business you've given me and I don't want to break our association. But in this particular case — well, I think I'd better pass it up."

"I find this rather difficult to understand, Mr. Mitchell."

"I know it doesn't make much sense but — well, I'd just rather not get involved with Lincoln Lord again, that's all."

"And yet you've maintained for the last hour that you've nothing against him."

"I don't."

"I see," the financier said, crisply cold. "Then you wouldn't be interested in taking on Coastal Foods as a client if Lincoln Lord were to be sales manager?"

Blindly he yielded to the instinctive demand for self-justification, asserting itself despite the sure feeling that there was nothing to gain, that he had already gone too far to retreat, that his position with Anderson Phelps was destroyed beyond redemption. He took a deep breath, steadying himself, and then said, "I'm not criticizing Lincoln Lord, Mr. Phelps. If I'm criticizing anyone, it's myself. I was tied up with him for a long time and — well, I've finally made the break and I'd rather leave it that way."

And then he was outside, leave-taking a barely endured formality, snatching up his coat, pacing the corridor as he waited for the elevator, down on the street before he felt the draining away of unbridled emotion, his mind an emptied pool, exposing the hard rock of truths that he had been too much of a madman to see before . . . *sales manager* . . . Lincoln Lord? Phelps asking him if Kassleman was a Jew . . . of course, of course . . . Coastal Foods was a Jewish Company. Good God, why hadn't he seen it? Was it possible to imagine Lincoln Lord ever taking a job as sales manager of a little Jewish cannery? He'd done it again . . . lost his head . . .

He let himself drift with the sidewalk crowd, carried into the backwater eddy behind a newsstand, feeling now the aftermath of madness, the wretching nausea of bitter self-recrimination. There was no strangeness in these symptoms. This was a sickness often experienced, this same terrifying realization that he had completely lost control of himself . . . throwing away what he wanted most . . . losing everything that ever mattered . . . no, not because of Lincoln Lord . . . blaming Lincoln Lord was a part of the madness. He had no one to blame but himself . . . going off half-cocked before he'd thought his way through . . . no reason why he shouldn't take the Coastal Foods account . . .

For an instant there was the temptingly dangled hope of recovery . . . "Mr. Phelps, I've been thinking this over and I'd like to change my mind" . . . no, he couldn't do that. The world didn't run that way . . . you had your chance and that was that.

6

Lincoln Lord was awakened by the speaking of his name, a sound that penetrated the deep sleep into which he had fallen. Groping through the foggy moment of returning consciousness, he thought that he was being paged. Then, picking up snatches of a distant conversation, he realized that he was being talked about by some member who was giving his luncheon guests a tour of the club and had stopped at the door of the reading room. Stealing a cautious glance over the high back of his chair, he confirmed his guess that the man with the booming voice was Nils P. Sampson, president of Alliance Surety, director of a dozen or more industrial concerns, and one of the most broadly influential members of the Greenbank Club.

Sampson and his two guests moved on for a quick look at the trophy room, an inspection so standardized that Lincoln Lord had no difficulty timing himself to bring about a seemingly accidental meeting in the corridor.

"Well, this is a coincidence!" Sampson said heartily. "Just talking about you, Linc. Saw your picture in the paper this morning. Want you to meet a couple of friends of mine from Pittsburgh — Sam Allaman of Metro Stores, Max Singmaster of Max-Mar-Co Chemical."

There was a round of handshaking, Singmaster recalling that they had met at a convention in New Orleans, the location a fortunate jog to memory, reminding him that Singmaster had been a member of the committee that had drafted an association code of ethics for the merchandising of household chemicals.

"Had your lunch, Linc?" Sampson asked. "How about joining us?"

For an instant he felt the secret embarrassment of having this contrived meeting pay off in a free lunch. It was a feeling easily enough put down, however, suppressed by the evident cordiality of the invitation and the no less apparent good fortune of this fine chance to get a little closer to Nils P. Sampson.

They were seated at a reserved table in the center of the grill-room, consideration of the menu delayed while Sampson got to the point of a story he was telling, another variation on the old one about the chambermaid and the big Texan, when a green-uniformed pageboy stopped at the table.

"Telephone call for you, Mr. Lord," the boy said.

"Get the number and I'll call back," he said.

"Katie said to tell you that it was a Mr. Anderson Phelps," the boy said in a voice that could easily be heard around the table. "And she said she thought it was something important."

He was still hesitant about taking the call, certain that all old Phelps wanted was a chance to compliment him again on his speech last night, but when he saw how impressed Sampson was at the mention of Anderson Phelps's name, he yielded and followed the pageboy to one of the telephone booths outside the billiard room.

7

Maggie Lord was returning to New York on the midafternoon train. Kip had offered to walk to the station with her, but she had sent him back to his classes and wandered alone down through the town, hoping that the strangeness of the scene, first the unfamiliar streets and then the deserted platform of the railroad station, would help her think clearly. She had accomplished the end that had brought her to Forgehill only to be confronted by an even more serious problem, one that seemed not only unsolvable but also a serious accusation that she had failed in her duty as both wife and mother. It seemed inescapable that she was somehow responsible for her son's attitude toward his father.

She had long since accepted the fact that Kip was not particularly bright — he had always had scholastic difficulty — and yet, today, more man than boy, he had shown a frightening keenness of perception. She had no idea how he had come to know that his father's speech last night had been one that Brick Mitchell had written for him three years ago; yet even if it were only a lucky guess, the fact that such a thought had entered his mind was proof that Kip regarded his father with shocking disdain.

Self-critically, she wondered if it were possible that she, in some un-realized way, had allowed her own doubts and fears to find their way into her son's mind and, once there, to grow to terrifying proportions. She was positive that there had been no occasion when she had said anything that Kip could possibly have interpreted as criticism of his father. On the contrary, she had frequently gone out of her way to encourage pride and respect. Could it be that Linc's weaknesses, so long her own closely guarded secret, had now become so evident that they were recognized by all, even a seventeen-year-old boy? Was that why no one would give Linc a job... because the magic of personality had worn so thin that it could no longer hide...?

No, no, *no!* Last night at the Chesapeake dinner... he'd never been more effective... the pin-drop silence while he was talking... all those men on their feet applauding him... signing pledge cards... "He was just wonderful, Mrs. Lord, just wonderful"... and it was true! If it weren't true, they wouldn't have said it... Dean Whittaker... Mr. Phelps... "You must be very proud of your husband, Mrs. Lord"... big men, smart men, pledging thousands and thousands of dollars that they would never have given if Linc hadn't talked to them... oh, why hadn't she been able to make Kip appreciate him!

Was it because...?

Terror snuffed out the question. She loved Linc! Of course she did! But did love demand blindness? Couldn't there be love and still a recognition of fault and weakness? Yes, yes, yes... you recognized and understood... and understanding was the very core of love. Or did there come a time after twenty years of marriage when you understood too well, when what you needed was not understanding but blind faith . . . that Linc would somehow get another job . . . start earning some money again . . .

She retreated hastily, shocked that she had let herself go so far as to think of love in such grossly materialistic terms . . . money wasn't important. And it was senseless to make it important . . . but it was to Linc . . . staying on at the Waldorf-Astoria . . . keeping Kip at Forgehill . . . an expensive lunch every day at the Greenbank Club . . . no, it was hopeless. Some men could adjust . . . not Linc. He'd go on and on. Where would it end? What did people do when they ran out of money . . . no, not ordinary people who could go to a relief agency . . . Lincoln Lord . . . ex-president of the Chemical Service Corporation, ex-president of the Luxor Pharmacal Corporation, ex-president of the Frazer Glass Company, ex-president of the Union Packing Company . . .

There was a tossed-away newspaper on the seat across the aisle and she reached for it, opening it to the want-ad pages, folding and refolding the paper until it was a tight packet exposing only the two columns of HELP WANTED FEMALE, a ritual that she knew she was performing without purpose. She had gone this far a dozen times in the last month, knowing that she could go no farther. Lincoln Lord would never be able to face the idea of his wife . . .

> SECRETARY to president big corporation
> Outstanding opportunity if experienced,
> responsible, versatile, able handle top-level
> contacts.

Yes, she could qualify for that one . . . experienced . . . twenty-one years with Lincoln Lord, president of five corporations . . . versatile . . . no one could argue that she hadn't been that. At least a job would be something to fill her days . . . no one would have to know who she was . . . Maggie Kipling again . . .

> SECY — GAL FRIDAY, small ofc, public rela-
> tions, 1 man. No routine. Oppty do some
> writing. 5 days, 9 to 5.

No, that couldn't be Brick . . . not nine to five . . .

Almost angrily, she dropped the paper and closed her eyes, feeling as if she had been tricked again by this conspiracy to keep her thinking about Brick. Last night it had been Mr. Phelps, insisting on asking her all those questions about the work that Brick had done all back through the years . . . and then it had been Linc, wanting to know everything that Mr. Phelps had said . . . Brick, Brick, Brick . . . and now Kip . . . even wanting to work for him . . . *Uncle Brick* . . .

Resolutely, she turned to the window. The train was back in the metropolitan area now, roaring through the apartment house canyons, the speed-blurred rectangles of endless windows inciting the memory of that first time she had come into New York, that very next day after she had graduated from Cornell, a brand new bachelor of science in Home Economics, so full of young-girl excitement about having won the *Hearthside* competition and a job on the magazine staff as an assistant to Beatrice Cullen, the most famous food editor in the country.

Her eyes searched the trackside for old landmarks. But there was no need for a stimulus to recollection. The memories of those first days in New York, twenty-five years ago, had been kept alive by the frequency with which her mind had gone back to them. They were more easily recalled than any others, less because they were nostalgically intriguing than because everything that had happened to her afterwards was directly traceable to that beginning. And, in this context, there was no prohibiting strangeness in thinking about Brick Mitchell. It was justified by normality, by repetition, by the realization that it was Brick who had given direction to her life. She would have been a very different person if she had never known him. It was Brick who had gotten her a job at Quincy Canning, and it was at Quincy Canning that she had met and married Lincoln Lord.

But there was more than that involved. It was Brick who had opened her eyes to reality, Brick who had given her the adult understanding that she had so badly needed when she had come down from Cornell, still a starry-eyed child living in a make-believe world. It was Brick who had taken her backstage and made her see that her castles in the air were only canvas scenery, that kings and queens and noble knights were only actors behind their grease paint, the puppets of an unknown director, their soaring words mouthed from a script that someone else had written.

Brick Mitchell had been one of the few men on the *Hearthside* staff, the only one who was eligibly single, the subject of constant interest on the part of all the questing females in the editorial offices. All this had been communicated to Maggie Kipling even before she had first noticed him on her third day at the office. He was escorting a group of advertising agency men on a tour of the *Hearthside* test kitchens and into a privileged personal conference with the famous Beatrice Cullen. He was a rumpled and rough-edged junior among slickly sophisticated seniors, his wiry thatch of red hair making him stand out from all the others, a look in his lazily narrowed eyes that seemed as if it should have been directed at a sweep of prairie and a herd of cattle instead of this little band of men so ponderously serious about making the American housewife overwhelmingly conscious of the merits of canned grated coconut. After he had gotten the coconut delegation safely installed in Beatrice Cullen's office, Brick had slipped out and wandered over to her desk, grinning down at her and asking, "So you're the new lady-in-waiting to the queen?" shocking her with what then had seemed cynical irreverence.

Even with Brick's hints, frequently repeated, it had taken her longer than should have been necessary to discover that her idol, Beatrice Cullen, was not all that she had imagined her to be, longer than would have been the case had she not been distracted by the endlessly exciting reality of living in New York and actually being a working member of the *Hearthside* staff, seemingly the total fulfillment of every dream that she had ever had. At first she had accepted Beatrice Cullen's eccentricities as glamorously appealing, her constant demand for praise and admiration no more than a justified request for what was due her. Every chance to do the great lady's bidding had seemed a queen-given chance to serve. Gradually, however, that feeling had faded as the invitations to Beatrice Cullen's Park Avenue apartment, so gratefully accepted at first, were revealed to be nothing more than orders to appear whenever there was work to be done. In the beginning she had been flattered when Beatrice Cullen had asked her to cook for what she referred to as "one of my famous little parties," a phrase as lightly used as her explanation that the drawing of food supplies from the *Hearthside* test kitchen was quite legitimate since every party was an "editorial project." There had been a pleasant excitement, too, when Maggie had found herself serving celebrities with recognizably famous names — there would have been more, she was sure, if she had only been able to read Walter Winchell more retentively — but, with increasing frequency as time went along, Beatrice Cullen's invitations were not for evenings when famous people were being entertained but for occasions when there was a basket of lingerie to be washed, a closetful of frilly clothes to be pressed, or a sink filled with a three-day accumulation of dirty dishes. At the slightest evidence of protest, Beatrice Cullen was always ready with an unanswerable question — "But, dear child, how can you possibly share our readers' point of view if you don't personally experience their annoying little problems?"

Long before the end of that first year she had begun to suspect that Beatrice Cullen was no more than a clever woman who hid an almost total lack of real ability behind a false front of bluff and pretense. Brick had laughed at her when she had first tentatively tested her suspicions. "Sure, old Bea's a phony. Haven't you noticed her in the test kitchen — so considerate, always asking for everyone's opinion before she sticks out her own neck? Don't you know why? The old fraud simply has no sense of taste at all. Blindfold her and she doesn't know what she's eating. Haven't you heard about the time that Mrs. Dempewolf mixed the cards on her and got her to approve a green turtle soup as a simply marvelous Beatrice Cullen improvement on ordinary chicken consommé? Of course, it was Mrs. Dempewolf who was fired when the story got out."

She had demanded to know then why Harvey Matrick, the editor, continued to put up with Beatrice Cullen.

"Don't you honestly know, Maggie? It's because he's a phony, too. Harvey's a frustrated writer who can't write a sentence that anyone in the world would want to read, so the only way he could get by was to let his hair grow and put on those big horn-rimmed glasses. Now he sits back and tells all the rest of us how we should write. You might as well face it, Maggie, they're the people who run the world — the phonies with the big fronts. We do the work and they get the credit."

Despite the ease with which she had accepted Brick's estimate of Beatrice Cullen, she had found it difficult to agree with him about Harvey Matrick. It was probably true that he could not write — after that night when Brick had talked about it she had noticed that the editor never attempted to compose even a single line caption for an illustration — and yet, strangely, she could always see a connection between the best things that Brick wrote for the magazine and something that Harvey Matrick had said in a staff conference. Once when Brick had an article that had been given featured position and a cover blurb, she had made the mistake of telling him how wonderfully she thought he had caught the editor's idea. He had flashed back angrily, arguing that what he had written bore no relationship to Harvey Matrick's original suggestion. And, seen through Brick's eyes, there was no doubt that his own creativity was dominant. Yet she could never accept Brick's premise that Matrick made no real contribution to the publication of the magazine. Somehow, in some undefined way, it was Harvey Matrick who made *Hearthside* the magazine that it was.

Beatrice Cullen's place in the scheme of things was much more easily seen as the months went by. There Brick had been right — Beatrice Cullen's basic talent was not editorial, yet there was real value to the magazine in her ability to impress advertisers and the representatives of their advertising agencies. They came to her constantly, soliciting her advice, bowing to her queenly judgment. Her best act, endlessly used, was to conclude a conference by announcing that the product in question, whatever it happened to be, held such fascinating possibilities that she simply had to be given time enough to work out its use in "one of my own famous recipes." That always got her off the spot, giving her a week during which someone on the staff — Maggie had drawn more and more of these assignments — could develop a recipe that would be branded as a "Beatrice Cullen original." The most amazing thing about her was that she had gotten away with it, not just once or twice, but time after time, year after year — except, of course, with Brick.

Yes, it was Brick who had seen through Beatrice Cullen . . . and Brick had known the truth about Linc, too . . . known it for so much longer than she had ever suspected . . . never hinting the way he really felt about him until that night on the boat coming home from the convention in Bermuda . . .

She flinched from the flame-hot edge of an inadmissible memory, hurriedly seeking retribution by grasping at the well-worn assurance that she had made the right choice when she had married Lincoln Lord, by-passing the small truth that Brick had never actually asked her to marry him. But she knew that it could easily have been managed. There had been a dozen times when the slightest encouragement would have produced a proposal, and she had more than once been tempted to offer it, coming closest of all on that night when they sailed across Chesapeake Bay in Mr. Quincy's old schooner, just Brick and herself, becalmed in the pre-dawn stillness and drifting up-bay with the flood tide. All that had held her back had been her doubt that she really loved him, a doubt resolved after she had fallen in love with Lincoln Lord. She knew then that she had never been in love before.

Confident as she was that she had never been in love with Brick, she had never been equally certain about his feeling toward her. The look that he had given her when she had told him that she was going to marry Linc had revealed something more than the disappointment of an adventuring male. There had been an instant when she had seen the sharp flinch from inner pain, quickly concealed and never again revealed, but it had haunted her for a long time afterward, troubling

63

her as she would have been troubled by any unwitting cruelty, causing her an indefinable embarrassment on the constantly recurring occasions when Linc had insisted on maintaining their old threesome relationship.

Years passed before she came to realize that her husband's desire to keep Brick close to him was something more than the continuation of an old friendship. She should have realized it right after the war, those first months at Rabson Foods, when Linc had told her that Brick was finally getting out of the Navy and that he was trying to hire Brick as his advertising manager. Her first impulse had been to object, a re-action aroused by her embarrassment at the way Linc had taken the Rabson job instead of going back to Quincy Canning, seemingly a disloyalty enhanced by the fact that she and her child had lived rent free in a home on Mr. Quincy's estate all during the war years. She had felt that Linc's position would be completely indefensible if, on top of everything else, he stole Brick Mitchell away from Quincy Canning. But when Linc had told her that Brick wasn't going back to Quincy in any event, and after she had realized how desperately Linc needed someone to help get Rabson's national advertising underway, she had withheld argument.

During those two years at Rabson, and almost as much so after the move to Union Packing, their home had been an annex of the office — recipes worked out and tested in her kitchen, copy written on the dining room table, displays worked out on the living room floor. She had been delighted with the chance that it gave her to participate in the excite-ment of her husband's life, yet she had sometimes felt an awareness of tension in Brick's presence, particularly on those frequent occasions when she was alone in the house with him, wishing that it were possi-ble in some subtle way to suggest to Linc that she would be more com-fortable if she didn't have to spend so much time working alone with Brick.

She had imagined that it would end when the move to Frazer Glass was made, almost welcoming the change for that reason. It was a big company, twice the size of Rabson and Union Packing combined, fully staffed, and since its business was the manufacture and sale of glass bottles and jars rather than food products, and since she had no special-ized knowledge or experience to contribute, she had thought that it would be the end of her participation in business affairs. Then, confus-ingly, she had felt herself left out and lonely, welcoming those evenings when Linc would bring Brick home with him, finding herself again drawn into the old threesome. There were more and more of those oc-

64

casions as the battle to get the new plant built had grown in intensity. Under the pressure of the need to help Linc, she had found herself trying to assist in any way she could, even learning to read blueprints and check cost estimates, studying textbooks on accounting, trying her best to make sense out of corporate finance and the involved maneuverings of the board of directors. More and more frequently she found herself knowing things that Linc did not. At first those occasions had given her some satisfaction. Then, however, pride in her own accomplishment began to be displaced by the disquieting fear that Linc was not digging into things as deeply as he should. Too often he accepted something that she and Brick had worked out without checking it himself or, in some instances, without seeming to really understand it. And yet she could never be sure. One incident had confused her more than any other. On the night before the directors' meeting where the question of whether or not a new plant was to be built had finally been decided, the three of them had been up until dawn — she and Brick in the dining room working on figures that would support the proposal, Linc in the living room supposedly writing the speech that he was going to make to the board. When she had finally gone in to give him some new figures, she discovered him sound asleep on the davenport. Awakened, he had sleepily glanced over what she and Brick had worked out, seemingly without comprehension. That next day she had lived through terrifying apprehension, positive that Linc would fail. Late in the afternoon, Brick had called her with the all but unbelievable news that the plant had been approved. "Linc was terrific, Maggie, just terrific," Brick had reported. "Had those guys spellbound. You know that stuff we worked out for him? He used every word and every figure — never slipped once. Don't ask me how he did it — I don't know — but he sure put it over!"

That incident and others like it made what she and Brick were doing seem worth while, a justification for the ever-increasing number of evenings that they spent together. Gradually, however, a disturbing change took place in their relationship. Before, Linc had kept Brick on a more or less even footing, accepting his advice and counsel as that of an equal. Then, slowly but noticeably, he began to exercise his presidential prerogatives, setting himself on a higher plane, demoting Brick to the status of an assistant left behind the scenes. It was, of course, thoroughly justified by corporate stature — Linc was the president of the company and Brick was his assistant — but it did mean that she and Brick, through a sharing of the same status, were joined by a common cause and interest. When the break-up came at Frazer Glass, it was Brick, not Linc, who told her what was happening — and it was Brick's fears and apprehensions that had wormed their way into her mind. That was the first time that Brick had ever openly cited Linc's weakness, on one of those nights during that last week when the Stacks crowd had finally gotten the battle for company control out in the open. "Maggie, you've got to do something to make Linc fight back," Brick had said. "He can't afford to go on changing jobs every time he runs into rough going. He's gotten away with it up to now, but it's going to catch up with him before long. No man can live with a record of having changed jobs every two or three years. This time he's going to have to stand his ground and fight. I've tried to make him see that but — well, I just can't. But you can talk to him, Maggie. He'll listen to you."

Out of loyalty to Linc, she had neither agreed nor disagreed, acknowledging nothing, but that had been the beginning of her realization of what was really wrong with her husband. There had, however, been no opportunity to do anything about it. That next day Linc had come back from New York and told her, a thunderbolt out of a clear sky, that he had been offered the presidency of the Luxor Pharmacal Company.

She had been surprised when Brick had finally decided to go along with Linc to Luxor Pharmacal, again Assistant to the President, but there was a marked change in personal relationship. Brick rarely came to their suite in the Waldorf Towers. Once, at Linc's suggestion, she invited him to a big party, but he had been obviously uncomfortable, having nothing in common with their new circle of friends, and she decided then that if Linc ever wanted Brick invited again, she would suggest that it not be for a big party. The suggestion had not been needed. Linc had never again asked that Brick's name be on a guest list.

As the months had gone by, there had been less and less mention of Brick's name, so pointed an omission from Linc's dinner table conversation that she began to suspect — with the hope that it was true — that he had finally broken the bondage of his dependence on Brick and was beginning to stand more squarely on his own feet. She could not be certain, however, because those occasions when Linc talked about what was going on at the office became progressively less frequent. She missed the sense of participation that she had had before, yet it had not seemed a calculated exclusion. Actually she and Linc were so infrequently alone that there was rarely a chance to talk about anything.

Almost every night there was a dinner party, every week end a social whirl — a life different from any they had ever lived before, but one to which Linc adapted himself with characteristic ease.

For her, however, those first two years in New York had been the loneliest of her life — and, in an increasing number of ways, genuinely alarming. Kip was in trouble at the Academy, giving her a concern that somehow she could not get Linc to share, any more than she could impress him with the certain fact that they were living beyond their income, a truth that he had dismissed with a shrug and a vague statement that there was something wrong if a man who made fifty thousand dollars a year couldn't afford to live decently.

Then, suddenly and without warning, she had been plunged again into a life that she had thought abandoned. One night, unexpectedly, Linc brought Brick home with him, asking her to cancel out a dinner party they were supposed to attend, telling her that he needed her to help Brick work out the speech that he was going to make at the annual sales convention in Bermuda. Despite the first flush of gratification at finding her help needed, a dangerous situation was suggested and then confirmed as she pieced together a picture of what was happening from listening to Brick and Linc attempt to plan a line of attack that would restore the confidence of the sales staff after a year in which, she gathered, almost the entire line of Luxor products had fallen off in sales because of a failure to match advertising pressure from competitive products. She did what she could to help Brick work up Linc's presentation, but she sensed from Brick's half-hearted attitude that he thought it was a lost cause, her own hope sustained only by the memory that Linc had so often managed to pull off a climactic miracle.

At the last minute, desperation unmasked, Linc had insisted that she go along to Bermuda to help develop any last-minute ideas that might occur to them. Hope had begun to fade the minute she walked into the hotel and sensed the atmosphere in which Linc was greeted by the older men on the sales staff, the branch managers and the key district representatives. When he rose to speak on the second day of the convention, there was only a polite spatter of applause, hardly that when he had finished. For the first time in her life, Maggie Lord saw her husband fail to sway an audience.

That night, in a wild flurry of suddenly changed plans, he had decided to fly back to New York alone, leaving her to return with Brick on the boat. Anxious to avoid facing the convention crowd, she had stayed in her suite. Late in the afternoon, Brick had tapped on the door, suggesting a drink. Rather than go out to the bar, she had invited him to come in and they had sat there for a long time in the gathering dusk. It was then, in an unguarded moment — or maybe it had been one drink too many — that she had let things drift to the point where Brick had been given an opening to say, "You don't have to ask me what's happened, Maggie. You know the score as well as I do. It's always the same old merry-go-round. You get on for a fast ride and then the music stops and you get off. But after a while you get tired of it. At least I do. He's in New York now, trying to grab off another job — resign instead of being sacked — and for your sake, I hope he can pull it off. But this time he'll need only one ticket on the merry-go-round. I've had all the Lincoln Lord I can take. Maybe you can stick it out, Maggie, but I can't."

And then he had sat there looking at her as if he were waiting for her to say that she, too, was ready to desert Lincoln Lord. She had known then that Brick had more than one drink too many, known it even more certainly when he had said, "If you think I'm letting you down, Maggie, maybe you'll forgive me if you know that I've stuck it out a lot longer than I would ever have done if it hadn't been for you. I wouldn't have gone along this last time except that — well, you know it anyway, so I might as well say it — I fell in love with you once and, like a dope, I guess I've never gotten over it."

The sense of guilt that was to later surround the memory of that evening was at least partly attributable to the recollection that she had offered no protest. Afterward she had tried to excuse herself by attempting to believe that she had been shocked into silence, a hopeless effort to banish the recollection that, at the moment, Brick's confession of love had seemed neither strange nor unexpected. What was to bother her most was the never to be answered question of how far she might have gone if Brick, shockingly, had not reached up to snap on the light. Afterwards there was only a blur of words, the memory of Brick standing at the door and saying that if she ever needed him, all that she would have to do would be to call him.

That was the last time she had seen Brick Mitchell, except for one glimpse that she had caught of him on the street, coming out of a Madison Avenue restaurant with a brassy blonde in a polo coat. Twice Linc had invited him to have dinner with them, once after he had finally made the Chemical Service connection and again just before they had left for Japan, writing him because he had been unable to reach him on the telephone. On both occasions Brick's response had been, as she had expected it to be, an almost formally worded note of regret. The second refusal had seemingly impressed Linc with the completeness of Brick's rejection, coupled as it had been with Brick's refusal to take on Chemical Service as a client for his new public relations agency. Last night, after overhearing her talking to Mr. Phelps, was the first time that Linc had mentioned Brick Mitchell's name in almost a year. Strangely, his attitude had not been at all what she had anticipated. There had been no evidence of resentment. Instead he talked about Brick as if he were an old friend who, entirely as their own fault, had been unfairly neglected. But there was no need to worry about it . . . Brick would never . . .

Suddenly a rattling thunder struck her ears. The train was underground now, making the homestretch rush into Grand Central. She took a handkerchief from her purse and dry-scrubbed a smudge of grime from the heel of her right palm which, without realizing it, she had rested on the window sill. She looked at her watch, seeing the position of the hands superimposed over the mental image of the hotel room. It was only three-thirty. Vaguely, without purpose or destination, she decided that she would walk over to Fifth Avenue before she turned north to the Waldorf-Astoria.

8

In the last hour, Brick Mitchell's progress toward a return to his office had been limited to a single city block. Around the corner from the Ashaway Building, he had stopped in a dingy little saloon, looking for a public telephone. Finding the booth occupied, he drifted to the bar and ordered a Martini. Now, his heels firmly hooked in the bottom rung of a high stool, his shoulders hunched, he sat staring down at the third glass that had been placed in front of him, empty, the glass shell a crystal ball in which he was seeing far more than he wanted to see.

The telephone booth was empty now, but he avoided looking at it, his field of vision circumscribed by the rim of the glass, a circular frame in which he saw, as if he were peeping through a round hole, the two-room suite occupied by Mitchell Associates, Inc. At the center of his vision, the vortex of his spinning thoughts, he saw the one person who, singlehandedly justified the plurality of the firm name. Wryly, not for the first time, he smiled at what had seemed, first spoken, an amusing wisecrack . . . "What do you mean — it's a phony name? I've got plenty of associates — six of 'em — and you're all of 'em."

And it was true. Tommy was all he needed — secretary, research assistant, consultant on public relations technique, advisor on feminine reactions, a knowing guide to the inner workings of most of the editorial offices in town, as good a second-string writer as the needs of any of his clients demanded — and, over and above all that, a reasonably good and more or less undemanding companion on those evenings when they rationed themselves to no more than two Martinis. The third was always one too many. And there had been a third and a fourth, and maybe even more on that night before the morning when she had gone to work for Mitchell Associates, Inc.

He had met her first when she had come to his office at Luxor Pharmacal, tough-minded and smart, knowing all the angles, swinging a big enough club so that she could get right to the top when she was digging a story about something that was going on in the pharmaceutical industry. As "Fanny Thompson" she wrote a syndicated mothers-and-babies column that could make or break any new product. As a second string to her strongbow, as "Dr. Frances P. Thompson" she did a new-products page for a medical magazine. To her personal acquaintances — there were, he had later discovered, an enormous number of them scattered all through the drug, pharmaceutical, medical and publishing worlds — she was invariably known as "Tommy," no one ever quite willing to accept "Fanny" as an appropriate name, much less to believe that she actually had, as he had since discovered, a doctor of medicine degree from Columbia.

She had come to his office several times during his Luxor Pharmacal days, but he had not seen her since until that day last year when, late on a rainy Sunday afternoon, he had gone into a little delicatessen up the street from the building where he lived. The only too evident fact that they were both buying something in an attempt to avoid eating alone in the week-end gloom of a restaurant had led to his picking up her packages along with his own. Then there had been the surprising discovery, so easily accepted as the workings of predestination, that she was living in an exact duplicate of his own quarters, the same number on the floor below, blank windows staring out at the same air shaft.

That evening had been, at least in its earlier stages, a matching of trials and tribulations — Tommy recounting her difficulties in attempting to write all day in the gray imprisonment of her apartment, he telling her about the trouble he was having to find a secretary whose range of talent was wide enough to encompass both making a clean draft of an already typed news release and answering a telephone without frightening away a prospective client.

He had awakened the next morning to the consciousness of a leather-tongued thirst, the odor of coffee and bacon, and Tommy's startling announcement that she had decided to take the job he had offered her. Very little pressuring had been necessary to make her admit that the offer was her own invention, an admission that did not, however, change her mind about its being a good idea. "It's the answer for both of us, Brick. You give me desk room and I've got a place to work. That's only an hour or two a day. The rest of the time I'm your gal Friday. Bad as I'll be, I'll be better than the ones you've had. Pay me what you've paid them and I'll feel like a kept woman, which is just about what my morale needs right now — only don't get the idea that there'll be any more little capers like this. From now on, you're the boss and I'm a gal who doesn't take her job home with her. Once in a while, maybe, I'll cook you a mess of spaghetti — but not on rainy Sunday nights with the boss mixing the Martinis."

He had known, although neither how nor why, that to agree would be a mistake, yet he had been as powerless to resist as, since, he had been unable to lessen his ever-growing dependence on her . . . that's what a man had to be afraid of more than anything else . . . needing someone else . . . had to stand on his own feet . . .

Tentatively he glanced right, momentarily substituting the long rectangle of the telephone booth's open door for the glassy circle of his cocktail glass . . . ought to call her . . . find out if anything had turned up . . . at least tell her where he was . . .

Why? He didn't owe her anything . . . nothing . . . no one . . . Lincoln Lord or anyone else. No point to calling her, anyway . . . she'd just want to know what happened . . .

"Hit it again, Mac."

The bartender's hand reached into the circle of his vision, breaking it, then restoring it.

9

Maggie Lord returned to their hotel room a few minutes after four o'clock. There was no recognizable sound from the other side of the door as she took the key out of her purse, yet some sixth sense told her that her husband was inside. She opened the door, surprised not to see him. Then, intuition justified, she heard the sound of running water and an instant later he burst out of the bathroom, flinging back a towel.

"Where in the world have you been?" he demanded, tight-reined excitement overriding a pause too short to permit her to answer. "Give me a hand, will you?"

She slipped out of her coat, anxiously asking, "What's happened, Linc?" fearing that she had let him down by being away from the hotel, pointlessly wandering the streets when, for the first time in weeks, there had been a chance to be of help to him. "I'm sorry, Linc. I could have been back an hour ago."

"Find me a clean shirt, will you, Mag?" he asked, no hint of recrimination in his voice. "You must have done quite a job on your boy friend last night."

"Who do you mean?" she asked blankly, quickly lifting a shirt from the top drawer of his dresser, then suddenly remembering that he had mentioned having a date this morning with Brooke Potter, the memory lost until now because she had given it no weight, thinking then that it had been no more than his excuse to get out of the hotel. "Did Potter have something that — ?"

He answered with a little burst of denying laughter. "I don't mean Potter." He snatched up a pair of shorts. "Phelps."

"Anderson Phelps?"

"He's after me to go into one of his companies."

"Oh, Linc, that's —" Her voice faded away, drained by her inability to find words that would describe this explosive release from the pent-up fears of a thousand nightmares.

"Or at least that's what it sounds like," he qualified.

"Tell me what's happened."

"He just asked if I was free to consider an important job — I said I was — and then he asked if I could see him at four-thirty."

"Four-thirty?" She shot an anxious glance at the clock on the bedside table. "How far do you have to go?"

"Go? I'm not going anywhere."

"Do you mean that he's coming here to see you? Oh, Linc, that does sound as if —"

"Look, Mag," he interrupted. "What did you tell him about me?"

"About you? Mr. Phelps? But we didn't talk about you, Linc. All we

72

talked about was —" She turned to find a pair of cufflinks, a diversion subconsciously grasped as an excuse for avoiding the mention of Brick Mitchell's name.

"You must have said something."

"Why?"

"He said that's what gave him the idea that I might be the man he was looking for — talking to you."

She shook her head, instinct blocking the acceptance of praise even before she consciously recognized the possibility that Anderson Phelps had tricked her last night, questioning her about Brick Mitchell's experience as a devious way of extracting information from her about her husband, a suspicion that started a hurried scanning of memory in a frantic attempt to recall anything she had said that might, in another context, leave her open to criticism.

"You must have said something about me," he repeated, even more argumentative, yet still without the slightest hint that there was a secret rancor hidden behind his apparent approval. "He seemed to know a lot about me."

"Why wouldn't he?" She forced an opening through the starch-stiffened cuff holes. "After all, you're not exactly unknown." The cufflink went through and she snapped it. "And he'd heard Dean Whittaker's introduction to your speech — your whole life's history."

"Someone must have told him about Sellcox & Lloyd. He called up there and got my résumé."

"Oh," she said, relieved. "If he had your résumé —"

"You know, it's a funny thing, Mag. This morning, on my way to the club, I just happened to walk by the building where they have their offices — Sellcox & Lloyd, I mean. It's hard to explain but I had the strangest feeling that I ought to stop in and see them — almost like a premonition. And do you know, I couldn't have been out of there more than ten minutes when Phelps called. He'd been trying to get me here at the hotel all morning."

"Oh, Linc, I'm terribly sorry. I've been out all day. I suddenly got the idea this morning of going up to —"

"Listen, Mag," he broke in, a welcome interruption. "When you talked to Phelps last night, did he mention any of the companies he's tied up with? Apparently he's quite an operator — in a dozen or more different businesses. I knew, of course, that he ran the Phelps Foundation but I thought that was about the size of it. I had no idea that he was as big a man as he seems to be. I talked to Nils Sampson about him after-

73

wards — I was having lunch with him when Phelps called, Sampson and a couple of men from Pittsburgh —" He stopped, abruptly returning to the question he had asked her. "Well, what did he tell you?"

"About — you mean the businesses that he's interested in?"

"Did he mention the names of any of the companies?"

"No, I — well, most of the time we were talking about this food-packing company —"

"Which one? What company?"

"Linc, you don't mean — ?" Again her voice drained away, again because of an explosive burst within her mind, now not the outrush of stored apprehension but the inrush of its return, the perpetually repetitious nightmare of endless wandering through a maze that always brought them to the same spot . . . it was the food company that had started Phelps talking about Brick . . . back in her life again . . .

Linc repeated his demand, seemingly blind to what was happening, asking her again for the name of the company.

"It might not be the same one," she said, the small-voiced expression of a desperate hope.

"What do you mean — the same one?" he demanded. "Tell me what he said — everything you can remember."

"Linc, I — I told you on the way home last night."

"I know, I know — about Brick," he said, brushing that aside. "But what company is it? If I know the name of the company I can check up and find out something about it before I talk to him."

Desperately she offered all that her memory volunteered. "The plant is somewhere in Jersey — I do remember that."

"Bridgeton? Vineland? Merchantville? If you can remember the town, I can make a pretty good guess as to what company it is. I knew all those Jersey canneries back in the Frazer Glass days."

She drove herself against the resistance of a mind subconsciously more anxious to forget than to remember. "No, it's not one of those towns. I'm sure it's over on the coast. I remember his saying that it was —"

"On the coast?" He gave her a puzzled scowl. "There aren't any canneries along the coast — at least any that are big enough to matter."

"Linc, do you remember — that time we were coming up from the canners convention with the Murdochs? We stopped there to see Betsey's folks."

"You don't mean Tern Beach, do you?" he said, driving ahead when she nodded. "There's no packing plant there. Tern Beach is out on an

74

island — nothing but a summer resort — like Barnegat and Beach Haven."

"But there's a town there just before you go across the bridge. Oh, it's right on the tip of my —"

"Goodhaven! And by golly, there *is* a cannery there! We made some special jars for them — something they were packing for the Gellman Stores. Don't you remember? It was that idea of Brick's, the jar with the big G blown into the side of it. We had some trouble getting it to work in their labeling machine. I remember talking to their production manager — what was the name of that company?"

She made no real effort to help him, knowing that the name would come to him in a moment, supplied as always by his incredible memory for anything and everything that had anything to do with a customer.

"Coastal Foods — that's it! Look, Mag — what did Phelps tell you about them? Try to remember everything he said. This is important."

"I know," she acknowledged, responding to the chance that he was offering to let her help him. "About all he said was that most of their business up to now had been packing private brands for one of the big supermarket chains —"

"That checks — Gellman Stores."

"But now they were going to bring out their own lines — advertise and promote them and build up a business for their own brands."

"Is that what Brick is doing for them — working on the promotion end of it?"

"I don't really know. Mr. Phelps did ask me a lot of questions about his experience in the food business —"

His wry smile was an interruption. "You know what it sounds like to me? All of those questions about Brick were just a cover-up. What he was really doing was pumping you about me. Don't you get it, Mag? Anything that you could say about Brick's experience was — well, everything Brick did was under my direction."

She nodded a grudging admission, the facing of fear.

He chuckled appreciatively. "Whatever you told him must have been right on the beam. He sounded as if he was really anxious to get me."

Startled, she saw his face suddenly darken, his smile extinguished like a blown candle. "What's the matter, Linc?"

"You don't suppose that's all he has on his mind, do you? Coastal Foods is nothing but — good grief, Mag, it's nothing but a little tin-shed cannery."

His exclamation struck with even more than its own weight, dislodging a memory that came crashing down upon her, recalling now that Anderson Phelps had said that his big problem was finding a sales manager ... *no, no, no* ... *sales manager of a little tin-shed cannery* ... *Linc back where he had started twenty years ago* ...

Vaguely, words lost, she was conscious that he was saying something about Coastal Foods, that it must have grown into a bigger company than it had been in his Frazer Glass days, a groping attempt to fight his way up from the depths. She rushed in with a helping hand, strengthened by desperation. "Linc, it must be some other company that he wants to talk to you about."

He nodded dully, agreement without belief.

"If it weren't a big job, Linc, he wouldn't be interested in hiring you. After all, he does know who you are and what you've done."

The light came slowly back into his eyes. "It doesn't necessarily have to be a big company. The important thing is — there are a lot of good opportunities with small companies, too."

"Of course there are," she agreed, then afraid that she was wrong in bolstering his hopes, making him all the more vulnerable to disappointment.

"And you know, Mag, it might be kind of fun to get my hands on an outfit that wasn't too darned big — small enough that I could get in myself and really make it run. If it was the kind of a company where there was a chance to — look, Mag, you'd better start getting dressed. You'll want to change, won't you? And he'll be here in ten minutes."

"You're not expecting me to talk to him?"

"Of course I am. Good grief, Mag, you're the one who really knows him. I've hardly met the man — just talked to him over the telephone, that's all. You were with him all evening. If you're there to break the ice —"

"Wouldn't you rather talk to him alone?"

"But he's expecting you — mentioned it two or three times. Look, Mag, you get dressed and I'll go down to check the suite to be certain that —"

"Suite?"

Startlingly, he snapped back, "What did you want me to do — meet him down in the lobby? Have him up here — entertain him in a bedroom?"

Bewildered by his sharply belligerent manner, she said nothing.

"What's wrong with it?" he demanded, his voice rising to an even higher pitch. "This is just temporary, isn't it — our being here? We always had a suite before, didn't we? All right, it's going to cost a few dollars. So what? Confound it, Mag, we have to take a few gambles."

"Of course we do," she said placatingly, relieved by the realization that his annoyance was self-centered, his argument directed not at her but at his own conscience, the sensitivity that was always aroused when he felt himself accused of pretense. "It won't take me long to change. What number is it? What suite did you get?"

She was momentarily blinded as she lifted her dress over her head, surprised when her eyes cleared to see him standing directly in front of her, his hands reaching out.

"I'm sorry," he said. "I didn't mean to blow off like that. It's just that — I guess I'm a little jumpy, that's all."

"It was my fault, not yours."

He shook his head. "I've been hard to live with lately."

"No you haven't."

"I know you've been worried, Mag. But this is going to work out. I know it. I can feel it. Things are breaking for us again."

"I know they are," she said earnestly. "But, Linc, if this particular job doesn't turn out to be what you want —"

"All right, maybe it isn't going to be something for the long haul. But it doesn't have to be. If it will just get us over the hump — tide us over until something better comes along —"

She stared at him, afraid to voice the protest that leaped to her lips ... didn't he realize the danger? He didn't dare take another job that wouldn't last ... his record was bad enough now ... another failure and no company would ever hire him again!

"Anyway, it will get us out of here," he said with a claustrophobic look around the bedroom's crowding walls.

Involuntarily she glanced toward the little desk, the pad corner stuffed with this month's bills ... maybe he was right ... face it ... he had to do something. But it would kill him ... sales manager of a little tin-shed cannery ... Lincoln Lord, President of the Luxor Chemical Company ... Lincoln Lord, President of the Frazer Glass Company ...

She sat on the edge of the bed, stripping her stockings, glancing up to see him lift from the window sill the framed photograph taken when he had visited the White House with the Japanese delegation.

His eyes caught hers and he said self-consciously, "I thought I'd take along some of this stuff — scatter it around so that the suite looks a little more lived in."

77

She looked down again. "You didn't tell me, Linc — what suite did you get? Where do I go?"

"Down at the end of the hall — the big one — 12A."

"I'll be there as soon as I can," she said, getting up from the bed and going to the closet for a dress, watching him in the door mirror, easily anticipating the other things that he would take . . . yes, the engraved sterling bowl that had been presented to him when he made that speech in Boston . . . the miniature replica of the Columbia Society plaque . . . and of course the brassy little statuette that a trade magazine had once awarded him . . . *Man of the Year in American Marketing* . . .

"Did you happen to notice what kind of cigarettes he smoked last night?"

"He doesn't smoke," she said over her shoulder in what was almost the voice of her subconscious, the response of a mind trained for twenty years to automatically register and retain such important bits of socially helpful information. "He drank Scotch," she added. "And he asked the waiter to be sure that it was Ballantine."

"Good," he said approvingly, opening the door, reaching back to pick up the collection that he had assembled on the edge of his dresser, a double handful of trinkets that seemed, as the door closed behind him, the pitifully inadequate stage properties of a silly charade.

Yet, letting her eyes wander around the room after the door closed, she was conscious of how much he had taken away. There was a strange barrenness now and her awareness of it made her realize how important that handful of souvenirs had become in their lives. That thin scattering of trophies was all that it took to give a hotel room the illusion of a home . . . but it would take more than that to fool Anderson Phelps . . .

A new fear flashed, grounded in the memory of what Phelps had whispered to her last night about some table-hopper who had greeted him too fulsomely . . . "Nothing but a four-flusher who thinks I'm fool enough to fall for his trying to butter me up" . . . if he got that impression of Linc . . . no, it wouldn't be true . . . but if he did . . . deciding against him and not offering him the job . . . rejected even by a little tin-shed cannery . . . the last straw . . . no that couldn't happen! If Linc lost his confidence in himself . . . no, no, no . . . Phelps had to offer him the job . . . he *had* to!

Escaping into a mind-blanking flurry of activity, she tossed away the dress that she had taken from the closet and, hurriedly fanning her

78

fingers across the top of the hangers, searched out the black sheath that she had bought in Hong Kong.

10

Slumped in the back seat of his ancient Rolls-Royce, Anderson Phelps felt himself pressed down by his years. He so frequently prefaced some personal observation by saying, "When a man gets to be sixty —," that he had almost accepted it as a perpetual truth, unchangeable by the passage of time. This afternoon he was all but ready to admit that two years ago he should have started saying, "When a man gets to be seventy —"

There had not been, he was positive, any deterioration of mental acumen, a fact pleasantly supported by the knowledge that he had made more money last year, even after tax, than in any year of his life. Physically, too, he was still capable of summoning, when it was needed, a full quota of driving energy. He had started work at six o'clock this morning and he was quite certain that no man of forty, or even of thirty, could have more vigorously pursued his day-long investigation of Lincoln Lord's record. What was now weighing him down with a consciousness of age was an awareness of the ever-heavier burden of accumulated responsibilities. There seemed to be some sort of natural law that for every success a man was forced to assume some balancing obligation. When you had lived so long and scored so many successes, the burden became almost too heavy to bear.

This was no new thought, nor was the situation in which he now found himself one that he had not tried to avoid. Years ago he had decided that before any company in which he had an investment reached the point where it might become a burdensome responsibility he would dispose of his interest. He had done so with Coastal Foods. Three years ago he had sold back all of his stock to Sol Zurich. Although he had made a handsome capital gains profit, cashing in had been an incidental consideration. What had motivated him to get out was his conviction that Coastal Foods was about to be attacked by the most dangerous of all small-company ailments. When a previously sound and sensible man — and Sol Zurich had been that — started building a fancy factory, the diagnosis was positive, the prognosis inescapable. Next there would be a burning fever to start national advertising. That would demand a big sales organization and all the other high-overhead trimmings, inevitably including that newest fad in profit-wasting, some-

79

thing that would be called a "research program." From then on out, what had been a first-class investment would deteriorate into nothing more than another listed stock paying a grubby little four or five per cent dividend.

Sol Zurich had died before matters had gotten to that sorry state — the cancer in his body had outrun the deterioration of his company — but he had, nevertheless, already completed his show-off factory, hired a young man to make a "market survey," and spent a sizable sum of money supporting a crackpot scientist who was supposed to be developing a new baby food.

Watching from afar after he had sold his stock, Anderson Phelps had found himself saddened that he had lost such a good friend — his investment in Sol Zurich had been one of the most profitable he had ever made — yet he had thought himself well out of it. He had not suspected that his escape was an illusion. Sol Zurich had outwitted him. In his will he had left instructions for his widow, telling her that if Coastal Foods ever got into trouble she was to call upon Anderson Phelps for advice and help. Sol Zurich had been no fool. He had known that if you were a Phelps, the son of George D. and the grandson of Thaddeus S., there was no way to shrug off an obligation to the widow of a man who had been, for over twenty years, such a profitable friend. A gentleman was a gentleman.

Burdened though he felt himself, Anderson Phelps had not thought that Mrs. Zurich would call so soon nor that her demand would be so great. Of all the difficulties he had imagined lying ahead of the Coastal Foods Company, he had never anticipated any such catastrophe as the loss of the Gellman Stores business. The company had been built upon that foundation and without it Coastal Foods was little more than a ghost, its substance lost. The only hope now was to find a man who could somehow fill the cannery with business again. The prospect was so poor that he would not have invested a cent of his own money on the bet that it might be done, yet he had promised Mrs. Zurich that he would do his best — and a Phelps promise, as three generations of Wall Streeters had known, was better than an AAA bond.

He had decided, immediately after his talk with Brick Mitchell, that if he could deliver Lincoln Lord to Mrs. Zurich, he would have discharged his debt, finally and fully, once and for all. The trouble, he now recognized, was that Lord was going to be a hard man to hire, the difficulty all the greater because he himself was so ill-fitted to the task of selling him the idea of accepting the presidency of the Coastal Foods

Company. In order to make a good deal with any man you had to understand him, and he knew that his understanding of men of Lincoln Lord's type was hopelessly inadequate.

Personally he would not have hired Lincoln Lord to be president of any company in which he had a substantial investment — but that was no argument against Lord, because the kind of company that needed him, as Coastal Foods obviously did, would never get a penny of Phelps's money. He had long ago decided, building upon inherited experience, that his investments would be confined to owner-managed small companies that made products so staple in character that they could be sold without gambling large sums on advertising, research, product development, or any of the other potential wastes of profit. He had no inclination to argue against such practices — for some companies they were obviously necessary — but since he had the right of choice, he would invest his money where he knew it would pay off. That was what he had done — and that was why, today, he found himself so handicapped by inexperience, so uncertain as to what might induce Lincoln Lord to accept the presidency of the Coastal Foods Company.

He had occasionally been called upon to select, or help to select, a new manager for one of his companies. The kind of men he had picked had always been the kind of men who had made the most money for him — square-jawed drivers who could bull their way through and get out production, tough enough to stand up to union organizers, shrewd enough to drive a good bargain with suppliers and customers; over-all, men who commanded respect through competence, personal force and the ability to do any job around the plant themselves. Such men were not always easy to find but, once found, they could usually be reached by appealing to their two primary motivations — a love of possession and a lust for power. The first could be satisfied with salary, bonuses, and a chance to acquire a substantial ownership through stock purchase; the second, by giving them a free hand to run and rule, a particularly tempting prospect to a candidate whose experience had been in some over-organized big corporation.

With a man like Lincoln Lord, however, Phelps was beyond soundings. He knew that there were such men around and that more and more of them were rising to high positions, not only in industry but in other fields as well. But their presence did little to reveal character. They were, he sometimes thought, a natural product of a world gone soft, an age in which "getting along" was all that really mattered, when

81

company presidents were no longer judged on their ability to strike fire in the hearts of their men as they led them into battle but rather on their talent for tranquillizing everyone into a state of nonresistant conformity to some scientifically determined pattern of human behavior. And it worked. He couldn't argue about that. He even thought he knew why — the welfare state, taxes, big government, big corporations, big unions, the enervating fat of too much prosperity — but what he could not comprehend was what motivated these new leaders. What did they want? If he could only understand that, there might be some possible approach to Lincoln Lord.

The car swung west now, off the East River Drive and heading for the Waldorf-Astoria. Anderson Phelps sat upright, his spine stiffened by a feeling of guilt for having gone as far as he had with Mrs. Zurich. When she had first called him he had told her that all Coastal Foods needed was a good sales manager. Now, almost unexplainably, he had gotten himself into this Lincoln Lord business. An hour ago over the telephone, he had reversed himself by telling her that what she really needed was a man of Lord's caliber, and that he would, of course, have to be given the presidency and full authority. She had not only agreed to that but also to his argument that matching the fifty thousand dollars a year that Lord had been paid at Luxor Chemical would be a cheap enough price to pay for getting Coastal Foods back on its feet again. If she had only argued with him, he would have an out — but she hadn't. Now he either had to deliver or be made to look like a fool — and all he had on his side of the bargaining table was a title and a paycheck — and it was almost certain not to be enough, not with a man like Lincoln Lord.

He slumped back again, wondering how he had gotten himself into this hopeless situation, trying to trace the origin of his mad behavior. As nearly as he could recall, the thought had first struck him last night at the Chesapeake dinner when Mrs. Lord had said, or at least implied, that she and her husband had spent the happiest days of their life when he'd been working in that little Quincy cannery down in Maryland. That was what had given him the foolish hunch that Lord might still be a small-company man at heart. After that, one thing had led to another. Every one of the business connections that Dean Whittaker had mentioned in his introduction to Lord's speech had opened up an avenue of easy inquiry, seemingly a conspiracy extended when Miss Peabody, whose memory was hardly notable, strangely recalled that they already had in their files a complete résumé on Lincoln Lord, sent down by Sellcox & Lloyd only a few days ago. The most damaging coincidence, however, had been the ready availability of Brick Mitchell, the best of all sources of information about Lord — and it had been Mitchell, more than anyone else, who had made him certain that Lord was the man he wanted to get for Mrs. Zurich.

Mitchell had convinced him that, despite surface evidence to the contrary, there must be some underlying strength in Lincoln Lord's character. If Lord were no more than he seemed, one of these keep-everyone-happy fellows, Mitchell would have given him unqualified approval. There was no surer indication of strong leadership than the grousing of assistants like Mitchell. He was an "idea man" and, like all of his kind, a natural boss-hater. They could never understand that their ideas, precious as they were to them, weren't worth a tinker's dam until a stronger man picked them up and did something with them — and that, obviously, was what Lincoln Lord had done.

11

The door of the suite stood ajar and Maggie Lord opened it cautiously, uncertain as to whether or not Anderson Phelps had yet arrived. Edging into the small foyer, she saw that her husband was still alone, the telephone instrument to his ear, silent except for an occasional acknowledgment, saying nothing that revealed who was on the other end of the line.

She moved to the center of the big living room, looking around her, amazed at how effectively the illusion had been created that this was their home . . . the White House picture on the window sill . . . the copy of *Business Week* lying open over the wide arm of a chair . . . waste paper in the basket . . . old letters stuffed in the pigeonholes of the desk . . .

Startled, she saw her own photograph standing on the gold-lacquered credenza that dominated the near wall of the room, unaware until now that it was one of the things that Linc had brought from their bedroom. It was the leather-framed photograph that he had long ago selected for his office, and in the days when he had had an office, she had sometimes thought of it standing on his desk and felt a warming sense of inclusion. Now there was the barely resisted impulse to snatch it up and hide it away, a denial of participation in this pretense of affluence . . . this cheap trickery . . .

Her mind froze in the cold terror of convicted disloyalty, a cessation of thought flow that forced her to see and examine the content of her irrational behavior. A moment ago, walking down the hall, she had blindly accepted the justification for everything that Linc had done, pledging unquestioning support, resolving to help him in any way that she could. And now, at the first test, there was this feeling of rejection and disassociation ... maybe it *was* her fault that Kip felt the way he did about his father ... *Uncle Brick never does anything just to make somebody like him* ... no, Kip was wrong! Everyone did things to impress people ... you had to! Linc was right ... they'd always had a suite like this until a few weeks ago ... there was no difference between renting a suite for a day ...

Behind her she heard the telephone receiver clatter down, the sound of a hypnotist's finger snap, the signal for release. She turned, her eyes searching for orientation.

"It's Coastal Foods all right," Linc said. "Phelps has been interested in it for years. The owner died about six months ago — a man named Zurich — Sol Zurich."

"Who were you talking to?"

"I called Sid Arnauth. You remember him, don't you — that chain store meeting at Hot Springs two or three years ago? He's president of Gellman Stores now. Married old man Gellman's daughter. Saw him a few days ago at an art auction."

"What did he tell you?"

"Funny thing," he mused, his brow furrowed. "Sid said it was a wonderful little company — one of their best suppliers. Told me what a close personal relationship there'd always been between Coastal Foods and Gellman Stores — his father-in-law and this man Zurich. But then he transferred the call to the man who handles their Coastal Foods contact — a fellow named Rubin — and he told me that they'd just cut off Coastal Foods and weren't giving them any more business."

"But why would Mr. Arnauth — ?"

"I don't know. But it sounds to me like Coastal Foods must be in some kind of trouble. That's probably why they're looking for a president."

President? Didn't Linc know that all Phelps was looking for was a sales manager ... hadn't Phelps told him ... ?

"Linc, if this doesn't turn out to be something you really want —"

The telephone rang and he answered it. "Yes indeed. Send Mr. Phelps right up."

She made another attempt to warn him, but again there was an interruption, the buzzer at the back door of the suite, and he jumped up as if it were a quickly grasped excuse for escape. "That's the boy with the whiskey and stuff."

"I'll get it," she offered.

"No, take care of Phelps for a minute. I want to make another telephone call." He started for the narrow hall that ran back to the kitchenette, tossing back as he reached the archway, "What's the name of Brick's outfit? Mitchell Associates, isn't it?"

"You're not going to call Brick?" she asked, an exclamation dangerously close to a cry of terror.

"Why not?" he demanded. "If Phelps has been talking to him, he'll know something about the company."

Her protest was cut off as he closed the door behind him, leaving her with the feeling of helplessness that had, over these last few years, become almost her normal state of mind . . . the same way it had happened before . . . Linc running away . . . the blind escape . . . the easy way out . . . always calling for Brick . . .

But would Brick help him? . . . no . . . *Maybe you can stick it out, Maggie, but I can't . . . I've had all the Lincoln Lord I can take . . .*

The doorbell rang, an explosion in her consciousness, and with the perversity of a mind spinning out of control, she found herself confronted again with the fear that Anderson Phelps would decide against Linc . . . if he couldn't get even a sales manager's job . . . if Phelps discovered that this suite was a four-flusher's bluff . . . no, she could handle old Phelps!

She waited through a poise-restoring moment and then, setting a smile, opened the door, anticipating the man she had come to know last night at dinner, the jaunty little spats-and-carnation dandy whose counterpart she had seen a hundred times on Sunday mornings, walking upper Fifth Avenue in a Chesterfield coat and a black Homburg, swinging a gold-headed Malacca stick. The man framed in the doorway was not that man at all. This was a different Anderson Phelps, unimaginable anywhere except on Wall Street, and even there he would have stood out as almost a caricature of the cautious banker, thin-lipped and suspicious.

"Oh, do come in, Mr. Phelps," she said, forcibly sustaining the brightness of her smile. "I had no idea when I left you last night that I'd have the pleasure of seeing you so soon again."

"Nor did I," he said, entering quickly, his manner that of a man steeled against distraction, averting his eyes, telling her that he was not fool enough to be taken in by guile.

"Linc had to step out for a moment but he'll be right back," she explained, starting to help him with his coat.

He rejected her assistance and she offered no protest when he draped his banker-gray topcoat over the bench in the little entrance foyer, deciding that it was wiser to risk a minor discourtesy than to take a chance on allowing him to see a completely barren coat closet. There were enough other clues to destroy the pretense that this suite was actually their own, a hundred little betrayals that Anderson Phelps would certainly see as he stood now, critically surveying the living room.

"Pleasant apartment you have, Mrs. Lord," he said, advancing to the window. "You must have a nice view."

It took a moment for her to orient herself before she could be sure of which direction the suite faced, an uncertainty that sharpened her awareness of Phelps's capacity for deviousness . . . last evening . . . all of those questions . . . pretending that he was interested in Brick . . .

Parting the glass curtains, Phelps said, "Yes, very nice indeed," turning then to confront her. "You've lived here for some time, Mrs. Lord?"

"Here in the hotel?" she asked. "Not so long this time — only since we got back from Japan."

Inadvertently, but not entirely without consciousness, she glanced toward the White House news picture and when she saw that Phelps's eyes had taken a cue from hers, she felt encouragement . . . perhaps after all, it would be possible to fool him . . . if Linc would only come!

"Yes, very pleasant," Phelps said, an abrupt return to the moment of his entrance, again surveying the room. "I imagine that this is quite convenient — an apartment right here in the city. I've a sister who's done it all her life — Gramercy Square. Insists that it's the only civilized existence. But then, of course, she's a confirmed New Yorker. Couldn't possibly imagine herself living anywhere else."

"I know," she acknowledged. "There are people like that."

"But you're not one of them?" Phelps stabbed, a quick thrust that could only mean that he knew this suite was a false front . . . or was he asking her if she was willing to leave New York?

"I like New York," she began, a knife-edge balancing of word and tone. "But I don't feel that — well, we've lived a number of different places and I've liked them all."

86

Too late she realized that she had given Phelps an opening to say, as he did, "Yes, you have done a bit of moving around, haven't you?"

She was groping for a reply when she heard footsteps in the back hall, giving her a welcome chance to avoid answering, saying quickly, "Here's Linc now."

Lincoln Lord stood in the arched doorway, hesitant for an instant, and she tried to catch his eye with a secret warning that Anderson Phelps was already suspicious and would have to be handled with extreme care. But his eyes avoided hers. He strode across the room, a stranger, not at all the Lincoln Lord who was so cleverly adept at making everyone like him. His greeting of Phelps was curtly clipped, his manner coldly disinterested . . . Brick had refused to talk to him! Yes, that was probably what had happened . . . Linc had been hurt . . . that was why he was so different.

Judged against expectation, Anderson Phelps's voice was surprisingly warm, almost solicitous. "Nice of you to be willing to talk to me, Mr. Lord."

"Not at all," he said flatly. "Sit down, Mr. Phelps. Wherever you're the most comfortable."

The financier made a strange choice, reaching for one of the small straight-backed chairs that flanked the credenza.

She sat on the edge of her chair, alerted to go out and make the drink that she fully expected Linc to propose. But he said nothing, his silence was as out of character as his slumped pose on the davenport.

"I don't want to waste any more of your time than necessary, so I'll get right to the point," Phelps said tautly, taking a small black notebook out of his inner coat pocket and fumbling it open, seemingly relieved to find a reminder of what he had planned to say. "I do hope, Mr. Lord, that you didn't think me unnecessarily secretive when I talked to you over the telephone. I would gladly have revealed the identity of the company that's involved had I felt myself free to do so. Unfortunately, my position was then that of an intermediary without authorization." He paused as if expecting the phrase to elicit a smile. Disappointed, he explained, "I couldn't place a proposition before you without approval — and yet, on the other side, it seemed quite pointless to secure that approval without at least some preliminary indication that you might conceivably be available. I do hope you didn't think that I was being stuffy about it?"

"Not at all," Lincoln Lord said again, the same words spoken in the same flat tone.

87

Phelps turned a notebook page, plainly an act of nervous preoccupation, because he did not look at it. "Even if I had been free to mention the name of the company, I'm afraid it wouldn't have struck a very responsive chord. It's not the sort of company that attracts a great deal of attention — privately owned, no advertised products or anything of that sort. I daresay you've never heard of it —" He hesitated, his voice suspended, the die about to be cast "— the Coastal Foods Company?"

Maggie Lord was watching for her husband's reaction. It was almost imperceptible, not the slightest change of expression around his eyes, only the movement of his lips as he asked, "Don't they have a plant down at Goodhaven?"

She shifted her attention to Anderson Phelps, catching his look of surprise and then the quick transition to relieved inquiry. "Then you do know something about the company?"

"I've heard a little gossip, that's all."

Apprehension raised the key of Phelps's voice. "Gossip? Recently?"

"They're in rather serious trouble, aren't they?"

"Trouble?"

"Haven't they lost the Gellman Stores business?"

The financier's face froze. "Where did you hear that?"

"Then it's not true?"

"It's true enough," Phelps said tightly. "But I had no idea that the gossips had gotten hold of it yet."

"Perhaps it was just speculation — someone's guess."

"I'd hardly think so."

"After all, Mr. Phelps, it wasn't too difficult to anticipate, was it? Gellman got a cannery of their own when they merged with Silver Crescent. You could hardly expect them to go on having their private brand specialties packed by an outside plant."

Again watching the financier's face, she saw the slow transition from shock to awed respect, the deferential smile that broke as his lips parted. "You're very well informed, Mr. Lord. I knew, of course, that you'd been associated with the food business at one time in your career, but I must confess that I'm surprised to find you so closely in touch with current developments."

There was something about Anderson Phelps's tone and manner — a quality of crumbling, of retreat, a bowing to superiority — that she found incomprehensible until, suddenly, awareness of her prior lack of understanding struck her like a crashing accusation of stupidity ... how could she have been such a fool! It was so easily seen now ... Linc was doing this purposely ... outmaneuvering Phelps in a struggle for the upper hand ... and he had won! There was not the slightest doubt now that whatever Anderson Phelps had to offer would be Linc's for the taking. But did he want it ... sales manager ... ?

She stole a glance at her husband, fearing that she might reveal how badly she had underestimated him, acknowledging the grossness of her error yet trying to find it excusable because there had been so few chances of late to see him in action when anything important was at stake. But the validity of that excuse was destroyed by the realization of how many times there had been when she had been too strongly tempted to underrate him ... last night, watching him dress for the Chesapeake College dinner ... the fishbelly whiteness of his soft-muscled body as he had stood in his shorts, fumbling his way through a halting rehearsal of his speech ... so willing to believe the worst of him that later, when she had seen him standing on the platform, lean and hard and sure-voiced, she had thought of it as the false face of deception ... yes, and when he had left the room only a few minutes ago, she had accused him of weakness, of running away, of taking the easy way out. No, that had been the false image ... this was the real man, the man she had fallen in love with, the man she had married ... *this was Lincoln Lord!*

Caught off guard, it took her a moment to respond when he suddenly spoke to Phelps, a victor graciously saving the vanquished from further groveling, glancing at his watch and asking, "Wouldn't a drink be in order? It's getting to be about that time of day."

On her feet, she asked, "What will it be, Mr. Phelps — Ballantine, one lump of ice, and just a little water?"

He blinked his surprise, making her feel that, if anyone were guilty of trickery, she was the one who stood convicted.

"Linc?"

"Thank you, dear — my usual," he replied, the code for a glass of plain ginger ale, all that he ever drank when he was engaged in an important negotiation, a positive indication that he was far more interested in Coastal Foods Company than he was allowing Anderson Phelps to know ... but was there ginger ale?

She found a bottle on the tray the waiter had left in the kitchenette, clinching proof that everything had been planned in advance ... Linc was amazing ... wonderful! But what would happen when he found out that all Phelps had to offer was a sales manager's job?

Hurriedly she filled glasses and rearranged the plate of canapés that he had ordered, returning to the living room as rapidly as possible, drawn not only by the realization that what was happening might reshape her life but also by a feeling of compassion for her husband, a desire to ease, by sharing, the decision that he would have to make, submerging his pride and taking a job that meant going back to where he had been twenty years ago . . . sales manager of a little tin-shed cannery . . . the gain of a whole lifetime lost. But there was no alternative . . . what else could he do?

Short though her absence had been, the atmosphere in the living room had changed pronouncedly. Anderson Phelps had moved to the davenport and, sunk low in the downy cushions, was looking up with abject pleading, shaking his head in advance rebuttal as he waited for a chance to speak.

An opening came and the financier leaped at it. "Quite so, Mr. Lord — granted — but if you don't mind my saying so, you're proceeding from two wrong assumptions. In the first place, Coastal Foods is not, as you put it before, in serious trouble. Yes, they've lost the Gellman Stores business — quite true — but Coastal Foods is still in a very strong position. This is not the situation that you so often find in a small company, Mr. Lord — having to start from scratch and lift yourself by the bootstraps. The factory's in excellent shape, one of the best small food-processing plants in the country. And it's fully operational, staffed with one of the best production organizations you'll find anywhere."

"So I understand," Lincoln Lord granted.

"Furthermore," the financier pressed on, "bringing out a line of Coastal products — their own brands — is not a desperation move. Please believe me when I tell you that it's something that's been planned for a long time. I'll grant you that it's suddenly become very important — quite so — but it's no new idea. So Sol Zurich was very much aware of the danger of having so much of his volume concentrated with Gellman Stores. As long as three years ago he hired a very able young man to study various market possibilities. For even longer than that he's supported a research program. One of the new products they've developed is a baby food —"

She had been waiting to hand the financier his drink, not wanting to interrupt him. Now he saw her and cut himself off in mid-sentence, thanking her profusely, then apologizing at some length for not taking one of the canapés. Finally, attempting to bridge the long gap, he had difficulty in picking up where he had left off.

"You'd mentioned a Mr. Zurich," Lincoln Lord reminded him. "I take it that he was the man who had been running the business for you?"

"For me?" Phelps said, startled. "Oh, no! I have given you the wrong impression, haven't I? It's not *my* company, Mr. Lord, not at all, not in any way. Yes, I did at one time hold some Coastal Foods stock, but the business was so profitable that Sol Zurich had no difficulty in buying me out. You may ask why I was willing to sell such a profitable investment — and also why I'm here talking to you. The answer is the same in both cases. You see, Mr. Lord, Sol Zurich was a friend of mine, the kind of a friend that —" He paused uncertainly. "I don't want to impose on your hospitality, Mr. Lord, but if I may be given time enough to briefly sketch the background —"

"Take all the time you want," Lincoln Lord said, the gracious host. "We've nothing on until dinner, have we, Mag?"

She shook her head, marveling at how skillfully he was keeping Phelps on the defensive.

The financier took the first sip of his drink, swallowing and then exhaling. "Thank you." He put the glass down. "My friendship with Sol Zurich goes back a great many years. It was right after the war — the first one, of course — the Kaiser Bill affair. I'd come back with a bit of lung trouble — a touch of poison gas at St. Quentin — the second battle of the Marne, you know? It was nothing really serious, but my father insisted that I spend the summer recuperating down at Tern Beach. Or at least that was his excuse for keeping me away from his office. He was an odd sort of man — my father. Had the most enormous ego. I must say that it was largely justified as far as financial acumen was concerned — yes, quite — but rather strangely he had no confidence whatsoever in himself as a father. It was inconceivable to him — or so he always made it seem — that he was capable of siring a son who had inherited even the smallest part of his own ability."

Maggie Lord found her husband's barely audible chuckle oddly bland, and she wondered why he didn't cut in to keep Phelps from wandering too far afield with what was plainly an old man's reminiscence, so often repeated that he could not bring himself to recount the story without all the detail.

"In any event," Phelps continued, "the circumstances were such that I was strongly impelled to prove myself an astute investor — on my own, of course. I had a little capital, no great amount but still enough to give me a bit of rope, and I started making some investments around

Tern Beach. The automobile was just getting reliable enough so that a week-end jaunt to the beach was a practical undertaking and I judged that there would be an inevitable appreciation in the value of shore property. So I bought a number of plots of land. One of them was down in the harbor area. It had an old crabhouse on it — nothing but a tumble-down shack, really — but after I returned to New York in the fall, I received a letter from a young man who wanted to rent it. He wrote that the hotel where he had been working during the summer had closed for the season, and that he was trying to tide himself over the winter by starting a little lunch counter for the commercial fishermen. There were quite a few winter workers around in those days — Tern Beach was something of a sea food center — and the idea of an eating place seemed sensible enough. So I wrote to the local bank that was acting as my agent and instructed them to tell this young man that he could go ahead — although, I must say that I had no idea how that old shack could ever be turned into a restaurant that even a Portuguese fisherman would patronize."

"And that young man was Sol Zurich?" Lincoln Lord suggested, skillfully guiding him back to the main line of his story.

Phelps nodded. "But some months were to elapse before I met him. He'd paid his rent regularly — ten dollars a month, as I recall — and there'd been no reason to go around and see him. Thus I was completely unprepared for what was about to happen." He took a punctuating sip of his drink. "Father always held court on Saturday morning at the breakfast table, a practice that prevailed whether we were in town or down at Tern Beach. Every Saturday morning without fail, all the members of the family were confronted with that week's accumulation of sins and transgressions. On this particular Saturday I was the prime offender. I was accused — and simultaneously judged guilty — of the most heinous of crimes. I had blackened our good name and sullied the family honor. What had I done? I had violated an unwritten law, a solemn pact between those honorable gentlemen who were the landholders of Tern Beach — I had allowed a Jew to get a foothold on the island!"

Maggie Lord flashed a glance at her husband, wondering whether or not he had known that Coastal Foods was a Jewish company. His poker face offered no evidence, one way or the other. But she did have the feeling that Phelps had made a purposeful maneuver, all the more certain of it when the financier said, "I'm ashamed to admit it now but I'm afraid that at the time I too harbored some Jewish prejudice. The name that had been signed to the original letter — S. *Zurich* — had not struck me as being inevitably Jewish. There'd been no warning from the people at the bank, and I'd never met the man. Naturally I made it a point to do so at once, fully prepared to tell him that he'd have to get out. He had no lease and it seemed a simple enough thing to do. But that was counting without Sol Zurich. He was a tiny fellow — not a dwarf but the next thing to it — an orphanage boy who'd been kicked around ever since he was born. This was the first chance he'd ever had to call his soul his own, and he was working like a demon to make the most of it. He'd done a really amazing job of fixing up that old crab-house — scrounged a bit of lumber here, a piece of tin there — goodness knows how he'd managed it but somehow he had. He was on the job twenty-four hours a day — all alone, no one to help him, catching what little sleep he got on a cot in the kitchen. If a fisherman came by and knocked on the door, Sol would bounce up and take care of him, even if it was two o'clock in the morning and all that was wanted was a five-cent cup of coffee."

"So you wound up letting him stay?"

Phelps nodded in rueful reminiscence. "Father was furious, of course. Now I'd committed an even worse sin. I'd not only defied him but the whole community. If there'd been a Ku Klux Klan in Tern Beach I'm sure they'd have burned a fiery cross for me. In any event there was a horrible hullaballoo. If there'd been less of a fuss, I'm sure I'd have found some way to save face and back down. As it was, I simply had to stand my ground. And then, too, I'd found out that there was more involved than just prejudice. Sol was making some wonderful clam chowder, magnificent stuff. Half the island people were going down there to buy it to take home with them, gallons and gallons of it. The hotel resented the business that Sol was taking away from them — and all the more so, of course, because the summer before he'd been one of their employees." He interjected a chuckle. "What I didn't know until I was too deeply involved to withdraw was that my father was the secret owner of the hotel!"

Maggie Lord joined in her husband's reserved laughter, admiring how adroitly he reset the tone of the narrative with his soberer observation, "I've often suspected that if it weren't for economic rivalry, most of the anti-Jewish pressure in the world would probably disappear."

"Quite so, Mr. Lord, quite so," Phelps said approvingly. "But I'd be sailing under false colors if I asked you to believe that my standing up for Sol Zurich was any magnanimous struggle against anti-Semitism.

93

It was not that at all. My fight was with my father, trying to prove that I had the guts — your pardon, Mrs. Lord — to be my own man and keep my word to Sol Zurich."

His apology had made him turn to her, and feeling the need for an indirect acceptance, she said, "This is a fascinating story, Mr. Phelps."

"I'm afraid I'm dragging it out more than I should?" he said, a pleading question.

"Not at all," Lincoln Lord assured him coolly. "The canning company, I take it, grew out of the restaurant?"

Phelps stared at his highball glass for a thought-collecting moment. "That next year — '21 — you're probably too young, both of you, to remember it, but we had a depression in the country, short but very severe."

"Oh, but I do remember," she protested. "I was raised on it — morning, noon and night until I left home. My father's business failed in the '21 depression."

"Then you do know," the financier agreed. "What business was that, Mrs. Lord?"

"He had a small textile mill. It was a family business, really — drapery fabrics." She was conscious of having broken her resolution to take no part in the conversation, afraid now that her participation had violated her husband's plan for handling the financier. "I'm sorry, Mr. Phelps. I didn't mean to interrupt your story."

"Not at all — very pertinent," Phelps said. "Textiles, foods, all sorts of consumer goods — that's where the '21 depression hit the hardest. Inventories had gotten too big and prices were too high. There had to be a shake-out and there was. Your father's business wasn't the only one that failed, Mrs. Lord. There were hundreds of them — thousands — all over the country."

"I know."

"And one of those companies that went bankrupt was a little cannery over in Goodhaven. It failed that winter and I picked up its physical assets at sheriff's sale the next spring. I don't recall exactly what I paid — six thousand, sixty-five hundred, something like that. In any event, no more than the land alone was worth. My point is that I had no intention of going into the canning business. There wasn't much to the cannery anyway — a corrugated iron shed and some old machinery that was ready for the scrap heap — but soon after I took title to the property, Sol approached me about buying it. He'd been putting up his

94

clam chowder in Mason jars for some of the summer residents to take home with them — Tern Beach had a lot of New York and Philadelphia society people in those days — and Sol had the idea of packing his chowder in tin cans so that he could sell it all over the country. I tried to discourage him, but he was a tough little terrier — when he got his teeth into something he wouldn't let loose — and I couldn't help but be impressed by the way he'd run his little restaurant. In three years he'd made and saved something over five thousand dollars. A man with that sort of character —"

"So you sold him the cannery?" Lincoln Lord said, prodding him along to the point of the story.

"No," Phelps said with a reminiscent twinkle. "I went into partnership with him. I put in the old cannery and he gave me a third interest in the business. And then, of course, the fat was in the fire! Father was simply infuriated. Renting Sol a building was bad enough. This was inexcusable! He simply couldn't understand why I would drag his name in the mud through an open association with — he always called Sol 'that little fishhouse Jew!' The names he called me —" He inclined his head toward Maggie Lord. "In a lady's presence, they're unrepeatable."

To her surprise, she heard her husband say, "He sounds a little like your grandfather, Mag."

She laughed. "More than a little."

"In what way?" Phelps asked.

"The way he felt about Jews," she explained. "The horror of my youth — he always came to our place for Sunday dinner — was being made to sit at the table for hours while he read the *Dearborn Independent* aloud to us."

"Ah, yes, the *Dearborn Independent*," Phelps chuckled reminiscently. "Yes, he and my father would have been bosom friends. The ironic circumstance in this case — unfortunately my father died before this came out, because I'd have loved the chance to tell him — was that Sol Zurich turned out not to be a Jew at all."

Momentarily stunned, Maggie Lord looked at her husband, her earlier question as to whether or not he had been concerned about Coastal Foods being a Jewish company seemingly answered by the taut tone in which he asked Anderson Phelps for an explanation.

"Or at least the odds are all against his having been a Jew," Phelps qualified. "As I say, this didn't come out until years afterward. By then,

Sol had become a director of Haven Home — a big contributor to its support — and he'd gotten access to the old records. I believe I did mention that he'd been raised in an orphanage."

"Yes."

"Haven Home is a quite different place now, but in those days it must have been really horrible. They raised children like draft animals. Got them big enough to be put out to work — twelve or thirteen years old — and then the Home collected their wages until they were of age. Sounds incredible now — this was fifty-odd years ago, of course — but that's actually what they did. And that's where Sol Zurich landed, poor little devil, a month-old baby left on the doorstep — and absolutely no valid evidence of parentage, race, religion, name or anything else. There was no proof whatsoever that he was Jewish."

"But his name?" Lincoln Lord asked incredulously. "Surely no one would have given a baby a name like that without being certain that —"

"Nevertheless, that's what happened," Phelps put in. "It's possible that someone at the Home may have thought him a Jewish child, although how they could have even imagined being able to tell at that age I've no idea. After all, Jewish babies aren't born with the Star of David stamped on their foreheads. It's a more likely possibility — Sol always suspected this — that they were trying to get rid of him. He was a sickly baby — didn't look like a very good prospect for a worker — and they may have been trying to palm him off on a Jewish orphanage. The Jews take care of their own, you know, and there was a place up near Asbury Park that made a practice of taking over Jewish children from other institutions. There may have been nothing like that involved. As I say, it's only supposition — but if it were true, even the Jews didn't accept Sol as one of their own."

"But the name?" Lincoln Lord repeated.

The financier nodded to acknowledge the prompt. "That was about as cruel a twist of fate as you could possibly imagine. In fact, it's unimaginable — incredible. But, nevertheless, it did happen." He raised a finger to beat out the words. "When they found this baby on their doorstep, he was wrapped in a woman's coat. The name on the label —"

"Oh, no!" Maggie Lord heard herself exclaim. "You can't possibly mean that they took his name from the label on that coat."

"That's exactly what I do mean, Mrs. Lord. No question about it at all. The old records make it perfectly clear. The label on that coat was the only clue they had that might conceivably have led to tracing the baby's identity and, quite properly, someone made a note of it on the form where the finding of the baby was recorded. But then someone else came along, gave the form a quick look, and obviously picked it up as the baby's name. At least that's the most generous explanation."

Lincoln Lord shook his head groggily. "When did he find out that he wasn't a Jew? How old was he?"

"Oh, it only happened a few years ago."

"And all his life he'd gone on thinking he was a Jew?"

"Yes, of course."

"And everyone else thought so?"

"Yes, naturally. Everyone around Goodhaven and Tern Beach had always thought of him as being Jewish. Most of them still do, I imagine. Sol never did anything to change their minds. How could he? You can imagine what the reaction would have been if he'd attempted it. And maybe he was, I don't know."

"Did he look Jewish?"

Phelps shrugged. "Possibly. But he could easily have been Italian — French — perhaps German. Almost anything. If you coupled the name and the face — yes, you could believe him a Jew. Afterwards, when I knew the truth and realized how heavily the odds were against it, I began to see how many people there are whose appearance is even more Semitic than many of the acknowledged Jews. I'm afraid it's the same way with some of the traits of personality that we attribute to them. When I first saw Sol I could always see what I thought were Jewish mannerisms. Afterwards, when I found out that he wasn't — well, it was a good lesson in tolerance."

Lincoln Lord nodded offhandedly, simple agreement to a self-evident truth. Then, as if he were ringing down the curtain, he said, "This has been very interesting, Mr. Phelps."

The financier was taken aback, glancing regretfully down at his notebook. "I've jotted down a few figures that more or less highlight the development of the company."

"Suppose we get to this Gellman business," Lincoln Lord said, a firm-handed order.

Phelps plainly missed the point and acted as if he had been reprieved. "Yes, that's very important — Sol's friendship with Mr. Gellman. You see, in those days, Abe Gellman had a little chain of delicatessen stores here in New York — four or five of them, all in the Park Avenue area — and the things that Sol was starting to can were just what Abe had been looking for. Nowadays, of course, all the stores are full of that sort of thing — these pre-cooked dishes that you just heat up and serve — but almost no one was packing them back in the early twenties. Sol Zurich was really a very forward-looking man, amazingly so in the light of what's happened since. He was almost the first canner in the country to see the possibilities."

"Really?" Lincoln Lord said, an expression of heightened interest that momentarily reflected itself as a warm glow on the financier's face. But it faded quickly as Lord added, "Shame he didn't capitalize on the idea."

"Why do you say that, Mr. Lord?"

"If he had, Coastal Foods might have become one of the big companies."

The financier's eyes narrowed and for an instant a sharp retort seemed imminent. Then, crumbling, he said, "Yes, of course. You're quite right, Mr. Lord. Yes, Sol might have built Coastal into a much larger business. That could still be done — easily enough, as a matter of fact, if the management were disposed to move in that direction." He paused, the shadow of resistance restored. "Personally, however, it's my own view that a lot of fine companies have been ruined because their owners have been deluded into imagining that there's some special merit in bigness. There's nothing wrong with a small company, Mr. Lord. Just because a company isn't a big national advertiser doesn't mean that it can't be a highly successful enterprise."

"Of course not."

Responding to encouragement, the financier inched forward. "I know there's no need to argue the point with you, Mr. Lord — you've been on both sides of the fence. But there are a lot of people who don't realize how much personal satisfaction a man can find in a company like Coastal Foods. I may be wrong — difficult to look into another man's mind — but I dare say that you yourself had more feeling of real accomplishment in some of your earlier associations than you did after you got into Luxor Pharmacal. I know something about what the president of one of these big corporations is up against — thousands of stockholders always on his neck, a board of directors with no real understanding of his problems, an organization so big that he couldn't possibly know what's happening. Yes, I know — there are men who like that sort of thing — but there are two sides to the story, Mr. Lord."

To her surprise, she had seen her husband nodding to Phelps's arguments, more and more vigorously as the financier's words gained strength. Then, suddenly, as if realizing that his guard had slipped,

98

Linc asked abruptly, "How important was this Gellman business? How much of Coastal Food's volume did it represent?"

Phelps squirmed. "A substantial percentage."

"More than half?"

"Yes, more than half," Phelps admitted.

She saw Linc shake his head, a gesture of bewilderment. "It's hard to understand how anyone could allow a business to get in a position like that, all its eggs in one basket."

"Not when you know the circumstances," Phelps said in cautious rebuttal. "As you say, Sol had a lot of eggs in one basket. Yes, that's true. But it was a very good basket, Mr. Lord — and for a great many years. Coastal Foods has made a lot of money out of the Gellman Stores business."

"That doesn't sound like the typical experience of a food packer selling to a chain store outfit."

"Quite so," Phelps said. "That's what I wanted to explain — the relationship between Sol Zurich and Abe Gellman. You see, the things that Sol was packing for the Gellman Stores — the Mother Gellman products —"

"That was their private brand?"

"Yes, for these ready-cooked dishes that Sol was packing for them. They were really the backbone of Gellman's success. Abe knew it. That's where he always concentrated his promotion. There was a catch-line they always used in their advertising —"

Maggie quickly quoted, " 'Why not let Mother Gellman cook your dinner tonight?' "

Phelps gave her a grateful smile. "Yes, that's it — and the real Mother Gellman, of course, was Sol Zurich. Everything with the Mother Gellman label on it was made in Sol's cannery. And of course the business grew amazingly. The more stores Gellman opened, the faster Coastal Foods had to expand to keep up with them. For quite a number of years, every cent of profit that Sol made had to be plowed back into the business, putting up more buildings and buying new equipment. Frankly, I was a bit concerned at first — the same point you raised, Mr. Lord, too many eggs in one basket — because there was no real guarantee that Gellman might not cut him off at any minute."

"Wasn't there a contract?"

"No, never. Sol and Abe did business for twenty years — millions and millions of dollars — and there was never the scratch of a pen. But there were other things that bound them together. One incident I

99

particularly recall because, at the time, it seemed to verify all the dire predictions I'd been making to Sol about what might happen to him. This was in 1929 — before the crash. Costs had been going up and up and Sol told Abe that he had to raise his prices. They squabbled for a few days, Sol wouldn't give ground, and finally Abe started shopping around to see if there wasn't a packer somewhere who could beat Sol's prices. And of course there was."

"There always is."

"Yes, quite so. In any event, Abe placed a big order with this other cannery. You can probably guess what happened. Their quality wasn't up to Sol's — no one could ever match his stuff for flavor — customers complained, demanded their money back, stopped buying at Gellman Stores. Abe told me afterwards that it was the most expensive mistake he'd ever made. He figured that it cost him a million dollars in lost good will."

"And Sol got the account back?"

"Yes, after that experience there wasn't much question about who got the Gellman Stores business. And there was even less after what happened in '34. That was really the tie that could never be broken — except, of course, by death. Anyway, it held them together as long as they lived. As I was saying, this was in '34. Gellman was a bold opera-tor. When the Depression hit, instead of pulling in his horns he ex-panded all the faster, opening one store after another, dozens of them. He was a clever financier, smart as a fox, but eventually he over-played his hand and his creditors started closing in. It looked as if he were licked, not a chance in the world to dig his way out. The man who saved him was Sol Zurich. Sol loaned him a hundred thousand dollars — no interest — and told him to keep it as long as he needed it. He didn't even ask him to sign a note. After that — well, no decent man would ever forget that kind of help."

"No, indeed," Lincoln Lord exclaimed, openly impressed. "You make them sound like a couple of wonderful men."

"They were," Phelps said, no less forcibly. "And a wonderful friend-ship developed between them. Sol wasn't the sort of man who makes friends easily and getting to know the Gellmans — Abe and Sarah and their children — was almost like having a family of his own. He used to go there —"

Lincoln Lord interrupted with a puzzled frown. "But Zurich was married, wasn't he?"

"Not in those days."

"But there is a Mrs. Zurich?"

"Oh, yes — yes, indeed. But they weren't married until — let me see — yes, it was about six years ago." Apprehension clouded the financier's face. "I imagine you've heard something about her?"

"I take it that she now controls the company?"

In her husband's eyes, Maggie Lord was certain that she saw a reflection of the same alarming memory that had risen before her own — the image of Cornelia Rabson, the old dowager whose matriarchal dominance had caused so much trouble at the Rabson Canning Company and, in the end, had given Linc his most plausible excuse for changing jobs.

Nervously Phelps said, "If that concerns you, Mr. Lord — the control of the company being in Mrs. Zurich's hands — please reserve judgment until you meet her. In the meantime, let me assure you that it's nothing to worry about. Her attitude is everything that you'd want it to be. Her only interest —" He stopped abruptly. "I can well imagine what people are saying — yes, easily enough. At first, I thought some of those same things myself. It was such an unlikely match — Kira was so much younger than Sol —"

Lincoln Lord cut in bluntly, "She's Jewish, of course?"

"Oh no, Mr. Lord — no indeed," the financier came back, his air of scoring a point revealing that his disavowal of Jewish prejudice was less sincere than he had tried to make it seem. "Perhaps, Mr. Lord, this will give you an indication that Mrs. Zurich is not the person you think her to be. After Sol died, Gellman Stores offered to buy Coastal Foods — and at a very fancy price. Frankly, I advised her to accept the offer. It would have made her a wealthy woman, very wealthy indeed. Instead, she chose to keep the company operating."

"But she did make herself president of the company," Maggie heard her husband say, reinstating the memory of Cornelia Rabson, whose lust for power was so strong that the old woman would sacrifice almost any amount of money rather than relinquish her personal control of the company.

"I'm responsible for that, Mr. Lord. It was my suggestion. And she only agreed to do it as a legal formality. A corporation must have a designated president. She's taken no active part in the management of the company, none whatsoever."

"Then who is managing the company?"

Phelps exhaled sharply. "That's the difficulty, Mr. Lord. They've been attempting to carry on with a sort of partnership management —

a man named Swann, who was Zurich's office manager, and a man named Kennan, who was his production manager."

"Oh yes — Frank Kennan," Lincoln Lord said in positive recognition. "Sandy hair — rather stocky?"

Phelps was slack-lipped with surprise. "You — then you know him?"

"Oh, just met him a couple of times, that's all," Lincoln Lord tossed back. "We made some special jars for Coastal Foods when I was at Frazer Glass. There was some difficulty about labeling, some design adjustments that had to be made. Kennan handled the whole situation in fine spirit. Impressed me very favorably."

Phelps swallowed and said, "Yes, he's an excellent man. Probably as good a production superintendent as you'll find anywhere in the industry. But I'm sure you'll agree that he's hardly the man — at least, as the situation has developed, I'm sure I was right in advising Mrs. Zurich not to give the presidency to either Swann or Kennan. If she had done so, she'd now have a very awkward situation. As it is, neither of them would have any feeling of being demoted if you were to step in as president of the company. In fact —"

...*president of the company!* The words echoed as a reverberant explosion in Maggie Lord's mind. Her ears blocked, she stared first at Anderson Phelps and then at her husband, her astonishment that the financier was offering the presidency of Coastal Foods fully matched by the all but incredible casualness with which that offer was being acknowledged ... Linc acting as if he had known it all along ... too modest to acknowledge how cleverly he had convinced Phelps that he was much too big a man for only a sales manager's job ...

"Let me assure you you'd have complete authority, Mr. Lord," Phelps was saying. "Your hands would be free to operate the company exactly as if it were your own. Yes, yes, I know — you'd want that assurance directly from Mrs. Zurich herself — and she'd be very happy to come to New York to talk to you. But I'm sure you'd want to see the plant, anyway — perhaps meet some of the key people in the organization." He took a deep breath. "Mr. Lord, would it be possible for you to run down to Goodhaven?"

Her attention was so intensely concentrated on her husband's reaction that she did not realize until Phelps went on talking again that Linc intended no response beyond a noncommittal shrug.

"As far as compensation is concerned, Mr. Lord — I'm sure there'd be no difficulty on that score."

Blinking, she heard Linc say, "That wouldn't be the most important consideration."

"No, no, of course not — naturally," Phelps said, quickly apologetic. "I was sure that's what your attitude would be. I only mentioned it because —" He let it drop. "I don't want to press you unnecessarily, Mr. Lord, but this is a matter of some urgency — not from your standpoint, of course, but from Mrs. Zurich's. She suggested — it may not be possible for you to fit this into your schedule, but she'd like very much to have you and Mrs. Lord come down and have lunch with her tomorrow."

"Tomorrow?" Lincoln Lord speculated, as casually as if he were considering the suggestion that he might have his ginger ale glass refilled. "Yes, I believe we could make that." He turned to her. "Unless you have something on, Mag?"

She shook her head, silent, not daring to trust her voice.

12

Brick Mitchell stepped out of the elevator and walked down the dark hall of the apartment house, grimacing at the six o'clock cooking odors that were being spewed out through the cracks around every door that he passed, a gagging conglomeration of smells that fed the belly-wrenching nausea that had started with his fourth Martini.

Approaching the door of his own apartment, he slowed his pace and lifted his heels, advancing on tiptoe. Tommy's apartment was directly below his. If she heard him come in, she would come up, wanting to know where he'd been all afternoon . . . none of her business! Didn't have to explain to her . . . nor anyone else! He was his own boss . . . do anything he damn pleased. If he wanted another drink, he'd have another drink! Who'd Tommy think she was? To hell with her! To hell with everybody! Sometimes a man had to do it . . . blow his top and get it out of his system . . . and, damn it, it worked! To hell with Linc Lord! He could say it now and mean it . . . you're damn right he could . . . hadn't thought of Linc now for hours . . . or Maggie either . . . licked it . . . damn right he'd licked it!

The key grated and the doorknob rattled. He listened. There was no sound from the floor below. Holding his breath, he opened the door, fearful that he would be betrayed by a haunted-house screech. The opening door was a black curtain, drawn aside to blind him with a blast of light, a fire haze that stung his eyeballs, a yellow cloud that slowly materialized into the swirl of Tommy's hair, her face fading in like a color print coming up in a tray of developer.

"How'd you get in here?" he said on the second try, too thick-tongued on the first attempt ... all right, she had a key ... damn it, she didn't have to tell him that ... what the hell, he knew she had a key ... "Got tied up — big afternoon."

"That's what I figured when you didn't come back to the office."

Office ... what about the office? Why didn't she tell him ... figuring he'd have to ask her ... to hell with that! He didn't need any favors ... Tommy or anybody else ... maybe Robbie had called about that tranquillizer piece ...

This time he took no chances, rehearsing the words before he spoke them. "Anything happen at the office?"

What did she mean, shaking her head like that? "No calls, huh?"

"Just one."

"Robbie?"

"No."

"Who? Somebody calls me, I got a right to know who it was."

"Lincoln Lord."

Something knocked her face out of focus ... all rubbery ... *Lincoln Lord.*

Tommy's face was needle sharp now ... too sharp ... needed a little diffusion ...

"What'd you tell him?"

"I said you were out."

Out? Yes ... very good ... very, very, *very* good ... "Good girl, Tommy. Wonderful. Just wonderful. Don't know what I'd do without you."

What was the matter with her now ... looking like he'd said something to make her feel bad ...

"Shut up, Brick!"

"Listen, Tommy —"

"Go get a shower. I'll make some coffee. That'll cure you of thinking I'm so wonderful."

What did she mean? Sure she was wonderful ... helping him ... telling Linc Lord to go to hell! Maybe she was right ... shower ... coffee ...

II

OVERNIGHT January had put on the false face of April. A warming wind had come in from the south, strong and fresh, sweeping away the rag-gray clouds of winter, burnishing the sky to a metallic springtime blue. The sun was a dancing fireball on the black-mirror hood of the Cadillac that Lincoln Lord had rented for the trip to Goodhaven.

They were off the New Jersey Turnpike now, well down the Garden State Parkway, the land flat and featureless, stretching away to a horizon line blurred by the violet haze of leafless trees. Looking to her right, Maggie Lord saw a clump of ramshackle farm buildings, the cedar trees in a winter-browned pasture an insistent prodding of memory. Most of what she had learned yesterday from Anderson Phelps had caused her to think of the Coastal Foods Company of Goodhaven, New Jersey, as a resurrection of the old Quincy Canning Company of Brighton, Maryland. Now the similarity of landscape between this part of New Jersey and the Eastern Shore country around Brighton heightened that impression, making her wonder if Linc's grim silence was induced by a recognition that what lay ahead was a back-tracking retreat to where he had been twenty-odd years ago.

Immediately she dismissed that possibility, finding it even more incongruous than the others she had tested in her search for some way to explain his startlingly strange behavior this morning. Last night she had been certain that he was going to turn down the Coastal Foods offer, so positive of it that she had put all thought of this trip out of her mind, not even dressing for it this morning. Then, an hour ago, he had called from the lobby and bluntly told her that he was ready to start,

105

impatiently annoyed when she asked for five minutes to slip into another dress. Although he had not said so — he had spoken hardly a dozen words since they had left New York — it was beyond all doubt that he had decided to take the job. She had no idea what had caused him to change his mind, and up to now she had made no progress in finding out. He had hidden what had happened during the morning behind a wall of silence and her too anxious attempts to penetrate it, fumbling and ineffectual because of her lack of understanding, had only made him more stubbornly resistant. She had never before seen him in a mood like this. If there had been anything to support the suspicion she would have thought him angry at her because of something that she had said or done.

She had, she knew, made one stupid mistake. Coming out of the hotel she had been startled to discover that he had rented a Cadillac and, not knowing then how radically he had changed his mind, thinking that the trip to Goodhaven represented no more than going through the motions of keeping his promise to Anderson Phelps, she had seen the limousine rental as an extravagant raid on their dwindling store of cash. She had caught herself in time to choke off open disapproval, yet with the supersensitivity that was a part of Linc's mood, he had guessed what she was thinking and sharply retorted, "If you were hiring a president for a company you controlled, would you expect to see him come crawling out of a day coach?" But her one slight slip was not enough to explain why he was acting toward her as he was — and in any event, his state of mind had been something set before that. Something had happened after he had left the hotel this morning and before he called her from the lobby.

All she knew was that he had gotten up early, dressing before she had awakened, already at the door when she had opened her eyes. He had said something about having breakfast with Otis Sellcox. Her mind had been too sleep-fogged to guarantee positive recollection of exactly what he had said, yet she had gained the impression that he wanted Sellcox to explain to Anderson Phelps why he couldn't take the Coastal Foods presidency, letting the employment agency handle his rejection of the job in order to establish a Sellcox-Phelps contact that might possibly result in the offer of a more desirable opening. At least she was sure that he had left the hotel with no intention of changing his midnight decision to turn down the Coastal Foods offer. She was no less positive that his mood, if not exactly cheerful, had been brighter than for the past several weeks, his spirits still lifted by having received an offer that, even though not one that he could accept, had raised his hopes and strengthened his resolve to stick it out until the right opening came along.

Now he was acting as if he were a man driven to do something against his will — and judging by his attitude, he seemed to feel that she was the one who was driving him. It was impossible to understand. She had made no attempt to influence him, none whatsoever. Last night, she had not made a single response until she was positive that it supported something that was already in his mind. She had been ultra-cautious even about the expression on her face. She had not argued with him, made no suggestions, agreeing with him constantly, following his every lead as his thinking had evolved. That was not difficult. At first she too had been elated, knowing how much it would mean to have the income that a job, any job, would bring them. Afterwards, her mind clearing with his, she had shared his question about whether or not he could really find happiness in so small a company. Then, logically — there had been no need for him to actually say it — her thoughts had followed his until she could see the dangerous situation that would lie ahead if he took another job that would have to be abandoned after a year or two. Another change might black-mark him forever. When he finally said, sitting on the edge of her bed, "Maggie, would you think I was crazy if I turned it down?" she had been fully ready to reply, "Of course not, Linc".... and that's all she had said, not another word ... no, it wasn't anything she had said or done. But something had happened this morning ... something ...

Or was it the money ... the money and the title ... Lincoln Lord, president of ... maybe it didn't matter what he was president of ... back on the top rung of the ladder again ... sending his son to Forgehill ... speeding down the Garden State Parkway at the wheel of a brand new Cadillac ...

PAY TOLL AHEAD

She opened her handbag and searched through the small coin purse. There were no more quarters but she sorted out two dimes and five pennies. Was it possible, despite her effort to hide it, that he had guessed how frightened she was ... all those bills piling up ... going to Forgehill yesterday? Was he thinking that this was something she wanted him to do? No, he couldn't possibly think that ... she didn't want him to take it ... unless ... yes, if it were something that would really make him happy, something that would last. But it wouldn't ... it couldn't ... a little tin-shed cannery ... no, not Lincoln Lord.

His hand reached out and she poured the coins into it as they stopped at the toll booth. He transferred them to the collector, asking, "Where do we turn off for Goodhaven?"

"Next exit," the man said, the voice of judgment pronouncing sentence.

With a snarl of released power, the car lunged forward.

Too quickly she said, "There's no hurry, Linc. We're going to be there in plenty of time."

His wince of annoyance told her that she had made another mistake, an error in the same category as the one she had committed before. And in the same tone that he had defended the renting of the car, he said, "It won't hurt to have a few minutes to look around the town — get our feet on the ground before we talk to Mrs. Zurich."

And again she nodded to the reasonableness of his explanation, hiding her conviction that it was, if not untrue, at least an excuse invented after the fact.

"How far is it after we come off?" he demanded.

She fumbled open the map on her lap, a delayed answer excused by an obscure mileage figure. "It's eight miles — but I can't tell whether that's to Goodhaven or Tern Beach."

"They're right together, aren't they?"

"Tern Beach is on the other side of the bridge — out on the island."

"That's right," he said, pedantic approval. "They were building a new bridge that time we stopped off with Lou and Betsy Murdock. You remember, don't you — coming up from Atlantic City?"

She looked at him sharply, grateful that he was at last beginning to talk, yet wondering if he had forgotten that it was she who, yesterday afternoon, had reminded him of that week-end stopover at Tern Beach.

"Remember that place they had?" he asked. "Might not be too bad living down here — get a house like that right down on the beach — close enough to New York so that you could run in any time you wanted to."

He was pulling out to pass another car and she waited to reply, waiting too long.

"What's the matter?" he asked, cutting back to the right lane again with a quick twist of the steering wheel.

"Nothing's the matter, Linc."

"Something is," he said, apprehensively positive. "What's bothering you?"

"Nothing's bothering me," she said, forcing a little laugh, yet knowing that it was a wasted effort. He could often be talked out of some reasoned conclusion but rarely, if ever, out of anything that he felt intuitively . . . but what could she say? What was he trying to do . . . convince her? Or himself? He knew that it didn't make any difference to her . . .

She saw the speedometer rise, the fever marking of a deep-seated resentment, and quickly said, "I'm sorry, Linc. Of course, I'd like living here. But that isn't the important thing." She paused, waiting a moment for a stepping-stone question. "What really matters, Linc, is whether or not it turns out to be something that you want."

"No," he said, a surprisingly sharp rejection. "You'll have to want it, too."

"Linc, you know that all that matters to me is —" She hesitated, blocked by the realization that she was sounding self-righteously noble, a soap-opera wife tearfully protesting that all she wanted from life was her husband's happiness . . . but it was true! And he could be happy if he'd only face up to it . . . if she could just make him realize that happiness had to be something solid, something that would last . . .

"If you don't want me to take this job, Mag, now's the time to say so."

"Linc, it's your decision to make, not mine."

"I know." His voice snapped and then exploded. "You don't want to take any of the responsibility."

Dazed, she groped for belief, unable to match this moment to any in the twenty years of her married life. There had been occasions when he had been openly irritated, even angry, but none when he had struck out at her like this. There must be some mistake . . . she must have misunderstood him . . .

There was no mistake. "Mag, we might as well settle this right now. There's no use going on if we don't. I'm not going to take it unless you agree that it's the right thing to do. This time you've got to stick your neck out, too. That's why I had you sit in with Phelps yesterday — why I brought you along today."

Self-justification pushed forward the counterattack of denial . . . this wasn't true! He'd wanted her yesterday because she was the one who knew Phelps . . . she was here today because Kira Zurich had invited her. This was a Lincoln Lord trick . . . explanation invented after the fact . . . but true or not, what difference did it make? He had made it true by saying it.

She dampened her dry lips. "Haven't I always gone along with everything you've decided to do?"

"You've got to do more than just go along. You've got to be with me all the way."

"And you don't think that I have been before?"

"Have you?" he asked quietly, a blow no less forceful because it was struck with a light hand. "What about Chemical Service?"

"Linc, I never said anything against your going into Chemical Service."

"No, you didn't say anything against it. Of course not. You wouldn't. But did you really think that it was the thing to do? I don't mean after we found out — I mean right at the start, that first night, after we'd had dinner with Brown. Do you remember on the way back to the hotel — I asked you what you thought of it? And all you would say was that I had to make up my own mind."

"But, Linc, you're the one who has to —"

"You said that, too," he broke in. "That it was my life and so I had to make the decision. That isn't true, Mag. It wasn't just my life then and it isn't just my life now. It's your life, too. How do you think I felt when the blow-up came at Chemical Service — knowing that you would have to take the rap, too — when you'd been against it from the start? I don't want to have to face that again."

EXIT TO TERN BEACH

He saw the sign at the same instant that she did, her warning cry wasted except as a release of pent-up emotion, a mind sound echoed in the screech of clawing tires as he whipped around the tight circle of the exit turn, his struggle to control the car matched to her own effort to give some direction to her madly driven mind. At first there was only the fight against credibility, the difficulty of believing that she had been so unperceptive that she had failed to sense what he was really thinking. Then there was the flashed realization that he was trying to escape the responsibility of decision by forcing her to share it. But what he had said was true ... it *was* her life, too! He was right. Or was he? Had she been wrong all these years ... ?

They were through the underpass now, heading down the road to Goodhaven, crossing a bridge over a marsh-bordered tidal creek. The air was heavy with the dank mustiness of low tide, an odor that inevitably forced her to recall her father. All through the years of her childhood and adolescence, every summer week end had meant a trip down the Eastern Shore of Maryland to their cottage on Fox Point.

Never once had her father approached the bridge at Brighton without slowing the car, his head turned to the open window, his nostrils searching out the first faint whiff of an odor that he drank in like a welcomed opiate, the smell of distant salt water subtly blended with the peppery aroma of marsh grass. Her memory was more vocal than visual, dominated by the sound of the deeply inhaled first breath with which he had always greeted the prospect of escape from the torture of his weekday life. Never had that sound been so deeply appealing as on those week ends, more and more frequent as she had gone through her high school years, when her mother had not been with them. It was during those last years of her adolescence that she had come to realize that her father's unhappiness was so largely the result of her mother's never-ending attempts to manage his life.

Much of what had gone before had been beyond a child's understanding, the more so because she had known so little about her father's business life. She had not been without curiosity — the lives that were lived by men had always had a special fascination for her — but she had shrunk from questioning the taciturn man who hurriedly ate every breakfast as if he were racing to avoid an inquisition and who, every night, came home gray-faced and worn, grimly resistant to his wife's nagging demand that he explain everything that he had done that day at the office.

Most of John Kipling's grudging responses had been meaningless — Maggie had never known precisely what his job had been — yet it was made inescapably evident by her mother that he had allowed the family textile mill to go into bankruptcy after the 1921 depression and that the only job he had then been able to secure was one that her mother, through her family connections, had gotten for him, an opportunity upon which he had apparently failed to capitalize. Inadequate as teenage understanding had been, Maggie's sympathy had been with her father, excusing him from any major fault, sensing that her mother's perpetually renewed attempts to manage his life were a crippling burden. And what she had sensed had been verified on that one occasion when he had finally broken down and talked to her. It had been during her last summer in New York, the long Independence Day week end when she had taken a four-day trip home as a substitute for a vacation. On their second morning at the Fox Point cottage, she had been awakened in the darkness before dawn by some unidentified sound. Looking out of the bedroom window, she had glimpsed her father's face momentarily illuminated by the flare of a match as he had stopped to light a cigarette on the path down to the dock. Hurriedly dressing, she had followed him, accepting his explanation that daybreak was the best time to find soft-shell crabs on the grassy shallows. She had offered to row for him, joining him in the dew-wet skiff, both silent as they watched the eastern sky lighten in the impressive minutes of the dawning day. Then, with no apparent provocation, abandoning the pretense that his early rising had been occasioned by anything other than his inability to sleep, he had started to talk to her about his work at the company, encouraging her questions and freely answering them, all a preliminary to his finally telling her that a younger man was about to be promoted over his head and given a vice-presidency. "They're making the right move," he said without rancor. "I couldn't argue with them, even if I had the chance. He's the best man for the job. But I know it's going to hurt your mother. She's always expected me to be an officer of the company — she can't understand why I haven't done better — and I can't blame her for that because I don't understand it either." He sat staring at the red ball of the rising sun, preoccupied, finally saying, "There's something a man has to have to get ahead, Maggie — not brains, nor working hard, nor knowing the business, nor anything else you can put your finger on. Whatever it is, I know now that it's something I don't have."

She had attempted a complimentary denial, but he had brushed it aside. "It's a difficult situation for a man, Maggie, when someone he loves is trying to turn him into the kind of a man he doesn't want to be, and couldn't be even if he wanted to. But I'm not blaming your mother. It's my own fault. I've never had courage enough to live my own life. I should have been a schoolteacher — that's what I always wanted to be."

Heart-touched, she had suggested the possibility that, even now, he might be happier in some other kind of work. "I'm not unhappy with my work," he had protested. "I'd be perfectly satisfied if only I weren't such a disappointment to your mother." It was then that he had reached out and clasped her hands in his, a rare gesture. "Promise me one thing, Maggie — when you pick out someone to marry, be sure that he's the man you want to spend your life with, not someone that you imagine you can make over into something that he was never intended to be. I want you to be happy, Maggie, happier than your mother has ever been."

Every word had been indelibly inscribed upon her memory, not only by compassion and the recognized rarity of the occasion, but also because he had touched a special sensitivity. The week before, in New York, she had gone out on two dates with Brick Mitchell and, in a tentative testing of the possibility, had been guilty of thinking that with the right kind of wife to manage his life Brick might someday become a successful writer, perhaps even a great and famous one.

Now, glancing left at her husband's profile, she re-established the association that there had always been between those last words of her father's and her decision to marry Lincoln Lord. She recognized that she was on dangerous ground now, venturing into the area where, for so many years, she had been assailed by the secret fear that what she had convinced herself was purely romantic love might have been tainted with a too coldly calculating estimate that Lincoln Lord was a young man unquestionably destined for success, the best long-range prospect of any of the six or seven or eight who, conceivably, she might have been able to maneuver into a proposal. Over the years she had outwitted her conscience with a subtle shift of attitude that permitted her to believe that any materialistic consideration that might have unwittingly influenced her falling in love with Lincoln Lord was canceled by the keeping of her promise to her father — that she would marry a man whom she would never attempt to change in any way.

Now, her mind slowing to a pace where conscious thought was possible, she asked herself if she dared accept Linc's criticism at face value. Was he really inviting interference . . . honestly willing to share his decision?

A test suggested itself. "What did you find out this morning, Linc?"

Significantly, he hesitated before he said, "Not too much."

She waited and the relevancy of her question seemed to impress itself more strongly upon him. He added, "Most of what Phelps told us checks out pretty well."

"What part of it doesn't?" she asked.

His resistance was stronger now, a longer hesitation before he said, "Nothing important. From everything I could find out, it's a fine company — not the biggest in the world, of course, but a good solid little outfit."

She decided to dig slightly deeper. "What did Mr. Sellcox think about it?"

The question rebounded from hard rock, evasion almost instantaneous. "That isn't the question, Mag — what Sellcox thinks. It's what you think that matters."

Was he laying the groundwork for escape . . . was that why he

wanted to shift the responsibility to her? No, that didn't make sense
... but what did? Was he afraid of the job? Or had it been fear that
had made him want to turn it down last night? Could this be the
courage of the morning ... but weakening now as he faced what it
would mean ... was that the answer?

Maybe nothing had happened this morning ... except what had
happened in Linc's mind. Did he honestly want her to share the
responsibility of deciding ... or was she to be his excuse ... the way
out?

2

In the months since he had become the acting head of Chesapeake College, Dr. Arthur B. Whittaker had learned a few lessons
about the functioning of the board of regents. One was that the real
decisions were made, not in the walnut-paneled board room in Quincy
Hall but in quiet little preliminary sessions in the downtown law
offices of Crockett, Bancroft & Crockett. That was where he had spent
the last half-hour and, now, was still closeted with Amos Crockett, for
twenty years Brighton's most distinguished citizen and, for the last
six, chairman of the board of regents of Chesapeake College. Judge
Crockett had proved himself, as Dean Whittaker had gratefully discovered, at least open-minded enough to listen to his plan.

"Yes, the idea may have some merit," Crockett granted, twisting a
curl into the wing of white hair that plumed out over his right ear.
"But are you quite certain, Arthur, that you may not come to regret all
this? There is the possibility, you know, that you may be making the
same mistake that I made when I was first called to the bench. I don't
mind saying that I was thoroughly frightened. I felt myself temperamentally ill-suited to be a judge. That lasted about a week. Within a
month, you couldn't have blasted me off that bench with dynamite. I
loved every minute of it — and have ever since. I've a notion you may
rather quickly come to feel the same way about the presidency of
Chesapeake College."

"Possibly," Whittaker said. "But if I did it would not be for the best
interest of either Chesapeake or myself. I've thought my way through
this, Judge, and I'm positive that I can best serve the college as provost. Believe me, this is no snap judgment."

"And you think Lincoln Lord is the man to bring in as president?"

"I'm convinced of it."

Judge Crockett shifted hands, twisting a balancing curl over the other ear. "And you want my opinion as to what the reaction of the board might be?"

"Very much — and any suggestion you might have as to how the whole matter can best be handled."

"As for the principle of your plan — a president to handle the college's business affairs and a provost to have a comparable responsibility for the academic side — my judgment, for whatever it may be worth, is that the board would approve that readily enough."

"I'm delighted that you feel that way, sir."

"As for myself, I'm inclined to think that your willingness to sacrifice the presidency and serve only as a provost would be accepted by the board as evidence of precisely what we would all expect of you — an act of most unselfish integrity."

"Thank you, sir."

The judge leaned back, the preliminaries disposed of, the verdict about to be delivered. "Now we come to this matter of selecting a president. I must say that I'm disposed to support you in thinking that Lord's the man. In what few contacts I've had with him, he's impressed me most favorably. However —" he paused for a magisterial throat clearing — "I do think you'd be unwise not to anticipate the possibility of some opposition. There is a board member, you know, who may have some rather strong personal feelings about Lord. I'm not saying that he does, only that he might."

"Who's that, sir?"

"You do know, don't you, that Lord was once employed by the old Quincy Canning Company?"

"You mean Jay Quincy?" Dean Whittaker asked, belatedly aware that the Quincy Fund was such an important source of Chesapeake's financial support that Jay Quincy's slightest frown had the power of a veto. "Do you really think that Jay would oppose it?"

"I'm only suggesting that it's a stumbling block that should be gotten out of the way before Lord's name is presented to the board. After all, you know, Lord did walk out on the Quincys — failed to return to them after the war — and that does raise the possibility that Jay's attitude might not be too friendly. On the other hand, Lord's relationship was with Jay's father — the old gentleman was still very much in charge in those days — and it may well be that Jay himself holds no resentment. Nevertheless, I do feel that you should test the wind in that direction before you put on full sail ahead. Half of wisdom, you know, is in being wise enough to find out in advance what the other fellow may do to make you look like a fool. I hardly need tell you that Jay's good will is very important."

Whittaker nodded, miserably conscious that he was guilty of a lack of financial foresight, yet aware that his fault was actually proof of his point that he did need someone to take care of this sort of thing for him.

"If I were you, Arthur, I believe I'd run out and have a little chat with Jay."

"Yes — yes, I suppose I should," the dean said, searching his mind for a loophole. "But it does seem a bit awkward — to do it myself, I mean. Don't you think it might be done with better grace by someone else? After all, it's still not official — my being asked to head the college. Might it not strike Mr. Quincy as presumptuous of me to —"

"No need for you to go that far," Judge Crockett decreed. "Suppose you were to have a little personal chat with him about — well, say, the endowment fund drive — how it's going and all that. Be perfectly natural to bring up Lord and the job he did at the New York alumni meeting, wouldn't it? That would give you a chance to put a damp finger to the wind without Jay even knowing what you were up to."

"I suppose that could be done," Whittaker granted, disturbed that he had not thought of the possibility himself, more convinced than ever that he would be misplaced in a position where the concoction of such cleverly devious plans would be constantly expected of him. "Yes, I'll take a run out there one of these days —" He paused, goading himself to courage. "The sooner the better, I suppose."

"Yes," Crockett agreed. "Be a shame to let Lord slip away from us. A man of that caliber won't be available for long."

3

Lincoln Lord's eyes roamed the roadside. There were houses now — a woman's face in a window, diapers flapping on a line, a boy on a bicycle, a hip-booted man working on a stranded cabin cruiser, the rhythmic clunking of a calking iron — and he felt himself a man awakening from a nightmare, a blind man who had miraculously re-gained the ability to see, a deaf man again able to hear. The world around him was reassuming normality, peopled again with human be-ings, no longer the lonely hell into which Otis Sellcox had driven him.

Last evening after Anderson Phelps had left the hotel and Maggie had gone back to their room, he had called Otis Sellcox from the suite and made a date to meet him at breakfast to discuss the terms of an employment contract with Coastal Foods. He had not told Maggie what he had done and, afterwards, when he'd finally thought it through and decided that taking the job would be a bad move, there had been no chance to call Sellcox and break the appointment without letting her know how foolishly impulsive he had been. It had then seemed better to go through with the breakfast date. At least, he had thought, it would give him a chance to call the turn on Sellcox, reasoning that if he, on his own and with no help from the agency, had been able to get as good an offer as he had from a man as shrewd as Anderson Phelps, surely Sellcox could hardly miss the point that with a little honest effort on his part an even better opportunity could be found.

Waiting at the restaurant — Sellcox had been a half-hour late — he had framed his explanation of why he was turning down the presidency of Coastal Foods, building upon his recollection of how Sellcox, on the occasion of their first meeting, had criticized him so caustically for having jumped in without adequate investigation when he had taken the presidency of the Chemical Service Corporation. He could, he had decided, honestly tell Sellcox that he had taken his advice.

All expectation of a reasonable hearing had been shattered with Sellcox's arrival. For a moment Lincoln Lord had thought that he was witnessing only his standard behavior, the vinegary face and acid tongue that set him apart from all other New York employment agents specializing in high-level executive personnel, an eccentricity that unaccountably but undeniably had made him the best known practitioner in his field. Then, quickly, Sellcox had outdone himself as a living legend, confronting him across the table with an all-knowing expression of supercilious cynicism, acting as if he disbelieved every word that he was hearing, unresponsive, making him squeeze out the last word of explanation, forcing him to say far more than he had intended. Only after Lincoln Lord had been driven beyond retreat, had Sellcox signaled him to silence.

"All right, Linc, you've told me your story. Now I'm going to tell you mine. If I've gotten anywhere in this racket, it's because I'm honest — and the only kind of a client I can help is the man that wants it that way. I'm no dope peddler. If you want somebody to give you a fix that will send you off into your own little private dream world again, you'd better get yourself another boy. But I think you've been on

117

the stuff long enough. It's time you took the cure. And the best cure in the world is facing up to the truth. If that's what you want, I'll give it to you. If you don't, let's call for a check and get out of here."

Fear-struck, Lincoln Lord had neither moved nor spoken and Sellcox had slowly lighted a cigarette, the endlessly prolonged act of a fiend bent on torture. "All right, Linc, let's get under the cold shower. This is the truth. I've been pushing you for months now, shoving that résumé of yours under the nose of anybody and everybody that's been looking for a company president. I don't know how many there've been — twenty or thirty, maybe more. And what's happened? Nothing. I haven't had a bite, not one. Not even a nibble. You think I haven't been doing a job for you because I haven't gotten you a lot of interviews. That's not my fault, Linc. It's yours. Face it, boy. Every time I go to bat for you — and don't think I haven't — I'm licked before I even get started. They take one look at that record of yours and, brother, that's it! Nobody wants a job-jumper."

And then Sellcox had slowly ground out his cigarette in the pink ash tray, fire against flesh, unfelt because the flesh had been numbed to insensitivity. "This is going to be a tough pill to swallow, Linc, but I'm going to hold your nose and shove it right down your throat. You've been slipping the knife to me because I haven't done anything for you — sure, I know, all very gentlemanly and you weren't really accusing me of letting you down — but still that was the general idea, wasn't it? No, wait! It's my turn now. You think you took old man Phelps into camp all by yourself, no help from me — that's it, isn't it? All right, Mr. Lincoln Lord, let me tell you what really happened. In the last six months Phelps has had two presidencies open in companies he controls. I pitched you at him for both of them. No go. Your name never even got on the first list. Yesterday he called up. I know — he'd heard you make a speech. That was your first lucky break. Your second was that he couldn't get hold of you and had to call me. Do you know what he wanted you for? Sales manager — that's all. And just who the hell do you think sold him on the idea of giving you a shot at the presidency? Do you know how long I was on the phone with him? Do you have any idea of what a battle I had? I never sold any man harder in my life. And I won't say I wasn't lucky, too. If it had been one of his own companies he probably wouldn't have gone for it. But it isn't. You know that, don't you? Coastal Foods is owned by the widow of some old friend of Phelps's. So he's on the hook. The only way he can get off is to find somebody to recommend to her."

He must have said something then, apology beaten out of him by the rain of blows, because Sellcox had said, "Don't blame me for giving it to you straight, Linc. You asked for it. If you want my advice, here it is — get down there today and charm the pants off that old widow. I don't care what you do, legal or illegal, moral or immoral, but grab that job. I mean it, Linc, *grab it!* All right, it's nothing but a little tin-shed cannery — forget it! Everybody thinks it's a Hebe outfit — forget that, too. Forget everything except getting your name on that payroll. And once you've got it there, for god's sake make it stick. You can't be this lucky again."

What had happened after that was uncertainly vague. Somehow he had escaped. And he must have started to walk, his feet in the rut of habit, because he eventually found himself far down Fifth Avenue, almost at Washington Square. Startled to discover where he was, his mind had cleared long enough to remember that Anderson Phelps had not been called, that he was still expecting him to go to Goodhaven today. That must have been when he had ordered this Cadillac, a telephone call made in an all but forgotten dream, a nightmare extended when he had finally gotten back to the hotel and called Maggie from the lobby, terrorized when he discovered that she hadn't been planning to go, seemingly final proof that she, too, was rejecting him.

That had been the low point, a nadir marked by a resurrection of his most deeply hidden memory — that one occasion when, the night after Maggie had gotten back from Bermuda, he had been so certain that she was planning to divorce him — but somehow he had talked her into going with him today, an accomplishment robbed of most of its validity when she finally came down and startled him by apologizing for keeping him waiting.

She had almost tricked him into admitting how desperately important it was to get the Coastal Foods job when she had seen the Cadillac, but he had managed to keep up a front, not letting her know ... but now she *had* to know. There was no other way. He had to tell her. He'd been a fool back there on the Parkway, trying to handle her as if she were a vice-president, attempting to plant the idea in her mind so that she'd think it was her own. He should have known better. Mag was too smart, too keen, too knowing ... and he'd been too fuzzy-brained and thick-tongued to get away with it. And even if he had, it wouldn't have lasted ... she'd know as soon as they got into town. Mag didn't realize it yet but she would when she saw the plant ... nothing but a little tin-shed cannery ... Quincy Canning ... back

119

to where he'd been when she'd married him. But if she would only agree that it was something that he *had* to do . . . if he could somehow convince her without being forced into telling her *why* . . .

Suddenly he realized that in giving her the power of decision he had handed her a double-edged sword. In his blindness, all he had seen was a chance to protect himself from her criticism. It had not occurred to him until now that the odds were all against her favorable decision. She would almost certainly think that it wasn't a big enough job for him, that he ought to wait for something better to turn up, not knowing that it never would . . . *he had to have this job!* There was only one way out . . . he had to sell it to her, make her believe that everything was wonderful . . . the town, the cannery, Mrs. Zurich . . . yes, Mrs. Zurich. And that might be a problem . . . if Mag didn't like her . . . or if she didn't like Mag . . .

"Do you know where to go, Linc?"

It took him a moment to realize that it was not his own question. "I'll stop somewhere and ask. Anyone will know. Coastal Foods is the biggest thing in town."

4

Waiting, Dean Whittaker transferred the telephone instrument to his other hand. But he could still hear the thumping of his heart over the low humming sound of the open line.

A voice exploded in his ear. "Yes?"

"Mr. Quincy, this is — Jay, this is Arthur Whittaker."

"Yes, Dean?"

"I —" He waggled his head, attempting to break the stricture that bound his throat. "I was just wondering — if you aren't too busy, would it be too much of an intrusion — ?" The binding band broke and the words rushed out. "I want to come out and talk to you."

"What's on your mind, Dean?"

He expelled his breath as if it were the abandonment of honor. "I've just come back from New York — the alumni meeting, you know? It was so successful — so very successful — I thought you might possibly be interested in hearing about it."

The moment of silence convicted him of gross prevarication. Then, amazingly, Jay Quincy said pleasantly, "Glad to see you any time,

Dean. Why don't you drop out this afternoon, fiveish, and we'll have a drink and a little chat?"

"Thank you — thank you very much," he said, hanging up, staring then at the damp fingermarkings, slowly evaporating, that his hand had left on the receiver. It had really gone quite well, amazingly so, much better than he had anticipated.

5

Maggie Lord felt the car slow and, glancing at her husband, saw that his eyes were on two boys who were standing outside the door of a beer joint, sideburned and black-jacketed, examining a parked motorcycle. He brought the car to a stop and ran down her window. The boys turned surly faces, eyes glinting as coldly as the nailhead ornamentation on their black horsehide jackets.

"Hello there," he called, only that and no more, yet she was not surprised to see the challenging scowls fade, the boys amble forward as if drawn by some irresistible magnet.

"Can you tell me how to get to the Coastal Foods Company?"

The shorter of the two boys whispered a hoarse prompt, "What he means is the cannery, Mickey."

"Crissake, I guess I know," the tall boy said under his breath, an angry rejection of assistance. "You go right into town, see? There's a red light just before you come to the bridge. Okay, you turn left and go down Main Street. Just keep going, don't turn or nothing. You cross the railroad track and there you are, see?"

"That's the Coastal Foods Company?"

"Sure, mister. You can't miss it."

"And would you happen to know where the Zurich home is — where Mrs. Zurich lives?"

"You mean the house, huh?" the tall boy said blankly, dry-spitting his embarrassment at being unable to tell him.

The other boy pushed forward. "You go the same way, mister. There's a road around the cannery and that takes you right down to the house."

"Thanks, fellows," she heard her husband say, conscious that he was starting the car again but not turning to him, still watching the faces of the two boys, their eyes lowered to catch a last glimpse of Lincoln

Lord through the window, their boyishly rapt attention filtering through an adolescent pretense of rough masculinity.

The car accelerated rapidly and she was left with the awareness that her inner mind, stealthily alert, had again pushed forward the old question of why Linc had always failed to exert upon his own son the attraction with which he so effortlessly drew to him every other boy of the same age.

"See those sideburns?" he said with a low chuckle, surprising her with what seemed a startling change of mood. "I'll bet Dr. Summerfield doesn't let the boys up at Forgehill get away with anything like that!"

She held firm to her decision to say nothing about yesterday's trip to Forgehill, certain that it would be interpreted as an admission of lost confidence, determination now added by the recollection that there had been so many occasions in her married life when, almost as a punishment, a low point of faith had been the preamble to a spectacular recovery, when by some miracle beyond reason, Linc had managed to prove her wrong.

He made the left turn at the traffic light and almost immediately said, "Golly, it's a nice town, isn't it?"

She looked ahead down the three blocks of the business section, puzzled by what had inspired a complimentary appraisal. By contrast with the decrepit shacks that had lined the main road, the stores and shops were solidly substantial; yet she saw nothing that lifted Goodhaven above the level of hundreds of other little towns . . . was Linc trying to talk himself into imagining that this was where he wanted to live?

A leaded glass clock jutted out from the corner building of the Goodhaven National Bank, and looking at it, she asked, "We're a little early, aren't we?"

"We still have to find where she lives. Anyway, I want to get a look at the plant before we talk to her." He had slowed the car to a crawling pace and was alternately scanning both sides of the street. "Reminds you of Brighton, doesn't it?"

"Yes," she said, wondering if the thought was fresh in his mind, if he was aware of all the implications of similarity.

They were out of the business section now, passing the last of the houses that had been false-fronted into stores and shops. Ahead on the right side of the road, were a half-dozen big old homes that faced the bay, wide lawns running down to the water's edge, almost a duplicate of Front Street in Brighton. Across the road, however, there was a structure incongruous to the scene, a sprawling modern building, jaggedly rectangular in outline, most of its wall area glassed. An unconsidered first glance made her think that it might be the office building of the Coastal Foods Company. Then she saw the line-up of yellow busses and the sign that identified the building as the Good-haven Consolidated High School . . . *they could bring Kip down from Forgehill!*

"That must be the plant," Linc said.

Thinking that he had committed her same error of too hasty iden-tification, she started to correct him, seeing then that he was looking, not at the high school building but directly ahead, beyond the warning sign of a railroad crossing to the bleak corrugated iron wall against which the road seemed to dead-end, a sight so perfectly duplicating memory that she braced herself for the right turn into the cannery yard, wrinkling her nose at the expectation of the sour smell of fermenting vegetable waste that, more surely than sight, had always identified the Quincy cannery. But the road turned left instead of right, circling the end of the building. A truck stood at a loading plat-form, *Coastal Foods* tastefully script-lettered in gold on its blue-lac-quered van body.

"This must be the old plant," he said. "Yes, there's the new one."

The circling road swung past a long brick building, single-storied except in the narrow central section, a low tower surmounted with a sign that duplicated the lettering on the truck. In other surroundings, the structure would have attracted no special attention — along any main highway, there were dozens of small industrial plants cast in the same mold — yet the contrast with expectation was so great that she found herself suddenly buoyant with hope.

"Doesn't look too bad, does it?" he asked.

"No, it really doesn't," she agreed, too quickly and too fervently, belatedly conscious of the danger of commitment.

"Anyway, it looks worth exploring," he said, a sober appraisal that ended with a teasing smile. "Or shall we turn around and go back to New York?"

"Not without lunch," she replied, light laughter quickly contrived.

"What time is it?" he asked, answering himself with a quick glance at the dashboard clock. "I don't think it's too early, do you? We still have to find the house. From what the boys said, it must be some-where down this road."

He accelerated, steering for a fork in the road, the apex of a triangle landscaped with low shrubbery that evidenced meticulous care. Beyond, there was a forest-thick planting of pine trees, seemingly impenetrable until an oblique cut through the trees was revealed as they approached. There was a moment of tunnel darkness, the boughs touching overhead to block the sun, and then they burst out into the light again. The car stopped in what seemed a demanded reaction to the beauty of the suddenly revealed scene. They were on a low rise, made to seem higher by the flat surroundings, the base of an arrowhead of land that thrust itself out into the summer-blue water of Barnegat Bay, sequin-sparkled by the sun. Beyond, in the haze across the bay, was the saw-edged outline of the buildings on Tern Beach and, more imagined than actually seen, the sweep of the ocean. The broad view was demandingly dominant, momentarily distracting attention from the house. Once seen, however, it became the focal point of interest, all the more so because it was so different from what she had expected. She had, for no good reason other than the location and the image of Sol Zurich that Anderson Phelps had fixed in her mind, imagined the Zurich home as being a rubber-stamp duplicate of the summer-home mansions built by turn-of-the-century millionaires all along the Atlantic coast. Instead, the house that lay ahead of them was startlingly contemporary in design, glass and stone and redwood, low-lying, so artfully integrated with the landscape that it seemed something that had grown out of its setting, not something built upon it.

Linc shared her surprise, saying, "Do you suppose that can be it?"

"It must be," she said, her eyes again searching the little peninsula, assuring herself that there was no other house in sight.

"Not what I'd expected," he said, lightly apprehensive.

She guessed that he, too, was thinking less of the house than of the woman whose home it must be. "Did you find out anything more about her — this morning, I mean?"

For a moment she thought he was evading an answer. Then he said, "No more than Phelps told us. She came down here right after the war — superintendent of that orphan's home he mentioned — married Zurich about six years ago." He paused, finally adding, "Looks like she did all right for herself."

"It's a beautiful house," she agreed.

"I don't mean just the house." He glanced back in the general direction of the cannery. "Not a bad payoff for six years of marriage."

He had spoken lightly, mildly cynical, but it seemed a thin mask for serious concern, and through it, she suddenly saw the image of old

Cornelia Rabson, who, although professing a hands-off policy in connection with the management of Rabson Foods, had actually controlled every move from behind the closed shutters of her King Street mansion house. Linc's most reasonable argument for not returning to Brighton after the war had been Admiral Rabson's promise of a freer hand than he could ever have hoped to have under Adam Quincy's one-man domination of the Quincy Canning Company. But the admiral's promise had been canceled by his mother. Cornelia Rabson had turned out to be, although not as openly dictatorial as Adam Quincy, even more resistant to change. Her husband had been dead for ten years but he was still running the company, management from the grave implemented by his widow's mad illusion that she could still hear him whispering instructions to her... if Mrs. Zurich proved to be another Cornelia Rabson... if Anderson Phelps's promise that she would turn over the company to Linc meant no more than the admiral's...

Suddenly, she remembered what Linc had said about the Cadillac ... *"If you were hiring a president for a company you controlled..."*

Realization came as the rush of air into a vacuum... this was why Linc had acted so strangely this morning! Now she could see her mistake, assuming that Phelps had the authority to offer Linc the job... of course he hadn't! No one would hand over complete control of any company so lightly, even a small one like Coastal Foods... and, actually, Phelps hadn't made a definite offer. Yes, that had been her error, imagining that the job was Linc's if he wanted it. It wasn't. Oh, why hadn't she seen it? It was so plain... Phelps not asking a single question about Linc's record or experience. All that was to come. If there was an offer to be made, Mrs. Zurich would make it... and Linc was afraid that she might turn him down...

"Mag, when you talk to her —"

Caught off guard, she said quickly, "I was just going to ask what you wanted me to do." She hurriedly corrected herself. "Is there anything I *can* do?"

"No, I don't suppose there is," he said uncertainly. "Except — well, a lot depends on her."

"Of course," she said, imagining she understood what he meant, startled when he added, "I mean, whether I take the job or not," revealing that he still thought the presidency was his for the taking... or was he only covering up?

"If it's another Cornelia Rabson situation — "

"I was thinking of that, too," she said, validity restored to her guess.

125

"But if she would —" His voice drifted off and she saw that he was leaning forward, his arms shaped to the circle of the steering wheel, his chin on his clasped hands. "Golly, Mag, this could be like a dream coming true — a chancè to really go ahead on my own."

In her mind his voice lost itself in the reverberant repetition of over-lapped memories . . . this was the way it had always been . . . so many dreams . . . a new one always ready when an old one was shattered . . .

She closed her eyes and in the false darkness the black Cadillac be-came an Essex touring car, the paved driveway to Mrs. Zurich's home a rutted back-country lane . . . "No, I'm only here at the cannery for the summer. As soon as the college opens they're going to appoint a new alumni secretary. I don't know how much chance there is that they'll give me the job, but if they'd give me a chance to go ahead on my own . . ."

"Well, we'll soon know," he said abruptly, breaking in on his own voice, easing the car down the long drive, coming to a stop in front of the house.

She got out, brushing at the wrinkles in her skirt, regretting her too-hurried choice of the suit that she had snatched from the closet when Linc had called.

"You're all right," he said, so obviously an attempt to generate self-confidence by transference that she smiled back at him in an oddly pleasant sharing of apprehension.

At close range the exterior of the house seemed even more attractive than it had from a distance. The wide steps were pebble-patterned concrete, beautifully fitted to the house, flanked by plantings of small evergreens that carried a strong reminder of the miniature gardens that had been, for her, the most attractive feature of Japan. There was even a pair of the verdigrised bronze ducks that she wanted so much to buy in Kyoto.

The doorknocker was another bit of Japan bronze, but when it was touched there was the distant sound of a muffled Oriental gong, the struck note still reverberant when the door opened, a response so rapid that she was unprepared for speech, caught in a blank moment of star-ing at the face of the woman in the doorway, seeing a smile of welcome that made her feel herself artlessly unpoised — an awkward predica-ment from which she was rescued by her husband's "Mrs. Zurich?"

"Yes, I'm Kira Zurich," the woman said. "And you're the Lincoln Lords, aren't you? Please come in."

Maggie Lord found herself included in the plurality of greeting, yet

quickly excluded by the duel of appraisal between her husband and
Kira Zurich, an exchange of glances that made them seem so intently
concerned, each with the other, that she was left as an excluded third
party, permitted only the privilege of observation. And yet it was a
role into which she slipped without resistance, the way eased by the
need of mental adjustment. Kira Zurich was not at all the person
that she had imagined her to be.

As loosely constructed as the frame of expectation had been, it could
not be made to fit Mrs. Sol Zurich. She had expected, if not eccentricity, at least the strangeness of someone who could logically have
married the little old Jew that she had visualized from Phelps's description. Instead, Kira Zurich seemed so ordinary that her normality
was almost bizarre. Even her surveillance of Lincoln Lord, intense as
it was, was made to appear no more than a frank exposure of curiosity.

Kira Zurich was younger than Maggie had expected her to be,
surely no older than herself; yet age offered no measure of personality.
She was the kind of person who would have been mature in adolescence and, unchanging, would show little aging with the years, her
whole life lived in the same fixed character. She was dark and olive-
skinned, small and light of stature, a physique suggesting a great store
of nervous energy, although there was no external evidence of tension.
She was much too plain to ever have been thought pretty, too ordinary-
looking to have ever been striking; yet it was difficult to believe that
she had been rejected in the marriage mart until her forties because of
any serious lack of physical attractiveness. It seemed a better guess that
she was a woman to whom a career had been more important than
marriage.

But the house was a warning, if one was needed, that Kira Zurich
might be a quite different person than she appeared. It was strikingly
modern, beautifully furnished, the perfection of taste and detail wholly
incompatible with a routine navy blue crepe dress, a strand of arti-
ficial pearls, and shoes that had been selected only for practicality and
good value. Her hair was long, drawn back into a tight roll that, once
made, could be forgotten for the rest of the day. Nowhere about her
person was there the slightest hint of the flair for smartness that was
reflected in every detail of the house and its furnishings. It had
probably been done by an interior decorator, yet, even so, it seemed
inconceivable that Kira Zurich had not imposed her own taste somewhere. But now, as they moved across the entrance hall, around a beautiful Japanese screen and into the big living room, there was not the

127

smallest thing, even an ash tray, that was compatible with her displayed character. There was almost the feeling — an impression that she dared not permit herself to trust — that Kira Zurich was a stranger in this house, and that the house itself had never been really lived in. There was a lifelessness, a sterility, that reminded her of the model rooms that, back in her *Hearthside* days, had been built and furnished only to be photographed as magazine illustrations.

"Golly, this is an attractive house," she heard her husband say and, cued by his glance, she offered enthusiastic agreement, thinking how easy it would be to make it truly that, how little would have to be done to give it the vital lived-in quality that it now lacked.

Kira Zurich's only reply was a smile that brushed both of their faces as she moved toward a circular game table, the geometrical tracery of a chessboard incised in its ebony surface. "Shall we sit here for a moment?" she asked. "There are one or two things that it might be well to clear up before the others get here."

Lincoln Lord's voice showed cautious surprise. "There's someone else coming?"

"Yes, I've asked Mr. Kennan and Mr. Swann to come over," Kira Zurich said. "I'm sure you'll have a lot of questions to ask about the company and I thought it would help to have the men here who could answer them. Frank Kennan is the production manager and Mr. Swann is in charge of the office."

"Yes, I know," he said blandly, his feelings so well masked that Maggie felt reasonably certain that Mrs. Zurich would not sense his resentment at being displayed for the judgment of some of her second-rung men.

"I hope you don't mind?" Mrs. Zurich asked, the first hint that her poise might be penetrable. "I was only trying to plan things to save as much of your time as possible."

"Of course not," he said, a denial almost withdrawn by adding, "But please don't be too concerned about saving our time. We're not at all pressed today."

"I was very pleased when Mr. Phelps phoned to tell me that you were willing to make the trip today. It was kind of you to come so soon."

"Not at all. Beautiful drive down here. A holiday for us, you know — a chance to get out of New York for the day. And we're delighted to have the chance to meet you, Mrs. Zurich."

She responded with no more than a quick-fading smile of acknowledgment. Her hand had reserved one chair for herself, an indication that she wanted them to sit in the two chairs that faced her. Then, as they did, Maggie noticed a file folder lying on the table, evidence that Mrs. Zurich had carefully planned what was about to happen.

Expectantly, Maggie Lord waited for her husband to say something that would establish his command of the situation. Surprisingly, he let the moment of interruptable silence pass, an opportunity shortened by the speed with which Mrs. Zurich moved to end it.

"Mr. Phelps was good enough to send all of this down with a special messenger this morning," she said, opening the file folder, exposing a letter that Maggie, reading upside down, could see was on the letterhead of Weeks, Phelps & Harrison. Under it there was the maroon cover of a Sellcox & Lloyd résumé, gold-lettered LINCOLN LORD, and as Mrs. Zurich fanned the pages off her thumb, it could be seen that they were so heavily annotated that there was no blank margin unfilled with Phelps's penciled comments. Inside the back cover there was a sheaf of clippings, too rapidly seen for all of them to be recognized, but no more than a glimpse was necessary to identify the *Wall Street Journal* account of the break-up of the Chemical Service Corporation, the *Fortune* article about Luxor Pharmacal, the *Business Week* piece that had appeared after they had gone to Japan, even the news story on the Chesapeake College dinner that had been in the *Times* only yesterday morning. The thickness of the file and the scope of its contents was a shattering destruction of the impression that Phelps, yesterday afternoon, had acted precipitously and without investigation.

Lincoln Lord smiled and said, "You seem to have quite a dossier on me, Mrs. Zurich."

Kira Zurich looked up as if uncertain as to how to react.

"But I imagine there are still a good many unanswered questions in your mind," he went on, still smiling. "And please don't feel the slightest embarrassment about asking them. I'll be only too happy to tell you anything that I possibly can."

Maggie was stunned to see Kira Zurich shake her head. "No, Mr. Lord, I have no questions about you." And now her hand was noticeably trembling as she twisted a paper clip and slipped the Phelps letter out of the file. "I think the important question, Mr. Lord, is the one that I know you have about me."

"I'm afraid I'm lost."

"This is a report that Mr. Phelps gave me on your talk with him

129

yesterday afternoon." She spread the letter on the table, turning over the first page to expose the second, "I'd like to read you what he wrote me —" She paused, waiting for his nodded approval before she picked up the page and read, " 'In my judgment, the only thing that could induce Mr. Lord to accept the presidency of Coastal Foods would be the chance to take over and run it as if it were his own company. I told him that you were prepared to offer him that opportunity, but I suspect that he may have questioned my authority to make so broad a commitment. In any event, I suggest —' " She cut herself off. "Is that the situation, Mr. Lord?"

"If I gave Mr. Phelps that impression, it was surely unintentional. I had no doubt that he was speaking for you, Mrs. Zurich, none whatsoever."

"But was he speaking for you?" Mrs. Zurich pressed. "Is that true, Mr. Lord? Is that what you would want?"

He hesitated for an instant but then his voice had the ring of struck metal, a positive, "Yes," unqualified and uncompromising.

Kira Zurich dampened her thin lips. "I do confirm what Mr. Phelps told you, Mr. Lord. I'd like nothing better than to have you take full responsibility for managing the Coastal Foods Company."

To her amazement Maggie heard him reply without the slightest hesitation or evidence of surprise, "That's very flattering, Mrs. Zurich. I appreciate your confidence in me — and all the more so because I know how difficult it must be for you to turn over to someone else the management of a company that must mean as much to you as the Coastal Foods Company does."

Kira Zurich regarded him so fixedly, so long silent, that Maggie Lord began to wonder if her suspicions had been aroused by Linc's too transparent desire to explore her attitude toward the Coastal Foods Company. When she spoke, however, it was obvious that her hesitation had been occasioned by nothing more than a search for words. "You say, Mr. Lord, that the company means a great deal to me. Yes, it does — but not, perhaps, in quite the way that you're thinking." She paused. "I hope you won't think me maudlin when I tell you this, but I know of no other way to explain my attitude. My husband died of cancer. He knew for several months that he had no chance to live. The thing that sustained him through those last awful weeks was the feeling that he had built something that would live on after he was gone. What frightened him, I think, even more than death itself, was that something would happen to his company. Perhaps he'd guessed that there was a danger of losing the Gellman Stores business — I really don't know — but the future of Coastal Foods meant much more to him than his own life."

"That's not difficult to understand," Lincoln Lord said sympathetically.

"Quite often during those last weeks he would ask me to promise him that I'd do anything I possibly could to keep the company alive and healthy. Naturally I promised that I would. But I had no idea what that promise would entail. Did Mr. Phelps tell you about his will?"

"Only in a very general way."

"You do know that he left full control in my hands?"

"So I understood."

"That came as a complete surprise to me," she said intently, almost as if it were a protest against suspicion. "He had talked to me of a quite different plan — of putting all of the stock in a trust fund for the benefit of Haven Home — and I have no idea why he changed his mind and left it all to me."

Lincoln Lord suggested, "Perhaps because he thought the company would be safer in your hands."

"Yes, that's the only conclusion I could draw," Kira Zurich agreed. "Of course, the end result would be the same — I'm sure he knew that I'd turn over all of my dividends to Haven Home, anyway — but personal responsibility for actually running the company was not something that I had expected. Nor was it anything that I wanted. But under the circumstances there was nothing else that I could do but attempt to keep my promise." She looked at the letter. "You do know that I've been president of the company?"

"Yes."

"That was a mistake," Kira said crisply. "Mr. Phelps had assured me that it was only a formality, that Mr. Kennan and Mr. Swann would go on running the company exactly as my husband had. I know now how impossible that was. They're both fine men, able and competent and loyal, but without leadership —" She smiled wanly. "I should have known — I've seen it so often in other organizations — no matter how good your people are, no matter how many committees you appoint or how many charts you draw, there has to be that one right man up at the top or it never works out. It's like a ship without a captain — sooner or later you run on the rocks. Sometimes you think that the captain does so little, that it would be so easy to take his place — I know better now." She paused. "No, Mr. Lord, if you're willing to take over, you'll not have to worry about interference from me. I've learned my lesson."

Maggie Lord could hardly believe her ears... the job *was* Linc's ... and on his own terms! If he really wanted it...

"I'd only ask your assurance on one point," Kira Zurich went on. "That you wouldn't blame Mr. Swann or Mr. Kennan for the trouble that the company is now in. What's happened is my fault, not theirs. And there are a number of other people for whom I feel a great sense of personal responsibility — all of the older employees who were so loyal and faithful to my husband. I recognize that it may be necessary to make certain personnel changes — I'd not want to tie your hands on that score — but I would ask that they be treated in a way that recognizes — well, I'm sure you understand how I feel."

"Of course."

"There is one rather special case," she said. "You'll not meet him today — unfortunately he's out of town — Dr. Perrill. For a number of years, he's been working on a baby food that my husband encouraged him to think the company might someday put on the market. Whether or not it has real commercial possibilities, I don't know. Perhaps it doesn't. But in fairness to Dr. Perrill I am anxious that it be given some consideration. If it turns out to be something that can't be sold successfully, well and good — I'd be quite willing to accept your judgment — but I do want to make certain that Dr. Perrill is fairly treated."

"Perfectly reasonable," Lincoln Lord said easily. Then, startlingly abrupt, he asked, "Are you really so certain, Mrs. Zurich, that I'm the man you want?"

Maggie Lord was shocked and puzzled by her husband's purpose until, watching Mrs. Zurich's face, it seemed revealed by result. Their eyes were locked across the game table, Kira Zurich's expression so obviously a pledge of complete surrender that Maggie felt herself, even more surely than before, an intruding witness — and then suddenly a detached observer, fascinated by the skill with which Linc had moved to clinch not only a solid offer of the presidency but also his complete control of the company if he accepted.

Kira Zurich sat motionless, her eyes unblinking. "There's no doubt in my mind, Mr. Lord, none whatsoever." She moved then, quickly, as if it were the breaking of a spell, glancing out of the window. "They're coming now — Mr. Kennan and Mr. Swann."

"I wonder if you'd mind telling me, Mrs. Zurich — ?"

She turned back to face him. "Yes?"

"It may be just a bit awkward if I don't know — have you told them why I'm here?"

"Of course," she said, puzzled, almost as if she were unable to understand how he could possibly have imagined that she might not have told them. She stood now, prepared to go to the door, waiting for the sound of the door gong, a moment idly filled by saying, "That's a beautiful car you have, Mr. Lord. What is it?"

"Cadillac," he said offhandedly — and then, no less casually, "But it's not ours. We just rented it for the day."

The gong rang, its sound amplified by the stillness. For a long moment Mrs. Zurich made no move to go to the door. Then she quickly left the room, leaving behind the impression of an odd bemusement. Seeing the after-image of her strange little smile, Maggie Lord realized that nothing that Linc could possibly have done would have so cleverly erased whatever last doubts about him that there might have been in Mrs. Zurich's mind.

Linc was beside her now, whispering, "What do you think of her?"

She started to express her good impression, stopped suddenly by the memory of his demand that she take the responsibility of judgment, an awareness that held her to a meaningless nod, doubly guarded by a shrug of her shoulders.

The voices in the hall were audible now, the two men easily identifiable even before they came to the doorway, the office manager's voice clipped and cautiously precise, the factory manager's rough-edged and rolling. It was even easier to know who was who as they stepped into the room. Except for the courtesy of introduction, there was no need for Kira Zurich's explanation that the thin-bodied man, graying and sixtyish, was Alfred Swann, the office manager. He could not possibly have been mistaken for anything other than what he was, the fine-print formality of his, "I am very pleased to meet you, Mrs. Lord," as much in character as was every aspect of his physical appearance.

Nor could there have been any doubt about Frank Kennan's identity, although he made himself seem momentarily out of character by being so overwhelmed by gratitude when Lincoln Lord immediately recognized him, stepping forward without waiting for Kira Zurich's introduction and saying, "Good to see you again, Frank."

133

"Good to see *you!*" Kennan exclaimed fervently. "I was just talking about you on the way over — wondering if you'd remember me."

"Of course," Lincoln Lord said quietly, his presidential tone such an obvious assumption of status that Maggie found herself wondering if his decision had already been made.

"Well, I didn't know — it's been such a long time," Kennan said, a self-conscious explanation.

Puzzled, Kira Zurich said, "I had no idea that you two knew each other."

She had directed the implied question to Lincoln Lord, but he deflected it to Kennan with a deferring silence that won an ear-to-ear smile of gratitude from the production manager. "Well, I didn't mention it last night, Mrs. Zurich, because I figured Mr. Lord probably wouldn't remember how —" He made another start. "This was back when Mr. Lord was president of Frazer Glass. He stepped in himself and helped us out of an awful jam — got us a jar that we could handle on those old Ross-Perry labeling machines."

"Oh, I see," Kira Zurich said.

"And you know, Mr. Lord," Kennan went on, "we haven't bought a case of anybody else's glass since. I've told a lot of people about that — salesmen from different suppliers, you know — telling them that what they ought to have was a company president who handled things the way you did when you were at Frazer Glass."

For a second Maggie Lord wondered if Kennan could possibly be sincere, deciding almost immediately that he must be, his open-faced honesty too evident to be questioned. Then, in almost the same instant of time, she found herself embarrassed by transposition, trying to imagine how Linc could possibly respond.

He solved the problem with amazing ease, saying nothing, simply letting his silence stand as an adequate answer, and her surprise faded into a renewed perception of an old error. She had been thinking of him as being facilely glib, his voice the prime instrument of his power to charm. Now, once again, she realized how often he used silence even more effectively than words, as if it were a language of its own, speaking it an accomplishment that set him above men like Kennan who, less gifted, nevertheless understood and accepted it as evidence of stature.

She listened now to the four-way flow of conversation, as amazed as if it were a new discovery that Linc, although giving the impression of being an active participant, was actually saying almost nothing, the vocabulary of silence inadequate only when Kennan suddenly addressed him with a startling question.

"Tell me something, Mr. Lord. This has been bothering me all morning, trying to remember his name. There was a chap you sent over here with those jar designs — I think he was your assistant — or at least that's the impression I had —"

"Oh yes — Brick Mitchell."

"Mitchell!" Kennan snapped his fingers. "Sure, that's it. Been right on the tip of my tongue, but for the life of me I couldn't remember that name."

Gratefully, Maggie Lord heard a voice behind them say, "Luncheon is served, Mrs. Zurich."

6

A thunderous cymbal roar beat against Brick Mitchell's eardrums, an agonizing sound that rose to a screaming crescendo, broke through the barrier to perception and then, abruptly, became only the ringing of the telephone.

Fireballs exploded in his eye cavities. And then he was staring up at the sun image that was burning a round-edged hole through the narrow slit in the down-slatted venetian blind.

He reached out for the telephone, failed to find it, discovering when it rang again that it was on the wrong side of the bed. He finally located it and lifted the receiver, awkwardly left-handed, a grumble of annoyance submerged in the dawning realization that he was not in his own apartment.

"Brick?" the voice in his ear asked, ending the guessing game, a reminder of the night.

"Yeah, Tommy," he said, the consciousness that he was still in her apartment negatively confirmed by his inability to remember having gone back to his own.

"Do you know what time it is?" she asked, irritatingly bright-voiced.

He nodded groggily.

"Did you hear me, Brick?"

"Sure, Tommy, sure," he mumbled, leather-lipped.

"Now listen, Brick. Robbie called and wants to talk to you about that article. I tried to stall him but the latest he can see you is three o'clock. Is that all right?"

"Why not?" he said gruffly, trying to counter her too tolerant concern. "Anything else?"

"Nothing important. The coffee's all made, Brick. All you have to do is turn on the stove and heat it up. And there's a jar of orange juice in the refrigerator."

"No other calls, huh?"

"No."

"Okay, Tommy, okay."

"You won't go back to sleep, will you? Shall I call you again?"

"No, I'm all right," he said, belatedly adding a forced, "Thanks, Tommy."

He hung up, letting his body follow the sweep of his arm, getting out of the wrong side of the bed, staring sightlessly at the strange cluster of cosmetic jars on the dressing table, groping through the fog of mixed memories, trying to separate illusion from the solid substance of valid memory. Hurriedly he gave up the attempt, not because it was too difficult but because it suddenly became too easy . . . off the deep end like a damn lush . . . months and months since he'd done anything like this . . . that Lincoln Lord business . . .

"To hell with him!" he said aloud, listening to the sound of his voice, still not satisfied, trying it again . . . sounded like somebody else . . . mouth full of cotton . . .

He stood, tentatively testing the stability of the room, finding the floor reassuringly solid . . . hell of a hangover . . . but it was worth it . . . out of his system . . . pressure was gone . . . drained . . .

The jar of orange juice was in the refrigerator, full to the brim, slopping out when he unscrewed the cap. He raised it to his lips and drank . . . Tommy was a good gal . . . wonderful . . . deserved a hell of a lot more than he'd ever given her. Maybe it would be different now . . . but, damn it, why did she have to keep acting as if he needed someone to take care of him!

7

Seated at the head of the luncheon table, Lincoln Lord was slowly recapturing some sense of confidence in the reliability of his judgment. He was aware of how anxious he had been, and experience had taught him that he was not immune to the danger of believing what he wanted to believe, yet now with every passing moment he was more and more certain that what was happening was not an illusion born of desire but a complete contradiction of all the charges Otis Sellcox had hurled against him.

Sellcox had said that he had ruined himself . . . *"They take one look at the record of yours and, brother, that's it!"* . . . and now that had been made a lie, that and everything else that Sellcox had said . . . stealing credit for selling Phelps . . . what had really sold Phelps had been his record, the very thing that Sellcox had said would kill him . . . *"Nobody wants a job-jumper"* . . . but Phelps knew his record, every twist and turn of it . . . everything had been in that file he'd sent to Kira Zurich . . . and, knowing everything, Phelps had recommended him without reservation. That must be true or Mrs. Zurich wouldn't have decided even before she saw him . . . and she, too, knowing all that there was to know, wanted him . . . more than anyone else had ever wanted him before . . . and Frank Kennan wanted him . . . and Swann wanted him . . .

Somehow it all seemed too dangerously pleasant, too perfect to be believed, so enticing that there must be a fault somewhere . . . but where?

Suspicion died for want of nourishment, caution sustained only by the apprehensive feeling that everyone was acting as if he had already accepted the presidency, as if he had sacrificed the right of decision when Kira Zurich had seated him at the head of the table, saying, "This is your place, Mr. Lord," putting Kennan on his right and Swann on his left, matching her own status to that of Maggie's, sitting across from her a long arm's length down the table from the men.

Tempted by normality, it was difficult to keep telling himself that he had still not made up his mind, and now he found himself forced to resort to a resurrection of last night's belief that if he had the courage to hold out and hang on, something even more desirable would turn up — but it was hard to imagine in what way desirability could be enhanced. It might, of course, be a larger company, but that was a questionable advantage — none at all financially, if he could believe what Phelps had said about Mrs. Zurich's willingness to match his Luxor salary — and never again, certainly, would there be another chance to start from scratch and build his own business, inheriting no one else's mistakes, everything in his favor, the whole situation so perfectly matched to his own abilities. So often before, he had been snarled in office detail or forced to waste himself on production problems. There would be nothing like that here. With a new modern cannery and as good a man as Kennan to run it, there'd be no production trouble — and Swann was that most valuable of all men, a real old-fashioned office manager, the best sort of right-hand man that any president could ever have ... another Paul Willis at Quincy, his head filled with a million miscellaneous facts that would always be on tap when you needed them, not buried in the onionskin pages of some unintelligible Comptrollers Department report ... there'd been a hundred times at Luxor when he'd have gladly traded a dozen big-time comptrollers like Sherman Chappel for one Alf Swann ... no, he wouldn't have to worry about the office, not with Swann ... and Kennan would go ahead on his own, too ... accept responsibility and not come running up to the president's office every time a decision had to be made. The only place where Coastal Foods was weak was on the sales side ... and that was where he himself could most easily supply the strength that was needed.

He caught a moment of silence and edged into it. "Tell me this —" He paused, uncertain as to where the question should be directed, fanning the table with his eyes. "How much of a sales organization do you have?"

Swann spoke. "There hasn't been much need for anything like that, Mr. Lord, not with so much of our business coming from Gellman Stores."

"You have no salesmen at all?"

A negative answer did not surprise him. Most food packing companies, many that were much larger than Coastal, sold their entire output through commission agents. "I suppose you use brokers?"

"Well, yes — yes, we did have a broker in New York — J. D. Feltsing Company."

"Feltsing was responsible for your contacts with Gellman?"

"Oh, no!" Swann said "No, we always handled that direct. About all that Feltsing ever did for us was — oh, job lots of this or that — sometimes a little contract business."

Surprisingly, it was Kennan who picked up the ball, evidencing a breadth that was not too common in production managers, "You see, Mr. Lord, we had an agreement with Gellman that we wouldn't sell competing products in the same area where they had stores. That takes in a lot of territory — as far out as Cleveland and Cincinnati and pretty well down into the Carolinas. When you get beyond that, the business isn't too desirable."

"Freight costs are against you?"

"That's right. We're filling an order now — a thousand cases of beef stew that we got from one of the Chicago chains — and we'll be lucky if we wind up with out-of-pocket cost. The only reason we took it was to keep one line running so that we wouldn't have to lay off our key people."

"That's all the business you have?" he asked, shocked, not having realized that the situation was quite this bad.

"That's about it," Kennan admitted.

"You're completely out at Gellman Stores?"

"As far as packing anything more is concerned — yes. We still have a lot of their stuff in the warehouse. How much of that they'll be willing to take — well, we just don't know what's going to happen."

"Wasn't there a contract? Weren't you operating against firm orders?"

Kennan shrugged, darting a suggestive look at the office manager, and Lincoln Lord turned, transferring the question.

Swann in turn glanced at Kira Zurich, who, after a moment of seem-ing reluctance to intrude, said quietly, "No, there was no contract. My husband and Mr. Gellman had done business together for so many years on a basis of mutal trust and understanding that there had never been any need for anything of that sort. After Mr. Gellman died — then of course, things were on a somewhat different basis. But there wasn't any real trouble until — at least there was nothing that I knew about until after my husband died." She looked at Swann. "There was no difficulty before that chicken à la king affair, was there?"

Again it was Kennan who took over. "Here's more or less what hap-pened, Mr. Lord. You see — well, I know I don't have to tell you any-thing about the way these supermarket chains operate —"

"I'm sure you can tell me a great deal, Frank. I've been out of the food business for several years now and I know there've been a lot of changes."

"Not too many," Kennan said wryly. "It's still about the same old story — only maybe a little more so. Almost all the chains have their own brands, of course."

"I know."

"But Gellman had played it smarter than most of the others — or at least that's the way it always seemed to me. Instead of using their own label just to fight the advertised brands, they made it a quality line that would keep the customers coming back to their stores. That's what we've always packed for them — absolutely top-end stuff — and they'd never cut-priced it. And I don't think anyone could argue that it hadn't been a pretty darned successful policy."

"Hardly."

"Well, after Mr. Gellman died, we got a letter telling us that all of

139

our contacts had to be through one of their vice-presidents, a man named Rubin — Irving Rubin. He'd been sort of an assistant to Mr. Gellman and we thought things would carry on pretty much as they had. But as soon as Rubin got in the saddle he started throwing his weight around. This chicken à la king business that Mrs. Zurich mentioned — well, Rubin had gotten into a hassle with one of the advertised brands over a coupon deal — I don't know what really happened, but, anyway, the story we got was that he was going to teach them a lesson by smacking them with a big cut-price special. He wrote us and told us what he wanted — so many cases at such and such a figure. It was a crazy price, just plain ridiculous. We couldn't begin to touch it without cutting our quality down to a point where we'd be packing nothing but junk. That was something that Mr. Zurich had never done — we've never put a can of anything through the plant that we couldn't be proud of — and so Alf wrote him and told him that we couldn't play along."

"And he blew his top?" he said, a possibility suggested by the recollection of Rubin's voice over the telephone yesterday.

Kennan shook his head. "No, we didn't hear anything at all. He'd been having these brainstorms at the rate of about three a week — the others had blown over and that's what we thought had happened to this one. Then we heard that the order had been given to some little outfit over in Newark. Even then we didn't think — well, I suppose we should have guessed what was coming. After that, Rubin started right down the line, one thing after another. Then — bang! We were out."

Swann broke in explosively. "You should read the letter he wrote when they cut us off."

Kennan said as a placating admission. "That letter was a little rough, all right."

"A little?" Swann demanded. "Is that the way you'd expect to be treated by a reputable company — cut off like that after thirty years?"

Kennan said, "We still don't know, Alf, whether or not that really represented the company attitude — hard to believe that it does."

"He's a vice-president, isn't he?" Swann shot back.

"I know but —" Kennan gave up. "I guess you're right — after your throat's cut, there's not much point in arguing about who held the knife."

Lincoln Lord said, puzzled, "But as I got the story from Mr. Phelps, the reason they took the business away from you was because they'd gotten their own cannery?"

There was an odd moment of silence, both Kennan and Swann looking at Kira Zurich, who for an instant seemed about to speak. But she settled back and it was Kennan who said, "Yes, that was Rubin's excuse."

Swann countered stubbornly. "But at least they could have given us reasonable notice. That's the thing that made it so bad, Mr. Lord."

"How much notice were you given?"

"Notice? None!"

"You don't mean —"

"'From this day forward —'" Swann quoted bitterly. "That was it, right then and there."

"That does seem strange," Lincoln Lord mused, thinking of Sidney Arnauth's polished urbanity, picturing him as he had seen him a month ago at an art auction, remembering his suave voice over the telephone yesterday afternoon. "No, it's hardly what you'd expect, is it?"

"With a man like Rubin, you can expect anything," Swann said.

"But if you were caught with a lot of stock on hand," Lincoln Lord said, "surely that was something that had to be taken into account?"

"Not by a man like Irving Rubin."

"But what did he say?"

"From this day forward," Swann repeated. "You ought to see that letter, Mr. Lord. It's really something."

"But when you talked to him?"

Swann said, "I tried to call him and he wouldn't even answer the phone."

"You didn't talk to him?" he asked incredulously, trying to keep from exhibiting how shocked he was.

"I tried at least a half-dozen times. His secretary would always ask who was calling and as soon as I'd tell her she'd say that Mr. Rubin wasn't in and she didn't know when he'd be back. I left word for him to call me. But of course he never did."

"Then you never did talk to him?"

"No," Swann said, almost belligerent as he added, "But it wasn't because we didn't try. I even sent Joel over. He wouldn't talk to him either."

"Joel?"

"Joel Morris," Kennan explained. "He's Alf's assistant."

Lincoln Lord looked down the center of the table, avoiding all eyes . . . was it possible that Gellman Stores had been this badly handled, only letters and telephone calls, no personal contact with the buyer upon whom the Coastal Foods Company was dependent for all of its business? No wonder they'd gotten into trouble! And when they had, Swann hadn't even gone to New York himself . . . sent his assistant . . .

"Joel seemed like the best bet," Kennan explained, apparently sensing what he was thinking. "He used to be with an advertising agency in New York that had the Gellman account — market research and all that sort of thing. He had a lot of inside dope on Gellman's operations and he'd worked up a presentation to show them how important it was to them to keep the Mother Gellman line up to snuff." He paused. "But, as Alf says, he never got a chance to use it. Rubin wouldn't even see him."

"And he *was* in his office?"

"Oh sure. Joel waited all day — nine in the morning until five in the afternoon."

Lincoln Lord nodded, shock giving way to the realization that Swann couldn't be blamed too much . . . the best office managers were never salesmen . . . even as good as Paul Willis had been, Mr. Quincy had never let him get near a customer. This wasn't anything to worry about . . . Coastal Foods' lack of a sales organization would be the easiest of all faults to correct. But there'd have to be something to sell . . .

He started to ask if Joel Morris was the marketing man whom Phelps had mentioned, but Swann spoke first, muttering, "We should have known that a man like that wouldn't stop at anything." His meaning was unclear, made even more obtuse by a strangely surreptitious glance at Kira Zurich.

There was an awkward moment, ended when Kennan said, more as an evasion than an explanation, "I guess what hit us so hard, Mr. Lord, was that we'd always felt so close to the Gellman people. We couldn't have been any closer if we were all in the same company. Their people would come down here to work out things with us just as if it were their own plant. And that's the way we'd always treated them — as if they were our own people. We were as married to Gellman Stores as if — well, when Alf came out in the plant with that letter from Rubin, I couldn't have been more surprised if my wife had walked in and told me that she was divorcing me."

Seemingly without instigation, Lincoln Lord looked at Maggie, and to his surprise, he saw that her eyes were fixed upon him. Although he had not been unaware of her presence, until now it had been a peripheral consciousness. She had taken almost no part in the conversation and there had been no occasion for him to allow his attention to drift farther down the table than Kennan, upon whose right Maggie was seated. A chilling thought shadow crossed his mind. But then he saw her smile and look down at her plate, asking, "Linc, isn't this wonderful?"

Food, too, had been something overlooked, eaten without consciousness of either substance or taste. Now, with his attention directed to it, he saw shoestring slivers of beef in a pinkish sauce that, tasted, had a creamy tomato flavor. "Yes, it's fine," he said. "Excellent."

Maggie asked Kira Zurich, "It's beef Stroganoff, isn't it?"

"Well, the label doesn't call it anything as frighteningly fancy as that," Kira Zurich said, "but, yes, that's what it really is — isn't it, Mr. Kennan? More or less?"

Kennan nodded and Maggie exclaimed, "You can't possibly mean this came out of a can?"

"Oh yes," Kira Zurich said. "And the soup, too. I thought it might be interesting for you folks to try a couple of the things that the company has been packing."

Maggie said, "It's wonderful, Mr. Kennan, it really is. And so was the soup. I had no idea."

"No credit to me," Kennan replied. "Same recipes we've been using for years."

"I shouldn't think you'd have any trouble getting people to buy things like this," Maggie said, concluding with an anxious glance up the table, a wifely inquiry as to whether or not she had gone too far, self-consciousness betrayed by repetition. "It is good, isn't it, Linc?"

"Top notch," he said, looking at Kennan, a silent request for an answer to her implied question.

Kennan either missed the point or chose to evade it. "We've got some other things that aren't too bad either."

"But they've all been packed for Gellman — nothing under your own brand?"

"All for Gellman. You see — well, as I said, we had this understanding that we'd never compete with them in any place where they had stores."

"But there's nothing to prevent you from doing that now?"

"No, indeed!" Swann answered for him, vindictively positive. Then, clearing his throat, he asked, "Is that what you think we should do, Mr. Lord — pack the same line under our own label?"

"At least it's a possibility worth exploring. Of course, we'd have to —"

143

He caught himself and started over again without the involving pronoun. "What you'd have to decide, of course, was whether or not the things you're putting up now would turn out to be your best bets for the long haul. It's a big job to establish a brand and build up consumer demand for it. You'd want to be very certain that you were starting with a line that would pay off in the end."

Kennan gave him a nod of sober understanding. "It'll be a battle, I know that."

"I'm assuming, of course, that you *do* want to build up a brand of your own?" he asked, the question general, directed to the table.

Kira Zurich, so long silent, surprised him by asking, "And you think that would be the thing to do?"

He hesitated. "I really don't know enough about the company yet to have any fixed opinion, Mrs. Zurich."

"Of course not," she granted, retiring, her tone apologetic.

"But in a general way — yes, something like that would seem to be indicated."

Kennan said, "I honestly don't see that we've got much choice. We can't live on private label business from the chains, not at the prices we have to bid to get it. And we aren't going to find another Gellman Stores setup."

"And even if we did," Swann said bitterly "where would it leave us? Right where we were before — another Irving Rubin."

Lincoln Lord saw that Kira Zurich's eyes were on him, apparently concerned that he was being unfavorably impressed by Kennan's and Swann's boldly expressed opinions. He gave her a reassuring smile, hoping that it told her that he had no desire to be surrounded by yes-men ... Swann might prove to be a bit irascible when he had his dander up, but that was a small price to pay for some spark and spirit. And there was no doubt that Kennan, too, had his own ideas and the backbone to stand up for them ... but a man who didn't have those qualities would never take responsibility. They were a good pair, Kennan and Swann ... be hard to find a better team.

He ate now, savoring the rich sauce, finishing his serving, his example followed around the table, the conversation undemanding, giving him his first chance to lower his guard and appraise the situation with detachment. Experience was his measuring stick, memory his standard, and it was impossible not to be favorably impressed by the contrast with comparable occasions. As anxious as they all were to get him to accept the presidency, they were being completely honest about the company's plight, holding back nothing, not even glossing over faults that reflected upon themselves, an approach reassuringly different from the web of deceptive half-truths that had snared him into Chemical Service. Nor were either Swann or Kennan harboring any of the secret resentment that had been held against him by the vice-presidents over whose heads he had been brought into Luxor Pharmacal. And there was none of the irrational ambition, petty jealousy and senseless antagonism that had been generated by the Coates-Stacks feud at Frazer Glass. Best of all, Kira Zurich was no Cornelia Rabson . . . he'd have no trouble handling her . . . no trouble at all.

The maid was serving dessert, a fluff of meringue with black cherries, and he heard Maggie say, "Now don't tell me, Mrs. Zurich, that this came out of a can."

"Hardly!" she said, glancing at Frank Kennan. "I had to give Viola a chance to show off, too." The remark brought a self-conscious smile to the maid's shining black face.

After Viola had left the room, Kira Zurich leaned forward and whispered, "She thought it was simply awful — here we were having these fancy people down from New York and all we were serving them was something out of a can."

Kennan said to Swann, "You know, Alf, I think we should resent that."

For once Swann responded to humor, smiling. But that was less of a surprise than Maggie suddenly saying with tongue-in-cheek laughter, "Linc, I think you and I should resent that, too. Imagine — being called fancy people from New York."

Caught up in the general laughter, Kira Zurich said, "I have put my foot in it, haven't I? Anyway, I hope you like Viola's meringues."

"It's wonderful, simply wonderful," Maggie said. "Isn't it, Linc?"

"Fine! Couldn't be better," he said, hurriedly correcting the fault of having consumed his first bite without consciousness of taste, then distracted by the strange rapport that was developing between Maggie and Mrs. Zurich. They were talking across the table now — food talk, woman talk, maid problems, female-to-female chatter that he hadn't heard for a long time. At first he thought that Kira Zurich was the aggressor, working on Maggie with the hope that it might be a roundabout way to pressure him into accepting the presidency, but after a moment it seemed that Maggie was no less anxious to win over Mrs. Zurich, raptly intrigued when she was listening, jewel-bright sparks flashing in her eyes when she responded. Suddenly, he remembered

145

that he'd told Maggie that this would be her decision. Alarmed, he tried to catch her eye . . . why was she driving ahead like this . . . forcing him into a corner, committing him before he was ready to decide? Did she think that this was the only job he could get? He had to find some way to stop her . . . break it up . . .

Kira Zurich saved him, saying abruptly, "Well, I imagine you're anxious to get over and see the plant, aren't you, Mr. Lord?"

"Yes, we are," he said quickly, the plural pronoun emphasized, a rebuttal of her obvious intention to make the factory inspection a manonly affair . . . get Maggie away from Mrs. Zurich . . .

Softly but positively, Kira Zurich made it bluntly clear that she was not to be circumvented. "I want to take Mrs. Lord over to Haven Home," she said, then adding as a concession, "If there's time, we'll stop at the plant afterwards."

For some unaccountable reason, Maggie seemed pleased with herself. She stood now with Kira Zurich, their forces seemingly joined, their combined weight against him.

The squaring of his shoulders as he stood up was the stiffening of his resistance. He waited out Kennan's protest that there was no need for Kira Zurich to accompany them to the front door and said, "Then I'll see you later," more to Mrs. Zurich than to Maggie, and led the way out of the dining room. Preoccupied, thinking of Maggie, he walked across the living room, unaware until he became conscious of the persistence of silence that Kennan and Swann were waiting for him to speak first, even more positive evidence that they had already installed him as president of the company. Resolutely, he refused final acceptance, clinging to the right of decision as a defense against what slight validity there might still be in Otis Sellcox's attack upon him.

Kennan found his topcoat for him in the hall closet and Swann, in a ceremonious sharing of the ritual, held it and then opened the outside door. They went down the wide steps together, three abreast, the silence still unbroken. But he was aware of a furtive exchange of glances between Kennan and Swann, a silent duel to determine who would speak up and reveal something that apparently both of them were anxious to have him know. Swann was the loser and, bowing to defeat, said, "I'm sure you know, Mr. Lord, that what we talked about in there isn't quite the whole story."

"So?" he asked curtly, not too surprised, recalling those awkward moments during the lunch table conversation when both Swann and Kennan had looked at Kira Zurich as if they were asking for permission to breach some secrecy.

"There are a lot of angles to this situation, Mr. Lord," Swann said nervously. "If someone didn't have all the facts it would be easy to get the wrong impression."

"In what way?" he shot back, curtness a cover for apprehension.

Kennan came to Swann's rescue. "It wouldn't be too hard to think that Alf and I were a couple of pretty stupid characters, just sitting around and letting things go to pot."

"Oh, I didn't get any such impression as that," he said offhandedly, an incomplete denial, keeping the pressure on. "I don't imagine that you had any reason to suspect that the situation was going to develop as it did. Hindsight is always —"

Kennan cut him off, stopping as they came to the curb, confronting him with a half turn of his body. "This isn't hindsight, Mr. Lord. We knew what Rubin was up to. But the hell of it was, our hands were tied."

"Yes, that's been the trouble," Swann murmured, opening himself to rebuttal.

"Then I must have misunderstood you, Mr. Swann. From what you said at the table, I'd gathered that the loss of the Gellman business came to you as a great shock."

Kennan started to reply but a glance held him back, leaving Swann to answer on his own. And he accepted the responsibility, more poised now, strength seemingly gained from Kennan's example. "It *was* a shock," he insisted. "We knew they were out to get control of the company, but we didn't think they'd go this far."

"We thought Rubin was bluffing," Kennan said. "That he wouldn't dare go through with it."

He hesitated, recalling what Phelps had told him about Gellman Stores attempting to buy Coastal Foods. "Are you implying that they cut you off as a way of forcing Mrs. Zurich to sell them the company?"

"We *know* it," Swann said positively. "I don't know why she wouldn't talk about it today —"

"Oh, I knew they'd made her an offer," he said.

Swann sighed his relief. "I didn't know whether you did or not."

"That's what kept us behind the eight ball," Kennan said. "We didn't know what she was going to do — whether she was going to sell or whether she wasn't. We didn't know until last evening. That's the

147

first word we'd had that she'd decided to hang on and battle it out —
when she called us over to tell us that you were coming down. Believe
me, it was good to hear."

"Yes, indeed," Swann said fervently.

"What I'm trying to say —" Kennan began. "We just want you to
know that we're behind you a hundred per cent, Mr. Lord, both of us."

"Absolutely," Swann echoed.

They were waiting for his response and, tempted as he was to accept their pledged loyalty, he felt himself forced to caution. "That's
very flattering — I appreciate your attitude — but right now, of course,
there's not much that I can say. I only came down today for a look-
see, trying to find out what it's all about. I really don't know whether
there's any contribution I can make."

"Well, *we* know there is," Kennan said. "I know what you did at
Frazer Glass —"

He saw a chance for escape as Swann opened the front door of the
Buick. "Maybe I'd better take my own car."

"No, no," Kennan protested. "I'll bring you back — no trouble about
that. And this way we can talk on the way over."

The production manager got in behind the wheel and, sitting beside
him, Lincoln Lord shifted to a sideways position in order to share his
attention with Swann in the back seat. "Tell me this — how active has
Mrs. Zurich been in the management of the company?" He waited
but there was no response and he went on. "As I understood it, she
took the presidency only as a formality. But I got the impression at
lunch that she's been rather deeply involved. At least, she seemed completely familiar with everything that was happening."

Swann began, "We have tried to keep her informed —"

"Look, Mr. Lord," Kennan took over. "This is nothing against Mrs.
Zurich — in her own line, she's a darned able woman, I guess — but
the point is that her real interest is Haven Home, not Coastal Foods.
As far as being president of the company is concerned — well, she just
hasn't been, that's all."

"But you do have to give her credit for her attitude," Swann protested. "The things she said last night — about wanting to keep the
company going for Mr. Zurich's sake —"

"Sure," Kennan agreed. "But as far as being president of the company —"

"No, you're quite right there," Swann agreed. "And of course that's
been one of our troubles, Mr. Lord. After this Rubin thing started —"

"I can see what a difficult situation that created," he granted, content to drop the subject now that he had confirmed his judgment that Kira Zurich would not renege on her promise to give him control of the company ... if she had given Kennan and Swann a free hand, there was no chance whatsoever that she would try to interfere with him ... no, there'd be no trouble on that score.

They were well away from the house now, starting into the tunnel through the pines, and the moment of semidarkness was a moment of silence ... but it *was* strange that she hadn't mentioned anything about Gellman's attempt to buy Coastal Foods ... or had she taken it for granted that Phelps had told him about it ... ?

They burst out into the sunlight again, the plant before them now, and Kennan said, "Here's how we'd more or less planned things, Mr. Lord — subject, of course, to your approval. We thought you'd probably want to see the cannery first, so I'm planning to take you through and show you our production setup. Then Alf can take over and carry on from there — show you the office operation and give you any figures that you want. Afterwards, we can get together again and cover anything that's been missed. But maybe you'd rather do it some other way?"

"No, sounds fine to me," he quickly agreed, reserving the question that he had been about to ask, guessing that Kennan would talk more freely about Kira Zurich when Swann was not present.

Kennan said over his shoulder, "Then we'll drop you at the office, Alf, and I'll swing around to the back of the plant so we can start at the beginning and come right up the production line."

Swann murmured agreement, edging forward on the seat, out of the door the moment the car stopped. "Then I'll see you later, Mr. Lord?"

"Right."

The car wheeled around in the drive and he caught only a fleeting glimpse of the entrance lobby behind the glass door before Kennan, speaking in a throaty whisper, demanded his attention. "Don't get any wrong ideas about Alf, Mr. Lord. He's solid as a brick. Just a little jumpy today, that's all."

"You seem to have a lot of worries about my getting wrong ideas."

Kennan gave him a concerned side glance until, seeing his smile, a self-conscious grin broke. "I guess maybe I'm a little jumpy myself. You don't know how much this means to us, Mr. Lord — getting you down here. This is what we've been praying would happen." There was a tight turn to make around the end of the building, a moment of silence extended until he stopped the car alongside a receiving platform.

149

"You're what this company needs, Mr. Lord — somebody to get things going down the right track again. What we've been trying — Alf and I double-teaming it — well, it just doesn't work. Maybe I'm wrong — you hear a lot of talk these days about group management — but for my dough, running a company has to be a one-man job."

He smiled. "I'm not certain that I'd go quite that far, Frank."

"Oh, I don't mean that the president of a company can't use everybody's ideas, sure you can — and he has to delegate responsibility — but unless you've got that one strong guy sitting up there in the driver's seat, you just aren't going to get anywhere. You can't run a company by compromise. Somebody's got to call the shots. You can think you're going right down the line, everybody pulling together and headed in the same direction, but sooner or later you come to a fork in the road. Then there has to be somebody to say whether you're going right or left — or maybe back up and turn around."

"That's not too bad a definition of general management," he said, appreciatively, finding himself more and more favorably impressed by Frank Kennan. "And I can see that you have had a difficult situation here since Mr. Zurich died. I know that —"

"Wait a minute, Mr. Lord. Don't get me wrong. I didn't say that because I've got any gripe against Alf Swann. I don't. We've been working together a long time."

"But I imagine you do have some ideas of your own — some things that you'd have done if you'd had the authority to go ahead."

Kennan shook his head vigorously. "I'm just not getting across what I'm trying to say. All I meant was — well, sure I've got some ideas. But they're in my own bailiwick. I'm no front office man, Mr. Lord. Give me a cannery to run and I'm happy. That's all I want. I figure that if a man is going to do a good job he has to be happy — and this is where I'm happy, running a plant. I had two years of the other side of it and — well, it taught me where I belong. I was with Century, you know?"

"Century Foods?"

"Sure. Eleven years. Came up through their production organization — New York State, out in Michigan, wound up as manager over in Camden. Then they picked me up and sent me to New York — assistant to the executive vice-president."

"Were you really?" he said, reminded that he had, from the beginning, rated Kennan as a big-time man. "How in the world did you happen to come down here?"

Keenan grinned. "I wish I could say that I was smart enough to get out on my own — but I wasn't. The truth is that Sally kicked me into it. You see — well, we used to have a cottage over on Tern Beach. Came down here for our vacation. This was my second year in New York. I'd been pushing like hell, bucking for a vice-presidency, and I guess I was pretty well beat — jumpy as hell, just couldn't relax, had to be doing something every minute. Used to get in the car and drive around just to keep from going nuts. Well, one day I happened to come down this road and I saw this cannery. I don't know what made me stop — busman's holiday, I guess — but, anyway, I wandered in and started looking around. Well, this funny-looking little guy comes up to me — sawed-off little shrimp, ugly as a board fence — you never met Sol Zurich?"

"No."

"Well, he wasn't much to look at, about the last man in the world you'd figure to be the owner of the place. But, anyway, we got talking about the canning business and — well, they were working on a new dicing machine, trying to get it running, and the first thing I knew I was down on my belly with a wrench in my hand. And then the next thing I knew, the whole afternoon was gone. When I got back to the cottage, I didn't say anything about what I'd been doing, but I guess it must have stuck out all over me — these damned women are too smart — so Sally pipes up and says that something must have happened to me because I'm acting like a human being for the first time in two years. Of course then I had to tell her and — well, one thing led to another and she started telling me that what I ought to do was chuck Century and get back in a cannery again where I could really have some fun out of life."

"Had Zurich offered you a job?"

"No, that's the crazy part of it. Nothing like that had even been mentioned. If anybody'd told me that night that I'd ever go to work for a little one-horse outfit like Coastal Foods — remember, this was ten years ago and it was a pretty junky looking plant in those days — well, I'd have told 'em they were crazy. But the next morning it was raining, couldn't get out on the beach, so I got in the car — I swear to god I wasn't even thinking of coming over here again, but the first thing I knew, here I was. Well, I got talking to Mr. Zurich again and — there's no use dragging it out. You know the payoff."

"And I gather you've never regretted it?"

"No, I've never regretted it, not for a minute. If I ever had, I wouldn't be here. I've had plenty of chances to change, a lot of offers —"

"I can believe that easily enough," he said, intending it as a compliment, surprised when he saw the production manager's stabbing glance, evidence that some unsuspected sensitivity had been touched.

For a moment Kennan sat picking at the corded edge of the upholstered seat-back. Then he looked up, some decision obviously made. "Maybe there isn't too much point in my telling you this — water over the dam — but I'd like to start with no cards under the table." He twisted his shoulders, facing him squarely. "You asked a while ago if we were certain that Gellman had a squeeze play on Mrs. Zurich?"

"Yes?"

"Maybe you ought to know that Rubin offered me a job — a hell of a lot of money and a juicy bonus to sign a contract."

"That's understandable enough, isn't it? Naturally, they'd want you. Why wouldn't they? If they're going to produce the Mother Gellman line in their own cannery —"

"That's a phony, Mr. Lord. They can't."

"But aren't they — ?"

"I went through that plant, Mr. Lord. They couldn't pack our line there — at least not without rebuilding the place from stem to stern. It's nothing but a seasonal vegetable cannery. And not a very good one at that. They aren't set up to handle meat processing — don't even have any refrigerated storage — and there isn't a man around the place that knows a damn thing about handling the kind of stuff we're packing here."

"That's all the more reason why they would be anxious to get you."

Keenan shook his head vigorously. "That isn't why they wanted me. They thought that if I walked out, Mrs. Zurich would cave in and sell them the company. That sounds egotistical as hell — I don't mean that it's necessarily true — but I do know that that's the way Rubin had it figured." He paused. "He practically said it, not in so many words but there was no doubt what he meant — after they got Coastal Foods I'd be back running this plant, everything I've got now plus a bigger salary and a hell of a juicy bonus."

He tried a testing smile. "Well, maybe you should have taken them up on it?"

"Maybe so," Keenan said with an ironic chuckle. "Maybe I was a damn fool — a guy does have to look after himself, I guess — but I'm just not enough of a bastard to go along with that kind of a deal. I owe too much to Sol Zurich."

"Well, I'm sure Mrs. Zurich is very grateful to you for sticking by her."

"She doesn't know it."

"You've not told her?"

"No. Nor Alf either. You're the only person I've told — except Sally, of course — and I'd like to keep it that way."

"But why? I should think that telling Mrs. Zurich would —"

"She'd have been all the more scared. And, anyway, I didn't do it for her sake. I did it because I couldn't have gone on living with myself if I hadn't. I don't know how to say it but — well, there's something a man feels toward a company like this —"

"A sense of loyalty," he suggested.

Kennan seemed doubtful. "Maybe — but it's something more than you usually mean when you talk about being loyal to a company. When I was at Century — well, I was a good company man, loyal as a man could be. That morning when I handed in my resignation — well, it was a hell of a wrench, believe me, it was. This is something else. I remember the first time I came over here. It was as different from what I'd been used to as you could possibly imagine — Sol Zurich, that crummy little office he used to have, a cannery that looked like our scrap pile at Century. Still I had a feeling the minute I walked in that this was where I belonged. It was like coming home. I don't know, maybe I'm just a small company man. I guess I am. Anyway, you feel closer to a little company than you ever can to a big corporation. With an outfit like Century you can feel you're a part of the company — sure you can — but here it's the other way around. Instead of you being a part of the company, it's like the company being a part of you. When you go into a company like this it's like getting married. You take it for better or worse, for richer or poorer —"

"In sickness and in health," Lincoln Lord supplied.

"That's right. And a decent man doesn't rat out on a wife that gets sick any more than he'd — well, I won't say that Coastal Foods is a sick company yet, but it could be if we don't get it rolling again."

"In other words, you're not going to leave?"

There was only the sound of Kennan's thumbnail picking at the upholstery. Then, looking up, he said slowly, "Let me put it this way, Mr. Lord — if you're going to be the doctor, I'll stick with the patient as long as there's a heartbeat left."

Lincoln Lord felt his throat constrict, an emotional reflex that made it impossible for him to express his gratitude. In the moment of embarrassed silence, he involuntarily closed his eyes. Light flashed in the darkness, the cold blue-white image of Otis Sellcox's bloodless face. He opened his eyes. Frank Kennan was looking at him, warmingly anxious, humanly concerned, saying now, "I guess maybe I've been talking too much — ?"

"No, no!" he objected. "This has all been very helpful, Frank, very helpful, indeed. I really don't know how to —" The lump was in his throat again.

Kennan opened the door. "Well, let's get a look at the plant."

Lincoln Lord merely touched the latch and, startlingly, the door beside him immediately swung open, almost as if it had been moved by some unseen hand.

8

Maggie Lord was not surprised that Kira Zurich had made no further reference to Haven Home. She had accepted it as Kira's device for letting the men get away by themselves and, approving that objective, had been concerned only that Kira might have the further purpose of separating her from Linc in order that she could talk to her about him. But there had been no prying questions to support that assumption, and as they wandered out into the living area, she had begun to feel that there was no more on Kira's mind than an anxious bid for friendship.

Response to that overture was not easy, handicapped as she was by the memory of the difficulties that had surrounded her relationships with all the other women, from Cornelia Rabson to Julia Wright, with whom friendship had always been a tightrope to be walked with a perpetual awareness of danger, never able to forget that anything she said or did might affect her husband's career. Upon occasion, she had been able to do something to help Linc, but there was no need of that with Kira — she could hardly be more favorably impressed with Linc than she had already shown herself to be — and there was always the possibility that she might inadvertently reveal something that would, at some future time, turn up to harm him. There was no way to tell how Kira's attitude toward Linc would change after he became president of her company — and, when it did, for whatever cause, she dared not let herself be at fault. The only safe course was to keep herself from being drawn into the friendship that Kira's manner proposed. That would not be too difficult. Kira Zurich was one of those women who, unaccustomed to intimacy, approached it with desire so obvious that it was self-defeating.

Maggie Lord was not unaware, however, that some of the fault lay within herself. This was not a newly born consciousness nor was it a reaction to this special situation. She had always found it difficult to achieve with any other woman that closely knit and deep-seated bondage that she thought must exist between true friends. There had once been, she had imagined at the time, something of that sort between herself and Peggy Lytton, with whom she had roomed during her first two years at Cornell, yet it had barely survived their junior year separation. Afterwards, surreptitiously watching Peggy and her new roommate wandering the campus, arm in arm, giggling over some whispered intimacy, she had seen her own shortcoming as an inability to return, in kind, the confidences that Peggy had been so anxious to exchange.

There had been what was, perhaps, a closer approach to true friendship with Blanche Galbraith, with whom she had lived in a Greenwich Village apartment that first year in New York; yet all that had survived had been a name on a Christmas card list, a loss probably accountable to the fact that, try as she would, and even with the help of some baldly invented episodes, she had never been able to match Blanche's uninhibited accounts of her amatory adventuring. Her most vivid memory of Blanche Galbraith was the sound of her voice when she would say, "All right, honey, if you don't want to tell me about it —"

Transient as her friendships with Peggy Lytton and Blanche Galbraith had proved to be, they had nevertheless been more intimate than any woman-to-woman relationship that she had experienced since Lincoln Lord had come into her life. Before her marriage, there had been only her own secret mind to hold inviolate. Afterward, his too had demanded her protection. In most instances, there had been the added difficulties that were accountable to status. The women that she had most often come to know best were the wives of men upon whom Linc was dependent for favor and support. With them, friendship had been defeated by the consciousness of purpose. And by simple transposition, she had always felt her own attitude reversed when she was approached by the wives of men in Linc's companies, that ever-changing parade of women who, professing friendship and seemingly courting intimacy, could not possibly forget that she was the president's wife, their sincerity suspect, a too close relationship with them as dangerous to offer as to accept.

There had been a few exceptions — women who had no company connections, most often the wives of other corporation presidents. With the same background and conceivably common problems, they had been the best prospects for solid and enduring friendships — and once she had come to what seemed to be within striking distance of that goal. For a few weeks she had spent more time with Sylvia Worth than with any woman in her adult life, often seeing her several times a week. They had met first in juvenile court, the mothers of two of seven boys, all sons of highly ranked Main Line families, who had been charged by the police with some childish vandalism. Nothing had come of it — Kip and Johnny Worth had been released with warnings — but she and Sylvia Worth had clung to each other, first because of the relief that was to be found in the sharing of terror, then for the more rational reason that both held the hope that, together, they might find the answer to a problem that neither had been able to solve alone. Unfortunately, they had in common not only sons who had proved difficult to manage but also a mutual reticence to discuss their husbands and their married lives. With that area blocked off, there was nothing else to hold them together. Both of their lives were so centered in their husband's careers that their peripheral interests were without substance.

Close friendships, Maggie sometimes thought, were only possible between markedly different persons, their attraction seemingly dependent upon each having qualities of character that the other admired but did not possess. In her own case, however, she rarely found herself drawn to anyone in whom she did not see a substantial mirroring of her own mind and heart. When she felt impelled toward making an effort to understand someone else, it was most frequently an urge to understand herself. She had been aware of this in other circumstances, but it did not occur to her that it might be valid observation now because, even though she knew almost nothing about Kira Zurich, what little she did know suggested almost no mutuality of outlook and attitude. Even with the most freely drawn transposition of character, she could not imagine herself having married Sol Zurich. But the question of why Kira Zurich had done so was the core around which growing curiosity was being constructed. She was anxious to ask Kira some questions about Sol Zurich, held back now only by the fear that in doing so she would open herself to similar questioning about Linc. Nevertheless, she edged toward it now by saying, "You must have had a wonderful time building this house."

"Not really," Kira said, her smile thin, embarrassment evident. "Actually, I had no part in building it. It was all done before I saw it, finished and furnished."

"Oh, then someone else built it," she said, thinking that this was the explanation why the house and everything in it seemed so mismatched to Kira Zurich.

"My husband built it for me," Kira said, adding, "— as a surprise," and her tone, although attempting to express satisfaction, left little doubt that the surprise had not been entirely pleasant.

Disregarding intuition, Maggie said, "How thrilled you must have been!"

"Yes, it did mean a great deal — his wanting to give it to me," Kira said. "He was a wonderfully kind and generous man."

Side-stepping the danger of sentimental involvement, she said quickly, "Well, it's simply beautiful. It's the most livable house I've ever seen."

"Then you like this modern style?"

"At least I like this. I used to think that modern houses were awfully cold and austere, but there's been so much change in the last few years." She felt herself chattering along to no purpose. "There's been a lot of influence from the Orient, of course. I don't think I really appreciated how much until we were in Japan last year. Linc was on the Far East Trade Mission, you know, and we were there for a month or more."

"Yes," Kira said. "The architect who designed this house — Mr. Lainson — spent several years in Japan. He was quite enamored of it, apparently."

"I can see that he was," she said, looking around her, her eye falling on the screen that separated the entrance hall from the living area. "They do such beautiful things. We saw some screens in Kyoto, none as beautiful as this one of yours, but I was awfully tempted to buy one.

But you do have to have a place to use one — the right place, I mean."

Kira looked at her oddly, almost as if she were finding her difficult to understand. "You like this house, don't you?"

"Like it? Oh, but of course I do!"

Even more oddly, Kira Zurich nodded to some secret prompting and walked ahead around the screen, opening a door, the strangeness of her manner seemingly explained as she said, "This was my husband's room."

Maggie stopped at the threshold, entranced. Here the Japanese influence was stronger than anywhere else in the house, and she felt again the charm that she had discovered in Japanese residential architecture, most positively in the Osaka home of a rich textile manufacturer who, quite believably, had characterized a room not unlike this one as the place where he kept his heart alive. There, for over an hour, deprecating their worth and value, he had displayed the priceless collection of old Japanese paintings that were hidden away in cabinets behind sliding wall panels.

By contrast with that aesthetically flavored memory, Kira Zurich's voice sounded almost coarsely plebeian as she said, "It's sort of an office — den — whatever you want to call it. My husband never used it very much. He wasn't the kind of man who would." She paused, a suddenly significant silence. "Do you think Mr. Lord would like it?"

She was lost in a maze of an untrustable anticipation.

"What I've been hoping," Kira Zurich went on, tautly poised now, "was that you folks might like this house enough to want to live here."

"To live here?" she said blankly, stunned.

"I didn't want to suggest it until I was certain that you really liked it. But you do, don't you?"

"Of course I do! It's the kind of house that I've — but surely you don't want to give it up?"

Kira Zurich's denial was a rapid vibrato movement of her head. "I've only stayed on here because it seemed the right thing to do, because I didn't want the men at the plant to feel that I had —" She made a gesture of abandonment, the completion of the thought. "You don't have to live here, of course — you may prefer something else — but it *is* the president's house and there'd be a certain rightness about your being here."

"But what about yourself?"

"Oh, I have my cottage over at Haven Home. It's where I lived when I first came, before we were married. It's a lovely place, really it is. And of course very convenient. I've taken over the management of Haven Home again, you know."

"No, I didn't know."

"I gave it up, of course, when I married, but now —" There was a sharply self-conscious smile, enigmatic, yet conveying the impression that she had embarrassed herself by a lack of restraint, quickly imposed again as she cut back to the original subject. "Anyway, this house is yours — that is, of course, if you do decide to come."

"I'm afraid that will have to be my husband's decision."

"Oh, of course," Kira Zurich said hurriedly. "And please don't think that I was trying to influence you in any way. I know very well that a house to live in will be the least of his considerations."

"I'm afraid that wouldn't be true if it were my decision to make," Maggie said, turning now and looking at the long vista through the living area.

Kira Zurich's eyes were penetratingly serious. "Then you wouldn't object to coming down here?"

"Object? Of course not."

"I've been afraid that you might not want to leave New York."

"But why would you think that?"

"From what Mr. Phelps said —" She paused. "Perhaps he got the wrong impression."

"He thought that I — ?" The force of denial spent itself in the realization that this might be an explanation of why Anderson Phelps had acted so strangely when he first entered the suite at the Waldorf. Hurriedly, she said, "Living in New York means nothing at all to me, Mrs. Zurich. The only thing that matters —" trite or not, she said it, "— is my husband's happiness."

"I understand," Kira Zurich said, her lip quickly bitten, a momentary break in the shell of poise. Then, as soon lost as glimpsed, the inner woman was gone and Kira Zurich was smiling again. "I really would like to take you over to Haven Home for a few minutes, Mrs. Lord. I told the men that I was going to and — but if you'd rather not — ?"

"Oh no, I'd love to," she said impulsively — and then no less so, "My name is Maggie."

"Thank you," came back as a low murmur of deeply felt gratitude — and then, almost as if it were the recollection of something long forgotten, she said, "And my name is Kira."

9

Despite the exterior attractiveness of the building and all that he had been told about the new Coastal Foods cannery, Lincoln Lord was unprepared for what he saw as he stepped through the firewall door and into the main processing area of the plant. Unreasonably but inevitably, his expectation had been related to his memories of the old Quincy cannery — sweet-sour steam swirling through half-lighted caverns filled with the tinny clatter of cans and the screech of machinery, hundreds of women frantically driven to keep pace with the production line. Now, stock-still and staring, it required a long moment to accept the reality of what he was seeing — a plant brilliantly lighted and gleamingly clean, glistening walls of pale green tile, the stainless steel processing machinery shining with a silvery glow. But the strongest challenge to credibility was the all but unbroken quiet, a strange lifelessness, unaccountable until he realized that most of the machinery was inoperative and unmanned. The only people in sight were a dozen or so white-clad women scattered along a packing line on the far side of the room. The almost deserted plant was a reminder that Coastal Foods was a company in trouble, his apprehension tempered only by the memory that the Quincy cannery, too, had been a ghost plant during the off season.

"By golly, Frank, this is a beautiful layout," he said, caution abandoned.

"About as nice as you'll find," Frank Kennan said, modesty strained. "At least I've never seen a better one."

"Nor I," he said, thinking then of Luxor's exhibition cosmetic plant on which a small fortune had been spent for far less ceramic tiling and stainless-steel machinery than was visible here. "You've got a lot of capital tied up here, Frank."

He had not intended it as criticism, but Kennan said defensively. "Maybe we did go a little overboard — I guess we did — but it was what Mr. Zurich wanted." An excusing smile broke. "And if we hadn't spent it here, he'd have spent that much over at Haven Home."

"I understand that was one of his big interests," he said, secretly reviving his objective of getting Kennan to talk about Kira Zurich. "But I suppose that's natural enough — his being raised there."

"That wasn't the real reason."

"You mean Mrs. Zurich?"

"She's the one who really got him to shell out," Kennan said freely. "I don't know how much of the story you know — or whether you're interested — ?"

"I know very little," he said, interest expressed by lounging against the side of a machine.

Kennan slumped into a half-sitting posture on the frame of a roller conveyer. "Well, you hear a lot of talk around town — listen long enough and you can hear almost anything — but I'm not inclined to criticize her. Sure, she got what she wanted for Haven Home — but I don't think Mr. Zurich got short-changed. She gave him a lot of happiness that he'd never have had otherwise — and what the hell, he had to do something with his money."

"My impression today has surely been favorable," he said. "Particularly her attitude toward the company."

"That's right," Kennan said, his agreement strong enough to indicate that this was what really mattered. "If money was all she was after, she'd have sold out to Gellman. But, of course, a lot of people don't know that."

"Am I to gather that the attitude around the community isn't too favorable toward her?"

Kennan hesitated. "No, I wouldn't say that exactly. But still — well, her marrying Mr. Zurich kind of set the town on its ear."

"But that was a long time ago, wasn't it — six or seven years?"

"Small towns have long memories."

"I know."

The door was half-open now and he pushed it the rest of the way. "Give me a little background on her, Frank. I believe Phelps said that she came here to manage Haven Home?"

"That's right."

"When?"

"Oh, it was two or three years after the war, '47 or '48."

"What had she been doing before?"

"Well, actually, I don't know too much about that. She doesn't talk about herself and — well, she's not exactly the social type."

"No, I gathered that."

"Most of this I've picked up from Doc Perrill. He used to know her in the old days. She was a nurse then, working in a hospital nights and going to the University of Pittsburgh in the daytime. That takes some stuff on the ball."

"It does, indeed," he said, making a mental note to come back to Perrill later. "What did she take at the university?"

"Social work — the health and medical end, whatever they call it."

"She got her degree?"

Kennan nodded. "And went to work for the government. What all she did, I don't know. Anyway, she must have gotten pretty well up the ladder. I know she was in Washington during the war, heading some kind of research project — developing a concentrated ration to feed starving kids in the war areas. After the war she went overseas. I think it was for the UN. Anyway, she was tied up with feeding refugees. She got sick over there, picked up some kind of a bug, and I guess she was in bad shape for a while. After she got back to this country she was convalescing over on Tern Beach and — well, they were looking for someone to manage Haven Home and she stepped in and picked off the job."

"Was Mr. Zurich interested in Haven Home then?"

Kennan smiled wryly. "Until she came along, nothing interested Sol Zurich except the Coastal Foods Company. Oh, maybe that isn't quite true — he'd given a little money to Haven Home now and then, I guess, but it was nothing compared to what he handed out after Kira got to work on him. You see — well, you've got to give her credit for being smart."

"I've no doubt about that."

"I told you that Mr. Zurich was a little guy, practically a dwarf?"

"Yes."

"He was very sensitive about it — blamed it on the way he'd been fed when he was a kid at the orphanage — so when Kira started this pitch about setting up a research program to study child nutrition, he was wide open and ready to be taken. Anyway, she got him to build their new research center — about a quarter of a million bucks."

"That was before they were married?"

"Well, no — actually, they didn't get started on it until afterwards. I guess that's what gave everyone the idea that she'd married him to get her building. Of course, there'd been the Doc Perrill business even before that."

"I was going to ask you about him."

"Doc's quite a character," Kennan said warmly. "You haven't met him?"

"No, I believe he's away today."

"Oh, that's right, he did say he was going to some meeting over at Princeton. I did tell you that he'd known Kira as a girl? I don't know whether there'd ever been anything between them, maybe not, but at least they'd kept in touch with each other. Doc had been out in the Far East for years — India mostly — doing research work on nutrition."

"He's an M.D.?"

"But he's got the other side of it, too. Practiced medicine for a couple of years and then went back and got a doctor's degree in bio-chemistry. Then he went into research. He's really quite a guy. Interesting as the devil when he gets talking about some of his experiences in India. But I guess he'd gotten a bellyful of rotting his life away out there in the jungle. And then, too, he'd married an English girl he met out there, and I suppose she had the whip on him to make some money. I know she did. Anyway, he'd worked up an idea for a baby food and came back to this country to try to sell it. He'd been all around the circle with it — Gerber, Heinz, Beechnut, I don't know where all. Nobody had given him a tumble and Kira finally got him to come down here. What she was after, of course, was to get him for her research center — he was a natural for that — but what Doc was trying to do was cash in on his baby food. Well, Kira tried to kill herself a couple of birds with one stone and got him together with Mr. Zurich. Well, actually it was three birds — this was right after I got down here and I was plugging pretty hard to get a plant chemist. Anyway, they made a deal. Doc went to work, part-time for Haven Home and part-time for us."

"Did he know anything about the canning business?"

"Well, not too much at first, but he caught on fast." He paused. "When you first meet him you'll think he's a crackpot scientist — in some ways he is — but don't underestimate him. He's keen as hell. I'd stack him up today against any food plant chemist in the country."

"He must be quite an asset to you?"

"He is, believe me! We haven't had a batch of anything go wrong in ten years, not once. I've still got my fingers crossed — you never know in this business — but, as you say, he's a terrific asset. I don't know what I'd do without him."

"He's still on this split basis — part of his time here and part over at Haven Home?"

"That's right. Actually, he's over there a lot more than he's here — that's where his lab is, over at the Home — but any time you snap your fingers, he's right here."

"Sounds like a good arrangement."

"It is. Wonderful. But to get back to this Doc and Kira gossip. Well, when Doc moved down here he brought along this dame he'd married out in India — Celia. How he ever got mixed up with her, I don't know. I guess it was just a case of anything white looking good out there in the jungles. For my dough, she was something tossed out of a cat house, a tramp if I ever saw one. But to hear her tell it, she'd been a hot-shot actress in London. And I will say she had a hell of an act. I don't know what it was — the English accent, I guess — that and a lot of crap about being a bosom pal of Noel Coward and Gertrude Lawrence and everybody else you ever heard of. Anyway, a lot of the gals around town fell for her. The big splash in the small puddle. Hell, she even had 'em drinking tea every afternoon."

Lincoln Lord chuckled understandingly, remembering the wife that one of the boys at Rabson had brought home from England.

"She was bleeding Doc white, every cent he made, and taking it out on Kira because there wasn't any more. She was really a bitch. But as I say, she had a lot of people around town fooled, so when she walked out on Doc it wasn't too hard for them to believe that it was Kira's fault."

"You don't think there was anything to it?" he asked, recalling now how Mrs. Zurich had singled out Dr. Perrill for special treatment when she had offered him the presidency.

"At least not what Celia claimed," Kennan said. "If you knew Doc — well, Kira's not the type either. But you know what small-town women are like — always all out to protect the institution of marriage — and to them Kira was a homewrecker. It didn't bother them at all that Celia was tramping it with some jerk actor on the beach. No, it was Kira who was in the wrong. Well, the gossip was still boiling — I don't know how long it was afterwards, maybe a year — and then right out of the blue, Kira married Mr. Zurich. Then the fat was really in the fire, everybody figuring that she was the designing female out to get his dough. And when he gave her the new building over at Haven Home and built her a big fancy house — well, of course that proved everything!"

Lincoln Lord nodded abstractedly, understanding easily enough, yet failing to see how the community attitude toward Kira Zurich could in any way affect the future of the Coastal Foods Company. There was the possibility, however, that if there was anything between her and Dr. Perrill it might be necessary to do something about Perrill's baby food. "Frank, you mentioned this baby food that Perrill had developed — what ever happened to it?"

"Oh, we have to run a batch for him every now and then. Damn nuisance — mess the place up for a hundred cases or so. Hellish stuff to sterilize. It's a thick viscous mess — hard to get heat penetration. Even with these little fruit juice cans that we're using now, we have to run it up to two-forty and give it seventy minutes. That does it — we're getting good sterilization now — but you can see how it gums things up to put a pack through. I'm glad that we don't have to do it any oftener than we do. A hundred or so cases every three months — that's about all it amounts to."

"Then you are selling it?"

"No, not selling it, just shipping it around to people that are running tests for Doc. As far as selling it — well, Doc's still hoping, of course."

Kennan broke off as a man approached, a stockily Teutonic figure, his face heavily featured but placidly inexpressive, the self-confident mien of a competent craftsman whom it was no surprise to have Kennan introduce as Mike Schlager, the chief engineer.

Schlager extended a knuckle-barked hand that seemed to mark him as an engineer more at home with a wrench than a drawing pen, but Kennan quickly lifted him above that purely practical category by explaining, "Mike's designed a lot of this machinery — built a lot of it, too — so I asked him to stand by and bail me out if I get over my head."

The engineer's thick-lipped smile evidenced a good working relationship with the production manager, a harbinger of high morale all through the plant. In Schlager's presence, however, Kennan's tone changed and he was more the top-rung executive again as he said, "Well, Mr. Lord, suppose I try to give you an over-all picture of what we've been shooting for with this plant. When you design a new cannery these days, the usual approach is to set up a specialized plant to pack one particular thing, or at least a group of products that are all processed in the same way. With your operations more or less standardized, you can keep your costs down — that's the theory. But we've gone at it the other way around. What we've tried to do is to get a plant so flexible that we can pack almost anything — within reason, of course — and still keep our costs within shooting distance of a specialized plant."

"That's quite an assignment."

"The guts of the problem," Kennan went on, "is the amount of equipment that you have to have when you're trying to cover the waterfront. Take spinach, for example. Here in Jersey, we've got about a three weeks' season. That means that you've got a spinach washer sitting around taking up space and depreciating its head off for the other forty-nine weeks of the year. Now let me show you what Mike's worked out."

They walked ahead, Lincoln Lord edgily apprehensive that he might not be properly appreciative. His production experience had been limited to that first summer at Quincy Canning and, with no special aptitude for mechanics and no urgent interest in processing methods, he was afraid now that he might not even recognize standard cannery machines. To his relief, he had no difficulty in picking out the spinach washer, nor did he have any trouble following Schlager's explanation of how this piece of equipment had been ingenuously adapted to perform a half-dozen other functions. With rising confidence, he again accepted a truth — when first discovered, a great surprise — that engineering, despite the mumbo jumbo with which its professional practitioners always attempted to cloud it, was really nothing more than the practical application of common sense.

Understanding did not, however, lower his estimate of Mike Schlager. He was undoubtedly a gifted machine designer, able not only to find mechanical solutions for production problems but, as was not always the case with creative engineers, to achieve his ends with simplicity. As they worked their way through the maze of processing equipment, there was example after example of how Schlager had designed, or redesigned, a machine in order to give it the versatility that made it usable for several different purposes. In more cases than not, the work had been done on the spot, the equipment built as well as designed within the plant walls.

"How big an engineering department do you have?" he asked Schlager.

With a rumbling chuckle, the chief engineer stabbed a thumb at his own chest, not at all displeased by the implied compliment.

"Mike's about it," Kennan confirmed. "We do have a couple of maintenance men that are pretty handy and Mike uses them to fill in when we're running light. But that's about all. You see, Mr. Lord, this is the way — well, you hear a lot of talk about a big company having all the advantages, but they can eat themselves up with overhead, too."

"They can indeed."

"I remember when I was with Century — I figured it out one time when I was in the Camden plant — we had to run one whole day out of every week just to cover what that fancy setup in New York was costing us — central engineering, central research and development, production planning, all the rest of the overhead departments."

"I know what you mean," he said wryly, recalling how much of his difficulty at Luxor Pharmacal had been accountable to the ever-mounting cost of perpetually expanding staff departments.

They were halfway across the floor now, and turning back, Kennan traced how the flow of production could be changed in order to accommodate the pre-processing preparation of a wide variety of raw foods, "I don't think there's another plant in the country — at least one that's anywhere near our size — that has this much flexibility. Of course, just having the equipment isn't enough. That doesn't mean anything unless you can jump from one thing to another without kicking your costs through the roof with a lot of down time for a clean-up. That's where we've really got something. Want to give us a demonstration, Mike?"

Schlager led the way to a nearby machine that, fortunately, Lincoln Lord recognized as a hammer mill used to reduce vegetables to a pulpy puree.

"See what you can do?" Schlager asked. "Supposing, for example, Frank is making pea soup. Okay, his run's over. We hit those valves — watch out now!"

Schlager turned two valve wheels and there was an explosive burst of steam and water inside the machine.

"It used to take two hours for a clean-up," Kennan explained. "This whole line — hammer mills through the finishers."

"Longer than that," Schlager insisted.

"Yes, if we'd been running something that was tough to clean," Kennan agreed.

"And now — twenty minutes!" Schlager said with bursting pride.

Responding to what the engineer plainly regarded as his prime accomplishment, Lincoln Lord reinspected the installation, a compliment that incited Schlager to a flood of specifications for pipe sizes, water pressure, and spray head design.

Kennan's summary was far more intelligible. "This is more than just a way to save down time, Mr. Lord. It changes the way you can run the business. To keep our costs down, we used to have to make long runs and then stack them up in the warehouse. This way — unless

167

it's something seasonal — when a big order catches us without enough stock, we can switch over and pack it as fast as we can get our hands on the raw material."

"Very interesting," he said, edging back now to cautious appraisal. "I can see that a plant like this would be very well adapted to handling the Gellman business."

Kennan visibly restrained a flashback. "Well, naturally, that's what we were shooting for. But don't get the idea that it isn't a darned good all-around plant. What I'm trying to say is that we can take advantage of what we've got here when we bring out our own line."

"For example?" he said almost automatically, a standard technique for the puncturing of generalities.

"Well, I'm not trying to tell you what to do, Mr. Lord — we're here to pack anything you want. All I meant was that we aren't limited to packing the same things we did for Gellman."

"What else could you pack?" he asked, a reiterated demand for a specific answer.

Kennan stood his ground. "Well, as one example — I don't say this is what we should do, you understand, but it'll show you what I mean. Suppose you decided to bring out a line of soups, not just the four or five specials that we've been making for Gellman, but a whole line. If you were starting with an ordinary cannery you'd have to spend a fortune on equipment because you'd have to set up to handle twenty or twenty-five different vegetables, not to mention your meats and noodles and rice and everything else that you'd have to use. Here, the way we're set up, you could start rolling this afternoon without spending a dime."

"All you need to do is give us the labels," Schlager added in a bass whisper.

"Very interesting," he opined, another cautious withdrawal, turning now to lead the way toward the one packing line that was in operation.

"We're running that pack of beef stew that I was telling you about," Kennan said, an explanation made redundant by the richly appetizing odor that permeated the area, a pleasant contrast with the surfeiting smell that Lincoln Lord associated with canneries. He saw now that there were more workers than had been visible from the far side of the floor. A dozen or so, hidden before, were seated at the moving inspection belts onto which diced carrots and potatoes were being fed from stainless steel hoppers, sliced onions from a fan-blasted chute.

Watching their flying fingers, he noticed that they were sorting the vegetables bit by bit, picking out every tiny piece that was blemished or off-color. Recalling the way that tomatoes, good and bad, had been poured into the hammer mills at Quincy Canning, he said in an undertone inaudible to the operators on the line, "You've got a lot of labor cost here."

"I know," Kennan acknowledged. "Maybe we're too fussy. But it's the way Mr. Zurich always did things and we've kept on in the same groove."

"I'll tell you this," Schlager put in. "You eat something we put up, you don't have to worry what's in it."

"I guess we could cut our material cost, too — if we had to," Kennan said with gritty reluctance. "I know darned well we're using better beef than anything we ever put into a stew at Century."

Schlager said, "You give somebody something good, they come back and buy it again."

"The better mousetrap theory," Lincoln Lord said with an understanding smile.

Kennan nodded ruefully. "I guess we're the ones that got mouse-trapped. All we did was build up a fine business for Gellman Stores."

"Yeah, and how long will they keep it?" Schlager demanded. "They give people a can of junk and they won't come back again. You know what I think we ought to do? We ought to run big ads in all the newspapers — tell people the truth — tell them that the good stuff they used to get in the Gellman Stores ain't there no more!"

Lincoln Lord joined Kennan in a chuckle, nodding as the production manager said, "Be a fine thing if we could, Mike."

"Why not?" the chief engineer stubbornly demanded, but now with a twinkle in his eyes. "Anyway, I say this — we don't want to start doing it, too — putting out junk. Mr. Zurich always said maybe we ain't the biggest but there's nothing to keep us from being the best. Don't you think that's right, Mr. Lord?"

Caution warned him against commitment, but the thought of Coastal Foods as a company worthy of pride was thoroughly appealing. "Yes, I must admit that my natural inclination is always in that direction — to make as good a product as you possibly can."

Schlager's heavy nod of approval told him that he need have no worry about the chief engineer's loyalty.

They had walked slowly along the moving belt as they had talked, conversation punctuated with Kennan's murmured greetings to the women, many of them raising their eyes for a darting smile at the production manager. Most of their faces suggested graying hair under their blue-piped white caps, middle-aged faces which seemed remarkably free of the grim resistance to authority that, in so many factories, characterized the older female workers. It seemed a point worthy of compliment and Lincoln Lord said to Kennan, "I'd guess that you have rather good morale."

To the production manager's credit, he seemed momentarily puzzled. Then, glancing back up the line, he said, "Oh, you mean those old gals on the belt. Sure, they've been wonderful about it. Most of them are supervisors, of course — forewomen and leaders. Tough to have to put them back on the line, but that was the only way we could hang on to them. Darned important to keep these key people."

"What's your normal employment?"

"The last few years it's run about two hundred. Those are regulars, the people we've always kept on right around the year. Of course, we have a lot of temporaries, too, in the vegetable season. You don't have to worry about them so much. It's the steady people that get under your skin. Wouldn't be so bad in the summertime — they can always get plenty of work over at Tern Beach hotels then — but this time of year there's not too much else around here that they can get to do. It's been tough, having to lay them off. Hits the town pretty hard, too."

"Yeah," Schlager said. "Last week at the meeting."

"Chamber of Commerce," Kennan explained. "Merchants around town, you know. They gave us a rough time, wanting to know when we were going to get going again. About all we could tell them was that we had hopes."

"Yes, I imagine it means a lot to the town," Lincoln Lord said, then swiftly changed the subject by stepping forward to examine the automatic scales that were ingenuously weighing ingredients as they were fed into the big stainless steel pans that were used to charge the batch kettles. His show of interest brought forth a long dissertation on the mechanics involved from Schlager, followed by a scarcely shorter explanation from Kennan on the necessity of small-batch cookery if flavor was to be maintained.

He began to feel himself surfeited by detail, a reaction that Frank Kennan must have sensed because he said abruptly, "Well, I don't know how much of the rest of it you want to see, Mr. Lord. From here on, it's pretty much a standard canning operation." He turned to the chief engineer. "Thanks, Mike."

"The new labeling machine," Schlager whispered, resisting dismissal. But he yielded when Kennan said that they would take a look at it on their way to the warehouse.

Schlager's horny hand closed in a crunching vise grip, unnecessarily emphasizing the urgency of tone in which he said, "I hope I see you again, Mr. Lord."

He caught himself in time and, evading a promise, said only, "Thank you, Mr. Schlager — and my congratulations. You have a fine plant here."

"I think maybe you'll want to take at least a quick look at the warehouse," Kennan urged. "That's one of our problems — the stuff we've got stacked up out there."

They walked on then, Kennan whispering after they were out of the chief engineer's earshot, "That's the most I've heard him talk in five years. What's been worrying him was that we'd get a president who wouldn't know what it was all about."

"I'd judge him to be a good man," he said crisply, walking past the filling machine with a knowing side glance but without breaking stride, nodding as Kennan called his attention to the magnetic lifter that packed the filled cans in the steel baskets that carried them into the processing retorts.

Short-cutting a corner of the big room, stopping only to allow him a brief inspection of the labeling machine, Kennan led him through a long passageway, following a conveyer belt as it carried filled cartons from the new building to the old warehouse, a sparsely lighted cavern that brought back memories of the old tin-shed buildings of Quincy Canning. The air was chilly, faintly fetid with the characteristic odor of cardboard cartons and glue. Except for the ghostly clatter of the conveyer chain, an ominous silence hung over the alleyways between the stacked cases of canned goods, finally broken when Kennan said, "This worries me as much as anything else — all this inventory and not knowing whether or not Gellman is going to take it out."

"It's all Gellman stuff?" he asked, a question already answered by the brown and gold identifying labels that he saw up and down the canyon-wall stacks of filled cartons.

"Yes, all of it," Kennan admitted.

"This rather surprises me, Frank, particularly after what you said about your being able to make short runs."

"Oh, this is no big stock," Kennan flashed back defensively. "Outside of the seasonal stuff that we can pack only once a year, there isn't more than a month's supply of anything here — I mean at the rate Gellman was buying when they cut us off. There are a lot of different items, Mr. Lord — thirty-five or forty at least. Just a regular stock adds up to a lot of cans."

"And a lot of money tied up," he added.

"It sure does. And the hell of it is that it's all labeled. If it weren't, it would be easier to dump. It's a devil of a job to unpack and relabel. You lose your shirt on it, particularly when you wind up having to sell it on a dump basis, anyway. Of course, if we were going to bring it out as our own line — well, that's why we've been standing by, waiting to see what was going to happen."

They had come now to the end of the aisle and, preoccupied, he automatically turned right, his wandering eyes unseeing until, suddenly, he noticed a break in the phalanx of brown and gold labels, a small stack of cases simply stenciled HAVEN HOME — 43B.

Kennan noticed his side glance and explained, "Oh, that's some of Doc's baby food."

"Tell me, Frank — does it have any commercial possibilities?"

Kennan stopped, alerted. "Did Kira talk to you about it?"

"Just mentioned it as a possibility, that's all," he said. "Something to consider."

Kennan scowled. "I've been hoping she'd forget it."

"I gather you don't think much of it."

"Oh, I don't say the stuff isn't all right. They're getting good results feeding it to the kids over at Haven Home, I guess. But for my dough it's never been anything that you could sell in volume. To begin with, it's got sort of an odd taste, not exactly moldy but — well, it isn't very appetizing. They claim babies will eat it, and I suppose they will, but no mother is going to feed something to her baby that doesn't taste good to her."

"No, I should think that would be quite a handicap."

"And then the whole idea goes against everything that mothers have been taught — giving their kids a little of this, a little of that. You know what big lines all the baby food people have to carry — forty or fifty items at least. They wouldn't do that if they didn't have to."

"Do you mean that you feed only this one thing?"

"At least that's the way I get it," Kennan said. "What you ought to do, Mr. Lord, is get hold of a copy of Joel's report. That's got the whole story in it. That's why he was hired, you know — to make a market study. Spent almost a year on it."

"And his recommendation was against trying to market it?"

"That's right. You see — well, maybe this is something I shouldn't say —"

"Say anything you want to as far as I'm concerned."

"Well, Kira had been pushing pretty hard to get Mr. Zurich to put the stuff on the market — he knew it wouldn't go — and I always figured that's why he hired Joel. Do you see what I mean — so that he'd have something to back him up and keep Kira off his neck."

"That's not the first time something like that's been done," he said, attempting lightness but not quite managing it . . . but all she had asked was that he consider it . . . *"I'll be perfectly willing to take your judgment"* . . . no attempt to pressure him. But it was strange that she was hanging on so stubbornly . . . unless she was trying to do it to please Perrill . . .

"Here we are," Kennan said, directing him toward the alleyway that led back to the cannery.

"What's Joel doing now?" he asked. "Did I understand you to say that he was Mr. Swann's assistant?"

"That's right."

"Is he still working on any market studies?"

"I really don't know. He's pretty much under Alf and I've stuck to my own bailiwick."

"A man like that should be valuable right now — depending of course on how able he is."

"Joel's a good bright boy — you know, the way a lot of these Jewish boys are —" He caught himself. "I didn't mean that as anything against him, of course. I've never been prejudiced against Jews. But I guess that goes without saying. If I had been I'd never have gone to work for Mr. Zurich."

"Oh, that's right — you did come down here before he found out that he wasn't, didn't you?"

Kennan broke stride, stopping, his eyes narrowed, silent through a long pause. "Maybe I'm sticking my neck into something that isn't any of my business —"

"What's on your mind, Frank?"

"I've been trying to level with you, Mr. Lord — nothing under the table."

"I appreciate that."

173

"That's one thing I've never been able to understand about Kira — that business about Mr. Zurich not being a Jew. I thought she'd dropped it — but if she brought it up again with you — ?"

"She didn't. Mr. Phelps told me the story. And he didn't say that Mr. Zurich wasn't a Jew, only that there was a question —"

"He was a Jew," Kennan said emphatically. "He was as Jewish as — well, I guess I'm off-base getting steamed up about it, but that yarn always has raised my hackles. In my book, Sol Zurich was a great man — he did a hell of a lot for me — and I've never liked the idea of somebody trying to apologize for him. He didn't need any apology from anyone."

Lincoln Lord found himself momentarily off balance, startled by Kennan's outburst yet finding it difficult to criticize him, either for the strength of his conviction or his loyalty to Sol Zurich, finally saying as they walked on, "It's always the man that counts, not the label you put on him."

"That's right," Kennan said. "I knew it didn't make any difference to you, but —" His voice faded off, lost in the clatter of the conveyer.

Lincoln Lord quickened his pace, anxious to get away from the depressing gloom that seemed to be closing in upon him, the passageway suddenly reverberant with Otis Sellcox's voice.

Back in the brightly lighted cannery, his spirits rose again as Kennan displayed the gleaming cafeteria and, beyond, gave him a surreptitious glance into the woman's rest room, pink-walled and chintzy. The men's room was furnished with individual steel lockers and tiled showers of country club quality. The first-aid room was a hospital in miniature.

"Well, that's about the layout as far as the plant is concerned," Kennan said as they came to a door marked OFFICE. "We've gone over it pretty fast but I hope you've seen enough to — well, all we need is a chance, Mr. Lord."

"I've no doubt of that, Frank, not the slightest."

Kennan hesitated as if groping for some more adequate conclusion, an effort abandoned as he pushed open the door.

Lincoln Lord stepped ahead, seeing ten or a dozen desks and, without thinking, asked, "What department is this?"

There was no immediate response and he side-glanced at Kennan. The production manager's face, caught in the instant of puzzled inquiry, made an answer unnecessary. He knew then that this was the entire office, all of it, and the magnitude of his error was measured by a

174

flashing succession of brain images, vistas of the four floors of block-long offices at Luxor Pharmacal. The presidential suite alone had been substantially larger than the entire office area of the Coastal Foods Company.

For a deluded instant he seemed to be seeing Otis Sellcox walking toward him, his lips twisted in an ironic smile of vindictive satisfaction, a demon about to claim his victory.

With a resolution born of fear, he fought against the illusion and, suddenly successful, raised his hand in a greeting to Alfred Swann, who had seen them through the glassed enclosure of his cubby hole office and was now coming out to greet them.

10

Dr. Arthur Whittaker was anxiously piloting his car through the late-afternoon traffic that crowded Brighton's six-block business section, feeling himself embarked upon a mission for which he was inadequately qualified and temperamentally unsuited. There were men, he knew, who would find it the simplest thing in the world to pay an informal call upon Jay Quincy, join him in a whiskey and soda, chatter along for a few minutes about this and that, and then casually toss off a simple little question to which Jay would reply with a clear statement of his attitude toward Lincoln Lord. Dean Whittaker was not such a man. He knew, with the clarity of a lifetime of introspection, that he had little capacity for informality, even less for whiskey, and almost none at all for artful deception. He would never be able to carry off the pretense, clumsily launched when he had called Jay Quincy on the telephone, that he had no purpose in wanting to see him other than the making of a friendly report upon the progress of this year's endowment drive. Nevertheless, having made the appointment, he had to keep it.

Narrowly escaping collision with a chicken farmer's truck loaded with empty crates and a brood of wide-eyed children, Dean Whittaker acknowledged that he had been guilty of a serious lack of foresight in having so impetuously revealed his plan to Judge Crockett. It would have been much better to have talked to Jay Quincy first. As the judge had suggested, Jay was a strange and difficult man, taciturn in board meetings, rarely speaking up unless his opinion was requested, yet quite capable of petulant obstructionism if his feelings were hurt by oversight. As the administrator of the Quincy Fund, he was a powerful regent. In this instance, he would be even more so. The mere fact that Lincoln Lord had once worked for the Quincy Canning Company would be enough to give Jay an expert's status in the eyes of the board. It would take no more than his frown to bar Lincoln Lord from the presidency of Chesapeake College, perhaps even to kill the whole plan.

Crossing the intersection of Front and Fourth, the end of the town's business section, Dean Whittaker sighed, less an expression of relief from the confusion of traffic than an acknowledgment that the affairs of the world were seldom decided upon the evidence of truth. Too often petty emotionalism was governing. Even among his faculty members, men supposedly trained in the scholarly approach, the triumph of truth over prejudice was rare enough to be notable.

Ahead of him now, he saw the iron-sheathed buildings of the old Quincy Cannery. Driving between them, glancing right and left, he noted the broken windowpanes, the loosened sheets of corrugated metal, the general air of neglect that confirmed the town gossip that Jay Quincy had given up and was letting the Quincy Canning Company rust away into oblivion. Surely there was no justifiable reason for Jay to be prejudiced against Lincoln Lord simply because he had been foresighted enough to anticipate that there would be no future in a little small-town cannery that had long since lost its ability to compete with the big corporations. Yet there was the possibility, unreasonable though it was, that Jay might still feel some resentment. There was always the potentiality of bitterness in any man who had seen someone else go onward and upward to a great success that he himself had failed to achieve. This, too, was a human phenomenon that Dean Whittaker had more than once observed in faculty members.

Beyond the cannery, across the Fox Creek swamp, he saw now the spreading lands of Kingdom Point, accessible only over the high-banked road that old Adam Quincy had built to connect the cannery to the great neck of land that had been his private empire. It was here on the eight thousand acres of Kingdom Point that he had founded his fortune, raising enormous acreages of tomatoes for his cannery. And it was here, after that fortune had been securely made, that Adam Quincy had poured back what was reputed to have been a million dollars in the complete restoration of My Kingdom Come, the seventeenth-century plantation that he had recreated as the seat of his twentieth-century barony. With this later phase of Adam Quincy's life, Dean

Whittaker had experienced an intimate and telling association, and now, despite his dominant concern with the old man's surviving son, he could not prevent the flooding return of all the thirty-year-old memories that were linked to Jay's father.

Arthur Whittaker had been only an assistant instructor then, just completing his first year at Chesapeake College, and he had grasped at the chance to spend a summer vacation working with Dr. Thomas Singleton Ruskin, who, even then, was beginning to make something of a reputation for himself as an authority on colonial American life. Some months before, a student in one of Dr. Ruskin's classes who was out on a Sunday hike on Kingdom Point had stumbled upon the almost buried foundations of some old buildings. He had reported his find to Dr. Ruskin, coupling it with the recitation of a local legend that Kingdom Point had once been the site of a great plantation. Jumping to a fortunate conclusion, Ruskin had guessed that there might be an association between the surviving name of the neck of land, Kingdom Point, and a lost plantation called My Kingdom Come which had been definitively described, except for precise location, in a London published collection of the 1664-1668 letters of Lord Wicklett. That was what had given rise to the summer project on which Arthur Whittaker had been employed.

From early June until late August, he had directed a crew of students working with pick and shovel, probing the earth for old foundations, mapping their outline and location. On his own, with only minimal direction from Dr. Ruskin, he had proved beyond doubt that Adam Quincy's tomato fields were indeed located on the lands of My Kingdom Come, the site of the old mansion house indisputably fixed by his personal discovery of two gnarled old English yews still surviving in the jungled growth of underbrush.

All through that following winter, existing on a half ration of sleep, he had continued to work on the My Kingdom Come project, endlessly digging through original source material, patching together every scrap of factual evidence that bore upon any aspect of the plantation. He had even made a rough perspective drawing of what the plantation buildings must have looked like in 1665, suggesting to Dr. Ruskin that his sketch might be developed into an illustration for the paper that would surely be written for one of the history journals. That had really been the beginning of the idea of restoration, that drawing that he had shown to Dr. Ruskin.

During that first year, Arthur Whittaker had learned a great deal about life in seventeenth-century Maryland. During the second, he learned even more about how, in the twentieth century, a man got to be as famous as Dr. Thomas Singleton Ruskin had eventually become. In the beginning he had admired the history professor for his scholarship. That high regard had slowly given way, however, before the mounting evidence that Ruskin's scholarly endeavors were largely carried out by eager young assistants whom he could charm into his service. The professor's real talents were, despite his carefully preserved pretentions of scholarship, those of a remarkably successful high-pressure salesman, abilities that he had demonstrated with telling effect upon old Adam Quincy.

That first summer, Arthur Whittaker and his digging crew had lived a touch and go existence, never knowing when they would be ordered to stop excavating by old Mr. Quincy, who, plainly enough, had little use for silly college professors who interfered with the far more important business of growing tomatoes. Exactly how Ruskin had won over Adam Quincy was not entirely clear, although some of the individual maneuvers had been so blatantly evident that it was hard to understand how as smart a man as Mr. Quincy had not realized that he was being taken into camp.

The most vivid of Arthur Whittaker's memories centered around the publication of *My Kingdom Come: A Seventeenth-Century Maryland Plantation,* the book that had eventually won for Dr. Thomas Singleton Ruskin the gold medal of the Academy of American Historians. Ruskin had written almost none of it, contributing no more than an outline and a final revision. Arthur Whittaker had not really expected his own name to appear on the title page as a co-author — he had come to know Ruskin well enough by then to keep his expectations within bounds — but he had hoped that his assistance would at least be acknowledged in the foreword. His name did not appear. Instead, the foreword was totally devoted to a paean of praise for Adam Quincy, who in the only paragraphs that Ruskin had written without assistance was pictured as one of America's greatest industrialists, an enlightened patron of scholarly endeavor, and a public-spirited citizen devoted to the preservation of our great colonial heritage. It was not a difficult deduction that Ruskin had somehow hornswoggled Adam Quincy into paying for the elaborate color plates and subsidizing the printing of a book so handsome that it had become a collector's item on the very day of its publication.

But that had been only the first important example of Ruskin's influence upon Adam Quincy. Somehow adroitly plucking every string that was in harmonic vibration with the old man's vanity, Ruskin had sold him the idea of restoring My Kingdom Come, a task unquestionably made easier by Adam Quincy's natural tendency to see himself as the lord of a great manor, a role to which he had been temperamentally attuned since he had struck it rich during the food-shortage years of the First World War. Ruskin had admittedly taken advantage of that situation but not, as he maintained, because of his devotion to historical scholarship. He saw to it that the restoration of My Kingdom Come was given nation-wide publicity, less importantly in the scholarly journals and annals of the historical societies than in the big magazines that were read and respected by the kind of men who served as regents and directors on the boards of colleges, universities, and well-financed foundations. The restoration work had hardly been completed before Dr. Thomas Singleton Ruskin had resigned from Chesapeake College and was on his way up the ladder.

Thereafter, whenever Arthur Whittaker read of some new upward step that Dr. Ruskin had taken, he felt a twinge of resentment that any man so lacking in real ability, so patently profiting from the work of others, should be so successful. Yet, set squarely against that feeling, there had later come a disquieting realization that Dr. Thomas Singleton Ruskin had really accomplished more for Chesapeake College than any of the more justifiably admired scholars who had graced the campus during the century and a half of the institution's existence. Had it not been for Ruskin's influence, Adam Quincy would never have set up the Quincy Fund. Without the Fund, and the other gifts that were traceable to its initial influence, Chesapeake would still be nothing but a little three-building college. Of late, Dean Whittaker had more and more frequently speculated upon this line of thought, wondering if perhaps some of his scholarly associates were right in the standards by which they judged a man's worth in this twentieth-century world.

But if his estimate of Dr. Ruskin had changed, so too had there been a revision of his initial opinion of Adam Quincy. He had never gotten to know the old man really well — characteristically, Ruskin had kept his assistant under cover — but after Ruskin had resigned and left the college, Mr. Quincy had occasionally called Arthur Whittaker out to My Kingdom Come for consultation on some detail of colonial craftsmanship. What had, on those occasions, so impressed him about Adam Quincy was that in two short years the old man had made himself, by driving application and an extraordinarily intense concentration of interest, a first-class authority on seventeenth-century life, so well informed that he could rarely if ever be bested in an argument. At the time, it had been highly disconcerting to find himself, despite his doctorate, no more than a match for a man who had not even finished grammar school. Later, particularly during these last few years when, as dean, he had come to have some influence in the selection of new members of the faculty, he often recalled Adam Quincy when confronted with some candidate instructor whose merit as a teacher seemed to lie principally in his accumulation of academic degrees. He often thought of Adam Quincy, too, when one of his associates made some categorically slighting remark about businessmen.

If it were true that Dr. Ruskin was entitled to some credit for having inspired the original interest in Chesapeake College that had eventually resulted in Adam Quincy's munificent gifts, the conclusion could hardly be escaped that Mr. Quincy deserved at least some respect for having accumulated the money that made those gifts possible. In academic circles, little progress could be made with this argument, the general attitude being that any man who was willing to abandon ethical conduct and resort to the distasteful tactics of money-grubbing could easily enough become rich. This argument Dr. Whittaker did not accept. Successful businessmen, he had come to believe, possessed some special genius, perhaps indefinable but nevertheless unarguably present. He had been almost the only faculty member who had defended Dr. Radcliff when Adam Quincy, before he died, had been awarded an honorary LL.D. and elected to the board of regents.

Although Jay Quincy had succeeded to his father's place on the Chesapeake College board, he had apparently inherited none of his father's genius. Jay had, so it was said around town, almost no head for business, being roughly classified by the gossips as the typically weak son of a strong father, victimized by an inferiority complex generated by paternal dominance, further explained by his odd taste for the life of a semi-recluse. He was believed to be financially solvent only because his father had left him, in addition to Kingdom Come, a great deal of property scattered all over the county, all of which had shown an enormous appreciation in value as a result of the influx of New York and Philadelphia people who were now coming down to the Eastern Shore and buying up anything that could be turned into a gentleman farm. Some of the local criticism of Jay Quincy for the kind of life that he had chosen to lead undoubtedly stemmed from the fact that his friends, such as they were, had been selected from this horde of invaders from the North. He had even married one of them and, righteously justified, Brighton had smirked when, two years later, the word had gotten around that Jay Quincy's Long Island wife had left Kingdom Come for Reno. Thereafter, more surely than ever, Jay had been locally regarded, not as a boy who had grown up on Front Street, but as one of the white-fence and station-wagon crowd who took their marriages lightly, their whiskey neat, and indulged in all sorts of wild carryings-on in their reconstructed manor houses.

Dr. Whittaker had no inclination toward criticizing Jay Quincy, neither for the way he was living his life nor, as did the town's shopkeepers, for his having failed to keep the Quincy Canning Company functioning as Brighton's only source of industrial paychecks. Business ability was, as the dean knew from his own case, something that every man did not possess; and again from his own experience, he knew that the irrational desires of a son were rarely explainable in terms of inheritance. His own son, Paul, for no discernible reason, had become so enamored of dentistry that he had freely chosen to spend the rest of his life poking around in people's mouths. And yet dentists were needed, as were practitioners of all of the other odd occupations to which men were so fortuitously drawn. Perhaps, he had concluded, it was all a part of nature's grand design, the life force of the community filling its needs in much the same way that the human body was so awesomely capable of sustaining itself. Somehow men were shaken and shuffled about until they found a niche that fitted them. And here again there was the evidence of his own life. He had never dreamed that, lacking in ability as he was, he would rise as high as he had. He was no Dr. Thomas Singleton Ruskin. He had achieved his own success, not by clever connivance and surely not by the force of his personality, but by being completely honest about his own shortcomings, not only with himself but with everyone else. He could not change. It would be ridiculous for him even to attempt to carry off the pretense, seemingly such a good idea when Judge Crockett had suggested it, that he had come out to Kingdom Come to make a report on the fund-raising drive. The only thing that he could possibly do would be to approach Jay Quincy in an honest and straightforward way, telling him truthfully why he was there. Strange as Jay might be, and even granting that some old prejudice against Lincoln Lord might still remain, Jay would surely be able to see that he was the man that Chesapeake College now needed as its president.

Diverted by the mental turmoil that led to this decision, he was unaware of the speed with which he was approaching the closed gates of the plantation. Only by throwing himself back against the seat, a stiff-kneed leg jamming down on the brake pedal, was he able to avoid collision with the ornamental wrought-iron barrier across the road. Exhaling relief, he slumped forward again while the old Negro gatekeeper hurriedly hobbled out and applied an enormous key to the great brass lock, its shining surfaces matched to the intertwined bronze initials worked into the decorative design of the wrought iron. They were K C for Kingdom Come, not MKC for My Kingdom Come, one of the innumerable concessions that Dr. Ruskin had made to Adam Quincy, who had decided to eliminate the possessive pronoun on the theory that this minor historical inaccuracy would save him from the accusation of being unduly immodest.

"Yes, suh, Mr. Dean," the gatekeeper said as the car slipped through. "Welcome to Kingdom Come, suh. Been a long time since you was here, suh."

"Yes, it has," Dean Whittaker acknowledged, easing the car through the gateway, his driving more cautious now as he started down the half-mile of cedar-bordered lane that led to the mansion house. It had, indeed, been too long since he had come to Kingdom Come. If he had only made a social call or two, his visit today would be less suspect. His wife had often suggested it, arguing ever since he had gotten his deanship that he had social obligations that must be fulfilled, although never without arousing the suspicion that her real purpose was deviously selfish. He knew what a feather in her cap it would be if she could only talk Jay Quincy into permitting Kingdom Come to be made a stop on the Spring Garden Tour of the Brighton Historical Society. Despite the high standards of her normal conduct, she was regrettably prone to deviousness in those instances where it could be excused by a charitable purpose. But perhaps she was right, the end an adequate justification for the means. At least the world seemed to be coming more and more attuned to that attitude.

The mansion house lay ahead of him now, a spearpoint at the end of the long lance of the lane, a reminder of the difficulty that he had experienced in getting his perspective just right in that first sketch he had made, unable to suggest the baronial magnificence of the house without unduly enlarging its proportions. The architect, too, had apparently encountered that same difficulty, because, in the final plan for the house, it had become a structure substantially larger than the Wicklett letters had suggested. Nevertheless, it was a beautifully designed house and, getting out of his car, studying the façade, Dean Whittaker felt a resurgence of creative pride. True enough, there had been certain compromises with historical evidence — whenever there had been a conflict between authenticity and Adam Quincy's desires, Ruskin had seen to it that Lord Wicklett's ghost was well laid — yet the end result was, in spirit if not in detail, remarkably successful.

Walking toward the main entrance from his parked car, he noticed that the gravel of the drive was as smooth as if it had just been hand-swept by slaves with broomstraw brushes, pleasant evidence that Jay Quincy, despite his neglect of the cannery, was not letting down Kingdom Come. The lion's head knocker was perfectly polished and the Negro maidservant who opened the door for him wore a crisply starched uniform, spotlessly clean and of precisely the primrose shade that Lord Wicklett had described as being such a pleasant contrast with the cocoa-shaded skin that he had made a qualification of all slaves chosen for his houseservants.

The maid escorted him to the library, telling him that Mr. Jay would join him there very shortly, a wait that Dr. Whittaker welcomed not only because it delayed the moment of confrontation but also because it gave him a chance to savor the atmosphere of the room. If not authentically 1665, it was nevertheless the complete fulfillment of what always came to mind when he had dreamed of having his own inviolate cloister, a room that his wife would not dare litter with the ravelings of her daytime sewing, nor his daughter use as the best of all places to park her offspring for at least two nights out of every week. It was a room too small ever to be invaded by the overflow from a faculty tea, yet large enough to house a handsome George Washington desk, historically anachronistic but most appealing, one of the few worldly possessions that Dr. Whittaker had always coveted. A small fire crackled pleasantly on the grate of the slate-faced fireplace, sensibly utilitarian. The walls were solidly bookcased, the shelves well filled. He could not help but notice as his eyes scanned titles that this was the library of an intelligent man with a wide-ranging and boldly active mind, not the Jay Quincy of rumor nor even the diffidently taciturn man who attended board meetings, but surprisingly appropriate to the man who suddenly appeared in the doorway, now offering a pleasant smile of greeting. He wore a country gentleman's sport coat, leather patched at the elbows, exactly the sort of garment that Dean Whitta-ker had long wished that he might dare to buy for himself, even if only to wear around the house.

"My apologies, Dean," Jay Quincy said, extending his hand. "I had a very persistent gentleman on the telephone. Somehow he'd gotten the idea that I might be willing to sell this house."

"I hope you're not —"

"Hardly! Sit down, Dean, sit down. May I offer you a drink?"

"No, no. I really — this is an imposition, I know, breaking in on you —"

"Not at all," Jay said, even more evidently now the assured master of his own house.

Dean Whittaker gathered himself for another start, recalling his resolution to abandon his planned approach, yet finding himself with nothing else to say. "I happened to be talking to Judge Crockett this noon — about the alumni meeting in New York — and I thought — *we* thought —"

"Yes, I saw a squib about it in the *New York Times* yesterday. Had Linc Lord for your speaker, I see. How is he?"

"Splendid!" he said, his exuberance partly accountable to his grati-tude that Jay's introduction of Lincoln Lord's name had saved him the necessity of bringing it up, giving a hopeful legitimacy to his now saying, "It was really an extraordinarily fine meeting, by all odds the best of that sort that we've ever had. You'd have been amazed if you'd seen that crowd react to Mr. Lord's speech."

Jay seemed vaguely amused. "Why would you imagine that I'd be amazed, Dean?"

"Well, I —"

"In a spot like that, I'd have counted on Linc to come through."

"You would?" he said blankly, scarcely able to believe this pre-cursor of a successful mission. "Really now, that's very encouraging."

"Encouraging?"

He had trapped himself. There was now no alternative to coming out with the truth. "What I came out to see you about — really, there's no point in my beating about the bush — I'd very much like your opinion of Mr. Lord."

"Opinion?"

"What do you think of him?"

"In what context? I'm not ducking an answer, Dean, but that's a rather broad question."

There was nothing to do now but to plunge in. "What I've been thinking of — subject, of course, to the judgment of the board — is that we might possibly bring Mr. Lord into the college in some capacity that would allow him to do — on a very much broader scale, of course — the same sort of thing that he did for us in New York. And a great many other things, as well. In fact — well, to put it quite bluntly, I'd very much like to see the board bring in Mr. Lord to direct all of that sort of thing."

Jay Quincy's eyebrows went up, stopped in that raised position. "As a full-time job — an officer of the college?"

"I realize that I may be overstepping the bounds of propriety in making a suggestion of this sort myself — I know that it's something that would normally originate with the board —"

"No reason why you shouldn't make any proposal you want to, Dean, no reason at all."

"Of course, I have been given to understand — informally — that I'm to succeed Dr. Radcliff —"

"No question about that, is there?"

"Not really, I don't suppose. Still one doesn't normally refuse a position that he's not yet been offered. If it weren't that time is rather of the essence —"

"Refuse? Dean, you aren't serious, are you? You're not actually thinking of turning down the presidency?"

Jay Quincy's surprise was a rich and warming compliment, an encouragement to continue in the same vein. "The plan that I've been pondering — and again let me say that I'm fully aware that this is something to be decided by the board, not myself — would call for giving Mr. Lord responsibility to manage all of the college's business and financial affairs." He paused, momentarily sizing up Jay's reaction, judging it to be, if not openly enthusiastic at least not forbiddingly adverse. "With a man of Mr. Lord's caliber — well, it would be quite unreasonable, I'm sure, to expect him to be interested if he were not given the presidency."

"And you'd be willing to give it up?"

"Oh yes — yes indeed."

"And go on as dean of the faculty?"

"Yes, if that were the decision of the board — although I had rather hoped —" He paused, recommitting himself to the honest approach. "Frankly, what I've been hoping is that the board might see fit to create a new position — *provost* is the title most often employed, I believe — for someone who would take complete responsibility for all matters pertaining to the college's academic affairs."

"In others words you'd have two top executives — Linc Lord on the money side and yourself on the educational side?"

"In essence — yes, I suppose you might put it that way. Although, as I say, this is only —"

"Well!" It was an explosive exhalation that propelled Jay Quincy to his feet. For a moment he stood with his back turned, his arms outstretched along the length of the fireplace's mantel. Watching him, Dr. Whittaker braced himself for an inquisition similar to the one to which he had been subjected by Judge Crockett, all of his answers suspect because it apparently seemed highly irrational that he would willingly give up the presidency.

"How widely have you discussed this, Dean?"

"I've talked to no one — no one, that is, except Judge Crockett."

"Then why are you telling me about it? Pardon my bewilderment but this isn't at all normal, you know. I've never before been consulted in advance about anything having to do with the college. As a matter of fact, until you started the practice of sending out an advance agenda, I've never known what was coming up at a meeting. Not that I've minded really — I know very well, of course, that I've been kept on the board only because I happen to control the Quincy Fund —"

"Oh, I'd not say that," Dr. Whittaker said in quick alarm. "Not that I have anything to do, of course, with the selection of regents —"

"Forgive me," Jay laughed, seemingly a recognition that he had been guilty of pettiness. "I was only needling you — and you aren't the one who deserves it. But you still haven't answered my question."

"I beg your pardon?"

"Why have you come to me?"

He waited until Jay sat down again. "Well, you do know Mr. Lord better than anyone else. At least better than any of the other board members. He did work for you, didn't he?"

"Oh!" There was a long pause. "What were you and Crockett afraid of — that I might cook Linc's goose with a bad recommendation?"

Dean Whittaker was no master of the evasive laugh, nor did he make a bad attempt better by blurting out, "Well, we thought if you were against the idea, it might be better to know it —"

To his surprise, Jay Quincy laughed, "Dean, you're a refreshingly honest man — and, bless your soul, I can see why that makes all this fund-raising business so distasteful to you. If I were in your place, I'd feel exactly the same way — all those horrible banquets, kow-towing to every old alumnus who might conceivably sign a hundred-dollar pledge — providing, of course, that the money is used only to support some worthy football player."

"Well, it's not that exactly," Whittaker said, an almost automatic response to his long-practiced habit of never supporting hackneyed academic criticism of the alumni. "The point is I'm not at all good at that sort of thing — the banquets and speeches and all that. And then — well, goodness knows, there's enough to do on the academic side, enough and more."

He was fully prepared to go on from there, ready with the detail of his plan to strengthen Chesapeake College as an educational institution, gradually molding the faculty into a body of men dedicated to the educational process, their ultimate goal the training of young minds and not the publication of monographs.

But he was given no chance to expound upon his dream. Instead, his host stood up again, his hands clasped behind his back, the fingers working with unanticipated nervousness, some inner turmoil well controlled as he said casually, "I've not seen Linc for a long time, only once or twice since he left here. How is he, anyway?"

"Oh, fine."

"Did you know him when he was here?"

Honesty had suddenly become a burden, forcing him to acknowledge that after his experience with Dr. Ruskin he had spent several years as a scholarly recluse, withdrawn from any real consciousness of what was going on around the campus. Unfortunately, those were the years when Lincoln Lord had been, first president of the Student Union and then, after graduation, an assistant in the alumni office. Tentatively, he began, "Well, I do recall his being on the campus, of course — but, at the time, I was rather fully occupied with a research project —"

"I don't mean at the college. I mean afterward — when he was here, working for the company."

"Well, as I say I was rather out of touch with —"

"They lived here, you know." Jay glanced toward the window, looking out at the plantation buildings that fronted upon the gardened oval behind the mansion. "After they were married, my father gave them one of the guesthouses — Linc and Maggie. You do know her?"

"Mrs. Lord? Oh yes — yes indeed," he said hurriedly, wondering if this were the opportune time to make the point that one of the strong arguments in favor of his plan was that Mrs. Lord was so perfectly suited to the role of the wife of the president of Chesapeake College.

Jay Quincy was looking at him but with an unfocused stare. "I've often thought about how differently things might have worked out if we could all have stayed together — Linc and Brick Mitchell and myself. It was one of those almost perfect combinations — the three of us working together. If Linc had only come back —"

His voice faded off into a silence that Dr. Whittaker felt as an oppressive weight, bearing down upon his lungs, preventing him from breathing. This was clearly the knife-edge moment. Did Jay's regret that Lincoln Lord had left the Quincy Canning Company mean that he still held him in high regard . . . or was his disappointment the key to resentment?

Jay Quincy went on, his voice detached, his faint smile inscrutable. "I suppose it was my fault, in a way — Linc's leaving — not standing up to my father a little more strenuously. But it was difficult to make him understand. And maybe I didn't understand then either, not really. I'd been raised on his point of view, of course — that the factory was the important thing, that that's where you made your success. It took me a long time to realize how business has changed — how the whole world has changed. It's the salesmen who are in the saddle now, you know. They're the boys who have inherited the earth."

"Very true," the dean murmured.

A convulsive lip movement signaled the breaking of Jay Quincy's mood. "That's what you've found out at the college, too, I take it — that a good director of public relations is worth more than a dozen professors."

"Well, I'd hardly say *worth more* —"

"Linc is available, is he?"

Dr. Whittaker hesitated, the rise of hope making it difficult to recall how he had phrased his answer to this same question when Judge Crockett had asked it. "Yes, it seems that he might be," was not it, close but not close enough, and he made another try. "I do know that he's still free as far as any other connections are concerned. He did tell me that. But as to whether or not he would be willing to accept a call —"

"You didn't ask him?"

"Oh no — no indeed! I hardly felt myself free to do that, not without some authorization from the board. And even then — well, I'd not be the one to approach him."

"But you did get a feeling that he might be interested?"

Regretfully, the dean shook his head. "No, I can't honestly say that I did. But it does seem reasonable. He's very much interested in Chesapeake — he couldn't possibly have done what he did in New York if he weren't — and the fact that he's recently spent several months on a government mission does seem to indicate a general interest in public service. And then, you know, it wouldn't be unprecedented. There are quite a number of businessmen who have come into the academic world these last few years — well, not precisely the academic world but at least the administrative end of it. After a businessman has enough money so that he doesn't have to worry about that sort of thing any more —" He hesitated, finally adding as if it were a fact recognized but not quite understood, "There seems to be something quite appealing about college life to a man of that sort — perhaps a chance to add a bit of stature."

Jay Quincy was whistling softly to himself, a speculative mannerism suddenly interrupted as he said, "Yes, I suppose it might appeal to her."

"To her?" slipped out as Dr. Whittaker felt the prick of fear. His alarm would have been less if, night before last, he had not briefly considered suggesting a rearrangement of the speakers' table in order that Mrs. Lord might be seated there, a possibility dismissed with the judgment that she was surely a woman too intelligent and well-balanced to be susceptible to such gauche flattery. It was a tactic that had often been effective with the wife of a prospective instructor — it was axiomatic that the best way to snare a good man for the Chesapeake faculty was to get to his wife — but he decided that a man of Lincoln Lord's caliber would be above being influenced by anything other than his own good judgment. Had he been wrong?

Jay had just said, "I can hardly imagine Linc taking it unless it was something that Maggie wanted him to do."

"You don't think she'd be for it?"

"I beg your pardon?" Jay was apparently puzzled by his obtuseness. "I just said, Dean, I thought the idea might appeal to her."

An odd acidity had edged Jay Quincy's tone of voice, a warning that put Dr. Whittaker on his guard. Quickly analyzed, however, all that Jay had said was that Mrs. Lord's influence would probably be in their favor and that, of course, was exactly what he wanted. And as he himself had been about to observe, having the right wife was a very important asset for a college president, a thought that he now tried to approach by saying, "Yes, I can well imagine that she's been quite a factor in his success."

Jay Quincy regarded him speculatively, seemingly a prediction of some highly important revelation. But all that he said was, "Linc would have been a very different man if he hadn't married her."

Dr. Whittaker fell back on a generality, "That's something, I imagine, that could be said of any man."

"But it isn't every man who married a Maggie Kipling," Jay said, his use of her maiden name a revealing indication that he was thinking of Mrs. Lord, not as she was today but as the young girl she must have been when she had come to Brighton.

The dean murmured agreement, suddenly conscious that anything he said on the subject of marriage had to be carefully weighed, recalling again that Jay Quincy had been divorced after an experience that, if the gossips were even half right, would have been enough to prejudice any man. The best course now seemed to be an abrupt change of subject — or, in lieu of that, to drive straight through to the point of whatever it was that Jay was getting at. Quickly deciding that the latter alternative was more safely forthright, he said, "I take it that you're not too favorably impressed by Mrs. Lord?"

For a moment, Jay Quincy seemed shocked, then only sardonically amused. "I hadn't meant to give you that impression, Dean. Not at all, no indeed. Maggie's a very capable person. I admire her greatly. Isn't that the temper of our time — that we must always admire anyone who wants something out of life and then goes out and gets it? Maggie wanted to be the wife of a big man — someone who'd get somewhere. And that's the way it worked out. With Maggie, it would."

"You think that she's been his — *inspiration*, I know, is the wrong word."

"Yes, it is the wrong word," Jay Quincy said curtly. "Maggie has been the whip on his back, the burr under his tail, everything that —" He cut off sharply. "Now don't get another wrong impression, Dean. What I'm saying is nothing against her — nor against Linc either. They're a great pair. What Linc didn't have, Maggie supplied." He paused. "You did ask me to tell you what I know about Linc Lord, didn't you? That is what you want, isn't it?"

"Yes indeed," he said, forcefully positive yet finding himself foggily bewildered by the way that Jay Quincy had so suddenly gone pinwheeling off in all directions, words flung like firecracker sparks tangentially launched, too briefly bright to be illuminating. Yet there was that same sensing of understanding that, as dean of the college, he had so often experienced in his private sessions with errant undergraduates. More often than not, what they failed to tell him was more revealing than what they said, not because they were consciously evading the truth but rather because they were able to see only the self-protective screen that their subconscious minds had erected to hide the truth from themselves. Jay Quincy was no undergraduate — he must be a man close to fifty — yet there was a boyishness about his petulant cynicism that gave validity to the guess that his attitude toward Lincoln Lord, and more particularly toward Mrs. Lord, had been distorted in much the same way a flunking student was so often inclined to blame his shortcomings on someone else. The difficulty in trying to read Jay Quincy's inner mind was that it lacked adolescent simplicity. There were too many possibilities, no one clearly indicated as being inevitably true. One was that there had been some premarital emotional attachment to Mrs. Lord, now rationalized into a critical attitude. The second, seeming ingrained in character, was a boyish jealousy incited by his father's superior attachment to someone other than himself. The third, even more strongly suggested, was that Jay was suffering from a guilt complex arising from his failure to keep the Quincy Canning Company going as a successful concern, the blame subconsciously transferred to Mrs. Lord for having deprived him of the services of her husband.

All this went very quickly through Dr. Whittaker's trained analytical mind, weighed for its possible pertinence and then set aside as he reasoned that even if he took everything that Jay Quincy had told him at face value there was nothing too disturbing about it. Although the fact that Mrs. Lord exercised considerable influence upon her husband did somewhat reduce Lincoln Lord's stature, there was the more than compensating realization that Lord's rather frequent change of association — he had been somewhat more concerned on this point than he had, up to now, admitted to himself — was chargeable to Mrs. Lord's driving ambition rather than to any inherent lack of stability in the man himself.

Abruptly Jay Quincy said, "Linc knows nothing about this?"

"No, I —"

"You've not talked to him? Not even a hint?"

"No."

"You're positive that he doesn't know he's even being considered?"

"I don't see how —"

"Suppose I were to do this," Jay Quincy said, his voice suddenly bright, an amazing change from what it had been only seconds before. "I'll be in New York next week. I'll give Linc a ring and have a talk with him. If this were presented to him in the right way —" Unexplainably he stopped, staring out of the window. "That is what you want, isn't it? You want my support?"

"Yes indeed," the dean said, enthusiasm somewhat dimmed by the prospect of slow development, yet recognizing that with Jay Quincy's sponsorship the board of regents could hardly avoid approving his whole plan.

"Where are they living?"

"The Waldorf-Astoria."

"That makes it easy." He was looking out of the window again. "There's only one thing —"

"Yes?"

"I want to handle this in my own way."

"Of course."

Jay Quincy looked at him with a vacant stare, his voice softly positive. "Yes, that's the best way." He paused through a long moment of silence. "Yes, this will mean a lot to Linc."

11

"I believe they're coming now," Kira Zurich said. "Yes, that's Frank Kennan's car."

Maggie Lord was on her feet instantly, reacting even before she caught sight of the automobile.

"Would you mind letting your husband in?" Kira asked. "There's a telephone call I should make."

It was a transparent excuse to give them a few minutes alone, thoroughly in character with the keenly perceptive woman that Maggie Lord had come to know in these last two hours.

"Of course," Maggie said, smiling as an attempted expression of gratitude, hurrying then to the door.

The automobile had already stopped in front of the house, but Linc had not gotten out yet and, waiting, she experienced a sensation neither new nor unexpected. In twenty years, she had rarely awaited his return after any separation, even one of only a few hours, without this same attempt to anticipate what good or bad had happened to him, this same hurried effort to prepare herself for any eventuality. The difference today was one of intensity, the grip of apprehension stronger, the awareness of consequence greater.

She was not expecting a positively stated decision as to whether he would or would not accept the presidency of the Coastal Foods Company. No matter what he found out in his inspection of the plant he would, as always, approach her with outward uncertainty. He would ask, "What do you think, Mag?" And then she would face the most dangerous of all moments. Given only the vaguest of hints, she would have to guess what he wanted to hear, attempt to echo what was already in his mind — a desire often so well hidden that she sometimes suspected that even he himself did not recognize its existence.

Waiting, she honed her consciousness to its sharpest edge, ready to make the most of the little signs and portents that would be her only guides. Usually they were enough. Often she could anticipate his mood just from hearing the sound of his footsteps coming down the hall, the metallic probing of the key in the lock, the rattle of the doorknob. Today, however, it might be more difficult. She would have only a few seconds of secret observation before he realized that she was watching him.

As yet she could see nothing — his face was hidden in the dark interior of the car — but in a moment he would get out and come walking toward her. Then almost instantly she would have to make her decision, allowed to know only what little might be learned from the intuitively sensed significance of the set of his shoulders, the cock of his head, perhaps an expression that might come to his face in an unguarded instant when he thought himself unobserved. Under normal circumstances that would be enough. But today it might not be. More than once since they had left New York this morning, he had said or done something that was completely outside the bounds of expectation, totally unanticipated.

Doubly incited, not only because it was an example of the strangeness that had come over him today, but also because there was the danger that it might now be reinvoked, she thought again of his accusation that she had failed him before through a lack of honesty, through not telling him frankly what she herself had really thought on similar occasions. At the time she had tried to protect herself by judging it to be no more than the excusable result of the tension that he was under. But she had been more deeply hurt than she had realized. The wound was still open, sensitive to the touch of awareness — the sting of pain no longer strong enough to spark the flashback of vindictiveness, yet so deftly penetrating that it found an untouched mind center, releasing a question that she had never before asked herself.

What would happen if, for once, she did tell him honestly and frankly what she wanted him to do? Maybe he was right . . . maybe she had been wrong. Maybe the time had come to speak up . . . tell him how much she wanted everything that was offered here . . . this wonderful house . . . no more hotel suites . . . no more furnished apartments, no more temporary shelters hastily rented and then as hurriedly abandoned . . . never buying a piece of furniture of their own without the secret reservation that next year it might have to be used somewhere else, or turned into another claim check from a storage warehouse. Yes, this was what she wanted . . . a home . . . roots . . . some one spot of earth that would be theirs and theirs alone . . . their own things . . . more than that little handful of trinkets that Linc had taken down to the suite yesterday . . . a refrigerator that had something in it besides canapés and soda water . . .

There was movement inside the car now, the flash of Linc's white hands across the window . . . no, he was still talking to Kennan. Did it mean that he was going to take the job? If he was . . . but what difference did it make? Why not tell him, anyway? Other women did . . . Agnes Braydon . . . "If Charlie thinks for one minute that I'm going to give up my home and my friends and move out to California . . ."

He was getting out of the car now, but on the other side, his face still hidden . . . *"Linc, I want you to take this job . . . I want this to be our home . . . I want to take Kip out of that awful Forgehill and bring him here to live with us. I want . . ."*

Suddenly his head appeared over the top of the car, his face strongly modeled by the low sun. Instantly, everything that had been in her mind vanished, a shadowy wraith dissolved by a blast of light, leaving only the consciousness of a horrible error barely avoided . . . no, she hadn't been wrong! Twenty years and he still loved her . . . that didn't just happen. It could never have lasted if she'd been wrong . . . no, not a word about Kira's offer of the house . . . not until she was certain that it wouldn't affect his decision, one way or the other. He had to make up his own mind. But what would she say when he asked her . . . ?

Striding toward her, he seemed a stranger, unknown and unknowable, offering not the slightest hint of what he wanted her to say. Blindly she guessed that he had decided against accepting the presidency, that his strangeness was attributable to fear, that he was thinking now of the consequences.

Hurriedly, almost frantically, she searched out the words that would support him . . . *"Don't worry about it, Linc . . . something else will . . ."*

He saw her. There was no smile, only a blink of blankness, the briefest possible acknowledgment of recognition and surprise. She opened the door for him, feeling it a gesture of sympathy. He stepped past her, starting to slip out of his coat. Pivoting, she caught his eyes. He froze, the coat half off, staring at her. She dropped her eyes slightly, seeing the slow rise of his chest as a deep breath squared his shoulders.

"Mag — ?"

She raised her eyes again.

"I don't know what you're going to think of this, Mag — it's going to be tough on you — but it's everything that Phelps said it was."

"You mean the plant?"

"Not just the plant — everything — the whole setup."

"Then you're going to take it?" she asked, already knowing the answer, realizing that she ought to be expressing her exultant support, yet so stunned by his having made a decision without even the pretense of consulting her that she was finding it impossible to react to reason.

He dropped the coat, freeing his hands, reaching out to her, "If you don't want me to do it — Mag, it's going to be tough, tough as the devil. It's going to take years to build this company up again — five years — ten years — I don't know how long. I know I haven't any right to ask you to —"

"Linc, that doesn't matter. Nothing matters except —"

His fingertips were lifting her face. "I know I can count on you. You're wonderful — you always have been. But I want you to know what this means. If I take this job, Mag — well, we might as well face it — we'll probably be here the rest of our lives."

She was in his arms then, his lips strong with the words they had just spoken, his body hard-muscled with resolution, a sustaining strength no less powerful because of its strangeness.

Kira's footsteps were approaching before she remembered to tell him about her offer of the house, quickly whispered as something that he should know, vaguely relevant but now unimportant.

195

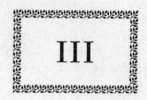

III

MAGGIE LORD had arisen in the grayness of first dawn, her bed made unendurable by the exciting prospect of further discovery. There had been time last night for only the briefest of inspections, leaving much of the house still unexplored, and even what had been once seen needed to be seen again to prove its reality.

Kira Zurich had called early yesterday morning to tell them that the house was now theirs and waiting for them, but for some unexplained reason Linc had clung to New York as if it were something that he could not bring himself to abandon, and it had been after dark last evening when they had finally arrived. Kira had turned over the house and everything that was in it, telling them that she had removed only her most personal possessions. At the time, however, that had meant little more to Maggie than relief from the necessity of spending any money for furnishings until their back bills had been paid. There had been no real anticipation of her discovery, still continuing this morning, that every drawer, every cabinet, every closet was a veritable treasure chest. The unknown person who had been commissioned to stock and furnish the house had plainly been someone with imagination, discrimination, and a virtually unlimited budget.

She was in the kitchen now, the very heart of a worldly paradise, knowing that she ought to be starting breakfast — Linc would have to get up soon — yet so intrigued with all that she was finding that she could not forsake the excitement of exploration. She opened another door, literally gasping at what she saw ... a butler's pantry ... a separate refrigerator for salads and desserts! And china ... china

... china ... oh, and it was lovely! Why hadn't Kira used these beautiful things that day they had been here for lunch?

She spun around at the sound of an opening door. A black face, orange-scarfed, was smiling at her. "Morning, Mrs. Lord. Case you don't remember, I's Viola."

"Yes, Viola, but don't you know — ?"

The orange scarf whipped off, releasing a chuckle. "Mrs. Zurich she called me last night and she says this the way it's supposed to be — me staying here with you folks. Course that is if you don't mind having me?"

"Mind? Oh, Viola, I'm delighted. But are you sure that Mrs. Zurich — ?"

Viola was out of her coat. "Ma'am, this is the way *she* wants it, and this is the way *I* wants it, so if this is the way *you* wants it, everybody's going to be happy." Her broad smile was both an acceptance and a prediction of that truth. "Now what we going give Mr. Lord for his breakfast?"

Maggie Lord took the quick plunge from pink-clouded exultation to the bedrock of reality, her feet on solid ground again ... Linc was so keyed up that he might not even want to eat ... "Well, he's having a big meeting this morning, Viola, and —"

"Yes'm, I knows. Everybody in town knows, I guess. They's inaugurating him, ain't they?"

Viola's chuckle of pleasure was too infectious to deny and she smiled back despite the recollection that one of the things that had gotten Linc so on edge last night was Kira's insistence upon making a ceremony out of introducing him to all the Coastal Foods employees this morning.

Viola suggested, "Maybe a nice light omelet?"

It seemed almost thought transference. "Well, if he'll eat anything at all —"

"That's what I was figuring," Viola said confidently. "And don't you worry none about him not eating it. First time I laid eyes on Mr. Lord — you know that day you was here to lunch? I says to myself — Viola, I says, you ain't gonna fool that man with nothing but the best. And don't you worry none, ma'am, that's just what he's gonna get."

"Thank you, Viola," she said, edging toward the door, thinking that she should warn Linc to be properly appreciative.

"Ma'am?" Viola's face had suddenly sobered.

197

"Yes?"

"Don't worry none 'bout my talking too much. This ain't the way I am regular. I'm just kinda all bubbly and excited this morning."

"So am I," she laughed. "It's that kind of a morning."

Viola's expression was still concerned. "And don't you worry none neither, ma'am, about my being the way some cooks is. Any time you feels like doing some cooking yourself, you just come ahead. I'll stay to help, or skedaddle right out'n your way, however you wants it. Nothing don't matter 'cept having things so you and Mr. Lord's going to be happy."

"Thank you, Viola," she said, honestly and earnestly. "I'm sure we will be."

She was across the dining room and out in the hall when she suddenly remembered that she still had those notes to type for Linc... so afraid that he didn't recognize everyone's name this morning...

2

Joel Morris stood on the platform where, an hour from now, Mrs. Zurich was scheduled to introduce Lincoln Lord to the key employees of the Coastal Foods Company. Examining the scene from what would be Mr. Lord's vantage point, he found himself confronted with the result of what now seemed a stupidly conceived effort to make a favorable first impression upon the new president. He was acutely conscious that it had been his idea, and his alone, to use the unfinished second floor of the office building for the meeting. Swann had given him only agreement, not approval. Pressing both janitors into service, he had spent most of the night getting the room ready. When he had left, long after midnight, fatigue had deluded him into a feeling of satisfaction with what he had accomplished. Now, in the cold gray light of this January morning, the meeting room could be seen only as a crude and clumsy makeshift, the effort expended upon it a foolish waste. Lincoln Lord, instead of being impressed, would surely think him a too eager young fool, lacking in both taste and judgment, not at all a man to whom the responsibility for sales management might be entrusted.

Shifting his weight, he tested the platform under his feet. A dull rattle betrayed the fact that it had been built up with cases of canned goods hauled in from the warehouse. The speaker's stand, hastily borrowed from the hotel, was emblazoned with an unremovable Chamber of Commerce emblem. The folding chairs would be recognized by everyone present as having come from the Halloran Funeral Home. Worst of all was the odor that pervaded the room. The tarpaulins that covered the mortar-splashed cinder block of the unfinished wall had overnight exuded an oily stench that, unnoticeable when they were first hung, had probably been released by the cooking blast of one of the portable space heaters that had been brought in from the warehouse to take the chill off the room.

For a moment, he considered the possibility of going down to Swann and admitting that he had been wrong, accepting the office manager's original suggestion that they just bring in some extra chairs and scatter them between the desks in order to provide seating for the people from the plant. Almost instantly he decided against it. Bad as it was, he had to stick to his guns and go through with it. Somehow he had to break away from Swann's domination, make Mr. Lord realize that he was Swann's assistant only because Sol Zurich had suggested it as a temporary assignment while he was learning the business, a job that would pay his way until the time was ripe to set up the sales department that the old man had promised him he would some day have a chance to manage.

That promise had died with Sol Zurich — no one knew that it had ever been made — and the only chance for fulfillment now lay with the man who was to become president of the company. The prospects were not bright. He had seen Lincoln Lord only once, a quick handshake and a few meaningless words on that day when Swann had taken him around the office. What he had seen had not been encouraging. Mr. Lord was undeniably a top-level man, polished and urbane, sophisticated, and knowing — and indisputably the kind of company president who might well decide that he did not want a Jewish sales manager.

There had been a time in Joel Morris's life when, seeing Lincoln Lord, he might have judged him to be too broad-minded for prejudice. Experience had taught him otherwise. There was, he had come to believe, no such thing as a total absence of anti-Semitism. The question was never one of presence, only of degree, and as he had long since discovered, that judgment by degree did not apply in the matter of Jewishness. Although the Jews themselves would not claim the son of a non-Jewish mother, he was no less a Jew to the rest of the world because his mother had been a Scot and a Presbyterian.

Once during his years at Wharton, one of his classmates had accused him of purposely dropping the last letter from his first name, wanting to be called Joe instead of Joel with the hope that it might help him to escape recognition as a Jew. Unfair as he had felt that accusation to be, it had nevertheless been deeply wounding, the more so because it had touched an area of secret temptation. He had been, at the time, in the throes of a love affair with a Christian girl who had put in his mind the possibility of eloping to some faraway little town where no one would suspect that he was a Jew. What had finally awakened him, in a fortunate moment when common sense had taken advantage of a temporary exhaustion of passion, was the realization that it was her suggestion, not his — in itself a crushing proof of her prejudice, not against him but against who he was. He had realized then, truly for the first time, that the two facts were inseparable.

Thereafter, he had accepted his Jewishness as the central fact of his existence, all-important and life-governing. In some ways it had worked out well enough. Had he not confined himself to dating only Jewish girls, it was easily possible that he might have married someone else before he had met Vicky. And it was his love for Vicky that had given a sustaining rightness to his whole life. Yet as true as that was, there were times when he wished, vaguely and hazily, always secretly, that since the fact of their Jewishness was inescapable, Vicky might have been just a little better Jew than she was. In his childhood home, there had been no manifestation whatsoever of the Jewish faith, a natural enough result of his father's having broken what slight religious ties there had been when he had married a Presbyterian. Vicky's parents, too, had largely abandoned their religious heritage, but without reason; and he had wondered sometimes, especially when an act of discrimination had hit him with unusual force, if some subscription to the old faith, even though tenuous, might give him the poise of strength. Although it was a corny old line, too often heard, it might still be true that the only way a Jew could armor himself against prejudice was by generating pride in his ancestral heritage. He had, however, never mentioned this subject to Vicky, largely because she showed no consciousness of the need, but also because he had more or less brought himself around to the point of view that his own sensitivity was unnecessarily acute. He could never quite believe, however, that the fault really lay within himself. Blocking the way to acceptance was the memory of what had happened to him before he came to Goodhaven.

He had finished Wharton with a graduate degree in marketing, the second-ranking man in his class, and he had won enough honors to make it seem certain that he would be able to pick and choose among a large number of job offers. On the résumé that he prepared for the placement office, he had outlined the kind of job he wanted in terms of his end-point ambition — two or three years in the field as a salesman, then into market research and the planning of merchandising and promotion, eventually into general sales management. He had been interviewed eleven times, fulsomely praised for his scholastic record and the foresight evidenced by his life plan, and not a single interviewer had brought up the matter of his being a Jew. But not an offer had resulted. All of the jobs he most wanted went to lower-ranking Wharton graduates. It was beyond coincidence that none of the men chosen were Jews, and he had finally accepted the truth of what his classmates had been telling him — that if you were a Jew, your only hope was a job with a Jewish company.

Finally yielding to the inevitability of prejudice, he accepted a salesman's job in the Philadelphia branch office of an electrical appliance manufacturer. The president of the company was a famous Jew, prominently identified with a national organization dedicated to the elimination of racial discrimination. Before the end of his first six months, Joel Morris had found a second side to the coin of prejudice. He discovered then that the company, although Jewish owned and Jewish managed, demanded Christian names and Christian faces in all sales executive jobs where there would be exposure to big-time buyers. Jewish boys were hired for the sales force in great numbers, but they rarely rose above a pavement-pounding level. Reluctantly, he had found himself granting some justification for this secret but rigidly governing company policy. His own most difficult experiences as a salesman were almost always with Jewish buyers, who, too often, accorded extra deference and respect to Christians. Time and time again he would be left waiting on the hard bench outside while a Christian salesman who had arrived later would be called in for his interview. His first notable sales accomplishment — breaking into an installment furniture chain hitherto regarded as impregnable — had been the result of a non-Jewish owner's agreeing to try out one of his promotion ideas. In his first year, he outranked all the junior salesmen in the Philadelphia office in the volume of new business produced. He had every reason to expect promotion to an area managership. The man selected was named McGinnis.

Even more disturbing than the revelation that anti-Semitic prejudice had some of its roots within the Jewish community itself was a growing feeling that he had made a mistake in planning his life. When he was with the other young Jewish salesmen he often felt himself an alien intruder. Most of them displayed, so blatantly that it seemed almost defiant, the worst of the characteristics that were so often cited as being objectionably Jewish. None of the Jews that he liked best were in sales work. His two closest friends at Wharton had both purposely avoided characteristically Jewish careers. Neither had gone into anything that smacked of buying or selling. One had turned down an excellent offer with a big New York department store and entered government service. The other, after having earned his way through college by door-to-door selling, had taken an office job with an economic research foundation.

Convinced that he had made a mistake, Joel Morris decided that the best thing to do was to correct it by changing not only his job but also the whole background atmosphere of his life. He moved to New York. His only connection was the editor of a trade magazine who had come to Philadelphia to write a story on the success of the retail furniture chain that had used his promotion idea. They had eaten lunch together and the editor had told him that if he were ever interested there might possibly be a job for him on the magazine staff. He clinched the position in an interview with the publisher, accepting a lower salary than he had been making, justifying himself because he was moving into a more satisfying participation in the intellectual creativity that he had come to think was, more truly than anything else, the real Jewish birthright.

He was slowly but thoroughly disillusioned. His own work, which was supposed to be economic and marketing research for the benefit of the editors, was actually used to no purpose other than the preparation of promotional material to sell advertising space. For ten and twelve hours a day, often seven days a week, he was holed up in an airless cubicle, sweating out facts and figures that, in order to do what was expected of him, he had to twist and torture to pull the wool over the eyes of the Madison Avenue space buyers. At first there was the excuse that his own involvement was minimized because he was doing what he was told to do by Van Albright, the advertising manager, who was a Christian. After a few months, however, he was completely on his own, unshielded from the guilt of trickery. A climax was reached when Albright, intending to compliment him for a portfolio presentation that he had just prepared, had said, "I've got to hand it to you people, Joel — nobody but a Jew could ever have juggled these figures as cleverly as this."

After a month of quiet brooding, he resigned without explanation, saying only that he was taking another job. Luckily it took no more than a single day to make that explanation true. He registered with an employment agent, outlined his experience and Wharton record, and after a short preliminary talk and a telephone call, was immediately sent to the Madison Avenue offices of McCutcheon & Paisley. He went only because he was asked, not because he had any hope of employment. He knew from the gossip of the space salesmen at the publishing company that the big advertising agencies maintained as tight a racial line as there was anywhere in New York, and as far as he was concerned, McCutcheon & Paisley was on the wrong side of the line. To his astonishment he was hired before the day was out, and at a salary that almost doubled his previous earnings. He was given a well-furnished office in the Market Research Department and designated as "Associate Director of Applied Marketing," a title that was ambiguously nondescriptive of the work that he actually did. His real responsibility was to gather background material for two vice-presidents who solicited new accounts. It was interesting work, exposing him to a wide variety of marketing situations and, although he felt a certain strangeness in being the only male Jew in the agency, he was kept too busy to be lonely, too frequently complimented to feel unwanted.

Now and then, often enough to give him a feeling of recognized stature, he was asked to attend meetings that were staged to impress manufacturers who might possibly become McCutcheon & Paisley clients. Once, called upon to outline a distribution plan that he had developed, he had the satisfaction of playing an instrumental part in bringing a three-million-dollar account to the agency. Almost a year passed before he suddenly awakened to the odd fact that every meeting he was invited to attend involved a company with Jewish management. Once his eyes were opened, everything that happened from there on out proved that the real reason for his employment at McCutcheon & Paisley was to provide a flesh and blood exhibit to refute the damaging rumor that the agency was anti-Semitic.

Even then he might not have changed jobs — he had married Vicky a few months before and was up to his neck in time payments — had it not been for the fortunate accident of meeting Sol Zurich. It had come about because of Gellman Stores. Previously, the Gellman account had been of no real importance to McCutcheon & Paisley because almost all its advertising space was placed locally, with no agency commission involved. Then suddenly the Gellman management expressed an interest in sponsoring a network television program. With millions of dollars in billings at stake, he was given the top-priority assignment of finding out everything he could about Gellman Stores. Discovering that the Mother Gellman line was one of the chain's more readily merchandisable assets, he had dug in to find out all he could about it. That was what had brought him to Goodhaven and the Coastal Foods Company.

Long before he had finished his first interview with Sol Zurich, he was convinced that he had at last found the pot of hope at the end of his personal rainbow. The relationship that he observed between Sol Zurich and his two key men, Kennan and Swann, came closer to being the perfect Christian-Jew association than anything he had ever seen — or, after his years in New York, had ever hoped to see. He decided then and there that he wanted to go to work for Coastal Foods.

Proceeding cautiously over the next four months — he was somewhat handicapped by loyalty to McCutcheon & Paisley until after Gellman Stores had finally made the decision that network television was too rich for its corporate blood — he pursued his campaign. He and Vicky spent their vacation at Tern Beach and, naturally enough after his original visit, called several times on the Zurichs. One evening Mrs. Zurich asked what he thought of the possibilities for marketing a new line of baby food. That had given him his opening. Over the next week, the last of their vacation, he had sold Sol Zurich on the idea of hiring him to work on the development and marketing of new products. His clinching argument had been the danger that Coastal Foods would face if, unlikely as it then seemed, the company was ever cut off as a source of supply by Gellman Stores.

Only once had he doubted the wisdom of his move, a doubt soon dissipated and subsequently turned into the strongest of all justifications. Shortly after he went to work for Coastal Foods, he picked up a rumor that Sol Zurich had recently found out that he was not a Jew, or at least that there was a good chance that he might not be. At first the implications were shattering. Gradually, however, he saw that this startling discovery made no difference whatsoever in Sol Zurich's manner, attitude, or viewpoint. He remained exactly the same man that he had been before. Nothing changed. As the weeks went by, Joel Morris came to feel for Sol Zurich something far beyond his initial high regard, bound to him then by a sense of unpayable debt for having proved that whether or not a man had Jewish blood in his veins was truly a matter of no real consequence.

He had now been at Coastal Foods for three and a half years, the three years the happiest he had ever known, these past six months a period of ulcer-breeding apprehension. Sol Zurich's death had left him with not only a great sense of personal loss but also the fear that he had been an incredibly stupid fool. It had never occurred to him when he had written a report advising against any attempt to market Dr. Perrill's baby food that Kira Zurich would some day hold his fate in her hands. What he had written had been his honest best judgment, based on factual evidence, and Sol Zurich had been obviously pleased. Nevertheless, his experience at both the magazine and the agency had taught him that if you knew in advance what you wanted to prove, the facts could always be molded by interpretation and selection, any conclusion justified by the certainty that merchandising was not an absolute science. The biggest successes were often the least predictable. At least it was never necessary for a marketing man to burn his bridges as he had done with the baby food report.

His initial fear that Mrs. Zurich might be hopelessly prejudiced against him had, however, somewhat subsided — six months had gone by and he still had his job — when he was suddenly struck with the proof of total failure. He had sold himself to Sol Zurich on the premise that his services would protect Coastal Foods against the possible loss of the Gellman business — the very thing that had happened — and, when it did, the company was no better prepared than it had been the day he had gone to work. Worst of all, last week, in the one chance that he had been given to redeem himself, he hadn't even been able to get by the receptionist's desk at the Gellman Stores headquarters in New York. But it had been too late by then, anyway. The groundwork should have been laid long before that.

Looking back, it was almost impossible for him to believe how little he had accomplished in three and a half years. There was, of course, the excuse that he had been kept too busy, that Swann had loaded him with far more work than he had anticipated when Sol Zurich had suggested that he serve as assistant office manager until there was need for a sales department — but that was just kidding himself, and he knew it. He could have worked nights and week ends as he had always done in New York, both at the publishing house and at McCutcheon & Paisley. He had spent a fair number of evenings at the office working on two major studies, one on the baby food business and the other on canned soup but neither had opened up an obvious opportunity for Coastal Foods, and his disappointment had, perhaps, somewhat dampened his enthusiasm. Afterwards everything had seemed to conspire against him. First there had been the house. With Sol Zurich loaning him the money to buy it, there had been no easy way to side-step his suggestion that he do some of the finishing work himself. Then the children had come along, only thirteen months between them, and trying to give Vicky a hand had made a lot of evenings slip away unnoticed, particularly after he had bought a Leica to get some baby pictures and allowed himself to become much too interested in photography. In retrospect, he fervently regretted that those evenings in his basement darkroom had not been spent at the office.

The Gellman news had blasted him out of what he could see now had been a frighteningly complacent rut. On the night after he had failed to get in to see Irving Rubin at Gellmans, he had gone back to the office for the first time in months. He had not missed an evening since. But he had accomplished far too little. For the first few nights it had been little more than blind atonement. Then, a week ago, with the word that Lincoln Lord was coming in as president, he had started a frantic search through old files and notebooks, hunting out forgotten ideas, attempting to bring his old studies up to date, hoping that somehow, somewhere, something would turn up to flux the forging of a close relationship with the new president.

Now, looking around him, he decided that all he had really done was to drive himself into an unbalanced state of desperate anxiety ... that was what had gotten him into this senseless business of trying to fix up this room. Or was it something in his blood? Was he the crazy Jew who could never keep his emotions under control ... the inner man revealed ... breaking out in this wild flurry of arm-waving and pointless activity?

He stepped down from the platform and walked toward the window, fighting for self-control, looking toward the pine grove that screened the Zurich house. In less than an hour now, Lincoln Lord's

Cadillac would break through the trees and come bearing down upon him. He stood transfixed by fear and hopelessness. There was a stinging sensation in his eyes, the threat of tears, a reminder that the only adult men he had ever seen openly weeping were Jews. He just didn't belong . . . he never would. There'd be no place for him now . . . Lincoln Lord would surround himself with men of his own blood . . . calm, controlled, poised, dignified, reserved, confident . . . men cast in his own image . . .

"Joel?" It was Miss Payne's voice calling from the bottom of the staircase.

"Yes?"

She came halfway, excitedly holding up a newspaper. "It's in the *New York Times* this morning — look, a picture and all!"

"I know," he said . . . she'd go on calling him by the first name as long as he was here . . . Mr. Lord, Mr. Swann, Mr. Kennan . . . but he'd always be Joel . . .

3

Brick Mitchell snuffed out a cigarette and looked at his watch, both acts automatic, neither quite consciously performed; yet the combined visual impact of seeing first, that it was almost nine o'clock and, second, that the ash tray was filled to overflowing was strong enough to break the spell of his preoccupation. Tommy would be turning up any minute now, all primed with another round of that you-smoke-too-much lung-cancer routine. Hesitant for only an instant, he dumped the ash tray in his wastebasket and, reaching down, ruffled the clutter of discarded yellow copy paper until the incriminating evidence had been sifted out of sight. Then, his wry grin fading, he ripped open a fresh package of cigarettes.

All that mattered now was the thin sheaf of yellow paper at the left of his typewriter . . . seven good pages . . . two thousand words. Another hour, another page and a half, and it would be in the bag. And it was good . . . fresh and clean and sharp . . . solid. Robbie wouldn't change a comma. You never had to worry about what an editor was going to think when it came this way . . . you knew when it was right . . . the way it felt . . . the way those words came running out of the end of your fingers, almost writing themselves.

Maybe this was what he ought to do . . . forget the damn public relations business and settle down to free-lancing magazine articles. Robbie wasn't the only editor who needed a writer who could do a job like this. And there was money in it, too . . . five hundred dollars since midnight. Be all right if it always went like this. But it wouldn't. That was the hell of it . . . weren't many days in a man's life when everything was clicking like this . . . the old brain running like a watch in a bucket of oil . . . no sleep and your head still as clear as a bell . . .

The door burst open. Tommy stood in the doorway, her polo coat bat-winged by the spread of her arms, the twine-tied bundle of morning mail slipping from her fingers, thudding on the floor. "Brick! What in the world are you — have you been here all night?"

"Most of it."

"But what — why — ?"

"Robbie called up last night. He's stuck his neck out with a lead article for his next issue — let the cover go to press with a big blurb — and then the piece blew up on him. He's had a gang of his staff guys on it and they fizzled out. He's got to have something that's at least printable."

"Oh, Brick, that's wonderful! But why didn't you call me? I'd have been glad to come down. You know that."

"It was almost midnight."

"That wouldn't have made any difference. At least I could have — how's it going?"

"Good. Just the windup left, that's all." He picked up the seven sheets.

"What can I do, Brick — give you a clean draft?"

"Yeah, maybe that would help — get a tight word count. The layout's all made, so I've got to hit it right on the nose — seventy-two characters, two hundred and four lines."

She flung off her coat. A tightly folded newspaper fell from its pocket. She retrieved it, holding it out to him, exchanging it for the sheets of the rough draft that he handed to her. "I thought you might be interested in that," she said offhandedly, starting for the door. "You said seventy-two characters, didn't you?"

He saw the picture first, then the headline:

LINCOLN LORD IS NAMED NEW
PRESIDENT OF COASTAL FOODS

"Brick, this is good stuff," Tommy was saying. "Awfully good!"

He stared at the sheaf of paper she had handed him . . . why was she giving it back...why didn't she get out of his office and type it? And then he saw that the paper was not yellow but white, the typed lines straight and clean, unmarked by corrections.

"You need forty-one more lines, Brick, that's all."

He nodded, staring at the blank yellowness above the keyboard... a minute ago all the words had been right there, just waiting to be written...now they were gone. Tommy...damn it, why had she come busting in on him! Why couldn't she let him alone...let him write! That's all he wanted...all he had ever wanted...just a chance. All the years of waiting for a break like this...and now she'd fouled it up for him!

Forty-two lines...forty-two lines...forty-two lines...

4

Late last night, Jay Quincy had checked in at the Waldorf-Astoria Hotel, a violation of normality — he had never before stayed at any New York hotel other than the Plaza — and the strangeness of his surroundings had been a plausible explanation of his inability to sleep soundly. Nevertheless, the gain was greater than the loss. This way, calling Lincoln Lord on the telephone could be made to seem something casually done, an act inspired by nothing more consequential than the coincidence that they both happened to be staying at the same hotel.

His plan had been carefully made. He would telephone at exactly nine o'clock, late enough so that Linc would surely be up and about, yet early enough to catch him before he left the hotel for the day. There was still a chance, of course, that Maggie might answer the phone and, recognizing his voice, would insist upon talking to him. He had, however, guarded himself against that possibility by, during the night, grossly mutilating the image of the face that he would visualize on the other end of the wire. In doing so, he had thought himself no more than reasonable. After all, she could hardly be the girl he remembered. The years would have taken their toll. She could no longer be as freshly beautiful as she had been that morning when he had discovered her in the cannery yard, wide-eyed with fear, a frightened fawn at bay in a forest glade...no, all of that would be lost. There would be a hardness now, a cold glitter where there had been a warm sheen, hinted at that night when she had told him that she was going to marry Linc, even more strongly evident that gray morning when she had come to the library to tell him that she was leaving Kingdom Come. And even that had been thirteen years ago.

Maggie Lord would be, in his carefully constructed visualization, an example of what happened to a beautiful girl when she became obsessed with ambition . . . the cocktail party wife of the big man . . . the glassy coldness of a beauty parlor face . . . the smile that flicked on and off like an indicator light on a lacquered instrument board . . . yes, even her voice would be changed. Now there would be that brassy hoarseness, forced a tone below its normal register, artificiality betrayed when you heard that rosin-stringed laugh . . . no, there was nothing to worry about even if Maggie answered the phone.

He looked at his watch and saw that it was already three minutes after nine. He picked up the telephone instrument. "Will you please connect me with Mr. Lord's suite — Mr. Lincoln Lord."

Yes, Maggie would probably answer . . . still managing Linc's life . . . deciding who he would talk to. She would want to know who was calling . . . but the thing to do was . . .

The operator said, "I'm sorry, sir, but we don't have a Mr. Lincoln Lord registered."

"Not registered? But I was told that he —" He caught a quick breath, steadying his voice. "Do you mean that he's left, that he doesn't live here any more?"

"Mr. Lord is not registered now, sir."

"Thank you," he said. The instrument slipped from his fingers, missing its cradle and clattering down on the desk top. Picking it up, he hesitated, wondering if he should call back and find out if there was anyone who could tell him where the Lords had gone, thinking that they must have left a forwarding address. But he replaced the receiver, deciding that it would be an inquiry better made in person than over the telephone. He would go to the mail desk after he had eaten his breakfast.

Five minutes later, on his way to the coffee shop, he stopped at the newsstand and bought a newspaper. As was his habit, he opened it to the financial pages. The first thing he saw was Lincoln Lord's picture.

5

"Just run down that list, will you, Mag?" Lincoln Lord asked, slipping a handkerchief into his breast pocket. "Help me get those names set in my mind."

Kira Zurich was due to arrive any moment now — she had insisted upon driving them to the office — but Maggie opened her purse without protest and searched out the narrowly folded sheet of paper upon which she had copied her notes on all of the Coastal Foods employees as Kira Zurich had named and described them last night. She started at the top of the list, skipping only Kennan and Swann. "Schlager?"

"I'm all right there. Go ahead."

"Morris?"

"Joel Morris — thirty-one," Lincoln Lord recited. "Been here a little over three years. Hired to work on new products but now assistant to Swann. Jewish. Master's degree from Wharton. Market research for McCutcheon & Paisley. Wife's name is Vicky. Two young children."

"Brown?"

"Henry Brown — close to sixty — bookkeeper. With the company almost from the beginning. Wife's dead. One daughter — married and living in White Plains." Scowling at the mirror, he pulled out the handkerchief and stuffed it in the back pocket of his trousers.

"Payne?"

"Miss Payne. Zurich's old secretary. Old maid. Swann's put her in charge of the girls. Keep her there. Travels a lot on her vacations. Mexico last year."

Maggie caught a blue blur with the corner of her eye and, looking out, saw Kira Zurich's car come up the drive. "She's here, Linc."

"All right, go ahead. I'll be there in a minute. I guess I've got most of them pretty well set."

"You're wonderful, Linc," she said sincerely, amazed again at his all but incredible memory, able now to recall everything that Kira Zurich had said last night, detail that she herself had been unable to fix in her mind even after a half-dozen reviews of her notes. "I don't know how you do it."

"It helps when you meet them — knowing who they are," he said, oddly argumentative, another revelation of tension.

"Of course it helps," she agreed, yet unable to understand why he was so concerned with the need to impress every little typist and bill-ing clerk. "Linc, are you certain that you really want me to be there?"

"Kira asked you to come, didn't she?"

"I know, but —"

"Better let her in."

She picked up her suit coat, slipping it on as she went out of the bedroom, the atmosphere of strangeness accentuated now by the anticipation of opening the door for Kira Zurich, whose home this had been until late yesterday afternoon.

Gratitude for giving her Viola was the first thing that she wanted to express and the words were ready as she approached the door, momentarily diverted by surprise as she saw that Kira was not alone. A man had gotten out of the car. He stood now lounging against the front fender as Kira left him to come up the steps — a big man, thin-fleshed but heavy-boned, his broad shoulders slouched, his bared head revealing a face dominated by a powerfully modeled skull, seemingly bone-bald, oddly winged with enormous ears. Far from handsome, he was nevertheless a striking man and Maggie knew instantly that it must be Dr. Perrill, a truth that Kira's explanation quickly confirmed.

And then, suddenly, Linc slipped up behind them and was saying what she had meant to say about Viola.

Kira responded to his gratitude with far more animation than she had shown at any of their attempts to thank her last night. "Viola really is a jewel — and a good cook is wasted on me. I always tried to show my appreciation but I'm certain she knew it wasn't sincere. I'm sure you won't have that trouble, Mr. Lord."

For an instant Maggie wondered if Linc would be caught on the hidden barb in the remark, a concern quickly lost as he said with an easy smile, "And without the slightest danger of jeopardizing my integrity, Mrs. Zurich. Her omelet this morning was magnificent."

Kira smiled. "And of course you told her just that?"

"No, as a matter of fact, I didn't," he said pseudo-serious. "I decided that it might be better if I took it a little easy at the start — sort of worked up to it. All I said, as I recall, was that it was a work of art."

Kira's laughter was far too bright to be anything but sincere and, as had happened so many times before, Maggie Lord found herself wondering why she had been so suspicious ... Kira hadn't been needling him ... and Linc had said nothing that wasn't absolutely true. But a minute ago, so tensely nervous, so tightly strung ... how could he be so perfectly relaxed now?

"Dr. Perrill was coming over to the meeting, of course, so I asked him to ride with us," Kira Zurich explained as they went out the door.

"Oh good," Linc said. "Delighted to have a chance to meet him."

But when Kira Zurich introduced them, Linc's effusiveness suddenly evaporated, apparently an instantaneous reaction to the scientist's coldly appraising stare, a guarded manner that made him appear not only a man who was ill at ease with strangers but, even more certainly, a taciturn man who suspected the motives of anyone less restrained than himself.

Maggie had been on the point of bursting out with something about how greatly impressed she had been with what she had learned about Dr. Perrill's work when she had visited Haven Home with Kira Zurich but, cued by the tone that her husband had set, she caught herself in time and said only, "I'm sorry that I missed you when I was at Haven Home, Dr. Perrill."

"You must come again," he said, formal and expressionless, evidencing a lack of warmth that drew an easily understood side glance from Kira Zurich. But she said nothing and they got in the car, Kira driving, Perrill beside her in the front seat, the uneasy silence persisting as they went out the drive.

Maggie was seated on the left side, which gave her almost a profile view of Dr. Perrill's face. Studying it, she wondered if there could possibly be any truth in the rumor that Linc had picked up that there was something beyond a professional relationship between Kira Zurich and this coldly austere man, so obviously the monastically dedicated scientist, at the moment too plainly annoyed that she had dragged him away from his laboratory to a meeting that he had no desire to attend. Then she heard Linc speak his name and, intuitively, she sensed from something about Perrill's resistant response that his grim manner was directed, not at Kira, but at the man whom he apparently had no desire to see installed as president of the Coastal Foods Company.

Linc said casually, "Dr. Perrill, I ran into a man in Tokyo a few months ago whom you may possibly know. From what he told me of his work, I believe you must have more or less the same interests. If my memory is right, he must have been in Burma about the same time you were in India."

Perrill's face was suddenly transformed into a battleground of emotions, curiosity warring with stubbornness, an expression that reminded

213

Maggie of her son when, as a small child, he had gotten into one of his moods of refusing to respond to any enticement. A convulsive muscle spasm ran up and down Perrill's throat. Then, slowly, his head turned. "You can't possibly mean — ?"

"Dr. Ichakuri."

The scientist's lips parted, a slackening of tension that slowly spread over his loose-skinned face. "You saw him — Dr. Ichakuri? He's alive?"

If Perrill was surprised, Maggie was no less so . . . and yet why should she be? It had happened so many times before, Linc reaching back in his memory to find some fragmentary recollection that perfectly served his purpose. She, too, remembered Dr. Ichakuri coming to their room at the Hotel Imperial, even his story of having worked with some American doctor in India, but the name had meant nothing to her and had been instantly lost.

"Oh yes indeed, very much alive," Lincoln Lord answered the scientist. "And unless I'm mistaken, he mentioned your name."

Dr. Perrill blinked slowly. "How did you happen to be talking about me?"

"You're much too modest, Doctor," Lincoln Lord said, flattery so adroit that Maggie was certain that Perrill would respond without suspicion.

He did, quickly making the effort required to reseat himself, then twisting his shoulders so that they were face to face. "I can't tell you how grateful I am to you, Mr. Lord — bringing me this wonderful news. I owe Dr. Ichakuri a great deal, more than I could possibly have known when we parted, and all these years I've never had a chance to thank him. There was the war, of course, and afterwards — well, I had no idea where to reach him. Do you, by any chance, have his address?"

"We do have it, don't we Mag?"

For once her memory served her well. "Couldn't he be reached through the drug company?" Then she saw her chance and grasped at it. "Dr. Ichakuri came to the hotel in Tokyo trying to get a research grant and Linc found a place for him with an American pharmaceutical manufacturer who's doing some research work over there."

"Did you really?" Perrill breathed, his long houndlike head waggling, his eyes flooded with gratitude. "I can imagine what it must have meant to him — a chance to keep going on. I don't suppose you know what he's working on these days."

"Only in a general sort of way," Lincoln Lord replied — and then, astoundingly, resurrected a phrase. "Protein metabolism, I believe — that and the enzymatic —"

He got no further, Perrill cutting him off with an enthusiastic drumbeat thumping of the seatback. "So he's still at it, is he? Wonderful of you to give him a hand, Mr. Lord. There aren't too many businessmen who understand these things — how important they're going to be some day."

"Oh, I did very little," Lincoln Lord said truthfully. "An introduction — that's about all."

Dr. Perrill's eyes thanked him for far more than a modest role.

They were approaching the office building now, and, as Kira Zurich glanced left, Maggie caught a glimpse of her face, a quiet little smile reflecting a satisfaction slightly tinged with awe that was not at all difficult to interpret. They got out of the car together, and, in the moment that they stood waiting for the two men to come around from the other side, Kira Zurich murmured, "Amazing that you should have run into the one man in the world that Dr. Perrill really worships." But her tone denied her words, almost as if she found it not amazing but almost certainly expected.

Dr. Perrill's great bear-paw hand clung to Lincoln Lord's arm, holding him back for a last precious word, and Maggie walked ahead, following Kira Zurich's lead, stepping into the entrance lobby. It was hardly more than a vestibule, surprisingly small but less shockingly so than the area beyond. She had gathered from remarks that Linc had dropped during the week that the offices were disappointing but she had not been prepared for anything as bad as this. The president's office, already identified by MR. LORD lettered on the glass, was separated from the rest of the room only by clear glass partitions, the enclosed area barely large enough to contain a desk and two chairs. For the first time, she realized that all of Linc's brave talk about how satisfied he was with the way everything had worked out was no more than whistling in the dark ... a big office had always meant so much to him ... and she had been so self-centered in her own happiness with the house ...

"Where is everyone?" Kira Zurich murmured to herself, making Maggie realize that the drab appearance of the office area was at least partly attributable to its lifelessness. There was not a soul in sight anywhere until, suddenly, hearing a protesting screech, she turned to see Alfred Swann pushing out through a heavy fire door.

He greeted them, flustered and out of breath, his little bow made all the more stilted by the tentative offer of a handshake, withdrawn once and then offered again as Lincoln Lord came up. His speech of welcome, patently rehearsed, lost itself in an explanation that everyone was waiting for them upstairs.

"Upstairs?" Kira Zurich asked, puzzled.

Nervously agitated, Swann said apologetically. "I suppose I should have called you — it was really Joel Morris's idea and I'm afraid it hasn't worked as well as — the second floor, you know? It's never been finished but —"

"Oh, of course," Kira Zurich said, her face clearing. "I'd almost forgotten." She turned to Lincoln Lord. "The architect's plans called for a suite of private offices on the second floor, but at the last minute my husband decided against finishing them. He was happier here with everyone around him. But it may well be something that you'll want to go ahead with, Mr. Lord. Things are a little crowded down here."

Swann put in, "Yes, I must say that it is a bit difficult here at times — the lack of privacy, you know."

Lincoln Lord cut him off. "We've a lot of problems to lick before we get to that one, Alf." A smile tempered the ring of decision in his voice, but it was none the less a rebuke and Swann hurriedly grasped at the chance to rescue himself with fervent agreement, then anxiously asked, "Shall we go up?"

Kira moved toward the fire door. "I hadn't expected a formal meeting. I really don't know what I should —" Her half turn shut Swann out of the conversation and, anticipating her desire, Lincoln Lord lowered his head, nodding through a whispered consultation so low-voiced that Maggie, sharing Swann's embarrassed isolation, was unable to hear until her husband concluded, "Yes, if they've made an occasion out of it, perhaps I had better say a bit more than I'd intended."

Again, Swann pushed his way in. "Indeed it is an occasion, Mr. Lord — a very big day for all of us. And I can assure you that everyone will be most interested in anything that you have to tell us."

The look that Lincoln Lord shot at Swann made Maggie wonder if the office manager was smart enough to realize that he was rapidly dissipating the good impression that he had made last week ... or had Linc's complimentary appraisal afterwards been still another example of his courageous acceptance?

A bare concrete staircase rose to the second floor, the enclosing walls nubbed with rough mortar. Kira Zurich and Lincoln Lord were in the lead, again in whispered consultation. Maggie heard her husband say, "Yes, I believe that it would be better to keep it all in general terms. Perhaps you might —" What he then said was lost as he brought his lips close to Kira's ear, hearing made even more difficult by Swann who, in clumsy mimicry, leaned close to her and said, "Too bad the factory people are going to miss this — the ones who aren't working at the moment, you know? But we do have all of the office people — not a single absentee this morning!"

Swann's voice was swallowed up in suddenly imposed silence, invoking the realization that there had been, unnoticed until it stopped, a background buzz of conversation and foot-scraping from the assembled crowd. The staircase was open to the room and the next step brought Maggie Lord's eyes above the floor level. She stopped for an instant, looking up at her husband. He stood for a surveying moment, height exaggerated by her angle of view, strikingly handsome. His level gaze met the stare of every pair of eyes in the room. Quickly, Maggie took the steps that brought her to his side. The welcoming touch of his hand on her arm was the sharing of a strangely transformed vision. Until this moment, the Coastal Foods Company had been a corporately impersonal name, an arithmetical problem in sales volume and profit dollars. Now it was fifty-odd pairs of eyes, fixed in tremulous anticipation, filled with an amalgam of canceling emotions, hope neutralized by fear, optimism set against despair, the hunger for leadership challenged by the resistance of pride.

It was an awkward moment, the silence climactic, suddenly broken as Lincoln Lord said, "Come on, Mag, let's meet these people," his voice low yet somehow carrying to the back of the room, moving like a swiftly running wave, its breaking edge relaxing every face that it touched.

"I'm Linc Lord," he said, advancing to the nearest man, who, quickly standing and murmuring his name, was greeted, "Of course! You're with Mike Schlager, aren't you? Say, you fellows have built some wonderful machines out there."

The whole crowd was moving as if mesmerically commanded, pushing forward, breaking the ranks imposed by the straight-lined chairs. Frank Kennan crossed from the other side of the room, gratefully accepting hearty recognition, quickly assuming a host's role.

At first Maggie acknowledged introductions with the murmured repetition of a name, dropping back then to no more than a smile and a nod as she became fascinated with Linc's brilliantly skillful use of her typed notes ... surely there would be someone he'd miss ... those white-capped women from the factory ... oh, why hadn't she gotten their names for him!

But there was no need for concern. He had something to say to everyone. And his simplest words seemed a magical incantation. Even those who had already been introduced still stood closely bunched around him, magnetically held, their eyes so firmly fixed upon him that she could stare directly at them without being noticed. This was no new phenomenon, she had seen it happen before; yet it was still difficult to understand why so many people would instantly pledge their loyalty and support to a man about whom they knew nothing except that he had recognized their names and offered some scrap of information about them. Their faces were charged with hope, with expectancy, with the promise of good fortune that everyone always seemed to find in Lincoln Lord's very presence.

Out of the corner of her eye, she saw Kira Zurich moving toward the lectern. Around her she heard the rustle of movement. Then she saw that Linc was sitting down and that everyone was so quickly following his example that it seemed the movement of a single man. His eyes looked up at Kira Zurich. Every set of eyes in the room followed his bidding.

The silence that now fell had a different quality. This was not awe but courteous submission to authority, obedient men and women doing what their acknowledged leader expected of them. A moment ago Maggie Lord had been concerned about what Mrs. Zurich might say in her introduction. Now it did not matter. Lincoln Lord was already president of the Coastal Foods Company.

IV

LINCOLN LORD sat at his desk, his eyes fixed upon the calendar. His stare was sightless but his mind was filled with a consciousness of the day and date. This was Thursday, the beginning of only his fourth day as president of the Coastal Foods Company. Two weeks ago today, in what now seemed the distantly hazy past, he had first talked to Anderson Phelps at the Waldorf-Astoria. Two weeks ago tomorrow he had first seen this plant, these offices, this tiny glass-walled cubicle in which he now sat. Then, his vision had been blurred in the climax of desperation to which Otis Sellcox had driven him, his eyes distorted to see only what had been good and hopeful. Now he realized how deluded he had been.

That first false hope, fear inspired, had been strong enough to carry him through his second meeting with Anderson Phelps, who, acting as Kira Zurich's agent, had negotiated with him the financial arrangement under which he had agreed to accept the presidency of Coastal Foods. Looking back now, the intensity of his delusion was measurable by the willingness with which he had accepted Phelps's proposal. It provided for a base salary of only twenty-five thousand a year but, more importantly it had seemed then, there was a bonus on total sales that would, as soon as he had brought Coastal's volume back to where it had been before the loss of the Gellman Stores business, lift his compensation to even more than the fifty-thousand-dollar salary that he had been paid at Luxor Pharmacal. The recollection of how hopefully he had imagined that it would be easy enough to reach that old level was a frightening indication of how blindly he had plunged.

Last week he had begun to suspect that he might be heading into trouble. Making use of the open days before he assumed the presidency — it had seemed necessary to insist that he needed time to wind up his affairs in New York — he had explored current conditions in the food and grocery field. It had been eight years since he had left Union Packing, his last direct contact with food merchandising, and he had not been aware of how much the situation had changed. Everything he had learned indicated that the big supermarket chains were becoming more and more dominant, the battle for shelf space more and more severe, the odds against success greater and greater when a little company like Coastal Foods tried to break in with a new line. By the week end, it was difficult to continue rationalizing his acceptance of the presidency of Coastal Foods as something done of his own free will.

The Monday morning meeting had, however, lifted his spirits again, the warmth of his reception a druglike stimulant that had temporarily dissipated doubt and fear and replaced it with a substantial restoration of his original delusion that handling any problem facing a company as small as Coastal Foods would be a simple enough task for a man who had directed the ramified, far-flung, and intricately involved affairs of a corporation as large as Luxor Pharmacal. That confidence had barely survived the night. The next day had demonstrated that his experience would be of little value, that there was almost no parallel between the Coastal Foods problem and anything that he had ever before been up against.

Always before, at Luxor Pharmacal and Frazer Glass, even earlier at Rabson Foods and Union Packing, his function had been more or less that of an expert mechanic called in to find and correct faults in a corporate machine which, inefficient though it might be, was still operating and making a profit. Here at Coastal Foods there had been a complete breakdown. The machine itself had to be rebuilt from the ground up, a job that could not even be approached, let alone undertaken, until a decision had been made as to the kind of products that were to be packed and how they were to be sold. Now the decision had to be made — *quickly* — and he alone had to make it. But how could a decision be made when he had been offered no alternatives between which to choose?

As Lincoln Lord practiced it, corporate management had been far more a matter of selection than of creation. He had never been, nor tried to be, a source of imaginative thinking. He could, perhaps, have trained his mind to work more naturally in that direction had he not noticed, as early as his student days at Chesapeake College, that the man of ideas usually had difficulty getting along with his associates. Later he had been warned by observation that a general management executive was rarely capable of fairly judging the worth of another man's idea when it had to be weighed against a brain child of his own. Thus he had come to accept the presidential function as that of a judge and arbiter who solved any given problem by selecting from all of the ideas that flowed up to his desk the one that promised to be the most practical and surely productive. It was a workable system and, applied with the skill that he had developed, a highly effective one. Its employment was, however, dependent upon one prime requirement — there had to be that flow of ideas. Without it, he was a craftsman with nothing to work upon, an arbiter with nothing to decide, a judge with no case before the court.

That was the core of his difficulty here at Coastal Foods. He had spent all of Tuesday on individual interviews, ostensibly to get acquainted with everyone and to give everyone a chance to get to know him. Unquestionably, he had accomplished something by way of getting off on the right foot as far as personal relationships were concerned, but he had gained not an inch of ground in his real objective of trying to ferret out, if not a full-blown plan of action, at least the glimmer of an idea that, nurtured by discussion, might grow into a concrete plan to replace the Gellman Stores business and get the plant running again.

A frightening aspect of the situation was that in a single day he had exhausted his plan of action. There were not enough people with whom to talk nor enough subjects to discuss. The contrast with his experience at Luxor Pharmacal was startling. There it had taken him all of his first month just to make the rounds of the department heads, a full week spent in the production department alone. Here he had found it difficult yesterday to use up another hour with Frank Kennan. He had already seen everything there was to be seen in the plant on his first visit, there was no point in talking about past production problems on products that might never again be packed, and the silent and empty plant was oppressively discouraging. Kennan had come up with no new ideas, nothing beyond his original vague notion that they could put their own labels on some of the old Gellman products and go out and try to sell them. What Kennan had not taken into account — although agreeing quickly enough when it was pointed out to him — was that the market was already saturated with lines of canned ready-cooked meals. Worst of all, the market itself was shrinking with the trend toward the purchase of frozen instead of canned foods. Through specialization and the long build-up of a demand, Gellman Stores had done a big job with the Mother Gellman line but, as he had been warned last week in New York, other supermarket chains would be much less interested in promoting such products unless they had a big advertising and promotion program behind them. Coastal Foods's financial resources would permit no such gamble.

Centered on his desk pad now was a half sheet of blue paper that had been, for the last ten minutes, the focalized essence of distilled fear. It was last week's operating report, only a simple mimeographed formed filled in with pencil; yet its very simplicity gave it more impact than any of the multi-paged volumes that had constantly flowed to his desk from the comptroller's department at Luxor Pharmacal. Plainly put, in terms of Alf Swann's old fashioned cash-in and cash-out accounting, last week's disbursements had exceeded receipts by $4,976.11. Coastal Foods was losing cash at the rate of almost five thousand dollars a week. Simple arithmetic made it all too obvious how rapidly the company's cash-on-hand, noted at the bottom of the sheet, would be dissipated at that rate. The company was rushing down the short road to disaster, its operating capital frozen in a big inventory of goods that Gellman Stores had no intention of taking out.

The financial situation was one that he had passed over too lightly on his first visit. Admittedly, Kennan had called the inventory to his attention, and Swann had shown him a balance sheet, but with Anderson Phelps's earlier assurance that Coastal Foods was amply financed, he had not noticed that the balance sheet figure for quick assets included inventory. It had to be liquidated before any capital would be available for the launching of a new line. Unfortunately, every can in the warehouse was already labeled with Gellman's private brand. Before the inventory could be converted to cash, thousands of cases would have to be unpacked, hundreds of thousands of cans put through the double operation of removing the old label and putting on a new one. The expense would be enormous, the gain small. Even after it was repacked and relabeled, the stock would have to be dumped at a low price in order to move it. There was little demand these days for canned goods with an unknown brand name. It would take years to build acceptance for a new brand. Long before that, Coastal Foods would be bankrupt.

Abruptly he decided that he would re-explore the whole inventory situation. But, looking up, he felt himself a cornered man, desperation revealed by exposure. In this little goldfish bowl it was impossible to raise his eyes above his desk without being confronted by the anxiously hopeful stare of everyone seated outside in the general office area, a dozen faces blurred into one, the composite face of the Coastal Foods Company, the superimposed image of all the faces that had been watching him so anxiously since the moment he had stepped into that meeting upstairs on Monday . . . everyone expecting him to perform a miracle, make some magical move, some great decision . . . why couldn't they realize that decision was impossible! How could he make a decision until there was something to decide?

He was on his feet now and, motivated only by the instinct of escape, he plunged out into the general office area, goalless until he saw the fire door. Driven, he threw his weight against it and forced it open, disregarding the attention that he knew he was arousing all over the office. The door swung shut behind him and he stood for a moment at the bottom of the flight of rough concrete steps, purposeless. But the promise of quiet and privacy drew him up the stairs. And then he remembered Kira Zurich's suggestion that he might want to go ahead with finishing this second floor into the suite of executive offices for which it had originally been planned . . . yes, that might help . . . a decent place to work . . . a place where he could *think!*

Reaching the top, he surveyed the big unfinished room. It was empty now except for a row of old transfer files and an attic collection of discarded office equipment. For a moment he embraced the relief of daydreaming. Then, abruptly, he cut himself off, a denial of nonsense, and turned to the window. He fixed his eyes upon the pine trees, black-green and shadowed, as impenetrable to sight as were the walls of the house hidden beyond, but he saw Maggie now as clearly as if that double barrier to vision had been suddenly made transparent. And he could hear her, too — the gay excitement that had been in her voice this morning. This was Thursday, she had exulted, Viola's day off, and she would have the kitchen all to herself. Ever since Sunday night, Maggie had been an eager Alice, wide-eyed in her own private Wonderland. He had told her nothing of how hopeless the situation at Coastal Foods was turning out to be, determined to preserve as long as he could the happiness that the house was so plainly giving her. But the pressure of his confined disappointment was rapidly building to the

223

point where containment would no longer be possible. Last night, when she had met him at the door with her bright, "Good day, dear?" he had been frighteningly close to confession.

Subconsciously directed he wheeled about, looking back into the room again. The tarpaulins were still hanging on the wall, a reminder of Monday's meeting, a quickly grasped association that brought Joel Morris into his mind again. Hurriedly speculative, he wondered if it might not be worth while to have another talk with him. Yesterday morning's interview had been almost unacceptably disappointing. His first impression of young Morris had been so favorable, his background and experience so promising, that it was still hard to believe that he had not come up with a single idea. Perhaps it was true, as Swann had suggested, that Joel was "a good boy but a little too much on the theoretical side" — that was often a shortcoming of young men who had learned their marketing and merchandising out of textbooks — yet the unmentioned fact that Joel was a Jew seemed to mitigate against his having a completely nonpractical point of view. True, there had been no positive evidence of a racially indicated talent for ferreting out a profit opportunity, yet there was still the possibility that it was there, suppressed perhaps by Joel's obvious consciousness that, all during their interview yesterday, Swann had watched them, his surveillance so intense that he could almost be suspected of lip-reading anything unheard through the separating glass. It was natural enough that Swann should be interested in what his assistant was saying to the president of the company — department heads always were — yet sympathy for Joel had kept him from digging as deeply as he had wished.

He started down the steps, deciding that he would bring Joel back upstairs, steeling himself against the suspicious gossip that doing so would probably start around the office. Halfway down, he became conscious that he had not seen Joel anywhere around this morning and, pushing open the door, he saw that his desk was still unoccupied. Thwarted, he hesitated. Instantly, seemingly triggered by his glance at Joel's desk, Miss Payne was on her feet. "He's back now and they're in the cutting room — Mr. Morris and Mr. Swann and Mr. Kennan. I'll show you the way —"

"I know my way, Miss Payne," he said, more pleasantly and less firmly than he intended, wishing that he could make her understand, once and for all, that he had no intention of restoring her to her former position as secretary to the president. At the moment he needed no secretary and, when he did, he would as resolutely resist Miss Payne as he had resisted all of the attempts that Swann had made to turn him into a resurrected Sol Zurich. He knew that he had shocked Swann on Tuesday morning when he had said that he had no desire whatsoever to read all of the mail before anyone else saw it, even more when he had told him that neither did he have any intention of participating in the daily ceremony in the cutting room, decreeing that Swann, Kennan and Joel Morris were to go on exactly as they had done since Sol Zurich's death, tasting sample cans drawn from the previous day's pack as well as older samples to be checked for any deterioration during storage.

Although his refusal to put himself on the tasting committee was honestly motivated by a recognized desire to avoid assumption of Sol Zurich's role in a dominantly dictatorial one-man management, there was also the underlying realization that he did not have a very discriminating palate. As early as his first months with Quincy Canning, he had learned that he had little ability to distinguish subtle variations in flavor. He had never been able to match Brick Mitchell's ability to catch an off-taste, nor Maggie's talent for identifying its source, much less to stand up against old Adam Quincy, who proudly exhibited a genius not unlike that of a skilled wine-taster, able to sip a tomato concentrate and not only name the variety of tomatoes that had been used but also, four times out of five, to correctly guess within a few miles of where the fruit had been grown.

The war years had somewhat educated Lincoln Lord's palate. His Navy duty as an aide to Admiral Rabson had involved the supervision of endless banquets and dinner parties, both official and private. His contacts with chefs and maître d'hôtels during that period had taught him at least the vocabulary, enough to impress Admiral Rabson, who fancied himself something of a gourmet. Lincoln Lord had always discussed proposed menus with the admiral and it had been one of those pleasant little chats that had directly led to his being offered the vice presidency of Rabson Foods. Supporting his reputation, he had served on the tasting committee at Rabson, but he had cautiously put other opinions before his own and, when he got to Union Packing, he had fully exercised the presidential prerogative of never giving a verdict until everyone else had spoken. When there had been a difference of opinion too sharp to be easily resolved, he had usually found some reason to delay his decision until he could get a set of samples and take them home for Maggie to taste.

None of this background was recognizably present in his mind as he walked quickly away from Miss Payne's desk, but as he pushed through the door to the factory and made the right turn down the short corridor that led to the recalled location of the cutting room, glancing at his watch and seeing that it was ten o'clock, the regular hour for the daily tasting ceremony, he almost turned back, fearing that if he opened the cutting room door it might give the impression of an unwarranted intrusion upon delegated authority.

But to his surprise he saw that the heavy refrigerator-type door stood open, negating its purpose of excluding even the faintest whiff of outside odor. Even more shockingly, he saw the outward drift of cigarette smoke, a never tolerated violation of cutting-room etiquette. Obviously this was no normally ceremonious tasting session, and his first glance inside the room confirmed it. Joel Morris, his head cocked to keep the smoke of a smoldering cigarette out of his reddened eyes, was emptying canned goods out of a Gellman Stores shopping bag, the last of several others that had been untidily tossed to the floor. Kennan was at the can opener, handing the opened cans to Swann, who was dumping the contents of each into a separate white porcelain tray.

Standing at the door, still unseen, he was conscious of an unpleasantly reminiscent smell, an odor of sourness and smokily rancid grease that reminded him of the catacomb kitchens under the dormitory at Chesapeake College where he had run a dishwashing machine during his freshman year. It was a smell that obviously came from the porcelain trays and, squinting at the identifying empty cans beside them, he saw that the labels were all alike — Mother Gellman's Vegetable Beef Stew. The stab of fear that shot through him was a reflex to which his brain had been conditioned during all the years he had spent in the food business. From Quincy Canning to Union Packing, an apprehensive anxiety had hung over every food-processing plant that he had ever known, the never to be escaped fear that sometime, somehow, something would slip up somewhere along the processing line and that a pack would go bad. He could never forget that night of terror at Rabson when there had been a suspicion that a mass attack of food poisoning at a Norfolk picnic had been caused by a jar of Rabson's Salad Dressing. That it had later turned out to be a false alarm had in no way softened the horror of the possibility of truth. Dry-mouthed, he now asked, "What's happened?" surprised when he heard his voice that he had kept it as calm as it was.

All three men froze for a moment in surprised awareness of his presence, suspended motion resumed as Frank Kennan said, "Oh, good —

glad you could come back, Mr. Lord. Joel's dug up the damnedest thing you ever heard of!"

He was inside the room now, the smell stronger and more positive. He looked expectantly at Joel Morris, seeing that his face was drawn with weariness, his clothes looking as if he had slept in them.

"Tell Mr. Lord the story," Swann commanded.

Joel's head rocked, half a nod, half the shaking off of fatigue. "Last night — well, Vicky has a sister living over in Atlantic City. Yesterday was her birthday so we drove down after work. Got there about six. We were sitting around before dinner having a drink when Max started to climb all over me about what lousy products we put out. I didn't think much about it at first — he's the kind of a guy that's never happy unless he's needling you about something — so I thought that's all it was. Then Stella backed him up and said that it was true — that they'd bought a can of beef stew at Gellman's Supermarket the day before and that it was so bad they couldn't eat it. For a minute that kind of threw me, but then I told them what's happened — that we aren't packing the Gellman stuff any more, that they're doing it now in their own cannery, and maybe they'd had a little trouble on their first run of beef stew. That more or less settled it for a few minutes — Max got off on something else — but I got thinking about what Stella had said about what had happened that morning when she'd gone back to the Gellman market and complained about this bad can of stew. She wasn't trying to return it, didn't even have the empty can with her, but she said that she'd no more than mentioned it to the manager and he started to write out a credit slip — didn't even question her."

"Apparently that wasn't his first complaint," Lincoln Lord observed.

"That's what hit me, too," Joel said. "And I sat there thinking about it, wondering if — well, I thought that if Gellman was having trouble getting their cannery going, we might get some of their business back, maybe not permanently but at least until they got themselves straightened out — maybe get rid of some of our inventory."

The same thought had flashed in Lincoln Lord's mind, but he caught Joel's implication that no such hope now existed and he said nothing, curbing impatience, realizing that the denouement of the story was still to come.

"Max disappeared," Joel went on. "And then in a minute or two he came up from the basement. What he'd done — he's the kind of a character who'd do something like this — he'd gone down and dug through the trash barrel for the empty can, trying to catch me off base.

And it looked like he had. Our name was on the label of this bad can of stew."

Frank Kennan picked up the last can that he had emptied into a porcelain tray, pointing a stabbing finger at a line of very small type along the lower border of the label: PACKED FOR GELLMAN STORES BY COASTAL FOODS CO., GOODHAVEN, N.J.

"That's one of the battles that Mr. Zurich won," Kennan explained. "Getting old Mr. Gellman to let us put our name on the label. Now the bastards are cutting our throat with it!"

Lincoln Lord asked incredulously, "You can't possibly mean that they're using this label on stuff that they're packing themselves."

Kennan picked up one of the filled porcelain trays. "Smell it! Do you think we'd ever let anything like that get out of this plant?"

The odor almost made him retch. "But how could they get hold of our labels?"

"They own the label plant," Kennan said. "Or at least control it."

"Of course I didn't know at first that it wasn't our pack," Joel explained. "All I had was the empty can — they'd thrown the stuff out — and I was afraid that — well, with a couple thousand cases of the stuff in our own warehouse, I thought that if something had gone wrong, I'd better find out in a hurry. It was Wednesday night — the stores were open until nine — so I went over to this Gellman super and bought a couple of cans off the shelf. I didn't say anything to the manager because — as I say, I still thought then that it was our pack. But as soon as I got it out in the car and opened it, I knew it wasn't. I've been in on the cutting of every run we've made and I knew that nothing as bad as this had ever gone through our plant."

"That's for sure," Kennan growled.

"I take it that you shopped some other stores?" Lincoln Lord suggested, glancing at the pile of cans that had been taken out of the shopping bags.

"Yes, I — well, for a minute or two I didn't know what to do. But the longer I thought about it, the more serious it seemed — this kind of junk being sold with our name on it. Anyway, I thought I'd better jump in as fast as I could and find out whether this was just a freak — maybe a bad case had gotten into Atlantic City. It was almost eight o'clock by then and I knew all the stores would be closing at nine, so I got on the telephone and called Vicky's brother in Philly and asked him to get out and shop as many Gellman Stores as he could. Then I called a couple we know in Trenton and asked them to do the same thing there, and then a cousin of mine in Newark. Then I got on the road and made the circle, picking up what they'd been able to buy. That's what this stuff is."

Lincoln Lord looked at the collection of cans. "You don't know yet whether they're all bad?"

"They're not," Joel said, picking up another filled porcelain tray. "This is all right. It's our pack."

"Look at the difference!" Kennan demanded. "But you don't have to look at it — you can smell it!"

"And you're certain that this bad can didn't come out of our plant?"

Kennan got a flash of resentment under control and picked up two emptied cans. "Look at this label — down here at the edge. See that little corrugated impression? That's one of the troubles we've had with this new labeling machine of Mike's. He's using a knurled feed roll and it marks the label, nothing serious but it's there if you look for it. This can has it, this one doesn't."

"Could this be old stock, packed before you started using the new machine?"

Kennan up-ended the can, indicating the coded date stamp. "That's two months after we started with the new machine." He squinted at the smeared black numbers. "And by god this is a fake! This was put on with a rubber stamp. Why those counterfeiting bastards — we've got enough evidence here to sue them for fifty million bucks!"

Lincoln Lord gave the production manager a sharp look, appreciating that his anger had flared out of his fierce pride in the quality of product that had always been packed under the Coastal Foods name, yet disturbed that he was not displaying judgment as calmly balanced as it should have been. "You don't really think that they've done this maliciously, do you, Frank?"

Kennan self-consciously retreated, but only a short step. "No matter how you figure it, it adds up to the same thing. This story'll be all over the country. And you know how it'll get twisted on the grapevine. They'll make it sound as if this was the reason Gellman Stores kicked us out — because we were giving them lousy stuff."

"We might have known it," Swann said as a muttered interjection.

"This will really cut our throat," Kennan added. "Fat chance we'll ever have now of selling a line of our own. From here on out, our name on a label will be the kiss of death."

Intemperate as the production manager's outburst was, Lincoln Lord saw that it had substantial validity. There was no business where rumor

229

moved more swiftly, nor with more killing effect. True or not, unjust as it might be, this story could easily sweep the country, blacklisting the Coastal Foods name with every broker, every wholesale house, every chain store buyer. Without a sales organization to fight back, Coastal Foods had no chance for justice. He picked up an empty can and stared at the label, seeing it as a climaxing final blow, striking down what little hope still remained that he would ever be able to get the Coastal Foods Company on its feet again.

Swann said bitterly, "After that letter from Rubin, I knew they were out to get us, but I never thought they'd go this far."

Kennan shook his head. "I've heard of a lot of scurvy tricks in my time — this tops them all." He turned, "You ever heard one to beat it, Mr. Lord?"

He felt himself too drained-out to reply, the loss of hope so weakening that his mind would not respond even for the framing of some pointlessly evasive remark. What little strength he had left was needed for the maintenance of an expression of deeply preoccupied thought. And then he heard an odd throat-clearing sound and looked up. There was a strange expression on Joel Morris's face, a peculiar compounding of intermingled courage and fear, hope struggling against doubt. And then he heard, "This is probably crazy —" and the strangeness was suddenly gone, lost in an instantly established association, the memory of Brick Mitchell using almost those same words, his face twisted into this same tortured expression of a mind in labor, an idea struggling to be born.

Given the encouragement of full attention, Joel continued, "You'll probably think I'm off my rocker — I don't know, maybe I am — but there's something about this that just doesn't check out."

"They're out to get us," Swann snapped. "If they can't do it one way, they're going to do it another."

"Go on, Joel," Lincoln Lord encouraged, disregarding Swann.

Joel's lips twisted, wringing out words. "When I had their stores shopped last night I figured that if they were using our name on their beef stew, I'd better find out what they were doing on the rest of the line. I couldn't cover everything but I did check the big sellers. They're all out of stock — everywhere. There wasn't a single can of any of the big items in any store we checked."

"Are they crazy?" Kennan exploded. "Don't they realize that they'll kill off the line? Good god, how stupid are they?"

"That's what doesn't check out," Joel agonized. "They *aren't* stupid."

"No, they're not stupid!" Swann said, acidly ironic. "They know what they're doing — exactly what they're doing!"

"Not the men up on top," Joel disagreed. "You know Mr. Arnauth, don't you, Mr. Lord?"

He nodded cautiously, doubtfully, making no more of an admission than was needed to support the memory that he had called Arnauth just before he had talked to Anderson Phelps, but Sidney Arnauth was only one of a thousand names catalogued in his mind, someone met somewhere at a convention, or a meeting, or a banquet, and thereafter classified as a man he *knew*, accessible when the need arose.

"I haven't met Mr. Arnauth," Joel went on. "But I know all of their other top men. I interviewed them when I was making the Gellman Stores study for McCutcheon & Paisley — Mandel, Blaustein, Harry Cohen, all of their vice-presidents. I just can't believe that men like that would get themselves into a mess like this. They're too smart."

Dead silence reigned. Lincoln Lord was hopeful that either Kennan or Swann would break it. Neither did. They were thinking the same thing he was ... Joel defending the Gellman crowd because they were Jews ...

Joel's face was drawn now, dull-flushed with embarrassment, and Lincoln Lord tried to avoid looking at him. But he demanded attention, speaking more vigorously now, "I know, that's three years ago. Maybe those men have changed. I don't think so. I don't believe it, but just for the sake of argument let's say they have — that they've all changed into a bunch of crooks with no ethics or morals or anything else. Does it make any more sense that way?"

Again there was silence.

"Put yourself in their place," Joel insisted. "Suppose that this is the executive committee of the Gellman Stores Corporation, and that we're sitting here listening to someone trying to sell us the idea of putting the squeeze on Coastal Foods. All right, here's the proposal — cut off the orders — no warning, no nothing, just cut them off like that!"

"Isn't that what they did?" Swann demanded.

"Wait a minute," Joel said, breathing hard. "If someone made that proposal wouldn't you want to know if Gellman Stores was ready for the break — if the cannery was ready to go, if there was a backlog of stock? Would you have approved cutting off Coastal Foods without checking up to find out if you weren't going to cut your own throat in the process? The Mother Gellman brand is worth millions. They know that. They've been building it up for thirty years. It's the backbone of their whole promotion pitch. Would they have said to hell with it — put out any old kind of crap — let all the stores run out of stock?" He faced Kennan. "Do you remember what happened only a few months ago when we let them run out — only one item, and only for a couple of days? All hell broke loose, didn't it? Do you think they've changed that much?"

If Kennan responded, Lincoln Lord missed what he said, all senses blocked as his brain suddenly became a machine forced to accelerate from dead slow to the peak of power, individual sense perception momentarily lost in the roaring maelstrom of pounding thoughts. He waited for the torrent to settle to controllable proportions and then he asked, "What are you suggesting, Joel?"

"Honestly, Mr. Lord, I just can't see how the top management at Gellmans could ever have approved it."

"You don't think that their decision to cut us off ever got to their executive committee? You think that someone went ahead without approval?"

Joel exhaled sharply, seemingly relieved that he had finally made his point. "Somebody must have gone off the deep end on his own."

"You mean Rubin?"

Swann was shaking his head. "No, no, Joel — that's too big a corporation — no, it just couldn't have happened." He turned, silently asking for confirmation.

Lincoln Lord understood Swann's attitude. He, too, back in the days when his experience was limited to small companies, had thought that big corporations were so highly organized and efficiently managed that everything was under perfect control. But he remembered only too well how difficult it had been to keep a tight hand on the reins at Luxor Pharmacal, how many occasions there had been when some fool had broken loose and gone off on a wild tangent, how often something had happened that he had known nothing about, concealed rather than revealed by the intricacy of organization . . . trying to explain to the board of directors how that purchasing agent could have been taking kickbacks for two years without being discovered . . . that plant manager in Chicago who had . . .

A flicker of movement attracted his attention to Kennan and, recognized, the production manager said, "Joel might have something. You remember my telling you about — ?" He hesitated, attempting a silent reminder, then quickly decided against secrecy and looked at Swann and Joel Morris. "I guess you fellows don't know this — I told Mr.

Lord — Rubin offered me a job managing their cannery. I went over to see it — not that I was ever really interested, but still I thought it wouldn't do any harm to take a look at the place. It was a damn mess. I knew they couldn't pack our line. I said so. Remember, Mr. Lord, that day out back?"

"Yes, very well."

"They didn't have the equipment, they didn't have the know-how, they didn't have anything. There wasn't anyone around except a couple of pea-packers, not a damn soul who had ever processed a pound of meat in his life. And that was only a week before they canceled out with us. They were still fumbling around trying to get going." He gave the nearest tray a disdainful shove. "Plain enough, what happened. They got panicky and had to shove out something — anything — no matter what it was as long as it got some cans on the shelves. That probably explains the label, too — so crazy to get going that they wouldn't even give Sunset Litho enough time to take our name off the plates."

Swann started to speak but Kennan cut him off, continuing, "And you know, this never hit me before, but it checks out. When Rubin first called me on the phone — I guess maybe I was a little suspicious right from the start. It just wasn't the way a big corporation operates. I've had enough other offers to know. They always feel you out under-cover — an employment agency, an attorney, some third party. And even if they approach you direct, they do it through channels — the personnel department. But I thought — well, what the hell, the guy's a vice-president and maybe he's got authority to operate on his own. Still I couldn't get over the feeling that maybe it wasn't on the level. So I asked him to write me — make it official — put it in a letter." He paused. "He never did."

Swann retorted, "He wasn't backward about writing us — cutting us off with no warning."

"That doesn't prove anything," Kennan countered. "Joel may still be right. How do we know that anyone up on top ever knew that he wrote that letter?"

"Or the first one, either," Joel added.

"What was that?" Lincoln Lord asked.

Joel deflected the question to Swann but he looked blankly puzzled until he was reminded, "The letter that he wrote us right after Mr. Gellman died — telling us that all of our contacts had to be through him?"

233

"Oh," Swann grumbled, acknowledgment without agreement.

"And there's something off-beat about that, too, Mr. Lord," Joel went on. "You know about my going to New York, trying to see him?"

"Yes."

"Waiting all day, I was about ready to blow my top. And I guess maybe I did. I knew it wouldn't do any good to ride the girls out front — it wasn't their fault — but when I sounded off, one of them broke down and told me —" He hesitated, changing tone. "She said that she couldn't understand why I had to see Rubin, anyway — that he wasn't even on the buying end — that he was supposed to be in charge of their bakeries. That's the way he got into Gellman's, you know — they bought a chain of bakeries that he owned and it was a part of the deal that he was to be kept on as a vice-president."

"Did you try to see someone else?"

"Rubin had things fixed up so I couldn't," Joel said. "You know how you register when you first come in? Then the girl at the desk takes your registration slip and checks it against your file card. There's a card for every company — the name of the buyer that you're supposed to see. Well, the girl checked the Coastal Foods card again — you know, to see if she could clear me to talk to someone else. There was a note on the card — I saw it — that no one from Coastal Foods was to see anyone except Rubin." He waited for a reaction, finally asking, "Doesn't that sound suspicious, Mr. Lord?"

He managed to say, "I suppose they do have a problem trying to keep salesmen from running all over the place," but it was rebuttal without conviction . . . if Joel was right . . .

Somehow an empty can had gotten in his hand and he stared down at the label, cautiously yielding to its full implication. Even if Joel was wrong, Gellman was completely off base . . . caught red-handed . . . but what the devil could he do about it? He had the trump card but how could he play it?

Habit-guided, he started to reach for the telephone, stopped by the realization that this wasn't Luxor Pharmacal. There was no legal department to call for advice. He put down the can, sensitive to the nervous chatter of metal against glass as it touched the table. And then he found another groove of habit, more deeply cut, and he said calmly in the long-practiced tone that he had used to bring hundreds of committee meetings to a conclusion, "Well, let's see if we can get a consensus here — decide on a course of action. What's your idea, Alf? What do you think we should do?"

Swann spread his liver-spotted hands in a gesture of helplessness. "You'd know better than I would, Mr. Lord."

He hesitated, wondering whether he should prod the office manager further, decision made unnecessary when Kennan said, "At least we ought to be able to clobber the bastards for using our name on this kind of garbage."

"Then you'd suggest instituting legal action?"

A moment of consideration led Frank Kennan to say, thinking out loud, "But whether or not it would get us anywhere — I guess that's the question. They've got a hell of a lot of money and they'd spend it, too — hire every damn shyster lawyer in the country. They'd break us before we even got close to licking them — and that would be playing right into their hands, just what they want us to do."

"What Rubin wants us to do," Joel corrected him.

"How do we know?" Kennan asked wearily, his face the face of the Coastal Foods Company, looking at Lincoln Lord with a lost man's hope for deliverance.

Only Joel remained and Lincoln Lord picked up the lead that he had given him. "You think the thing to do is to get to Rubin?"

Swann missed the point, obtusely asking, "How can Joel get to him? He won't even see him."

"I don't think I could," Joel said, his eyes rigidly confined to Swann's face. "But Mr. Lord could call Mr. Arnauth."

The suggestion slipped into Lincoln Lord's mind, no more than a catalyst inducing mental reaction, speeding the crystallization of a thought that had already begun to form . . . yes, that was probably the thing to do . . . standard procedure . . . the quiet little off-the-record call . . . president to president. Sometimes it worked . . . that was the way he'd gotten an armistice in the vitamin price war that had threatened Luxor Pharmacal . . . just a friendly little call to Marty Goodman. But that had been a different situation . . . he'd had a big corporation behind him. What would have happened if little Marty had tried to threaten him? No, he'd have laughed him off. But if it should turn out to be true that Sid Arnauth didn't know what was going on . . . all the Gellman stores out of stock . . . and a warehouseful of the stuff that would fill those store shelves . . .

The mind fog settled and he said, a general statement, undirected, "It seems to me that the first thing we must do is to decide on our own objective — what do we want to accomplish?"

Joel was looking down, his long fingers nervously working a jagged

235

tear down the side of a shopping bag. But he finally looked up, "Maybe I'm off base but — well, this does give us a club — don't you think, Mr. Lord, that we might get them to take out the stuff we've got in our warehouse?"

Kennan flared, "You aren't going to let them off that easily, are you? Good god, that would be doing them a favor — getting some stuff back on their shelves again." Anger faded. "But if we could clean that warehouse —"

Small-voiced, Swann said, "It would be an enormous help, no doubt about that. There's almost a half-million dollars tied up out there."

"The thing that hits me —" Joel began.

"Yes."

"If we're right about this whole thing being something that Rubin did on his own — maybe their top management doesn't even know that we've got this inventory."

"You mean that bastard didn't even tell them," Kennan asked, but not as a question.

Joel's eyes were fixed on Kennan. "It seems to me that if Mr. Lord could talk to Mr. Arnauth —"

Why not? He might not even have to use a club . . . just give him a call . . . tell him that they were about to start relabeling a lot of Gellman stock with their own brand . . . just occurred to him that before he actually gave the order to go ahead, it might be a friendly gesture to see if Gellman might possibly need some of it. If that didn't get a rise . . . yes, there was another opening . . . one of his men had picked up a rumor that a lot of Gellman stores were out of stock . . . just a tip, president to president . . . thought he might want to check up and see if it was true. But it was hard to handle something like that over the telephone . . .

He said, "Well, I was planning to run up to New York this afternoon. I might give Sid Arnauth a ring —"

Joel's hand had moved, pointed now toward the telephone, his fingertips a runner's feet set to their marks.

His curt nod was the starter's gun. Joel's hand shot out. "I'll put through the call."

There was the ratchet twist of mounting tension, the alternation of action and waiting as the call went through — the office operator, the Goodhaven operator, the New York operator, the Gellman Stores operator — "The president's office, please — Mr. Arnauth." Another wait. "Mr. Arnauth's office? May I speak to him please?"

Muscles tensed, charged to move ... what if Arnauth wouldn't talk to him ... wouldn't see him ... ?

Joel answered a question, unheard but obvious, saying with the triumphant tone of a magic password confidently given, "Mr. Lincoln Lord."

"Here you are, sir."

Joel was handing him the instrument and he took it, strong-fingered and outwardly calm, braced against embarrassment as he heard a feminine voice say, "I'm awfully sorry but Mr. Arnauth is in a very important meeting and simply can't be disturbed. Could I take a message for him?"

Joel's eyes were on him ... Frank Kennan's eyes ... Swann's eyes ...

"I'm leaving in the next few minutes from Goodhaven, New Jersey. It's extremely important that I see Mr. Arnauth as soon as I arrive."

He heard her say, "Just a moment, Mr. Lord," his pulse quickening as he sensed her response to command. Her voice faded, pretense lost, then suddenly re-established. "If you could be here by twelve, Mr. Lord, I think I can get you in for a minute or two."

"Yes, I should be there by twelve," he said, handing the instrument back to Joel, trying to avoid seeing the awed respect that was now sparkling in his black-amber eyes ... Joel didn't know that it was only one of those five-minute brush-offs that a smart secretary squeezed in at twelve o'clock ... Alf didn't know ... Frank didn't know ...

Kennan said, "If you want my car, Mr. Lord —"

He remembered then that he hadn't bought an automobile yet ... *damn* ... he should have gone ahead, even if he didn't have the money in hand ... Maggie so worried about those old bills ...

"I'll drive you, Mr. Lord," he heard Joel say excitedly, an undeniable demand, weariness thrown off ... Brick ... Rabson Foods ... that trip to Washington the time they'd made that wild pitch to the Quartermaster Corp on a specification change and knocked off a half-million-dollar order ...

"We've got to hurry if you're going to make it by twelve," Joel warned.

He stood quickly. "I'll have to call Mag — tell her I'll not be there for lunch."

Joel's hand was already on the phone. He dialed the number. The line was busy.

2

This was the last Thursday of the month, the day designated by the by-laws of Chesapeake College for the regular meeting of its board of regents. Outside the meeting room in Quincy Hall, Dr. Arthur B. Whittaker stood listening to Jay Quincy's whispered explanation of what had happened in New York. The dean's shoulders were deeply bent, his eyes down, his mechanical nod an attempt to convince himself that Jay Quincy's negligence in having waited so long to get in touch with Lincoln Lord was, if not excusable, at least forgivable.

"Yes, I'll grant you — unfortunate that we couldn't have gotten to him a bit sooner," Jay was saying. "On the other hand, I can't see it as anything to be too concerned about. After all, you know, it's going to take a bit of time to work this thing out — convince the board — "

"But if Mr. Lord has taken this other job — ?"

"If Linc's still the man you want, he'll be available again before too long."

"You really think so?"

"Of course," Jay Quincy said, quietly confident. "I got the whole story in New York. The man I talked to — this is confidential, Dean."

"Yes, of course," he said abstractedly.

"But I don't mind telling you that he's one of the biggest food brokers in the country — Art Gerhart — and if there's anyone who's really on the inside of what's going on in the industry, it's these big brokers."

"Yes, I suppose that's true."

Jay Quincy dropped his voice. "As I got the story, the little Jew that owned this cannery — Zucker or some such name — died suddenly a few months ago and left the business to his wife. Apparently, she was anxious to cash in fast — probably needed the money for inheritance tax. Anyway, Linc beat everyone else to the draw, jumped in and got hold of the property. The story is that he picked it up for a song — ten cents on the dollar. Whatever he paid, he obviously got a bargain. Wouldn't be bothering with it if he hadn't. What he'll do now, of course, is hold it for six months, establish a capital gain, and then sell out. Probably make himself a million dollars net."

"No doubt," the dean agreed, making no attempt at comprehension, knowing that the way clever men made enormous sums of money was a mystery that his mind would never be capable of penetrating. He was content with this additional evidence of Lincoln Lord's financial skill, now more convinced than ever that he was the man that Chesapeake College needed. Six months was a long time to wait, but if Lincoln Lord became available by midsummer he would be on the job soon enough to take over before next year's endowment fund campaign — and, with an extra million, it would matter even less that the presidential salary would seem like no more than an honorarium.

Jay Quincy was smirking at him. "You weren't really imagining, were you, Dean, that he'd let himself get stuck away in that kind of spot — president of a little Jewish cannery — Lincoln Lord?"

"It did seem a bit strange," he agreed. "Yes, I must admit — a man of Mr. Lord's caliber — hardly what you'd logically expect, is it? Yes, I really must confess it — I was wondering if I'd overestimated him."

He looked for tolerance in Jay Quincy's smile, not entirely certain that it was there, doubt heightened as he heard him say, "Don't worry about it, Dean — you didn't. But if you don't mind a suggestion — ?"

"Yes?"

"Don't lose contact."

"Contact?" the dean asked, the question genuine, uncertain of all the meanings this word had taken on of late in the outside world.

"You're having some more of these alumni meetings, aren't you?"

"Yes — oh, yes, indeed. Philadelphia next week. But if you're suggesting that I have Mr. Lord talk again — unfortunately, he's not available."

"You asked him?"

"Well, not personally. I thought it something better handled, perhaps, by Mr. Potter. The fund-raising agency, you know?"

Jay Quincy's smile had become discomfiting. "Dean, if you don't mind my saying so, I'm afraid you were guilty of an error in protocol."

"Really?"

" 'The king's ears hear only a king's voice,' " Jay quoted.

"You think I should have called him myself?"

"Of course."

"Perhaps you're right."

Jay glanced at the meeting room, still open. "If I were you, I'd do it right now. It's Goodhaven, New Jersey."

"You don't happen to know where he's living — his address?"

"The operator will know, don't you think? After all, he's been there for four days now. Lincoln Lord?

"Yes — yes, of course," he said. "Of course she will."

239

Excusing himself, he started for his office. It was really quite amazing how simple these things were when you thought of them. But it did take a certain kind of mind. The discouraging thing was that so many men had them — even, as he had now discovered, Jay Quincy.

3

Perched on the kitchen stool, Maggie Lord waited impatiently for the return of the long-distance operator's voice. It seemed that there was some diabolical conspiracy afoot this morning to keep her away from the stove. This was Thursday, Viola's day off, the first day when the kitchen had been completely her own, and all she had been able to do up to now was answer the telephone.

Actually, this was only the third call, but all three had been so coincidentally grouped, one right after the other, that there had been no time between them for a dissipation of annoyance. First it had been the warehouse company in Philadelphia, telling her that the delivery of the things that they had held in storage since the Frazer Glass days could not be managed until next Monday. That was unimportant. There was nothing she really wanted in those old boxes anyway, except her recipe files and her cookbook collection. She wouldn't need them for another seven days. There was only one Thursday in a week.

The receiver had hardly been back on the hook when the phone had rung again, this time a Mrs. Peters who identified herself as the president of the Goodhaven Garden Club, the wife of a man whose name was Fred, the mother of five wonderful children who were a terrible care but worth every minute of it, a sufferer from a form of arthritis so rare that it could be described only by recounting every word that had ever been uttered by an uncountable procession of doctors — and then, just when it seemed that Mrs. Peters was finally getting around to an invitation to join the Goodhaven Garden Club, she had additionally identified herself as the Goodhaven representative of a simply wonderful line of foundation garments, so exclusively fashionable that they were sold only on a personal basis by certified graduates of a twelve-week correspondence course, every lesson so fascinating that it demanded description from the moment of the arrival of the postman to the despatch of the written examination, a seemingly interminable accounting finally climaxed by the arrival of the simply beautiful diploma that Mrs. Peters would, without fail, bring along for her to see when she had her first fitting.

There had been a minute of grace after Mrs. Peters, hardly more than that, scarcely enough time to start a search of the freezer shelves, and then there had been this call, long-distance from somewhere, someone trying to locate Linc. She had told the operator that he could be reached at the Coastal Foods Company, Goodhaven 4040, but there had been a suspending, "One moment, please," and then this long wait.

Now, finally, the operator spoke again. "When do you expect Mr. Lord to be available at this number, please?"

"He'll be coming home at noon," she said. "I can't tell you exactly when but he should be here by twelve-thirty."

"One moment, please."

Ten-thirty already, half the morning lost . . . not time enough now to defrost a chicken breast . . . maybe there wasn't one in the freezer, anyway. And without a car she couldn't drive into town to buy anything . . . they *had* to buy some kind of car . . . but there was Kip's Forge-hill tuition . . . if Linc would only be satisfied with a small car . . . but, of course, it would have to be another Cadillac . . .

"When Mr. Lord comes in, will you please have him call Operator Number Four in Brighton, Maryland?"

"Brighton? Who is it that's calling?"

"One moment, please," the voice said, less tape-recorded now, uncertain.

Strange . . . she'd just been thinking about Brighton . . . Mrs. Peters so like old Mrs. Thompson at the boardinghouse . . . you had to be so careful in these small towns not to offend anyone . . .

"The call is from Dr. Whittaker at Chesapeake College," the operator said now. "And you will have Mr. Lord call back as soon as he comes in — Brighton, Maryland and ask for Operator Four?"

"I'll give him the message," she agreed and hung up, reaching now for the chained pencil and a slip of paper from the note box . . . Dr. Whittaker . . . another speech. And Linc would probably do it. But he *shouldn't* . . .

The pencil point broke. She decided against bothering to resharpen it, certain that this was nothing that she would forget. She needed every minute. Today was important. Somehow she had to make Linc realize that this was really their house now. Always before he had settled down so quickly, but there was something wrong here. Even after

241

three full days, a frightening aura of temporary intrusion still hung over the house, almost the feeling that Linc wasn't expecting to stay.

She had awakened this morning with the vibrant awareness that today would be her chance to banish the still persistent strangeness, insisting that Linc come home for lunch, reminding him that he had almost always done it when they had lived in any small town before, mentioning the days at Brighton, certain that he would remember those wonderful first months of marriage when he would drive out to Kingdom Come at noon. At least he would remember what that chicken dish had come to mean after that first unforgettable association. But it was probably a silly idea ... no chicken in the freezer ...

But there was, a dozen packages grease-penciled CHIKN in purely phonetic Viola-language, and she could feel the unmistakable wedge of a whole breast through the ice-crackled parchment. Hesitant, anxiously glancing at the clock, she unwrapped it, deciding that it did not, after all, have to be defrosted if she was going to poach it. She penetrated the mystery of the stove's controls and the coiled burner glowed red. Effervescent bubbles quickly leaped upward from the silvery bottom of the tinned copper pan, gay assurance that her competence in the kitchen had not been lost with five years of hotel living.

There was the giddy feeling of joyous recapture now, self-induced and yet not insincere, as genuine as the tears that, as a child, she could bring to her mind by recalling the sight of a kitten crushed under a coal truck's wheel. And now she felt the positive stirring of physical arousal ... silly! Of course, it was silly ... the bedroom was so much farther away from the dining room here than it had been at Kingdom Come ...

The telephone rang.

What might have been, released, the girlish giggle that had risen in her throat, now became the pseudo-laughter of incredulity, annoyance turned to farce by repetition.

"Mrs. Lord? This is Miss Payne — at the office, you know? Mr. Lord tried several times to call you but your line was busy and he asked me to give you a message."

"Yes?"

"He had to go to New York, Mrs. Lord — a twelve o'clock appointment with Mr. Arnauth of Gellman Stores —"

She clicked off the burner dial. The bubbles stopped, champagne suddenly gone flat. There was only one thing Sid Arnauth wanted ... to buy Coastal Foods! Linc had given up already ... only four days

this time ... not even the few months that it had taken at Chemical
Service ...

4

During the hour and twenty minutes that it had taken Joel Morris
to drive him from Goodhaven to the Gellman Building, Lincoln Lord
had kept him talking almost constantly, exploring every aspect of the
relationship that had existed between Gellman Stores and the Coastal
Foods Company. Joel had proved a fertile source of information,
able to draw not only upon his perceptive observation during the last
three years, but also upon the store of detailed factual data that he had
assembled for the study of Gellman Stores that he had made while he
had been at McCutcheon & Paisley. His respect for Joel had risen
tremendously. Nevertheless, the longer he had listened, the more he
had suspected that the conclusion to which Joel had leaped had been
substantially influenced by the bitter resentment that he felt toward
Rubin for having refused to see him.

Now, stepping from the elevator on the sixth floor of the Gellman
Building, he found that animosity even more credible. A whole day
spent in the atmosphere of the over-sized entrance lobby where salesmen waited to interview Gellman buyers would be enough to warp
anyone's judgment. Even now, in what should be a noontime lull, the
long double rows of depot benches were filled, the overflow crowd
leaning against every foot of open wall space. Stale tobacco smoke hung
in a stratified cloud against the low ceiling, stagnant and eye-stinging,
stirred now and then as the raucous loud-speaker system barked a
number and some salesman, anxiously rechecking his pass-button,
fumbling his samples, leaped for the door that guarded the entrance to
the buying offices.

But there was more to be sensed here than the breeding of frustration, and responsive as always to the environment in which he found
himself, he felt the enormous pressure concentrated within this room.
The sales volume of Gellman Stores was, according to Joel, rapidly approaching the all but incredible total of a half-billion dollars a year.
Every working day more than a million dollars' worth of orders flowed
out of these buying offices. This waiting room was the staging area for
a tremendous battle, the never-ending warfare between thousands of
manufacturers, processors, brokers and agents. A nod of favor from a
Gellman buyer often meant the difference between survival and failure.

There was nothing unusual about what had happened to Coastal Foods. Many a manufacturer had heard a death sentence delivered from one of the judgment cells beyond that guarded door, a verdict from which there was no appeal.

Glancing around the room, he wondered how many of the waiting salesmen were there to bid on items that Coastal Foods had once packed, how many more had already left with orders in their pockets. With the situation having developed to the point that Joel had discovered, it was hardly believable that Gellman Stores had not already moved to correct it.

As a blind denial of hopelessness, he side-stepped the two men who had gotten off the elevator with him and started for the reception desk. A uniformed woman confronted him, blocking the way, demanding, "Register and get your number."

"I'm Lincoln Lord," he said, his voice low, trying to keep from being overheard by salesmen within earshot. "I have an appointment with Mr. Arnauth."

She looked at him now as if, before, she had not actually seen him, and there was something close to grudging apology as she said in a policewoman's voice, "I gotta check you," and turned to the reception desk to ask, "Got a Lord for Arnauth?"

"Check," a weary voice responded.

The door was opened for him and he stepped through, feeling every pair of eyes in the room as a knife at his back, sharpened by resentment, then blunted by the closing of the door. He listened to instructions and then strode rapidly down the long corridor, for a moment feeling himself a runner ahead of the pack, then a tail-ender hopelessly outdistanced, already defeated, burdened by the heavy package in his hands, the two cans that Joel had wrapped for him to bring along, one drawn from the Coastal Foods stock, the other a sample of what Gellman Stores had packed for itself. He was tempted to drop the package — he had always disliked carrying things, even a briefcase — and now, recollection by association, he remembered toting Quincy samples all over the Chicago territory, flinching to the memory of a day when he had opened a can of tomatoes in a wholesale grocer's cutting room, sour and rank with spoilage ... *what if there was no difference in these two cans of beef stew!*

He had taken Kennan's word for it ... but could he be sure? Wasn't it possible that the cans Joel had brought back had been packed by Coastal Foods? Things went haywire in every factory ... incredible, unexplainable, but still they happened . . . and no production manager would ever admit that he was in the wrong. And that's all there was to support the whole fantastic structure of Joel's imagined plot . . . one shaky clue . . . a wild guess . . .

But he strode ahead, his feet on the path that had carried him through his whole life. This was not the first time that he had felt this fear of dependence, this often terrifying demand that he rely upon others. This was the president's lot . . . you had to take the word of your men . . . not lose faith . . . on and on, on and on . . . and when they were wrong, the fault was not theirs but yours. But that was something you had to forget.

He turned right, following an arrowed sign lettered EXECUTIVE OFFICES, pushing through glass doors and entering a wood-paneled corridor, the sound of his footsteps lost in deep-piled carpet . . . here were the offices of some of the smartest merchandising men in the country . . . BLAUSTEIN . . . COHEN . . . POLSKY . . . MANDEL . . . Joel couldn't possibly be right . . . these Jews were too clever . . . too cold-bloodedly calculating . . .

The door to the president's suite was in sight now and he raced his mind in a last-minute attempt to decide how he would open the interview, an effort made all but hopeless by his memories of the man he would be facing. He had vague recollections of having seen Arnauth at least a half-dozen times, but his sharp memory was confined to two occasions. One, the more important, had been at a supermarket convention in Hot Springs. Arnauth had been a member of the program committee and had written to him, asking him to speak at the banquet. He had been under no obligation to accept — Luxor Pharmacal was committed to drugstore distribution and had no fish to fry with the supermarkets — and under the circumstances it had seemed that Arnauth might have been more appreciative of his acceptance. The most acceptable explanation had charged his lack of warmth to a personality in which it was possible, perhaps, to mistake the taciturnity of shyness for less appealing attributes of character.

Someone had once told Lincoln Lord — it was a memory that traced back to that year in Chicago when he was getting his first experience as a salesman — that there were two kinds of Jews. Whoever it was had called them the "jolly Jews" and the "brooding Jews," a generalization that had not stood up too well over the years; yet it was something remembered and often grasped as a handy first step to quick classification. Without doubt, Sidney Arnauth was in the second group, almost a caricature of the type, his every mannerism suggesting accentuated introversion, physically evidenced by his greyhound thinness and the intellectual cast of his darkly Semitic face. He dressed with exaggerated conservatism — black cloth and white linen — yet there was about him an air of too polished elegance that gave him, caught in some lights, an air of arrogant self-esteem, conceivably as much his personal response to anti-Semitism as the too loud laughter and the dialect jokes of the sport-shirted jolly Jews among whom Arnauth had seemed so uncomfortably misplaced at the Hot Springs convention. At the pre-banquet cocktail party, he had stood withdrawn and alone until Maggie had gone out of her way to talk to him, her thoughtfulness unrewarded except for the discovery of how Sidney Arnauth had gotten into the supermarket business — he had, after a long bachelorhood in international banking, married Abe Gellman's daughter.

Lincoln Lord's second set of memories of Sidney Arnauth was more recent. Only a few weeks ago, wandering the streets aimlessly searching for something that would fill an empty hour of an empty day, he had gone into an art gallery on Fifty-seventh Street where a collection of modern paintings was being dispersed at auction. An usher, mistaking him for a well-heeled bidder, had opened the way to a seat in the crowded room. He had no particular interest in the paintings that were being sold, but the auction atmosphere had caught him up and he had begun to follow the bidding. After one fast round had carried the price of a smallish painting to seventeen thousand, five hundred dollars, the bang of the auctioneer's gavel had been followed by a mass eye movement toward the successful bidder. It was Sidney Arnauth. Thereafter, he had watched Arnauth through the rest of the auction, fascinated by his ability to maintain an absolutely expressionless face. He had bought two more paintings, one for an even twenty thousand dollars, another for thirty-one thousand, one hundred fifty dollars — the last after a spirited bidding battle that raised an audible buzz of excitement in the crowded room; yet not the slightest reaction had been visible on Sidney Arnauth's face, no hint of either the tension of struggle nor of the satisfaction of victory and possession. And that was the man that he now had to face, the coldly brooding Jew, unresponsive to any normal emotions, his chill austerity impenetrable by any argument that was not legally enforceable — and there was no contract with Coastal Foods.

But he stepped forward and pushed open the door of the reception room in the president's suite, untempted by retreat. This was what he

246

had been doing all of his life, pushing through closed doors, facing down the fear of failure . . . those first weeks in the Chicago territory, so fear-struck that no wholesale grocer would ever give him an order, and then that night when he talked to the old drummer at the Hotel Radisson in Minneapolis . . . "There's only one thing that ever really licks a salesman, son, and that's letting himself get scared of what he's going to find on the other side of a closed door . . . the quicker you push, the less time you're standing around scaring yourself to death."

If anything, the door to Sidney Arnauth's private office opened too quickly. "Please go right in, Mr. Lord — he's waiting for you," a secretary said instantly, her voice a hurrying thrust, and he imagined her standing by to snatch him out in a moment or two with a reminder to Sidney Arnauth that he had a twelve-fifteen luncheon appointment.

Arnauth was not seated at his desk. He stood beside it, silent and rigidly immobile, taller than memory, thinner than memory. His face did not perfectly match that of the man of the art auction, but the difference offered no encouragement.

Instantly judging that he was not even to be allowed to sit down, Lincoln Lord stopped. The package was still in his hand, not left outside as he had planned. Boldly deliberate, he turned and placed it carefully on a side table, handling it as if it contained heavy explosives. Stalling for time, he tucked a loose ear of wrapping paper, reminding himself of the futility of resentment. Then, prepared to offer a warmly normal greeting, he turned with the expectation of confronting Sidney Arnauth's coldly leveled eyes.

To his surprise, he discovered that Arnauth had moved toward him, that he was standing now at his side and reaching for his hat. Still without a word spoken, Lincoln Lord slipped out of his coat and Arnauth took it, turning away to hang it up. Then, his face averted, he finally spoke, saying, "Good of you to come, Mr. Lord," the words tortured out of meaning, yet carrying the unintelligible implication that this was not an interview granted but a visit requested.

Lost and groping, Lincoln Lord waited, instinctively positive that he had some strategic advantage, yet completely baffled as to what it might be. It was possible that Arnauth had guessed what was in the package, and equally believable that he was embarrassed at finding himself in an awkward position, but it was hardly credible that the threat of a lawsuit over a labeling error could have changed the Sidney Arnauth of the Hot Springs convention into the badly unpoised man who now held out his hand, a gesture so belatedly made and so clumsily performed that it could be accepted only as the surrender of the last shred of sophistication. Now, closely seen, his face had lost even a superficial resemblance to that of the man at the art auction. His skin color, recalled as warmly brown, deeply sun-tanned, had now taken on the ashen cast of illness, so tightly drawn over his set jaws that the knotted muscle pattern stood out as if it were cast in some gray metal.

Abruptly, Arnauth walked to his desk chair. He found a cigarette and lighted it, so preoccupied that there seemed no discourtesy in his failure to offer one across the desk. Suddenly the tension snapped. He broke his fixed stare at the desk top for a nervous glance at the package on the side table. The tremor of his hand corkscrewed the thin trickle of smoke that rose from his cigarette. Hoarse-voiced, he said, "Under the circumstances, Mr. Lord, the least I can do is to spare you the necessity of telling me why you are here. There's no need for it." A deep breath rasped in his throat. "For whatever it may mean to you — Irving Rubin is no longer with this company."

Rubin out . . . was Arnauth admitting . . . ?

"And I'm sure it's unnecessary to tell you that it was by request. Or at least I hope that it's unnecessary." Arnauth paused, waiting anxiously. "Surely, Mr. Lord, you're not imagining that what has happened was supported by the management of this company?" Again, he waited. And then he shuddered, the death of hope. "I see."

Lincoln Lord had not meant his failure to respond as an accusation — he had remained silent only because of this stunning confirmation of Joel Morris's long-shot guess about Rubin — but now the suspicion arose that Arnauth was attempting to evade corporate responsibility. Clamping his lips, he said nothing, attacking Arnauth with his own weapon, pressing him with the steel-cold force of unbroken silence.

Arnauth's eyes flickered uncertainly, finally coming to rest on the tip of his cigarette. "You may not believe this, Mr. Lord — I've no reason, I suppose, to expect that you might — but when you called, I was at the point of calling you. As a matter of fact, I did place the call. And then at the last minute I canceled it. I couldn't bring myself to face the possibility that you might think — " The spell of introspection broke, sight regained, and he looked across the desk, studying his face now with searching intensity. "You weren't thinking, were you, Mr. Lord, that my telling you about Rubin's resignation was an attempt to excuse myself?" He paused. "It is true that no one knew what he was doing — no member of the executive committee, no general officer of the company, least of all myself — but I'm well aware that ignorance gives me no excuse. I *should* have known. The responsibility is mine. I accept it. Believe me, this is not a pleasant situation — to have to admit to you that I've allowed this company to be put in a position —"

"I know," Lincoln Lord said, aware too late that he had broken his pledge of strategic silence, the words drawn out by the strong tug of transposition, remembering how many times he had found himself in Arnauth's place, bearing the burden of some betrayal of trust . . . but this was no time to go soft . . . Arnauth was assuming full responsibility . . . there'd have to be some kind of a payoff . . . yes, he could clinch it in a moment now . . . get Arnauth to agree to buy every can in that warehouse . . . a half-million-dollar order! But he had to be careful . . . take it easy. This was too big to fumble . . .

He set a fixed smile and said with calculated informality, "If you want me to be frank, Sid —"

"I do."

"I can understand, of course, that you were anxious to get your hands on Coastal Foods —"

Arnauth looked thunderstruck. "No, Mr. Lord — no, no —"

"But you did offer Mrs. Zurich — ?"

"That offer to Mrs. Zurich wasn't from Gellman Stores — it was Rubin, trying to buy Coastal Foods for himself."

"I'm sure that Anderson Phelps told me —"

"Yes, I talked to Phelps." Sidney Arnauth's eyes closed and, for a moment his face had the look of a death mask, finally restored to life with a shudder. "I finally remembered your having mentioned Phelps's name. That's what first tipped me off, you know — your telephone call."

"My call?"

Arnauth seemed not to have heard his question. "How much do you know about the past relationship between Gellman Stores and Coastal Foods?"

"A fair amount."

"You do know that the business was handled on a very personal basis, between Mr. Gellman and Mr. Zurich?"

"So I understand."

"Even during his last years, when Mr. Gellman was rather inactive as far as the rest of the company was concerned, he held on to Coastal Foods — that and a few other things — the coffee roasting plant —the bakeries."

A memory clicked and he asked, "The bakeries, I understand, you bought from Mr. Rubin?"

Arnauth looked up with sharp surprise. "Then you know the story?"

"No more than that."

"Perhaps I should tell you this," Arnauth said. "It does have a bearing on what's happened. It had always been Mr. Gellman's policy to stick to retailing, not engage in manufacturing or processing. When there was something to be packed under our own brand, he always preferred some such arrangement as the one with Coastal Foods — buying from a source owned by someone else but nevertheless closely enough tied to him so that he could maintain close quality control. That's how we had handled our baked goods — two bakeries in New York, one in Jersey, one up in Connecticut, and so on. Until a few years ago, it had been a quite satisfactory arrangement. Then we started to run into some quality trouble, particularly with some of our older bakeries that had changed hands. The situation got so bad that Mr. Gellman finally felt it necessary to buy these bakeries." He paused. "They were owned by Mr. Rubin."

Arnauth was obviously implying something beyond what he'd actually said, but Lincoln Lord was unable to guess what it might be. "Mr. Gellman, I understand, brought Rubin into the company as a vice-president."

"Yes — although not in the regular line of organization," Arnauth agreed hesitantly. "Rubin functioned more or less as a personal assistant to Mr. Gellman. It was sort of a bastard arrangement —" A bitter smile flickered. "No double meaning intended — applicable enough, god knows, but in all fairness I can't say that I objected to it. Mr. Gellman was getting old — needed someone with him — and I was so tied up with trying to finance the opening of thirty new supermarkets that I couldn't give him too much of my own time. I was opposed to buying the bakery chain — I felt that we needed the capital too badly for store expansion — but as far as Rubin himself was concerned —" He spread his thin-fingered hands. "I must admit that I saw no reason not to accept him as Mr. Gellman did — as a trustworthy and honorable man."

Arnauth reached for another cigarette, this time offering one across the desk, a gesture made with something approaching the polished urbanity that evidenced a return to normal behavior. But there was still the abnormality of his willingness to talk so freely, a sign that the stress under the surface was still there. Lincoln Lord's acceptance of the cigarette with an easily informal, "Thanks, Sid," was no less a betrayal of his own inner tautness — he rarely smoked.

"As Mr. Gellman's assistant," Arnauth continued, "Rubin was familiar with the things that Mr. Gellman had kept under his own wing, so after his death I called him in to discuss the Coastal Foods Company relationship. I had learned that there was no contract and I felt it important, now that Mr. Gellman was gone, that there be some formalization of the relationship. Rubin argued that Mr. Zurich would be greatly disturbed by any such proposal, that he would have suspected our motives, and that it was better to let things ride along as they had."

"I didn't know Mr. Zurich personally, but from what I've heard, I'm inclined to think that he would have welcomed a contract."

"I should have insisted upon it," Arnauth ruefully agreed. "In any event, a few months later, when I learned that Mr. Zurich had died — I was in Europe at the time — I sent a long cable to Rubin, asking him to contact Mrs. Zurich immediately and determine what her plans were for the continued operation of the company. The Mother Gellman line was extremely important to us — we'd made a great promotion feature of it — and I felt it essential to ensure a continuing source of supply, and the maintenance of the same quality standards that we'd had in the past."

"But you didn't tell him that you were interested in buying Coastal Foods?"

A headshake of denial was abruptly cut off. "Well, I did go this far — I told him that if Mrs. Zurich was not going to carry on, that if she was forced to sell control — I was thinking, of course, that she might be in a difficult inheritance tax situation — that we *might* consider buying the property. But only if it became absolutely necessary — that is, if there was a serious danger of its falling into hands that would jeopardize our interests."

"Perhaps Rubin took that as authority to make an offer."

"Absolutely not!" Arnauth said sharply. "When I returned, he reported that Mrs. Zurich was quite prepared to carry on, that all of the key plant personnel were staying with her, and that there was no reason whatsoever to be concerned. Until you called me two weeks ago, I had no suspicion whatsoever that there had been any change."

"You can't mean that you didn't know that Coastal Foods had been cut off as a source of supply?"

"Incredible as it may seem to you, I didn't." His cigarette stabbed out, an insistent pointer. "Do you remember what I told you when you called?"

"Very well."

"You asked me my opinion of the Coastal Foods Company?"

"Yes."

"I don't recall my exact words but I believe I told you, in substance, that I thought it to be one of the finest small food-processing plants in the country, and that we'd had excellent relationships over a great many years. Wasn't that the sense of what I said?"

"Almost word for word."

"And then I told you that I was tied up at the moment but that I would transfer your call to the man who handled our Coastal Foods account."

"That's right."

"Would I have done that if I'd known what the situation really was?"

"I'll have to admit it was a little confusing — your attitude set against Rubin's."

Sidney Arnauth cocked his head. "If you don't mind telling me — what did he say? Did he tell you that we were no longer doing business with Coastal Foods?"

"Yes —" he began, the rest of his answer cut off.

"But you knew it anyway, didn't you? Of course. Phelps knew it. Everyone did apparently — everyone but me. I didn't find it out until the next day — Friday, I believe. You called on Thursday?"

"That's right. Two weeks ago today."

"Your call disturbed me. Not at the moment — I was up to my neck in our new debenture issue — but I got thinking about it afterwards, wondering why you were interested. I knew your background, of course — president of Luxor Pharmacal and all that — and I couldn't understand why you'd be attracted to a little company like Coastal Foods. The only possibility I could imagine was that Mrs. Zurich had changed her mind about selling out and that you were contemplating buying the company."

Silence seemed the best response.

"The next morning I called in Rubin," Arnauth continued. "It was only then that I finally learned that we'd broken off with Coastal Foods. I was very much put out and criticized him for not having consulted me before any such drastic action had been taken, particularly in view of the kind of relationship that there'd been between Mr. Gellman and Mr. Zurich. However, Rubin maintained that he had been thoroughly justified in what he'd done. He had his alibi ready.

We have a system under which every store manager must make out a report on every complaint made by a retail customer. We keep a running summary here of those complaints for each source of supply. Rubin's defense was the record on Coastal Foods. It was incredibly bad — something over five hundred complaints in a month — and they were serious ones."

Fear hit Lincoln Lord a smashing blow, his vision blurred, his eyes finally settling on the package of wrapped cans . . . why hadn't Kennan admitted it . . . told him the truth? Swann must have known too . . . all those complaints . . .

Arnauth had gone on talking and, wildly groping, Lincoln Lord fastened on something that he thought he had just heard him say, "You said that you didn't know then — ?"

"Even if someone had told me the truth, I couldn't have believed it. It was too incredible! It still is. How anyone could stoop so low — the man's really a criminal. We're letting him off too easily, just kicking him out. But at least we finally caught up with him — thanks to Harry Cohen and Milt Blaustein."

Completely lost, unable to conjure up even a logical guess as to what Rubin had done, Lincoln Lord said as blandly as he could manage, "Yes, I was wondering about how you managed to trip him up," hoping that it might be enough to provoke Arnauth into revelation.

"We had a bit of luck there," Arnauth said. "On the Monday after I got Rubin's story, I brought the matter up at the executive committee meeting. I had no reason then to question his justification for having dropped Coastal Foods — the facts were there, the complaints record backed him up — but it did raise a serious question as to why our testing laboratory hadn't stopped this junk from getting into the stores. The lab boys were caught off base. They'd gone so many years without a single complaint on anything Coastal had packed that they'd stopped routine testing. That put Blaustein on the spot — he's responsible for over-all quality control — and he immediately wanted to know why standard procedure had not been followed in referring these complaints to his department in order that they could be followed up at the Coastal Foods plant. It developed that not one of these complaints had been sent to Blaustein. I thought, of course, that it was due to Rubin's lone wolf way of operating. He'd been carrying on pretty much as Mr. Gellman had done — outside the bounds of standard routine — so I made a note to see that he changed his tactics. Blaustein, however, didn't stop there. After the meeting, he started hunting through the files. He discovered that not only had he not been advised, but also that there was not a scrap of evidence to indicate that anyone at Coastal Foods had ever been told about these complaints. All he found was a brutal letter telling them that we were cutting them off as a source of supply."

"I know the letter."

"What aroused Blaustein's suspicion was that there was not a word in that letter about complaints. If that was the reason for cutting off Coastal Foods, why wasn't it mentioned? It seemed so illogical to Blaustein that he brought the letter to me. I was horrified. No matter what the circumstances, that just wasn't the way Gellman Stores did business with anyone, let alone a supplier that had been as close to us as Coastal Foods had been for so many years. I tried to call Rubin. He was out of town — supposedly working with this cannery that he'd picked to pack the Mother Gellman Line. When I called him there, he couldn't be reached. That was probably fortunate — if I'd talked to him, he might have concocted some sort of an explanation to throw me off the track. Anyway, I called a meeting and we sat around here most of Friday evening — just brain-storming the possibilities. Finally we hit something. Just as a wild stab in the dark, Blaustein asked if there was any possibility that anyone other than Coastal had ever packed anything under the Mother Gellman label. That sparked something in Harry Cohen's mind. He remembered that some weeks ago he'd been reviewing the label account — for some reason he'd gotten out the invoice file — and he'd noticed a no-charge memo-invoice covering some Mother Gellman labels that had been sent to some address in Newark. Maybe it was perfectly all right — we didn't know — but we played a hunch and had a couple of the boys follow it up. The address turned out to be a little Italian restaurant, a rathole of a place down in some industrial district. It looked like a dead end — a wrong address — but the boys snooped around. Out back they found a shed. When they looked in the window they saw a little can-filling machine and a double-seamer. This restaurant owner had been putting up his own spaghetti sauce. There was a junk heap and there our boys hit pay dirt — a bunch of Mother Gellman labels had been spoiled and thrown out."

"Good god, you don't mean — !"

A sigh of admission tore Sidney Arnauth's lips apart again. "I couldn't believe it! It's still like some crazy nightmare. How any hu-

254

man being could be so depraved as to deliberately pack up the filthy mess that Rubin had him put in those cans —"

"The man must be insane!"

"He is! Believe me, he is!"

"But what did he think he was going to accomplish?"

Arnauth shuddered. "He'd had this junk packed — every can a guaranteed complaint against Coastal Foods — and then somehow he got it fed out through our regional warehouses to our stores, never more than a case at a time into any one store. How he managed that, we don't know. He must have bribed some warehouse employees. We have a firm of private detectives working on it now. But, anyway, it happened. And then, of course, he had his complaint record against Coastal Foods. That was his alibi for changing sources."

Groggily, Lincoln Lord asked, "And he went that far just to force Mrs. Zurich to sell the company to him?"

"Apparently. At least we know this — sweated it out of him last night — as soon as you went into Coastal Foods, he bought into another cannery as a silent partner. You've probably guessed it by now — that's the cannery that he'd given the Mother Gellman business to."

The race to keep pace with Sidney Arnauth's revelations had, until now, been such a pell-mell dash that Lincoln Lord had been struck with only major implications. The climax reached, he looked back now at the jigsaw jumble of bits and pieces of information, trying to fit what Arnauth had told him to what he had picked up from Swann, Kennan, and Kira Zurich, even more pointedly from Joel Morris's astoundingly perceptive feat of deduction. The most easily seen misfit was what he had been told about Gellman Stores' desire to operate their own cannery, and he quickly phrased a question to Arnauth.

Astonishment predicted Arnauth's answer, "So that's the way he kept Coastal Foods quiet? Yes, I suppose they would accept that explanation. That's one aspect of this affair that I hadn't been able to figure out — why someone at Coastal Foods hadn't fought back."

"They tried. One of our young men — Joel Morris — spent a whole day in your waiting room trying to talk to Rubin. He wouldn't see him."

"Why didn't he see someone else?"

"The girl at the desk told him that she had instructions that no one from Coastal Foods was to be allowed to see anyone other than Rubin."

A groan escaped Arnauth's lips as he reached for a note pad.

255

Watching him write, Lincoln Lord asked, "I take it then that you didn't intend to operate the cannery that you got with the Silver Crescent merger?"

"Never! We put it on the market the day we got control. If we can sell it, we will. If we can't, we'll scrap it."

"It might interest you to know that Rubin offered our production superintendent a job as your plant manager."

"He what?" Arnauth crumbled as if struck a final blow. "Where in god's name is this thing going to stop? It's like a wormy apple — the deeper you dig, the rottener it gets." He sighed. "Yes, I suppose that was a part of his plot, too — keeping your man from suspecting."

Lincoln Lord chuckled, surprised at his ability to do so. "He'd have been in a tough way, wouldn't he, if both sides had started checking stories? With one hand, he kicked out Coastal Foods because of bad production and then, with the other, offered a job to the plant manager who turned it out."

Wearily, unable to see any humor in the situation, Arnauth said, "The man was simply insane. There's no other possible explanation. Even his basic plot was completely mad, frightening away customers from the very line that he was trying to cash in on. Complaints like that are murder — one bad can of anything in the line and you can lose business from a whole neighborhood. Thank god, we caught it in time and got the stuff off the shelves."

"When did you do that?"

"The moment we were sure what had happened. Fortunately, we had complaint records so we knew what the bad stuff was — chicken à la king, chicken and noodles, corned beef hash."

With sudden decision, Lincoln Lord rose and walked to the side table, ripping the wrapper of the package, quickly checking Joel's crayon marks. "This can of beef stew was bought last night about seven-thirty in your Atlantic City store."

Arnauth's thin body shot up from his desk, a lance hurled upward. "You don't mean that's bad, too? I thought we'd caught it all. I issued an order that not a can was to be sold that didn't come out of our old Coastal Foods stock. This must mean that there's still some of Rubin's junk scattered through our warehouse." A shuddering sigh broke in on his voice. "Is there any way to tell the good from the bad?"

"No easy way. But there is a difference in the way the label's put on. On our pack, there's a little mark that the rollers of the labeling machines make."

Embarrassedly, Arnauth asked, "Could your men tell the difference — show our inspectors what to look for? I know we've no right to ask favors after what we've done to you — but this brand is worth millions of dollars to us. We can kill it off in a hurry if we don't get stock back on those shelves and be certain that it's right. Could I possibly induce you to help us sort what we have in stock?"

"Well, it would be quite a job," he said cautiously, aware that the climax had suddenly been thrust upon him, the whole point and purpose of being here dependent upon the next move that he made, yet he found himself surprisingly clear-headed, quickly able to say, "Wouldn't it be more practical to get those store shelves filled from our stock?"

"Your stock? You don't mean that you've got — ?"

"A few thousand cases. I had planned to relabel it with our own brand —"

Almost frantically, all reserve lost, Arnauth reached out. "For god's sake, Linc, let us have it! I know that you're anxious to get your own line out — you have no interest in supplying us, you'd never have gone into Coastal Foods if you were — but can't you see what it would mean to us? We're going to be in a bad enough spot as it is. Naturally, we've canceled the contract that Rubin placed. We've still got to line up another source of supply. Even when we do, it's going to be weeks before — name your own price, Linc — we'll pay anything you ask — anything!"

"Oh, that won't be necessary, Sid. If we can help you —"

"Does that mean that you will? Thank god! At least this is one break. Let me call Mandel to get things rolling." His hand was on the telephone. Then he froze, "You did say, didn't you, that you were planning to relabel some of our stock and put it out as your own line? Does that mean that you're going to keep on packing the same kind of products? I thought, of course, that you had something else in mind — ?"

"Give me time." He smiled. "After all, I've only been president for four days."

"But if you were even considering —" He took a deep breath. "I know this is a long shot, Linc — you'll probably laugh at me for even suggesting it — but is there any chance, any chance at all, that you would consider taking back our business?"

His heart seemed to have stopped, his mind suddenly inanimate, fixed on a single memory . . . that night at Kingdom Come when he had been so afraid of rejection that he had been unable to ask Maggie to marry him . . . "Linc, I know you're not thinking about marrying me now, but is there any chance that you might ever ask me?"

5

The darkness of night had come early on this last Thursday of January. At noon, staring out across Barnegat Bay as she ate a lonely lunch, Maggie Lord had noticed that the blue sky of the morning had lost its pristine polish, scummed to grayness by a cirrus film. Later she had seen a cloud bank rolling in from the sea. Within minutes everything had been shrouded in gray-green mistiness, the sun blotted out. Then the wind had come in from the northeast, lifting the fog from the land but only to tree-top level, a low-hanging scud, ominous and depressing.

Sometime late in the afternoon she had thrown herself across the bed, never imagining that she would fall asleep. But she had, as deeply as if she had been drugged, and the telephone had only half-awakened her. She knew that it was Linc, and that he was telling her that he was back from New York, something about Gellman Stores and trucks and the warehouse stock and what a wonderful job Joel Morris had done; but by the time she had gained full comprehension he was saying, "Golly, Mag, it's too much to tell you over the phone — be home as soon as I can — but you'd better not hold dinner for me." And that had been the end, all that she could remember with any certainty, nothing beyond the vague feeling that he had said something about having a surprise for her. And then, after he had hung up, there had been this still-persistent feeling that she must have disappointed him with such a dull and lifeless response to whatever it was that he had been telling her.

The darkness into which she had awakened had shocked her into imagining that she had slept longer than she had, hardly able to accept the clock's reassurance that it had been less than an hour. She had showered and re-dressed in panicked haste, her mind occupied with the planning of a dinner that could be quickly prepared after Linc got home from the plant. She had found the chicken breasts in the refrigerator, the sauce finished and waiting, her luncheon plan quickly revived. But a half-hour in the kitchen had been more than enough to do what little else could be done in advance and then, loose-ended, still bothered by the feeling that she had failed a wifely duty because of the way she had answered the telephone, she had groped for some special offsetting attention, finally making canapés, fussing over their arrangement on a lace-doilied silver tray, arousing an induced gaiety that too quickly foundered on the accusing realization that it had been a long time since she had gone to the trouble of turning their pre-dinner cocktails into the pleasant little ceremony that Linc always enjoyed so much.

Going into the hall to be certain that there was Scotch in the liquor cabinet, her attention had been attracted to the big living room window by oddly eerie blades of light that were sweeping across the black sky. Studying them, she decided that she must be seeing the headlights of automobiles coming into the cannery, their high beams lifted as they came up the low hill from the railroad crossing, fanning the sky as they turned into the parking lot. She stepped out through the front door, listening, and once she thought she heard the roar of a truck motor over the sound of the wind; but her vague sensing of excitement seemed more logically explained by the atmosphere of impending storm than by anything that could possibly be happening at the plant.

Back in the house, slamming the door against the wind, she heard what seemed a distantly percussive echo. Then there was a second sound, unrelated, and she hurried toward the kitchen with a skipping run, thinking that Linc must have come in the back way, surprised when she flung open the kitchen door and saw Viola wiping her wind-watered eyes with a corner of the bright red scarf that still half-covered her head.

"Oh, Viola, you wouldn't have had to come back," she said, a not too successful hiding of her disappointment at being robbed too soon of her Thursday kitchen privilege.

"Wasn't nothing I could do 'cept come when I could," Viola said, with an out-of-breath chuckle. "First they call Big Charley and then it was Rita's man, he's gotta come to work too, and that's the last car anybody's got and I wasn't hankering none to walk all the way from Lizzie Pearl's. As 'twas, Rita's man couldn't get no closer'n the other side of the cannery, all them trucks jamming up the road, and I had to walk from there and that sure don't do these old feet of mine no good. But ain't it just wonderful, ma'am, Mr. Lord getting everybody's job back for 'em?"

"What did you hear, Viola?" she asked blankly, quickly rephrasing the question, substituting, "What are people saying?"

"You mean what they's saying about Mr. Lord?" Viola loosed a blues song moan of helplessness. "Ma'am, there just ain't no way to tell you all the things they's saying — everybody — down to Lizzie Pearl's and over at the beer place and all them men on the road, just everybody. They say it's a plain miracle, that's what, Mr. Lord being here only four five days and already they's all working again. You know what Lizzie Pearl does when that call comes 'bout Big Charley? She just throws herself back like she been took by the power and yells, 'Glory be to the God Jehovah!' And what I says to 'em is that they better be singing 'Glory be to Mr. Lord!' "

"Now, Viola —"

"I wasn't taking no name in vain," Viola protested. "You'd be mighty proud, ma'am, just hearing all they's a saying 'bout your husband." A giggle soared like a rising clarinet run. "Guess maybe I was putting on a little myself, Lizzie Pearl telling everybody I's the one that's cooking for you folks, and 'bout how I been saying it right along. You 'member that first day you folks was here? Lizzie Pearl was helping me here in the kitchen that day and right after I come back out from serving that soup I says to Lizzie Pearl that she don't have nothing to worry 'bout no more. Soon's I see Mr. Lord I says there's a man going get all them folks working again right away quick."

For a moment Maggie Lord suspected that Viola's unusual loquacity was traceable to that beer place she had mentioned, but her bubbling excitement seemed genuine enough and then, almost as if she had intuitively sensed suspicion, Viola's face sobered. "You just can't 'preciate what it means, ma'am, nobody having no pay, Rita's man and Big Charley and all them folks. 'Course now they got the unemployment, but that don't do more'n take care of them 'stallments they got, and a man ain't working he's just a pack of trouble, beerdrinking and fighting and all such. Lizzie Pearl she says I'm supposed to thank Mr. Lord for what he done, 'cause 'bout one more week and they'd been bad, all them menfolks would. That's the truth, ma'am, and Lizzie Pearl she just wants me to tell him so."

"I know Mr. Lord will be very pleased," Maggie said.

Viola was out of her coat now, reaching for an apron. "You folks ain't had no dinner yet, have you, ma'am?"

"No, but you don't have to worry about it, Viola. I've something all ready to cook as soon as Mr. Lord comes."

Without hesitation, Viola snugged down her apron strings. "Least

I can do is do what I can, ma'am. 'Tain't much compared to what Mr. Lord's doing for all my folks."

"But he's still at the office, Viola, and I've no idea when he'll get home."

"Midnight or not, don't matter to me," Viola said cheerfully. "You just show me what 'tis you got fixed to have and I'll be waiting with it whenever he comes."

Maggie gave up without further argument, showed her the chicken and the sauce in the refrigerator, hurriedly gave her directions, and escaped to the dining room window, curiosity rising higher and higher. After only a moment of hesitation, she snatched her coat from the hall closet, ran back to the bedroom for a scarf to tie over her hair, and then out into the darkness.

The night had turned colder than she had realized, the northeast wind driving a stinging spit of sleety snow, but the wind was half behind her, coming over her left shoulder, and with her head cocked to protect her face, she hurried on up the long drive, feeling herself exhilarated by the drama of the stormy night. Finally, at the break in the trees, she saw the plant as a skyrocket burst of light blazing at the end of a fiery shaft of headlights, trucks backed up so far that the end of the line was lost behind the unseen bulk of the high school building. This was as far as she had planned to go, stopping here at the trees, but she hesitated only long enough to remember that she had the excuse of messages for Linc . . . the long-distance call from Brighton . . . Kira Zurich's luncheon . . .

Closer now, the scene ahead of her brought back the memory of a circus being moved at night — floodlights blazing, trucks roaring, the black figures of distantly seen men scurrying about with anthill frenzy. Still closer, what she saw was resolved into an understanding, vague though it was, that all of Coastal Foods warehouse stock was being moved out in a mad overnight rush. Why it was happening she had no idea, and her lack of understanding rose as an accusation that she had failed to learn as much as she should have about what was going on at the company. She tried for a moment to shift the responsibility to Linc, blaming him for not having told her more, but the fault was too inescapably her own. She knew that he would have talked to her if she had shown more interest, if starting over again with another company had not been so wearisomely repetitious.

She was at the edge of the parking lot now, the office ahead of her, and through the big windows she could see that it was crowded with people, the flurry of activity less physically evident than out at the shipping platform, yet it was a scene no less supercharged with drama, immediately reminiscent of nights when she had shared the excitement that communicated itself through the windows... the nights when *Hearthside* went to press... the first night of the strike at Quincy Canning... all those nights when she'd been working with Linc and Brick...

Someone was coming out and, seeing her, held the door open for her, eliminating the need for final decision. She was inside the little lobby then, side-stepping the group of men clustered around the switchboard operator, slipping past before she attracted their attention, into the bigger office, suddenly aware of how windblown she must be when she found herself the focal point of glances from all over the room.

"Why, Mrs. Lord!" a feminine voice said beside her and, turning, she confronted a set smile that, although no more than hazily remembered, could be no other than Miss Payne's, identification made certain as she added with a heavy-handed attempt at jocularity, "I'll bet you've come over to help us, haven't you?"

She shook her head, unavoidably cool, yet a moment later when she saw Linc coming toward her, anxiously expectant, the call from Brighton and Kira Zurich's luncheon invitation seemed excuses so artlessly contrived that there was nothing left to say but, "I don't know that there's anything I can do to help, Linc, but if there is I'd be glad to."

"Golly, Mag, that's wonderful," he said, and she was completely unprepared for the look of gratitude that came into his eyes, an expression almost forgotten until this instant of welling association with the best moments of their life together. "Come on and give Joel a hand," he whispered, guiding her with a hand on her elbow. "Frank Kennan's all tied up trying to get those trucks rolling and Joel's taken over to call crews for tomorrow — that's the bottleneck now."

She wanted to ask him what had happened but was hesitant because of her embarrassed consciousness that she had not heard what he had told her over the telephone. They were beside Joel Morris's desk before she could say anything.

Joel shot to his feet, fumbling at his loosened tie, running a self-conscious hand through his tousled black hair, blinking his disbelief when Linc said that she was going to help him, then breaking into a smile of pleasure that was no less openly genuine for being more than slightly tinged with incredulity.

Linc left them and, slipping out of her coat, the way opened to questioning, she grasped at one of the few things she could remember from Linc's telephone conversation. "My husband told me that you've done something quite wonderful."

"Me?" Joel shot a glance at the president's office. "What I did was nothing, nothing at all — I mean compared with what he did. All I was hoping — gosh, I thought maybe we could get them to take some of the stuff we had in the warehouse, but I never imagined that we'd get *all* of their business back. He's really wonderful, isn't he, Mrs. Lord? I guess that's no news to you but — well, he's just terrific, that's all you can say about him."

She murmured an acknowledgment, asking no more questions for the moment, overwhelmed by the realization that by some miracle, as yet unexplained but momentarily unimportant, Linc had gotten back the Gellman Stores business. Her first reaction, conditioned by the fact that everything that Linc had said about the future of the Coastal Foods Company had been tied to the necessity of bringing out their own line of products, was that there had been an abandonment of objective. As Joel went on talking, however, she picked up from little remarks interjected into his explanation of their job tonight, a strong feeling that getting back the Gellman Stores business represented a rescue of the company from a situation far more dangerous than Linc had ever permitted her to know existed. And she learned, too, what was happening in the warehouse. Using a fleet of trucks that had been mobilized during the afternoon, drawn in from as far away as Trenton, more than two hundred Gellman Stores were being restocked overnight with a supply of Mother Gellman products, the trucks bypassing Gellman's slower system of regional warehouse distribution, making deliveries direct to stores in order that their shelves would be full tomorrow morning for the Friday crest of the consumer buying week, an operation so boldly conceived that even the two Gellman men who had come down from New York to draw up shipping schedules on the spot had thought it unworkable until they'd seen empty trucks come pouring in from the whole countryside and go rolling out again loaded with canned goods.

There were dozens of questions still unanswered but, with the main outline sketched in, Maggie quickly became absorbed in the job of rounding up a cannery crew for tomorrow's second shift. The first shift, already called, would be no more than a clean-up and break-in crew to get the plant turning over and ready for full production by the time a full second shift came on at three o'clock.

"If you don't mind doing it, Mrs. Lord," Joel suggested, "it would be a terrific help if you'd do the telephoning," explaining that while she was making one call he could be setting up another, checking names against personnel records and seniority lists, frequently soliciting the advice of the factory forewomen, who were all waiting in the check-in room, voluntarily standing by to be helpful in any possible way.

On the telephone, Maggie first began to feel the full impact of what this sudden turn of events meant to Goodhaven. What Viola had told her had not been, even in implication, an overstatement of the jubilant excitement that gripped the town. On almost every call, the ringing sound was instantly cut off by the receiver being snatched from the hook. Apparently there was not a home of any Coastal Foods employee where, tonight, someone was not sitting by the telephone. Even where the worker had no telephone, where the call had to be relayed through a neighbor, there was no delay — "Yes, ma'am, she's right here at my place waiting."

On the first couple of calls, automatically and without thinking, she had identified herself, starting off, "This is Mrs. Lord, calling from the Coastal Foods Company —" The reaction had been so fulsomely personal that, conscious of it, she stopped using her own name. But Joel had noticed it and, although shyly and tentatively, had insisted that she continue. "Gosh, Mrs. Lord, you just don't know what that means in a small town like this, the wallop that they'll get out of having you call them. They'll never forget it."

And so she had gone back to doing it, embarrassed, yet warmed as she had never been before by the outpouring of gratitude to her husband. She had often heard him praised, frequently in extravagant terms, but almost always before by people who had fallen under the unexplainable spell of his personality. These people who were singing his praises tonight had never even seen him, judging him entirely on results. Admittedly, they were influenced by material self-interest, yet it was after the fact rather than before it, gratitude freely given with no expectation of further future favor. So often in the past what Linc had done had seemed to be forgotten after the moment of accomplishment.

She was seated with her back to most of the rest of the office, able to see her husband only by turning her head, and now and then she glanced back over her shoulder as she listened on the telephone, hopeful as she heard some bit of praise, direct or indirect, that she might be able to convey its essence to him. Once or twice, he returned her smile but more often he was looking away from her, engaged in conversation with someone who had come into his office, and after a little time she stopped trying to catch his attention, storing appreciation for later when they would be alone together. But then, consciously attempting to remember remarks that could be quoted, she became aware of how difficult it would be to match those expressions of appreciation with any that she herself had voiced for a long time. In retrospect, she felt herself accused of having done almost nothing to keep alive the courage and spirit with which he had battled his way through this awful last year... he was really wonderful! And she wasn't a good wife at all... negligent... self-centered... doubting...

"Well, I guess that's it," Joel said suddenly. "This has been a terrific help, Mrs. Lord. If it hadn't been for you, it would have taken hours longer."

It was ten minutes to eight now. Aware that she had been sitting too long in a cramped position, she stood up and looked around the office. The crowd had noticeably diminished, most of the girls gone, and the atmosphere of tension had slacked off into an easy camaraderie. Linc was sitting on the corner of a desk, talking to Swann, who stood in the door of his office, and Frank Kennan, whose cold-flushed cheeks indicated that he had just come in from the shipping platform. Self-consciously, she looked away, thinking that she might search out the woman's rest room and do something about her still windblown hair but Linc called to her and, turning back, she saw Kennan and Swann step apart to make a place for her, not with the president's wife deference that she always found embarrassing but with an easy acceptance that she instantly sensed she had gained, fortunately if unwittingly, through having stepped in and gone to work with them.

Linc was talking about what had happened in New York, apparently having waited until the first-things-first rush was over to give them any of the details. She had missed the beginning and, obviously, the others had some background that she did not possess — something about Joel having discovered some cans of horribly counterfeited Mother Gellman products — but it was not difficult to pick up the thread of the story, her inability to comprehend Linc's account of what this man Rubin had done less disconcerting after she saw that her incredulity was shared by the others. During the years that she had been either in the business world herself or close enough to it to have an insider's vantage point, she had been exposed to scattered examples of ever-reaching greed, of men unbalanced by ambition gone wild, but she had never heard of anything even approaching the insane behavior evidenced by Rubin's mad plot. It was a story so shocking that she could easily understand Linc's motive when he concluded by saying, "I've told you about it because I think you've a right to know — there'll undoubtedly be situations where you won't be able to act intelligently without knowing what happened — but I do think it's important that it stop right here. We can do a lot of harm both to Gellman Stores and ourselves by ever letting this story get out." He paused, drawing a smile from Kennan as he added, "Particularly now that we're packing the Mother Gellman line again."

"I still don't see how they could possibly have let him get away with it," Swann said, vindictively grim.

She heard Linc explain, "I know how you feel, Alf — and I felt the same way myself until after I'd talked it out with Sid Arnauth. Strange things happen in business organizations, Alf, things that are hard to believe — and all the more so when they happen to you —"

"Remember your old pal Sterling," Kennan said to Swann in a hoarsely humorous whisper, bringing a self-conscious flush of admission to the office manager's face.

Linc went on, "The worst thing that any of us could do now would be to go on harboring any ill-feeling or resentment toward Gellman Stores. They were tricked by an insane man — they took a beating because of it — so did we — but that's water over the dam now. We've got a big job to do, a lot bigger than it was before, and we aren't going to get that job done if we go into it with any holdbacks or reservations of any kind."

"I'll buy that," Kennan said.

Swann asked suspiciously, "What do you mean, Mr. Lord — a bigger job than it was before?"

"We're no longer prohibited from selling in the same territory where Gellman has stores," Linc replied, a calmly tranquil revelation, his perfect poise made all the more evident by contrast with Swann's thunderstruck face.

"You mean we're free to pack their stuff under our own label?" Kennan burst out. "How in the name of — man, you must have really done a job over there!"

"After all, it was never a very reasonable requirement — a recipe for beef stew or chicken and noodles isn't exactly patentable — and Mr. Arnauth is a very reasonable man." But there was a twinkle in Linc's eye. "And of course he *was* just a little anxious to get this stuff we've got in the warehouse rolling out to those stores."

Kennan's rough chuckle was far more an expression of awed admiration than an appreciation of humor.

"Well, you fellows still have some work to do," Linc said. "And there's not much I can do to help, so Mag and I will get out of here and let you get at it."

Unnoticed, Joel Morris had been standing behind her and, brief as the moment of general leave-taking was, it gave him time enough to find her coat and bring it to her.

"You've had a big day, boy," Linc said to Joel over her shoulder. "You'd better knock off and get a little rest."

"Before long," Joel promised — and, then, his throat moving with the muscle movement of swallowing, he made an embarrassed attempt at compliment, fumbling words that Maggie heard cut off by Linc's laughing refusal to listen. Her husband's modesty was understandable and praiseworthy, yet she felt instant sympathy for Joel, knowing the torture of being unable to say what needed to be said — a failure of expression that plagued her again now as they crossed the little entrance lobby and stepped out into the night. The spirit of her heart made her want to flood her husband with an outpouring of gloriously blended love and appreciation, but all that came out of her lips was a soul-sickening little, "My, it's getting cold."

"Over here," Linc said, turning her with an arm thrown around her shoulders, reaching out toward a blacker black in the shadow of the building, opening a car door. There was an orientating flash of memory ... yes, Joel had said that he'd come back ahead of Linc ... maybe he'd rented a car again. But this was no Cadillac ... one of those expensive foreign cars ...

In the seconds that it took Linc to go around to the door on the other side, she was battered by the recollection of the extravagant spending that had always been triggered by Linc's optimism every time he had started on a new job, so often recalled during these last months when it would have meant so much if they had only saved a small part of the money that he'd so blithely tossed away. She had been imagining that this time it would be different ... all their back bills paid before ...

In the instant when Linc's face was illuminated by the light that flicked on when the door opened, she caught a change of expression on his face ... Kip's face when he'd squandered his whole allowance on some silly extravagance ... this car wasn't rented! He'd bought it!

"Told you I had a surprise for you," he said in the darkness.

"But, Linc, what in the world is it?"

"Pantheon," he said. "Italian. You've seen their ads, haven't you — 'The Car You'll Drive the Rest of Your Life'?"

"Well, I knew it wasn't a Cadillac —"

"I thought it was time for a change," he said, strangely sober. "Five Cadillacs in ten years —"

Suddenly she felt her body propelled as if incited by a compulsion so long lost that flinging her arms around his neck was an act expressly invented for this moment, and the fiercely driving press of his lips was a full forgiving of her secret sin, a glorious release from all her love-destroying doubts and fears.

V

DEFYING the prediction of the weather-wise, the winter storm that had begun late Thursday had blown itself out ahead of schedule. Instead of turning into the three-day northeaster that the local citizenry had knowingly forecast, there had been an overnight wind-shift, the gale quickly abating. A gray overcast had persisted through most of yesterday but this Saturday morning had dawned bright and clear, the trees quickly freed of sleet, the snow melting rapidly. Coming out of the office building at noon, Lincoln Lord felt the springtime warmth of the sun and his pace slowed as he crossed the parking lot. There was no hurry. He had more than enough time to stop by the house, pick up Maggie and drive out to Haven Home to keep their luncheon date with Kira Zurich.

Although the weather was perfectly attuned to his mood, his state of mind was not a product of what had happened in the vast reaches of the sky but rather of what had gone on during the past two days within the four walls of the Coastal Foods Company. These last forty-eight hours had opened an entrancing vista, a prospect so appealing that he was only now beginning to accept its implications. He had lived so long with fear that it was still difficult to comprehend all that it meant to be freed of any concern about the future. Under the terms of his employment contract, his earnings could hardly drop below sixty thousand dollars a year as long as the Gellman business could be retained, and with the lesson that Sidney Arnauth had been taught, the chance that Coastal Foods would ever again lose the Gellman Stores account was extremely remote. All that had to be done now was to keep the company operating with reasonable efficiency. From what he had observed since Thursday night, that was going to be an almost unbelievably simple task.

Driving back to Goodhaven from New York, he had been afraid that the Coastal Foods Company, understaffed and without the benefit of the modern organizational structure that he had not yet had time to develop, would almost certainly prove inadequate to the task of fulfilling his bold promise to Sidney Arnauth that, overnight, every Gellman Store from Connecticut to Maryland would be restocked with at least a representative selection of Mother Gellman products. Yet somehow that promise had been kept, the fact of final accomplishment no less astounding than the apparent ease with which the job had been done.

Joel's idea, telephoned from New York, that a fleet of local trucks might be mobilized had been quickly implemented through Frank Kennan's personal acquaintance with every truck owner within fifty miles of the plant. By the time Lincoln Lord had driven into the parking lot, the shipping platform was jammed with a line-up of waiting trucks. No less amazingly, Kennan had somehow assembled a small army of warehouse workers and, under his quietly confident direction, the stuff was being moved out to the platform as fast as the trucks could take it away. Even Swann, who had heretofore seemed inflexibly frozen against innovation, had stepped in with a hastily devised system that had turned what might have been paper-work chaos into an effective control procedure.

Although it had seemed on Thursday night that Kennan was totally occupied with his personal direction of the warehouse activities, he had pulled off an amazing feat of left-handed legerdemain by somehow managing to issue all the orders that were necessary to get the cannery operating again. Mike Schlager, the chief engineer, had quietly slipped into the role of acting superintendent, moving ahead in perfect accord with a schedule that apparently existed only in Kennan's mind, transferred to Schlager by extrasensory perception. This same method of communication seemed to exist all through the company. Nothing was committed to paper and there were no committee meetings, yet everyone seemed to know what to do and how to do it. Raw materials had started flowing into the receiving dock before daybreak, and within three hours after a full crew reported for the morning shift, filled cans were already coming off the first line. This morning, all three lines were running smoothly, and Kennan had reported that, barring accident, the total pack would come within a hundred cases of plant capacity.

The speed with which Coastal Foods' seemingly unorganized organization had moved off the dead center of a complete shut-down and accelerated to almost capacity production had called up in Lincoln Lord's mind a contrasting circumstance during his last year with Luxor Pharmacal when it had suddenly become necessary to reopen the Brooklyn plant. There, with all of the meetings that had been necessary to ensure the co-ordinated action of eleven different departments, fifteen days had elapsed before the plant was back in production. To his amazement now, that had then seemed a creditable accomplishment, possible only because of efficient organization and reported to the board of directors with honest pride. Coastal Foods had accomplished that same end in less than two days.

Lincoln Lord could now see that he had made a most fortunate escape from a serious delusion. Until Thursday night he had thought of Coastal Foods as an out-dated company, a product of Sol Zurich's old-fashioned operating methods, and he had visualized his own function as that of introducing and applying the scientific principles of modern management. This morning, reviewing what had happened, he had decided that the wisest course he could possibly follow would be to leave everything exactly as it was.

This conclusion had not been easy to accept. Over the years his mind had been conditioned to the belief that constant change was the demanded measure of accomplishment. He had trained himself into a state of perpetual dissatisfaction, the reaching of one goal only a signal that another had to be set, more distant and more difficult. He had long since accepted the creed that any company president who, for more than the briefest of passing moments, permitted himself to luxuriate in relaxed satisfaction with the status quo was yielding to professional sin. Yet, rising against that code, there was now the feeling — largely subconscious but nevertheless governing — that this wonderful sense of well-being that he was now experiencing was his reward for having endured all those years of strain and tension. Never had he known what it meant to walk out of his office, as he had just done, without a mind loaded down with problems to be solved and decisions to be made. Never before had he left his desk without the feeling that it would surely become, the moment his back was turned, the storm center of some new disaster.

There were, of course, decisions that would have to be made — Joel

271

had been something of a nuisance this morning with his eager-beaver anxiety to get going on their own line — but nowhere, even looking years ahead, was there any potentiality of real trouble, no problems that would even remotely approach the seriousness of those that had been thrust upon him in ever-mounting numbers over the years. Here at Coastal Foods there would be no multimillion-dollar gambles on television programs, no bond issues to pilot through the wolf-denned canyons of Wall Street, no shock troop of tax lawyers to direct in the never-ending warfare with Internal Revenue, no harassment from gangster-led unions, no strength-sapping struggles between vice-presidents, no more anxiety over sharp-tongued stockholders — and, most important of all, no more board meetings where he would have to confront cold-eyed directors to whom nothing mattered but the net profit figure, a drop of a penny a share excuse enough for the gut-twisting torture of disapproval. That could never happen here. Coastal Foods did have a board of directors but its existence was no more than the filling of a legal requirement of incorporation, a meaningless entity shorn of power by the way Sol Zurich's will had put all control in his widow's hands — and Kira, even more certainly than had been true before Thursday night, had transferred that authority to him. For the first time in his life, freed of all fear, he was truly in control of a company.

He could smile now at the recollection that he had imagined, before he had met her, that Kira Zurich might turn out to be another Cornelia Rabson, a thought incited now by parallelism of circumstance. But this luncheon today would be nothing like those horrible noons when old Cornelia would insist that he come out to share her rye crackers and grated carrots, sipping green tea made all the more bitter by her perpetual suspicion that he was in league with her incompetent sons — all of whom she was sure were banded against her — robbing her of her marriage right to pile up capital as rapidly as had been done by her rapaciously money-hungry husband. Kira was no Cornelia Rabson. The only reason that she was inviting them to lunch today was to give herself a chance to express, more adequately than she had been able to do when he had called her on Thursday night, her appreciation for the speed with which he had made good on his promise to restore to the Coastal Foods Company the security of a guaranteed future. If this luncheon produced any problem it would arise from the truth being almost indistinguishable from pretentious modesty . . . and yet, confound it, it hadn't been all luck either! If he hadn't handled Sid Arnauth as well as he had . . .

Commandingly, his sense of sight took control of his mind. The Pantheon was directly in front of him now, sleekly black and blatantly foreign, and he felt an insistent shudder of embarrassment at this evidence of behavior so wildly impetuous that, were it not for this physical evidence of guilt, he would scarcely have been able to believe that he had done what he so plainly had. In his present state of mind it was impossible to credit the full intensity of the madness that had burst upon him as he had come out of Sidney Arnauth's office. He could see the man involved only as someone other than himself, an errant underling to whom he owed the effort of attempted understanding . . . yes, under certain circumstances, a man might possibly do something of this sort . . . the sudden release of anxiety . . . all those months of worrying about money . . . never buying anything for himself, not even a new necktie . . . counting the small change in his pocket . . . going bareheaded to duck hat-check tips . . . charging his lunches at the Greenbank Club . . . yes, it was credible that if a man who had been tortured by that sort of humiliation were suddenly to hit the jackpot . . . walking blindly down the street . . . seeing that phony Englishman with the blonde mustache looking at him through the window of the Pantheon showroom . . . daring him to step inside . . .

His hand closed over the door latch, a dream-matched action, and the opening of the car door was the shattering of objective detachment. A smile broke as he got in the car, secret and self-conscious, and now there was no temptation to dissociate himself from the scene, no disposition to deny himself the amusing memory of the way the needle-pointed ends of that silly mustache had trembled as he strode past, right back to the manager's office . . . sure, it had been a foolish thing to do . . . crazy! But why not? He could afford it, couldn't he? Had to have some kind of a car, didn't he? After all, it hadn't cost much more than a Cadillac . . .

The force of argument drained away, thinned by the hothouse warmth that the sun was pouring in through the glass, and he settled back with the contented realization that there was no point now in attempting to rationalize something that didn't need to be rationalized . . . Maggie understood. And she hadn't been criticizing him, anyway . . . he'd taken it the wrong way, that strange look on her face when she had first seen it . . . his own conscience . . . but why? There was

273

nothing foolish about the Pantheon . . . cheaper in the long run . . . a car that would last a lifetime . . .

He started the motor and the bee-buzz hum filtered into his brain, the lazy sound of a misplaced July day, hot and still. For a long moment he sat looking out at the blue water of the bay, watching a fisherman's boat as it cut a slowly curling wake across the glassy surface . . . maybe they could pick up a sailboat this summer . . . Maggie had always liked sailing . . . that skipjack of Brick's . . . the night they had sailed out to the island . . .

Suddenly, as if the car were thought-directed, it spurted up the drive, quickly leaving the plant behind. Then, mood sensitive, it slowed itself as it broke through the cut in the trees, coasting contemplatively down the long lane to the house. And now the warmth that surrounded him was not the false heat of summer but the flesh warmth of Thursday night — and the slow approach was a purposeful savoring of the mystery of love.

What had happened at the plant, surprising as it had been, was tangibly explainable. He could not understand, however, except in the most vague and inadequate of terms, what had happened in his relationship with Maggie. Of the two miracles, this was in every way the greater, all the more astonishing because he had not realized how much had been lost, how much there was to be regained. He had thought that a state of passion high enough to blank all other consciousness had been, if not something lost with the years, at least a possibility so dimmed by time that he would never again experience a peak of climax beyond all comprehension — and then, no less wonderfully, the slow flooding of this still persisting sensation, this feeling of tension forever released, his whole being bathed in this all-pervasive warmth that was, as the only certainty, something that Maggie had given him as a gift of love.

There had been no need for words, for the whispered ritual of question and answer that had become their long-practiced rite for the arousal of passion — and that wordlessness had been a part of the wonder of the moment. It had been a time of truth, unspoiled by the asking of any question that could not be answered without recourse to some trite response that would have been, if not untrue, at least a distortion to fit sentimental convention. Maggie might have asked him, as she so routinely did, to describe the exact moment when he had first known that he was in love with her and, as always, he would have been forced to repeat the answer that he had given her the first time when, fearful that the truth would be misunderstood, he had fallen back on a romantically acceptable citing of that moonlight night when they had taken Brick Mitchell's little Chesapeake skipjack and sailed out to the island off Kingdom Point. Once told, that story had been forever unchangeable. But the true moment of first love, never mentioned but more surely marked than any other, had been on that evening of a hot August day at the Quincy Canning Company when Maggie had come back to the office to help him with the talk that Mr. Quincy had asked him to make to a wholesaler grocers convention. He had stood watching her as she sat at her typewriter that night, her soft hair damp-ended with perspiration and impatiently pushed back from her ears, a smudge of carbon black on her cheek, so intent upon helping him make a success of his first speech that she had been surely oblivious of any way that he might have evidenced the first sensation of rapture. That had truly been the beginning of love, yet admission had been made impossible by the fear that if he were to tell her so, she would think his love no more than gratitude for something that might have been done as well by a clever clerk and a neat typist.

That had not been the only time when there had been an association between the sharing of some enterprise and the rise of a passion so far beyond all ordinary bounds that it could only be credited as a manifestation of love. The first time that they had achieved a consummation that was something above and beyond the satisfaction of physical need had been one night in Chicago, months after their marriage, when Maggie had worked until long after midnight on some charts that he was going to use the next day in a sales-meeting presentation of the Quincy line. Neither then nor afterward had he ever been able to tell her that when she was doing something to help him — coming to the office as she had night before last — that she was satisfying a hunger that lay very close to the core of his being, something that had been there since childhood.

Although the relationship of boy to man was unrecognized, Lincoln Lord's memory of his mother was nevertheless dominated by the recollection of the times when he had gone to her for help with some homework school problem only to have her tell him, as if she thought it was a compliment, that he was perfectly capable of doing everything himself. His mother, like so many of the people who had later come into his life, judged self-sufficiency to be the most desirable of all traits of male character. To him, it had never been worth the price of loneli-

275

ness. If he had ever been able to tell Maggie that love had begun when loneliness had ended, he would have been close to essential truth. She was the first person who had ever understood that he wanted to be helped, that there was a need within him that could be satisfied only when he was.

But there was another need, too, and these last ten years had been tortured by the conflict that had been aroused when this second need could no longer be satisfied without sacrificing fulfillment of the first. As much as he had needed Maggie's active participation in his work, less for what she actually did than for what was implied by the doing, there had also been a demanding need for her unwavering approval. What she gave him was something quite different from the applause that came at the end of a speech, the sycophantic congratulations of a vice-president, the mass smile of a board of directors when he turned in a good earnings report. That kind of praise, momentarily pleasant though it was, had too often turned out to be only an acknowledgment that he had lived up to expectations. Disillusionment had taught him that Maggie's approval was the only reward that had any meaning, and it had been the urge to ensure its unwavering continuance that had made him sacrifice, after the Union Packing days, the strength that had always come from having her share his business life.

He had not been required to make any such decision — it had come about naturally enough when he had made the move to Frazer Glass, where there was no longer any direct application of Maggie's experience in the food business — but he had, nevertheless, welcomed the chance that it had given him to compartment his life, building a wall between his home and his office that would keep his wife from getting so close to the business that she would be blinded from seeing his real accomplishments. Maggie would not have been able to understand that when you got into a big company so many problems flooded the president's desk that no man could make the right decision on every one of them; that you had to gamble, trust other people's judgment, back your hunches, play the percentages, hope that you would be right more often than not. One of the troubles, of course, had been his mistake in letting Maggie work too closely with Brick Mitchell. In the beginning it had gone well enough, but then Maggie had lost sight of the fact that what he had wanted from Brick — criticizing everything he did, searching out every flaw, questioning every judgment he made — was not at all what he wanted from her. What he needed from Maggie was the strength that came from her approval . . . believing in him

... and this time she had believed! That was the amazing thing, the way she'd been so certain right from the beginning that Coastal Foods was going to work out ... accepting Goodhaven as her home ... "Oh, Linc, I could live here the rest of my life" ... yes, Maggie had believed ... and that was what had carried them through. No, it wasn't luck ... it was Maggie's faith ...

Almost as if it were the materialization of a vision, he saw her now, tripping down the steps of the house as he let the car glide to an easy stop, her figure still so wonderfully youthful, her smile as brightly anticipatory as it had been when she used to run out to meet him when they had been living in the guest house at Kingdom Come.

"I tried to catch you at the office but just missed you," she said, leaning down to the window. "Kira called a few minutes ago."

Hope leaped. "The luncheon's off?"

She understood. "Oh, I wish it were. It's much too glorious an afternoon to waste. But no, she wants us to come as early as we can — right away. You're all right, aren't you? You don't have to change or anything?"

"No, I'm all right."

She came around and got into the car. "Maybe we can get away early."

"Hope so. Such a beautiful day. I wish we could run out and look over the beach."

"Oh, Linc, let's!" she said eagerly. "This shouldn't take too long. It isn't a party or anything, just the four of us."

"Four? Who else?"

"Dr. Perrill."

For an instant a thought-shadow of apprehension fell on his mind. But it was quickly gone, the sun-warmth brought back by Maggie's voice. "Oh, Linc, I've had such an exciting morning! Do you know what I discovered? There's a storage room behind the den. I didn't even know it was there until Viola showed it to me. And, Linc, it's just full of the most wonderful things. There's a whole set of summer draperies and slip covers — simply beautiful! And Kira never even had them out of their boxes. Can you imagine? And Viola — honestly, I think she's having as much fun as I am. She's so proud of the house and apparently Kira just — well, anyway, Viola says that she's mighty happy with her new white folks."

He chuckled at her mimicry of Viola's accent. "Well, you can just tell Viola that her white folks are mighty happy, too."

"I did." Her laughter was the sound of joy.

"So you think you're going to like it here?" he teased, whipping the car around in a tight turn.

"Like it? I love it! Oh, Linc, you were so right to take this job, so wonderfully right!"

"It was a lucky break," he said, fishing for denial, pleased when he saw her shake her head.

But she said only, "You deserve it, Linc," warmly yet somehow disappointingly, and before he could say that the credit was more hers than his, she had asked, "Everything still going all right at the plant?"

"Fine," he said, hesitating for the moment that it took to banish the suspicion that there had been an odd overtone of concern in her voice, silence extended then as they drove up the lane toward the pines, conscious that starting to give her a detailed report on what was happening at the plant would be the unlatching of a door that, once opened, could never be closed — but he could imagine no reason why he would ever again want it to be. "Frank got the third line going this morning. Started right off without a hitch. We're running all-out now. Oh, there are a few little bugs here and there — some new girls that have to be broken in — lost a few of the old gals with the shutdown — but by tomorrow we'll be right up to capacity."

"You're working Sunday?" she asked, picking up his businesslike tone.

"Have to. No other way we can catch up. Frank's juggling shifts to give everyone a day off during the week. Nothing else we can do. We'll have to run seven days for at least a month. Maybe longer. It's going to take quite a while just to get those Gellman shelves filled again. After that, we'll still have to build up our own inventory — get in a service position again."

"How long will it be before you can bring out your own line?"

For an instant he regretted his decision to talk business with her. "Golly, I don't know, Mag. Depends on how fast we can get some stock ahead."

"But you're still planning to do it?"

What was the matter with her today...pushing him...as bad as Joel.

"Aren't you?" she insisted.

"Of course. But it's going to take time to get things worked out. We have to pick the line — get a brand name — labels — lot of things to do. Have to build up a distribution organization, too. And you don't do that in a day."

"How are you going to sell — through brokers?"

"I suppose so," he said impatiently. "Oh, we'll probably have to have some men of our own, too. I don't know. Haven't had time to think it through yet. After all, it's only been two days —"

"I'm sorry," she said, pleasantly apologetic. But then she spoiled it by asking, "Are you going to make Joel your sales manager?"

He made no reply, excused by the road fork ahead of them. "Which way do we go? Down through town?"

She gestured toward the road that swung past the plant. "You turn right at the high school."

He drove ahead, wishing that he could recapture the lightheartedness that had somehow been lost . . . Mag was wonderful when she was herself . . . Thursday night . . . if she would just forget business! But it was his own fault . . . telling her too much . . . shouldn't have told her about bringing out their own line. Now if he decided not to do it, she'd think . . .

"Here's the road, Linc."

He braked hard to keep from overshooting the half-hidden corner, the sideroad angled back sharply to clear the glass-walled wing of the new high school building. Then, the turn negotiated, he had to brake quickly again to avoid hitting a stalled car, a sign-plastered jalopy that a crowd of boys in bulky orange and black athletic sweaters were trying to push off the road. Maggie looked back as they passed and he saw her face go enigmatically taut.

"What's the matter?" he asked.

"Nothing." The mask broke. "There was a letter from Kip this morning."

"Anything in it?"

"Nothing special."

"Oh." He guessed what she was leading up to, annoyed, yet knowing that if he didn't settle it right now, she'd go on worrying about it. "That last tuition payment is due, isn't it? Overdue, I guess. Have to get a check off." Her lack of response made him look squarely at her. "You did get a bill, didn't you?" She was avoiding his eyes. "What's wrong, Mag?"

Suddenly she burst out, "I walked over here yesterday afternoon and — oh, Linc, it's a beautiful school. I don't know what you'll think — maybe you won't agree at all — but I can't help but believe it would be better for Kip if we brought him down and put him in school here. I know you want him to be at Forgehill —"

Her questioning pause, oddly argumentative, caught him unaware. "I don't hold any special brief for Forgehill. It's a good school but —"

A burst of exultant joy exploded. "Oh, Linc, Linc, Linc — please let's do it! It would be so wonderful to have him here with us."

"Well, if it's what you want —"

"It's not just a question of what I want, Linc. It would be so much better for Kip. And we do have room for him now. There's that bedroom —"

"All right," he said quickly . . . Maggie was herself again . . . so wonderful . . .

"Do you mean that you wouldn't mind?"

"Why should I? Don't you think — ?"

Her hands were suddenly on his shoulder, her lips pressed hard against his cheek.

He caught the steering wheel as the car, momentarily out of control, bumped the grassy shoulder of the road. "Hey, you're a dangerous gal to —"

"I'm sorry," she said, quickly contrite, but her eyes were dancing, a little girl's apology, free of any fear of punishment.

"Happy now?" he asked.

"Completely!" She wriggled down into the soft leather of the body-cupping seat. But after a moment she asked, "Do you think I ought to run up there Monday morning? Dr. Summerfield was so nice about taking Kip —"

"Maybe we ought to leave him there for the rest of the term, finish out the —"

"Oh no!" Her alarm startled him. "All I meant was that — I suppose we do owe Dr. Summerfield some kind of an explanation. And there is an early morning train that gets to New York in time to catch the nine-ten up to —" She stopped. "What's funny?"

"You."

"What about me?"

"The way you had everything all set — even the train picked out. Doesn't sound like you were worrying very much about my letting you down."

Her hand reached out to the steering wheel, covering his, gripping hard. "You've never let me down, Linc."

He felt suddenly sobered. "That's not true, Mag. I've let you down — plenty. Lots of times."

"Never!"

"Sure I have." Strange how easy it was to talk to her now . . . Thursday night . . . even *wanting* to say it . . . "I'm not kidding myself, Mag. These last couple of years — I don't know, sometimes I've felt like I was completely off the beam — wasting so much time — that Japanese business —"

"Linc, that wasn't wasted."

"Oh, we had a trip that we'd probably never have gotten otherwise, but as far as accomplishing anything —"

"You've never heard anything from Washington about your report, have you?"

"No, not a word."

"But still it wasn't a waste, Linc. Things do work out. Even little things. If we hadn't gone to Japan you'd never have met Dr. Ichakuri. Did I tell you that Dr. Perrill had cabled him?"

"No," he said, feeling again that chilling mind shadow of apprehension, positively associated now with the mention of Perrill's name. Only half-listening to Maggie's explanation that Kira had told her that Dr. Perrill had cabled to Tokyo and that an answer had come back from Ichakuri, he searched his mind until he found a sensitive spot that, touched, made him ask, "You don't suppose do you, that that's why Kira's inviting us over to lunch — to give Perrill a chance to go into his baby food pitch?"

He heard first the wordless sound of puzzled inquiry, then Maggie's concerned voice saying, "But I told you Thursday night, Linc. Don't you remember? I said that she'd invited us because she wanted you to have a chance to hear Dr. Perrill's story."

"But that was before we got the Gellman business back," he said. "We don't need it now."

"You wouldn't want to put his baby food in your own line?"

"Start out with a product that's sure to flop? That would be the worst thing we could possibly do."

"You don't think that there's any hope that it would sell?"

"Not a chance."

"What's wrong with it, Linc?"

"Everything." He was aware that his voice had raised to a sharply argumentative pitch, and he quickly lowered it. "Joel spent a whole year making a study of the marketing possibilities — beautiful job, absolutely professional, as good a report as you'll ever see — and he came to the conclusion that there wasn't a chance in the world that you could ever put it over."

"But why?"

What the devil was the matter with Mag today . . . fighting him . . . trying to prove that he was wrong . . . had Kira sold her a bill of goods . . . ?

With the sudden exercise of tight self-control, he forced his brain to flash the image of the summary sheet of Joel's report, unseen since Wednesday but still photographically sharp, in perfect focus. "The basic fault — the thing you just can't get around — is the way the stuff tastes."

"But they are feeding it to babies, aren't they? Kira told me when I was over here before —"

"You don't sell baby food to babies, Mag. You sell it to mothers. And when a mother tastes something that she thinks is spoiled, something that tastes as if it were moldy —"

"Is it really as bad as that?"

A direct retort was blocked by self-conscious awareness that he had not actually tasted it himself. "It isn't only the taste. You'd have to sell a whole new concept in child nutrition. In order to get people to accept it, you'd have to unsell them on just about everything they believe now about the way children should be fed. You'd have to sell the whole medical profession — doctors, nurses, hospitals — Mag, it's just hopeless. You could spend ten million dollars for advertising and it wouldn't be a drop in the bucket — or at least that's what Joel says."

"But doesn't Kira realize that?"

"How do I know? I haven't talked to her about it — except that first time we were down here. What did she say to you?"

"Nothing more than she said then, just that — well, I think she feels an obligation to Dr. Perrill. He's spent so many years working on it."

"But if all she wants is to do something to please him —"

"Maybe I'm wrong," Maggie broke in. "Maybe she isn't really pushing it. But even if she is — Linc, that doesn't mean you *have* to do it. She's given you complete authority to run the company. And she means it, I know she does. All she asked you to promise that first day we were here was that you'd consider it. And that's all you *did* promise, Linc. She admitted that she didn't know whether or not it had any commercial possibilities —"

"I know, I know," he interrupted ... it was happening again ... always some crazy idea ... Coates and his wild dream that something could be done with the hand-blown department at Frazer Glass ... K. C. Wright wanting Luxor to sponsor the Philharmonic broadcasts ... *"I'm just suggesting it, Linc — use your own judgment."* But they never really meant it ... no, they wanted you to go ahead regardless ... damned if you do and damned if you don't. If it flopped, they could blame you ... your judgment ... but it was even worse when you didn't. When they got a bug in their bonnet, it burrowed in like a tick ... festering ... a sore that never healed ... K. C. killing the advertising budget when it got up to the board. Maggie didn't know anything about that ... no, he'd never told her ... she wouldn't understand anyway. She didn't realize that you had to play the game ... try to get along ... humor them. Kira was going to be like all the others ... this yen for Perrill ... old Cornelia Rabson and that banker ...

He heard Maggie warn him that the turn was just ahead, a whisper against the suddenly heard sound of Otis Sellcox's rasping voice ... *"Forget everything except getting your name on that payroll ... and once you've got it there, for god's sake make it stick ... you can't be this lucky again."*

2

Absent-mindedly exploring the faint trace of fuzz on his bone-bald head, Henry Lee Perrill, M.D., Sc.D., sat watching a male cardinal at the feeder outside the laboratory window, speculating upon the adaptation to environment that had so well equipped *Richmondena cardinalis* to nourish itself upon man's foible of judging worth by external coloration. Strip that gaudy red plumage and what did you have? Would the girls in the laboratory be feeding it sunflower seeds at twenty cents a pound if it weren't for those fancy feathers?

As if suddenly aware of a critical presence, the bird took off, a flash of red against the pines, and Dr. Perrill found himself with no better excuse to postpone getting back to the job in hand than the forced recollection that somewhere he had once read a paper on the nutritional value of sunflower seed oil, reminded then that he himself, long ago, had done some work on it and crossed it off as being of no special interest.

Grimacing as he shifted his heavy-jointed body — he had been bothered with an arthritic-like tenderness of the bursae ever since his bout with breakbone fever in Bengal — he again turned his attention to the battered old scrapbook that lay before him on his desk. Kira had said that it should not be shown to Lincoln Lord, arguing that it would make entirely the wrong impression — business men were most interested in *new* scientific developments, not in something that had kicked around for years and years — and he was forced to admit that this scrapbook did look like something exhumed from dead storage. He had been shocked to see how badly it had deteriorated when, last night, he had dug it out from the old trunk where he had stored it away nine years ago. That was the last time he had used it, when he had shown it to Sol Zurich. Time had taken a heavy toll. The cover was riddled by silverfish, the earlier photographs were faded and brown as a result of that bad lot of sodium hyposulfite that he had been sold by a Marwari in Calcutta, most of the clippings were yellow-edged and many of them had popped loose from their brittle bedding of aged flour-and-water paste. Still and all, it *was* an interesting story. Once he'd started to tell it, no one had ever stopped him ... the men at Gerber and Heinz and Beechnut and Clapps had all been fascinated. True enough, nothing had come of it ... they'd all turned him down ... but they had been *interested*. And this man Lord would be, too, if Kira would only give him the chance ... but of course she wouldn't.

Dr. Perrill sighed his submission. He owed everything to Kira Zurich — this wonderful laboratory, this fine equipment, all of the staff who were employed to help him — and if bowing to Kira's every whim and foible was the payment that she demanded, he had no choice other than to pay it.

Regretfully, still resisting her admonition against showing the scrapbook to Lincoln Lord, he slowly turned the pages, fanning to his nostrils the odd scent of India that still clung to them, an odor that brought back those nights in Calcutta when he had put this portfolio together, telling Celia that it would surely make him a wealthy man, promising her that if she would only return to the United States with him, he would be able to buy her even more fine dresses and precious jewels than she would have, so she said, if she went back to the London stage. He had been certain then that this scrapbook would be his touchstone to wealth, that some American baby food manufacturer would surely give him, as soon as he heard his story, a fabulously lucrative contract for the rights to manufacture and market the baby food that he had developed.

That, of course, had not happened. Sharp as his disappointment had been, it had nevertheless faded quickly after Celia had walked out, divorced him, and married a man who, so she had written, owned a big motel near a race track in Maryland and was giving her everything that her hungry heart desired. After receiving that final letter from Celia he had stopped worrying about having his baby food marketed — he no longer had any obvious need for a large sum of money.

Now, suddenly, it came into his mind again, not as something resurrected from the past but rather as an idea newborn and full of the promise of life . . . if Lincoln Lord *could* be interested . . . and if he *did* make a great deal of money . . .

The prospect of escaping Kira Zurich's domination was so entrancing that he could overlook the argument of improbability. As heavily as the odds were against him, there was still the chance that Lincoln Lord might make it possible for him to pay his own way. Then he would no longer be dependent upon anyone — and the breaking of that bondage suddenly became an enormously important goal.

All of his life, it seemed, he had been a beggar forced to bow and scrape before those men and women who had somehow acquired the unjustified right to award or deny everything that he had ever needed — the scholarship that had paid his college tuition, the half-pay sweatshop job that finally had gotten him through medical school, the grades that professors had handed out as if they were favors bestowed rather than honors won. He had imagined that once he had his degree, he would finally be free. That had not proved to be true. Afterwards it had been worse than ever — appointments and fellowships, money grants and research funds, always the supplicant condemned to beg for what should have been freely given, finally reduced to this ignominious kow-towing to Kira Zurich . . . but this might be the end. If he could only convince Lincoln Lord . . .

His brain tricked him. He had attempted to fix the image of Lincoln Lord in his mind, but the face that he now saw was that of Dr. Horace Cleaveland. It was discouraging confusion, all the more so because it was so readily explainable by their striking similarity of appearance. Cleaveland, too, had once seemed a last lone hope.

Even before Lee Perrill had entered medical school, he had decided upon a specialization in pediatrics — he had originally been drawn to medicine by the compassionate feeling that an ill child had always evoked within him — but the achievement of his goal required a residency that had proved extremely difficult to obtain. He had graduated high in the top tenth of his class, but academic accomplishment had been more than offset by a disastrous physical loss. Early in his last year at medical school, his hair had started to fall out, first in irregular patches and then, as the areas spread and linked, he became totally bald. By the time he received his degree, even his eyebrows were gone. Unfortunate as he felt himself, he did not realize how severely he was to be handicapped until he discovered how hard it was to get an internship. He had hoped for one of three, all in hospitals with outstanding pediatric sections, but was forced to settle for any berth he could find. He had spent two awful years in a grimy hospital in Pittsburgh where, because of his stature and strength — and, he suspected, his frightening appearance — his almost standard assignment was the subduing of violent drunks and dope addicts. His applications for assistantships in pediatrics were unavailing, his picture seemingly enough to cancel every opportunity. Desperate, he had stayed on for another year at the hospital, working with a doctor who was doing the clinical testing of a new sedative that was being developed by one of the pharmaceutical houses. A representative of the drug firm, discovering that it was he who had done all of the work and written the final report, opened the door to an assistantship in pediatrics under Dr. Horace Cleaveland of the Cleaveland Clinic in Los Angeles.

Hitchhiking to California had seemed a pilgrimage to the fountainhead of his chosen specialization. Almost every month, one or another of the medical journals carried a paper by Horace Cleaveland, M.D., as authoritative a name as there was in the whole field. To his astonishment, he soon discovered that Dr. Cleaveland's medical competence was about on a par with that of Leslie Howard, who had been cast to play the role of Dr. Philip Carey in a filming of Somerset Maugham's *Of Human Bondage*. Cleaveland's fame was no less a product of histrionic ability. He was a truly great actor. All he needed was someone behind the scenes to tell him what to do and say. For the two years of his assistantship, Lee Perrill served in that capacity. Most of his time was devoted to a money-coining scheme that opened his eyes to unimagined aspects of medical practice. Because of Cleaveland's high standing in the profession, coupled with an ability to charm corporation executives no less effectively than he wooed the mothers of goldspooned babies, he was constantly being given supervisory power over grants of money allotted for the clinical testing of new pediatric drugs. The most efficient aspect of Cleaveland's supervision, Lee Perrill had quickly learned, was making certain that a lion's share of that money found its way — with ethical indirectness, of course — into his own bank account.

Dr. Perrill, like other eager young assistants before and after, managed as much clinical work as Cleaveland's penny-pinching would permit, ghost-writing the long statistic-studded papers for the medical journals that the famous doctor, with the host of friends that he had carefully made in editorial offices all over the country, could always manage to get published on a date conveniently co-ordinated with the sales promotion plans of the drug manufacturer. Much of Dr. Cleaveland's popularity with the grant-makers was due to his reputation as a sensible man with a well-developed sense of co-operation.

With the calmly objective outlook of the born scientist — and this, from the beginning, had handicapped Lee Perrill's human relationships even more than his startling baldness — he had found it disturbingly difficult to understand Dr. Horace Cleaveland's great success. His only asset seemed to be his appearance, a handsome face and a luxuriant shock of thick curly hair. Professionally, he could hardly be judged as anything but a charlatan, worthy of no respect, interested only in the accumulation of wealth; yet it was confusingly impossible to blackmark him with the evidence of any instance where anyone had felt defrauded. Those who paid him his big fees always seemed satisfied that they had received full value for their money. He was undeniably clever. Working with the pharmaceutical manufacturers, all of whom gave him first choice in the selection of drugs to be clinically assayed, he guaranteed their continuing high regard by exercising great caution in the new drugs that he chose to test, rejecting any that might conceivably necessitate an unfavorable report and thus jeopardize a corporate friendship.

His medical practice was no less wisely managed. He rarely failed to effect a cure in any case that he personally handled, a record maintained by his open-handedly turning over incurable cases to other practitioners — thus managing to make himself many friends in the profession — and he was no less generous in sharing all diagnostic problems with the younger men in the clinic, who, although necessarily aware of his lack of competence, nevertheless were grateful to him.

His patients loved him. Everyone around the clinic was aware of his awesome ability to charm children — he could quiet a screaming child with a smile, break up a tantrum with no more than a hypnotist's murmur — and it was this talent that, in the end, had most seriously disturbed Lee Perrill. After observing Cleaveland in action, he finally came to realize the full extent of his own handicap. He had noticed, of course, that some of the children with whom he worked in the charity wards of the hospitals where the clinical work was done were plainly frightened by his appearance, yet it had been difficult to believe that the loss of his hair had turned him into such a terrifying ogre that he could never hope for success as a children's doctor. It was a verdict all the harder to accept because it was so unfair — he loved children and wanted nothing more than a chance to help them — but somehow his face seemed incapable of reflecting his heart. His eventual acceptance of the fact that he was physically unfitted for the practice of the specialty toward which he had devoted so many years of total effort was a trauma so severe that it was much more the real cause of his decision to abandon medicine than the more acceptable explanation that he was sickened by professional conditions under which a man like Horace Cleaveland could rise to wealth and fame, and earn the coast-to-coast plaudits of his colleagues. Nevertheless, there was an unbreakable association between this period of tumultuous mental upheaval and the person of Dr. Horace Cleaveland.

The final episode of his association with the Cleaveland Clinic had been especially trying. Having abandoned his plan to go into private practice, and faced with the necessity of earning a living, he had started out to find a job in the research laboratory of some drug manufacturer where, hidden away, his appearance would surely be no handicap. In those depression years, there were few openings in pharmacological research, all the fewer for men with no more academic qualification than a medical degree. A round of letters produced not even an opportunity for an interview. In some way, however, one of those letters found its way back into Dr. Cleaveland's hands and, defeating Lee Perrill's intention to slip away without explanation, he had been forced to explain himself. With his natural antipathy to personal revelation, heightened by what he felt to be an unjustified invasion of privacy, he had come close to telling Cleaveland what he really thought of him and his clinic, close enough so that he had fully expected an angry flashback and immediate dismissal. Instead, Cleaveland had listened to him with unruffled tolerance, finally offering his calmly stated opinion that he was unquestionably making the right move, advising him to go back to some university and add a Sc.D. to his M.D. It was advice so firmly supported by his inability to get a job with only an M.D. that it had been difficult to disagree, and he had argued only that it was financially impossible. Thereupon, Cleaveland had picked up the telephone and, as casually as if he were calling a pharmacy to order a prescription, had placed a long-distance call to one of his innumerable friends, this one a university president who just might be able to dig up a research fellowship. He was. In three minutes, two of which were largely filled with first-name banter, everything was settled. Lee Perrill's momentary shame at having had intemperate criticism rebuffed with kindness had made him express embarrassed gratitude, but his after-feeling toward Dr. Cleaveland had been in no way improved, arousing as it did the conviction that there was something wrong in a world where ability counted for nothing, impotent without the intercession of a Horace Cleaveland.

Lee Perrill's doctoral thesis was based upon the amino acid research that he had done under his fellowship. A carbon copy, submitted with no more than a brief letter of transmittal, had been enough to get him a job in the laboratories of D. R. Page & Sons, a pharmaceutical house for which he had gained a high regard while testing some of its products at the Cleaveland Clinic. Although Page was not one of the largest drug firms, there were more than a hundred employees in the research laboratories alone, a group so big that Dr. Perrill had no difficulty losing himself in it. Except for Dr. Martin Sampster, the director of research, who occasionally called upon him to make a verbal progress report, he had little contact with his fellow workers beyond the exchange of data or the borrowing of equipment required by some particular project on which he was working. Once, soon after his arrival, he did eat dinner with the two men, Welk and Keiffer, with whom he shared laboratory space. As he had suspected from their gossipy chatter during the day, neither was an acceptable candidate for close friendship. The only thing they ever talked about except girls — Welk, particularly was genitally obsessed — were the maneuvers of intra-laboratory politics. Who had been invited out to Sampster's house for dinner was, for both of them, news of far greater import than anything that was ever published in the technical journals. Their greatest concern, however, was over the assignment of research projects. They both shied away from work of real scientific value — what they called "brain busters" — willing to go to any ends to get their hands on some simple project that would quickly result in a commercially marketable product.

Perrill had thought it only more of their silly chatter when he had first heard Welk and Keiffer maintain that the front office judged a research worker only by how much profit he brought into the company till. Toward the end of his first year, however, he found that it was shockingly true. He had been making one of his reports to Sampster, expecting to be complimented for having gone far beyond his assignment and broken into some new ground, when the director of research had suddenly said, "I'm afraid it's about time that you and I had a little talk, Dr. Perrill. The scientific quality of your work is quite satisfactory. You're an excellent technician — we have no complaint whatsoever on that score — but you seem to be having a hard time fitting in here. This isn't an endowed institution, you know. We have to pay our own way. We do as much basic research as we can afford, and now and then we're able to bring out something that gives us prestige even if we lose money on it, but there has to be a limit on that sort of thing. I know you'd like to forget the commercial side. So would I. Who wouldn't? But if we did, we'd bankrupt the company, the lab would close, and then where would we be? Suppose we were to do what you suggest — set up a special project on this work you've started. It would cost, I'd guess, close to a hundred thousand dollars. And suppose you were lucky enough to find what you're after. How much of it would we sell? How many babies are there with that particular allergy? We couldn't possibly get our research money back, let alone make a profit. Can't you see that? Your trouble, Dr. Perrill, seems to be that you can't keep your feet on the ground. Maybe you don't belong here. Maybe you ought to find a place with one of the foundations, or go back to the university. If you still want to stay on, we're willing to give you another chance — but you'll have to promise me to take a more practical point of view from now on. When we give you an assignment, you'll have to stick to it, not go wandering off into the blue. I'm sorry, Dr. Perrill, but we'll have to consider you as being on probation. Keiffer may be able to help you — we're making him the chief of your section — but if your record doesn't improve in the next six months —"

Before that six months had ended, he was in the hospital, not as a physician but as a patient, a perforated duodenal ulcer less serious than what had happened to the rest of his being. Surgery took care of the ulcer and his digestive system began to function again with reasonable normality, but there was no medical treatment that could reactivate his brain nor restore hope to his heart. It was then that he had met Kira. She was working as a night nurse and, without the hospital authorities knowing it, trying to keep up with a full schedule at the university in order to get her degree in social service work. At the time he had not stopped to think why she had confessed her secret to him, nor did it dawn on him until long afterwards that when she would slip into his room to ask for help with some class assignment, she might have been doing it as much for his sake as for her own. In any event, it was Kira who had helped him, as a long-bedded invalid must sometimes be retaught to walk, to again use his mind. And it was Kira who had sent him, after he had left the hospital, the mimeographed bulletin from which he had learned that the Inter-Church Mission Board was looking for a doctor to go to India.

There, working in a village of mud huts in Bengal, he finally found satisfaction for the hunger that had first sent him to medical school. Wherever he went, he was followed by a pack of children, dirty and ragged but always jewel-eyed with awed respect. They called him "Doctor Sahib" — and made him, with their freely given love, the man that he had always wanted to be.

Marveling at his good fortune, he had attempted to write a letter to Kira expressing his gratitude for her help. But there was, as always, the feeling that she had aided him because she pitied him, and before he could complete his letter, one had come from her, telling him that she had not only gotten her degree from the university but also a field supervisor's job with the public health administration, all of which she credited to the help that he had given her. It was a reversal of role that he found extremely gratifying.

Every year after that she had sent him a Christmas card, usually with a note telling him of her latest promotion and he always replied with a January or February letter describing his work in India. Once he had written her in August, when the *Journal* had taken his first paper and there was no one else with whom he could share his elation . . .

OCTOBER 1943 . . .

He stared at the date on the clipped pages that he saw now in the scrapbook, finding it difficult to believe that it had really been so long ago. Fifteen years had slipped away. And now, as he had not done before, he faced the full memory of what had happened when he came back to the States. Knowing how much he had changed, he had imagined that everything else had changed, too. But it hadn't. Everywhere he had gone with this portfolio, everywhere he told his story, there had been always the echo of Sampster saying, "Unfortunately, Doctor, your work doesn't seem to have any commercial application. This is all very interesting, and undoubtedly an important contribution to the science of nutrition, but you see —" And then they would say, "We can't afford to put out a product that won't get us volume sales in the mass market" . . . and that's what Mr. Lord would say today. There was no hope. Kira was probably right about telling the India story . . . Mr. Lord would think what all of the others had thought . . . nothing but a crackpot . . . running off to Bengal . . . not what a practical man would do . . .

He got heavily to his feet, working his broad shoulders, flexing muscles to take the stiffness out of his joints, and then with a delicacy of touch incongruous with his huge heavy-knuckled hands, he picked up the scrapbook and carried it across the office, putting it in a file drawer, closing it as if he were shutting the door on the past.

There was a flash of polished black across the window area and, looking out, he saw a car drive past. Watching, he saw it stop at Kira Zurich's cottage. The man who got out was, even at this distance, unmistakably Lincoln Lord. Perrill gave his watch a panicked look, checking it against the wall clock, frightened that he had absent-mindedly let the time slip away. But it was only twelve-thirty. He was not late . . . the Lords were early.

Lincoln Lord had gone around to the other side of the car now, but his face was still visible over the top, and Dr. Perrill fought against the same hallucination that had struck him before. The disembodied face made the impression even stronger . . . Dr. Horace Cleaveland . . . picking up the telephone . . . a few words and he'd had his research fellowship . . . yes, that was what Lincoln Lord had probably done for Dr. Ichakuri . . .

He stared ahead, unseeing now, his eyes empty sockets in his great skull-like head . . . why did there have to be Lincoln Lords? . . . why was a truly great scientist like Dr. Ichakuri dependent upon help from someone like that . . . why?

The cardinal was back at the feeder again.

3

On her earlier visit to Haven Home, Maggie Lord had seen only the exterior of Kira Zurich's cottage, pointed out as they had driven past as the place where Kira said she had lived before her marriage to Sol Zurich. It had been closed then, the shutters blanking the windows, suggesting an emptied interior. Looking around her now, Maggie was certain that Kira had only turned the key in the lock, leaving everything as it was. This was not a house that had been furnished in a week. Marriage had plainly been no more than an interruption, a temporary excursion into another world. When it had ended, Kira had come back and picked up her life exactly where it had left off.

Maggie Lord's first reaction was one of relief, released as she now was from any further feeling that Kira had deprived herself by giving up the president's house. This was her true home. She was as perfectly placed here as she had been misplaced before. Considered, it seemed a startling revelation of character. This was the home of a woman to whom her career was an all-sufficient obsession, the furnishing of a house little more than a concession to conformity.

Seeing Kira Zurich in this light was a contrast to Maggie's original appraisal, yet she was quick to see that it was a far more logical characterization. Her marriage to Sol Zurich, something of a mystery before, could now be seen as the act of a woman to whom the end was far more important than the means of its attainment. She was obviously a strong and purposeful person, far stronger than she had seemed before, and that strength revealed a potential danger that Maggie Lord now knew her husband faced. Before, she had thought his concern about what might happen today to be pointless. Now she knew differently. But what she could not know was whether or not Linc realized that there was a way to handle Kira Zurich . . . he would have no trouble with her as long as he could hold her respect. He still had it . . . Kira's manner as she had complimented him on his recapture of the Gellman business left no doubt about that . . . but it would be almost certainly lost the moment he showed the slightest sign of weakness. If he made the same mistake that he had made so many times before . . . so anxious to please that he refused to stand by his own judgment . . . giving up . . . not fighting back . . .

Her mind recoiled, stung by the realization of how quickly she had slipped back into the rut of habit, so ready to think the worst of Linc that she had almost instantly overridden the appreciation that he deserved . . . she'd been wrong so many times about him . . . she might even be wrong about Kira . . .

Almost as if it were denial, Kira Zurich said bluntly, "I asked you to come early because I wanted to talk to you about Dr. Perrill," an abrupt dropping of any pretense that this was to be a purely social occasion, a warning that she had some objective in mind and that she intended to drive through to it without delay, letting nothing stand in her way.

Maggie shot a glance at her husband, unavoidably fear-filled for an instant by his expression of easy nonchalance, then finding herself wonderfully lifted as she heard him say calmly, "Yes, I'm anxious to know a bit more about Dr. Perrill and the setup over here. Swann tells me that we're paying him a rather substantial retainer fee for the laboratory work that he's doing for us. Naturally, I'm anxious to know what we're getting for our money."

Maggie thought it a beautifully contrived response, a positive reminder to Kira that she had given Coastal Foods its own corporate identity and that he intended to hold her to her promise to give him complete control over its affairs. Nevertheless, she wondered as she saw the momentary blankness on Kira's face, for an instant the expression of a woman thwarted, if Linc might have gone too far, too quickly.

But Kira was clever, too. "Yes, I'm sure that's something you'll want to consider — whether or not you wish to continue the arrangement to have your laboratory work done here at Haven Home. I do know that Mr. Zurich always thought it very worth while. But perhaps he was overly sensitive. He'd had a frightening experience once. Something that he'd packed — clam chowder, I believe — made a number of people ill. I don't suppose there's much chance of anything like that happening these days, not with the kind of controls over processing that you have in the plant now —"

"But it's still every food processor's nightmare," Linc conceded, soundly enough, yet it seemed that he was going farther than necessary when he added, "Oh, I've no thought of changing the setup. We need laboratory control, no doubt about that — and I know, too, that Dr. Perrill has done more for us than just testing. Frank Kennan tells me that he's been very helpful in working out some of our processing problems." His smile was a question. "Dr. Perrill seems to be a very versatile man."

Kira looked at him fixedly. "Yes, we're very fortunate to have him here at Haven Home."

"I understand that he was a medical missionary in India," Maggie said, mainly because she felt herself called upon to take some part in the conversation, yet hoping, too, that a slightly more personal discussion of Dr. Perrill might reveal Kira Zurich's objective.

"Yes, he was in India for some years," Kira said, but her tone made Maggie's question seem a scarcely warranted intrusion.

Linc asked, "Well, he was in Burma, too, wasn't he? That's where he met Dr. Ichakuri, I believe?"

Maggie said, "I told Linc about the cable Dr. Perrill got back from Tokyo."

"Yes, that's where the preliminary work was done — India and Burma," Kira said quickly, now obviously dropping the subject, justifying an impatient desire to push ahead by glancing at her wrist watch, which was, Maggie noticed, of the plain-cased utilitarian sort that nurses usually wore. "But, of course, the really important developments have all come since he's been here at Haven Home." She paused, oddly belligerent, almost as if she were expecting argument. "The unfortunate thing is that there's been so little recognition of all that we've done. Dr. Perrill's papers have been published — that sort of thing — but that's about all. Oh, there was some talk a couple of years ago about his being given an honorary degree — not that that would have meant too much either — but still nothing ever came of it. You know how those things are — the logrolling that goes on. Scientists have their little cliques."

"You scratch my back and I'll scratch yours," Linc suggested. His smile offered full understanding, but Maggie could not help but feel that he must be as puzzled as she was by Kira's purpose . . . could it be that she was going to ask Linc to pull some strings to get Dr. Perrill an honorary degree?

Kira went on, "Of course, he's handicapped by being here at Haven Home. It would be different, I'm sure, if he were associated with one of the big research foundations. They have the connections to see that their work gets publicized. We don't. There was an article in one of the magazines just a few weeks ago — *Time,* I think, or it may have been *Newsweek* — about all of the new developments in the field of child nutrition. Not a word, of course, about all that we've done here at Haven Home."

"Yes, I can see how that must be a little discouraging," Linc agreed.

"It's so unfair!" Kira burst out. "We've done more important work on child nutrition here at Haven Home in the last few years — more truly significant work — than anyone else has done anywhere in the world. But what does it mean if nothing comes of it? That's the discouraging thing. Oh, of course there's some satisfaction just in the search for knowledge, but it would mean so much more if it were only being put to some use. She paused, her thin lips tightly drawn for an instant. "You do recall, don't you, Mr. Lord, that I asked you to consider the possibility of putting our baby food on the market?"

"Of course," Linc said, his puzzled smile making it seem a surprise that Kira would even suggest the possibility of his forgetting.

A slight flush warmed the olive cast of Kira Zurich's cheeks. "Please don't misunderstand me when I say this, Mr. Lord — but I do hope that you've not been prejudiced against it."

"Why would you imagine that I had been?"

Kira's hand went to her throat, her fingers closing the already narrow gap of her white-piped collar, "I'm assuming that you've seen Joel Morris's report?"

There was a missed heartbeat before Linc's "Yes," time enough for Maggie to sense his well-hidden disappointment that Kira did not intend to back down in face of the arguments that Joel had assembled.

Kira's hand was still at her throat, but now she leaned forward in a posture of intent concentration. "That report must be read, Mr. Lord, with an understanding of the attitude that prevailed in the company at the time it was written. Please don't misunderstand me — I'm not criticizing Mr. Zurich — but the fact does remain that he was never really interested in having the company bring out any products of its own. He was perfectly satisfied to go on just handling the Gellman business. And I'm not criticizing Joel Morris either. I'm sure that he did as honest and conscientious a job as was possible under the circumstances."

"I'd not have the slightest doubt about that," Maggie heard Linc say positively, his instant support of Joel gratifying assurance that he meant to stand his ground. "Believe me, Mrs. Zurich, there's no one in the company who's more anxious to get started with a line of our own than Joel is. He's champing at the bit to get going. As a matter of fact, I spent the better part of an hour with him this morning, going over a preliminary selection of the products that we might have in our line."

Kira's hand dropped from her throat. "Then you are going to bring out some products of your own?"

"Of course," he said, again with that same puzzled smile. "You weren't imagining, were you, that we'd be content to stop with getting back the Gellman business?"

"No, I — well, I was sure you wouldn't be."

"No, indeed. We'll move ahead as rapidly as we can. We do have to take care of the Gellman business first, of course — get the shelves in their stores filled again and build up our own warehouse stock. That's basic. But as soon as we —"

"You mentioned the selection of your line," Kira interrupted with another anxious glance at her watch. "Please don't think that I'm questioning you with any idea of interfering in your management of the company, Mr. Lord. I have no such intention —"

"Ask any questions you wish," Linc said with an open-handed gesture. "As far as details are concerned — of course we're still in the preliminary planning stage. After all, I've only had forty-eight hours since —"

"I know," Kira said, an apologetic interjection.

"In a general way, however, I think that our most logical move is fairly obvious. As I told you over the telephone on Thursday night, we're completely free now to put out the same products under our own label that we're packing for Gellman Stores."

"And that's what you plan to do?"

"Well, as I say, this is all preliminary thinking — nothing definitely set — but it is difficult to conceive of any other course that would be less of a gamble. As far as the products are concerned, there's no question whatsoever about their salability — they've all been market-tested in the Gellman Stores —"

Kira broke in to ask, "You say it really wouldn't be much of a gamble?"

"No, I'd not think so. We'd not have to invest —"

Again Kira interrupted. "Since you're not taking any real gamble there, Mr. Lord, would it be too serious a risk to take a small one on our baby food? I realize that if it didn't sell, the company would sustain a certain amount of loss. I don't think that would happen — or at least I'm hoping that it wouldn't — but if worse came to worse and it did, I want you to know that I'd be quite prepared to have my dividends reduced by whatever amount had been lost. In other words, the gamble would really be mine, wouldn't it?"

Maggie stared at her husband, wondering if he had been taken in by Kira's trick . . . claiming that she wasn't interfering in the management of the company . . . if this wasn't interference, what was it! If Linc let her get away with that kind of reasoning, there was nothing in the company that would ever be safe from her meddling . . . everything affected dividends. If he didn't stand up to her now . . .

"I'm glad you've told me how you feel about it," he finally said, his tone enigmatic and unrevealing, neither strong nor weak. "But I'm assuming, Mrs. Zurich, that when you speak of your willingness to assume whatever loss might be involved, you're not thinking of any very large sum of money?"

Kira dampened her lips. "Joel Morris said in his report that it would cost somewhere between fifteen and twenty thousand dollars."

Linc's voice strengthened as he said, "Yes, I do recall that figure. But unless I'm mistaken, that was only for what you might call preliminary expense — labels, cartons, cans — the factory cost that would be involved in getting ready to put a first run of the product on the market."

"Well?" Kira demanded, waiting.

"If you'll remember, Mrs. Zurich, Joel went on from there to outline what he felt would be necessary by way of a minimum advertising and promotion campaign if the product was to have any chance at all of being accepted. Even then —"

"Do you agree with that, Mr. Lord — that it would take that much money?"

"Frankly, I have no idea. Until I've had a chance to dig in and find out what it's all about, I'd surely not hazard a guess. I do know this — a million dollars doesn't go very far these days if you're trying to put across a product that —"

The doorbell interrupted him. Kira did not rise. "That report was written two years ago, Mr. Lord. Joel Morris knows nothing about all the progress we've made since — the wonderful results we've gotten. It's a very different story now from what it was then. All I ask is that you don't make up your mind until you see what we have to show you over at the laboratory."

Then, without waiting for a reply, she was on her feet and moving toward the front door.

Maggie glanced at her husband, tempted to whisper what had just occurred to her, but the room was so small, the front hall door so close to where they were sitting, that the risk of being overheard by Kira was too great to take. But she was positive that she was right, even more so as she saw Kira re-enter the room with Dr. Perrill. Whatever reason there might be behind Kira's all-out attempt to get the baby food on the market, her objective was not what she had maintained it to be . . . and the gossip was wrong, too . . . there was nothing between Kira Zurich and Dr. Perrill except the relationship of a determined woman to a man who was not strong enough to stand up to her

298

domination. Kira wasn't interested in getting recognition for Dr. Perrill ... she was trying to justify herself for having married Sol Zurich to get the million dollars that she had spent on Haven Home ...

4

A pang of hunger knifed through to Joel Morris's consciousness, making him suddenly aware of the passage of time. Everyone else had slipped away, leaving him alone in the Saturday afternoon isolation of the deserted office.

Now that he had broken his concentration on the figure-filled sheets that covered his desk, he realized that the throbbing headache of hunger was already pounding away behind his eyeballs ... all he'd had for breakfast had been a seven o'clock cup of coffee. It would be midnight again tonight, maybe even later before he had everything wrapped up and tied down ... but, it would be worth it. Once he had the Gellman sales charted, item by item, territory by territory, month by month, it would be easy to pick the best items to pack under the Coastal Foods label. Tomorrow he could start working out his distribution plan. But he had to have food to keep going ...

He pushed through the swinging doors of the cafeteria, seeing that the stainless steel counter had already been emptied and washed clean. But one of the old-timers, Cora, was still there, up on a stool scrubbing out a coffee urn. "Oh, for goodness' sakes, I didn't know you was still here," she said, getting down quickly, surprising him as much by her troubled concern as Miss Payne had done yesterday by suddenly starting to call him "Mr. Morris," instead of "Joel."

"What can I get you, Mr. Morris?" Cora asked anxiously.

"Suppose you could dig up a bottle of milk?" he asked. "Maybe a few crackers?"

"Oh, I can do better than that, Mr. Morris. There's still soup and I'll make you a ham and cheese. I guess you'd like it toasted, wouldn't you?"

"Please don't bother."

"It's no bother, Mr. Morris. You just go sit down there with Mr. Kennan and I'll have it for you in a minute."

Frank Kennan was hidden from view until Joel rounded the cash register at the end of the chromium-piped runway. He saw him then, sitting alone at the alcove table that tacit understanding had always reserved for top management, the Coastal Foods equivalent of an executive dining room. Joel had often eaten there but never without being asked. Today, Kennan's manner made it plain that an invitation was no longer necessary.

Kennan stumped out his cigarette in a coffee-splattered saucer. "What are you doing here? Saturday afternoon — I thought Vicky'd have you baby-sitting."

"Not today." He sat down. "Too much to do to get ready for the meeting. Miss Payne told you, didn't she — Monday at ten?"

"What's it all about?"

He paused, savoring the pleasure of having a confidence that could be shared. "We're going to pick the items that we'll have in our own line."

Kennan lit another cigarette. "Kind of rushing things, isn't he? It's going to take at least a month just to get on top of the Gellman business again."

"It'll take longer than that to get our own line set up. It's a big job."

Kennan nodded agreement. "Kind of fools you, though, doesn't he?"

"Mr. Lord?"

"You know what I mean — taking it so easy, acting as if he was just letting things drift along, almost as if he didn't know what he was going to do next."

"I wouldn't take any bets on that, Frank."

"Oh, I know it isn't true. But he makes it look so damned easy. That's what I was just sitting here thinking — a week ago today we were flat on our can, not a damned order in the place. Then he walks in and — wham, we're back in business again."

"He's terrific, all right. You just can't get away from it."

"You can take a little credit yourself, boy. If you hadn't found that crap at Atlantic City —"

"Oh, that was just a lucky break. It wouldn't have meant anything if it hadn't been for him — the way he handled it."

"Yeah, he's got what it takes," Kennan said soberly. "I don't know what it is but he's sure as hell got it."

Overhead, there was the raucous squawk of two long blasts on the call system.

"Oh, hell," Kennan said, rising wearily. "Now what!"

"You better get out of here, Frank," he said. "Get yourself a little rest."

The production manager shrugged, heading quickly toward the door to the cannery. Watching him, Joel Morris heard the echo of his own voice, struck suddenly with how much he had sounded like Lincoln Lord . . . he'd have to be careful of that . . . it had happened before, unconsciously slipping into mimicry of someone he admired . . .

Cora came around the corner, carrying a tray that bore not only his soup, sandwich, and a cup of coffee but also a heaping dish of rosy-tinted ice cream.

5

Lincoln Lord had more than willingly acceded to Kira Zurich's request that he reserve judgment until he saw what they had to show him at the research center — at that point any delay had been all to the good — but now, walking along the winding path from Kira's cottage to the laboratory building, every step was carrying him closer and closer to the unpleasant necessity of decision.

He had learned little from their lunch table conversation, nothing that detracted from his earlier conviction that Kira was not going to be as easy to handle as he had imagined. His one best hope was that whatever they had to show him would support her claim that the product had been greatly improved over what it had been at the time of Joel's study. If that proved to be the case, he might be able to satisfy her with a test marketing. Even if the stuff didn't sell — and Joel was probably right in saying that it didn't have a chance unless there was a tremendous advertising campaign behind it — Kira would at least give him credit for a good try and, finally convinced, would forget it. On the other hand, if the stuff was still as bad as Joel said it was, even a market test would be dangerous. The way rumors flew around in the food business, everyone in the trade would know within twenty-four hours that he had been fool enough to test a product that didn't have a chance. If Coastal Foods tried to sell a baby food with such an unappetizing taste that no mother would ever give it to a child, anything else that the company ever packed under its own label would be black-marked by every buyer from Boston to San Diego.

Grimacing, he admitted his negligence in not having opened a can and tasted the stuff himself . . . but, confound it, he hadn't known that this was coming up today! Maybe it was true that Mag had told him on Thursday night . . . yes, she probably had . . . but she might, at least, have reminded him this morning.

Subconsciously prompted, he glanced back over his shoulder. Maggie was walking beside Kira Zurich, a half-dozen paces back. They were talking animatedly, so far away that what they were saying could not be clearly heard, but he did pick up one word . . . *Kip* . . .

The question that he had been about to ask Perrill was lost in the quick-rising fear that Maggie was making the mistake of opening their personal life to Kira Zurich. Almost as quickly, however, alarm was snuffed out by appreciation. Maggie had Kira actually smiling, briefly but unmistakably, the first time that it had happened since they had arrived.

Maggie saw him watching her and, flashing a smile, quickly walked up to him, explaining, "We were just talking about the high school. And do you know what — Kira's on the school board!"

He expressed pleased surprise, prepared to go on, but Kira gave him no chance, closing the subject by saying, "I'm happy to know that you've decided to bring your son to Goodhaven, Mr. Lord." And that was that.

As he and Perrill moved ahead again, Lincoln Lord quickened the pace, hoping that if he could get the scientist safely beyond Kira Zurich's earshot, Perrill might open up enough to give him some hint of what to expect, some anticipation of the decision that he would have to make. Perrill had been peculiarly unresponsive during lunch. Twice it had seemed that he was about to rise to a conversational bait, once when he had tossed out a mention of Dr. Ichakuri and again, even more positively, when he brought up the subject of India; but on both occasions Perrill had glanced at Kira and curbed himself to no more than monosyllabic response. Now again Perrill gave him the impression of wanting to talk, yet of being afraid to do so because of some prohibition that Kira had imposed. On the other hand, that impression might easily be a false one. Research scientists were, Lincoln Lord had long since learned, often subject to strange inhibitions — most of them would go to almost any end to avoid positive commitment on anything — and Perrill's startlingly stark appearance offered no encouragement that he was the normal man who, if properly incited, could always be made to talk about himself.

The graveled path was now a concrete sidewalk, and as they walked on, the research center came into full view. It was easy enough now to accept Kira's statement at lunch that almost a million dollars had been spent on physical facilities alone during the last five years. What had seemed a relatively small building from a vantage point down the path was now revealed as being considerably larger, actually two low structures connected by a covered walkway across an open court. As a first reaction, he found himself encouraged to believe that so large an operation would surely have made substantial progress in the two years since Joel's study, but memory offered the warning that fancy buildings were no guarantee of results. The K. C. Wright Research Center, erected as a monument to the chairman of the board's twenty-two years as Luxor Pharmacal's chief executive officer, had been a multimillion-dollar white elephant, the research workers it housed far less productive than they had been in the old converted schoolhouse where they had formerly been quartered.

Nevertheless, he exclaimed, "By golly, you've got yourself quite a setup here," his own words inciting the thought that Perrill, despite his seeming subservience to Kira Zurich, must have somehow learned how to handle her in order to get what he wanted. "I imagine this represents a dream come true as far as you're concerned, Dr. Perrill. I know a good many research men who —"

Unexpectedly, it was Kira Zurich who answered, "Yes, it means a great deal to all of us, Mr. Lord." She had slipped up behind them and now made it plain that she was ready to take over as their guide. Gesturing toward the bronze plaque beside the entrance door they were now approaching, she said, "This building we call the Haven Home Health Center. Here we provide medical and psychiatric care on a more or less temporary basis for those children that we hope to be able to bring along to the point where they can be placed in foster homes."

"You keep no children here?"

"That's correct," Kira said, formally precise. "Haven Home hasn't been a residence orphanage for some time now. All of our children are placed in foster homes. However, we follow them up almost as actively as if they were directly under our own care. We have five field-workers who spend their full time checking on our children and the homes in which they are living. This assures us that the children are not only being properly cared for but also gives us a chance to secure detailed reports, not only on diet but also upon every environmental factor that might conceivably affect the development of the child involved. Then at regular intervals, usually once a month, the foster mother brings the child in here to the Health Center for a physical examination. The nature of that examination varies with circumstances, but at the very least we secure a detailed record of physical development. The co-ordination of those growth records with the diet and environmental reports of the field workers gives us some very solid background for Dr. Perrill's work."

"Most valuable," Perrill dutifully agreed.

Lincoln Lord said, "I had no idea that you went into it this deeply."

"You're by no means alone," Kira said, crisp almost to the point of acidity. "There are very few people anywhere who have any concept of what we're doing here at Haven Home." She gave a curt nod to Perrill, who, as if he had been waiting for a cue, stepped forward and opened the door for them.

Inside, Kira said, "This, perhaps, is starting at the end rather than the beginning, but we do have some of the children in today for their monthly check-up and I thought you might be interested in seeing them."

She led the way down the long center corridor of the building and Lincoln Lord dropped back beside Maggie, exchanging quick secret glances, almost certain now that she was as disconcerted as he was by the discovery that Kira Zurich, on her home ground, was a person so different from what she had seemed on first acquaintance.

Twice they passed open doors, children in hospital beds briefly glimpsed, but Kira walked on without stopping, her silence broken only when she tossed back a crisply grateful, "Thank you," to acknowledge Maggie's comment on how attractive the building was. Then, suddenly, she came to a full stop, facing a cross corridor, waiting until everyone had reached her side before she directed attention to a wide glass window part way down the side wall, enclosing an area that was being used as a reception room. Several children could be seen with a number of women who were apparently foster mothers. A nurse in a white uniform was standing by, seemingly waiting for their arrival because, when Kira stepped forward and tapped on the glass, the nurse immediately began to remove the coat of one of the boys, making it evident that activity had been held up pending their arrival.

The scene was as prosaically dull as any pediatrician's waiting room, surely nothing to explain the tensely dramatic tone in which Kira said, "I think you're going to find this very exciting."

"The glass," Perrill said as a whispered prompt.

"Oh yes," Kira acknowledged. "There's no need for you to feel self-conscious about watching them. That's a one-way window. We can see in but they can't see out."

Maggie said, "I was wondering why no one was paying the slightest attention to us."

"We set up this area for psychiatric work," Kira explained. "But we use it for a waiting room, too. It's very handy for an occasion like this. Do you see that boy over on our left, Mr. Lord, the one wearing a blue-striped shirt?"

"With the woman in the red coat?" Maggie asked.

Kira nodded to Maggie but her eyes were still on him. "Mr. Lord, that boy — his name is Neil — is six years and four months old. What would be your general impression of physical development for a child of that age?"

He hesitated, resisting his natural inclination toward compliment, uncertain as to what lay behind Kira Zurich's question. "Golly, I wouldn't know what to say. I'm afraid the only standard I'd have would be our own son —"

"Would you judge him to be small for his age?" Kira persisted. "In any way underdeveloped?"

Maggie came to his rescue. "He surely doesn't seem to be."

"He's not," Kira affirmed. "He's what any pediatrician today would call a normally developed child of that age."

"Actually a little above the median," Perrill put in, puzzling Lincoln Lord as to the point that was being made.

"Now look at another boy," Kira went on. "The one behind the screen. Miss Hedrick is taking off his shirt, getting him ready to go in for his examination."

He found himself in the same situation that he had been with the first boy — another perfectly normal-looking youngster, a year or so older. Again Maggie saved him from taking the lead, surprising him when he heard her ask, "Are they brothers? They look so much alike."

"Yes," Kira said. "And how much older would you think this second boy to be?"

Kira had turned from Maggie again, directing the question to him, and he took a gamble and said, "A year — maybe a little more."

Beside him, he heard Perrill's pleased chuckle as Kira said triumphantly, "They're exactly the same age. This second boy's name is Noel. I didn't tell you that before because I thought you might guess if I did — Neil and Noel."

Astounded, he exclaimed, "You can't possibly mean that they're twins!"

"Yes, they're twins."

Maggie asked, "But surely not identical twins?"

"Oh, yes, indeed. That's true, isn't it, Dr. Perrill?"

"Yes, they're single-egg twins," he affirmed. "No question about that, not the slightest. If it had not been for a difference in diet, I dare say that today they'd be almost indistinguishable. As it is, the second boy — Noel — is roughly two inches taller and weighs eleven or twelve pounds more. At least that was the difference that we had last month."

Lincoln Lord muttered an expression of incredulity.

"You were very close to the mark with your guess, Mr. Lord," Kira said. "At this age — between six and seven — the differential is usually of just about that order. In other words, at six years we reach what is generally accepted as the normal development of a seven-year-old child."

Groggily, he asked, "And it's all because of their being started on this baby food of yours?"

"Well, hardly —" Perrill began, interrupted then by Kira Zurich who carried on. "It's really a misnomer to call it a baby food, Mr. Lord. It's much more than that. One of the things that Dr. Perrill has so clearly established is that the nutrition of a child is no more important during infancy than it is in the years afterward."

"Less important," Perrill put in forcefully, obviously blocking another interruption. "We don't do too bad a job of feeding babies in this country. Oh, a few silly fads turn up now and then, a bit of nonsense here and there, but generally speaking, infant feeding is usually adequate. It's afterwards — eighteen months on up — that's where we start to fumble. And that's when a child is really growing."

Maggie was staring at the glass. "And those two boys — the only difference was diet?"

"That's right," Kira affirmed. "But please don't imagine that Neil has been underfed. He hasn't. He's been fed in a perfectly normal way, actually better than the average child. Our field-worker has been checking every week since he was four months old to make certain that his foster mother was following what the pediatricians now regard as the optimum diet for a child of that age." She paused. "Noel, of course, has been given Dr. Perrill's food."

Perrill cocked his head, his expression that of an artist savoring the joy of creation. "You may not be able to fully appreciate this without a chance to examine the boy a little more closely. But still I think you

306

can see what I mean now that he has his shirt off. Notice that there's no evidence of overnourishment, none of the surplus fat and general flabbiness that is usually associated with overfeeding. That's why weight figures alone are so meaningless. Here we've gotten the gain where it counts — in skeletal structure and muscular development."

Kira asked in a climactic, "Well, Mr. Lord, does that interest you enough to make you want to hear some more?"

He mumbled something, the words unimportant, knowing that his astonished agreement would come through no matter what he said . . . this was a hundred times better than he could possibly have expected! Joel hadn't seen this . . . no, if he had he could never have written that report . . .

The boy in the blue-striped shirt had slipped away from his foster mother's hold and dashed across the room, peeking behind the screen. Quickly, the nurse shooed him back into the capturing arms of the woman in the red coat. But for an instant the two boys had stood together, side by side, the contrast in growth even more startlingly evident then. And it was that picture that fixed itself in Lincoln Lord's mind . . . full pages in all the women's magazines . . . golly, what a job Brick could do with this . . . !

The thought struck and rebounded . . . no, not Brick. He'd had his chance . . . called him three times last week in New York . . . always out. He'd left his name and Brick had never called back . . . but he didn't need Brick. Joel had plenty of advertising experience . . . Mc-Cutcheon & Paisley, one of the best agencies in New York . . .

Caution overtook his racing thoughts . . . this was only one case . . . and Joel had admitted that the stuff did a job. There was still no proof that it was salable. If Perrill hadn't licked some of the objections . . .

"And now shall we go over to the research center?" Kira Zurich asked confidently.

6

Stretched out on the south side of the sheltering rock ledge, Brick Mitchell felt the seeping warmth of the winter sun, and his lazy yawn was soft with the sound of contentment. This was the first time he had breathed air scented with snow-dampened pine needles since that last deer hunt before he had left for college, the first time in many years that he had worn a flannel shirt and leather boots, one of the few times in his life that he had ever reached out for a woman's hand when there was no desire other than the comfort of presence.

And the feel of Tommy's hand was right, the pressure of her fingers neither too light nor too strong, the response of desire without the demand for possession. He opened his eyes and looked up, seeing her sitting close beside him, her face turned away, her hair burnished bronze against the blue sky. Involuntarily, the muscles of his hand contracted and the turning of her head was as the reflex movement of his own body. But her eyes were something apart and he had to keep them that way. He doubled his right knee and dug a boot heel deep into the pine needles, again and again until the heel struck hard against the bedrock.

"Lucky that Mike and I wear the same size of boots," he said.

Tommy looked away. "You don't."

"What do you mean — we don't? These fit perfectly."

"They're not Mike's."

He sat up. "Hey, what goes?"

"I'm confessing," she said. "I called Selma yesterday and asked her to borrow them from someone."

"I don't get it."

"That's what I'm trying to confess. I've been a conniving bitch."

"But why?"

"I wanted you the way you really are."

"With my boots on?"

"Yes."

"You should have told me last night."

"This isn't last night — it's now."

The feel of her hand had changed. It was warm flesh now, feminine and demanding, and he crushed it with the grip of passion, reaching out with his other hand.

Tommy pulled away. "Don't you understand?" Her laugh was brittle. "I'm giving up — cleansing my black heart with a full confession."

"There's a connection, huh — the black heart and wanting a guy with his boots on?"

"I just thought it might be a change. I'm funny that way. I have a lot of ideas. Mostly bad."

"Not that I've noticed."

"You're not that much of a fool." Suddenly, she turned on him, her voice fiercely vibrant. "Oh, damn it, why aren't you! Why couldn't you have just relaxed and let me pull the wool over your eyes."

"I'm lost."

"Oh no, you're not! You knew what I was doing right from the beginning — three Martinis and then the big shanghai act — the smart female. Oh, I was the clever gal. I had it all figured. Let him see how happy Mike and Selma are. This was just the ticket — get him up here in the woods and he'll be the kind of a crazy young kid again that could be fooled into —" Her voice broke and tears flooded. "You're just too damned smart to be tricked."

She struggled against his attempt to take her in his arms, a Tommy that he had never known before, and the shock of discovering that she could cry was, even more than what she said, the motive strength of the force with which he drew her toward him, pulling her down to the bedding of pine needles. "I'm not so smart," he whispered hoarsely. "Not smart at all."

For a long moment every fiber of her body was limp, as if there was no life left anywhere except in the fierce drive of her lips. Then, suddenly, it was her lips that were limp and her body that was strong and she broke away from him, on her feet before he could stop her, running down the path without looking back.

He stood then, watching her until she disappeared at a turning of the path. He kicked deep into the pine needles, again and again until the hobnails of his boots struck fire from the flint-rock underneath. "I'm a bastard," he muttered. "And I don't know why."

7

Lincoln Lord was not surprised that there was a noticeable change in Dr. Perrill as they entered his private office — no man was ever quite the same in his own four-walled kingdom — and there had already been more than a hint that the scientist was chafing under Kira Zurich's domination. They had come into the research center building through the back door and, as they had made a wandering inspection of the laboratory areas on their way to the director's office, Perrill had been noticeably annoyed by her proprietary attitude. She had stepped in to introduce his assistants, taken the lead in pointing out apparatus and equipment, even assuming for herself the privilege of describing the work that was being done in each section.

Dr. Perrill had not, however, accepted a subservient role without resistance. Several times he had interrupted her to take over himself, and once he had stepped in to correct her, mincing no words in a quick reversal of some statement that she had made. This latter show of strength had been particularly encouraging to Lincoln Lord because it evidenced a scientist's adherence to objective truth, a welcome safeguard against the bias that had shown through everything that Kira Zurich said. He had heard enough now to know that her fierce pride in Haven Home would keep her from exposing anything but the best side of all that was being done here. She was not to be blamed — it was the high-pressure saleswoman's expected approach — but it was Perrill who had to be cultivated if the full truth were to be known.

He felt that he had made a certain amount of progress in establishing a good personal relationship with Perrill — the Ichakuri business had been a lucky strike — but he could still sense an indefinable resistance, perhaps only the discomfiture that scientists always seemed to feel in the presence of a layman invasion of their cloistered world. Whatever the cause, it was something that had to be broken down if Perrill were to be induced to speak as freely and frankly as he wanted him to do. The obvious need was to get him talking about himself, not only to prevent his slipping too quickly into the jawbreaking jargon of biochemistry — a danger suggested by the technical journals and research reports stacked upon his desk — but also to open the way to a better understanding of Perrill as a human being. Although this latter objective was not something reasoned to the point of full awareness, Lincoln Lord had less faith in his ability to judge facts than in his talent for weighing them in terms of the man who offered them for judgment.

As they found seats around the research director's desk, Lincoln Lord waited to sit down until Kira and Maggie chose chairs together on the right side. Then he said, "Dr. Perrill, I'm very much impressed with what we've seen so far, but I must admit to being a little lost, too. Would it be too much trouble — perhaps this is what you've planned, anyway — but I'm sure it would be most helpful if you'd go back to the beginning and trace this whole development step by step. From what I've picked up, I gather that it started during your days in India?"

"Well, if you really want to hear the India part of it —" Perrill began, oddly flustered. But his embarrassed smile seemed no more than a modest acceptance of a pleasant invitation until he glanced at Kira Zurich. Then his expression assumed an I-told-you-so cast, that meaning instantly confirmed by the tightening of Kira Zurich's lips. For a moment, Lincoln Lord felt himself guilty of error, lost because he had no idea of what he had inadvertently stepped into, worried now that he might have offended Kira. Quickly, he said to her, "But if you've planned this another way —"

She started to speak and then shook her head. But there was still the feeling that she was going along only because it was too late to resist, Perrill having already gotten heavily to his feet and opened a drawer in a file cabinet beside his desk.

From the cabinet he took out what seemed an oversized photo album and brought it back to the desk, placing it on the pad in front of his chair with an air of defiance. Lincoln Lord was more positive than ever that he had gained ground with Perrill by opening the India subject, but there was the fear that he had lost even more with Kira Zurich. He glanced at Maggie but she was looking away, seemingly a purposeful avoidance of his eyes, and his apprehension increased, all the more so because he still had no idea what his error had been — except that, for some unexplained reason, Kira apparently didn't want Perrill to talk about what had happened in India.

Resolutely, the research director opened the battered cover of the scrapbook, exposing a blank flyleaf at which he sat staring thoughtfully. Then, raising his eyes he said slowly, "All of this came about — this chance to go to India — because of Mrs. Zurich."

Kira's eyes snapped up. But her expression was unreadable.

"Of course she wasn't Mrs. Zurich then, this was a long time ago," Perrill went on. "But even in those days she was the same sort of person she is now — very understanding and most generous."

"Oh, come now, Dr. Perrill," Kira broke in with an embarrassed little laugh, turning to Maggie as if it were an escape. "I really didn't do a thing in the world except send him word that there was an opening."

Maggie said something to express her surprise that Kira and Dr. Perrill had known each other as long as they apparently had, and Lincoln Lord let Kira's answer slip past without hearing it, his consciousness dulled by amazement that Kira was so susceptible to blatant flattery. He had, he saw, been right about Perrill's capability in handling her.

Perrill plunged ahead. "I went out as a missionary doctor. You see, I'd been ill for some time, badly in need of a change of scene, and going to India was about as complete a change as you could possibly imagine." He had turned the flyleaf now, revealing a photo-

311

graphic print so faded that, seen upside down from the opposite side of the desk, it was no more than a brown blur. Perrill did not turn the book to display it. Seemingly, the only purpose that he intended the scrapbook to serve was an aid to his memory, and the old picture must have set a pleasant scene, because there was a richly reminiscent quality in his voice as he said, "I'd been here for a year or more — medical officer at this mission station — when a runner came in one evening with the news that there'd been a disaster at a coal mine about fifty miles away. I was the nearest doctor and they demanded that I come. The head of the mission was opposed to my going, arguing that the mine was out of our territory and that we had plenty of illness in our own area — all true enough — and then, too, the monsoon had started and the roads were very bad, very bad indeed. Nevertheless, I felt myself called upon to go. I rounded up a man with an ox cart and we set out." He turned the page. "That was the beginning."

The picture on the second page was again badly faded but apparently not to Perrill's eyes. "I'd heard something about these mines — gossip — listening to the wind, as they say out there — and most of what I'd heard proved to be true. They were being operated by a managing agency in Calcutta and, from all accounts, the men who ran it were a rather bad lot. Of course, that was said of all the British in those days. That was the Ghandi period — India fighting for its independence — and there was anti-British feeling everywhere. Personally, I'd had the impression that most of the British had handled themselves rather well — at least better than the Indians ever gave them credit for doing — but no one could possibly defend what had been done at those mines. To begin with, they were in protected territory. The area had been reserved for one of the aboriginal tribes — the Tokalis — and there were regulations forbidding the settling of any other people. Originally, I'm told, the mine owners had gotten in under the guise of providing employment for the Tokalis, but that hadn't lasted long. Not too difficult to understand, the way they'd treated them, paid them little or nothing and exploited them horribly. The Tokalis were a very proud tribe — wonderful people as I was later to learn — and they'd rebelled in rather violent fashion. After that, the mine managers had kicked out the Tokalis and brought in two hundred or so families from Bihar."

"As strike-breakers, I take it?"

"No, as a permanent labor force," Perrill said. "The owners drove off the Tokalis — shut them out of the mining area with a high fence. As I say, this was all being done on land that was supposed to be reserved exclusively for the Tokalis, so, as you can imagine, considerable animosity developed. Some of the Tokali men had learned to use dynamite while they'd been working in the mines and so, every now and then afterwards, they'd somehow slip through the fence and blow up this or that around the place. That had been going on for months. Whether that's what happened in this instance, I have no idea. In any event, it was a horrible affair."

He turned another page. "It was a surface mine — just a great pit. On this particular day, all of the mineworkers were down in a deep cut opening up a new seam of coal. Every adult man and woman in the village was working there, every child large enough to carry even a tiny basket of coal or earth. Suddenly, there was a great roar and the earth walls around them collapsed. They were all caught like rats. Most of them were killed outright, buried alive. Not more than a half-dozen escaped." He stared at the photo. "I shall never forget standing here on the edge of this pit and looking down upon what was the grave of some four hundred living souls."

Lincoln Lord finally broke the silence by saying, "I take it that there wasn't much left for a doctor to do."

"No, not as far as those poor devils in the mine were concerned," Perrill said. "But there was something else that I'll never forget either — walking back from the edge of the pit and hearing the cries of starving babies. There were almost seventy of them. What had happened, of course, was that all of the women had brought their babies to work with them — common practice out there — and they'd left them in sort of an improvised nursery in a little grove of trees. Don't let my calling it a nursery give you a false impression. There was no building, nothing of that sort, just the underbrush cleared away. A couple of the older women stayed with the babies and, at intervals, the mothers had come up from the mine to nurse them."

"Then they were all tiny babies?" Maggie asked, plainly horrified by Perrill's description of the scene and circumstances.

"There were a few that were as old, perhaps, as a year," Perrill went on, the very flatness of his tone suspensefully dramatic. "Out there, of course — at least in those days and I dare say there's been little change — breast feeding is almost invariably continued until the mother's flow of milk is stopped by an ensuing pregnancy. In any event, all of our babies were still nurslings, dependent upon their mothers for sustenance. And the mothers were dead. Worst of all, there was no cow's milk to be had. The mine owners had prohibited the Bihar people from bringing in any animals — saved themselves the nuisance of having cows wandering about the working area, I suppose — but it put us in one devil of a spot, trying to find some way to keep those babies alive. Standing by and watching seventy tiny babies starve is not a pleasant prospect."

There was a shuddering tremor in Maggie's wordless agreement.

"We'd already lost a few," Perrill went on. "You see, some forty-eight hours had elapsed between the accident and my arrival — ox cart is a slow method of travel and the roads, such as they were, were in horrible shape." He sighed deeply. "If the message they'd sent me had only given some inkling of what the situation was to be, I could easily enough have brought in a supply of canned milk from the mission station. But I'd been told nothing and so I'd loaded down the cart with medical supplies, the sort of things that I'd naturally expected I'd need most. After I got there, I'd gladly have traded the whole mission hospital for a few cases of tinned milk. But then it was too late. Even if we'd sent back to the mission station for a supply, it couldn't possibly have gotten back to us in time to do any good. The survival capacity of an unfed nursing infant is not high at best, you know, and it's all the lower when you're dealing with babies that are seriously undernourished to begin with, even prenatally."

"Wasn't there any place around that you could get fresh milk?" Maggie asked. "I suppose I'm wrong — I've always thought of India as being full of cows."

"Yes, in most parts of India that would have been true — cows everywhere," Perrill said. "And, naturally, that was my first hope. I thought surely that somewhere not too far away there must be a village where there'd be cows and goats enough so that we could get our hands on at least a little milk. There wasn't. As I've said, we were in Tokali territory, surrounded by them, and the Tokalis kept no cows, no goats, no water buffaloes, no domestic animals of any sort. You see, they were strict vegetarians. They ate no flesh of any kind, not even animal products — no milk, no eggs, nothing that was even secondarily animal in origin." He changed tone. "In the light of what's to follow, that's a point that should be particularly noted — the complete absence of any source of animal protein in the Tokali diet."

Now for the first time, Perrill turned the scrapbook to display a photograph, a reasonably clear picture of a gaunt man with a scraggly beard, wearing a battered topi and a bush jacket. "Here's the man who was really responsible for saving the lives of most of those babies. His name was MacIntosh — Evan MacIntosh. As you'd guess from his name, he was a Scot. Really quite a remarkable man. I can't tell you too much about his personal background — he was a secretive sort, not given to talking about himself — but according to gossip he'd come out to India with the British colonial service as a young man, gotten himself involved in a scandal of some sort, and disappeared into the bush. I do know that he'd lived with the Tokalis for some years, at least long enough to have learned their language — and that, believe me, was not something that he could have done in a short period of time. Afterwards, I had a go at it myself, so I know what I'm talking about. It's fantastically difficult, full of strange nasal sounds — no language on earth quite like it. But as I say, MacIntosh had mastered it and the mine owners had employed him as a liaison man with the Tokalis. As long as they were working in the mines, MacIntosh was the only white man who could talk to them. And, afterwards, the mine manager had kept him on to keep negotiating with the Tokalis, trying to get some sort of truce in the guerrilla warfare that they were carrying on against the mines. MacIntosh hadn't been too successful — I rather suspect that his sympathies were more with the Tokalis than with the mine owners — and the mine manager, a man named Bowser, was very much down on him. He was certain that the cave-in had been caused by the Tokalis sneaking in and setting off a dynamite blast and he blamed MacIntosh for not having done something to prevent it. In any event, Bowser warned me against MacIntosh as soon as I arrived, telling me that he was not to be trusted, and that I wasn't to take seriously anything that he told me. Unfortunately, I believed him — a mistake that cost me several hours and the lives of at least a half-dozen babies. Eventually, however, I listened to his story. By then I was desperate, ready to grasp at any straw no matter what it was, and I must admit that at the outset I didn't believe a word of what MacIntosh claimed — his story that the Tokalis had some sort of a special tribal food that they cooked up to give to their children. He insisted that he had seen it fed to babies no more than a month old and they'd thrived on it. He was positive that if we could get our hands on some of this food, the babies could be saved. Bowser pooh-poohed the whole idea — he regarded the Tokalis as the worst sort of savages and, after what had happened, refused to let MacIntosh outside the enclosure. Eventually, however, I convinced him that there was nothing to be lost by giving MacIntosh a try. We had to do something. Anything, no matter what it was, would be better than standing around and watching the rest of those babies die."

Kira was looking pointedly at her wrist watch. Perrill saw her and said apologetically, "Yes, yes, I know — afraid I am dragging this out —"

"Not so far as I'm concerned," Lincoln Lord said, responding to the appeal in Perrill's anxious expression, then saying to Kira Zurich, "If you're concerned about me, please don't be. I've plenty of time."

Plainly pleased, Perrill said, "Well, you do have to have a bit of background if you're to understand all this. Now, let's see —"

"Your man MacIntosh was about to get some of this baby food from the Tokalis," Lincoln Lord prompted. "And I don't imagine that was too easy to do, was it? From what you've said, I'd gather there wasn't any love lost between the Tokalis and these strike-breakers who'd been brought in."

"No indeed," Perrill said. "They were mortal enemies — the Tokalis and the Biharis —"

"Oh, but not those tiny babies?" Maggie protested.

"Yes, that may have been the way MacIntosh appealed to them," Perrill conceded uncertainly. "In any event, he came back about two hours after he'd slipped out through the fence, bringing with him four or five Tokali women carrying brass pots filled with this food of theirs." He paused, grimacing. "I shall never forget my first smell of the stuff. Simply horrible. And it looked as bad as it smelled. It was a watery sort of gruel, a dirty gray with a greenish cast, a sourish fermented odor that was absolutely revolting. I was sure that it was putrid — couldn't see how it could be anything else — but MacIntosh insisted that it was all right and the Tokali women backed him up, claiming that it was what they always fed their babies. Something of an argument developed and I finally attempted to settle it by agreeing that we would *try* to feed a little of it to one of the older babies. I was positive that even a starving child wouldn't be able to stomach the stuff. I was wrong. One of the Tokali women dipped her finger in the jar that she was carrying, put it in the nearest baby's mouth, and the little rascal went to work as if it were the finest thing he'd ever tasted in his life."

"But wouldn't a starving baby eat anything?" Maggie asked.

"Yes, that's what I was afraid was happening," Perrill said. "But it was too late then — the Tokali women were feeding one baby after another. All I could do was hope for the best, trying to comfort myself with the realization that our Western standards of wholesomeness are by no means accepted all around the world. Nevertheless, I was thoroughly frightened of the consequences, fully expecting that we'd wind up with gastroenteritis all over the place. But as I say, what else could we do? And at least we were getting something in those little bellies. The cry of a starving baby is one of the most awful sounds on earth."

"I should think it would be," Maggie whispered.

"Well, it was after dark by the time all of the babies were fed," Perrill continued. "I'd not closed my eyes for almost two days — the whole night before in that jogging ox cart — and I finally fell off to sleep. How much I actually slept, I have no idea. Awake or asleep, it was all the same horrible nightmare, imagining what I was going to find in the morning. I awoke about dawn. The first thing that struck me was the absolute silence. There wasn't a sound, not a single baby crying. You can imagine what I expected to find." A faraway look came into his eyes. "There are moments in every man's life, I suppose, that remain with him forever. This was one such moment for me — standing there in the cold morning mist, the sun just coming up, turning down the ragged blanket that covered the first baby I came to. I fully expected that when I reached down I'd touch a cold cheek. But the little tyke was just as full of life as he could be, happily sleeping off a tummyful of the first food that he'd had in almost three days. And that's what I found all around the circle. I couldn't believe my eyes. Or my ears either."

"It must have seemed like a miracle," Maggie said.

"It *was* a miracle!" Perrill exclaimed. "Within twenty-four hours, we had those babies coming along in astounding fashion. Three days later, they were as chipper as could be. Oh, not all of them, of course — there were a few who were too far gone to save — but the rest responded amazingly. If I'd had all the milk in the world I couldn't have brought those babies along as well as we did on that Tokali food."

"What in the world was in the stuff?" Lincoln Lord asked.

"That's what I spent the next year trying to find out. I knew that the base was some sort of cereal — that was obvious — but beyond that I had the devil's own time finding out anything about it. Mac-Intosh had lived with Tokalis for years — knew more about them than any white man who'd ever gotten into their villages — but still he didn't have an inkling of how they were preparing their food.

You see — well, there's a bit more background that I really should give you."

Kira looked at her watch again, her little sigh sharp with the sound of disapproval, but Lincoln Lord carefully avoided any evidence that he had noticed it, continuing to give Dr. Perrill the encouragement of full attention.

"As long as I was at the mine," the scientist continued, "I saw no Tokalis except the women who came every evening to bring us a new supply of food. They were fine-looking women, well developed and noticeably taller and heavier than the average Indian woman, but it wasn't until after I'd seen a group of their men that I could fully appreciate what MacIntosh had been telling me about what extraordinary physical specimens the Tokalis were. The first time I saw any men was on the way out. MacIntosh took me over to one of their villages so that I could thank their headmen for helping to save the babies. We were met at the edge of the village by a delegation of men, twenty or thirty of them, and I could hardly believe my eyes. There wasn't a man under five-ten and most were six feet or more. Almost all of them were powerfully built, big-boned, heavily muscled, absolute superb specimens. Up to that time, I'd never seen such a group of men anywhere in India. Afterwards, I got to know the Sikhs and I'd say they were more or less in the same class as far as physical development was concerned. However, the typical Sikh physique was explainable in terms of their excellent diet — or at least what I'd been taught to regard as an excellent diet. The astounding thing about the Tokalis was that, once their babies had been weaned, they ate absolutely no animal protein of any kind."

"But what *were* they eating?" Lincoln Lord asked.

"That was their secret," Perrill said. "Naturally, I tried to find out what it was. They'd tell me nothing."

"But *why?*" Maggie asked.

Perrill waited through a thought-collecting moment. "MacIntosh's hypothesis — and he was by way of being a very creditable amateur anthropologist — was that some time in the distant past, hundreds of years ago, perhaps even thousands, the tribe had somehow managed to discover how to prepare a food that made their children grow into bigger and stronger men than those of any of the other tribes with whom they were always battling for existence. You can understand, of course, how enormously important an advantage that would give them."

"And also why they'd want to keep it secret," Lincoln Lord added.

318

"Exactly. And you can understand, too, how their food preparation would become a secret religious rite," Perrill added. "That's a standard technique in primitive societies, you know — the secret rite as a means of hiding your magic from your enemies. And then, too, all of the world's religions have always been greatly concerned with food practices. The Jewish faith is perhaps an outstanding example, but even we Christians —"

Kira interrupted sharply. "I'm sure the Lords would be interested in hearing about your experiences when you were living with the Tokalis."

Perrill was taken aback by the abruptness of her demand, his momentary fumbling with a scrapbook page obviously an attempt to keep from showing resentment, successful enough so that when he spoke again his voice was well controlled. "Yes, I finally managed, some months later, to get a leave from the mission station and went to live in a Tokali village. I'd arranged it through MacIntosh, of course, and with his sponsorship the Tokalis received me in quite hospitable fashion. And then, too, I did a little medical work now and then, and of course they appreciated that." He paused. "There was one incident that helped me particularly. One of the young men of the tribe — he was the son of Napi, their chief headman — fell from a tree and impaled himself on the stub of a broken limb. It was a horrible wound, his whole belly ripped open, but I sewed him up and somehow he managed to survive. I'm sure it was his rugged constitution rather than my rough and ready surgery that pulled him through, but still it opened the way for a good relationship with old Napi."

"After that, I should think that you'd have been right on the inside."

"I thought so too," Perrill said wryly. "But still it took a long time. Napi wasn't an easy man to get around. Sorry I don't have a better picture than this — I'd gotten hold of a bad lot of photographic chemicals — but you see something of the sort of man he was."

Lincoln Lord squinted at the brown-blotched print, seeing little more than the blurred features of an old man's face, character established more by ear than eye as Dr. Perrill went on to describe him. "Napi was well over sixty at the time — the average life expectancy in India then was somewhere in the thirties — and he was no less remarkable as a physical specimen. He was six feet three, must have weighed a good two hundred pounds, and even at his age he had as powerful a set of arm and shoulder muscles as I've ever seen on a human being. And he was no fool. He knew what I was after and, grateful as he was to me for having saved his son's life, he wasn't giving away any tribal secrets.

But the more I saw of the Tokalis, particularly their children, the more determined I became. Nowhere in India — and here I'll not even except the Sikhs — had I seen children grow the way those Tokali youngsters did. And the survival rate was almost unbelievable. Down in the mission station area, even with hospital facilities available, less than half of the babies got through their first year. The Tokalis lost less than ten per cent. The incidence of disease was so low that — well, perhaps that's enough to tell you why I couldn't give up trying to find the secret of that Tokali food."

"But if you were living right there in the village, how could they keep you from knowing what they were eating?" Lincoln Lord asked.

"Oh, I found out easily enough what their raw materials were. They couldn't keep that from me. As I'd guessed already, the base was a meal made out of one of the pulses — they're legumes, you know — and I found out, too, that they were also using considerable quantities of sesame seed. Both are excellent sources of vegetable protein but neither had the nutritive qualities that somehow got into the finished food. I knew they were adding herbs and roots — I could see the women bringing them in from fields and woods — but that led me nowhere either. There was nothing that even suggested a reasonable hypothesis as to why, after they cooked up the stuff, it became what was apparently a perfectly adequate milk substitute. And the most amazing thing of all was that it was tolerated by the tiniest of infants. I'd seen that at the mine, of course, and there was still more evidence in the Tokali village."

"Then the secret was in the cooking — the processing — whatever they did to it?"

"Yes, that became evident very soon," Perrill said. "But knowing where the secret was and getting your hands on it were two very different things. All of the cooking for the entire village was done in one building. I suppose you might call it a temple. At least it was their holy of holies. Once a day, they'd stew up a new batch — the fire always lighted with the first rays of the sun — and no one was allowed to come anywhere near except the three village elders, Napi and his two other headmen, plus a half-dozen women who did the actual work. I did get the idea that there must be something like a fermentation process involved — the odor made that almost unmistakable — and then, too, there was a waiting period before it could be served. What they cooked up one morning was never served before the following day. Beyond that, I couldn't find a thing. And it began to seem that I never would. Then, finally, I got a break. And it came just in time. That very morning MacIntosh had told me that he couldn't possibly stay on any longer. Without him I'd be lost. I still hadn't picked up enough of their language to be able to carry on alone. Even with MacIntosh translating, I was having a hard time getting across the idea that Napi would be doing a great service to humanity by giving me the Tokali secret."

"He just wasn't interested in service to humanity," Lincoln Lord observed. "All he wanted to do was keep the Tokalis alive."

Perrill's smile took on a wry cast. "As it turned out, what he was really interested in was keeping himself alive. He called us to his hut on this particular evening, barred the door, and after a long and wandering preamble — neither of us had any idea what he was leading up to — he finally got around to the point. He made me a proposition. If I'd sew up his belly in the same way I'd sewed up the belly of his son after he'd fallen out of the tree — and if he, too, recovered — he'd let me watch what went on in the temple cookhouse."

"Sew up his belly?" Lincoln Lord puzzled. "Had he been hurt?"

"He had a hernia," Perrill said. "Or so I discovered when he finally permitted me to examine him. And it was a rather bad one. Oh, I don't suppose it would have been too difficult a job for a competent man working with good hospital facilities, but I'd never been any great shakes as a surgeon, and all the facilities I had were my own two hands and a rather skimpy bag of instruments. MacIntosh was the only person who could possibly assist me — there was no one else who understood a word of English —" The doctor stopped, his face contorted into a worried scowl. "I'm sure you realize, Mr. Lord, that Napi's proposition had nothing to do with my decision to operate. As badly as I wanted that secret —"

Quickly Lincoln Lord supplied, "Your professional obligation as a doctor was still the paramount consideration."

"Exactly," Perrill said gratefully. "Actually, the decision was unavoidable. That next morning, when there was light enough so that I could make a thorough examination, I saw definite evidences of strangulation and, in that climate, gangrenous complications develop in a hurry. As heavily as the odds were against a successful operation, the prognosis was even worse if I didn't operate. So I went ahead — and somehow I got through it."

"And it was successful?" Lincoln Lord asked, the answer a foregone conclusion.

Perrill's fingertips explored his bald head. "Do you remember the fable about the man who was promised that if he could work a riddle, he'd be able to find a great treasure chest — and he did — and then when he opened the chest, all that he found inside was another riddle? That was about my situation."

"Do you mean that Napi still wouldn't tell you the secret?"

"Oh, he kept his promise. He let me spend a whole day in the temple cookhouse. But he couldn't tell me something that he didn't know. As far as he was concerned, what was happening inside those cooking pots was the work of the gods. All he was doing was carrying out the ceremony that had been passed down from generation to generation. After that, the gods took over. Who could explain the magic of the gods?"

Perrill flipped a scrapbook page but did not look at it. "Goodness knows how many times I went back over all this afterwards trying to find out where the secret was hidden." His eyes narrowed as if to sharpen the image of memory, but they were twinkling, a warning that this story was a guessing game. "I should tell you one thing at the outset. The sacred tree of the Tokalis is the papaya. All of their religious rites are tied up with it and it plays a big part in this cooking ceremony. The temple itself was really an enclosure for a little papaya grove — a swampy sort of spring, papaya trees all around it, and all that enclosed by the temple, buildings on two sides, walls on the other two. Sorry I don't have a decent picture, but it was almost impossible to get one. The trees were so thick that almost no light got in, even in the middle of the day."

"I can visualize what it must have been like."

"The ceremony began with the building of a fire — papaya wood, of course — and this was accompanied by a rather elaborate ritual of chanting. Then brass pots were brought out of the building and scoured with a special earth brought from somewhere up on the side of the hill." As an aside, he explained, "I later determined that this earth had a very high calcium content," then continuing, "water was then dipped from the swampy spring and the pots filled to a certain mark. All this was being done, as I've said, to the accompaniment of chanted prayers to the gods."

Maggie said, "It must have been a fascinating sight."

"Oh, it was! Unforgettable. And all the more so, of course, because I was trying so hard to determine the significance of every move that was being made. Let's see now, where was I?"

322

"The water."

"Oh yes. Well, while the water was heating, the women ground the meal — pulse and sesame principally but there were little dashes of other things, too — nine different kinds of seeds and nuts."

"Could you identify them?"

"Yes. At least afterwards. While I was there, I picked up sample grains from the ground around the grinding stones. All of this meal was mixed together — more chanting — and then it was ladled into the pots of hot water. While the women stirred, the men kept up the chant, every now and then tossing in a handful of herbs and papaya leaves. Finally, the whole mess was cooked into a thick porridge. Then came a very important part of the ceremony. The pots were watched carefully, the headmen leaning over them and listening for the voice of the gods. When they heard it — a thick gurgling sound — the fires were immediately put out. The pots were taken off and plunged into the swamp water to cool them quickly. Then papayas were taken from the trees — the ripe fruit — and crushed into a pulp that was stirred into the mixture. Finally, the pots were carried to a certain spot in the temple where they were allowed to stand for about eight hours. By then, the mixture was giving off a yeasty sort of odor, gas bubbles coming up through it. Have you ever seen a setting of old-fashioned buckwheat pancakes?"

Maggie said, "Yes, many times."

"Well, that's what it looked like — a buckwheat pancake batter with a little scum of green mold over the top."

Maggie said, "It doesn't sound very appetizing."

"It wasn't," Perrill said. "If the mold didn't develop, by the way, it was a sign that they'd somehow displeased the gods and the magic wasn't working." The scientist stopped and asked with a tongue-in-cheek smile, "Any guesses as to what was happening in that pot?"

"I'm afraid I'm completely lost."

"So was I," Perrill acknowledged. "But I thought I could dig out the answer in my lab. I'd set up a little laboratory at the mission station — nothing elaborate, but still I had facilities enough to run a reasonably reliable food analysis. I found nothing, absolutely nothing, no reason whatsoever why this Tokali gruel should have such remarkable nutritive qualities. As far as my analysis revealed, I might have been testing any cereal porridge into which you'd mixed some chopped-up spinach. I knew I was missing something — I'd seen too much to believe otherwise — but what was it? My first guess was that it might

323

have had something to do with vitamins. This was in the late thirties, you see — the big vitamin discoveries were just being made, the journals were full of the subject, and I thought the answer might be somewhere in that area. But I had no facilities for vitamin analysis. There was a biochemist in Calcutta who had done some work in the field — Dr. Chokuri — and so I took him samples. He ran a vitamin assay for me. There was a high concentration of thiamine — from the pulse and sesame seed base, of course — but that was hardly enough to account for the results. Chokuri was very interested, however — he'd been working on a project to develop a synthetic milk substitute — so he offered me the facilities for his laboratory."

"You'd left the mission by then," Kira prompted, her manner and tone now giving Lincoln Lord the impression that she had changed tactics, no longer resisting the scientist's reminiscences, perhaps because he and Maggie were so obviously finding them interesting.

"Yes, I'd left the mission," Perrill said. "I'm afraid I'd been something of a misfit there from the beginning — my interest was more the body than the soul — and then, too, I'd become so obsessed with this Tokali thing that I could think of nothing else. I simply had to follow it up. The first year was discouraging — one dead end after another. The worst of it was that I couldn't match the Tokali food in the laboratory. I'd started animal work, of course — I'd get terrific growth with their stuff but I couldn't match it with anything I cooked up, even though I thought I was duplicating everything they did. Every month or so I'd make a trip back to the Tokali country to get more samples, trying to find what I was missing. For a while I thought it was bacteriological — or maybe a strain of yeast mold — something that they were picking up in some raw material that I wasn't getting when I bought what I thought were the same things on the Calcutta market. But I couldn't check that out either. I began to suspect that there was something that Napi hadn't let me see — you know, the old trick of the cook who gives you the recipe for her prize dish but leaves out the most important ingredient?"

"I was wondering about that," Maggie said.

Perrill shook his head. "No, Napi wasn't holding out on me. Actually — the truth is that I never *have* been able to completely duplicate the Tokali food."

Lincoln Lord felt himself suddenly propelled into emptiness, the tricked victim of a story without a payoff, yet the first instant of conscious thought made him realize that he must be wrong.

324

And the twinkle in the scientist's eyes proved that he was much too good a yarn spinner to have worked himself into a dead end. "But it was the Tokali food that gave me the lead — and one day I happened to run onto a paper in one of the British journals."

Surprisingly, Kira Zurich broke in and said, "I'm glad you made that point, Dr. Perrill. I was afraid that we might be leading the Lords astray — letting them imagine that all we have now is just a duplicate of that foul-smelling stuff the Tokalis were making."

"Oh, I was hardly imagining that," Lincoln Lord said, pleased at this evidence that Kira was conscious of what Joel Morris's report had raised as the prime objection to the marketing of Dr. Perrill's baby food.

Kira said, "As a matter of fact — correct me if I'm wrong, Dr. Perrill — what we have now is so far away from what you originally started with that it bears almost no relationship to what you had when you first came back from India."

"Well, yes, we have made some progress —" Perrill began.

"And particularly this last year," Kira said forcefully, her eyes on Lincoln Lord, the argument too plain to be missed that Joel's report was no longer valid.

Had he been forced to reply, he would have said something to try to make Kira Zurich realize that he was not resisting her, but before he could say anything, Kira said, "I'm sorry, Dr. Perrill. I didn't mean to interrupt your story. I just thought that it was important to —" She broke off with an anxious little laugh. "You'd just found that enzyme article in the journal."

For an instant Perrill seemed reluctant to go on, although it was impossible to know whether his resistance reflected disagreement or only his annoyance at not having been allowed to tell his story in his own way. His tone was flat, petulant as he finally said, "The paper covered some work that had been done in Burma on the use of *papain* as an enzymatic agent in the production of food stuffs from high protein cereals. What caught my eye, of course, was the use of papain. As you probably know, papain is an enzyme that is produced by the papaya tree."

Maggie said, "Isn't that what they use in a lot of these meat tenderizers?"

"Exactly," Perrill said, brightening noticeably. "Yes, that's the active ingredient in a good many of them — papain. When you put it on meat you get — you might call it a pre-digestive action — breaking

325

down some of the protein molecules. I was familiar with that, of course, and since both the crushed papaya fruit and the leaves of the papaya tree were ingredients of the Tokali food, I'd even considered the possibility that we might be getting an enzymatic reaction from the presence of papain. There was nothing in the literature, however, to indicate that papain had any such effect upon vegetable proteins as I'd been observing — that is, until this paper of Dr. Ichakuri's came along."

"Ichakuri?" Lincoln Lord exclaimed. "So that's how you got to know him?"

"Yes, that was my first contact with Dr. Ichakuri," Perrill said. "I wrote him as soon as I read the paper — through the editorial offices in London, of course — and so it took a couple of months before I finally got a reply. Well, to make a long story a bit shorter, I finally went to Rangoon to see him. Thank goodness I did. It was Dr. Ichakuri who finally put me on the right track. You see —" He hesitated, groping for something that seemed beyond expression.

"I was hoping you were going to mention that," Kira said, taking over. "The thing that so impressed me about Dr. Perrill's whole attitude toward nutrition — after he came back from India, I mean — was this positive approach of Dr. Ichakuri's. So much of the nutritional work had been from the negative side, just the correction of deficiencies. Dr. Perrill, I'm sure you can express it very much better than I can."

Perrill seemed by no means confident of his ability to fulfill her expectations, but after a moment he said, "Well, yes, that has been rather generally true, I suppose — what you might call, perhaps, the medical point of view toward this whole subject of nutrition. So many diseases, so many abnormalities of human development have proved to be traceable to dietary deficiencies that it's only natural that most of the research work has been in that direction."

Kira stepped in again. "The old approach, the negative approach, was almost limited to the identification of dietary deficiencies and then finding a way to correct them. The objective, of course, was normal development. We wanted every child to grow and develop in a *normal* way. Isn't that true? We say, don't we, that we want our babies to grow into good, healthy *normal* children. But what's our standard for normality? It's the other children we see around us, isn't it? If your child is as well developed as your neighbor's children you're satisfied. But why should you be? Why shouldn't we set ourselves a new goal? Why

326

shouldn't we provide the nutritive means by which we can develop the human body into something over and beyond anything that we've ever thought possible?"

Lincoln Lord's smile was meaningless, no more than an acknowledgment of surprise, but Kira took it as a challenge. "Does that sound fantastic, Mr. Lord? It isn't at all. Surely you've noticed what a change there's been in our children over the past fifteen or twenty years — how much taller and stronger they are?"

"Of course."

"And it's a result of improved diet. So —" She caught a quick breath. "We've gone that far, why can't we go farther? Is there any indication that we've reached the optimum capacity for human development? No, indeed. We've raised the normal line — true — but we can raise it still farther."

"Yes, I suppose it's theoretically possible."

"It's beyond the theory stage," Kira said, crisply conclusive. "We're doing it. You saw Neil and Noel."

"That's a very convincing case, no doubt about it," he replied, caution aroused by the vehemence of Kira's drivingly argumentative tone. As a purposeful diversion he turned to the research director and said, "That's a very clever idea, Dr. Perrill — using identical twins. Fortunate that you had them available."

The satisfied smile that Kira gave the research director indicated that there was more involved than good fortune, the smile fading as Perrill said modestly, "Oh, there's nothing unusual about using monovular twins for experimental purposes. The literature goes back a long way — Galton in 1876, for example. Hundreds of people have done it. The classic work, I suppose, is Newman's — Chicago, you know. And then there were the Germans — Siemens and Von Verschuer and Korhaus. And, of course, the Russians have been at it on a simply fantastic scale."

Lincoln Lord smiled. "Now don't tell me the Russians are ahead of us on this, too."

"Oh, we're not in it at all with what they've done! Do you know — at one time they had eight hundred pairs of twins in the Maxim Gorky Research Institute in Moscow? Imagine — eight hundred pairs of identical twins — and all of them right there in that one institution where they could maintain absolutely controlled conditions!" The research director shook his head as if overcome with envy at such riches. "Dr. Ichakuri was more or less following the Russian lead in Burma. Not

327

on as large a scale, of course, but still using their general method."

"Then he was working with twins, too?"

"Oh, of course! That's why he'd gone there. You see, there's a great difference in the incidence of twins. Japan has a very low twinning rate, something like two-thirds of one per cent as I recall. It's not as low as the Annamese in Indo-China — twins are virtually unknown there — but Burma has one of the highest rates in the world. That's why Dr. Ichakuri had come down from Japan."

Kira said, "Don't you think it might be interesting to the Lords if you told them something about the general objective of Dr. Ichakuri's project?"

Perrill gave her a questioning side glance and Kira took over on her own. "As I recall — correct me if I'm wrong, Dr. Perrill — the Japanese were intrigued with the idea of building up a body of very strong and powerful men for their army. Dr. Ichakuri had already proved that it was possible to add considerably to their stature through raising children on a different diet, and they'd started the Burma project as a way of speeding up his research program through having lots of twins available for experimental purposes. Isn't that right, Dr. Perrill?"

"Yes, I suppose so — perhaps that was their objective — super-soldiers for their army. Dr. Ichakuri never actually said so —"

"Well, that part of it's unimportant," Kira said. "Maybe it was just their feeling of inferiority because they were a small people. Anyway, it was a big official project with all sorts of government support behind it. I am right about that?"

"Oh yes, Dr. Ichakuri had plenty of support, no doubt about that. But as far as he himself was concerned — oh, I don't mean that he wasn't trying to do something for his country — of course he was — but I really don't think it was a purely nationalistic thing. He was much too sincere a scientist for that."

"But it is true that he'd proved that they could materially change the Japanese physique with a different diet?" Kira insisted.

"Oh, definitely. That's what had first attracted the attention of the Japanese government to his work — why they'd backed him in setting up this Burma project."

Lincoln Lord asked, "Was there a relationship between your Tokali food and what Dr. Ichakuri had discovered?"

Perrill hesitated. "In a broad sense — yes."

Kira objected, "But he never did get it worked out on a practical basis, did he?"

"No, that's true," Perrill agreed. "He never really got beyond papain. But if the war hadn't come along — the British drove him out of Burma, of course — ruined everything for him. I wasn't even certain that he'd gotten away with his life. I did hear, after I got back to Calcutta, that he'd managed to escape, but I'd never been sure of it until you brought me this word from him." He looked up, reminding himself of the question that had gone unanswered. "As for the relationship of Dr. Ichakuri's work to the Tokali food — yes, as I say, the basic concept was there — the enzymatic approach. So after I got back to India, that's the direction I took. And I was very lucky, very lucky indeed. Pure coincidence, of course — no credit to me — but the Bengalis have the highest twinning rate in the world, even higher than the Burmese. You had no trouble getting your hands on twins in Calcutta, no trouble at all. And the people were so poor that they'd gladly let anyone feed them who wanted to. No, my trouble there wasn't finding twins to work with — it was trying to find food enough to feed all of them that were brought to our door. But it was a wonderful opportunity and I did make a lot of progress as far as — well, here's my first publication."

He twisted the scrapbook now, opened to a four-page clipping, three pages solidly packed with the fine-print type of a scientific report, the fourth illustrated with paired photographs of dark-skinned twin boys pictured at four-month intervals over a year of growth. One was clearly out ahead of the other and Lincoln Lord commented, "Very convincing." Then, noticing the yellowed paper, he asked, "When was this, Doctor?"

He was unprepared for Perrill's reaction, a gruffly grumbled, "Forty-three," that was unaccountably close to belligerence.

Kira Zurich put in quickly, "There've been fifteen years of very productive work since then, Mr. Lord."

Quickly Perrill accepted her suggestion for a way to circumvent whatever it was that had embarrassed him. "Yes, yes, we've come a long way since then — yes, a very long way," suggesting the guess that his raw-nerved response might be related to what Kira had said before lunch about his having worked for so many years with so little tangible recognition of accomplishment.

Lincoln Lord leaned forward, reading the picture captions and searching his mind for some comment that could be made, grateful when he heard Maggie change the subject by asking, "You're still using twins here, Dr. Perrill?"

"Oh yes, indeed — every pair we can possibly get our hands on."

"But where do you find them? I mean — well, are there enough twin orphans?"

"It isn't finding them that's the difficult part of it," Perrill said. "You see, we have a fairly high twinning rate here in the United States. Not up to Burma or Bengal, of course, but still not too bad — not bad at all really. Many people don't realize how many twins we have here in the States. About one child in every forty-four is born as a twin. Roughly, that's eleven pairs of twins in every thousand births. Of course, the incidence of identicals is less than that, and the survival rate is lower than on single births, but still there are a fair number of them around. No, finding them isn't the problem. Making them available for controlled feeding experiments — that's where the rub comes." He looked at Kira and, for the first time, Lincoln Lord saw what might pass for an expression of affection. "That's where Mrs. Zurich has done such a wonderful job."

"Oh, I've done little enough," she said, modestly proclaimed with that slightly overdone quality that indicated she would be more than willing to recount her accomplishment with a little encouragement — and Lincoln Lord gave it to her with an earnestly asked, "How in the world do you manage it?"

"It really isn't so difficult," she said. "In the beginning — well, in my work with the government I'd had contact with a great many institutions and organizations that were dealing with homeless children. Naturally, I'd gotten to know some of the directors rather well. So after I saw the exciting possibilities in Dr. Perrill's work, I simply contacted some of these people and asked them to advise us whenever they ran into a pair of identical twins that were to be separated and placed in different homes."

Maggie asked, "But why would they have to be separated?" and then quickly answered herself with a second question, "Oh, I suppose both children would want to have the same things to eat, wouldn't they?"

"It isn't the children so much as whoever is raising them," Kira said. "If the children are together in the same home, as soon as the foster mother sees that the child that's getting Dr. Perrill's food is growing so much better than the other — then of course she thinks that the twin that isn't getting it is being terribly deprived."

"It's really as noticeable as that?" Maggie asked.

"Oh, definitely. If you start with a pair of six-month-old twins, there'll be an easily seen difference inside of four or five weeks, often even earlier than that. And, of course, if the twins are together so that you can see the contrast — well, that's when we raise the bugaboo that we're always up against — someone thinking that we're using poor little orphan children for experimental purposes."

"Even if the second twin is being fed as well as any other children?"

"Better," Kira said. "Much better in most cases. But it's one of those emotional things that we have to be very careful about. Of course, when the twins are separated — and that happens quite often — then we don't have that complication. That's the kind of case we're always looking for. And we really do find quite a few. Most twins are split up for adoption, you know."

"But how do you get the parents — adopted parents — to go along?"

"It's really quite simple. In the case of one twin — the control — we tell them that we're making growth studies and simply ask them to help us by keeping a daily record of what the child is fed. To compensate them for their trouble, we agree to supply free medical care. If it's in this area, we serve them from here. If not, we pay a pediatrician and he gives us the monthly growth and development report that we want."

"I shouldn't think you'd have much trouble getting parents to co-operate on that basis," Maggie observed.

"We don't," Kira Zurich said.

She paused for an instant and Lincoln Lord stepped in, seeing an opening to test the validity of Joel Morris's conclusions on mother-resistance. "I imagine that you have more difficulty with the other family — getting the mother to accept this food of Dr. Perrill's?"

Kira Zurich stiffened as if she sensed a trap. "By no means as much trouble as we had in the beginning," she said in measured tones. "At the start, the formula was rather unappetizing, but Dr. Perrill has made a lot of progress in that direction." She looked at the scientist, "And we're hoping to make even more."

Perrill dutifully picked up her cue, although evidencing some reluctance and plainly side-stepping support of her hope. "Yes, we've made some progress, I think. Of course our American mothers have been conditioned to a certain taste pattern —"

Kira interrupted. "You do have to educate the mothers — yes, that's true. But when you can show her the wonderful things that it does, the way all of these other children have grown —" She turned abruptly. "Why don't you show them some of these case reports, Dr. Perrill?"

"Yes, yes, I have them right here," Perrill said, obviously nervous.

"At least those that have been carried along over a sufficient period to be of any significance." He reached out for the nearest of the three piles of stacked reports.

As a quick guess, Lincoln Lord judged that there were between forty and fifty of them and asked, "Do you mean that you have that many pairs of twins under test?"

"Some of these have been stopped now for one reason or another —"

"But we still have twenty-three current ones," Kira interrupted. "Isn't that right, Dr. Perrill — fourteen of our own, the four in New Orleans and Dr. Kaloff's five in Los Angeles?"

"That's right," he agreed.

"I think the Kaloff group is particularly interesting —" Her pause was a suggestion, almost an order, and Dr. Perrill quickly sorted one of the piles, separating five reports that Kira took as he handed them to her. "One of the first men that I got in touch with when I came here was Dr. Serge Kaloff. He'd been trained at the Maxim Gorky and had been carrying on some work in California — more or less as a hobby — trying to study the nature-nurture relationship, attempting to determine the degree of correlation between the intelligence factors and nutrition. Of course, that was made to order for us — we could get our growth comparisons at the same time that he was carrying on his work — so we made an arrangement with him. We thought at first that the twins he had available were too old to be substantially affected as far as mental development was concerned. However, that surely hasn't proved to be the case."

Lincoln Lord had resigned himself, until he began to comprehend what she was saying, to repetitious recounting of cases that only proved over and over again what he had already accepted. Now, however, he found himself no less shocked into attention than he had been when he had been hit by the revelation that Noel and Neil were identical twins, differentiated only by diet. "Are you implying," he demanded, "that the children who are fed on this food are mentally superior?"

Kira broke in with a confident little laugh. "Well, I don't know what you'll accept as proof, Mr. Lord — but look at this." She opened the report, displaying first the photographs of two nine-year-old girls, then thumbing through pages until she located a block of tabulated figures that she explained were the contrasting results of three different types of intelligence tests, regularly given to both girls at six-month intervals. There was a positive difference in favor of one girl and, as Kira pointed out, the disparity between her and her twin sister was

332

growing wider and wider, the margin almost doubled since the first tests had been given at the age of six.

The second report — twin boys of nine — showed somewhat less of a difference. The third case, however, evidenced an even greater advantage for the Perrill-fed twin. It was almost matched in the fourth. The fifth report was a different story, almost no difference showing up between the two twins. "I don't know what happened here," Kira said. "Dr. Perrill thinks that there might be an explanation in the fact that apparently there's a strong hereditary predisposition toward high mental development."

Perrill said, "It's only a guess, of course, but you'll notice that both of these boys rate way up. I don't know whether or not that sets up a reasonable hypothesis, but it does seem that better nutrition has its most pronounced mental effect when you have the opposite situation. At least that's borne out here in these other two cases. Where you have the biggest differential, the control twin rates quite low." He reached for the folder on the third case. "Here's what I mean. This twin is just a notch or two above being a moron. He's in the lowest group in his class at school and barely getting by. Now look at his brother. He's no mental giant but at least he's in the middle group and his teachers give him a satisfactory rating."

Maggie said, "In other words, you probably can't feed a basically smart boy into being an outright genius, but at least you can lift the low-mentality ones above the moron level."

Perrill hesitated and Kira said, "Well, I'm not sure Dr. Perrill would want to make any claim as broad as that —"

"No, no," Perrill said. "Much too early to draw final conclusions. But it is significant, don't you think — even four cases out of five?"

"And I'm sure it's going to be the same story with our children here," Kira said. "They're too young yet for intelligence tests to have very much meaning, but still you can see a difference, just in the way that one child learns more quickly than the other."

"Golly, I must say," Lincoln Lord began, floundering until his thoughts found direction. "I suppose it's perfectly reasonable — of course, it is — but I've just never thought of intelligence as something that you could pack in a can and feed out with a spoon."

Kira's smile was appreciative but brief. "After all, why should we be surprised that there's a relationship between nutrition and intelligence? I know — we're inclined to think of the *mind* as being something disembodied and nonphysical — but, of course that isn't true at all. The brain is a purely physical thing, essentially no different than any other organ of the body — more complicated, perhaps, but still only a collection of cells that have to be produced out of nutrients that the body takes in during the growth process. Isn't that true, Dr. Perrill?"

Perrill nodded. "Yes, yes, of course. Although I do think there's more to it than just initial growth. Really, we know so little about the biochemistry of the mental process that we're groping in the dark. Still there's been some very significant work done. Harrell opened up a whole field when he established the relationship between the thiamine intake and mental performance. And then, of course, there's all the work that's been done with glutamic acid. Now all the journals — just last night I was reading a very interesting paper on MAO — monoamine oxidase, you know. It's an anti-amine enzyme that apparently has a very important part to play in the functioning of the brain and the whole nervous system. This whole amine-enzyme relationship — well, there's just no telling where it's going to lead us. But we do know that there's a very close linkage between nutrition and mental performance."

Kira Zurich's voice knifed into the first opening. "To me this is the most exciting possibility of all. This whole idea of realizing a potentiality for human development beyond anything that we'd ever even visualized wouldn't strike me as being half as important if it were only physical. In this day and age, stature and strength aren't too significant. There's really no great point in turning ourselves into a race of giants. Maybe we've gone as far as we need to go in that direction — and, of course, that's where all the nutrition work has been concentrated until Dr. Perrill started — physical development was the only index of results. But if we could improve brain capacity —"

"It's a fascinating possibility!" Maggie exclaimed.

For an instant, Lincoln Lord found himself responding to her suggested appreciation . . . yes, it was a terrific . . . fresh, too . . . different . . . if you could promote a baby food with the sales argument that it would . . .

The summary page of Joel Morris's report flashed in his mind, seven paragraphs as solidly constructed as a stone wall, a barrier that blocked the forward rush of excited speculation . . . no matter how good the stuff was, it still had to be sold. Joel had raised no arguments against the results that Perrill was getting . . . he was even feeding the stuff to his own kids . . . no, that wasn't the point . . .

Suddenly he was conscious of silence, everyone looking at him as if some unheard question had been asked. He saw that Dr. Perrill had closed his scrapbook and he knew that he was, if not actually facing the moment of decision, so close to it that he had to be prepared for it. "Tell me this, Dr. Perrill —"

"Yes?"

He discarded the question that he had been about to ask and said instead, "I wonder if you'd have a can of this food of yours around."

"Here? Well, yes — back in the laboratory."

Maggie said eagerly, "Oh, I'd like very much to see it. I don't suppose you can tell too much just tasting it, but after hearing all these wonderful things —"

Lincoln Lord's eyes had been on Dr. Perrill, aware of the reluctance with which he rose from his chair, and it was not until he caught sight of Kira Zurich's face that he realized why Maggie's voice had cut off so abruptly. Kira's expression had changed as if she had suddenly been struck a death-dealing blow. Where, a moment before, there had been ebullient confidence, now there was something akin to anger. But it was a face in transition and, an instant later, he realized that what he had seen as anger had been only an automatic flashback against sudden defeat. Kira stood up, stiff and straight-spined for a silent moment, then moved quickly toward the door, seen now as if she were an actress caught in that disillusioning lapse between the ending of a role and a hurried exit from the stage.

Perrill followed, calling after her, "I'll get it, Mrs. Zurich, I'll get it," but she was already ahead of him, disappearing from sight without looking back.

They were alone then, he and Maggie, and her deeply troubled expression told him that there was no need to interpret what had happened. She knew as well as he did that Joel was right . . . Perrill still hadn't licked the taste problem . . . the stuff was as unsalable as it had always been . . . and Kira knew it, too. She'd been running a bluff . . .

Maggie whispered, "What are you going to do, Linc?"

He shrugged, silent.

"Linc — ?" Maggie waited, forcing him to look at her before she continued. "I don't think that Kira really wants what she thinks she wants — putting it on the market, I mean. Maybe I'm wrong but —" She waited again.

"What are you thinking?"

"At least I'm sure of this — there's nothing between her and Dr. Perrill." She paused. "And I don't think what's bothering her is getting recognition for *him*."

"Maybe not," he said, agreement supported by an instinctive conclusion that had not been consciously realized until Maggie had voiced it.

"And it isn't because she's trying to make money on it."

"No, of course not," he muttered, remembering what Kira had said about her willingness to absorb what loss there might be.

"Then what else could it be but — oh, Linc, I'm certain that what she really wants is recognition for Haven Home."

He looked at her with a puzzled scowl, the silent expression of his lack of understanding.

"Can't you see why she'd feel that way, Linc? She has to have it. It's the only way she can justify herself. I don't know whether or not she married Sol Zurich just to get the money to build all this — I mean, I don't know whether she did it *consciously* — but that's what it adds up to, Linc. How much did she say they'd spent here?"

"Close to a million," he said, now beginning to sense what Maggie was driving at.

"And that was before she got him to leave her all the company stock."

"Right."

"Maybe it wasn't anything that she *made* him do — I mean, I'm not suggesting that she tricked him into doing it. He might have done it anyway."

"Still it was her idea — building up Haven Home into a research center."

"Yes, that's what I mean."

"And now she has to justify herself," he said, the repetition of her words a weighing of validity.

"Maybe that's the wrong way to put it but — Linc, she can't help but feel something like that — pouring in all this money for years and years now and nothing's happened — I mean, nothing that's given Haven Home the kind of recognition that she has to have to clear her conscience. Remember what she said about that article in one of the news magazines — a survey of all the work that had been done on child nutrition —"

"— but not a word about all they'd done here at Haven Home," he supplied.

336

"And when Dr. Perrill was talking about what happened in India —"

"I know, I know," he put in, understanding coming with a rush now. "She didn't even want him to talk about that part of it. All she wanted us to get was the story of what's happened since — what's been done here at Haven Home. Maybe you're right, Mag, maybe that is what she's after."

"Oh, Linc, I'm sure it is. That's why she wants their baby food put on the market, just because it's the only way she can think of to get recognition for Haven Home. Do you remember what she said about how much it would mean to Dr. Perrill? She wasn't really talking about him, Linc, she was talking about herself — about Haven Home."

"But if the stuff's a flop — ?"

"She's desperate, Linc! If there were a better way to get what she wants —" She broke off with her voice significantly suspended and he looked at her, wondering what she had in mind.

"Linc, maybe — I know that if someone had come to us at *Hearth-side* with a story like this —"

Recognition burst like a star shell, the way ahead suddenly illuminated. "Golly, Mag, that might be it. If we could just get some publicity for Haven Home, she'd forget about trying to force us into putting the stuff on the market. And it might be that —"

"Oh, Linc, I'm sure that you could get one of the big magazines interested."

He nodded vigorously. "It's a terrific story — this story of Perrill and the Tokalis."

"Well, maybe —" Maggie began.

"I know," he hurriedly acknowledged. "She'd want it slanted so that it was Haven Home that got the build-up. But what they've done here with these twins. Golly, if we could just show some of the pictures in these reports to the *Post* — *Life* — they'd go for it, I know they would."

"Even if you couldn't get it in one of the general magazines — Linc, I know one of the women's magazines would run an article on it. Just the idea that you can affect a baby's mentality by the way you feed it — Linc, there isn't a mother in the country that wouldn't hang on every word of it."

For a moment he let himself be swept along. "If there were enough publicity it might even break down prejudice to the point where you could sell it." Caution overtook his racing thoughts. "But that wouldn't be the important thing. As you say, if we could just get some publicity for Haven Home — if we could plant a big story in one of the good magazines, Kira would probably forget all about everything else."

"I'm sure that's all that matters to her now."

"It would have to be handled just right, though. If you got the wrong slant — the thing to do would be to get a good man on it, some-body who knew his way around these big magazines."

"Couldn't you just contact the editors for her? They all have staff writers and if you gave them an outline —"

He shook his head. "No, I don't want to get involved in it myself. And she said she'd be willing to lose twenty-five or thirty thousand, didn't she? All right, for half that, we could get her a good public re-lations outfit to take over the whole job — research the story, get to some editors —"

The sound of footsteps interrupted him. And then Perrill was stand-ing at the door, two yellow plastic dishes in his hands, his expression that of a condemned man. "Mrs. Zurich will be here in a moment or two," he explained in a gruffly evasive whisper. "She had to make a telephone call."

Lincoln Lord saw his opening and moved, instantly on his feet . . . yes, the thing to do was to catch Kira alone . . . before it was too late . . . before she got wrong ideas about him . . . keep his own hands out of it . . . *Brick?* Of course! Brick would be perfect . . . the best stuff he'd ever done had been right down this alley . . . popularized science. And he'd appreciate it, too . . . having an account like this tossed his way . . .

VI

IF THE TRAIN from Goodhaven had arrived at Pennsylvania Station on schedule, Maggie Lord would have had a full forty minutes to reach Grand Central, more than enough to catch the nine-ten to Forgehill. But twenty of those minutes had been lost while the train sat motionless on the Jersey meadows and, when she had finally arrived and fought her way through the Monday morning crowds to the taxi-stand, more minutes had been squandered on a long wait for a cab. There would still have been time enough if the slushy streets had not been snarled with the bumper-to-bumper traffic of Manhattan on a bad weather morning, and if the taxi driver had not attempted to go crosstown on Thirty-eighth Street and jammed himself into immobility.

Resignedly, she now accepted the situation, knowing that she should have taken the shuttle subway instead of a cab, yet not truly blaming herself for having failed to struggle against a tide of fate that had already proved itself unstemmable. She could criticize herself for her initial mistake — and she had, a thousand times since that unthinking moment in Dr. Perrill's office — but once she had suggested to Linc that Kira Zurich might be placated by getting an article about Haven Home into one of the big magazines, there had been no escape. That one misstep had plunged her into a nightmare millrace that had carried her on and on and on.

Over and over again she had reviewed those minutes after Linc had finally come back to Perrill's office with Kira Zurich, searching for some place where she might have saved herself. Even in retrospect, she could not find a single such point. She had been trapped from the outset by her foolish insistence on going up today to take Kip out of

339

Forgehill, so firmly committed that there had been no chance to escape when Linc had said, "Mag, since you'll have to stop over in New York on Monday, anyway, why don't you drop in and talk this over with Brick?" Stunned and fumbling for words, she had allowed herself to appear so disturbed that she had almost forced him into asking, "There's no reason why you can't, is there?"

And then the memory of that night on the boat coming home from Bermuda had flooded down upon her, engulfing her with a sense of guilt, tearing from her lips a denial of the accusation that had seemed to be forming behind Linc's eyes during that terrifying moment when he had waited for her to answer, his questioning stare so deeply penetrating that he would surely, in the next moment, have discovered that there *was* a reason why she never wanted to see Brick Mitchell again.

Struggling, she had still attempted escape, trying to suggest that there might be a public relations agency better suited to the assignment than Mitchell Associates, defeated when she discovered that Kira already knew about Brick — Anderson Phelps had, for some unexplained reason, already talked to her about him — and the almost fantastically unfortunate coincidence that Brick apparently had on his staff, so Phelps had told Kira, a Dr. Thompson who was a specialist in child nutrition and therefore eminently qualified to do exactly the kind of job that needed to be done for Haven Home.

There had been no satisfaction in learning how right her guess had been that Kira's real interest was in publicizing Haven Home rather than securing personal recognition for Dr. Perrill; nor afterwards had there been any of the buoyant pleasure that she would otherwise have found in Linc's gratitude for the way she had helped him side-step the dangers that would have been inherent in an attempt to market an unmarketable product.

As a last effort, she had tried yesterday to ask Linc why Kira, if she wanted to retain Brick's firm as a public relations agency for Haven Home, could not approach him herself. Fortunately, she had stopped short of asking that foolish question. A moment later Linc had mentioned how great Kira's appreciation would be if Mitchell Associates could be induced to take the Haven Home account, a prospect of gratitude that had made Linc look to her with an undeniable appeal that she help him gain this windfall of good will.

Somehow, Linc seemed to have completely missed Kira's implication that Brick had already been offered the account and turned it down ... and maybe that wasn't what had really happened. It was true that

Kira had acted as if the idea of publicizing Haven Home had never occurred to her before. But then, why would she consider it such an accomplishment to get Brick to accept a ten-thousand-dollar retainer fee for a job that he could do in a couple of weeks?

No, it just didn't make sense . . . nothing did! Maybe it was Coastal Foods that Anderson Phelps had talked to Brick about . . . but if that was what it had been, it must have happened before Linc came into the picture.

She tried to clamp down on the flow of thought, attempting to stop short of the fear that it was Linc, not Kira, who was anxious to bring Brick to Goodhaven . . . Linc weakening again and doing what he had done so many times before, calling for Brick the moment he got in trouble . . . and he had tried to call him that day when Anderson Phelps had come to the Waldorf-Astoria . . . and Brick had never returned his call. Linc didn't know why he hadn't . . . he couldn't know what Brick had said that night on the Bermuda boat . . . *"I've had all of Lincoln Lord I can take."* . . . no, Linc didn't even suspect it. If he did, he would never have recommended Brick to Kira. But still it was true . . .

Yes, that was going to be her problem today, trying to convince Brick that this didn't have anything to do with Linc . . . that there was no connection between Haven Home and the Coastal Foods Company, that there'd be no need for contact with Linc. And she'd never see Brick again either . . . only this once . . . today . . . this afternoon . . . after she got back from Forgehill . . .

Out of nowhere a new fear slashed across her consciousness, all the more frightening because she thought she had already exhausted every potential of terror . . . what if Brick refused to see her? How would she ever explain to Linc . . . no, no, no . . . he'd see her . . .

She clamped her gloved hands over her ears, trying to shut out the sound of Brick's deep voice, low against the distant throbbing of the ship's engines, telling her that if she ever needed him all that she would have to do would be to call him. But she dared not remind him . . . no, no, no . . .

"This too cold for you, miss?" the cab driver asked, grinding up the glass in the open window through which he had been inspecting the jam of trucks.

"No, I'm all right," she said, quickly dropping her hands. "But I've missed my train now, so there's no use going to Grand Central. You might as well drop me —"

341

But where could she go? No stores open yet . . . raining again . . . horrible slush . . .

She looked out, seeing the crowded sidewalks, girls on their way to work pouring into the building entrances . . . stenographers and typists who had to punch in before nine . . .

"Take me up Madison," she said suddenly, hurriedly opening her purse to search for the address of Brick's office . . . he wouldn't be there yet . . . he'd never gotten to any office before ten o'clock in all his life. But this Dr. Thompson might be there . . . or at least she'd arrive before Brick did . . . yes, she could talk to Dr. Thompson . . . maybe not have to see Brick at all . . .

As if she had finally cleared a path through the maze of fears, the cross-parked truck suddenly moved and the cab made a rattling plunge toward Fifth Avenue, caught the tag end of green light and burst through the line of pedestrians that were already streaming across from the far corners.

"You might still make it, miss," the driver called back with moronic good cheer.

"No," she said positively, deciding that this was still the best plan . . . this afternoon she'd have Kip with her and he'd insist on going along . . . that terrific crush that he'd always had . . . "Uncle Brick" . . .

"That's around Fifty-second, huh?" the driver asked, a delayed reaction to the street address she had given him.

"I don't know," she said, then remembering that she had been crossing Fifty-second Street when she had caught her only glimpse of Brick since that night on the Bermuda boat, seeing him coming out of a little restaurant with a brassy blonde in a camel's-hair polo coat . . . Brick's type . . . strange how much alike they'd all been, every girl he'd ever gone out with, always that Babs Patton look . . . the bachelor gal with money somewhere in the family . . . tweeds and linen and hunky gold jewelry . . . always knowing when you asked her what she wanted to drink that it would be a dry Martini . . . those gray-green eyes that were always looking at some other woman's husband as if she were wondering what he would be like in bed . . . or remembering what he *had* been like! That night in Baltimore . . . hearing Brick and Babs Patton through the thin-paneled door in the hotel . . .

Without realizing it, she had let herself slip into an old mind channel, worn deep by all the times she had purposely aroused revulsion as a way of proving to herself that she had been right in marrying Linc . . . no, she'd never loved Brick . . . she was no Babs Patton . . . love

342

couldn't be something without meaning . . . three Martinis and a strange bed . . .

"Okay, miss."

The taxi had stopped and she got out, strangely weak-kneed, the fare paid before she saw that she was standing in front of the restaurant where she had caught sight of Brick. Then she saw the number that she was looking for on the side-door entrance to the floors above . . . they'd probably been coming down from Brick's office . . . yes, that's what Babs Patton would have done, gone up to his office to get him . . .

"Up?"

"Mitchell Associates?"

"Fourth."

The door of the cage slid shut and she was trapped, surrounded by bars, released only into the narrow confinement of a musty corridor. The operator did not close the cab door when she got out, watching her, waiting to make certain that she did not yield to the temptation of a last-minute escape.

"Right there in front of you," he challenged.

MITCHELL ASSOCIATES, INC.
Public Relations

She opened the door, tentatively stepping inside. There was no one in sight, not a sound to be heard. She looked around her, seeing a small reception room that did double duty as a secretary's office. There was no evidence of how many offices lay beyond, yet there was the immediate impression that Mitchell Associates, Inc. was a much less successful enterprise than Anderson Phelps had led her to believe when he had talked to her at the Chesapeake College dinner. There had been no reason then to disbelieve him, validity supported by her high regard for Brick's facile creativity, yet now there was that same sensing of the atmosphere of failure that always hung over a shop that was about to go bankrupt, a restaurant that had somehow failed to capture public favor.

She stood for a moment with the corridor door still open, noticing now that there was a cigarette smoldering in an ash tray on the secretary's desk. Suddenly she heard approaching footsteps down the corridor, a voice behind her asking, "May I help you?"

Startled, stepping back to clear the doorway, she found herself face to face with a woman so instantly recognizable that she must be, if not

343

the girl in the polo coat, at least proof that Brick was still running true to form . . . Babs Patton's green eyes . . .

"Is Dr. Thompson in yet?" she asked, judging from the woman's superior air as she turned to stub out the cigarette that Brick had made the mistake of letting his personal relationship with his secretary give her an upper hand around the office, accounting for the amused smirk that was on the woman's face when she finally looked up from the ash tray to ask, "Would you mind telling me who wants to see her?"

"Maggie Lord."

"Mrs. Lincoln Lord?"

Her surprise at recognition was overwhelmed by the greater surprise of hearing, "I'm Dr. Thompson, Mrs. Lord. What can I do for you?"

Everything that she had planned to say went out of her mind, blanked by the boldness with which she found herself being examined by this woman who, despite her claim of identity, seemed all but incredible as an expert on child nutrition.

"I've been told, Dr. Thompson, that you specialize in pediatric publicity."

The green eyes were still measuring her. "Yes, I do a column for one of the baby magazines."

"Oh," she said, letting the sound of disappointment pave the way for retreat.

"But since you've heard of me as Dr. Thompson, I suppose you mean my new-products page in *Modern Pediatrics*. That's the by-line I use there. Won't you take off your coat?"

"No, thank you," she said too quickly, missing the chance for a momentary respite from those searchingly curious eyes. "But I will sit down if you don't mind."

"Please do."

She seated herself so that it was possible to keep a guarding eye on the corridor door. Then, plunging, she asked, "I don't suppose you've ever heard of Haven Home?"

"Haven Home? No, I'm afraid not."

"Or of Dr. Lee Perrill?"

"Lee Perrill?" Her head cocked, her eyes narrowing, the name repetitiously whispered. "Was there a paper of his in one of the medical journals — oh, five or six years ago — some work that he'd done in India?"

"Yes, that's the man," Maggie acknowledged, impressed by a feat of

344

memory that suddenly disassociated Dr. Thompson from Babs Patton and all the others for whom, a moment before, she had appeared a physical counterpart. Re-examined, that resemblance was largely lost, seemingly a delusion induced by expectation. Now she was a New York career woman, caste-branded first by the smile that looked as if it had been bought at a cosmetic counter, and then by the imitatively masculine voice in which she said, "Am I to understand that Dr. Perrill is connected with — I believe you said Haven Home?"

"Yes, he's director of research."

"From the name, I'd take Haven Home to be an orphanage?"

"No, it's not an orphanage," she said, perversely pleased by this chance for contradiction, then quickly realizing that it was a pleasure too petty to be relished. "But, yes, that's where the name originally came from. At one time it was an orphanage. Now it's a research center specializing in child nutrition."

"Oh, really? Somehow I've missed hearing about it."

"That's quite understandable, Dr. Thompson. So have a great many other people. That's what I'm here to talk to you about."

There was no response beyond a look of silent inquiry, and Maggie Lord felt annoyance rise to the point where it threatened to break into unreasonable anger, self-control possible only because her instinctive reaction to personal challenge was an icy calm that chilled her voice as she asked, "You've read none of Dr. Perrill's more recent papers in the medical journals, nothing since that old one on his work in India?"

"No, I'm afraid not. I can't possibly keep up with everything that's being published these days. And there's really no need to try. I can always run a subject research if there's something I need. It isn't as if I were in practice."

"Of course not," she granted. "And perhaps some of the Haven Home work hasn't been reported, even to the profession. I really don't know whether it has or not. But I do know this — the general public hasn't been given even a hint of the amazing things that they're doing down there. At least it was all new to me. And I think I'm as well-informed as the average layman. After all — well, I was a home ec. major in college and I've had a special interest in nutrition. When I was on *Hearthside* —" She clipped off her voice ... why was she trying to defend herself?

"You were there when Brick was, weren't you?"

Side-stepping, she said, "Of course that was a long time ago, and I know there've been a great many new developments since" ...

how much had Brick told her? Probably plenty . . . and she had called him *Brick* . . . no, that didn't mean anything . . . everyone always had . . .

"There haven't been too many real developments," Dr. Thompson said, almost as a concession. "There's been a lot of work done, of course, but as far as the public is concerned — nothing that's ever kicked up the stir that the vitamin discoveries did back in the thirties."

Suddenly it seemed that a wall had broken down and Maggie Lord pushed through eagerly. "If you could see what Dr. Perrill has done at Haven Home, I'm sure you'd agree that it's as big a story as the first vitamin discoveries were. Let me give you one example. They showed us two boys — identical twins. One of them had been fed on what everyone accepts now as an ideal diet for a growing child. The other had been fed on this new food of Dr. Perrill's. The difference between them was so obvious that — they were actually six years old but it would have been easily believable that the second twin was at least a year older than the first."

Dr. Thompson seemed no more than mildly impressed and Maggie drove ahead, recounting as much of the detail as she could recall, finally rewarded with sharp interest when she said, "And the gain isn't only in physical development. The most amazing thing is that these children that have been raised on Dr. Perrill's food are way out ahead in mental development. And it's not one freak case. They have records now on twenty-one pairs of identical twins. I may be wrong — you'd know better than I would — but I don't think anyone has ever before come up with any real proof that you can increase a child's mental capacity by the way you feed it."

For an instant, Maggie thought that she had scored, the green eyes momentarily wide. Then they narrowed, crinkled as that faintly cynical smile settled into place again. "And your husband is about to put Dr. Perrill's baby food on the market — right?"

She was able to suppress resentment only because there was a release of pressure in being able to say, "No, Dr. Thompson, you're wrong."

"Oh?"

"There's nothing like that involved."

"But I am right, am I not — he has just taken over the presidency of a food company, hasn't he?"

"Yes, that's true enough" . . . there was no doubt about it now . . . Brick had talked to her . . . she knew the way he felt about Linc . . .

346

"But my coming here today has nothing to do with my husband's business interests, Dr. Thompson, nothing whatsoever." She hesitated, wondering if there was any point in continuing.

"I'm sorry, Mrs. Lord. I'll stop jumping to conclusions. Please go on."

Although not an apology, it was at least an indication that this Thompson woman's armor was penetrable, encouragement enough to make a last try worth while. "I happened to be coming through New York — I'm on my way to Forgehill to pick up my son — and Mrs. Zurich asked if I'd mind stopping in to see if you would be interested in writing an article about what's happening at Haven Home — and, of course, getting it published in one of the big magazines." She paused. "That's why I'm here, Dr. Thompson."

"And you want *me* to do this article?"

"This has nothing to do with what *I* want. All I'm doing is delivering a message from Mrs. Zurich. If you're interested, she'd like to have you come down to Haven Home and spend a couple of hours seeing what's been done. After that, all of your contact would be with her, of course."

"She's — ?"

"I'm sorry. I should have explained. Mrs. Zurich is the managing director of Haven Home."

"But isn't she — there is a connection with your husband's company, isn't there? I saw the newspaper story when he took over as president and I thought that was the name of —"

"Yes, she's the widow of the man who owned the company," Maggie Lord said, resenting what seemed a continuation of suspicion, yet determined now to clinch her victory. "Mrs. Zurich was the director of Haven Home before she was married — she's the one who brought in Dr. Perrill and converted Haven Home to a research center — and since her husband's death, she's gone back and assumed active direction again."

"What's the pitch, Mrs. Lord — a build-up for a fund-raising drive?"

"No, I'm sure she has nothing like that in her mind. Her husband left her most of the Coastal Foods Company stock and her dividends are enough to keep Haven Home going."

"Do you mean that she's supporting the place herself?"

"There is an old endowment fund, I believe — some money that was left over from the orphanage days — but, yes, the principal support has all been given by the Zurichs."

347

"How big a setup is it?"

"I think you'd be quite impressed," she said, confidence mounting now. "They've built a new research center — houses for the staff — oh, I don't know how many but there must be a dozen or more. In any event, it's no small operation. I don't know what their operating budget is but there's a staff of about twenty people —"

"Honestly, Mrs. Lord, I've never heard of Haven Home."

"That's the situation that Mrs. Zurich wants to correct. And under the circumstances, I'm sure her attitude is quite understandable. They've poured a lot of money into Haven Home, she and her husband — Dr. Perrill and his staff have gotten some wonderful results — it's quite natural that she'd feel they're entitled to some recognition."

"Cigarette, Mrs. Lord?" The package was offered as if it were a surrendered sword.

"No, thank you," she said.

Dr. Thompson lit her cigarette. "Would you mind telling me this, Mrs. Lord —"

"I'll be glad to tell you anything I can," she said, certain now that success was within her grasp . . . but she had to hurry . . . get out of here before Brick appeared . . .

"How did Mrs. Zurich know about me?"

"From Mr. Phelps, I believe."

"Well, that's a surprise." Her smile was brief but genuine. "I had no idea he even knew I existed."

"And Dr. Perrill recognized your name, too," she added for good measure. "I suppose from the things you've written." She paused. "And this would be right in your field, wouldn't it?"

There was a curt agreement in the flick of her cigarette. "That's all that would be involved — this one article? There wouldn't be a continuing campaign — general public relations?"

"I really don't know. Yes, I suppose there's a possibility that something like that might develop. For the time being, however —" She cut herself off, seeing a point that she'd missed before. "But this first assignment would be a fairly substantial one. It's something Mrs. Zurich is extremely anxious to have done, and she's quite willing to pay a fee that would be commensurate with its importance to her." She waited long enough to be certain that interest had risen to a peak and then said, "She's thinking in terms of a ten-thousand-dollar fee. I don't know how that strikes you — ?"

There was no need to complete a question that had already been answered by a brassy exclamation of surprise, a cymbal crash quickly damped, yet not before there had been the ringing revelation of character, fitting neither the Babs Patton prototype to which Maggie Lord had first matched her, nor the smugly professional cynicism that had afterwards seemed a more than skin-deep shell. Having been twice wrong, however, Maggie Lord was cautiously aware of the danger of misreading the complexly fluid expression of the face that she saw across the desk, constantly changing as Dr. Thompson studied her cigarette tip.

Suddenly she looked up, her face drawn by what could only be the torture of some difficult decision. "This is a hell of a thing to have to ask you, Mrs. Lord — but you do know Brick, don't you? He's so — all of this means so much to him, trying to make a go of it on his own —" She stopped as if she had exhausted the possibilities of evasion. "I suppose you've already guessed what I've been thinking. I know now that it isn't true — you've already told me — but I do have to ask you."

"Yes?"

"This isn't something that you're doing to help Brick, is it — just a handout?"

Maggie Lord's relief broke through as a little burst of laughter, a quick release from the fears that had fumed up in her mind until, at the last moment, she suddenly realized that she was in no way implicated. "Please believe me —"

"Oh, I do! But I had to make certain. You can understand that, can't you? You know how Brick —" There was a quick recapture of lost poise. "This isn't a job that I could do on my own, Mrs. Lord. I'd have to bring Brick into it."

"I'm sure you'd want to talk to him."

"Look, Mrs. Lord, this has been a hell of a boost to my battered old morale, just finding that there's somebody who even knows my by-line. But I'm not kidding myself. And I'm not going to try to kid you. As a writer, I'm strictly back-of-the-book. I know what I can do and what I can't do. I can rewrite publicity handouts, and I can translate medicalese into English, and no editor has ever had to kick my tail because my facts didn't add up — but when it comes to busting my way into the front of the book —" She shook her head vigorously. "I know where I belong. If this is as big a story as you say it is — and I know you wouldn't be here if it wasn't — you don't want me, Mrs. Lord. You want Brick."

Her last words reverberated dangerously and Maggie Lord said, quickly, "Please, Dr. Thompson, it isn't a question of what *I* want —"

"I know — Mrs. Zurich. But you can tell her. You know Brick. You know the way he can write —" She spun her chair, picking up a magazine that lay on a small table behind her desk. "Have you seen this?"

She shook her head, surprised to see Brick's by-line.

"It's just out today. And he's working on another one. That's where he is this morning, seeing some of their editors. It might even turn into a series. At least, that's what they're talking about. This is what Brick should have been doing all the time. He's too good a writer to be grinding out publicity handouts." She stopped, seeming fear-struck. "You don't mind, do you?"

"Mind?"

"If I toss this into Brick's lap? I don't mean that I wouldn't be in on it, too. I would. I'd dig the story for him, get him all the background — you'd get everything I could give it — but Brick is the one who'd have to —"

"Please, Dr. Thompson —"

"I know — Mrs. Zurich."

"But I'm sure that would be a very satisfactory arrangement with her. So if you want to talk to Mr. Mitchell about it, and then call Mrs. Zurich —" She stood up. "I don't have her telephone number, but it's Goodhaven, New Jersey, and you can reach her easily enough through Haven Home."

She had been talking to a head bent over the desk as a note was being made, suddenly raised to reveal eyes that were no longer green, but gray-misted now, a lower lip bitten for the instant before she said, "Brick ought to be back before long, Mrs. Lord. If you want to talk to him yourself —"

Maggie Lord's breath caught, but a smile covered it and she said calmly, "No, there's no need of that. I'm sure you can tell him enough about it to find out whether he's interested. And I do have a train to catch."

A hand reached out to her. "I guess I owe you an apology, Mrs. Lord, but I'd only mess it up if I — anyway, thanks."

"Not at all, Dr. Thompson."

There was the feeling of victory until she had dropped her hand and turned to the door. Then, too quickly, it began to fade. Out on the street again, she wondered if she might have let herself be too diverted by her triumph over this Thompson woman. Somehow there was the feeling of a need unsatisfied, almost as if she had forgotten something

350

that she had planned to do, a lapse that bothered her until she decided that it was no more than her concern that when Brick turned it down she would have to tell Linc that she hadn't actually talked to him ... but that would be easy enough to explain ... and there were dozens of public relations agencies. Anyway, it was done and over. Now all she had to think about was Forgehill and Kip ... plenty of time to walk to Grand Central ...

2

Brick Mitchell stood at the corner of Forty-fourth and Madison, his coat winged out to protect the thick file folder that he was carrying from the spurting splashes of slush, alert for the top light of an empty cab. Suddenly his eyes froze ... *Maggie* ...

She turned the corner and now all he could see was a mink coat headed toward Lexington ... no, it couldn't be ... Maggie wasn't in New York. Damn it, how long was this going to go on? ... two years and he still saw her a half-dozen times a day ... only it never was ...

"Cab!"

The taxi stopped ... lucky! Maybe this was a good sign ... finally getting the breaks ... Tommy had been right as hell about striking while the iron was hot ... Robbie had gone for the idea like a catfish after a doughball. Now all he had to do to sew it up was bat out an outline for the editorial board to see. But it was as good as in the bag ... Robbie wouldn't have let him use their own morgue files if there was any question about it. A thousand bucks ... get this next one and then he could hit Robbie with the series idea ... a thousand bucks a month ...

"Fifty-second," he said without interrupting himself ... twelve thousand a year. He'd have it made then ... get the overhead covered and anything else would be velvet. But he'd sure as hell have to give Tommy a raise. If it hadn't been for her ... no, that couldn't have been Maggie ...

3

Lincoln Lord had driven Maggie to the station to get the New York train and then, early as it was, had gone directly to the office instead of returning to the house. Outside, sitting for a moment in his parked Pantheon, he had questioned the wisdom of what he had just done — or, more precisely, what he had failed to do. All day yesterday, and even more certainly this morning, he had been conscious that Maggie was becoming increasingly tense. It was understandable — she was beginning to realize the responsibility that she was assuming in taking Kip out of Forgehill — but try as he had, and with as many openings as he had given her to do so, she simply would not admit that she had been carried away by an impetuous impulse, and that it might be better to let Kip finish out the term at the academy. What he should have done, even as late as this morning, was to have taken that positive position, and he would have done it if Maggie had given him half a chance, if she hadn't so stubbornly refused to admit that she was in any way aware of the questionable wisdom of what she was setting out to do.

Sitting there in the car, he had excused his noninterference by deciding that he had followed the only course that had been open to him. To have opposed her would probably have done more harm than good. Maggie had a streak of stubbornness when it was aroused by opposition and, this way, by suggesting only that she make a final decision after she had talked to Dr. Summerfield, he had left the way open for her to change her mind.

It was only seven-thirty when he got out of the car, an hour before the office was scheduled to open, and he had been surprised to find the front door already unlocked and the lights on, even more so to have an unrecognized young woman jump up from a typewriter desk as he stepped into the general office, obviously startled and plainly embarrassed.

"I'm Vicky Morris — Joel's wife," she introduced herself. "We don't have a wide-carriage machine at home and Joel was so anxious to have these things ready for your meeting this morning —"

Joel had suddenly appeared then, coming in through the back door, at first almost as embarrassed as his wife, and it had taken Lincoln Lord longer than it should have been necessary to put them at their ease, handicapped as he was by his momentary inability to remember having called the meeting that they were both talking about. He finally recalled that he had, on Saturday, stalled off Joel by telling him that they would get together this morning to talk about selecting the Gellman items that they might pack under their own label as a Coastal

Foods line. He had not expected that Joel would take it so seriously — obviously, his preparation for the meeting had been a day-and-night job through the whole week end — but this was not the first time that some eager underling had read more into his words than he had intended and, once he had seen what was happening, he had offered the encouragement of keen interest in what Joel had worked up. He did not, however, make the mistake of looking at any of the charts that were scattered around desk tops, compassionately aware that prior inspection would blunt the climax of revelation that Joel was so plainly anticipating.

Vicky had left soon afterward but, during the few moments that he had watched the two of them through the glass wall of his office, there had been a rich resurrection of memories, recalling all the times during his own early years in business when Maggie had stepped in to help him, a parallel that subconsciously reinforced his growing conviction that Joel was going to be his most valuable assistant. Joel's guess on the Rubin situation at Gellman's had been so perfect an anticipation that even a discount for luck still made it seem an act of genius.

He did, for a moment, consider the fact that Joel was a Jew — it was even more obviously true of Vicky than of Joel — but it was an awareness submerged almost at the instant of recognition, and watching them go out together when Joel left to drive her home, he again felt the bond of transposition, remembering an occasion when he had taken Maggie home from the old Quincy Canning office in the first hour of a winter dawn, almost embarrassed then by the erotic arousal that the memory induced, hurriedly side-stepped by transposing the past to the present, picturing Maggie's arrival at Forgehill this morning. He wondered then if it might not be a good idea to call Dr. Summerfield sometime before she got there and pave the way by letting him know that she was coming. Even at first thought, however, it seemed a questionable thing to do, and since it was too early to call then, and since Maggie would not be arriving at Forgehill until ten-forty, there was plenty of time to consider it. By then, too, people had started coming into the office, Swann one of the first, and when the office manager stopped to offer a surprised greeting he had said, "Come in a minute when you get your coat off, Alf."

After Swann's hurried return and a few moments of preliminary conversation, he said, "Alf, how badly do you need Joel as an assistant? I know you're snowed under now, and that you will be until we get squared away again, but how much would you be handicapped if we put him full time on another job?"

"Just what did you have in mind?" Swann asked stiffly, evidencing again, as he had too many times, a lack of adroitness.

"As I understand it, Mr. Zurich brought Joel in to do a sales job," he said, counting now on Swann's demonstrated deference to every wish of Sol Zurich's. "And there's something that badly needs doing, Alf. We've got to get a lot closer to Gellmans than we've ever been before. We ought to have someone in their New York office at least once a week, really get to know them, not just our buyer but everyone else around the place. And we ought to be getting into some of their stores, too — I don't mean real sales coverage — but we should have enough contact to know what's going on."

"I see," Swann said. "And you're proposing to turn all that over to Joel?"

"As far as sales contact is concerned — yes, that's what I had in mind," he said. "And if we're going to bring out a line of our own, we do have to make a start at building up a sales organization."

"Wouldn't that be enough to give Joel?"

"But keeping on top of the Gellman account is first priority, Alf. That's still the backbone of our business and it's going to be for a long time to come." Swann's resistant silence was trying his patience. "If you don't think Joel is the man to handle it, what's the alternative?"

"Oh, I don't say that he might not be able to handle it," Swann said. "With the right kind of supervision, that is. But he is rather inexperienced — and those people do take some special handling. I've always kept an eye on the Gellman account myself, you know — that is since Mr. Zurich died.

He was tempted to remind Swann of the near-catastrophe that his so-called supervision had brought on, restraining himself to a dry, "I believe I'll be able to give Joel all the direction he'll need."

"Oh, in that case —" Swann said, a quick but forced repentance. "Yes, I suppose I'll be able to get along."

"And if you can't, we'll pick up another assistant for you," he assured him. "But don't say anything about this to Joel yet. I'll want to talk to him myself first. By the way, he's setting up a meeting for this morning — ten o'clock — back in the cutting room. Afraid there's not room here for the four of us" — he injected a smile — "and all the charts Joel seems to have worked up."

"Yes, we do need some decent offices, don't we?" Swann said humorlessly. "I don't suppose you've had a chance yet to think about going ahead with the second floor, have you?"

"No, I really haven't," he said, seeing Swann now as a narrow-gauge old man, his stature marked by the pettiness of his objection . . . strange how many men there were like him, measuring themselves by the size of their offices . . .

"You do know, don't you," Swann asked anxiously, "that the plans are already drawn? They're around here somewhere."

"Yes, I know," he said, deciding that it might be better not to reveal that Joel had already turned over to him not only the architect's original plans but also the names of three competent contractors from whom competitive bids might be secured.

With Swann out of his office, and after a delaying perusal of the morning mail — still more letters congratulating him on his assumption of the presidency of Coastal Foods, most of them from prospective suppliers — he walked briskly back to the cannery and finally located Frank Kennan, who was personally supervising the repair of the conveyer into the warehouse. He listened for some minutes to Kennan's proposal that a new control unit be installed, approved its purchase, and then worked his way around to asking for Kennan's opinion on Joel's ability to handle the Gellman account. Kennan pleased him by evidencing substantially more breadth than Swann had shown, not even prefacing his opinion by saying, as he usually did, that the sales end of the business was out of his bailiwick, mincing no words in his general approval of Joel. "That was a smart piece of work Joel did last Thursday — not that I'm minimizing what you did, Mr. Lord, not for a minute — but for my dough, Joel was damned fast on the uptake."

"He was indeed," he said heartily. "And by the way, Frank, I'd appreciate it if you'd drop the formality and stop calling me Mr. Lord."

"Sure, you bet — thanks," Kennan said solidly. "As far as Joel is concerned — well, I think he's got a break coming to him. That's why he came down here — hoping that it was going to lead to a sales manager's job — and he's never really had a fair shake. The cards were stacked against him from the start."

"I don't get your point."

"Well, Mr. Zurich had him on that baby food study for a long time. That was a dead duck from the beginning — I mean as far as ever making a commercial product out of it."

Kennan's voice had cut off on an odd up-note, his open-faced expression failing to conceal that there was some purpose behind his having

355

so quickly twisted the conversation to the subject he had raised. The reason was not too difficult to guess and Lincoln Lord said with a secret smile, "We were over at Haven Home on Saturday."

"I heard you were," Kennan said with engaging frankness. "I happened to call Doc while you were there — wanting to check something — and they told me that he was tied up with you and Kira."

"She invited us over for lunch and a tour of the place."

"Quite a layout, isn't it?"

"It is indeed," he said. "You were right about Perrill, he's a very interesting man."

"Get him talking about India?"

"Oh yes. He told us the whole story."

Kennan hesitated. "Maybe this isn't any of my business —"

"What's on your mind?"

"Did Kira make another pitch to have us put the stuff on the market?"

He hesitated, considering the possibility of telling Kennan exactly what had happened, quickly deciding that it would be better to wait until everything was all set with Brick ... he'd take the job, of course he would ... no matter how well Brick was doing, he wouldn't turn down a ten-thousand-dollar fee for nothing but planting a magazine article ... but still there was always a chance for a slip-up ... Brick might even have a competing client ...

Concerned now by his silence, Kennan began, "I didn't mean —"

"Yes, I'm sure Mrs. Zurich would like to see something come out of all the work they're doing over there," he said carefully. "And it does deserve some recognition, there's no question about that. They're getting some really astounding results."

Kennan asked earnestly, "You've seen Joel's report, haven't you?"

"Oh, yes," he said. "Went over it again yesterday afternoon."

"I suppose the situation has changed some since Joel made his study —"

"Not too much," he said, noting Kennan's evident relief. "Joel's still right in his basic premise — it's not something for Coastal Foods to tackle."

"That's what I've always thought," Kennan said. "Some big outfit might be able to put it over, somebody that had ten million or so to plow into advertising —"

"It would take that," he said. "And maybe more."

"Anyway, I'm glad we're not getting into it," Kennan said. "Kira's worried me a little —" He paused. "I guess this sounds like a workout on the old apple, but it's a good feeling to know that you're the guy in the driver's seat, Linc."

"Thanks, Frank," he said, suppressing the rise of emotion, wishing again that it were possible to tell him why there was no longer any need to worry about Kira . . . but no, the thing to do was play it safe . . . wait until after Maggie had seen Brick this afternoon on her way back from Forgehill . . .

4

Brick Mitchell was staring over the top of his typewriter, his head so tightly clamped in a vise of stubborn resistance that it was impossible to raise his eyes high enough to see Tommy's face. She had stopped talking now and the only way that he could be certain that she was still standing in front of him was the section of her skirt that could be seen between the front edge of his desk and the top limit of his vision. Her skirt was a drumhead, stretched taut by the stance of anger, her feet planted apart as if she were bracing herself to strike another blow.

Suddenly the skirt came alive with rippling folds, moving, not out of the door but to the left. His head was still clamped but his eyes followed, strained in their sockets. He saw her coat whipped off the clothes-tree, then the stabbing thrust of her hand into the welt-edged pocket. His eyes were not quick enough to follow the movement of her hand but they did catch a blurred flash, and then he heard the dulled tinkle of a small metallic object striking the linoleum top of his desk. He knew before he looked at it that it was her key to the office, seeing it then as a saw-edged dirk twisted deep inside him, cutting strained tendons. His eyes snapped up and his throat shaped a cry of protest to the sound of her name.

She stood in the doorway, pinpoints of fire in her eyes. "What do you expect me to do — stay here and take it?"

He swallowed and it seemed as if there were no bottom limit, as if the words in his throat had fallen into disemboweled emptiness.

"I know what the score is now," she said bitterly.

"Tommy, we don't need that job."

"We?" Her laugh was the sound of a cracked bell. "You can leave me out of it from now on."

357

"All we need —"

"All you need is a bottle of gin."

"Tommy, listen to me —"

"What do you want me to do — go out and buy it for you? Hold your head? Pour it down your throat?" She wheeled away. "Or do you want me to get Maggie Lord and bring her back to you?"

"Tommy, you're crazy. I —"

"No, you don't want that, do you? You wouldn't have the guts to face her. You might find out that she isn't that gal in the gin bottle."

"Tommy — last night —"

"Sure! Last night! It was wonderful, wasn't it? A jug of Martinis and you went to bed with her. Only this morning you woke up and it wasn't her at all. It was me. I've had it, Brick. I've been a stand-in long enough."

"That's not true!" He was on his feet. "You don't believe that."

"You're the one who's lying, Brick — and they're the worst lies of all — the ones you tell to yourself."

"Are you crazy enough to think Maggie Lord means anything to me? For god's sake, Tommy — listen to me. It isn't true. It never has been true."

"No?" Her lips were a curved blade, slashing. "Then why are you afraid of this job?"

"I'm not afraid of it. Can't you — ?"

"Why won't you even consider it?"

"I've told you."

Her voice was sardonic mimicry. "You don't want to have anything to do with Lincoln Lord."

"No, and I'm not going to," he said, but not as the exclamatory explosion that he wanted it to be. His lips had gone slack at the change of expression on Tommy's face.

For an instant he thought he glimpsed understanding, almost sympathy, but then she said bitterly, "You poor, dumb, blind, stupid fool! You don't even know, do you?"

His stare was vacuous, open to the emptiness of his mind.

Tommy's lips curled. "Don't you know why you can't face Lincoln Lord? Because you hate his guts — he's sleeping with your dream girl and all you've got is the dregs at the bottom of the bottle."

He was stunned, speechless, unable to even shake his head.

She pounded words at him, not into his blanked ears but down his throat, into the emptiness. "Who did you think you were kidding — me?

Good old Tommy? All right, damn it, I *was* a fool for a few minutes last night. I thought you were telling me the truth. I know better now."

"It was the truth," he muttered hoarsely. "It still is."

"You don't know what the truth is. You don't even tell it to yourself. How blind can you be? Don't you ever look in a mirror? Try it some time. You'll see something you don't see in that gin bottle, buster. You'll see yourself. You'll see what I saw when I mentioned her name — Maggie Lord — that's all it took, just her name. And then I saw what you really are — just a damn fool who's wasting his whole life carrying a torch for a dame that he can't ever have."

He mumbled something, again trying to say it wasn't true ... but, oh god, it was! And maybe it was even true about Linc, too ... and he'd never known ... never! But it was too late now ... Tommy wouldn't believe him if he tried to tell her that he'd never realized ... only prove that what she'd said about him was true ... dumb ... blind ... stupid ...

"I'm sorry if that hurts," she said, then instantly correcting herself, "No, I'm not. You've got it coming to you. All right, maybe I am a bitch — maybe I was asking for it —"

"No, Tommy, no." He moved toward her. "Listen to me —"

She backed away, matching him step for step. "I did — last night."

Yes, he was blind ... drunk and crazy ... but never as drunk as this ... hang on, hang on ... if you fall, you'll never get up ...

"Good-by, Brick."

He lunged for her and his fingers caught the edge of her coat as it swirled around her, a death-grip hold on the narrowest of margins, almost lost as she tried to pull away from him. The rip of fabric was something tearing in his mind. She flinched and he caught her arms in that off-guard instant, pinning them to her side. "Now you listen to me!"

She fought against him, turning her head away.

"Call this woman at Haven Home," he demanded. "Tell her that we're coming down."

"What will that prove?"

"Maybe nothing to you," he said, cold sober now. "But it will prove something to me."

"That I'm wrong?"

"No, I can't prove that. I *have* been a damn fool, Tommy. But maybe it'll prove —" His grip on her arms relaxed but she didn't move away from him ... there was still a chance ...

"You don't have to prove anything to me."

"Yes, I do."

"It doesn't matter."

"If this doesn't matter, there's nothing in this crazy damn world that does. Tommy, I've got to prove to you that I wasn't lying last night."

"Forget last night." Her voice broke. "I was a bitch — the whole week end. Forget it. I made you say it."

"You aren't making me say it now. And this isn't gin talking, Tommy — and I'm not lying — to you, or myself, or anyone else." He expected a choke in his throat but the words came through clear and sharp. "I love you, Tommy."

Her clenched fist came up as if she were going to beat his chest, and then suddenly her fingers opened, in the instant of first touching as soft as her lips, then suddenly steel-strong again, digging into his muscles, tearing through as if to prove that the emptiness was gone. He finally whispered, "You do love me, don't you?"

She was crying. "You know I do — I couldn't have been that cruel if I didn't. Oh, that doesn't make sense —"

"Sure it does. If you hadn't — maybe this doesn't make sense either, but if you hadn't said it, I'd never be able to love you the way I do now."

Afterwards he said, "Aren't you going to make that call?"

"You still want me to?"

"Of course."

"You'll go down to Goodhaven?"

"Sure. Why not?"

She hung up her coat again and, passing his desk on the way out, picked up her key. Without looking back as she went out, she said, "I'll set it up for the end of the week. That'll still give you time enough to change your mind."

What was the matter with her . . . did she still think that. . . ?

His hand was trembling but he spun a doubled sheet of yellow paper into his typewriter.

5

Using the cutting room wall cabinet as an improvised easel, Joel Morris displayed the first of the exhibits that he had prepared for the meeting, a bar chart comparing the total annual sales of the twenty top-selling items in the Mother Gellman line.

Listening with approval, Lincoln Lord noted that Joel's voice was stronger now, his manner easier, his confidence in himself more evident. For the first few minutes he had been obviously nervous, suggesting a lack of poise that had seemed to justify Swann's doubts about his ability to head the company's sales activities. Now, however, he was beginning to get his feet on the ground. There was added encouragement as he explained the manner in which he had analyzed sales on each of the Gellman items, assurance that the plan he was to propose would be solidly underpinned with factual data.

"Since our objective is to establish a line of our own without taking any substantial gambles," Joel went on, "the obvious thing to do is to pick products that have already proved themselves in the Gellman stores, items that we know *will* sell because they *are* selling. On the other hand, it may not be wise to make our selection purely on the basis of total Gellman sales. Suppose, for example, that we were to pick their six best sellers. All right, here's what we'd have — Beef with Gravy, Roast Beef Hash, Beef Stew with Vegetables, Chicken with Noodles, Corned Beef Hash, and Chicken à la King. They're all staples that are found on the shelves of every grocery store in the country — that's what you get, of course, when you pick big-volume items — and that's why everybody and his brother is packing them. Here's the competitive picture."

He changed charts. "This is Beef with Gravy. The *Canner's Directory* lists forty-two competitive brands. That's the worst case but the others aren't too far behind. Against that kind of competition I think we'd have a rough time getting anywhere with a line that didn't have anything in it but the same old staples."

Kennan's eyebrows went up and Joel reacted instantly. "Oh, I know — our quality is way out ahead. I'm not afraid of what would happen after we got on the store shelves — once people tried our stuff, they'd come back and buy again — but before they can try it, we have to get on those shelves. That would be a real battle. We don't have a big advertising campaign — that's out of the question — and with the kind of competition we'd have, there's no hope of being able to buy shelf space with cut-price deals."

Kennan nodded. "It's tough to get into those stores these days."

"I think we'd have rough going even before we got that far," Joel amended. "It would be hard to line up the right brokers to represent us. Oh, we could get brokers — there's always some hungry guy who's willing to collect his five per cent — but the really good ones, the boys who could do a job for us, already have competitive lines." He paused as if anticipating objection, hesitating through a moment of silence, then going on. "Now let's consider the possibilities of some other products — items that are in substantial demand but still not in the staple class — less competitive. Here we run into some situations that I wasn't aware of until I started to break down our shipments by geographical areas. The variation in regional demand is rather surprising — or at least it was to me."

He flipped back the cover on another chart. "This is Hungarian Beef Goulash. It was seventh in total volume last year, eighth the year before. But look where the business is coming from — almost eighty per cent of our shipments were to the New York metropolitan area. I don't know why, maybe it's the garlic, but it just doesn't sell in the outside territory. So unless we want to try cracking that tough New York market, it's not a good bet for our line. Now here's the reverse situation — Chicken Fricassee with Noodles. It's twelfth in total volume, but when you get outside of New York, the sales jump substantially. It was fourth out of the Harrisburg warehouse and sixth in Albany. In other words, it's a strong item in the territory where we'd have the best chance to break in."

"This is damned interesting," Frank Kennan said, glancing at Swann for agreement and getting no more than a minimal nod.

"Extremely interesting," Lincoln Lord said pointedly, looking directly at Swann who, as if forced, finally said, "Yes, there are a lot of things that have to be taken into account."

Step by step, Joel went on building his story, sometimes going into more detail than seemed necessary yet always pushing ahead, finally displaying the chart on which he revealed the six products that he was recommending as an initial line, each checkmarked against a listing of desirable characteristics. He was now beyond the support of the statistics that had been developed from the Mother Gellman sales figures, moving into an area where opinion and judgment had to be called into play, yet even here he had assembled a surprising amount of supporting data, making it obvious that this whole presentation was more solidly grounded than something dreamed up over the week end.

Several times, Lincoln Lord shot questions at him, as much to see how Joel would react as to test the validity of his reasoning, and he found himself increasingly pleased on both scores. Joel's analysis of the competition between canned and frozen prepared foods was particularly sharp, crystallized as he showed several sketches, rough but graphic, of store displays that cleverly capitalized upon the special appeal of products he was recommending.

Joel had already turned to the next chart when Swann suddenly spoke up, the first question that he had asked. "Those posters and streamers, all that display material — you'd supply that to the stores?"

"Yes, of course," Joel puzzled.

"How much would that cost?" Swann asked.

"Well, that would depend on how many stores we lined up. The more we got, the lower the unit cost would be."

"But there would be a certain minimum?"

"Yes, if we —"

"How much?" Swann demanded. "I'm sure you've set up a budget?"

"Yes, I've made a budget," Joel said with a commendable patience.

"And there'd be more expense than just this display material," Swann pressed. "You'd use some demonstrators, wouldn't you — buy some locations — co-operative advertising — ?"

"I have all of those things covered," Joel said tightly, fingering the thin sheaf of charts that he still had not shown. "I thought I'd go through the whole plan first and then we could go over the budget."

Seeing that Swann was in no mood to give up, Lincoln Lord was about to come to Joel's rescue but he decided against interference, interested to see how Joel would handle himself under pressure.

Unrestrained, Swann pressed on. "What would it cost us the first year — two hundred thousand?"

The flash freezing of Joel's expression indicated that Swann had struck close to the mark, suggesting that perhaps he had stolen an advance look at some of the charts that had been lying around the office the first thing this morning. Joel finally admitted, "Somewhere in that neighborhood."

Swann had his pencil out. "And what volume would you expect to do?"

"I don't know," Joel said, his poise beginning to slip away now. "That would depend on a lot of things."

"A million dollars gross would be an outside figure, wouldn't it?"

"Yes, I suppose so," Joel said, flushed now. "At least the first year."

"That's twenty per cent," Swann said, tapping the table top with his pencil. Add five for brokerage and it's up to twenty-five per cent. And you mentioned putting on a couple of specialty salesmen of our own, didn't you? Add that and you're up to twenty-seven or twenty-eight per cent. Do you realize what that means?"

Joel's eyes appealed for direction and Lincoln Lord finally stepped in. "Alf, aren't we getting ahead of ourselves here? I'm not necessarily approving Joel's plan — I want to hear the rest of the story first — but I do think we'd be wrong in basing our final judgment on what our first-year sales and advertising ratio might turn out to be. It's bound to be high until we've had time enough to build up volume. But even then, twenty-five per cent isn't too frightening. There are plenty of food specialties that run even higher."

"But they have the margin to cover it," Swann said evenly. "We don't. We might get away with five per cent brokerage — yes, I suppose that's possible — but I don't see how we can go beyond that."

"Oh, come now, Alf —" he interrupted, covering annoyance with a quick little laugh.

Swann stopped him, his pencil a poised dagger. "We're proposing to sell the same products that Gellman is selling, aren't we? And in the same towns where they have stores?"

"We have that right."

"Yes, we have that right," Swann agreed. "But do we have the margin? Let's take an example — Chicken Fricassee with Dumplings. You can buy it in a Gellman store, I believe, for fifty-nine cents a can. Now let's see what we'd have to sell it for to the store across the street." He made a rapid calculation, talking as he figured. "We'd have the same costs that we have on what we're packing for Gellman, of course — plus this twenty-five per cent advertising and selling expense. On that basis —" He drew a line and struck a total. "Our wholesale price to the store across the street would work out at about sixty-one cents a can. In other words, it would be cheaper for them to buy from Gellman's. Their retail price would be lower than our wholesale price to the store that's trying to compete with them."

"But how — ?"

"There's not one penny of advertising or sales cost in any of the Gellman prices, Mr. Lord. There never has been. There was never any reason why there should be. We just didn't have any sales expense — and, of course, there was no advertising cost. Even our general overhead has always been very low. That was Mr. Zurich's policy — as he used to say, to put all the value inside the can. That's how we were able to hold the Gellman business, Mr. Lord. And that's the big reason they've been able to build up so much volume on the

Mother Gellman line. Other stores just haven't been able to compete. No canner could ever pack as good a product as ours, add a lot of sales and advertising expense to his cost, and still sell to other retailers at a price that would allow them to match Gellman's."

Lincoln Lord looked around him for some hint of rebuttal. Kennan was nodding agreement, murmuring, "That's about it, I guess." Joel seemed crushed into silence, a man stunned by the collapse of his world.

Swann said with a bad imitation of apology, "I'm sorry to have to bring this up now — all this work that Joel's done — but of course I'd never been told that you were considering anything like this."

There was more than a hint of vindictiveness in the office manager's voice and Lincoln Lord found it hard to suppress anger, able to do so only because his mind was diverted by the sharp sensing of his disappointment in Joel. Instead of replying to Swann, he turned to Joel asking, "What about it — what's the answer?"

"I don't know that there is an answer, sir," Joel said without looking up. "Unless it might be possible to adjust the Gellman prices."

"And if we do, we'll lose the business," Swann said smugly.

"What are you suggesting, Alf — that it's impossible to bring out a line of our own?" Lincoln Lord asked, seeing now the hollowness of the victory that he had thought he had scored in getting Sidney Arnauth to permit Coastal Foods to pack and sell Gellman products under its own label.

"No, I don't say that it's impossible," Swann said. "All I'm saying is that I've never been able to figure out a way to do it. I don't see how we can have our cake and eat it too. If we had a completely different line — you remember, Joel, what Mr. Zurich used to say — that anything we'd ever bring out ourselves would have to be something that we didn't sell through Gellman Stores?"

Joel retorted, still without looking up, "But every time something new did come along, he'd turn it right over to them."

"Because that was the most profitable thing to do," Swann said. "After all, that's why we're in business, isn't it — to make a profit? Mr. Zurich may not have been —"

Lincoln Lord cut him off. "I don't think we're going to get anywhere with a post-mortem on past policies. This is a new day and we're starting from scratch. What happens from here on out —" He hesitated, false courage exhausted... what the devil *could* they do? Maybe Swann was right... maybe the thing to do was just sit back and be content with the Gellman business. Why not? What did he have to gain? He was making plenty of money, as much as he'd ever made in his life ... Maggie liked it here ...

He was in strange territory now. Never before had he consciously made any decision upon the basis of what it meant to him personally. Always he had thought of the company first — and now it was the company that was watching him, waiting for what he was about to say, watching with Frank Kennan's expectant expression, pleading with Joel's eyes ... he had to do something, find some way out ... he'd gone too far to turn back ...

"You may be right, Alf," he heard himself say, blindly, still not knowing where he was going. "It's possible that we may not be able to carry a high promotional cost —" Suddenly he saw a faint glimmer of light. "But as you said a moment ago, we would be able to pay a brokerage commission and still compete. If we could get one of the big general brokers, someone that had broad sales coverage all over the East — enough power and prestige to force some distribution —"

"Someone like National Distributors, or J. C. Harten & Company," Swann said quickly, as if this had been his objective all along. "You don't happen by any chance to know Mr. Harten personally, do you, Mr. Lord?"

"No, I don't," he said. "The only one of the big brokers I've ever known was Art Gerhart — Gerhart & Gerhart. We used them on one of our lines at Rabson."

"Well, they'd be even better," Swann said. "The only reason I didn't mention G & G was because I didn't think there'd be any chance of getting them to even consider taking us on. But if you know Mr. Gerhart —"

"Oh, that was a long time ago," he said, suspicious of Swann's motive ... but still it might work ... this wasn't too far from the kind of job that Art Gerhart had done for him at Rabson ... getting distribution for those salad dressings ... Brick's idea ...

Joel had finally shaken free from the lethargy of shock and was hurriedly leafing through the exhibits that he still had not shown. "This isn't something that I didn't consider, Mr. Lord. I did. I know we've got to get brokers to represent us — of course we do — but if we turn over the whole sales management job to one of the big national outfits —"

Joel's eyes suddenly lifted, fixed on the door and, turning, Lincoln Lord saw Miss Payne.

"I'm sorry, Mr. Lord," she said. "I know you said you didn't want to be bothered with any calls —"

He was on his feet immediately . . . Maggie was calling from Forgehill . . . she'd changed her mind about Kip . . .

But after he was outside the door, Miss Payne said, "It's Mrs. Zurich and I thought you'd want to talk to her."

When he picked up the receiver, Kira said, "I hope I haven't taken you away from something important?"

"No, no," he protested, hurriedly trying to reorient his mind.

"I just want to tell you how grateful I am to you for getting to Mr. Mitchell so quickly. Dr. Thompson called me a few minutes ago. Perhaps you know already — they're both coming down on Friday, Mr. Mitchell and Dr. Thompson."

"No, I didn't know," he said, looking at his watch . . . Maggie couldn't possibly have gotten back to New York from Forgehill . . .

"Of course, they haven't said yet that they'll take it on," Kira continued. "But Dr. Thompson sounded very interested —"

"Oh, I'm sure he will," he said, fighting distraction.

"Well, I just wanted to thank you, Mr. Lord."

"You've nothing to thank me for," he said quickly. "Maggie's the one who arranged it."

"I thought perhaps you'd called him."

"No, I —"

"You will tell her how grateful I am, won't you?"

"Yes, of course. And thank you for calling, Mrs. Zurich."

Maggie must have gone to Brick the minute she got in New York . . . was that why she had been so keyed up, seeing Brick again . . . but why?"

There was no answer in the torrent of thoughts that swept through his mind, driven by a chill wind that came out of nowhere.

6

Maggie Lord's luck seemed to have changed — the train from New York arrived at Forgehill on schedule, there was a taxi immediately available, and she caught Dr. Summerfield before he left his office for lunch. Surprisingly, he was neither resistant nor unpleasant, professing quick understanding of why she wanted to bring her son to Good-haven, even agreeing that it might be a good thing for Kip. The mood of apprehension clung to her mind, however, and as she left the headmaster's office the unexpected ease with which she had with-drawn her son from Forgehill Academy raised the suspicion that Dr. Summerfield had welcomed the chance to relieve himself of the prob-lem of handling Kip.

She had a long wait in Dr. Summerfield's outer office while his secretary tried to locate Kip, and the fact that he was apparently somewhere off the campus seemed to support her earlier opinion that Forgehill was a badly managed school, impossibly slack in discipline and control. Then, suddenly, a Mr. Reggley had appeared, out of breath and hurriedly apologetic, introducing himself as her son's sci-ence teacher and explaining that Kip and another boy had been taken to the pathological laboratory of a local hospital as part of a vocational guidance program. Word had been sent to Kip that she was waiting for him and he should be back on the campus within ten minutes, a wait that Reggley had insisted upon sharing with her.

The message that had reached Reggley had not told him why she was there and when she finally disclosed it, his concern was too gen-uine to be mistrusted. "I'm sure you have sound reasons for your decision to transfer your son," he had said, "but I'd be less than honest if I didn't express my disappointment. We've had some difficulty with Kip, of course — perhaps as much our fault as his — but during the last week or two we've somehow managed to get through to him. I really don't know what was the matter before. The adolescent mind is often difficult to penetrate, and all the more so in a boy like Kip, particularly at this period in his life. Most boys feel something of the sort — this need to find themselves — but Kip strikes me as a boy to whom it's peculiarly important to have some positive purpose, some definite goal. He may abandon it later in favor of something else — he probably will — but in the meantime it does serve as a steadying in-fluence that's vitally important to his development. Our trouble with Kip was that we just couldn't find the touchstone — or at least we hadn't been able to until a couple of weeks ago. Then our science course got into biology. Somehow that got through to him. That's why I had him sent over to the hospital today, fanning that spark. I really do think we've made a breakthrough now, Mrs. Lord, and I hope that you'll be able to follow it up."

She found it frighteningly difficult to share that hope, no longer able to suppress the question that was now fully exposed, confronted with the realization that Foregehill Academy, despite Dr. Summerfield, was doing something for Kip that she would have a hard time matching at Goodhaven High School ... and if she failed, the blame would be entirely her own ... Linc had agreed to take Kip out of Forgehill only because she had made him feel that it was something she wanted ... he'd never shown enough enthusiasm for the idea so that there would be an honest sharing of responsibility if it didn't work out.

Crossing the campus after word finally came that Kip was at Hawthorne Cottage, even the academy grounds seemed more attractive, the bare earth and unsightly litter hidden under a white snow blanket. And when she got to the house, the door was opened not by Mrs. Grandon but by a pleasant and well-dressed woman who introduced herself as Mrs. Carpenter, the wife of the new housemaster. But it was Kip himself who most seriously shook her resolution. She had never before seen him come down a flight of stairs so quickly, nor had he ever before greeted her with what was, if not actually a smile of welcome, at least an amazing improvement over his usual blankly suspicious expression. And then she told him why she had come, and now he stood staring at her, his eyes wide, his lips slack.

"But you did say that you hated it here," she said, attempting to keep herself from thinking how difficult it would be to go back to Dr. Summerfield and explain why she had changed her mind.

"Yeah, I guess I did," Kip said, nodding as if it were an ancient memory only vaguely recalled.

"But now you've changed your mind, is that it?"

He shrugged, hunching his shoulders, burrowing his chin into the heavy roll collar of his sweater. "I just quit thinking about it, that's all. You know — Dad and this new job."

"How could that change the way you feel about Forgehill?"

"You know — what it costs here."

Her heart threatened to choke her. "Oh, Kip, was that the reason you said that you didn't like it here — because you thought your father couldn't afford it?"

He was looking down, digging at the carpet nap with the toe of his worn loafers. "No, I guess all I was thinking was — I don't know."

"What were you thinking, Kip?"

"He got another job so I figured you could afford it again — you know."

"No, Kip, I don't know. What are you trying to say — that you'd rather stay here?"

He shook his head. "I thought if Dad was making a lot of money again — I guess what I thought was that you wouldn't be taking me out of here if you didn't have to."

"Kip, please listen to me." She paused, hoping that he would look at her. "Will you?"

"Sure."

"This doesn't have anything to do with money, Kip. We can afford to keep you here. Everything's working out wonderfully at the company. They've gotten the Gellman Stores business back and that means your father will be making — well, as much money as he ever made before, perhaps even more. There's no question of our not being able to afford it."

"Then why are you doing it?" he asked, his voice so muffled that she could not be certain that it was not an accusation.

"Because —" She stopped, afraid that he might not believe her, and quickly said instead, "We thought you might like it better at Goodhaven. There's a wonderful new high school right near our house and — oh, Kip, it's such a beautiful house. There's a great big room for you, all your own, even your own bathroom. There's your own door to go out on the terrace. It's almost like having your own apartment. It isn't really fixed up yet — not the way you'd want it — Viola and I did the best we could with what we had, but I didn't want to buy anything new because I thought you'd rather pick out your own things." She paused. "Wouldn't you?"

He seemed to nod but then he said, "I guess you know — Mrs. Grandon isn't here any more. We've got a housemaster now — and his wife lives here, too — Mrs. Carpenter."

"Yes, I know — I met her."

"She's pretty nice," he said, avoiding her eyes.

"Does that mean — ?"

"I just said it, that's all. If you want me to come down there —"

"Oh, Kip, I do want you," she burst out, no longer able to hold back what she had started to say in the beginning. "It's the first chance we've ever had to really be together. You've been away from us so much — another year or two and then it'll be college, and then we'll never be together again —" She stopped, realizing how terribly unfair she was being, subjecting a child to the full force of sentiment at the same time that she was asking him to assume the adult responsibility of independent decision. "Kip, I'm sorry. I shouldn't have said that. I was being selfish. All I was thinking of was myself — how wonderful it would be to have you with us."

"You mean you really want me there?" he asked, guardedly incredulous.

"Oh, Kip, of course I do. But that isn't what really matters. If you've gotten to like Forgehill —"

"What about Dad?"

"Whatever you decide will be all right with him."

"I didn't mean that. I meant —"

It was only too plain what he meant and she dared not let him say it. "Your father wants the same thing I want, Kip. We both want you to go to school wherever you're happiest."

"You mean I can make up my own mind?" he asked, his voice strangely lowered in tone, surprisingly manlike, and as he straightened up from his slouched position against the stair rail it seemed that he had grown another head taller in the last three weeks.

"Yes, it's your decision to make," she said, frightened by the gamble she was taking.

"I don't know," he muttered, avoiding her eyes again, her apprehension in no way eased by the feeling that he was not weighing Forgehill against Goodhaven High, that he was wondering if he could trust what she had told him.

Quickly she said, "I know it isn't a fair decision to ask you to make, Kip. You haven't seen Goodhaven, or the high school, or anything else down there. If you want —"

"I guess they'd have science, wouldn't they — you know, biology and stuff like that?"

"Oh, I'm sure they do," she said, wishing that she could be as certain as she tried to make herself sound, then suddenly remembering that Kira Zurich had said something about the influence that she had exerted to have the science curriculum expanded. "Yes, I know they do. Mrs. Zurich is on the school board — she's the director of the Haven Home — and they're doing a lot of research over there on all sorts of things that are — well, it's all really biological. Is that what you're interested in, Kip?"

"I guess so — kind of." He shifted uneasily. "Maybe I better pack up, huh?"

"If it's what you want to do."

He nodded and started slowly up the stairs, turning back when she called his name. "Yeah?"

"I want to call your father and tell him what train we'll be on."

"It's right there — the phone."

"How long will it take you to pack? There's a train to New York from here at two-fifty. Do you think we can make that?"

"Sure." And then he turned and plodded up the rest of the steps.

The telephone was at the foot of the stairs and she placed the call, person to person, then suddenly realizing that if she talked to Linc he might ask her some question that would force her to admit that she had avoided seeing Brick. "Operator —" she called. "I've changed my mind. Don't bother to make it person to person. Just get me the Coastal Foods Company."

"You'll talk to anyone?"

"Yes"... she could leave a message for Linc... wait until she got home to try to make him understand about Brick... she didn't dare try to do it over the telephone...

The call went through. "Coastal Foods. May I help you?"

"Yes, if you will, please. I want to leave a message for Mr. Lord. This is Mrs. Lord and I'd like to have you tell him —"

"But he's right here, Mrs. Lord, and I know he wants to talk to you."

Her protest was useless, the connection dead until Linc's voice burst in upon her. "Golly, Mag, where are you? New York?"

"No, I'm still at Forgehill. I didn't get here until —"

"I know," he said. "You went to see Brick first."

His tone was cool and, for an instant, she was choked by unreasoned fear. "I was so late getting into New York that I missed the first train up here. I had almost an hour to kill so I —"

"Oh, that's it," he said. "I was wondering what had happened. I knew you must have talked to Brick early. He called Kira back before noon. You must have really done a job on him."

She was momentarily stunned, and it was fortunate that she was because it gave her a chance to suppress an expression of astonishment, time enough to get her voice under control before she asked, "Do you mean that Brick's taking the job?"

"Well, at least they're coming down to look it over."

"When?"

"Friday. Brick and this Dr. Thompson, Kira's walking on air. She's really grateful to you for setting it up."

372

"I'm glad it worked out," she said flatly, screening astonishment from her voice, still bewildered, unable to imagine how that Thompson woman had ever been able to convince Brick.

"What about Kip?"

"Everything's all right. That's why I called, to tell you what train —"

"No trouble with Summerfield?"

"No."

"And Kip's coming back with you?"

"Yes, we're leaving here on the two-fifty —"

"How is he?" Linc asked, bridging her hesitation by driving ahead. "Look, Mag, this is why I've been hoping that you'd call. I've got to go into New York. I'm leaving in a few minutes — got a date to meet Art Gerhart at the Greenbank Club for a drink at five. Sorry not to be here when you get home, but Art's leaving for the West Coast tonight. That's why I have to catch him before —"

The rest of what he said was lost. Looking up through the railing around the second-floor landing, she caught a glimpse of Kip's loafers and the shadowed whiteness of his wool socks, the rest of his body cut off by the overhang of the ceiling. He had been listening and she could see, as plainly as if his face were visible, the reflected emptiness of his heart . . . Kip would never believe that his father really wanted him if he weren't there to meet him when he got to Goodhaven . . .

"Linc?"

"Yes?"

She caught a quick breath, grasping at the hope that he would guess that she was talking for Kip's ears. "We'll be getting into New York about four-thirty — I do want to get into one of the stores for a minute — but we could meet you anywhere you say."

She waited through the short silence of seemingly lost communication, separated by all the miles that stretched between Goodhaven and Forgehill. Then the gap flashed shut, sound out-speeding itself as Linc said, "Sure, Mag, why don't you come by the club? I won't be tied up too long with Art and if you'd want to, we could have dinner —"

"Oh, Linc, that would be wonderful. I know Kip would love it. You are going to drive, aren't you?"

"He'll probably get a kick out of the car, too — driving home."

"Oh, I know he will."

"There's a waiting room, Mag. When you go in, just tell the doorman."

"I know, I know," she said hurriedly, not knowing — she had never set foot inside the Greenbank Club — but all that mattered now was the need to make Kip believe that his father was coming to New York to meet him. "Good-by, dear. Thanks so much for thinking of it. And Kip will thank you when he sees you."

She hung up, quickly calling "Kip!" louder than was necessary to carry her voice to the top of the stairs, expecting that he would wait before answering, pretending that he had been in his room. But he spoke immediately and without the slightest attempt at deception, leaning down over the rail so that his face was visible.

"Your father's meeting us in New York," she called. "And you'd better put on your good suit. He's taking us to dinner at the Green-bank Club."

Kip was actually grinning. "I guess I was crazy, wasn't I? I mean what I was thinking about Dad and Uncle Brick."

She was too surprised to mask her momentary lack of comprehension, a failure that twisted the smile off Kip's face. Anxiously, he asked, "Isn't that what Dad said — about his taking the job? He is coming to Goodhaven, isn't he?"

"Yes — yes, he's coming to Goodhaven," she groped. "But he isn't working for the company. He's writing an article about Haven Home — all the research they're doing over there."

"But he is going to be there, isn't he?"

"Yes, I suppose he'll have to be."

The smile came back. "I guess I better get packed."

And then there was the sound of his footsteps running down the hall, the excited banging of a door, the dull thump of a suitcase hurriedly hauled out of its hiding place and tossed on the floor.

7

Preoccupation with the problems that crowded his mind had made Lincoln Lord's drive to New York seem far shorter than it was, so short that there was hardly time enough to give more than a passing thought to his five o'clock meeting with Arthur Gerhart. Although the strangeness of Gerhart's attitude over the telephone had puzzled him, he was not particularly concerned. Calling him had been a long-shot gamble. If nothing came of it, Gerhart & Gerhart would be a name crossed off a salesman's prospect list, nothing lost but a bar check for a couple of rounds of drinks . . . a man had to play the percentages, keep pushing open those doors . . . you never knew what might happen. You could never outguess luck nor anticipate trouble . . . a problem was something to be faced after you knew what it was.

He could remember Adam Quincy saying, "The only serious problems are people-problems — never forget that, boy — and the only serious mistakes in judgment are when you misjudge men." After this morning's meeting, it had seemed that he had misjudged everyone, Alfred Swann as much as Joel Morris, Frank Kennan no less. Yet now as he plunged into the Lincoln Tunnel, he found himself in the accustomed middle ground of compromise and accommodation. All men were a blending of good and bad, of strength offset by weakness, of breadth narrowed by pettiness. You struck a balance and that was your man, always less perfect than you had optimistically hoped, never quite as bad as you feared in your moments of disappointment.

He could see now that he had overweighted Joel Morris's cleverly creative mind, but there was the balancing realization that he had, at first, downgraded Joel too sharply for having failed to check through on the price situation. He should have anticipated that Joel would slip somewhere — Brick, too, had often been so carried away by some big idea that he neglected some practical considerations — and, in the end, Joel's basic concept of a merchandisable line still stood up, no less sound because it would have to be sold through a national brokerage organization without the sales promotion operation that Joel had so much wanted to set up under his own personal direction — Brick, too, had always had that same yen to be the head of a big department — and Joel's weakness was no more than the common one, shared in some degree by all men, of judging success against the wrong set of values.

Swann's weakness was no less understandable — he was every old man who feared that his own precious status would be depreciated by the rise of an assistant and the loss of some of his own authority; yet, for all his tactlessness and lack of diplomacy, as petty as he had been and as badly as he'd handled himself, the fact remained that without Swann's intervention, a serious flaw in Joel's plan might have been missed.

Together, Joel and Alf were a good pair, each man's weaknesses offset by the other's strengths, and Lincoln Lord could now see that his problem was going to be that of keeping that complementary relationship from being destroyed by Joel's obvious feeling that Swann

375

was cutting his throat, and Swann's no less evident fear that Joel was a challenge to his own standing in the company. And it was here, in the handling of that knife-edge situation, that Frank Kennan had revealed himself in a quite unexpected role. Until today, Lincoln Lord had accepted Kennan's self-estimate at face value, even thinking that he was wise to limit his ambition to the production side of the business. After what had happened at lunch, however, Kennan was clearly a bigger man than he thought himself. He had proved himself a master diplomat, first suggesting that they recess the meeting and go down to this noon's Chamber of Commerce luncheon, then insisting that Joel accompany them — it was the first time Joel had ever been asked — and, finally, with the adroitly skillful way that he had maneuvered things in the hotel lobby so that it became Swann's privilege to introduce the new president of the Coastal Foods Company to all of the businessmen of the community.

When they had reconvened in the cutting room after lunch, there was a new air of compromise and co-operation. Kennan had said almost nothing, and Lincoln Lord had followed his lead by restraining his own comments, but somehow Joel and Swann had found common ground, gradually evolving a plan that combined a limited amount of promotional expense with the services of a national broker, Swann agreeing that it would be wise to cut their profit margin to help balance selling prices, Joel conceding that the final plan was an improvement over his original concept.

A faint smile warmed Lincoln Lord's face as he recalled how Frank had nudged him into calling Art Gerhart. The smile faded, however, with his memory of what had then happened. He had put through the call without hope, wanting only to sustain the spirit of the meeting, and his anxiety had thrown him off balance . . . he'd made a mistake in pressuring Gerhart into meeting him for a drink at five o'clock despite the fact that he had a plane to catch at seven . . . the whole atmosphere would be completely wrong. But he was into it now and there was nothing to do but keep driving ahead . . .

UPTOWN

He turned right on Fortieth Street, the New York scene reminding him that he had, just before he left the office, called in Joel and given him the assignment of handling contacts with Gellman Stores' headquarters. He was by no means certain that he had been right in doing so, but if he had not gone through with it, both Kennan and Swann might have gotten the idea that he had lost some of his faith

376

in Joel — and, until he had talked to him, he had. But as always there was good to offset the bad, a gain to weigh against the loss. He was sure that he had accomplished something with this evidencing of his faith and confidence in Joel's ability ... and he *was* a good boy. No, he was no Brick Mitchell ... that was a mistake he'd made too often, thinking of Joel in terms of Brick ...

The thought of Brick reminded him that he was coming to Goodhaven on Friday and he made a mental note to suggest to Maggie that they have Brick and Dr. Thompson over for a drink after they'd finished at Haven Home ... maybe for dinner if there was time enough before they had to return to New York ... but it was the obvious thing to do .... Maggie had probably already invited them ...

He turned left up Sixth Avenue, found the parking lot fortunately unfilled, and entered the Greenbank Club with eight minutes to spare before his five o'clock date with Arthur Gerhart. At the reception desk, after making the demanded inquiry about the health of old William's granddaughter, he said, "I'm expecting a Mr. Gerhart in a few minutes. Page me as soon as he gets here. If I'm not in the washroom, I'll be in the English Bar."

He was halfway across the lobby, already responding to Frank's welcome from the hat-check counter, when he suddenly remembered something forgotten and abruptly turned back. "Oh, William?"

"Yes, Mr. Lord?"

"Mrs. Lord and my son will be coming in later. Take care of them, will you? Have them wait in the small lounge."

"I'm not to page you, sir?"

"No, I'll be having a little meeting with Mr. Gerhart. But I don't imagine it will take very long."

"Very good, sir — and I'll see to it myself that Mrs. Lord and your son are made comfortable," William said, a generous attitude in view of his jaundiced disapproval of the club's recent action in allowing the premises to be invaded by women guests.

"Thank you, William," he replied gratefully, the promise of special attention to Maggie a slight salve to his conscience for having even momentarily forgotten that she and Kip were to meet him here. Since her reassuring call from Forgehill, there had been no need to be concerned about her, but now his thoughts picked up where they had been broken off and he let them dwell there for a moment in a pleasant respite from tension, smiling at the memory of how adroitly Maggie had gotten around to the idea of their having dinner with him here tonight, warmly aware that she had done it not for her own sake but for Kip's, and he wished now that it was something that he had thought of himself . . . Kip would probably get a wallop out of having dinner here at the Greenbank Club . . . yes, and driving home afterwards in a Pantheon . . . all these kids were car crazy . . .

Too quickly he found anticipation diffused by uncertainty, remembering how often he had been disappointed by his son's reaction. Somehow, he had never been able to outguess Kip. Almost invariably, the farther he had gone out of his way to please him, the more perversely his son had reacted. But the whole subject of his relationship with his son presented a problem that could not be solved by thinking about it and, characteristically, he put it out of his mind and walked toward the washroom.

He anticipated that Gerhart would be late — as reluctant visitors usually were — and it was a distinct surprise to have a pageboy almost follow him into the washroom, telling him that a Mr. Gerhart was waiting for him. Quickly, he returned to the lobby, hoping that there would be no one else at the front desk to confuse his recognition. There was not. But he need not have worried. Seeing Arthur Gerhart again, the face came back clearly enough so that he would surely have recognized him, yet the matching of memory to the man he saw was a rather startling reminder of how many years it had really been since the last time he had seen him. His hair was gray and he'd put on weight, but he was still the same Art Gerhart, recognizing him instantly and driving toward him like a challenged bull seeking the joy of fierce combat, a great personal salesman who was still proving to the world that there was no door that he could not break down, no man who could stand up against the onslaught of his personality. The heartiness of his greeting would have been more reassuring if Lincoln Lord had not known that it was habitual, the standard act of a self-made man who was afraid to abandon the technique by which he had raised himself in the world from a route salesman for a Buffalo wholesale grocer to one of the most powerful men in the whole food industry.

Back in the late thirties, Arthur Gerhart had recognized that, with national distribution becoming more and more important, there were many food packers who were having difficulty finding the right brokers and controlling them after they were found. Thereupon he had set himself up as super-broker, building up a network of associated smaller brokers, offering food packers much the same facilities that they would have had with their own national sales organizations. He

378

had been enormously successful — he was reputedly a major stockholder in a half dozen of the firms he represented — but now, gripping Lincoln Lord's hand, he was still a peddler hungry for a commission.

This was not at all what Lincoln Lord had expected after Gerhart's reluctant agreement to meet him and, searching for solid ground, he said, "I know this is an imposition, Arthur, asking you to meet me here when you're —"

"What the hell, Linc, wonderful to see you again!" Gerhart exploded. "Where can we talk?"

"I thought we might slip upstairs and —"

"Good!" Gerhart agreed, offering no resistance, again a surprise because he had anticipated that Gerhart might want to stay downstairs where escape would be easier.

The elevator door closed in front of them and the big broker said, "Just occurred to me after you called, Linc — you were in Japan, weren't you? Some sort of trade study — economic relations between us and the Japs?"

"Yes, I was chairman of the Far East Trade Mission," he said, but without the pride that acknowledgment would normally have given him, recognizing Gerhart's strategy as one that he himself had often used. There was no easier way to avoid an unwelcome subject than by substituting another, no better way to stall off a pest than by sidetracking him on something that he would talk about.

"Tell me this, Linc," Gerhart said as the elevator started up. "Did you get into the tuna business at all?"

"Tuna? Oh yes. That's been one of the real sore points, you know — Japanese tuna coming into this country. Yes, we dug into it rather thoroughly."

"Talk to any of the Japanese operators?"

"Oh, of course. I don't recall exactly how many interviews we had but I'm sure we covered every big factor in the business."

"Don't know why I didn't think of you before, Linc. Been looking all over hell for someone who could help square me away. Canned tuna is a big item with us, you know. We're handling one of the top lines. Better than a million cases last year. That's a hell of a lot of volume, and it looks like we're getting into trouble fast over this Japanese import situation. Matter of fact, that's why I'm going out to the Coast tonight, trying to figure out what we're going to do if we lose our source of supply. The damned union is threatening to strike the cannery and close it down tight."

379

"Because of Japanese imports?" Lincoln Lord asked as they stepped off on the second floor, beginning to wonder if his guess had really been right.

Gerhart went on talking and the longer Lincoln Lord listened, the more certain he became that Gerhart's desire for information was sincere, all the more so after he said, "I know this isn't what you want to talk about, Linc, but it's damned important to G & G and I'll be grateful as the devil for anything you can tell me."

Gratitude was not a mean force to have working in his favor and he made a definite effort now to recall the detail of testimony from leaders of the Japanese fisheries industry. It was not a difficult task, one recollection leading to another, and by the time the bar waiter came to serve their drinks, he was talking freely.

Vigorously stirring his highball, Gerhart asked, "Has your committee made its report?"

"Oh yes, several months ago."

"Where can I get a copy of it? Or hasn't it been released?"

He hesitated. "To be perfectly frank, I don't know what's happened to it, Art. There was a terrific push on it for a while — as long as the trade bill was being debated in Congress — but after they voted an extension, the interest died down. Of course, there may be some work going on behind the scenes —"

"I don't want to ask you to violate any confidences, Linc — if I'm out of order here just say so — but does what you've just told me represent the viewpoint you expressed in the report?"

"Yes, I'd say so," he replied after a thoughtful pause.

"What's your own view, Linc? Do you think the union has a case against the Japanese?"

He hesitated, not at all certain that the committee's findings in Japanese fishery products would get a sympathetic hearing from the food broker, yet aware that his future relationships with Arthur Gerhart would be seriously jeopardized if what he told him now did not agree with what he would read if and when the report was made public.

"This isn't my own view particularly," he said cautiously. "Actually, it's the committee consensus. Yes, I'd say the union has a case. But not against the Japanese."

"What do you mean by that?"

"I don't know how typical this company is that's packing tuna for you, but it seems to be fairly common practice for our packers to use

380

Japanese tuna as a club over the head of the American fishing fleet. They use every means at their command to break the price —"

"As a threat against our own fishermen?"

"That's right," he agreed. "I don't say that there's anything basically wrong about it — the fisherman's union is a tough gang, I understand, and I suppose the packers have to fight them in any way they can — but from the union's point of view it's easy enough to see why they're so anti-Japanese. Every time they try to get a raise, the American packers pass the buck to the Japanese, claiming that they can't pay any more because of Japanese competition."

"So the fleet operators and the fishermen's union head for Washington and start screaming for an embargo against Japanese tuna?" Gerhart asked perceptively.

"Well, if not an embargo, at least they want to enforce the anti-dumping law. And that's an absolute phony."

"Tell me this, Linc — damn it, I know you've got something you want to talk about, too, but you're the first man I've found who can see this whole picture objectively."

And that question was followed by another, and then another and another, and it was ten minutes to six when Arthur Gerhart, finally draining his third highball, leaned back in his chair and said, "Linc, I can't tell you how much you've helped me. I've got a real line to follow now. Damned shame the way I've hogged all of your time, and I do have to stop by the apartment on my way to the airport, but what can we do for you? You said over the phone that you wanted some advice?"

"Well, this is pretty small potatoes compared to a million cases of tuna —"

Gerhart laughed him down. "I know damn well that if it's something you're tied up with, Linc, those little potatoes are going to start growing into big potatoes pretty damned fast. What have you got on your mind?"

As rapidly as possible, he sketched in the Coastal Foods situation, compression aided by the food broker's general familiarity with the business. Gerhart had not heard, however, that the break with Gellman Stores had been mended. "You mean that you've gotten the business back again? Well, I'll be damned! I hadn't heard that. The boys that are running my grapevine must be slipping. Have to jack 'em up." A knowing grin spread over his face. "Say, you're sitting with a pat hand, aren't you, boy? That's a smart one — pick up a cannery for a song when it's flat on its back, load it up with business, and you've got yourself a damned salable property. And I might just be able to find a buyer. But you'll have to hang on for six months, won't you — establish it as a capital gain?"

It took a moment for him to realize what Gerhart was thinking, another to decide on the best tack to take. "That isn't quite the way it adds up, Art."

"You don't mean that you're going to go on operating it?"

"Yes, I —"

"Well, I'll be damned!" Gerhart said explosively. "But I won't say you're wrong. I understand it's a hell of a nice little plant."

"It's a nice little company," Lincoln Lord said as a broadening qualification. "And it's going to be a whale of a lot of fun to take hold of it and build it up into something. I started in the food business, you know — a little cannery down in Maryland —"

"With old Adam Quincy, weren't you?"

"That's right. And I've always —"

"You know, you surprise me, Linc."

"How so?"

"I've always thought of you as — well, I don't know how to put it — but damn it, boy, you're doing the smart thing. Get yourself a nice little company and settle down and operate it. You take care of it and it'll take care of you. There's nothing in this big corporation rat race. I see plenty of those boys. And what the hell do they get out of life — a diamond service button and a coronary."

"I know."

"Sure you know. You've been through it. And, Linc, I'll just say that it increases my respect for you a hell of a lot to find out that you're smart enough to — don't misunderstand me, Linc, I've always had plenty of respect for you — if I didn't before I would now — sure appreciate the way you've squared me away on this tuna situation! Where was I? Oh — Coastal Foods. Yessiree, boy, you're just smart as hell, getting your hands on something like that while you're still young enough to get some fun out of life. I envy you, Linc! You're doing what I always wanted to do — get the hell out of New York. But there's one thing you ought to do."

"What's that?"

"You asked for my advice — okay, I'll give it to you in a nutshell." Gerhart leaned forward, tapping out the rhythm of his words on his knee. "Getting back the Gellman business is fine, Linc. Hell of a nice backlog to have. But you never want to have all your eggs in one basket. You lost it once, you could lose it again — right? Now don't get me wrong, Linc. You may think I'm just playing my own game here. But you know me too well for that. Hell's bells, we aren't looking for another line. We've got plenty now. This is for your own good, Linc. What you ought to do is get a brand of your own established. I mean it. You may not think you need it, but I'm telling you, Linc, you ought to have it. This chain store business is fine while you've got it, but sooner or later they start putting the squeeze on you and unless you've got an ace of your own up your sleeve — man, they've got you right by the short hair. And hell's bells, Linc, it would be easy enough to do. You just pick out six or eight good items, get yourself a real snazzy package —" He stopped short. "You're free to do it, aren't you? You weren't damn fool enough to let 'em tie you up so you couldn't bring out your own line?"

"No, we're in the clear now," Lincoln Lord said cautiously, resisting the temptation to say more, frightened that he might lose the advantage of having Gerhart think that the whole idea was his own. "You may be right, Art."

"You damn betcha I'm right. Seen it happen too often."

Guardedly he said, "Well, we could get a line together easily enough. There are some good items —"

"Do it, Linc, do it!"

"The problem would be to get enough distribution to make it worth while. We don't have a sales department —"

"Distribution!" Gerhart burst out. "Hell's bells, Linc, that's what I'm trying to tell you. Just give us a line and we'll get it distributed for you."

"Do you think you could —?"

"With our setup?" Gerhart laughed. "You've been away from the food business too long, boy. You don't realize what we've built up. Let me just give you a quick idea. First, we've got our own direct branches — nine of 'em. That covers all the big metropolitan markets — New York, Boston, Philadelphia, Pittsburgh, you know what I mean. On top of that, we've got twenty-seven sub brokers that are tied up with us so tight that all we've got to do is give 'em the word. We'll get you distribution, don't worry about that. Oh, I don't say we're going to sell you a million cases the first year. It takes time to get a brand established — you know that — but if you just get it started and let it grow —"

"Yes, that would be the thing to do."

"Good god!" Gerhart had looked at his watch and bounded to his feet. "Linc, I've got to get going or I'll miss that damned plane. Look, why don't I do this — you going to be in your office tomorrow?"

"Yes, I —"

"I'll have Johnny Keating down there to give you a hand lining this thing up. Now don't worry about it, there's no obligation. I mean it, Linc. This is what we've got Johnny doing all the time — helping our accounts develop new items, working out promotion ideas, all that kind of stuff."

"Art, I —"

"Now, don't try to thank me, Linc. I'm the one who ought to be thanking you. And I do, Linc, I sure as hell do. This steer you gave me on the tuna situation — yessiree, you really squared me away. Good to see you, Linc. And I'll have Johnny down there tomorrow. Call him from the airport."

There was the crushing grip of his handshake and then he plunged toward the elevator. Lincoln Lord made no attempt to follow him . . . let well enough alone . . . but what a terrific break, Gerhart thinking it was his own idea! His luck was really riding with him today . . . but of course it wasn't all luck either . . . that Japanese business . . . no, it really hadn't been luck at all . . . just keeping on the ball, pushing ahead . . . yes, that's what a man had to do . . .

Suddenly he remembered Maggie and Kip and, not waiting for the elevator to come back, he walked rapidly toward the staircase. There was a telephone booth on the landing and he hesitated for a moment, debating the possibility of calling Goodhaven and giving Joel the news . . . get him started on revising his presentation . . . a million things that had to be done . . . pick a brand name . . . label designs . . . price lists . . . if he only had Brick! And he *was* coming down to Goodhaven . . . but not until Friday . . .

No, the devil with Brick! He didn't need him . . . Joel was a good boy, better in a lot of ways than Brick had ever been . . . and, anyway, Brick had had his chance. He'd called him that day in New York, left his name and Brick had never called him back . . . cocky now that he was getting by on his own. Yes, there'd always been a little streak of that in Brick . . .

But maybe he was wrong . . . messages did get lost . . . Brick might have been out of town. Anyway, there were no hard feelings as far as he was concerned. Brick would call up to thank him when he came down to Goodhaven on Friday ... of course he would ... no matter how successful he was, a ten-thousand-dollar fee wasn't something that you picked up every day in the week ...

Rapidly, he walked down the last few steps, his mind lightened, an anticipatory smile breaking as he imagined Maggie's gleeful surprise when he told her that G & G was going to distribute the new line ... she'd know for sure now that he hadn't made a mistake when he'd come to Coastal Foods!

And then he thought of Kip and his mind clouded ... but bringing him to Goodhaven would work out, too ... everything did if you just kept pushing ahead ...

VII

"GOOD NIGHT, JOEL," Lincoln Lord had said, only that, not another word, and then he had walked out of the front door.

One by one, slowly and deliberately, Joel Morris snapped the four switches and, gulp by gulp, the Friday dusk swallowed up the office. Groping his way through the gloom, stumbling over a wastebasket, he found his way back to his desk and picked up his briefcase. Suddenly there was an explosion of light, the whole office seen as if revealed by a lightning flash. A double fireball swept across the windows that faced the parking lot. Again there was darkness, even more impenetrable now, broken only by the disappearing red taillights of Mr. Lord's black Pantheon.

Something had happened today. Somehow, somewhere, he had done something to alienate Mr. Lord. He had no idea what it was, the mystery all the greater because everything had started off so wonderfully this morning when Mr. Gerhart had called Mr. Lord and told him that G & G was definitely taking on the new line. And then Mr. Lord had said, "Joel, you can really be proud of what you've done. Art Gerhart says it was the most impressive market study he's ever seen."

The first hint that something was wrong had come after lunch when he had gone in to tell Mr. Lord that the trademark agency couldn't clear either of the two names that they had picked for the new line . . . but that couldn't be it . . . Mr. Lord had said from the beginning that they were sure to have difficulty finding a name that hadn't already been registered . . . and *"Goodhaven"* wasn't too bad a brand name. But something was wrong . . . maybe Mr. Lord was remembering Monday, the way Swann had tripped him up . . . no . . .

Wearily, Joel groped his way toward the front door, giving up as hopeless another review of everything he had said and done in an attempt to discover why Mr. Lord had so mysteriously turned against him. And it had gotten worse and worse as the afternoon had worn on, the chill more pronounced, the distance constantly growing greater between his desk and the door of Mr. Lord's office. Twice he had tried to talk to him about hiring two promotion men . . . yesterday he'd been pushing for fast action, this morning he hadn't even seemed to be listening . . .

He saw the lighted clock in the entrance lobby now, an unneeded reminder that he'd promised Vicky that he wouldn't be late tonight . . . Anne's birthday party . . . but he must be mistaken about what he'd thought Mr. Lord had said yesterday about this Brick Mitchell who was coming down today to gather background material for an article on Haven Home . . . that note on his engagement calendar . . . *Brick & Dr. Thompson* opposite 5:00 on the Friday page . . . no, Mr. Lord hadn't actually said it . . . he'd just guessed that the Lords would be having them over for cocktails at five . . .

As an act of impulsive contrition, he picked up the telephone on the reception desk, dialed the number of his home, and when Vicky answered he said quickly, "I'm sorry, dear — got tied up and couldn't call you before. I'm leaving right now."

"Oh, I was afraid that something had gone wrong," Vicky said, her tone still half-questioning, as if it were impossible to so quickly throw off her concern.

"No, everything's all right," he said firmly.

"You don't have to go back tonight, do you?"

"No, not tonight."

2

Lincoln Lord had been in the shower so long that the sting had gone out of the spray, his body insensitized by exposure to the blast of water made hotter and hotter, the door so steam-fogged now that he could see only the faintest shadow of Maggie's figure as she rapped on the glass. "Don't you think you've had about enough of that, Linc?"

He mumbled watery agreement, throwing back his head to let the shower beat on his upturned face, a last effort to achieve that misty state of euphoria where his nerves would finally start unwinding . . . he

387

needed a let-down, needed it badly ... been off his pace all day ... too tense, not able to concentrate the way he should ... too many times when his mind had wandered. Tired, that's all. Thank goodness, he'd been able to stall off Joel ... another night session would have been too much. And there'd be no point in it, anyway ... everything was moving along faster than he had any right to expect. Joel was really doing a fine job ...

"Linc?"

"All right," he said, spinning the control handle, abruptly cutting off the water, giving up, aware that he was accomplishing nothing by way of dissipating the strange feeling of apprehension that had hung over him all day.

Maggie cracked the door and handed in a giant towel. "I was beginning to get worried about you."

"Worried about me? Why?"

"I just wanted to be sure that you were all right."

"This was what I needed" ... so Maggie had noticed it ... "Feel fine now."

She opened the door more widely, holding up a woolly robe, and his spirits lifted as they always did when he found himself the focal point of her undivided attention.

She moved toward the door to the bedroom. "Why don't you stretch out for a few minutes?"

"A drink would do me more good," he said, surprising himself.

"You can have that, too. Scotch?"

"Oh, don't bother," he said as she started for the door. "I'll get dressed and be out in a minute."

"Let's have it here," she said, and the flick of her eyes made him notice that, while he had been in the shower, two chairs had been drawn up before the bedroom hearth. The red glow of the burned-down charcoal in the Japanese *hibachi* was evidence that this was not something as casually unplanned as she was trying to make it seem. He felt the pin-prick of suspicion, unidentified but somehow related to the shadowy apprehension of the day.

"What about dinner?" he asked, picking up his watch from the dressing table, seeing that it was almost seven.

"There's no hurry." She had the hall door open now. "Viola's not going out and she said that it didn't make any difference what time we ate. And Kip's not going to be here."

"Not going to be here? Where — ?"

388

"I don't know. I didn't talk to him. I was in the shower and he left a message with Viola that we weren't to wait for him. He was here after school, polishing his car, so maybe he has a date. Oh, Linc, he's so proud of that car — you were so right to get it for him."

"I hope so," he said uneasily.

"You were," she said positively. "And please don't worry about his not coming home to dinner. After all, he's seventeen. And he drives beautifully. He took me into town this noon. I imagine he's with some of the boys from school."

She closed the door and he picked up the thought of his son and weighed it as a possible clue, wondering if what had been bothering him today might have been the sub-surface realization that this was his first week end with Kip, the first time in so many months when they would be alone together for more than the few minutes of parting and greeting, subjecting him again to the odd discomfiture that he had so often felt in his son's presence.

But that was a thought out of orbit, unnatural, and he quickly abandoned it for the more tangible memory of what had happened on Tuesday, disconcerting proof of the ineptness that had always seemed to curse his attempts to get close to his son. The idea of buying Kip a car had occurred to him on Monday night, driving home from New York after they had left the Greenbank Club. Kip had been withdrawn and remote during dinner, talking very little, and what few remarks he initiated had all been directed at his mother. When they had started home, however, the Pantheon had broken the ice and there had been a few minutes of automobile talk, Kip actually asking him questions, talking then about the cars that some of the boys had at Forgehill, obliquely suggesting that his heart's desire was centered in the possession of "some kind of an old wreck that a fellow could fix up the way he wanted it." He had decided then to buy it for him and the next morning had slipped away from the office and driven out to the used car lot of Lou Sessions who, as a vice-president of the Chamber of Commerce, had sat with him at the head table the day before. He had been almost ready to buy a '52 Ford convertible when Sessions had said, "Mr. Lord, maybe I'm being a darn fool, sticking my nose in where it isn't wanted, but I got a couple of hot-rod brats of my own and — well, I'm nobody to tell a man like you what to do, but I'm just wondering if maybe it wouldn't be a good idea to let this boy of yours pick out his own car?"

Lou Sessions had been only too right, of course, and he had been all the more grateful to him after he felt the warmth of Kip's "Holy creeps, you mean I can go buy it myself?" But neither his son's appreciation, nor Maggie's approving gratitude, had erased the consciousness of how close he had come to making a stupid error. Again, as had happened so many times before, he had been frightened by the realization that his instinctive reactions, usually so trustworthy with everyone else, were so unreliable in his relationships with his son.

Lincoln Lord was not, however, a man who dwelled long on past mistakes and, conscious as he was of the warning that the car incident had given him, his thoughts quickly slipped past the word-bounded area of tangibility and into the cloudy region beyond. If he had been inclined to do so, he would have been easily capable of remembering how Kip's birth had changed his life — he could, upon demand, recall almost anything that had ever impressed him — but his talent for total recollection was, perhaps fortunately, coupled with the ability to put out of his conscious mind all of the memories that, otherwise, would have constituted a self-destroying burden. Thus, much of what he felt about his son was on the dark side of the threshold of realization.

Kip had been born while Lincoln Lord was in the Navy — Maggie had discovered her pregnancy the month after he had been commissioned — and although he had managed a few extra leaves because of his closeness to high command, he had seen his son only at long intervals. Each time he had come home, the change in his son had been so great that, again and again, it had seemed as if he were being forced to accommodate himself to another strange intruder in his life. Somehow, an association had developed between Kip's presence and the changes that, step by step, had come over Maggie during the years that he had been away in the Navy. Before, their love had been something unshared and its very exclusivity had been part of its magic. He never knew quite what had happened, never consciously resenting that he was no longer the focal point of Maggie's total interest, even less aware of the effect upon himself of a sharing of love. As far as he had ever gone was to blame the war for having lost him his chance to get as close to his son as Maggie had been able to do during the years when he had been away. That was what his lieutenant-commander's stripes had cost him.

Afterwards, so busy during Kip's early childhood, so desperately anxious to clinch the almost unbelievably good opportunities that had opened up before him, first at Rabson Foods and then at Union Packing, he had never had time enough to regain what he had lost. Marriage, like his job, had demanded a delegation of authority and, inevitably, raising Kip had been one of those things that had fallen to Maggie's lot.

In somewhat the same way, although by no means to the same extent, Brick Mitchell had taken over doing some of the things for Kip that Lincoln Lord would have liked to have been able to do himself if he had been less busy — and, too, if he'd had Brick's aptitude for catching the interest of the kind of boy that Kip had turned out to be. Brick had been raised in the West, living an outdoor life, and there were endless things that he could do, and stories that he could tell, that had fascinated Kip. Lincoln Lord had always felt himself handicapped because his own boyhood had been so contrastingly lived. He had never camped out in the wilds, never caught a trout in a mountain stream, never stalked an elk, never known a real redskin Indian. Nor had he ever ground the valves on a Model T motor nor built anything with a hammer and saw. His life had been that of a minister's son, his boyhood world a succession of parsonages, and most of what he had been taught had been concerned with the ever-demanding need to make new friends in a new congregation. Thus, again as a delegation of authority — although not always wittingly made — he had let Brick do, at home as he had at the office, some of the things that he could not do so well himself.

There had been times when Lincoln Lord had felt something like jealousy over the attachment that his son had shown for Brick Mitchell — on a few occasions it had struck him sharply enough to be deeply painful — and as Kip had grown older it had more and more seemed that his expressed feelings toward Brick were, as was true of so many of the other things he did, a manifestation of his strangely perverse personality, a reason to excuse his almost sullen resistance to any attempt to draw close to him. Kip's insistence upon calling him "Uncle Brick" had often carried the feeling that he was doing so as a taunt.

None of this was recognizably present in Lincoln Lord's mind as he sat now close to the hearth, seeking warmth to offset the loss of the heat that his body had drawn from the scalding shower; yet he was still faintly suspicious that there might be something behind all this attention that Maggie was giving him tonight. For no apparent reason, the thought flashed that it might be somehow connected with the fact that Brick was in Goodhaven today ... maybe Brick had called her ...

For an instant, almost as if he had caught sight of something recognizable through the fog of apprehension in which he had been trapped since morning, he wondered if what had been bothering him had been Brick's failure to call. But it was inconceivable that so small and unimportant an expectation could have disturbed him so greatly. Then, suddenly, it occurred to him that Maggie, neither last night nor this morning, had said a word about this being the day that Brick was coming to see Kira Zurich, an omission that now seemed oddly significant. Could it be that . . . ?

Quickly he put this suspicion in the same class as the one that had leaped into his mind when he had learned that Maggie had gone to Brick the minute she had arrived in New York, feeling again the embarrassment of injustice . . . her train had been late . . . it had meant no more than that . . . nothing. No, Maggie wasn't worrying any more about that silly idea that he couldn't get along without Brick . . .

Maggie came in the door, shouldering it open, both hands needed to carry the big tray. He started to help her but she said quickly, "Don't get up. I'm all right. And you're tired." She put the tray down in front of him on the low black lacquer table, displaying a plate of canapés much too elaborate to have been made and arranged in the very few minutes that she'd been gone . . . yes, she had something on her mind. Or was this one of those times when, knowing that he'd been hurt, she was trying to distract him by being especially attentive . . . Brick must have called her . . . yes, and said something that she didn't want to tell him. He'd probably turned down Kira . . .

"Long or short?" she asked.

"Here, let me do it," he said quickly, taking the whiskey bottle from her hand, gaining command of the situation.

"You do feel better, don't you?"

"Where'd you get the idea that I feel bad?" he asked, thumping ice into their glasses.

"Oh, I don't know — you just looked so low."

"You're seeing things," he laughed. "I'm not in the least low."

"I don't mean now. I meant when you first got home."

"Just a little tired, that's all. Been a long week."

"Too long," she said, taking the drink that he handed her. "You shouldn't work so late, Linc."

"Well?" he raised his glass.

"To love and life," she responded, smiling dutifully, and he wondered if she was remembering that this routine observance of a set

392

ceremony dated back to Brighton and the Quincy Canning Company ... Brick's toast at their wedding supper ...

"To us and ours," he corrected, surprising her with a departure from formula, pleased when she echoed his words with a grateful little laugh, yet concerned when he saw her take her first gulping drink, a sure sign that she was tensely concerned about something. "No, I'm not low," he said reassuringly. "Everything's going fine. Art Gerhart called up today. They're taking the line. He was tremendously impressed with the dope Joel had worked up."

"Oh, I'm glad," she said, but she seemed to have missed the point.

He made it more obvious. "I used to think Brick was clever — and he was in his own way, of course — but Joel's got what it really takes on a job like this." He sipped his drink, watching her, and when he saw that there was to be no response beyond her nod, he said as casually as he could manage, "Isn't this the day that Brick was supposed to come down here to see Kira?"

"Yes — yes, I think so," she said, a surprisingly clumsy pretense of uncertainty.

"He didn't call you, did he?"

"Call me?" It took her a moment to select a canapé. "No. Why would you imagine that he would?"

"I wasn't imagining it. I just thought — well, you did go to some trouble to toss the job his way. He might have called up to thank you."

"He doesn't owe me any thanks," she said flatly, reminding him of how strangely reluctant she had been to discuss just what she had told Brick. "Is this going to mean a lot of extra work for you, Linc — G & G taking on the line?" Then, suddenly apologetic, she said, "I'm sorry, dear. I didn't mean to start talking business."

"Why shouldn't you?"

"Because I've made all kinds of resolutions that I wouldn't." She smiled nervously. "That's my job — to help you forget it for a little while."

"Well, if you're interested in what we're doing — ?"

"Oh, Linc, you know I'm interested. But don't talk about it now when you're so tired."

He laughed at her over the top of his glass. "You get a lot of crazy ideas about me, don't you?"

"You *are* tired," she insisted.

"Sure," he admitted. "But not the way you mean. You think I'm jumpy, don't you? Well, I'm not. Everything's going beautifully. I mean that. It is."

"Everything?"

"Everything!" He ate another canapé. "Of course there'll be problems — plenty of them, I suppose, before we really get going. G & G will do as good a job as any broker could, but their men are handling a lot of different lines and we can't expect them to do the kind of specialty promotion that we've got to have if we're really going to get anywhere. We'll have to hire a couple of men of our own."

"But isn't that going to —" She broke off, quickly apologetic. "I'm sorry, dear."

"What were you going to say?"

"Nothing. I just — well, I was just being silly."

He repeated his demand.

"Oh, Linc, please. It wasn't anything, really it wasn't. I was just hoping that you wouldn't have to — well, you did say that you weren't going to have to worry too much about this new line, that you were just going to put it out and let it build itself up. And you do have the Gellman business, Linc. It isn't as if you had to —"

"But if we're going to do it at all, Mag, we've got to do it right."

He sensed that she was not agreeing with him, a feeling confirmed now when she changed the subject by asking, "What have you decided to do about the second floor?"

"Well, I don't know what to do," he said, not quite honestly, conveniently forgetting that he'd already made his decision. "Alf got the bids this morning."

"High?"

"Right through the roof. They were really a jolt. Even the low bid was twenty-one thousand over what I'd figured for a top."

"But you'll have to do it, Linc. You just can't go on in that awful little cubbyhole. And if you're going to be hiring more people —"

"It isn't just the first cost. We'll have to furnish it, too. Golly, when you see what's happened to office furniture prices! I was just looking at some catalogues this morning. Remember that desk that I had at Luxor, the one you found at Sloane's? Of course, I'm not thinking of anything as fancy as that —"

"Why not?" Her smile was oddly challenging. "If you figure the cost over all the years that you'll be using it — well, it isn't as if it was something temporary."

394

Suddenly it became clear, and he laughed at himself for having let his imagination run away with him ... all that was bothering Maggie was the same old worry that Coastal Foods wasn't going to work out. "Maybe you're right, Mag. Maybe that is the way to figure it."

"What are you laughing at?" she asked anxiously.

"You."

"Just because I want you to have a decent office?"

He reached out for her hand. "You're a funny gal."

"Am I?"

"Coming down here hasn't turned out as badly as you were afraid it was going to, has it?"

She was out of her chair in an instant, kissing him, suddenly, impetuously, almost fiercely. "I never thought that, Linc. Never! You do believe that, don't you?"

"Kiss me like that again and I'll believe anything."

"Even that I love you?"

"Might be worth trying," he said suggestively.

She twisted away from his exploring hand, loosing a little burst of oddly giddy laughter and, involuntarily, he glanced at her glass, seeing that it was drained. She saw him and boldly thrust the empty glass toward him, a brazen act that he found an erotic stimulant to which he immediately felt himself react. It was a long time since she had asked for a second drink, even longer since she had done it without warning him to make it a light one.

He gulped the last of his own drink and then poured two more. Maggie was still sitting on the arm of his chair and when he leaned back he found the circle of her arm waiting for his shoulders. She took the drink with her free hand and clinked his glass asking, "What this time?"

"Maybe we ought to drink to the Coastal Foods Company," he suggested.

"To the *president* of the Coastal Foods Company," she corrected.

He protested, "But I can't drink to that."

"I can," she laughed — and did. But it was only a token sip. And then she put the glass down. "I really don't need this."

"Won't hurt you."

"I just don't want anything to change. I'm too happy the way I am. Oh, darling, it is wonderful, isn't it? Everything's working out so well — the company, this house, having Kip here —"

395

"You sound as if maybe you like it," he teased her.

"Like it? I love it!" Her voice suddenly sobered. "You do too, don't you, darling?"

"Sure. Why not?"

"I mean it, Linc — you do, don't you?" She held his head, forcing him to look into her eyes. "You don't regret coming here, do you?"

Seriously he said, "I think it's the best move we ever made."

"Oh, Linc, so do I."

Her lips met his with a little rush, hard-pressed and clinging. Almost instantly, he felt the quick rise of passion, not as the sense-blinding thing that it had once been but now as something infinitely more satisfying. As a younger man, sexual desire had been a physical need that had built up entirely within himself, like water behind a dam, the pressure rising and rising until there was an explosive outburst that could only be linked with love through a basely elemental rationalization. Those days were past and there had been, over the last few years, a certain disquietude as he had come to realize that the cyclical build-up of desire was less and less reliably automatic. However, what had been lost had been substantially offset — most recognizably since they had come to Goodhaven — by the feeling that passion was no longer something generated within himself, a personal need to be satisfied, but rather that it was something transmitted, originating not within himself but with Maggie, and her capacity for stimulus had become proof, no less important than the reliability of his quick response, that what there was between them now had been refined to the pure essence of love.

Suddenly he felt the tensing of the softness under his hands, an alarming resistance that made him whisper, "What's the matter?"

"That must be Kip," she said and, listening now as he had not done before, he heard the sound of a motor raced and then cut off. Hurriedly, Maggie murmured, "It doesn't matter," kissing him again. But the moment had been lost, the spell broken, and knowing that it could not be recaptured, he said, "Time I got dressed anyway." And then he saw her questioning discomfiture and added as a kindness, "Maybe you'd better see if he's come home for something."

She kissed him fiercely, "I love you, Linc. More than anything in all the world. You know that, don't you?"

"And I love you," he said, realizing that his tone made it sound too much as if he were forgiving her for leaving him, yet vaguely aware after she had gone that there was a deceptive contrast between her

396

momentary reluctance to leave and the quickened sound of retreating footsteps after she had closed the door behind her. He stood, feeling for a moment the emptiness of drained desire, the loneliness of desertion. Then he dressed much more quickly than was normal, grabbing a pair of flannel slacks and the first sport shirt that his hand touched.

Maggie and Kip were in the living room when he came out, both standing, his son facing him, stiffening to attention as their eyes met. Without turning, Maggie said over her shoulder, "Kip's been over at Haven Home."

"Oh," he said, clamping down on the reaction of shock, rigid until it was dissipated, then waiting for Maggie's lead to give him some indication of what had already been said.

Kip shrugged defensively. "If you didn't want me to go — holy creeps, I didn't know it was something I wasn't supposed to do. I was just driving past and I saw the sign and — well, you said this morning that Uncle Brick would probably be so busy that he wouldn't have time to get over here and so — holy creeps, I didn't think there'd be any harm in just stopping in and saying hello to him."

Lincoln Lord's mind leaped over this evidence that Maggie had discussed Brick with their son earlier in the day, shattering her pretense that she was barely aware of his presence in Goodhaven. His concern was centered now on the old problem of trying to support her, right or wrong, in whatever stand she had taken with Kip. But she remained silent, giving him no indication, and he said the only thing that seemed safe. "You probably shouldn't have bothered him, Kip. If he was too busy to come over to see us, he was too busy to be interrupted."

"But he was glad to see me," Kip protested. "He said so. And, anyway I didn't waste much of his time. I just talked to him for a little while and then he had to talk to Dr. Perrill again, so Mrs. Zurich wanted to know if I didn't want to see the research laboratory. Gosh, it's sure a keen place. You know this laboratory we went to see up at Forgehill? That just wasn't in it with Haven Home. But I guess you've seen it, haven't you?"

Kip's eyes went to Maggie, and quickly Lincoln Lord stepped in to say, "Yes, we were over last week. It's a fine laboratory — excellent."

"And Mrs. Zurich — gosh, isn't she swell! You know what I mean — just nice. And she said —" His rare enthusiasm was suddenly lost in an expression of apprehensive questioning. "Maybe you won't want me to do it. I guess maybe you won't. But, anyway, she said that they'd like to have me over there."

Maggie shot back an anxious glance and Lincoln Lord said, "Yes, Mrs. Zurich is a very nice person. And I'm sure you'd find it interesting to visit Haven Home now and then. But, of course, those people do have their work to do."

"I wouldn't be bothering anybody else," Kip argued. "I'd have my own work to do."

"Your own work?"

"Sure," Kip said impatiently. "Holy creeps, there's all kinds of things that I'd have to do. You know, like washing up glassware and taking care of the place where they've got all the guinea pigs and white rats and stuff. There's just this one old guy doing it — Amos — and if I could just help him two hours every night after school — holy creeps, that's twelve-fifty a week right there. And then if I worked eight hours on Saturdays, that would be ten more dollars. That what she said they'd pay me — a dollar and a quarter an hour."

"Do you mean that Mrs. Zurich offered you a job?" Lincoln Lord asked.

"Sure — only she said I'd have to have your permission." Kip's eyes narrowed, unblinking. "I guess you wouldn't want me to do it, huh?"

"Oh, Linc —" Maggie was looking at him now, appealing.

"Did you ask her for a job, Kip?"

Kip looked down, scuffing the rug with his shoe. "All I said was — I guess I did say it would be something I'd like. But I didn't really ask her. We were just talking about different stuff when she was showing me around —"

"Mrs. Zurich showed you around? Herself?"

"Sure. And then afterwards when we were having dinner — no, I guess it was when I was getting ready to take Uncle Brick and Dr. Thompson to the railroad station — well, Mrs. Zurich was thanking me for doing it and that's when she said I could have a job if I wanted it."

"You took them to the station?" Lincoln Lord asked, caught off guard.

"Sure. Uncle Brick thinks I did okay on my car. Only he says I've got a valve sticking. But he's going to show me how to fix it when he comes back next week. If I'm over there anyway — well, what I was figuring — Mrs. Zurich said I could start Monday if I wanted to."

The question hung over them, demanding decision, and after an unrewarded glance at his wife, Lincoln Lord said, "Well, Kip, I don't think this is something you'd want to jump into without giving it some thought."

398

"You mean I can't?"

"No, I don't mean that at all. But if you do take a job at Haven Home they'd have to be able to count on your being there."

"Sure."

"And there'll be a lot of evenings after school when you'll have other things that you'll want to do. You may not think so now but you will after you get better acquainted."

Maggie finally spoke up. "And, Kip, there'll be things you'll want to do on Saturdays, too, especially after the weather gets better."

"She knows about things like that," Kip protested. "And she said it wouldn't matter. She said I could just let Amos know I wasn't coming and then I wouldn't have to. Gosh, she's sure swell, isn't she? I mean — well, holy creeps —"

"All right," Lincoln Lord broke in. "I'll make a deal with you."

Kip's set face was humorlessly expectant.

"Here's the deal — if your mother agrees —"

"Whatever you think, Linc," Maggie whispered.

"We'll give you our permission on one condition."

Kip waited.

He allowed a smile to break. "You'll have to agree not to say *holy creeps* oftener than once in every ten words."

A flush of deep embarrassment seemed to rise out of the squirming of Kip's shoulders. "Yeah, I know — okay." He started away and wheeled back. "Thanks. What I mean is —"

"Well, holy creeps, what else could I do?" Lincoln Lord asked, and the sound of his son's quick little laugh was the sound of his own suddenly found happiness.

Maggie came to his side as Kip ran out of the room. "Do you remember what I was telling you when we were interrupted — that I love you?"

"Still?"

"More than ever. You were wonderful with him, Linc, just wonderful."

She was in his arms when he heard Viola's throat-clearing snicker. "I begs your pardon —"

"It's all right, Viola," he laughed, and Maggie whispered, "There's a conspiracy against us tonight, dear."

"Dinner's ready whenever you folks is," Viola said.

They followed her into the dining room, his arm still around Maggie. They separated then, silent until Viola served the consommé, still silent until he said, "Well, from what Kip said about Brick coming back next week, it sounds as if he must have taken the job."

Watching her face, he saw the tension break and, strangely, her quick smile was almost as gratifying as Kip's laugh had been.

3

On the train that was taking them back to New York, Brick Mitchell sat alone in a double coach seat, mining his pockets, digging deeper and deeper, finding more and more of the crumpled slips of paper on which, during this amazing day, he had scrawled notes to remind him of all that he had seen and heard at Haven Home. Across the aisle, alone in another double seat, Tommy seemed too absorbed to be distracted, studying a laboratory report that Dr. Perrill had given her, one of the toppled stack that all but filled the facing seat.

The day had been an astounding one, all the more so because he had approached it with no expectation beyond the thin hope that he might, if he was lucky, find the subject matter for a salable magazine article. That prospect had, however, been a secondary one. He would not have made the trip if a refusal to do so had not been made impossible by what had happened on Monday, when Tommy had slapped him into the realization that, stupid and senseless and unrealized though it was, it might nevertheless be true that he had been half in love with Maggie Lord. He had been forced to prove to Tommy that whatever it had been, love or not, had been completely destroyed when she had dragged it out from the dark of his mind and exposed it to the harsh light of realization. And he was certain now that it had been destroyed. On the way to the train, he had asked Kip Lord about his mother and there had not been, neither in the asking of the question nor in listening to Kip's answer, the slightest recurrence of that strange tension that had always charged his mind when he had thought of Maggie Lord. If he had been unaware of its nature before, there was no lack of awareness now — freedom was more telling than subjection — and he felt himself a man who had been freed of a crippling obsession.

Gratitude welled up within him and he looked across the aisle, wishing that there was some way that he could express his appreciation to Tommy for what she had done for him. But he could think of no way to open the subject. Tommy had not mentioned the Lords, either Linc or Maggie, since she had walked out of his office on Monday morning ... but he'd find some way to thank her tonight ... after they got back to the apartment ...

His plan foundered immediately, challenged by the strangeness of Tommy's behavior over the past several days. Until Monday night, there had been no restraint between them, never a barrier to even the ultimate intimacy, yet now that it would have a meaning that it could never have had before, she would probably close the door in his face as she had done every night this week ... what the devil was the matter with her, anyway? She knew he loved her ... hadn't he told her that on Monday? And he would have told her again if she had ever given him the chance ... "Brick, let's wait" ... damn it, what was there to wait for! It didn't make sense. Yes, he'd been a fool not to have married her when it would have been easy ... she'd practically asked him last Saturday night up in Connecticut ... *damn it, why couldn't she believe that there had never been anything between him and Maggie Lord!* And even if there had been ...

His mind instantly rejected the counter-accusation that there had been other men in Tommy's life, too, blanking out everything except the hope that he might, by example, generate the same feeling in her mind that now dominated his own, the positive conviction that this could be the beginning of a new life for both of them. But if she wouldn't give him a chance ...

Impulsively, he reached across the aisle, sliding the palm of his hand over the page that she was reading. "Take it easy," he said. "You can't soak it all up in one day."

She gave him the encouragement of taking off her glasses, whipping back her brass-glinted hair with a toss of her hand. "This is terrific stuff, Brick."

"So are you," he said, a clumsy grasping at a phrase. "Look, Tommy, I've got to tell you how great you were today. You did a wonderful job down there."

"The job's just beginning," she said crisply, not clearing the seat beside her.

"I mean it, Tommy. You *were* wonderful." He bunched the reports she had put down and tossed them on the facing seat, sitting down next to her.

Her glasses went on again and she picked up the report she had been reading. "You ought to dig into this, Brick. It's heavy going but it comes closer than anything else to explaining what those enzymes are doing — what's happening to those protein molecules."

"I'm more interested in trying to find out what's going on inside that head of yours."

She evaded his reaching hand. "The only trouble is that these reactions are so terribly complicated. I don't know how you're going to simplify them enough to make people understand."

"Let's forget enzymes for a minute and talk about us." She refused to look at him. "Tommy, what's the matter?" He pulled the report from her hand and tossed it across to the facing seat. "Ever since Monday —"

"Don't," she said, choked.

"You've changed your mind?" he asked. "Is that it?"

"No, I — yes, I've changed my mind."

"About what — us?" he demanded, waiting until she answered with a silent nod. "You're a damned poor liar, Dr. Thompson."

"No, Brick — please. Let's just — we've got a big job to do, let's just do it and forget everything else."

The coach swayed, screeching a protest as the train rounded a curve. He waited until the sound had settled back to the heartbeat click of the rails. "Would it make any difference if I asked you to marry me?"

Her hands went up to her face, muffling her denial. "No, Brick, no — please don't."

"Okay, if that's the way you want it — all right, that's the way it is."

"Oh, Brick, it isn't the way I want it! Can't you see — oh, god, why did I have to be such a fool — such a *bitch!* If I hadn't done it —"

"Done what?"

"Monday."

"What about Monday?"

"Oh, Brick, I was so unfair — all those things I said about you. I don't know what got into me. It was just that — when I saw her and she was so smart and clever and I — I suppose I was just hunting for some way to excuse myself for not being able to make you love me —"

"But, Tommy, for god's sake, I told you —"

"You didn't mean it. You couldn't have meant it."

"I did mean it. I do mean it."

"No, Brick, no. You only said it because I'd hurt you —"

"Does that make sense?" he demanded. "If that were true, would I be asking you to marry me?"

"There has to be some reason."

"You can't believe that it might be because I'm in love with you?"

"How could you be? I'm such a fool."

He grinned. "Thank god you are. If you weren't, I'd be out of luck.

402

No one but a fool could ever be in love with me — and damn it, Tommy, you are, you know you are. Aren't you?"

"I must be," she said, and this time it was her hand that reached out for his. "If I weren't, I wouldn't be so desperately afraid of losing you. But maybe that isn't love, maybe it's just fear."

"Of what?"

"Of how terribly empty my life would be again if it weren't for you. You don't know how much it's meant to me, Brick — just having someone to work for, someone to help, someone who — until you came back I was so lonely that there were times when I —"

He felt the shudder of her body through the tight grip of her hand. "You don't have to tell me anything about loneliness. I know."

She shook her head. "It's not the same, Brick. No man can ever know a woman's kind of loneliness. A man can do something about it, a woman can't — not if you've made the kind of a mess of your life that I have. When I think of what a fool I've been, what a crazy sense of values I had, all that I threw away —" She finished with a bitter laugh. "I wrote a piece once, a very clever piece, all about how women victimized themselves by believing all the nonsense that male psychologists wrote about them — the urge for security, the dependency complex, the need to be needed. Oh, it was a wonderful piece. Very convincing. I even convinced myself. Arise, you females of the world! Throw off your inhibitions!"

"There are a million women who'd trade places with you any day in the week — Dr. Frances P. Thompson, columnist, writer, *Who's Who of American Women* — page 1273."

She looked at him with astonishment. "How did you know that?"

"Kira mentioned it," he said.

"Yes, I suppose she would." She looked away from him, out into the speed-blurred night. "She's there, too, you know."

"No, I didn't know." He waited for her to turn back to him but she kept on staring out of the window. "You did a beautiful job of handling her today."

"We're two of a kind."

"I don't buy that."

"No, you're right. We aren't. She's honest — I'm a phony. A career really means something to her. Haven Home is the most important thing in the world. To me — I'm just a tomboy who got old without ever growing up. At fifteen, it's cute. But when you're a beat-up forty-two with bags under your eyes —"

"Cut it," he demanded, smiling. "You're slandering the woman I love."

She finally faced him again. "If this were twenty years ago —"

"It couldn't have happened then. We weren't the same people. That was a couple of other guys."

"Oh, Brick, I don't know."

"Look, Tommy, are you worrying because — damn it, love isn't just something that happens to kids. Sure, it's wonderful then, like hitting the jackpot on a pinball machine, lights flashing and the bells ringing. But that isn't the payoff, Tommy. That's just the signal — so a couple of dumb kids that don't know any better will realize that it's happened. We're not kids any more. We don't need any signals. We know it's happened."

"How?"

"Because we need each other."

"Is that enough?"

"Isn't that what love is — knowing that there's some one person that you need more than anything in the world. That's it, Tommy — that's what it's all about."

"But it seems so selfish, so one-sided. I need you — oh, god, I do need you, Brick."

"Don't you think I need you?"

"That's what I've been trying to make myself believe — today — every day, every night. You're wrong about love, Brick. It isn't just needing someone. It isn't just taking. There has to be giving, too. And there's so little I can give. Oh, Brick, I want to do things for you, I want to help you, I want to be a part of you —"

"You do — you are."

"Today —"

"I'd have been lost without you. And I'd be lost now if it weren't for you. Look Tommy, if I didn't have you, I'd turn this thing down right now. It's too big for me. I'd be a mile over my head the minute I started to wade in."

She glanced toward the litter of notes that covered the seat across the aisle. "You've got plenty of stuff to do a magazine piece."

"On Doc Perrill — sure, I could do a piece. I could do a couple of pieces. Maybe even a three-parter profile for the *New Yorker*. He's a juicy character — Yul Brynner playing Dr. Schweitzer in the Indian jungles with lyrics by Rudyard Kipling — all you need is the MGM lion and Technicolor. For a couple of hours this morning, that's what I thought it was going to turn out to be — a magazine piece with a Brick Mitchell by-line."

"But aren't you going to write — ?"

"That isn't the story, Tommy, not the big one. For every reader who'll buy the Doc Perrill yarn, there'll be a thousand mothers who'll be soaking up every word in print about a new way to feed their kids. This is no one-magazine story, Tommy. This is right across the boards. They'll all use it. There isn't an editor in town who won't grab at it. It's too big to pass up. Just the idea that we can make kids grow so much better than anyone ever imagined — good god, Tommy, a half-dozen pairs of those twin pictures on a double spread, just that and a headline, and you'd grab off the damnedest readership any magazine page ever had. And this whole idea that you can affect a child's mentality by the way you feed it —" He stopped, suddenly concerned as he saw her look down, her lower lip caught. "What's the matter? Is there a bug that I've missed, a hole that —"

"No, no, Brick, you're right. Of course you are. It's a big story, an awfully big story."

"But you think I'm wrong about giving it a general release, is that it? I don't see how I can do anything else. Sure, I'd like it as a by-line piece — what writer wouldn't? But if we're taking Kira Zurich's dough to get all the space we can for Haven Home —"

"Please, Brick, I'm not arguing with you."

"Then what — look, Tommy, don't you see what this can mean to us? If this goes the way I think it will, we'll wind up with a scrapbook a foot thick and Mitchell Associates will be the hottest outfit on Madison Avenue. Tommy, this is the break I've been waiting for — a chance to handle something that was big enough to —" Suddenly, an unbidden image materialized out of nowhere, unexplainable except as thought transference, and even that explanation was so deeply buried in his subconscious mind that he did not know why he said, "Are you still worrying about Maggie Lord?"

She looked up as if struck, silently asking how he had known.

"You were, weren't you?" he demanded.

She nodded with her eyes tightly closed. "I just wish — I know it's what you've always wanted — oh, Brick, why couldn't I have been the one to give it to you?"

He was stunned, momentarily unable to think, knowing only that this was a crucial moment, that he had to resist the impulse to take her in his arms, that this was something that had to be settled here and now. Once buried, it would fester away in darkness for the rest of their lives. And then he said slowly, words laid down as if they were steppingstones, "Yes, she's the one who gave it to us — and we'll be grateful to her — and to Linc, and to Kira Zurich, and to Anderson Phelps. But gratitude doesn't have anything to do with love —"

And then she was in his arms, and the train plunged into the Hudson tunnel and he heard his own words echoing above the roar, and he wondered if he, too, until this moment, had not been confusing gratitude with love.

VIII

FEBRUARY had slipped off the calendar and this was the fourth day of March. Brick Mitchell had gone as far as he could without a decision from Kira Zurich. That was why he had come to Goodhaven today and was sitting now in her office at Haven Home, Tommy beside him, waiting for Mrs. Zurich's first reaction to the heavy black-bound notebook that evidenced what had been accomplished during the month since Mitchell Associates had taken on the Haven Home Research Center as a public relations client.

Brick Mitchell's approach to any important job had always been one of total immersion, plunging in with his mind blanked to everything else, and never had he driven ahead more single-mindedly than during the past four weeks. Impelled by a powerful combination of mixed motives, paced by Tommy's seemingly inexhaustible energy and harried by his own innate perfectionism, every facet of the Haven Home story had been explored and recorded in the volume that Kira Zurich was now examining. There were more than two hundred pages, tab-divided into eleven chapters that ranged all the way from a prefacing twenty-page section on the current state of scientific knowledge of enzymes to an almost literal transcription of Dr. Perrill's reminiscences about his years in India. As an appendix, there was a thick folio of photographs, most of them picturing the contrasting physical development of identical twins.

Time ticked by as Kira Zurich slowly turned the pages, reading a paragraph here and a paragraph there, stopping to examine a chart or a diagram, finally turning back to the first chapter. At last she looked up. "This is really amazing, Mr. Mitchell. I had no idea that anything like this could be done — that something so complicated could be made so clear and understandable."

"That's largely Dr. Thompson's contribution," Brick said.

"But with a very big helping hand from Mr. Mitchell," Tommy said, preserving the formality that they had decided to maintain in their relationship with Mrs. Zurich, successful in her case as it had not been with Dr. Perrill, whom both of them had slipped into addressing as "Doc" after their first visit to Haven Home.

"Whoever did it — it's beautifully done — all of it," Kira Zurich said, now fingering the book's thickness. "But is there really a chance that any magazine will publish all this? It's awfully long, isn't it?"

"Oh, this isn't anything to be published, Mrs. Zurich," he said. "It's only a press book, something to get editors interested."

She blinked her incredulity. "Just to get them interested?"

"Well, it's a little more than that, actually," he explained. "It's sort of a dope book, too — all the facts pulled together for any writer who's doing a story. You see —" He checked Tommy with a glance and then went on, cautious now. "Mrs. Zurich, the thing you commissioned us to do was to get an article on Haven Home in one of the big magazines?"

"Yes?" she said, alarmed to alertness.

He leaned forward, an elbow on his knee. "We haven't talked to you about this before — we wanted to be sure of our ground first — but Dr. Thompson and I have felt from the beginning that this could be a lot bigger than just a one-magazine story. This last week — well, as soon as we got this press book done we started checking around to get some sort of an idea of how much interest we could arouse. I don't mean that we had any real doubts — we didn't — but we've both been so wrapped up in this that we wanted to get some cold reactions from people who hadn't been personally involved. Naturally, we picked pretty carefully — we didn't want to open up to anyone we couldn't absolutely trust to hold the story until we were ready to release it. Dr. Thompson's handled most of this so —" He turned to her. "Why don't you take over and tell Mrs. Zurich what's happened."

"Here are the five people we've talked to," Tommy said, indicating the notes in her hand. "The first one is an editor who happens to be a very good friend of mine — he was on both *Time* and *Life* for many years and he's now chief editor for a book publishing house. The second is a free-lance writer who specializes in popularized medical stuff — a lot of his articles have been in the *Reader's Digest*. This third man is the publisher of one of the big baby magazines. Then there's a science editor for one of the newspaper syndicates, and a producer at NBC who's doing a series of television programs on new scientific developments. I'd say it was a group that would be quite representative of the kind of editors and writers we're going to be counting on."

Kira Zurich sat silent, tensely anticipatory.

"Not a one of them had ever heard of Haven Home before," Tommy went on. "And all we did was just hand them this press book and ask them to read. As soon as they got into the story, particularly after they saw the twin pictures — honestly, Mrs. Zurich, they were just bowled over. They all agreed that this is a very big story, one of the biggest in years."

Her glance was a cue and Brick picked it up. "If this is a fair sample of the editorial reaction we're going to get — and I'm sure it is — we aren't going to have the slightest trouble finding a magazine to carry an article about Haven Home, not the slightest."

"All we'd have to do is pick up a telephone," Tommy interjected.

"But," Brick continued, "if we do that — give it to only one magazine — we can't help but feel that we're going to sacrifice a lot of coverage. If one magazine has an exclusive, it's only natural that the others aren't going to play it as big, particularly if there's a long publication lag. The women's magazines, for example, need at least a couple of months. If we gave the story to the *Post*, let's say — and *McCall's* and *Good Housekeeping* knew nothing about it until the *Post* appeared —"

"What is it you're proposing?" Kira Zurich asked.

"Well, we feel that this ought to be handled just like any big news story — which, of course, it is. We think we should open up and release it to everyone at the same time — newspapers, magazines, radio and television, the trade and technical press, everyone."

Kira seemed doubtful. "Then you wouldn't have an article in one of the big magazines — the *Post?*"

"We might and we might not. There's the possibility that if it gets big spot news coverage, the *Post* editors might pass it up. On the other hand, there are so many angles — for example, if *Time* and *Newsweek* played the scientific side, the *Post* might still use a personality story on Dr. Perrill."

There was an instant cooling of Mrs. Zurich's expression, plainly an unfavorable reaction to personal publicity for Dr. Perrill. Tommy must have noticed it, too, because she said quickly, "We may not get as much space in any one magazine, Mrs. Zurich, but I'm sure the total would be greater. And, of course, we'd reach more people."

Brick had been somewhat restrained up to now by the recognized selfishness of his own objective — the broader coverage that the story got, the bigger scrapbook he'd have to show to other prospective clients — but he brushed aside selfconsciousness and put on the pressure. "If you'd prefer one big feature story in one magazine, I'm sure we can get it. On the other hand, if we handle it as a news break, drop the bars and let everyone in, we'll get newspaper coverage all over the country, plus radio and television, plus the news magazines — and there'd still be an excellent chance of getting some good solid stories in the general magazines."

"I know the women's magazines will all use it," Tommy said. "They'll have to. It's just too important to pass up." She paused and then added as a clincher, "It's really much more in the professional tradition, too — simply release it as news and make all the facts available. It's what all the big research centers would do —"

"I'm sure you're right," Kira Zurich agreed, looking down at the press book. "What would you do — give everyone a copy of this?"

Brick nodded. "It wouldn't be too expensive to reproduce two or three hundred copies."

"No, I wouldn't think so," Mrs. Zurich agreed. "And I'm sure it would be very worth while."

He paused now, gathering himself for the final push. "But there's one thing we can't do with a press book, Mrs. Zurich. I've no idea how you'll feel about this — there'd be some expense involved and a fair amount of time and trouble — but we don't think anyone can really get the feel of what a wonderful job you're doing here at Haven Home until they see the place with their own eyes. I know that was true in my own case. It wasn't until I got down here and actually saw —"

"What are you suggesting, Mr. Mitchell — that we try to get some reporters to come down here?"

"We'd like to go beyond reporters. We want to get some top level people — editors, publishers, television producers —"

"But would they come?"

Tommy said, "As soon as we release this, Mrs. Zurich, you'll be swamped. They'll be down here in droves — reporters, writers, photographers, everyone. That's why this plan of Mr. Mitchell's —"

Hurriedly, he explained. "What we're thinking of, Mrs. Zurich, is one big affair to give them all a look-see — get them down here and then get them out of your hair. It wouldn't be too hard to handle. Most of them would be coming from New York, so it would be fairly simple to charter a bus or two and bring them down. We could leave New York about nine-thirty, get here about eleven, take them through the research center, have some exhibits set up with the lab people to explain them, maybe a short talk by Dr. Perrill —"

"And every pair of twins you could get your hands on," Tommy put in. "That's the real clincher."

"Then we could give them lunch," he went on. "Hand out these press books — maybe a question and answer session —"

Kira Zurich broke in to ask, "How many people would there be — how many could you get to come?"

"Well, that would depend," he said cautiously. "I really don't know, Mrs. Zurich, but I'm reasonably certain that we could get twenty-five or thirty."

"Oh, I'm sure we could," Tommy amended. "Particularly if we gave them enough advance information so that they'd have some idea of how big a story it really is. I'd say we could count on fifty — newspapers, magazines, radio and television — oh, I'm sure we could."

An abstracted stare had settled on Kira Zurich's face and Brick guessed that she was thinking about expense. "It wouldn't be too costly, Mrs. Zurich. Transportation wouldn't run more than ten dollars a person. We could give them a good lunch for no more than —"

"We'll not worry about that," she cut him off. "Have you talked to Dr. Perrill about this?"

"No, we thought we ought to come to you first," he said, quickly but cautiously. "He's spent so much time with us already — I'm afraid we've pretty well wrecked this last month for him —"

"I'll speak to Dr. Perrill," she said crisply, a note made. "If you'll tell me the things that need to be done here, I'll follow through to make certain that they are. When would you propose that we do this, Mr. Mitchell?"

"Well, I'd say the sooner the better. We've selected a more or less tentative date —"

"When?"

"The seventh of April. Maybe that's too fast — we'd have only a month to get things set up — but if we wait too long —"

"I'd think that would give us enough time," Kira Zurich said, another note made. "You'll take care of the New York end, of course — inviting the people you want and getting them down here?"

"Oh yes," he said. "And we'll help you all we can on this end, too. Dr. Thompson has worked up some suggestions of what might be done —"

Tommy's portfolio was already open and she handed the outline to Kira Zurich, who began immediately to read it, murmuring approval as she read. Finished, she sat silent for a moment, finally saying, "Yes, this should be very effective."

"From here on out, Mrs. Zurich, I don't think there'll ever again be any question about Haven Home getting the recognition that it deserves."

"Yes, this should mean a great deal to Dr. Perrill and all of our people here," Kira Zurich said, but she spoke as if it were repetition by rote, staring past them. "Of course, it would mean more if —" Suddenly, her eyes focused on him. "You've had some experience in the food business, haven't you, Mr. Mitchell? Of course you have. You were with Mr. Lord, weren't you?"

He guessed what was coming and tried to prepare himself for the question that she would almost certainly ask, the same question that had been in his own mind ever since Perrill had told him that Lincoln Lord had turned down the marketing of his baby food.

"Don't you think, Mr. Mitchell, that all of this publicity will make a great many mothers want to start feeding our food to their own children?"

He had to say, "Yes, I'd think so."

"And you do know, don't you, that Mr. Lord was considering the possibility of having Coastal Foods put it on the market?"

"Yes, I — well, Dr. Perrill did mention that it had been up for consideration."

Kira Zurich nodded curtly. "And at the time, I'm sure Mr. Lord's decision was a sound one. He felt that it was completely beyond the company's financial capacity to do enough advertising to get the story across to the general public — but now that we'll be getting all this publicity with no expense to the company — don't you think that Mr. Lord might want to reconsider his position?"

"Well, I'm sure there are a lot of things involved that I don't know about —"

"You've not talked to him?"

"No, I — well, I've meant to give Linc a ring, but I've been so busy every time I've been down here — so many things to do that I haven't had a chance."

Kira asked, "There's no reason why Mr. Lord shouldn't be informed about what we're planning, is there?"

"No indeed, Mrs. Zurich — no reason at all why you shouldn't tell him," he said quickly, thinking that he had found a loophole.

Kira Zurich blocked it. "Would you be willing to do that for me, Mr. Mitchell? You know so much more about it, you and Dr. Thompson, and I'm certain that he'd have questions to ask that I wouldn't be ~ble to answer." She paused. "Would you be good enough to talk to him for me, Mr. Mitchell?"

He felt the pressure of Tommy's demanding stare . . . if he tried to duck it, she'd think he was still running away from Linc . . . because of Maggie . . . *"Don't you know why you can't face Lincoln Lord? Because you . . ."*

"If there's any reason, Mr. Mitchell, why you'd prefer not to talk to Mr. Lord —"

"No, I'll talk to him," he said, a decision that seemed impossibly difficult until he had made it — and then, suddenly, he found himself looking at Tommy with the feeling that she had been expecting him to refuse . . . but why? There was no reason why he couldn't talk to Linc . . .

"I believe you'll find him working at home today," Kira Zurich said. "I know he was there yesterday. They're all torn up at the office — starting to remodel the second floor. But Kip should know. I just saw him go past the door. I'll ask him."

She left the office and for a reminiscent instant he felt the racing of his heart . . . if Tommy went with him to their house . . . watching his face when he saw Maggie . . .

Tommy said quietly, "Do you want me to go with you?"

Breath-held, he asked, "Why not?" and then, gratifyingly, he found himself breathing freely again, as easily as if his expression of surprised inquiry had been completely honest. And now it was . . . there was no reason to be afraid of what Tommy would see in his eyes when she watched him meet Maggie Lord . . . there would be nothing to see . . .

A faint smile had broken around Tommy's eyes, an edging of sunlight on dark clouds. "There's no point in my going, Brick. You go ahead. Kip can drive you over. I'll get things started here and pick you up in half an hour."

Kira interrupted from the door. "Yes, Kip thinks he's at home but

413

he's calling to make sure. He'll let us know in a minute." She walked back to her desk. "I've just been wondering — do you suppose it might be worthwhile to invite a few people other than the press?"

For a moment he couldn't imagine what she was talking about. By the time he had gotten himself oriented again, Tommy had taken over ... god, she was wonderful! She was so damned smart, letting him go alone ... there wasn't another woman in the world who would have understood ...

2

With great caution, Maggie Lord cracked the bedroom door and stood listening, quieting the sound of her breathing, trying to hear what was being said, annoyed when Linc's first words were muffled by the snorting exhaust of Kip's car as he started back for Haven Home. But then it faded off and she heard Linc's voice again, distantly reverberant as he said, "Golly, it's good to see you, Brick! Almost gave up — thought you'd deserted us for good."

Although she strained her ears to the limit of sensitivity, she was unable to resolve Brick's reply into distinguishable words. All that came through to her was an overtone, untrustworthy because it made him seem so pleasantly friendly ... but Linc would probably be taken in ... he'd always been such a fool about Brick ...

She closed the door, guiltily attempting to muffle the betraying click of the latch, and sat down at her dressing table. She had exhausted the excuse that she had to change her clothes — she had finished changing ten minutes ago — and the recognized needlessness of rebrushing her hair was another accusation of pointless delay. She dropped the brush and slammed the drawer, the noise somehow relieving. But then there was silence, and she got up and slowly paced the length of the room, window to window, wearing away the minutes, exposing the memory of another day when she had paced a bedroom ... Kingdom Come ... listening for the first note of the wedding march ... and then she would have to walk down the stairs ... Brick standing there with Linc ... not daring to look at him ...

Angrily she shattered the memory, a glass bauble smashed, but the fragments had a cutting edge as sharp as the annoyance that had struck when Kip had called ... oh, why did it have to be today! And just when Linc had finally started to tell her about what had happened yes-

terday at the G & G meeting... Brick again... spoiling everything
... *always!*

Thinking about it now, it seemed that Brick Mitchell had always been a harbinger of unhappiness, his appearance associated with every crisis, and the thought was no sooner formed than it took on substance, fleshed with memories... Brick coming to the house that night to tell them that there was going to be trouble with Cornelia Rabson... Brick turning up with the bad news that old Kasselman was coming back to take over Union Packing again... Brick warning her that she had to keep Linc battling the board of directors at Frazer Glass... yes, it had always been Brick. He'd been clever about it, of course, making it seem that he was trying to help Linc... until that night on the boat. And then he'd revealed what must have been in his mind all the time... *wanting* Linc to fail... imagining that she might leave him if he did... and now he was back again...

For an instant, anger sustained the resolution that she would not leave the bedroom until Brick was out of the house, a decision dissolved by the realization that the only way she could protect herself was to make certain that he wasn't coming back into their lives again... Linc had always been so blind, thinking that he needed him... and he *was* worried about the reaction that he'd gotten to the new line from the G & G men...

She flew to the door, the eternal protectress, the primitive female responding to the elemental urge of self-preservation, ready to rout the invader — but this house was no aboriginal cave and, as instinctively as she had reacted to basic danger, her mind now picked up the sophisticated coloration of the house's atmosphere. She stopped at the kitchen door, half opening it. "Viola?"

"Yes'm?"

"I imagine we'll be having a drink —" She saw then that a tray was already being prepared. "Oh, good."

"The menfolks, they's gone into the den," Viola said. "But I guess they won't be wanting no drinks in there while they's talking business, will they, ma'am?"

"No, just put the tray in the living room," she said, letting the door swing shut again, realizing that Linc's action in taking Brick into the room that he had been using as his private office for the past several days gave her a valid excuse to avoid seeing Brick... but if Linc got talking to him...

She waited, not moving toward the den until the magnetic pull of

415

attraction seemed logically explained by the need to make certain that Linc didn't try to charm Brick into going back to work for him again ... Brick always so weak ... and Linc imagining that Brick was loyal to him ... if he only knew what Brick had said that night on the boat ... *"I've had all the Lincoln Lord I can take"* ...

The door of the den stood open and, too suddenly to give her a chance to achieve poise, Brick was coming toward her — and what, a moment before, had been fear and suspicion and mistrust, was instantly transformed into a sensation that hovered somewhere between the idea that she had done him an injustice and the even less credible belief that something had happened to change him into a stranger that she was meeting now for the first time, his murmuring of her name hardly more than an awkward pretense of familiarity.

"Hello, Brick," she said, striking a wrong note with the first attempt, trying to remedy it by repitching her voice as she asked, "How are you?"

"Fine, fine," he said, seemingly having the same trouble she was having, his tone uncertainly experimental as he went on. "Sorry I missed you that day in New York. But I — well, I do want to —"

She knew that he was trying to thank her and she was grateful that Linc prevented it, his quickly intruding voice not only cutting off Brick but also giving her a chance to drop his hand and bring her eyes back to the safe haven of her husband's face.

"Sit down, Mag, sit down," Linc said, his voice high-keyed with excitement. "Brick, go back and catch her up — tell her what you've told me."

"No, no, please," she protested. "Just go ahead. I only —"

"Tell her, Brick," Linc demanded, unusually animated, too plainly pleased that Brick had finally come to see him. "Listen, Mag, you've got to hear this." He turned to Brick. "You know this whole publicity idea was really Mag's?"

"Oh, but it wasn't," she denied, yet feeling herself strangely lifted and warmed.

"You'll get a kick out of this, Mag," Linc said. "Just listen."

Brick was looking directly at her now, his expression oddly unfamiliar. She had never seen him appear so sure of himself, so calmly confident as he asked, "You did meet Tommy, didn't you — Dr. Thompson?"

"Yes, of course," she said, the words fortunately launched before she

416

was aware of the implication of Brick's strangeness, and now it was much more difficult to say, "She seemed a very competent person."

"That's what I've been telling Linc," Brick said. "She's the one who's really carrying the ball on this whole job."

"Now, now," Linc protested. "This has the Brick Mitchell trademark all over it. You can't fool me about that. Here — look at this, Mag."

She had not noticed the black-bound volume that Linc had been holding, and now as he handed it to her she voiced her first thought by asking, "What in the world have you done, Brick, written a book?"

"By golly, it would *make* a book!" Linc said enthusiastically.

Brick's failure to register gratitude for Linc's approval was added evidence of how much he had changed. Without even a glance of acknowledgment, he fixed his eyes on her. "You were right about this being a great story. It really is."

"It was much more Linc's idea than mine," she said, prepared to face down the faintly cynical smile that she expected to see crinkle Brick's eyes.

But it never came. His expression was unchanged as he said, "As soon as we started to dig in, it was obvious that there was a lot more here than just one article, so we decided to shoot for the moon and give it a general release. There are so many angles, so many possibilities — well, we couldn't boil it down into a two- or three-page poop-sheet. Anyway, this is what we wound up with."

She read the cover label, asking with surprise, "Then this isn't a book — I mean, not a book to be published?"

"No, this is all background dope for editors and writers — Dr. Perrill in India, the Haven Home research program, the identical twin story —"

"And they did all that in a month," Linc marveled. "Less than a month."

"Well, it's been a day and night job for both of us —" Brick began, his voice going on, but she heard it only as if she were still listening from the bedroom door, Brick's words less vivid than the memories they evoked ... all those nights when she'd worked with him on that first advertising campaign at Union Packing ... the presentation on the factory expansion for the Frazer Glass directors ... that night in the hotel room in Atlantic City when they'd rewritten Linc's speech ... that silly house detective ...

"Did you hear that, Mag?"

"Yes," she said, barely aware that Brick was saying something about bringing editors down to Haven Home. "Yes, it sounds wonderful."

"We don't know yet how it's going to work out," Brick was saying. "But even if — well, good or bad, I don't see how we can miss getting a hell of a lot of space. Tommy's done a terrific job with —"

"Now, now, Brick," Linc laughed. "Don't start pulling that old modesty act. I know you too well, boy."

Maggie looked at her husband, wondering if he could really mean what he said . . . modesty? Couldn't he see what was happening . . . Brick making a fool of himself over this Thompson woman? But, of course, Linc didn't know her . . . he hadn't seen her. If he had, he'd know that she was just another of Brick's . . .

Suddenly she was conscious of silence. Linc had asked a question that she had not heard and was waiting for Brick's answer.

"But she must be pleased?" Linc insisted, revealing that his earlier question must have been about Kira Zurich. "She wouldn't have asked you to tell us about it if she weren't. And she did ask you, didn't she? That is what you said, isn't it?"

Brick nodded reluctantly. "I don't know what's gone on before, Linc, so I'm sort of in the dark — how you feel about it — but, anyway, it's her idea that with all this publicity breaking — well, I think she feels that you might want to consider putting the stuff on the market."

Maggie Lord felt herself stunned by sudden catastrophe. A moment ago she had been basking in her husband's gratitude for having thought of the idea that had diverted Kira Zurich from forcing him into putting Dr. Perrill's food on the market. Now it had backfired. Instead of helping Linc, she had hurt him . . . with all this publicity, Kira would be impossible to handle! Oh, why hadn't Brick let well enough alone and done what she'd suggested! One article would have been fine . . . yes, that had been her idea . . . but, no, Brick hadn't been satisfied with that! This had always been his trouble . . . no judgment . . . a lack of balance . . . never knowing when to stop. Maybe he was even . . .

"This does put a different light on it," she heard Linc say and, snapping her head around to face him, she was horrified to see that he was nodding in sober agreement, now adding, "With all this publicity to get the story across — yes, it might work." He saw her looking at him but he completely missed her silent warning and turned back to Brick. "What do you think?"

Brick shrugged off the question.

"But you've got an opinion," Linc insisted. "You know darned well you have. Never saw you when you didn't. What do you think — is there a chance of the stuff selling?"

"Gosh, I don't know, Linc. It does a terrific job, there's no doubt about that — but whether you could ever sell enough mothers on feeding it to their kids so that it would turn into a volume item — maybe, maybe not. I just don't know. It does have some promotion angles —"

"That's what I've been thinking," Linc said vigorously, ignoring Brick's plain intention to keep from being involved. "And that's what we need. Let me give you a quick rundown on what we're up against. You know that we've got the Gellman Stores business?" He leaped over Brick's pointed lack of response. "But we can't stop there, of course — have to build up a line of our own. That's what we're doing. Almost ready to kick off now." He reached down in the carton beside his chair and picked up one of the sample cans that he had used yesterday at the G & G sales meeting, the *Goodhaven* brand name black-accented against the white and gold background. He handed the can to Brick, who accepted it with evident reluctance. "I know — the name's a little awkward — longer than I wish it was. We had some others that I liked better but you know how hard it is these days to hit on a name that someone else hasn't already registered. But still it doesn't have too bad a sound, do you think — *Goodhaven* Chicken Fricassee, *Goodhaven* Vienna Goulash, *Goodhaven* London Beef Hash? The more you say it, the better it sounds."

Brick said, "It's a perfectly good name," obviously side-stepping, yet Maggie saw that he was looking at the label now and, almost against her will, she found herself sharing her husband's desire for Brick's approval.

"Looks all right," he finally said. But he put the can down on the corner of the desk.

Linc took another tack. "Look, Brick — you are certain, aren't you, about all this publicity breaking?"

Brick shook his head. "You've been wound up with enough publicity campaigns to know how it is. Editors are editors. You can never be sure what they're going to give you until it's in print and out on the newsstands."

"I'm not asking you to guarantee anything, Brick. All I want to know —"

Forced, Brick said, "Yes, I'd say we're going to get a lot of space."

"And all of it will be a build-up for Dr. Perrill's baby food? It would have to be, wouldn't it?"

"Well — yes, it would have to go down that line — that's the story."

"And when a mother reads about the stuff, she's going to want to try it, isn't she?"

Brick squirmed. "I don't know what to say, Linc. Sure, if it hits —"

"You remember what happened at Luxor when the *Digest* ran that article?"

"Look, I'm not saying that it couldn't happen, Linc. Sure it could. I'm not underrating what publicity can do. Why should I? It's my bread and butter. When something catches fire, it can make or break a business overnight. An article turns up on lung cancer and half the country starts buying filter-tip cigarettes. It's happened dozens of times, everything from tranquillizer pills to yogurt. But there've been a hundred times when it hasn't happened. It isn't anything you can count on, Linc. When it hits — sure, it hits like a ton of bricks. All I'm saying is that you can never be sure."

"I know," Linc said briefly, making it only too plain that Brick's warning was wasted. "Golly, it would mean a lot to us right now if we had a really hot promotion item in the line. That's our battle — trying to get those salesmen steamed up enough to —"

"Sorry," Brick broke in, suddenly standing. "There's Tommy and I'm afraid I'm going to have to dash."

Linc was up, too, clutching his arm. "Now wait a minute, Brick, you just hop out there and bring her in. You can't dash off like this — first time we've seen you in over a year. You can spare time enough to have a drink."

Brick shook his head stubbornly, edging toward the door. "Make it a rain check, Linc, and we'll cash it in when I get off the wagon. Sorry, but — look, I do want to thank you for what you've done, both of you. This is a break that Tommy and I — well, I just can't tell you what it means."

"Forget it," Linc said. "If this works out, we'll owe you a lot more than you owe us." But now he dropped his restraining hand, abandoning hope of holding him. "You will keep me posted on what's happening, won't you?"

"Well, nothing much will happen until after we have this gang down at Haven Home," Brick said, through the doorway now.

"Good-by, Brick," Maggie said, but he was already out of the door, and her farewell seemed something said more to herself than to him. She walked toward the window, catching sight of his last long steps as he hurried toward the car at the curb.

Behind her Linc asked, "Do you suppose he really meant that — about being on the wagon? Be a different Brick if he did."

She nodded without answering, seeing him now as he opened the car door . . . yes, a different Brick . . .

There was a glimpse of brass-blonde hair and the shadowed whiteness of a face waiting to greet him, an apparition suddenly lost as the car door closed and Brick's arms reached out, his broad shoulders blanking the window. A shivering flinch racked Maggie Lord's body and she twisted away, fighting down the flash fear that Linc might have noticed. She saw then that he was dialing a telephone number and, realizing that he had not seen her, the pace of her breathing so quickly slowed that her fear seemed as foolish as it was unaccountable.

He was calling the office, asking for Joel Morris, finally acknowledging, "Oh, that's right — he's in New York today, isn't he?" He hung up, after saying, "Yes, see if you can locate him and have him call me back."

She said, hoping to divert them, "Joel's doing a fine job with Gellman, isn't he?"

His nod was automatic, unrelated to what she had said. "If this thing works — Mag, you really started something when you dreamed up this publicity idea. I never imagined that it would build up into anything like this."

"Neither did I," she said, half to herself, then quickly raising her voice, "But Linc, this isn't what we started out to do. All we were thinking of was some way to satisfy Kira —"

"I know," he broke in with the impatience of high excitement. "It's just one of those lucky breaks."

"But Linc, you still don't know —"

"You think Brick's too optimistic about all the space he's going to get?"

"No, not necessarily. But even if he does get it, it's still going to be the same product it was before. Publicity isn't going to change the way it tastes."

"Oh, it's not so bad," he said stubbornly. "It doesn't taste any worse than baker's yeast. And you remember a few years ago how everyone was gobbling that stuff down. You even ate some yourself."

"I know, Linc, but a baby food —"

"Mag, I'm not kidding myself. I don't think we're ever going to sell a lot of the stuff. That's not the point. No matter how much publicity it gets, it isn't going to be big volume. I know that. But it could turn out to be a terrific promotion item. That's what we need. Golly, what a different story it would have been over at G & G yesterday if we'd had something like this."

"But I thought Art Gerhart was so pleased with your line?" she said, literally truthful, yet probing for the reason why he had been so obviously concerned all last evening.

"I don't mean Art," he said. "I mean the boys that really know what the score is — the men in the field."

"And they don't like your line?"

"Oh, as a line — sure, they're crazy about it. We had a sample table set up and they dug in like a bunch of kids at a picnic. But when we told them that they were going to have to go out and sell it without national advertising, no big promotion — oh, Art made a hip-hip-hurray speech and they all applauded, but that was just buttering the boss. They haven't got their hearts in it, Mag, and it isn't too hard to see why. This is a promotion business these days. A salesman has to have some kind of a gimmick, something he can use for a hook. He's got a dozen lines to sell and he's lucky if he can get enough of a store manager's time to talk about one of them. Unless he's got something that's really hot, something that's going to make them perk up their ears and listen —"

"But, Linc, if it doesn't sell after the store has it in stock —"

"Any store will sell enough of it to get rid of a case — the publicity will do that — and by then they'll have the rest of our line on those shelves. That's what this can do for us, Mag — give us a wedge to drive in and get distribution. Look — suppose you could walk into a store — every magazine and newspaper in the country all full of articles about this miraculous new baby food that's been developed at Haven Home — and suppose you've got a big banner sign that says, '*Here it is — we've got it!*' With bait like that, don't you think you could convince a store manager that he ought to give us enough shelf space for the Goodhaven line? And Mag, that's all we need. Once we get on those shelves, our stuff is going to sell. All it needs is a chance." His voice changed key. "What's the matter — what's worrying you?"

"Nothing," she said, aware that she had foolishly let her face reflect all the vague but virulent apprehensions that it was impossible to banish from her mind.

"Even if we didn't make a penny on it, we'd still be ahead of the game. Can't you see that?" He paused, scowling. "Mag, what's worrying you?"

"Nothing," she repeated. "I was just thinking — all this publicity for Haven Home — it's a shame that you can't take advantage of it without —"

The pistol-crack snap of his fingers cut her off. "Mag, that's it! Of course, of course! Why didn't I think of that before — it's a better name, anyway — *Haven Home* Chicken Fricassee — *Haven Home* this, *Haven Home* that — Mag, that's terrific! Look —"

He wheeled away from her, giving her an instant to realize that he had completely misinterpreted what she said . . . but he was right. It *was* a better name . . .

"It's perfect!" he exclaimed, back now with a sample can in his hands. "We'll have to make new label plates but that's easy. The design doesn't even have to be changed — *Haven Home* fits right in, almost the same number of letters as *Goodhaven*. Golly, Mag, this is what I've been wracking my brain to find — some way to get a real tie-in with all of this publicity. Honestly, Mag, I don't know how to thank you."

Embarrassment made her search for a change of subject. "You don't think that Kira might object, do you — using the Haven Home name?"

"Object?" He laughed. "Oh, I'll check with her, of course, but when she hears that we're going to bring out her baby food — you don't really think she'll object, do you?"

"I hope not," she said, the words meaningless until she heard herself speak them. Then, echoing, they rasped like a chalk squeak and the false sensation of a chill ran through her body, suddenly stopped by force as Linc's hands clenched over her shoulders, gripping hard. "Mag, you're terrific! I don't know what I'd do without you!"

She was torn between warring emotions, wanting to respond to his praise and gratitude yet terrified by the possible consequences . . . if Linc took this crazy gamble because he thought it was her idea . . . her fault when it failed . . .

Strain broke the bonds that held her mind within the limits of normality and for a horrifying instant she found herself wondering if Brick had purposely lured Linc into another trap. Then, madness recognized, she threw herself into the saving shelter of his arms, murmuring, "Oh, Linc, I just hope it works out."

3

Joel Morris was walking rapidly toward the climax of what had been an enormously gratifying day. This was only his fourth week, the fourth Wednesday that he had come to New York to spend a day in the headquarters of Gellman Stores, yet he was already being treated as an insider, almost as if he were a Gellman man himself. He had been afraid, when Mr. Lord had originally suggested the idea of spending a full day every week in the Gellman offices, that he never would be able to penetrate more deeply into the Gellman headquarters than the office of Paul Sachs, who, since the abrupt termination of Irving Rubin's association with the company, had been designated as Coastal Foods regular contact . . . but Mr. Lord had surely been right . . . all a man had to do was keep pushing those doors open.

Of course, Mr. Lord's call to Mr. Arnauth had helped to open a lot of those doors . . . and Paul had been wonderfully co-operative, too . . . but still no one could say that he hadn't accomplished a lot himself . . . Sam Mandel taking him in this noon to eat at the vice-presidents' table in the executive dining room . . . inviting him to sit in on the meeting of the Merchandising Board when they were discussing their new Mother Gellman promotion . . . and now this . . . "If it wouldn't be too much trouble, Mr. Morris, could you stop in and see Mr. Arnauth for a minute or two before you leave today?"

Walking down the carpeted corridor toward the president's office, he felt himself floated along on a wave of elation, his spirits all the more buoyant because what had happened today had lifted him so far above the depression into which he had been dropped yesterday by the disappointing response of some of the G & G men to the new Goodhaven line. Despite what Mr. Lord had said on the way home about the reaction being all they could reasonably expect, there had still been the feeling that somehow he had slipped up, that there was a missing something that he might have supplied if he'd only been clever enough to come up with it.

Now there was no such feeling of questionable competence . . . and this was what counted, the Gellman business . . . this was what kept Coastal Foods going . . . and he'd really done a job here today! But it wasn't all to his own credit . . . part of it was the kind of men you had to work with here at Gellman's . . . every name on every door . . . MR. BLAUSTEIN . . . MR. COHEN . . . MR. POLSKY . . . gosh, they were a smart crowd! This was a wonderful company . . . MR. MANDEL . . . Sam talking about Israel at the lunch table ... that's what a Jew ought to be, proud of his people. And you *could* be in a company like this ... the way they'd faced up to what Rubin had done and made good on it. A lot of outfits would have bluffed it through and admitted nothing ... and not Jewish companies, either ...

MR. ARNAUTH

Through the glass door of the reception room, he saw a painting that he was certain was a Picasso and, inside, when the president's secretary left him alone to announce his arrival, he confirmed the identification with a quick look at the signature, recalling that Sidney Arnauth was a collector of modern paintings and prompting himself to mention it if he needed something to say.

But there was no such need. Sidney Arnauth met him at the door and immediately took over, instantly putting him at ease with his simple and straightforward greeting, a man upon whom the polish of culture had not raised an impenetrable glaze. "I understand you were just leaving, Mr. Morris," he said solicitously. "I hope I haven't made you miss a train?"

"No, I'm driving. And I'm delighted to have this chance to meet you, sir."

"Cigarette?" Arnauth offered. "And please sit down. I'll not take much of your time — I know you're anxious to get away — but I did want this chance to thank you. Sam Mandel has just told me how helpful you were at our promotion meeting today. There aren't many suppliers we can count on for that kind of contribution."

"Well, I don't know that I made much of a contribution —"

"Sam says you did — and Sam's a rather good judge," Arnauth said. "But I've another reason to thank you, too. Perhaps a bit more personal. I am right — you were with McCutcheon & Paisley at one time, weren't you?"

"Yes, sir — just before I went to Coastal Foods."

"And I believe you made a study of our company?"

"That's right, sir. They were considering a television program and —"

"That was just prior to my coming here. I'd been in banking, you know — a long way from the retail grocery business — and I had the problem of orienting myself. May I tell you, Mr. Morris, how very valuable I found your report. It helped me a great deal, almost more than anything else I found. It was a beautiful job."

"That's good to hear, sir. Thank you."

"This might possibly interest you," Arnauth said, pausing with a quizzical smile. "I was so impressed that I asked our personnel people to contact you and see if you might be interested in a place on our staff."

"You did? But I —"

"No, the offer was never made. They reported back that you'd left McCutcheon & Paisley and gone to work for Coastal Foods. Of course, we could hardly approach you then — Coastal Foods being one of our big suppliers. But there's no harm in your knowing it now."

"I'm sorry I didn't know it then," he said, fearing for a moment that he might be sounding too sorry. "But thank you, anyway, sir. It's very flattering to know that you wanted me."

There was something odd about Arnauth's expression now, a speculative silence that flashed the impression that he was about to renew that offer of a job — but Arnauth quickly proved him wrong, so wrong that he felt a twinge of secret embarrassment as he heard him say, "I must admit to being a bit surprised at the time — your leaving McCutcheon & Paisley. That's a big agency. With your ability, I should think you'd have had quite an opportunity there?"

He hesitated, still uncertain as to what reply he should make when he heard himself say, "No, I really don't think I did — at least not the kind of an opportunity that I wanted."

"Because you were a Jew?" Arnauth asked, the stab of his words no less deep because they were spoken softly, tempered with a smile.

"Yes, I suppose that was a factor," he said as an admission, strange only because he had never made it aloud before, even to Vicky, and the strangeness colored the self-conscious laugh with which he added, "At least I couldn't look around and see any Jewish vice-presidents."

Sidney Arnauth smiled. "And if you can't make vice-president in an advertising agency — that is discrimination, isn't it? The advertising business is almost as bad as banking — everyone who has any contact with a prospective client has to be a vice-president."

"Well, it wasn't that the title meant anything —"

"I understand," Arnauth said quietly. "And I dare say you've not regretted your move?"

"No, sir, I haven't — particularly now that I'm getting into the kind of thing that really interests me. It's meant a lot to be able to work with some of your men here. You have a wonderful company, Mr. Arnauth."

"Thank you." Again there was that strange little smile. "How are you and Linc Lord getting along?"

"Oh, fine, sir. I've never known anyone who — well, it's made a big change in the Coastal Foods Company, having him there."

"I'm sure that's true," Arnauth said, his long-fingered hand reaching out to touch the ash from the end of his cigarette. "Just what is your organizational setup? Mr. Lord is president, of course — who are your vice-presidents?"

He found himself fumbling through an unaccountable hesitation before he could say, "Actually, there aren't any vice-presidents. Mr. Swann — Alf Swann — is in charge of the office operation and Frank Kennan has the production end."

"And you're in charge of sales?"

"Well, more or less," he said, cautiously uncertain. "Of course, we're just getting squared away. I know that Mr. Lord has some organizational ideas in mind —"

"Oh, I'm sure he does," Arnauth said, pushing back his chair, an indication that the interview was over. "And I'm sure, too, that there'll be no need for you to worry about your future."

"I hope not, sir," he said, taking the president's hint and rising from his chair.

"So do I," Arnauth said, his black eyes intently sober for an instant. Then he, too, got to his feet, smiling broadly as he said, "Well, Joel, if Linc Lord doesn't treat you right, you just tell him that you've got a spot all ready and waiting for you at Gellman Stores." He quickly extended his hand, blocking a reply. "Thank you for stopping by, Joel. Do it again, any time at all. My door's always open to you. It always will be."

"Thank you, sir," he said, trying to keep the grip of his hand from being too strong. "I'll remember that."

His mind was racing as he went out the door, stopped suddenly by the president's secretary, who said, "There's a message for you, Mr. Morris. You're to call Mr. Lord right away — at his home — and your operator said that it was important."

"Oh, thank you," he said, blank-minded for a moment.

"May I put the call through for you?"

"Well, if it wouldn't be too much trouble —"

"No trouble at all. Mr. Lerner is out. You can take it in his office."

The call went through almost immediately, so fast that there was

427

not time enough to decide which of a half-dozen catastrophic possibilities was most probable, all of them momentarily banished with the sudden burst of Lincoln Lord's voice.

"Golly, I'm glad I caught you before you left, Joel. Brick Mitchell was over here this afternoon and it looks very much as if we ought to jump in and get this Haven Home baby food on the market just as soon as we can. Brick is kicking off a big publicity campaign —"

His brain choked, gagged by the words that were pounding down upon him . . . Mr. Lord was rejecting every recommendation he'd made . . . his whole report thrown out . . . bringing this Brick Mitchell into the company . . . turning over everything to him . . . of course . . . he should have known! He was always talking about him . . . Brick this, Brick that . . .

"Joel, did you get that?"

"No, I —" he said, fighting for self-control. "I'm sorry, sir. This must be a bad connection, but it's all right now. Just tell me again what it is that you want me to do."

"The first thing to do is to get in touch with the label company — I'd do it myself but I don't know who to call — and tell them not to run any more Goodhaven labels."

"No more Goodhaven labels," he repeated dully . . . Mr. Lord was dropping the line . . . rejecting that, too . . .

"Then call G & G and tell them to hold up anything they're doing — that we'll be in touch with them in a day or two, maybe tomorrow."

"Maybe tomorrow," he repeated, bracing himself, then asking, "Anything else?"

"No, not for now. But you'd better see me the first thing in the morning."

"All right," he said, hanging up, Lincoln Lord's voice still ringing in his ears. But as he listened, it faded away and then he heard another voice . . . *"Because you're a Jew?"*

4

Brick Mitchell leaned forward, his arms over the top of the steering wheel. "All I want to know is *when*. There's no point in waiting." Tommy's long silence frightened him. "Look, if you're trying to figure out some way to get out of it —"

"Oh, Brick, I don't want to get out of it. You know that. I want to marry you more than I've ever wanted anything in all my life. It's just that — oh, I don't want it to be city hall or some grubby old justice of the peace. And I — you'll probably think I'm being awfully silly about it but — oh, Brick, I don't want to have to get up the next morning and start pounding a typewriter. I don't want it to be like it's ever been before."

His smile died on his face, a chuckle choked back by the lump in his throat. "It won't be," he promised. "What do you want to do?"

"Would you mind terribly if I asked you to — Brick, I want to go back home."

"You mean that you want to be married in Dover?"

"Do you mind?"

"No, but — well, I thought you said you didn't have anyone there any more?"

"I don't really. Only my cousin Mary. It's just that —"

"Forget it," he said quickly, intuitively prompted. "You don't have to explain. If you want it — that's all the reason there has to be."

There was the wonderfully mingled sound of joy bursting through a vibrant sob. "Oh, Brick, if I hadn't loved you before, I would now! Thank you, my dear."

"I just happen to love you, that's all."

"Oh, Brick, I know you do. I'll never doubt that — never! And I *will* be a good wife for you."

"And I'll never doubt that." His little laugh was the breaking of an unsustainable pitch of emotion. "I just want to know when, that's all."

"May I ask another favor?"

"I said I loved you, didn't I?"

"Brick, let's wait until we can — oh, I know it's silly, and that it doesn't make any sense — it's corny and sentimental and you'll laugh at me — Brick, I want a honeymoon."

He nodded, unable to trust his voice until he finally managed to say, "I guess that's what I want, too."

"I don't care where we go — and it only has to be for a few days. But I want those days, Brick. I want you all to myself — no telephones, no typewriters, no Kira Zurich —"

"No amino acids and no enzymes," he concluded, smiling again, then suddenly alarmed. "But if we wait until we get this job licked — good god, Tommy, we can't wait that long! It'll be —"

"Only six weeks. Brick, listen — I've got it all planned. The open house will be five weeks from yesterday. We'll need another ten days to get squared away afterwards. Then we go. We've got to hire a girl, anyway. She can keep the office open — take messages. We could leave New York at noon — be married at five. Then we could leave for —"

"For where?"

"I know you'll think I'm mad — this *is* crazy —"

"Don't tell me Niagara Falls."

"No, there are too many people there. Brick, I want it to be the most all-alone spot in the world — some place where no one else will even know we're alive."

Something made him say, "New York."

"Oh, Brick, would you mind? Let's get a great big wonderful suite at the — oh, I don't care where, just so it's plush and glorious and ridiculously expensive — where no one in the world could possibly imagine that either of us would ever be."

"All right," he said. "I'll make a reservation."

And then he knew she was crying but when he reached out his hand she pushed it away. "Oh, quit it, Brick! I'm not used to it — oh, damn it, why do you have to be so good to me."

IX

DR. LEE PERRILL stole a furtive glance from the open door of his office, hoping that he might catch a glimpse of Brick Mitchell somewhere in the crowd. Before his eyes could focus, however, the frightening spectacle of what had happened to the Haven Home Research Center made him snap back his head . . . it was even worse now than it had been when he had escaped ten minutes ago . . . much worse!

Kira Zurich had told him that there might be twenty-five or thirty people, fifty at the most, and here there were at least two hundred, maybe more. There were five New York busses parked outside, another from Philadelphia, and the paved lot was so full of private cars that they had spilled over on the lawn and halfway down the drive. Across the parking area, gaudily bright under the brilliant noonday sun, stood the big candy-striped tent where lunch would soon be served, setting a circus atmosphere that now pervaded all of Haven Home. The entire research center was jammed with a milling throng, shoving their way from laboratory to laboratory as if they were touring a side show . . . any moment now, they'd be shouting for him . . . the prize exhibit . . .

He still felt himself half-blinded by bursting flash bulbs, yet he could see clearly enough the stark image of his bone-bald head in the finders of all those cameras . . . "Just a little smile now, Doctor" . . . a grinning skull that would be staring out from newspapers all over the country . . . it wouldn't have been so bad if he'd only had his white lab coat on . . . they'd caught him unaware, wearing a dark jacket . . . made him look like an old bald eagle . . .

Desperation drove him back to the door. He had to find Brick . . .

he'd never be able to get through his talk after lunch if those photographers kept blasting away at him ... Brick would take care of it ... if he could only find him without going out there and running the gauntlet again ...

Suddenly he saw him and a hoarse call burst from his lips, frighteningly loud, but still not loud enough to carry over the crowd noise. He called again, relieved now to see that Brick had heard him and was signaling that he would be there as soon as he could break away from the man to whom he was talking.

Leaving the door ajar, Dr. Perrill waited, the prospect of support already acting as a predictable sedative ... Brick was the only person who would understand ... yes, Dr. Thompson could be very understanding, too, but it was Brick he could count on ...

Gratitude mingled with embarrassment as he again acknowledged how wrong he had been about Brick Mitchell. He had been concerned enough when Kira Zurich had first told him that she had retained Mitchell Associates — the whole idea of hiring a press agent had been so distastefully unprofessional that he could hardly imagine even Kira doing such a thing — but his visualization of Brick Mitchell had been even more disturbing. He had expected a flamboyant character, addicted to alcohol and extravagant inaccuracies, the loud mouthpiece of a grossly materialistic and anti-intellectual world. Dr. Thompson had contributed to his sorry misjudgment because, knowing that she had her M.D., he had imagined that it was Mitchell's bad influence that had turned her into one of those renegades who catered to the public's depraved appetite for popularized medical information.

His eventual discovery that Brick Mitchell drank not a drop had been no more surprising than the revelation of his quite remarkable knack for expressing a great deal in a very few words. On one of the first days that they had worked together, Brick had taken a seventeen-page scientific report and compressed it into a single paragraph that, although regrettably unprofessional in style and tone, was nevertheless a clear and accurate statement of everything of any consequence that the report had contained. That a lay person should possess such understanding and capability was a surprise of much the same order as some of his discoveries about the unsuspected knowledge and talents of the aboriginal tribes of India.

Almost as surprisingly, Dr. Thompson had proved herself a thoroughly professional person and extraordinarily well informed. She was conversant with all of the important new work in child nutrition, more fully grounded in enzymology than most of the specialists he met at conventions, and the only M.D. he had ever known who was intimately familiar with everything that he had published. She, like Brick, was a very competent person.

Nevertheless, the affection that he had come to feel for both of them could not be accounted for in terms of professional competency, and that alone was enough to make it a disturbing emotion. It was impossible to understand why it should give him such pleasure to have Brick Mitchell chuck a feinting fist into his ribs and call him a "crazy old coot" — or even something worse — nor could he explain why, on three separate occasions, his own tongue had slipped so badly that he had inadvertently addressed Dr. Thompson as "Tommy." The last time was, perhaps, explainable if not justified. Somehow, she and Brick had discovered that Thursday was his birthday, and when he had gone back to his cottage he had found a new silk dressing gown in a tissue-packed box. It was the most luxurious garment that he had ever owned, a red plaid that he would never have felt free to choose for himself, and the only birthday present that he had been given by anyone since his mother had died when he was thirteen.

The behavior pattern to which Dr. Perrill had shaped all of his mental processes provided no easy response to personal friendship, and now as Brick Mitchell threw open the door of his office, his face was so undeniably that of a good and close friend that the scientist found himself floundering, momentarily unable to recall why it was so necessary to talk to him.

"Anything wrong, Doc?" Brick asked, his eyes narrowed with concern.

Suddenly it all came clear, order out of confusion, and he looked down at the speech notes that he had, unknowingly, picked up from his desk. "Do you still think I ought to say all these things?" he asked. "All this about not giving too much weight to some of our results — the intelligence tests?"

"What are you worrying about, Doc, that you're going to sell yourself short? If that's it, forget it. That crowd out there needs something to bring them back to earth. After they saw those twins — Doc, if you don't cool them off a little we're going to get some wild stories. They're going to make this stuff sound like black magic — two cans of it and any mother can turn her little darling into a cross between Paul Bunyan and Albert Einstein."

"Really?" he asked, genuinely frightened.

433

"Oh, they'll simmer down — we've got the press book loaded with warnings not to overplay it — but it isn't going to hurt to sprinkle a little cold water around."

"I do have to give them an honest picture —"

"Absolutely," Brick said. "Give them the bad with the good. Tell them the truth. You've got nothing to worry about. You're not trying to sell them anything."

"No, no, of course not," he said too quickly, forced then to correct himself. "But I wouldn't want — all of those men that Mr. Lord has brought over —"

"Oh," Brick interrupted, seeming to understand until he said, "Sure, Linc's got some people out there — three or four from Gellman Stores and half a dozen from Gerhart & Gerhart — but just forget them. We aren't putting on a show for their benefit. We didn't set up this affair to plug the Coastal Foods Company. We aren't selling baby food, we're selling Haven Home — the Haven Home Research Center and Dr. Lee Perrill."

"No, no," he protested. "I don't want —"

"Look, Doc, I know how you feel. Or at least I think I do. You've put twenty years of your life into this thing — it's good and it's solid and it's important, and you don't want to see it messed up with a lot of commercial ballyhoo. But, Doc, that isn't happening. And it isn't going to happen. I told Linc from the start what we wanted — a high-level scientific press conference — and he's played ball right down the line. There aren't any Coastal Foods exhibits out there. There isn't even a can of the stuff standing around. These press people don't even know yet that it's going to be put on the market, and they won't know until Kira makes her announcement after your speech. And all she's going to say —"

"But these people of Mr. Lord's," he broke in. "They are the men who are going to go out and try to sell it, aren't they?"

Brick's face was frighteningly blank.

"I wouldn't want to do anything to discourage them," he blurted out. "If it doesn't sell — if people won't buy it —" He had said it now and there was no turning back. "This is my only chance. I've got to have my own money. I can't go on like this — dependent on Kira."

Brick cocked his head. "Let me get this straight, Doc. Have you got some kind of royalty deal?"

"Yes, yes, of course. Mr. Zurich promised me —" Fear struck. "You don't think they'd keep that promise, is that it?"

434

"Do you have a contract?"

"Contract? No, I — but Mr. Zurich did promise me — yes, I'm sure that's what he said — ten cents a case." His heart seemed to have stopped. "You don't think they'll pay me?"

Brick's pause stretched over a fear-filled eternity. "Have you said anything about this to Mrs. Zurich?"

"No. She'd try to stop it. She wouldn't want me to get away from her."

Brick's eyes narrowed. "Doc, you've got me a little groggy. I don't get this. I thought you were happy here at Haven Home?"

"Oh, I am. It isn't Haven Home. I've everything here that I've ever wanted. But I can't go on like this, being dependent on Kira. I've got to be on my own — pay my own way. Can't you understand how I feel?"

For an instant he thought Brick was going to laugh at him but it never got beyond an eye-crinkling smile, and even that was almost instantly transformed by an oddly abstracted stare, suddenly broken as he said, "I guess that's a bug that bites all of us sooner or later — worrying about being dependent on someone."

Understanding was enough, all that he had counted upon, and he quickly gave up the attempt to solve the puzzle of Brick's strange smile. "Do you think Mr. Lord would try to get out of it — not pay me?"

Brick hesitated, finally shaking his head. "No, I wouldn't worry about that. I've known Linc a long time, a good many years. Sometimes he gives you the impression of being — well, a lot of people think he's —" He stopped, staring past him, suddenly smiling again. "No, Doc, if you had an agreement with Sol Zurich, I'm sure Linc will honor it."

"You understand, don't you — it isn't that I want the money for myself. I'd put it right back into Haven Home. It's just that —"

"I know," he cut him off. "Look, Doc, I've got to get back out there. And so do you. They're starting to go over to lunch."

"And you think it's all right to say these things?"

Brick's hand shot out, a tight fist closing over his lapel. "Listen — the worst thing you could possibly do would be to get up there and say one damn thing that isn't absolutely and completely true. And when they start shooting questions at you — Doc, there are a hundred people out there who've spent their whole lives smelling out phonies. If they get one whiff that you're faking it up —"

435

"No, no, I couldn't do that!"

"Of course you couldn't." Brick's fist dropped, punching into his ribs. "Now come on, you old coot, let's get out there and give the common people a look at the famous Dr. Perrill."

He felt a flush and, his eyes dropping, he saw that Brick's grip on his lapel had pulled his coat open. He started to rebutton it, hesitated, wondering if he dared. Then, boldly stripping his coat, he reached for his white lab jacket. "I always feel more comfortable —"

"Sure," Brick grinned, winking. "Why not? Might as well give them the full act. You know, Doc, damned if I don't think all of you big-shot scientists have got a streak of ham in you!"

He laughed, not as an appreciation of humor but as an expression of enormous gratitude for the comfort of true friendship.

2

Whispering to Frank Kennan, telling him to go ahead with the G & G men, Lincoln Lord breasted the crowd that was streaming out of the Research Center building. He pretended to be looking for someone but his mind was tuned to his ears rather than his eyes, listening to the comments that were being made by the magazine and newspaper people, and what he heard convinced him that there was not the slightest doubt now that all and more that Brick had set out to do would be accomplished. Beginning with tomorrow morning's newspapers, there would be a tremendous outpouring of publicity on Haven Home . . . and tomorrow morning the Coastal Foods Company would start selling *Haven Home Wonderfood!*

There were only three thousand cases in the warehouse . . . nowhere near enough . . . but Frank had pulled off a miracle to get even that much ahead. And three thousand cases meant three thousand stores . . . no more than one case to a store on the first round . . . and every case of Wonderfood meant six cases of the regular line. That was going to be a problem, too, trying to steal enough production from Gellman Stores to get distribution on Haven Home Foods. That was probably what was bothering Joel . . .

Suddenly he smiled, the faint outward reflection of inner laughter at his own expense, recognizing now that he was searching much too hard for something to worry about, less clearly aware that his mounting tension was grounded in the abnormality of this fantastic run of good luck. Everything that he had done this last month, every decision that he had made, every step that he had taken, was paying off here to-day.

The crowd chatter told him that he had even been right in agreeing to Brick's stipulation that not a single commercial note be injected until the very end of the program. Many of the comments that he was picking up reflected the question that seemed to be on everyone's mind — would it be commercially available? A moment ago he had heard some newspaper man say, as an indignant generality, that the trouble with all research institutions was that they had their heads so high in the clouds that they never thought about marketing their developments. Now, when Kira made her announcement, the whole audience would feel that she was acting in response to its mass demand ... Brick was clever ... that new announcement was perfect ...

Turning away, out of the crowd stream now, he fished from his pocket the flimsy carbon of the revised paragraph that Brick had, this morning, added to Kira's closing remarks.

> In response to the many questions that have been asked, I would like to announce that the Coastal Foods people, who have co-operated with us for so many years in the processing of the special food that we have used in our experimental work, have agreed to pack it for general sale. Because of limited production facilities and the care and control necessary in processing, only a relatively small amount will be currently available. It will be sold, I understand, under the trade name of Haven Home Wonderfood.

He folded the paper, put it back in his coat, and started looking around for Brick. Searching the crowd, he saw Kip carrying a box of something toward the tent and moved to intercept him, asking if he knew where Brick was.

"Sure, he's right over there with Dr. Perrill," Kip said, his eyes uncommonly bright. "I guess it's going all right, huh, Dad?"

"Couldn't be better," he said. "I saw your display — the one you made. Good work, Kip."

"Gee, thanks, Dad," Kip said, his eyes even brighter now. "Want me to get Uncle Brick for you?"

"No, I'll find him. You've got more important things to do."

For a moment Lincoln Lord's eyes followed his son, and again there was the difficulty of believing that everything could possibly be working out so perfectly, a feeling that made him instantly respond to the look of concern that flashed on Brick's face when he finally caught his eye.

Brick pointed to a rendezvous spot, catching his arm as he joined him, turning him away from the crowd. "Linc, Doc's kind of worked up — a little jittery. It's going to be a tough enough assignment as it is, all those sharpshooters plugging questions at him — I don't want him to get up there with anything else on his mind."

"What's the matter, Brick?" he asked, apprehension aroused by the certainty that sooner or later something had to go wrong.

"Maybe nothing. But I'd like to ease his mind before he gets up on that platform. Do you know anything about a promise that Mr. Zurich made to pay him a royalty on Wonderfood?"

"Royalty? Yes, I —" He was almost afraid to accept the relief of believing that this was all that was worrying Brick. "Just a minute. Alf Swann's over here — I'll check."

He saw Swann and called to him, welcoming the opportunity, hoping that the flattery of consulting him would help offset the resentment that he suspected Swann was harboring because Joel had been assigned the responsibility of guiding the Gellman Stores delegation on their trip through the research center.

There was, however, no relaxation of Swann's grimly tight-lipped expression as he listened to a repetition of Brick's question, and there was an unpleasantly sharp edge in his voice as he said, "Of course, I included the royalty in our costs. Perhaps you've forgotten, Mr. Lord, but I did mention it to you."

"No, I've not forgotten," he said patiently, suppressing annoyance. "As I recall, I suggested that you check with Mrs. Zurich to make certain that the royalty arrangement had not been superseded by any subsequent agreement."

"If there'd been any change, I'd have known about it," Swann said. "I was always very close to Mr. Zurich. He never did anything without telling me about it."

"But you did talk to Mrs. Zurich?" he insisted.

"Yes, I talked to her."

"And she understands it?"

"Of course," Swann snapped. "Why wouldn't she?"

He overlooked the question and turned to Brick. "Well, I guess that clears it."

438

"Fine," Brick said. "Look — is it all right if I tell Doc? Or would you rather do it?"

"I'd see no reason why you shouldn't tell him, Brick," he said. "Do you, Alf?"

Swann shook his head.

"This will help a lot," Brick said, moving quickly toward Perrill.

"Thanks, Alf," he said, pushing away then to avoid any further conversation, deciding that this was neither the time nor the place to do something about Swann's increasingly difficult attitude. It had gotten worse and worse over the past month. At first it had seemed directly related to the old office manager's resentment of Joel being given more and more responsibility as the marketing plans for Wonderfood and the new line of Haven Home Foods had been developed. These last few days, however, Swann's behavior had gotten to the point where it was as unexplainable as it was inexcusable. One of these days, he was going to have to sit down with Swann and tell him off . . . tomorrow . . . the next day . . . as soon as he had the right opening . . .

Someone called his name and, turning, he saw Kira Zurich standing with Anderson Phelps. He knew that she had invited him but he had never expected that Phelps would attend.

The financier's greeting was surprisingly hearty, his smile almost free of blue-blooded restraint as Kira said, "I've just been telling Mr. Phelps how grateful I am to him for having sent you down to me, Mr. Lord."

Phelps said to Kira, "I'm delighted that it's all worked out so well," and then to him, "And I trust, Mr. Lord, that you have no regrets?"

"No indeed, none whatsoever," he said, smiling, secretly amused by the memory of how clever Phelps had obviously thought himself with the terms that he had written into his employment contract, imagining that the financier was now regretfully calculating how big his bonus on sales volume was going to be.

One of the caterer's employees came up to ask Kira a question and she nervously excused herself, hurrying away.

Phelps said, "She's very keyed up about all this, isn't she?"

"Yes, it means a lot to her."

"And it should mean a lot to you, too," the financier said archly. "All this publicity should bring you a lot of business."

"We're hoping so."

"I've been listening to some of these press people. My, but they're enthusiastic."

"Yes, the reaction seems very good."

"When all this gets out in the papers and magazines, you should sell tons and tons of — what is it that you're calling it?"

"Wonderfood."

"Ah, yes. Quite so. Good name."

"I don't know how much Wonderfood we'll sell — that's still a question mark — but at least it should help us get distribution on our other products. I suppose Mrs. Zurich has told you — we're bringing out a line under the Haven Home trademark."

"Yes, so she said. Sounds like a ten-strike. Don't see how it could miss. That one of Mitchell's ideas?"

"No," he said with satisfaction. "Actually, it was Maggie's."

"Your wife's? Really? Now that is interesting. She's here?"

"Somewhere around. I saw her a moment ago with one of the magazine —"

"No, please don't call her," Phelps interrupted. "I'll see her later. And there is something I'd like to tell you, Mr. Lord. I mentioned this to Mrs. Zurich but she said that it was all in your hands." He cleared his throat portentously. "I trust you'll not misinterpret this — please don't feel that you're under the slightest obligation to me, either personally or because of my past relationship with the Zurichs." Again he cleared his throat. "At the rate you're expanding, I imagine you'll need some additional working capital before too long."

"Possibly," he said, well short of an admission of the danger that he had spent two unpleasant hours discussing with Swann yesterday.

"If you have any difficulty getting what you need from your regular banking sources, I'll be glad to see you through," Phelps said. "Against my principles really — usually avoid putting money into merchandising businesses — but in your case, I'll be glad to go along."

He was nonplused for a moment, then voiced the gratitude that welled up in his mind. "That's a real vote of confidence, Mr. Phelps."

"I meant it that way."

"Thank you, sir. I appreciate it. And I'll probably be in touch with you in a few days."

"Whenever it suits you," Phelps said, smiling drily. "Got you into this, you know — have to see you through. By the way, Mrs. Zurich tells me that you've made a tie-up with Art Gerhart's outfit."

"Yes, they're distributing for us. As a matter of fact, I was just looking for some of his men when I caught sight of you. They're around here somewhere with Frank Kennan."

440

"Gerhart here himself?"

"No, unfortunately he couldn't make it today. He's tied up down in Washington."

"Goes in for a lot of that sort of thing, doesn't he?" Phelps asked, his tone leaving no doubt of his disapproval.

"I suppose someone has to do those jobs," he said cautiously, anxious not to betray his annoyance that Art Gerhart had chosen to go to Washington today instead of coming to Goodhaven. "I take it that you know him."

"Somehow he got into my country club," Phelps said. "Don't suppose you can really blame the membership committee — they do have a difficult time these days. But I imagine he's a good man for you — just what you need, no doubt?"

"He does have a good organization," he said, keeping his approval within safe limits, thinking now that even Art Gerhart's non-appearance was probably all to the good, that he'd be a bull in a china shop here, an unsuppressible high-pressure salesman who would put the wrong atmosphere on the whole affair. "And we do have all of their top men here. Frank Kennan has them in tow."

"Kennan? Oh, really? You've got him over on the selling side?"

"No, he's just pinch-hitting. Joel's taking care of the Gellman people."

"Ah, yes. Quite a feather in your cap, getting Sidney Arnauth to come down. Mrs. Zurich tells me it's the first time he's ever been here. And I believe she said you've two of their vice-presidents as well. Glad to see you've re-established the old relationship."

"It's Joel Morris who's really responsible. He's been spending a day a week over there. He's a very able boy."

"And being a Jew rather helps, I imagine."

He hesitated, irked without quite knowing why, and Phelps continued, "I am right — he is the Jewish boy that Sol hired?"

"Yes," he said, quickly changing the subject. "How about a touch before lunch? We've a little bar over here —"

"No, no," Phelps objected. "When you get to my age — past sixty, you know — stimulation leads only to frustration."

Lincoln Lord chuckled dutifully, again thanked Phelps for his generous offer, and agreed with the financier's suggestion that there were other people around to whom he should talk. One of them was Maggie. He finally saw her standing just inside the entrance of the tent, but Kira Zurich was with her now and he immediately changed

441

course, letting himself be caught up in the crowd that was pressing down upon the bar. Kennan saw him, waved, and then there was no alternative to rejoining the G & G delegation. He guessed that by now they would have become seriously worried by the scientific-report tone of the morning's program and, fishing in his pocket for the script of Kira Zurich's closing remarks, he prepared a defense against their expected criticism, ready to explain that it would have been a serious mistake to scare off the press by doing anything that might make this Haven Home open house appear to be a publicity stunt for a commercial product.

His concern was immediately proved unnecessary. Earl Canning, the leader of the G & G delegation — and plainly enough the real operating head of the firm now that Art Gerhart had been so badly bitten by the Washington bug — greeted him obliquely by saying to Kennan, "All right, Frank, if you won't give us enough production, we'll have to go to work on the boss." Canning dropped his voice then, perceptively aware of being overheard by the newsmen around him, and said earnestly, "I mean it, Mr. Lord — three thousand cases isn't going to be a drop in the bucket."

"Oh, let's not get too optimistic," he smiled, the warning more seriously intended than his tone indicated, directed as much to himself as to the others, yet aware that Canning's natural conservatism made his enthusiasm far more significant than Art Gerhart's would have been. It was Canning who had been largely responsible for the cool reception that had been given to the line they had first proposed.

"If this doesn't go over," Canning said, "I'll turn in my crystal ball."

"You can never be sure," he replied, again a warning. "But still a small toast to Haven Home might not be too much of a gamble — if anyone could dig up a round of drinks."

"Make mine a double," Canning said positively, and the explosive burst of laughter from the others made it seem an extremely humorous retort.

The long delay until Kennan finally started passing highballs back over the heads of the crowd gave Lincoln Lord more than enough time to say everything that he dared say to the G & G men, and by then he saw Joel Morris coming out of the door of the research center building with Sidney Arnauth and the Gellman Stores delegation. Excusing himself as gracefully as he could, he slipped away in that direction, putting down his untouched drink, alerting his mind to handle what he was afraid might turn out to be a prickly situation. If the Gellman group reaction to Wonderfood was as enthusiastic as everyone else's, they would demand the right to sell it in their stores — and every case that Gellman took would mean one less entering wedge that might be used to force the Haven Home line into another store. He wished now that it had not been necessary to invite the Gellman top management, yet there had been no way to counter Joel's argument that they would find out about it sooner or later, and that there might be a serious loss of good will if they were excluded — and, too, he had never expected that two vice-presidents would accept, let alone Sidney Arnauth. But here they were — and it was undeniably true that the Gellman Stores business still dominated the Coastal Foods Company, and would continue to do so for a long time to come. No matter how successful the Haven Home line turned out to be, it could hardly be expected to pile up more than a fraction of the Gellman volume.

The Gellman men were standing apart from the crowd and as he came up to them there was an instant when their expressionless faces gave him the impression of an unfavorable group judgment on the possibility of successfully merchandising Wonderfood. Then he realized that all he was seeing was vice-presidential mimicry of Sidney Arnauth's habitually enigmatic mask.

"Got around, did you?" he asked Arnauth, keeping his voice flat, purposely avoiding any attempt to influence the Gellman president's reaction.

"Very interesting," Arnauth said, signaling a background murmur of general agreement. "I knew, of course, that the Zurichs had been putting money into Haven Home, but I had no idea that it had grown into anything this substantial. Very worth while, I should say."

There was the momentarily awkward pause of a dead-ended conversation, adroitly bridged by Joel, who quickly asked, "Could I get you a drink, Mr. Arnauth?"

"No, thank you, Joel," Arnauth said. "But you fellows go ahead."

Lincoln Lord was pleased by the first-name familiarity that Arnauth accorded Joel Morris, assuring evidence of the effective job that Joel was doing in his handling of the Gellman account, yet he was alert to the fact that Arnauth had purposely maneuvered things to be alone with him . . . now he'd make his demand . . .

"Very able young man, isn't he?" Arnauth asked.

"Joel?"

"Yes," Arnauth said, his crisp tone seeming to indicate that this was not a small-talk introduction to some other subject. "We appreciate

443

your letting him spend so much time with us these days. He's been very helpful."

"I'm glad to hear that. I thought at first that it might be more than you'd want him around — a full day every week."

"No indeed," Arnauth replied, a thin smile slowly forming. "I'd be quite agreeable to making it five days every week. As a matter of fact, if it weren't for the corporate relationship, I might even try to hire him away from you. Joel fits in very well at our place."

"He fits in very well here, too," he said with a laugh that he hoped would not only cover his surprise but also close the subject.

"Oh, I'm not thinking of trying to steal him away from you," Arnauth said, not too convincingly. "But we do have a vice-presidency opening up in a month or two. Be a great opportunity for him."

He felt himself forced to say, "Well, I'd never stand in any man's way —"

"No, of course you wouldn't," Arnauth agreed. "I've always had the feeling that it's rather pointless. Men tend to find their own level. Or to put it in the common idiom, you can't keep a good man down." His smile was meaningless. "And I suppose that's a problem that's inherent in the very nature of a smaller business, isn't it — the difficulty of offering a really attractive future to an outstanding young man?"

Timing himself carefully, he asked, "Am I to take it that Joel has indicated to you that he's unhappy?"

"Oh no, not at all, no indeed," Arnauth said hurriedly. "And I'm sure he's not. He's a great admirer of yours, by the way. Said some things about you that I'd be very pleased to know that any of my boys had said about me."

"I'd not judge loyalty to be any problem at your place either," he said not intending it sharply, yet not displeased when he saw Arnauth blink as the thrust went home. "Well, I see they're starting to sit down. Shall we go over?"

He made the first move and Arnauth followed, pointedly dropping the subject of Joel Morris. His own mind could not, however, be so easily diverted . . . Joel was underpaid, no doubt about that . . . be a good idea to give him a raise . . . yes, and he should settle who was going to get what office when they moved to the second floor . . . the logical thing to do would be to give Joel the office right next to his . . . most of the things he'd want to get into himself would be on the sales side . . . but that would kill Swann . . .

Startled, he realized that he had missed a question that Arnauth had

444

asked and, embarrassed by the necessity of having to ask to have it repeated, he quickly imposed the discipline of complete concentration, excluding everything from his mind except Sidney Arnauth and Gellman Stores, wondering now why Arnauth was avoiding bringing up Wonderfood ... had the Gellman crowd decided that it wouldn't sell ... that it would be a flop ... ?

3

Maggie Lord had done her best to keep from becoming involved with Kira Zurich — Linc had made it plain enough that the open house was to be entirely a Haven Home affair — but Kira had started coming to her for advice early in the forenoon and sympathetic concern over her almost neurotic fear that something might go wrong had forced her into offering continual assurance that Kira could safely rely upon Brick's advance planning and the caterer that he had brought in from Philadelphia to handle the luncheon. To prove Brick's reliability, she had mentioned some of the big conventions and sales promotion meetings that he had staged so successfully in the past, calming Kira but calling up in her own mind the reservation that, in those days, she had been at Brick's side, helping him in a hundred ways, always taking over full responsibility for luncheons and dinners.

Now there was almost the feeling, hardly recognized and surely not admitted, that nothing but fantastically good luck could possibly account for the way that everything was going. Brick had taken a dozen long-shot gambles and all of them had paid off. Putting on a big luncheon in a tent during the first week in April had surely been tempting fate — a cold, rainy day would have wrecked everything — but the sun was bright, the air warm, and the general atmosphere that the tent created was admittedly right for the occasion, brightly informal and yet not detracting from the seriously scientific tone of the program. Brick's decision that the caterer could employ local waitresses had seemed a gamble, too, but all of them had turned out to be summertime employees of the Tern Beach hotels and the service had been amazingly fast, the food hot when it reached the tables. The menu gamble — barbecued beef — had been no less than an all-out success.

A few minutes ago the press books had been passed out and, all around her now she was hearing praise for the job that Brick had done on it, his name more often than not coupled with Dr. Thompson's — everyone seemed to know her as "Tommy" — and Maggie Lord sat back now with an odd sensation of anonymity, of being lost in the crowd. Because it was a feeling that could not be acknowledged, she transposed it to Linc's mind, wondering how he was reacting to the strange situation of being completely out of the spotlight. She knew that he had said it was what he wanted, that he had insisted upon not even being introduced . . . but had he really meant it?

There was a sudden burst of sound, a massive hammering that rattled the loud-speakers, quickly brought under control by whoever was monitoring the public address system. Looking toward the speakers table, she saw that Kira Zurich had risen and was rapping the lectern with a gavel. She was obviously nervous, her face so tensely drawn that speech seemed all but impossible, and for an instant it seemed that this was going to be one of those horrible moments when a speaker's voice froze. Words finally came, but they were dry-toned and too highly pitched, and Maggie Lord felt the panic that must be in Brick's mind . . . this was to be the climax of his whole program, everything dependent upon this closing impression . . . even a few minutes of this and an audience could be lost.

Kira's voice finally eased down into its normal register but she was still obviously reading and her monotone recital of Dr. Perrill's record and accomplishments was too dull to hold an audience. A buzz of inattentive whispering spread over the tent. Brick's script, if read by almost anyone else, would have accomplished its purpose of arousing a high pitch of interest in the scientist's appearance on the platform, but Kira was not only reading it in an inexpressive voice but there was a damning hint of insincerity, almost as if she were being forced to praise Dr. Perrill against her will.

Maggie Lord shuddered as Kira fumbled her last line, lost the point, and then transferred her discomfiture to Dr. Perrill by brusquely motioning him to his feet. Sympathetically, Maggie's eyes searched for Brick, catching sight of him at the back of the tent. Even in the orange light that filtered down through the canvas, his face was an ashen gray. There was, however, a look of intense anticipation that made her turn back toward the speakers table.

Perrill's bald head glowed like a polished skull, eerily lighted by the reading light on the lectern, his face seemingly unfleshed and incapable of expression. There was not the slightest hint of warmth or humor in his formally intoned, "Mrs. Zurich, ladies and gentlemen."

446

He paused, sorting his notes. Again, there was the frightening sound of a lost audience. Then, suddenly, his eyes lifted and he said solemnly, "In case Mrs. Zurich's introduction left you under any misapprehension, perhaps I should announce — unnecessary as it may be — that I am not a long-haired scientist."

For an instant, there was a dead hush, everywhere the question of whether he had meant it humorously. Then his eyes crinkled and the roar of laughter burst like a storm. Glancing back, she saw that Brick had not been taken by surprise. His elation was unmistakable. He looked like a man who, gambling his last penny, had hit the jackpot.

Dr. Perrill began to talk now, his voice low and vibrant, seemingly warmed by radiation from the audience. His tone was informal, yet somehow it carried great authority, an impression enhanced by the frankness with which he admitted that there were still shortcomings that had not been corrected. Kira, sitting beside him, glanced up anxiously as he admitted that many mothers would find the taste rather unappetizing, but Maggie Lord's instinct told her that nothing would so surely clinch the scientist's hold upon this audience as the impression of unwavering honesty. Even the last skeptics would be won over now, the last doubters convinced, and as that realization formed in her mind it became an admission that she herself was finally agreeing that Linc had probably been right in going ahead with the marketing of Wonderfood.

Thought-directed, her eyes searched him out. He was sitting at a long table on the other side of the tent, the Gellman group on his right, the G & G men on his left, but seemingly he had lost all consciousness of their presence. Like everyone else, he was transfixed by Dr. Perrill. In his case, however, there was a difference. His expression evidenced not surprise but confidence, as if he had never for a moment doubted the outcome, and Maggie Lord felt herself suddenly accused and instantly convicted of having done her husband a serious injustice in having given so much of the credit to luck. But if it hadn't been for Brick . . .

4

Lincoln Lord was beginning to feel nervous about Dr. Perrill's long stand behind the microphone. He had been there for almost an hour now, answering one question after another, and the danger was increasing that he might dissipate the extremely good impression that he had so obviously made. Perrill, too, seemed to be aware of it. Twice he had tried to shut off further questioning by saying that almost anything that anyone wanted to know could be found in the press books. But still the questions came.

Far back in the tent, someone rose to ask, "If it's true, Dr. Perrill, that enzymes are destroyed by heat, then why aren't the enzymes that you're using destroyed by the high temperature that you have to use to get sterilization during the canning process? I am right, am I not, that you are canning this food?"

"Yes, we're canning it," Perrill said. "And because of the heavy viscosity it's true that we do have to use high heat, and for a rather long time period in order to get adequate penetration. I might say in passing that we had considerable trouble with that problem during the early stages of our work over at the Coastal Foods Company."

This was the first time that the name of the Coastal Foods Company had been mentioned — he knew that Brick had warned Perrill against it — but this casual introduction of the company's name would serve as the perfect build-up for the announcement that Kira would soon be making and he was surprised to see her critical glance dart up to Perrill's face.

"Now as to the effect of that heat upon the enzymes —" Perrill continued. "Yes, enzymatic action is inhibited by heat sterilization. But here's the point — the principle involved is *not* the introduction of enzymes into the digestive tract. The enzymatic action takes place during the processing of the food rather than after it has been eaten. In other words, we're getting what you might call a kind of pre-digestion. We're releasing these nutrients and putting them into a directly consumable form prior to ingestion by the child. You might say that we're letting the processing kettles in the cannery do a part of the job that would otherwise have to be done by the digestive tract." He hesitated. "To get back to your point — here's what I'm trying to say — the high heat necessary for sterilization is applied *after* the enzymatic action has taken place. Thus, it's no handicap. Actually, it's a help, because by careful timing we can inhibit the activity of the enzymes at exactly the point where we want the action to stop."

A tweedy woman was already on her feet waiting with the next question. "Doctor, we've been hearing a great deal lately about the use of hormones as growth regulators. Is there anything like that in your formula?"

"Absolutely not," Perrill said. "We are using no hormones, no drugs, no chemical additives of any kind. This raises a point on which I want to be very explicit. What we have developed is in no sense a pharmaceutical preparation. Our research objective has not been a treatment for glandular malfunction, nor any other physical shortcoming that might affect a child's general growth pattern. This is simply a superior food for a normal child, that's all. Perhaps I can explain in this way — ordinary cooking increases the effective nutritive value of certain raw foodstuffs — all we've done, in effect, is to develop a better method of cooking. That's putting it a bit too simply but, nevertheless, I believe it makes the point."

A hand was already up for another question. Perrill nodded and the man asked, "Doctor, this is a question that I'm sure is on all of our minds — when is this food of yours going to be on the market? Have you made any arrangements with anyone to produce it and sell it?"

"Yes, we —" Perrill began, his voice cut off as Kira made a quick move to get to her feet. Flustered he said, "I'll let Mrs. Zurich answer that — so if there aren't any more questions — thank you."

There was sustained applause as he moved heavily away from the lectern, and then a further delay until the flashing lights of the photographers had died down. Kira was waiting at the microphone and, watching her, Lincoln Lord prayed that she would be perceptive enough to use that last paragraph immediately. Fortunately she did, and even though she read it word for word there was enough continuity with the question that had been asked to give it impact. The applause that broke had almost the quality of a mass cheer. There was no question now that all of the publicity would include an openhanded reference to the Coastal Foods Company, perhaps even a mention of the product name . . . this was the payoff!

Surprisingly, Kira made her first departure from the prepared script, leaning into the microphone as she said in a loudly amplified voice, "Mr. Lincoln Lord, the president of the Coastal Foods Company, is here with us today and I'd like to thank him for all the help that he has given us."

He sensed the demand for response, rising instinctively, yet catching a moment for consideration before he said, "All of us at Coastal Foods are very happy, indeed, to do anything that we can to further the great work that's being done here at Haven Home." He anticipated the applause before it came and cut himself off with a little wave, fanning the audience with his eyes as he sat down, at the last minute catching sight of Kip standing against the side wall of the tent. His son's face was unsmiling, set with deep concern, and for an instant he thought it disapproval, feeling a chill that took all the warmth out of the audience's reaction. To his relief, he then saw that Kip's raised hand held a note for him. Signaling him to stay where he was until Kira adjourned the meeting — she had only two short paragraphs to read now — he waited through the final round of applause before beckoning Kip to push through to him. Everyone was getting up now, hands clutching at his arms, but there was something about the expression on Kip's face that urged him to immediate action. He leaned far out, taking the note with his fingertips, and even as he was telling himself that his apprehension was surely as groundless as all of the other worries that had come to nothing, the words on the message blank struck home:

TO: *Mr. Lord*
FROM: *Switchboard*
There is a long distance call for you from Senator Trew's office in Washington, D. C. I told them you were in a meeting but they said it was very urgent and asked that you call back at once.

Sidney Arnauth was trying to talk to him but it was impossible to make sense out of what he was saying, all power of reason lost in the flood of madly mingled thoughts that writhed around the suddenly resurrected image of Senator Albert Trew's face, a ghost that he thought securely buried with all of his other rigidly suppressed recollections of the Chemical Service Corporation. Once, for a climactic hour, he had thought Senator Trew his great and good friend — that afternoon in his suite at the Carleton when he had called someone at the White House and received final assurance that he, Lincoln Lord, was to be named Chairman of the Far East Trade Mission . . . god, what a fool he'd been, never realizing that Trew was nothing but a cat's-paw for that gang of crooks who were setting things up to make their fast buck millions by liquidating Chemical Service . . . getting him out of the way by shipping him off to Japan . . . buying his appointment with a big contribution to Trew's campaign fund. One of those investigating committees had probably caught up with Trew . . . bribery of a White House official . . . a subpoena to testify. No one would ever believe that he'd known nothing about it, so stupid that he hadn't realized what was happening . . .

450

Mumbling a general promise that he would be back in a moment, he shouldered his way to Kip.

"Gosh, Dad, I didn't want to bother you —"

"No, you were right," he said, slipping out through the tent flap that Kip held open for him, committing himself to haste by adding, "This is very important," yet torn by the instinct to slow down the onrush of catastrophe.

Skirting the tent, leaving Kip behind, he strode across to the research center building and found a telephone in a deserted laboratory. He closed the door and stood for a moment, trying to think, his body wracked by a massive shudder that subsided only as his brain seemed finally drained of even the stored energy for an involuntary reflex. The telephone instrument was almost too heavy to lift, his words leaden as he said, "This is Mr. Lord. I understand you have a Washington call for me."

"Oh yes, Mr. Lord. I'll get it right away."

He let the receiver slide down to his shoulder . . . he should have known that all this was too good to last . . . yes, he *had* known . . . the way he'd felt all day . . . the premonition of disaster hanging over him. This was the way it had always happened . . . right at the peak, just when he'd thought everything was going so wonderfully . . . Mag . . . she'd be the one it would hit the hardest, so happy here in Goodhaven . . . oh god, why did it always have to end like this! But it always had, it always would . . . Otis Sellcox was right . . .

A voice exploded, so loud that he recognized it even before he lifted the receiver to his ear . . . Art Gerhart? There must be a mistake . . . the operator had given him another call . . .

"Sorry as hell to have to drag you out of your meeting," Gerhart said, interjecting a quick question about how everything was going, then roaring on without waiting for an answer. "Linc, how fast can you get down here to Washington? I know you've got that meeting, but can you slip off — no, I don't mean *can* you — damn it, boy, you've *got* to! As soon as they get a White House release, every reporter in town is going to be in on it. The committee hearings are starting in the morning and with the trade bill coming up —"

"Wait a minute, Art" . . . trade bill . . . White House . . . could it be that the committee report was finally being released . . . ?

"Didn't you see the *Times* this morning, Linc?"

"No, I've been so tied up —"

Gerhart's sharply expelled breath rattled in his ear. "Oh, then you

451

don't know, do you? Here, let me try to fill you in. You remember that time you got me squared away on the tuna situation — you told me about this report of your committee?"

"Yes, of course."

"Well, that's what I've concentrated on for the last month, Linc — making a damned nuisance of myself around here, trying to get that report blasted loose and out in the open where it could do some good. The Senator here's been with me all the way — wonderful support — but we had to get through to the White House. Well, he's pulled a real dilly — clever as hell — got somebody over there really steamed up about it and now it's tied in with the whole foreign aid program — you know, the old trade instead of aid idea? Well, at yesterday's press conference, there was a direct quote from your report — even mentioned your name. That's what made the *Times* this morning. That's why it's so — damn it, Linc, there's just too much of this to cover on the phone. How soon can you get down here?"

"I can't possibly make it today, Art," he said, even the effort of speech made difficult by the limp weakness that followed the collapse of terror. "We've got the Gellman crowd coming over to the house."

He could hear Gerhart repeating what he had said and then a distant senatorial voice demanding the privilege of speaking to him. "Mr. Lord, this is Albert Trew."

"Yes, Senator."

"Allow me to say first, Mr. Lord, how very greatly I admire the splendid job that you and your committee have done on this Japanese study. It's one of the finest things of its sort that I've seen in my fourteen years in the senate — fair, balanced, objective — exactly what we need to help us make some sense out of this foreign trade mess. We owe you a real debt, Mr. Lord, the whole country does."

"That's very nice to hear, Senator, but —"

Senator Trew was a practiced master of debate. "And surely, Mr. Lord, you'll somehow manage to give us enough of your time to help my committee frame a bill that will implement your recommendations. That's what we really want, Mr. Lord — why we need you so badly. Now how soon can you get down here?"

"I'm sorry, Senator, but I simply can't make it today."

"What about tomorrow? We're starting our hearings at ten o'clock. If you could be here then — I know this is short notice, Mr. Lord, but it's really vitally important. The only way the nation can possibly get full value out of your splendid work in Japan is to have you here in person. Can you make it by ten o'clock?"

"Yes, it might be possible."

"Can I count on that?"

"I'll be there."

"Here in my office," the senator decreed. "And let me say again, Mr. Lord, how grateful I am to you."

Gerhart came back on the line again. "Listen, Linc, I know I don't have to warn you about this — you've been through the mill before — but these newspaper reporters will probably be ten deep around here tomorrow. You'd better brace yourself." He chuckled. "And don't forget to bring that handsome mug of yours along. It's going to look awfully good on a lot of front pages in the next few days."

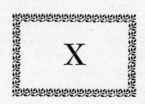

X

ARTHUR BELL WHITTAKER'S long service on the faculty of Chesapeake College had conditioned him against precipitate action. This morning, however, the restraining shell of academic behavior had been shattered. Fifty minutes ago, sitting down to breakfast, he had found Lincoln Lord's picture on the front page of the *Baltimore Sun*. Unmindful of the madly bubbling percolator — he passionately hated over-brewed coffee — he had read the two-column account of yesterday's testimony before the Trew Subcommittee. That alone would probably have been enough to stir him into unusual action. But there was more. On the editorial page he discovered a short but pungent paragraph commending Lincoln Lord for exemplary service to the nation.

With lesser provocation he would never have telephoned Jay Quincy at twenty minutes after eight, and less inured by righteous indignation, he would have been greatly embarrassed to find that Jay had apparently been awakened while still in bed. Under the circumstances, however, he felt no compunction about demanding an immediate audience, offering no explanation of what was on his mind other than the suggestion that Jay look at this morning's *Sun*. That alone should be enough to prove that there was no longer the slightest vestige of legitimacy in his ridiculous claim that the board of regents would look unfavorably upon Mr. Lord because he was, as Jay had so horribly misjudged him, "nothing but the president of a little Jewish cannery."

As the gates of Kingdom Come swung open, Dean Whittaker plunged ahead down the long cedar-bordered lane to the mansion house, the urgency of immediate action sustaining the force of in-

454

dignation. His original suggestion that he be made provost had been only a tentative proposal, plainly made conditional upon Lincoln Lord's acceptance of the presidency. Nevertheless, it had been evident at the last meeting of the board of regents that either Jay Quincy or Judge Crockett had violated his confidence, and that everyone was already thinking of him as no more than the new provost. Unless Lincoln Lord came to Chesapeake, he was a trapped man, forced to relinquish the presidency without gain — and, from what he had read in the paper, Mr. Lord was already being considered for a high post in either the International Cooperation Administration or the State Department. There was no indication, however, that he had accepted. If someone drove to Washington right away . . . this morning . . .

The strength of a desperate resolve was in his hands as he thumped the lion-headed door knocker . . . Jay would probably vacillate, say that they'd have to wait for the next board meeting . . . but they dared not wait! Even an hour might be too long. It would be easy enough to canvass the regents by telephone . . . yes, that's what he had to force Jay to do!

The maid admitted him and escorted him back to the library. To his astonishment, he discovered that Jay Quincy was not alone. Judge Crockett was seated across the desk from him, the telephone instrument in his hand, and as Dean Whittaker stepped into the room he heard the chairman of the board of regents say, "No, there's no doubt about Lord being the man we want — and the point, Mr. Phelps, is that if we don't move fast, somebody's going to snatch him right out from under our nose."

2

Now at last there was silence along the committee table and Lincoln Lord started to rise from the witness chair.

Senator Trew lifted his hand in a restraining gesture. "Mr. Lord, since you've already given us so much of your time, may I presume upon your generosity to ask for one more minute — and I ask it, sir, in order that I may express to you not only the thanks of this committee but also my personal admiration. If my notes are correct, you have been in that chair for a total of more than five hours — almost three hours yesterday afternoon and well over two hours this morning. Quite frankly, Mr. Lord, I have been amazed by your extraordinary grasp of this whole foreign trade situation. Never has anyone appeared before any committee of which I have been a member and conducted himself more admirably. I only wish that more of our American business leaders had the breadth of your viewpoint, and the temperate and balanced judgment that you have displayed throughout these long hours of questioning. You have earned, sir, our admiration and gratitude. We owe you a genuine debt for the contribution you have made to our understanding of these complex and difficult problems."

Lincoln Lord attempted a response that would give recognition to the other members of his committee, but the chairman's gavel thumped down and his brusque announcement of an adjournment for lunch triggered a convulsive crowd movement. Nevertheless, there was a substantial spatter of applause and, as Lincoln Lord looked out over the crowded room, he saw a dozen or more men pushing their way toward him. The first to reach his side was Art Gerhart, a heavy hand extended. "Put her there, boy! Say, that really hit the nail on the head."

"Hope I didn't cross you up with what I had to say about the tuna situation," he whispered, less concerned than he would have been if the food broker had not so baldly claimed credit for having used his influence to exhume the Lord Committee report and have him called as a witness.

"Cross us up? Not for a minute! What you said was right down our alley. This is all we've ever wanted, Linc — just the truth, nothing more, just the truth."

There were other hands to shake, more congratulations to acknowledge, flash bulbs blinking, a knot of reporters blocking his progress toward the door.

"Mr. Lord, I'm Mart Seigel of the *Tribune*."

"Yes, Mr. Seigel?"

"We've picked up a rumor, sir, that you're on your way to the White House. True?"

"Untrue." He smiled. "I'm on my way to my home in Goodhaven, New Jersey."

"But you have been offered an appointment to ICA?"

"No."

"How about the State Department?" another reporter asked.

"No, gentlemen, I've been offered no government post of any kind."

A third reporter pressed through to his side and, identifying himself, asked, "Mr. Lord, my paper carried a story yesterday about some terrific new baby food, and unless I'm mistaken the name of the company that's selling it —"

"Yes, it's my company," he broke in, reaction speeded by the suddenly self-censoring realization of how long it had been since any thought of the Coastal Foods Company had crossed his mind. Almost as retribution, he quickly added, speaking to the whole group, "As far as my personal plans are concerned, perhaps this will answer all of your questions. I am, as you know, the president of the Coastal Foods Company. That's a big enough job to keep me fully occupied. We're just starting an expansion program that demands every bit of attention and energy that I can possibly give it. Beyond that, I have no plans, none whatsoever."

"Then you have no intention of going into governmental service?" the first reporter asked.

"No indeed."

"That's definite?"

He smiled. "Yes, that's definite."

"Thank you, Mr. Lord," they chorused.

"Not at all."

And then, suddenly, he was looking into a face that seemed, for an indecisive instant, a porthole to the past . . . but, no, it couldn't be . . . Adam Quincy had been dead for years . . .

Recognition came with a rush, supported by the belated realization that Jay Quincy's face had, over the years since he had last seen him, aged and weathered into a remarkably accurate replica of his father's, a likeness shattered only when Jay spoke, his voice thin and reedy as he said, "Linc, it's good to see you again."

"Jay! By golly, this is a surprise! Don't tell me you've been here all morning? With those confounded lights in my eyes —"

"No, we just got here a few minutes ago. Drove over from Brighton this morning — the three of us —"

As Jay Quincy's backward glance suggested, he looked toward the door, catching sight of Dean Whittaker first, positive recognition of the other man delayed until Jay's whisper identified him as Amos Crockett, chairman of the board of regents of Chesapeake College.

"I know we should have called you for an appointment," Jay apologized. "But we couldn't reach you this morning, so we took a chance and came over, just hoping that we might be lucky enough to get to talk to you for a few minutes. I suppose you're tied up for lunch?"

There was something about Jay Quincy's expression, even more positively evident in the pleading anxiety of Dean Whittaker's fixed stare, that made him feel that this was something far more than another attempt to get him to make a fund-raising speech. "Golly, Jay, I had planned to get on the road right away — but I do have to pick up a bite somewhere —"

"Wonderful!" Jay exulted, directing a beckoning gesture at Whittaker and Crockett, who were still waiting just inside the doorway. Both responded instantly, beaming with gratitude, walking quickly toward him, yet he sensed an odd deference that, although only intuitively recognized, warned him that whatever it was that they were about to propose would precipitate a crisis of decision.

3

Maggie Lord was eating her lunch from a tray, grateful to Viola for having suggested the terrace. Bright with sun and sheltered from the wind, there was a summertime warmth in the air, daffodils dancing along the flagstone border, a pair of bold robins searching the lawn and coming closer and closer to her feet with each darting foray. She had spent the morning with Gus, the company gardener, planning the flower beds along the drive, knowing that it was a waste of time — Gus would plant them his own way in the end — yet welcoming the chance that it gave her to divert her mind from more pointless speculation about what was happening this morning in Washington. At ten, and again at eleven, she had come inside to hear the radio news broadcasts, learning nothing new. A plane had crashed somewhere in Nevada and the rest of the news had been briefly brushed, no word of Linc, not even a mention of the Trew Subcommittee hearing.

He had told her when he had telephoned last night that, although he had been asked to stay over and take the stand again this morning, he should be on his way back to Goodhaven no later than noon. Now, hearing a car coming up the drive, her heart leaped to the thought that he might already be home. Almost instantly, however, reason denied that possibility — the committee had not been scheduled to meet until ten — and then, closer now, the sound identified itself as the barking exhaust of Kip's car. But that, too, was a challenge to reason. Although the high school was less than five minutes away, Kip always ate at the cafeteria, never coming home at noon.

The door to the living room stood open and she called when she heard her son come in the house. "I'm out here on the terrace, Kip."

But he came as if unbidden, a packet of rolled newspapers in his hand, and the way he thrust them toward her made her remember a bashful neighbor boy who, long ago back in Millburgh, had brought her a crushed bouquet of field flowers.

"I thought maybe you'd want 'em," Kip said. "You know — the stuff about Dad."

"Oh, Kip, how nice of you!" she exclaimed, greatly pleased, actually less by his thoughtfulness than by the hope that this was evidence of a newly found pride in his father. "What did you do, drive into town for them?"

"Sure," he said, shrugging. "Only they didn't have any more left — the *New York Times*, I mean — so I got — well, the principal had one and he said you could have it."

"Oh, do thank him for me, Kip. And thank you for being so thoughtful!"

"Yeah, well —" He bent down, the conquering of self-consciousness, and opened the *Times* to what she saw was almost a page-long transcript of yesterday's testimony, barely glimpsed before Kip, opening another paper, found the editorial page and pointed to a long paragraph from which *Lincoln Lord* leaped out from the gray type. Her eyes snatched at words, fastening on a phrase here and there, enough to make her certain of the editorial's favorable tone.

"Kip, have you read this?"

He nodded. "I guess it's pretty good, huh?"

"It's wonderful," she said eagerly, trying to draw a smile to his face. "Aren't you proud of your father?"

"Sure," he said flatly. "How come he knows so much about all this stuff — foreign trade and all that?"

"But, Kip, he was chairman of the committee," she said, knowing that it was not an answer, adding, "and he was in Japan for over a month, studying the situation there."

"Sure," he said doubtfully.

"And most of the men on the committee were specialists in the area — Dr. Solbeck and Louis Gerslau — the men from State and Commerce —"

"Sure," he said again, but now with an entirely different connotation. "Then I guess it's so, huh?"

"What's so, Kip?"

He flipped pages, quickly finding a columnist's paragraph, the near margin of the page thumb-marked by much handling.

The buzz around the capital cocktail circuit tonight has Lincoln Lord all set for that empty big desk at ICA. The handsome Mr. Lord had them eating out of his hands on both sides of the aisle in today's Trew Committee hearings, and with nobody but nobody needing a Congresscharmer more than ICA does these days, it's a better than even bet that the chit-chatters are right.

The pretense of slow reading gave her an extra moment, less time than she needed to stem the surge of fear that raced her heart, yet long enough to achieve the self-control that allowed her to say, "Oh, I don't think there's anything to this, Kip."

"I guess you'd know if there was, wouldn't you?"

She hesitated, remembering all the times in the past when she had not known, but the danger of losing Kip's confidence was too great to permit disagreement. "If it were true, don't you think your father would have said something about it when he called me last night?"

Kip shuffled his feet, kicking out at a chair leg. "Anyway, even if you are going to move to Washington, I guess maybe I could still stay here — you know, over at Haven Home?"

She laughed at him. "I don't think I'd start packing yet, Kip."

"I guess not," he said. "But I just got thinking about what if it was true. They've got plenty of room over there and — well, lots of nights, you know, I could be helping Dr. Perrill."

"Let's wait until your father gets home, shall we?" she said, her smile difficult to maintain, her basic concern overlaid now with this new evidence that Kip, instead of losing interest in Haven Home as she had confidently expected he would, was making it more and more the center of his life, Dr. Perrill far more his hero than even Brick had ever been. "Kip, you've not had your lunch, have you? Viola can make —"

"Sure, I had something," he said, backing into the living room, gone so quickly that he was out of the front door before she could thank him again for having brought the papers.

When she finally lifted her cup, the tea was cold, strangely colder than the air, and she put it down after the first sip, unconcerned, giving her total attention to the transcript of Lincoln Lord's testimony in the *Times*. She read rapidly at first, translating words into sounds, hearing his voice. Before she was halfway down the first column, however, she was reading as a proofreader, matching the printed word against the committee report that she had typed and retyped so many times that every sentence was engraved on her memory. The farther she read, the plainer it became that everything he had said on the witness stand yesterday was lifted directly from the report, so perfectly duplicated that it seemed he must have been reading, yet the news report said that he had appeared before the committee without even a note before him. She was not truly surprised — it had happened before — yet she could not help but be impressed anew. Months had passed since the report had been finished and Linc had not seen it since — except for a brief fanning of the pages night before last after the party had broken up — and because he had driven to Washington, there had been no chance to reread it on the way down.

But what surprised her most — and the more so the longer she thought about it — was that the Lord Committee report had apparently been without meaning to the dozens of men who must have read it before, significance achieved only when those same words had been heard from Linc's lips. Until then, it had been a hundred and eighty-three pages of typing buried in a file. Now it was front-page news all over the country, and the pictures were not of Dr. Solbeck who had planned the committee program out of his lifetime study of Japanese economics, nor of Louis Gerslau who had distilled the evident truth from such an incredible mass of statistics, nor even of that wild-haired little man from Columbia, whatever his name had been, who had originally conceived the trade balance concept...no, there was only one picture...Lincoln Lord...

> Lincoln Lord's proposals are a wholesome example of the application of common sense and business sense to a problem too often before approached only through an academic haze or a political smoke screen. Mr. Lord's clear-headed thinking has substantially clarified the problem surrounding future Japanese-American relationships. We would welcome a broader application of the same approach to the whole international scene.

Fear was no longer manageable, no longer an emotion that could be shut away. In the darkness of delay it had grown to an overpowering force, impelling her trembling hand to reach out for the thumb-marked page...*that empty big desk at ICA....*

461

4

Lincoln Lord burrowed the point of his chin into the hard mass of his double-clenched fists, staring into his coffee cup, only half listening as Judge Crockett stubbornly reiterated all the arguments why he, Lincoln Lord, should accept the presidency of Chesapeake College. He had listened for almost an hour now, first to Jay Quincy, then to Dean Whittaker, so stunned when Crockett had finally made their offer that he had sat since without response, trying to hear his own mind over the sound of their voices as, over and over again, the three of them had massed their arguments against his refusal.

He had sensed in the Senate hearing room that they were about to make him some sort of proposal, guessing as they had driven downtown for lunch that it would be the offer of an honorary degree in exchange for a commencement speech, shifting to the likelier possibility of membership on the board of regents after Jay had dropped a hint on the way into the hotel dining room, never suspecting the truth until it had suddenly burst upon him. The only steppingstone to credibility was the memory that once, months ago, he had wondered if there might possibly be a chance for him to take over direction of the college's endowment program and fund-raising activities. But that had been only one of those wild dreams that had plagued him during those last days before Coastal Foods had finally rescued him from more desperate imaginings. Never, not once, had the possibility even brushed his mind that he might ever be offered the presidency of Chesapeake College.

"Mr. Lord, I don't know what more we can say," Crockett said, the tone of conclusion a warning that he was about to press for a decision. "We appreciate the fact that you undoubtedly have other committments. As I said a moment ago, however, your actual installation in office could be delayed, if necessary, until the beginning of the fall term in September. That would give you time enough to —"

He lifted his head, and the board chairman, taking it as a signal of response, immediately cut off his own voice. Silence hung over the table, insistently demanding. He relaxed his doubled fists, letting his hands fall away in a gesture of hopelessness. "Gentlemen, I don't know what to say. There just aren't any words to express how honored — how grateful I am to you for even thinking of me. In all frankness, it's hard to believe that I'm the man the board really wants."

Crockett said, "It was unanimous, not a single dissenting vote."

He took a deep breath. "If this were three months ago, my decision would be an easy one. I was free then. But now —" He saw Dean Whittaker glance accusingly at Jay.

But it was Crockett who stepped in to block immediate rejection. "Don't give us your answer now, Mr. Lord. We're not asking that. All that we want you to tell us today is that you're willing to consider it. A quick decision would be unfair to us — and if I may say so, Mr. Lord, unfair to yourself. It would be most unfortunate for everyone concerned if some temporary and transient situation were permitted to stand in the way of your acceptance. So often, you know, an obstacle that seems insurmountable at the moment can be worked out with a little time and patience. Do tell us, Mr. Lord, that you'll at least consider it. Take a week and think it over."

He wavered between immediate rejection and the easier course of writing a letter in a few days, quickly deciding that it would be unfair of him to waste the time that they'd need to find another president. "Unfortunately, gentlemen, I'm afraid that a week won't alter the situation."

"How long would you need?" Crockett demanded, misinterpreting his meaning. "Suppose we were to give you a month?"

"Oh, that would be far more time than I'd have any right to ask," he protested. "After all, you do have the problem of finding a president."

"Our problem isn't getting *a* president," Crockett countered. "It's getting the *right* president. Yes, if you'd turn us down in the end, we'd lose a month — quite true. But if your decision were favorable, we'd have you as the president of Chesapeake for — well, how long would it be? You're not fifty yet, are you? At least fifteen years until you reach retirement age. We'd be gambling a month against fifteen years. At those odds, it's a chance that I'm sure we'd all be willing to take."

Jay responded to the chairman's glance, quickly smiling. "That's better than a hundred to one. I'll take those odds on almost anything."

"Yes indeed," Dean Whittaker said in turn. "And I've just been thinking, Mr. Lord — if your acceptance is at all contingent upon your relationship with me — as Judge Crockett explained, we have been contemplating a division of responsibility in which I, as provost, would be in charge of the academic side. However, if you feel that your authority would be too limited under such an arrangement, I'd be quite willing to stay on as dean."

"No, no," he protested. "Any contribution I might be able to make would surely be on the general administrative side, anyway. But thank you, Dean. That was a fine and generous thing for you to suggest."

"We do need you," Whittaker said earnestly. "We need you very badly, Mr. Lord, very badly, indeed."

Crockett asked, "Shall we leave it that way then — a month — a month from today?"

"Well —"

"Splendid!" the chairman exclaimed, snatching agreement out of the air.

They got up from the table then, Crockett seeming to feel as if any further delay might hazard a victory already won, moving ahead to the checkroom with a hurrying hand on Dean Whittaker's arm. Jay held back, obviously with purpose, saying as the other two moved beyond the range of his low voice, "Linc, I haven't said much — had to let old Crock carry the ball — but this is a dream I've had for years, ever since you left — getting you back to Brighton. I've always felt that — well, if things had been in my hands, Linc, you'd never have left. I'd have found some way to keep you there. Still, maybe this is better, the way things have worked out. And it is where you belong, Linc — up at the college. Chesapeake's always meant a lot to you, and you've no idea how much it would mean to Chesapeake to have you there. As for myself — damn it, I've missed you, Linc, more than you'll ever know. I think about those old days a lot — you and I and Brick. And Maggie, too, of course."

"So do I," he responded, validity supplied by the memory of how many times a parallel with the old Quincy Canning Company had asserted itself during his first few weeks at Coastal Foods.

"Why don't you do this, Linc — come down for a day or two? You haven't been back since — well, you haven't seen the place since all the new buildings have been put up. It's a beautiful campus now, Linc."

"I know."

"You ought to see it, Linc. You owe it that much consideration. What would you say to next week end? Come down and stay with me at Kingdom Come. It wouldn't have to be an official visit to the college. No one would even have to know that you were there. And it would mean a lot to me, Linc. Be like old times again, having you there — and Maggie, too, of course."

"Let me see what I can work out," he said, the only possible escape. "I am pretty badly jammed up."

"But you'll have a whole week to clear your desk," Jay Quincy protested. "And after all — Linc, I know you've got this cannery on your hands and you have to get it operating — but that's a temporary situation. And I know you too well to believe that you're going to go on in business for another fifteen years. Why should you? What do you have to look forward to? What can you do that you haven't done already? But if you took over Chesapeake College — Linc, promise me you'll come down for the week end."

"I'll have to let you know, Jay," he said, using Crockett and Whittaker's long wait as an excuse to move toward the exit.

But as they parted in the lobby, Jay whispered insistently, "You will let me know?"

"Yes, I'll call you," he promised, wishing that he hadn't as he went up to his room to finish packing his bag. Then he remembered another promise and put in a call for Goodhaven.

Maggie answered at the first ring, her voice eagerly impatient as she said, "Yes, yes," to the operator's demand that she agree to accept the reversed toll charges. "Oh, Linc, where are you?"

Her disappointment was sharp when he told her that he was still in Washington. "But you will be home for dinner, won't you?"

"I'm leaving right now." He looked at his watch. "I ought to be there by six — six-thirty — depends on how bad the traffic is. Sorry I got held up but there wasn't much I could do about it."

"Have you been testifying all this time?"

"No, I got off about noon. But I had to stay over for lunch. Saw an old friend of yours."

"Of mine?"

"Jay."

"Jay?"

"Jay Quincy."

He was ready to tell her what had happened but her flat, "Oh, really," failed to give him the opening he expected, and then she changed the subject, excitement in her voice again as she asked, "You've seen the morning papers, haven't you? Oh, Linc, aren't they wonderful? I'm awfully proud of you, dear."

"They've given it quite a play, haven't they?" he said. "But it's over now. Back to work again. Heard anything from the plant?"

"They've been calling all day, trying to find out when you were getting back. You don't want me to tell them, do you?"

"Who called?"

465

"Oh, everyone. Joel just called again a few minutes ago, wanting to know if I'd heard anything from you yet. He's terribly anxious to talk to you — something about Gellman Stores."

"Maybe I'd better give him a ring," he said doubtfully, finding it difficult to bring his mind into focus . . . Gellman Stores . . .

"But you won't stop at the office will you, Linc?"

"No, I'll come right home," he promised. "I'm too whipped down to get into that tonight."

"I should think you would be. But you are all right, aren't you?"

"Sure, I'm fine."

"I'll have a drink waiting for you."

"I'll need it. And don't worry about hurrying dinner."

"All right." Her little laugh cut off. "Oh, Linc, if Kip should be here — well, you ought to know before you see him —"

Something in her voice alarmed him. "What's wrong, Mag?"

"Oh, there's nothing wrong. It's just that — well, he saw something in one of the papers about your taking a job in Washington — the State Department or something — and he was terribly upset about the idea that he might have to leave Goodhaven."

For an instant he found his voice oddly blocked. But a little laugh broke through, clearing the way, and he said, "Well, you can tell him we're not moving to Washington."

"I did," she said, the lightness back in her voice again. "I thought you ought to know before you see him, that's all."

He murmured agreement. "I'd better get rolling."

"Good-by, dear," she said. "And I'll be waiting for you. I'm terribly anxious to hear all about it."

"Well, there's a lot to tell you," he said, wondering after he'd hung up if he had let an overtone slip into his voice that betrayed just how much he did have to tell her.

With his hand still on the telephone instrument, he debated placing a call for his office, attempting anticipation, trying to imagine what had gone wrong at Gellman Stores, again conscious of how difficult he was finding it to concentrate. He tried to tell himself that it was only fatigue, no more than the let-down that always came when he'd been too keyed up . . . one thing on top of another, no break, the Haven Home open house and then Washington . . . and now this Chesapeake College thing . . .

Reason failed to bridge the gap of the last two days. Coastal Foods still seemed a once-known world that had slipped away from him, blue-fogged and distant, something vaguely recalled from a forgotten dream. Suddenly, startlingly, he realized that he hadn't even searched the newspapers to see what, if anything, they had carried on Haven Home and Dr. Perrill. All he had seen had been the stories on the hearings . . . *himself* . . .

Conscience struck hard and, almost as a physical reflex, his hand lifted the telephone instrument. But the force of impulse faded away rapidly and, waiting for the hotel operator to answer, the voice he heard was Jay Quincy's . . . "Another fifteen years . . . why should you . . . what do you have to look forward to . . . what can you do that you haven't done already? But if you took over Chesapeake College . . ."

"Order, please."

His lips parted but for an instant he was speechless . . . *oh, why hadn't this happened three months ago . . . if Whittaker had only talked to him that day in New York* . . .

"Order, please," the voice repeated, more insistently now.

He took a deep breath, steadied himself, and then said, "I'm sorry," quickly replacing the telephone instrument in its cradle.

5

After twenty-one years of marriage, Maggie Lord felt herself capable of anticipating her husband's reaction to almost any circumstance. Tonight, however, she found herself disconcertingly wrong. She had expected him to be high-keyed and effervescent, super-charged with nervous tension, her problem that of easing him down from the emotional peak to which he had been raised by the Washington hearings and the brilliant glare of nationwide publicity. She could not, it seemed, have been more wrong. He had come in as if bone-tired and heavily depressed, dropping his briefcase and slumping into the first chair; and yet there was something intuitively sensed that made her suspect that this was no simple case of fatigue, suspicion raised close to certainty when she saw him drink his highball, not meditatively sipping it as if he were truly weary but gulping it as if he were quenching the thirst of fever. It was then that she had decided that today must not have gone as well as yesterday, that something had surely gone wrong. But her cautious probings found no tender spots. Finally, when her concern became too obvious, he told her with an air of irritated finality what the chairman had said at the end of this morning's hearing.

She made him another highball, her own first drink little more than tasted, wondering now if there might, after all, be something to the story of his having been offered a government job, recalling that he had not actually denied the offer, only that he was not moving to Washington . . . could it be that this strange mood was the depression of regret?

She felt herself forced to find out, yet alerted to the need for a cautious approach. "Kip's not coming home to dinner," she said, adding when she saw that Linc hadn't even looked up, "He's over at the plant."

"Plant?" His eyes raised, the first show of interest in anything she had said. "What's he doing there?"

"He called up about an hour ago — something about Dr. Perrill coming over to check some change in the way they're processing Wonderfood. I wanted Kip to be here for dinner, but he was so excited about being asked to help —" She paused, searching for direction, a seemingly pointless quest.

His eyes had dropped and she was wondering if his depressed mood might be the result of something he had heard when he had called the office in Washington, when he suddenly asked, "What was that you said about Kip being afraid that I was taking a job in the State Department?" The question was so unexpected that she didn't realize for a moment that it gave her the opening she wanted.

Eagerly she capitalized on it. "Oh, he'd seen this thing in the paper about your being offered something down there. But I told him what you said — that there wasn't anything to it." The faint question mark that she traced with her voice was not uncalculated.

"If I were looking for a change it wouldn't be that — not Washington." And now it was his voice that left a suspended question mark when he asked, "I told you that I saw Jay, didn't I?" and she guessed that he had adopted her strategy of the circuitous approach.

"Yes, you told me," she said, forced to follow his lead. "How is he?"

"All right," he said, his tone perceptibly brighter. "Funny thing — when I first caught sight of him, all I could see was his father. I never used to think of them as looking alike —"

He stopped unexpectedly, catching her in the act of resolutely block-

468

ing her mind to the memory of their years at Kingdom Come, a pause unavoidable before she could say, "Neither did I."

"He sent you his best."

"What did you do — just run into him?"

He looked at her as if surprised by her obtuseness. "No, they came over to Washington to see me — Jay and Dean Whittaker and Judge Crockett."

"To see you?" she said, so innocent a repetition that she was completely unprepared for shock, and when it struck she was unable to believe that he had actually said what she thought she had heard him say.

Unknowingly, she must have asked for confirmation, because now he said, "Yes, the presidency." And then startlingly, he smiled, "I don't blame you for being surprised. I was, too. When they asked me to go out to lunch with them — I knew they had something in mind, but I never for a minute imagined that they were going to offer me the presidency of Chesapeake College."

Staggered, she groped for belief, finding nothing more substantial than the memory that, always before, taking a new job had meant that he was running away . . . or was there something wrong at Coastal Foods? No, there couldn't be . . . Joel had said that the orders were pouring in . . .

Her mind cleared . . . there'd been offers before that he hadn't taken, dozens of them over the years . . . "What in the world did you say to them?"

"I didn't know what to say. I was so flabbergasted that about all I could think of was —" He exhaled sharply. "All I could say was that I wished they'd come to me three or four months ago."

His regret was alarmingly evident. "You did turn it down?"

"What else can I do?" he asked, pointedly changing tenses.

"You didn't tell them?"

"I tried to. But they insisted on my taking a month to think it over." Dangerously, she asked, "Would you have taken it — I mean if they'd come to you before?"

He looked at her as if unable to believe that her question was really serious. "Do you mean if I'd had a choice — Coastal Foods or Chesapeake College?"

"You'd have taken the college?"

"Wouldn't you? Golly, Mag, when you think of —" He slumped,

469

recovering with a wan smile. "Do you remember that morning when Dean Whittaker called me in New York, the morning after that talk I made to the alumni meeting?"

"When he asked you to make some more speeches?"

"That was just that fool Potter. Apparently he flubbed it — either that or Whittaker did. Anyway, putting two and two together and counting back — when Crockett was explaining why the thing had dragged on so long, he mentioned talking to Whittaker about me the day after he got back from New York." He shook his head ruefully. "If they'd only told me then. Or if I'd been smart enough to guess what was in the wind."

"I suppose Dean Whittaker was still hoping that he was going to get it."

He shook his head. "No, all he wants is to be provost. His attitude is wonderful. Perfect. He'd take over the academic side — curriculum, courses of study, all of that. Suits him perfectly. And from the president's standpoint, it would be ideal — free his hands and give him a chance to really concentrate on the over-all job. It's a good plan, Mag — if you've got the right president, of course. That's going to be the rub — finding the kind of man they need. And they know it. That's why they've made it so hard to turn down."

"I'm sorry, Linc," she said, hoping that sympathy would be an antidote for his disappointment. "But it must make you feel good to know that they wanted you."

He seemed not to have heard. "They're really all out to get me, no doubt about that. They offered me everything in the book. Even agreed to stall off my taking office until September — if I needed that much time to get squared away here."

Fear cut in, slashing away at his claim that he had already made up his mind to turn it down. She saw no alternative to asking bluntly, "Linc, are you still considering it?"

"How can I?" he demanded. "If I hadn't gotten in so deeply here — this new line and everything. Or if there was only someone who was strong enough to carry on. And I don't know, maybe he could. I'd have everything pretty well set and rolling here by September. If he had Joel to back him up —"

Desperate, she broke in, "But, Linc, you said just the other night that he was still trying to treat Joel as if —"

"Good grief, Mag, I don't mean Swann. Of course not. Frank Kennan's the only possibility."

"Would he want it?" she asked, remembering what Linc had once told her about Kennan's complete lack of interest in general management.

"Frank's changed in the last couple of months," he said in a thinking-out-loud tone. "He's a lot bigger man than he was. If there were the right kind of an organizational setup — Joel in there to back him up as his vice-president in charge of sales — yes, that's a move I ought to make — get Joel up there on the same level. That would be the first step — make them all vice-presidents. Then it would be easier to make the next move."

As frightened as she was of what the answer would be, it was impossible not to ask, "You have changed your mind, haven't you, Linc?"

"About what?"

"I thought you were happy here."

He scowled, demanding, "What do you mean by that? Of course, I'm happy here. Why shouldn't I be? Everything's fine. For a small company, it's as good as you can find." He stood abruptly. "Look, I feel as grubby as the dickens. I'm going to grab a quick shower. Viola can hold dinner, can't she?"

By the time she could bring herself to answer, no answer was necessary. He had turned away from her and was striding off toward the bedroom. Subconsciously directed, her eyes darted around the room, her hands digging into the upholstery of the chair as if she felt herself being bodily torn from this haven of shelter.

"Oh —" Linc had stopped at the turn of the hall. "I forgot to tell you — Jay's invited us down for next week end. But there's no need to decide now. We can talk about it later."

Her hands fell away into emptiness . . . there'd be no need to talk about it later . . . Linc had already decided . . .

471

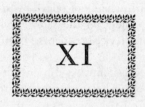

XI

Lincoln Lord's promise to himself that he would put Chesapeake College completely out of his mind was proving a pledge easier to keep this morning than it had been during the long hours of a largely sleepless night. Arriving at the cannery a few minutes before nine, he was almost immediately confronted with a situation that demanded total concentration on the affairs of the Coastal Foods Company.

Heavy rain was whipping in from the sea and he had driven into the shelter of the warehouse instead of parking in the open lot. Walking through the cannery on his way to the office, he saw a vacuum kettle uprooted from its foundation and, nearby, Mike Schlager and a crew of men were working on the stainless steel piping of another piece of production equipment. Kip had told him at the breakfast table that Dr. Perrill had been checking some changes in the processing of Wonderfood, but Kip had been vague and uncertain as to why it was being done and now, seeing what was happening, he guessed that some trouble had been encountered. Searching out Frank Kennan, he found him with Joel Morris and quickly discovered that the changes were not being made to correct a production difficulty but as a way of speeding up production of Wonderfood. That was his first hint of the crisis that had developed over the last twenty-four hours.

Day before yesterday, the morning after the Haven Home open house, Joel had driven to Manhattan for a G & G sales meeting and had made a presentation to the New York metropolitan sales force on Wonderfood and the new line of Haven Home Foods. The salesmen had gone out that afternoon, so Joel said, and with no more to back them up than clippings of the stories that had appeared that morning in the New York newspapers, had made a surprisingly successful start on getting distribution. Yesterday's sales had raised surprise to the level of astonishment. Today the G & G branch offices would swing into action. On Monday morning all of the affiliated food brokers would be turned loose. A simple projection of the New York metropolitan area sales over the rest of the Eastern seaboard was all that was needed to prove that the available supply of Wonderfood would come nowhere near satisfying the initial demand.

"And the real publicity hasn't even started yet," Joel said. "If *Newsweek* and *Time* break their stories next week — and if *Life* comes out with a picture spread — we're really in trouble."

"Well, if you have to have trouble, Joel, this is the kind to have," he said with the laughter of relieved tension. "No one ever went broke from being oversold."

"I know, sir, but how are we going to take care of Gellman Stores? That's the problem. I don't know whether you talked to Mr. Arnauth about Wonderfood when he was down here — ?"

"Only in a casual way," he said, searching his memory, finding that anything that had happened after the telephone call from Washington was hazy and indefinite. "I gathered that they weren't particularly interested."

"I didn't think so either," Joel said. "I mean when they left here on Tuesday — or even when I stopped in on Wednesday after the G & G meeting. But that night Sam Mandell called me at home — almost ten-thirty — and said they'd just decided to go ahead with a big promotion on Wonderfood and wanted to place an order for two thousand cases."

"Two thousand cases!" he turned to Kennan. "How much do you have in stock?"

"That would just about clean us out," Kennan said. "Take us right down to the bottom of the barrel. The orders are coming in faster now than we can turn the stuff out. If we take this Gellman deal we'll have to back order on G & G."

"We can't do that," he said decisively. "After all, the whole point in bringing out Wonderfood is to use it as a wedge to get distribution for the Haven Home line."

"I know that, sir," Joel said.

"If we sell a case of Wonderfood to Gellman, that's all it amounts to — one case — but if G & G sells it as a part of the Haven Home deal, we get six cases of other stuff to go along with it."

"But Gellman has an argument, too," Joel said quickly. "And it's a little hard to answer."

"What's that?"

"They say that for every six cases we'll be getting from someone else, they're already giving us a hundred cases of exactly the same stuff — except for the label, of course. And it's true. They are."

Lincoln Lord hesitated, beginning now to sense the outline of crisis. "You didn't agree to do it, did you?"

"No, of course not," Joel said hurriedly. "But I didn't think I ought to give them a flat turn-down either. I told them I'd check with you. I did promise that we'd give them a decision before eleven this morning. That's the deadline on their big ads for next week."

"They're planning to advertise it?"

Joel nodded. "They've got the layouts all made. I saw them yesterday. It's their regular Thursday double truck, the one they run in all of the cities where they have stores. There's a big banner on Wonderfood right across the top of both pages." He paused. "That's an awful lot of space, Mr. Lord, and they're willing to do it all on their own. They're not even asking us for an advertising allowance."

"From what you've said about the way orders are coming in, it doesn't look like we're going to need much advertising," he argued, less a statement of conviction than a device to test Joel's reasoning.

"That's true, sir, but we've still got the job of getting the public to come in and buy. No matter how much publicity Haven Home gets, the newspapers and magazines aren't going to plug the Wonderfood name. The Haven Home trade mark will help some, but it will still mean an awful lot to have some retail advertising to pinpoint it right down to a specific product. Gellman would get the jump, of course, but their advertising would do a job for other stores, too. It would be almost as good as having a campaign of our own."

"And they're willing to foot the whole bill?" he asked, finding it difficult to believe.

"More than willing," Joel said. "They've really got the pressure on to get us to let them do it. And it's right up to the top. Mr. Arnauth had me in his office for almost an hour."

"They seem to have a lot of confidence that it's going to go over."

"They do."

"Do they know what the stuff's like? Have they tasted it?"

Joel nodded vigorously. "I don't think there's anything they don't know, Mr. Lord. They've really dug in. They've got a copy of the Mitchell Associates press book and they've checked it from every angle. The whole crowd over there has been on it for two days. They even brought in a couple of big-shot pediatricians and talked to them about it. They're not jumping in blind, Mr. Lord."

"Why are they so anxious to give it such a big play?" he asked, responding now to a vague suspicion that Gellman Stores might be making a tactical move to block Coastal Foods from launching out and building its own independent business.

"That's what I kept asking myself," Joel said perceptively. "I thought at first that they might be trying to tie us up. But I don't think that's it. I'm sure it isn't. All they're looking for is a big promotion. They're positive that the Haven Home story is going to get a lot of publicity — I'm sure they've even checked through with some of the magazine people — and they want to jump fast and take advantage of it. If they can get Wonderfood in stock before the other chains have it — the supermarket business is rough these days — they don't get many chances to get out ahead with a big promotion boost."

"But if we give them an exclusive —"

"They're not asking for that," Joel protested.

"That's what it would amount to though, wouldn't it — if we give them all the production we've got?"

"Oh, I'm not thinking of doing that," Joel said. "We'd have to give some to G & G — we can't call them off completely — but if we could just slow them down enough so that we could give Gellman the stock they'd have to have in their stores to back up this first big push —"

"Then you're recommending that we do it?" he demanded.

"No, sir, not necessarily. If you want to stick to the policy of only selling Wonderfood to a store that's stocking the rest of the Haven Home line —"

"But that wouldn't be *your* policy?"

Joel gave him a twisted grin. "It would be if you said so."

"What if it were your own decision to make?"

"If it were my own decision — yes, I think I'd go along with Gellman — at least part of the way."

"How far?"

"That's what I've been trying to work out here with Frank, trying to see how much production we can squeeze out. I've been hoping that we'd have enough so that we could take care of Gellman and still have a pretty good slug to sell through G & G. But from what Frank says —"

"What's the story?" he demanded of Kennan.

The production manager shrugged. "We'll get this changeover made some time this afternoon. That'll give us an extra hundred cases a day. Beyond that — well, that's about all we can do."

"Why? Raw material?"

"No, we're all right there," Kennan said. "Or at least I hope we are. It's machine capacity that's got us licked. We've only got one filling line where we can handle these small cans. And we've got to use that for other stuff, too."

"We'll need more equipment, is that it?"

"If we really want to roll the stuff out," Kennan said, "we've got to have a separate production line."

"What are you talking about in terms of money?"

"Depends on how much old equipment Mike Schlager could adapt," Kennan said. "But I'd say we'd have a hard time getting by for much less than fifty thousand."

Lincoln Lord's first reaction was one of relief that the amount was so small. Before he could express himself, however, he was caught up by the realization that his mind was still conditioned by the multi-million-dollar figures that he had been tossing around in Washington, flashing back then to the difficulty that he'd had ever since he had come to Coastal Foods in scaling his sights downward from Luxor Pharmacal levels.

"And that's a lot of money to sock in," Kennan concluded. "Particularly when we don't know that the stuff's going to keep on selling."

"Yes, that's the problem," he agreed.

"Would you — ?" Joel began, then paused to reframe his question. "If you were sure, Mr. Lord, that it *was* going to keep selling — that the mothers who bought it the first time would turn into repeaters — would you consider making that kind of an investment?"

"Of course," he said. "But that's not going to solve your problem now, not if you have to give Gellman a decision by eleven o'clock. It's going to take several weeks just to find out what kind of buyer reaction we're getting — whether or not it's really catching on."

"But we could speed that up," Joel said anxiously. "We could check it pretty fast with this market research setup that Gellman has. I don't know whether Mr. Arnauth told you about it — ?"

476

"No."

"What they're doing is this," Joel said. "They take three or four stores where they have a controlled market — you know, some big real estate development where Gellman has an exclusive shopping center location and is getting eighty-five or ninety per cent of all the grocery business? And that would be a perfect place to get a concentrated test on Wonderfood, because such a high percentage of the people in these new developments are young couples that have babies. What Gellman would do — this is their standard technique — they'd saturate the whole buying area with Wonderfood — maybe with coupons, maybe a free can to every mother at the check-out counter, maybe even door-to-door sampling. Anyway, they'd get a can of Wonderfood into every home where there was a baby. Then they'd move a buyer research crew into the store. Every time anyone went through the check-out counter with a can of Wonderfood, there'd be someone there to make certain that she was a repeater — get her reaction on the first can she tried — you know, all the usual questions. It's a terrific operation, Mr. Lord. I saw the results of a test they ran on instant coffee — six days and they had all the answers. It would be even faster than that with Wonderfood. A can only lasts two days. By the end of the third day we'd really know what was happening. And if it looked good enough, and if we could get started right away on a new production line — how long would it take you to get a new line set up, Frank?"

"Three weeks," Kennan said after a moment's thought. "Everything we'd need is pretty much standard equipment."

Joel went on, "In a month, Mr. Lord, we could be all set. And we'd still be ahead of the publicity that's coming out in the women's magazines — that's where we're really going to get our big push, anyway — *Good Housekeeping, McCall's, the Journal.*"

"It's an interesting idea," he said guardedly, afraid to trust his own enthusiasm.

"A fast check like that would be worth a lot," Joel pressed. "And if we tried to do it ourselves — hired one of the regular market research outfits —"

"You think Gellmans would be willing to do it for us?"

"I haven't talked to them about it," Joel said. "But, yes, I'm almost certain they would. I don't think there'd be any trouble about it at all. If you want me to call Sam Mandel —"

477

"No, not yet. We'd better know where we're headed before we go that far."

The cannery noise, unnoticed before, was now roaring in his ears. The jumble of sound seemed to be scrambling his thoughts, defeating his attempt to counter all the arguments that favored going ahead with the Gellman plan ... there had to be some drawbacks, there always were ... G & G wouldn't like being held up ... no, of course not, but it would only be temporary ... and they'd all be better off in the end ... the Gellman promotion would pre-sell every grocery store in the country ... and Joel was right about the best publicity not breaking for over a month. They could really cash in if they had a production line ready to roll ... fifty thousand dollars ... have to get a loan but there'd be no trouble about that ... Anderson Phelps ... hadn't told Swann about that yet ...

"We'd better get hold of Alf," he said. "This is an important decision and we want to make certain that we're all thinking alike."

His words struck a wall of silence, both Joel and Frank Kennan avoiding his eyes until the production manager finally volunteered, "We had a session with Alf last night."

The implication that there had been trouble was too plain to be missed, and Kennan's surreptitious side glance at Joel made it no less clear that Swann's opposition had been personally directed.

"I'll call you in a few minutes," he said, remembering Swann's attitude at Haven Home and his own decision to do something about it. Sooner or later, Swann had to be caught up and brought into line. Unpleasant as the prospect was, it was something that could no longer be delayed.

As he walked toward the office, however, the thought crossed his mind that Swann might have found some flaw in Joel's proposal that he himself had failed to discover, remembering then that it was Swann who had saved him from approving Joel's original plan. Negative though Swann's contribution had been, it was nevertheless true that if it had not been for Swann, the far more effective merchandising plan that they were now following would never have been developed.

2

This was a holiday for Kip — Goodhaven High was closed because of a district teachers' conference — and Maggie Lord had hoped to keep him at home, his presence enough to lighten this dark morning.

478

But now he was off to Haven Home, insisting that Dr. Perrill needed him today, and she again felt herself victimized by submission to convention, her son's silent demand this morning that she be a good and understanding mother no less onerous than her husband's no less demanding expectation last night that she be a good and understanding wife...oh, why couldn't she ever be herself...honestly say what she really thought...what a fool Linc would be to give up all of this for that little jerkwater college!

The rain-bleared window was a screen for the projection of memory. She knew that what she was seeing was no longer valid — time and time again she had seen pictures of all the new Chesapeake College buildings that had been erected since the war — yet the insistent image was still of the campus she had known in those years when she had lived in Brighton, three old ramshackle structures, each more surely dated by the worst taste of the era in which it had been built than by its cornerstone, all made doubly ugly by the barren plot of foot-beaten earth from which they rose. The people had been no less unattractive than the campus, the student body dominated by turkey-necked farm boys who had come to Chesapeake because it was the cheapest college they could find, the faculty salted with a strange collection of backwater oddballs. Against her own then recent memories of Cornell University, Chesapeake College had seemed hopelessly third-rate, not even up to Millburgh Normal. And yet for some unexplainable reason, Linc had always regarded Chesapeake College with a starry-eyed respect that had been, from the very beginning, a challenge to her understanding.

She could still recall with almost the vividness of first shock that he had taken it for granted that they would be married in the college chapel. Mr. Quincy's fortunate insistence that the wedding be in the mansion house at Kingdom Come had saved her from that, yet Linc's disappointment had been so evident that she had felt herself called upon to suggest that the ceremony be performed by Dr. Dunwoody — as was true of all pre-war Chesapeake presidents, he had been an ordained minister of the Gospel — and Linc had seemed almost as gratified by Dr. Dunwoody's acceptance of the invitation as he had been by her agreement to marry him.

Linc had always been a fool about Chesapeake...the money he'd given, the time he'd wasted...alumni meetings...speeches...oh, why couldn't he see how crazy it would be to give up all he had here. Everything was going so wonderfully...

479

Or was it?

The wind seemed to have driven the rain in through the window and she felt herself suddenly chilled to the bone . . . had something gone wrong at the plant? Was this the same thing it had always been before . . . Linc running away from trouble? No, no, no . . . it couldn't be . . .

After Linc had left for the office, she had pressed home the questions that he had asked Kip at the breakfast table about what Dr. Perrill had been doing at the cannery last night, and she had finally gotten Kip's positive assurance that nothing was really wrong . . . "It's just that they got so many orders they have to make it faster . . . so what they're going to do is use this big kettle kind of thing . . ."

"Ma'am?"

Startled, she wheeled, "Yes, Viola?"

"I was just wondering, ma'am — it's so kind o' mean and ugly out — you think maybe Mr. Lord he'd like some good hot soup tonight, maybe like a fish chowder or something?"

"Oh, I'm sure he would," she said too quickly, too enthusiastically, forgetting until it was too late to withdraw agreement that Linc would be inescapably reminded of Chesapeake College . . . those horrible fish chowder parties that he'd always thought were so wonderful.

3

Lincoln Lord's office offered no haven from noise. The ceiling overhead was thunderously reverberant, a drumhead on which an army of demons seemed to be beating out a rhythmless percussion against the piercing wail of a power saw screaming its way through metal. Only too obviously, the contractor's crew had finally gotten around to installing the prefabricated partitions for the second floor executive offices.

The environment was enough to induce irritation and, recognizing that, he was doing his best to discount the significance of Swann's highly nervous mannerisms. It was not easy. He had anticipated resistance, even open antagonism to Joel's proposal that they accept the Gellman offer, but he had not expected that Swann would stoop to the attack by innuendo that he launched by saying bitterly, "Joel seems awfully anxious these days to please that Gellman crowd."

"What are you implying, Alf?"

"Nothing that isn't obvious," Swann snapped, his eyes oddly fixed in an unblinking stare.

"I must be a little dense this morning." He forced a smile. "I'm afraid that it isn't obvious to me."

The long fingers of Swann's liver-spotted hands twisted into a double-tied knot. "One day he's all out to build up our own line — break away from Gellmans. The next day he wants to hand them everything on a silver platter. Why?"

"Well, Alf, there may be some drawback that I don't see, but if Gellman is willing to give us all this advertising and promotion —"

"All right, if that's what you want to do," Swann muttered, grimly tense.

The preservation of patience was becoming more and more difficult. "Alf, I'm asking for your help. I can see the advantages — frankly, I can't see the disadvantages. What am I missing? Tell me."

"Wonderfood!" Swann snorted. "He's all for it now, isn't he? Why? You read his report, didn't you? It was horrible stuff then. Wouldn't sell. Not a chance. But now — oh no! Everything's fine. What's so different about it?"

There was no longer any doubt that he was dealing with a wildly distraught man, no longer any hope of getting a sane judgment. There was, however, an evident need to quiet Swann. His raised voice had carried through the glass partition and the girls outside had already had their attention attracted. Fortunately, Joel had not yet come in from the cannery. "Alf, I'm afraid I don't quite get your point. Yes, Joel recommended against marketing Wonderfood — and so would I on the basis of the situation that then prevailed. But the circumstances have changed. With all this publicity —"

"You don't have to tell me that things have changed!" Swann exploded. "Nobody has to tell me that. I know it now. I saw it."

"Now, Alf, let's calm down," he said, softly but firmly, positive now that Swann's mind had slipped its moorings.

Instead of being quieted, Swann's face suddenly contorted as if a storm of fury had burst within his brain. His thin lips trembled violently, the power of speech seemingly lost until he burst out with an exact repetition of what he had last said, "I know it now. I saw it."

"You saw what, Alf?"

"You know what I saw!"

481

"I haven't the slightest idea what you're talking about," he said quietly.

Swann's eyes darted about the tiny office, an animal caged. Suddenly, he was on his feet and out of the door. For a moment, he seemed a madman running away from himself. But then he shouted back, "Come up here and I'll show you," and plunged toward the hanging tarpaulins that covered the unfinished staircase to the second floor, whipping back the gray canvas and disappearing behind it.

Lincoln Lord hesitated. Everyone in the outside office was watching him. He set an easy smile on his face, took a moment for a blank glance at something on his desk, and then sauntered over to the hanging canvas and pushed his way through. Loose boards had been put down to protect the new rubber tile on the steps and he slowly picked his way to the top. He had no idea what Swann intended to show him nor did it particularly matter. This was, he knew now, a serious case of mental derangement. Although this was by no means the first time in his life that he had been called upon to cope with such a problem, he was uncertain as to how he should proceed. Violence was not in the typical pattern . . . that fellow Collins who had cracked up at Luxor . . . bursting out crying in the middle of a budget meeting, sobbing like a child . . . but still there had been Ferguson at Frazer Glass . . . vowing that he was going to kill that girl in the accounting department . . .

The power saw screamed, snatching his breath away, and he stood for a moment at the head of the staircase, waiting for the emptiness inside himself to be filled by the slow seepage of courage.

Swann was nowhere in sight, lost somewhere in the maze of partitions. The construction noise had stopped now. Two workmen were staring at one of the open doorways. Taking that hint, he cautiously stepped through and into what he recognized as his own office. He heard a sound and wheeled right, facing the doorway that opened into the adjoining office. Swann stood with his feet planted apart, his shoulders hunched forward in a posture of physical defiance so incongruous with normality that it was a final proof, unneeded, that sanity was too far gone to be regained with no more than the calming effect of a quiet manner and a low voice. Nevertheless, it was the only possible approach. "Alf, what's the matter?"

"Don't try to deny it," Swann said with an unmistakable hiss of warning. "You thought you could get away with it, didn't you?"

With the movement of a cornered man stooping to snatch up a weapon without lowering his guard against attack, Swann's hand darted down and came up with a blueprint that had been lying on the floor. He held it out, stabbing at it again and again and again with his forefinger, the wild thrusts matched to his voice as he shouted hoarsely, "There — there — there — there!" He flourished the paper as if it were a battle banner. "Do you think I'm a fool? Do you think I can't read? Do you think I don't know what you're trying to do to me?"

Cautiously, he stepped forward and took the blueprint, still unaware of what Swann was talking about, knowing only that he himself was not responsible. The construction plan that was being followed was the one that the architect had drawn at the time the building was erected.

"You won't get away with it," Swann threatened.

And now, suddenly, he saw it. The architect, as architects usually insisted upon doing, had lettered names into each of the spaces indicated as private offices and, adjoining the one marked *President,* connected by the indicated open doorway in which Swann was now standing, was the cryptic legend: *V.P. Sales.*

"Oh, Alf, this doesn't mean a thing," he said, a little laugh breaking through. "I haven't even thought about who's going to have which office. This is the old plan that Mr. Zurich had drawn —"

"That's a lie!" Swann screamed. "Do you hear me — a lie! Mr. Zurich would never have done this to me. I was always closer to him than anyone else." A paroxysm jerked his lips into a twisted slash. "You think you've got me, don't you? You don't think there's anything I can do. We'll see about that! There is something I can do!"

There was a madman's crafty gleam in Swann's eyes, a madman's superhuman quickness of movement as he suddenly broke past him, evaded his automatically outstretched arm, and went dashing down the stairs, a headlong plunge so wild that Lincoln Lord fully expected to hear the crash of his body at the bottom. But there was only the clatter of the loose boards on the steps. By the time he reached the top of the staircase and looked down, the canvas flapped emptily behind Swann's flying exit. He controlled the impulse to hurry after him, waiting until the force of anger was neutralized by compassion, revulsion by understanding. There still remained, however, a snake's-nest of small fears, the most readily identifiable an automatically aroused criticism of himself for having let a personnel problem rise

483

to this frightening state. He did not know what he had done wrong, nor how he could possibly have prevented what had happened, only that he had failed in a situation with which the president of a company was supposed to be able to cope.

Standing at the top of the stairs, he visualized Swann at his desk, their offices separated by only a pane of clear glass, and alive to the embarrassment that would strike Swann when he came to his senses after this emotional blast-off, he decided not to return to his own office but to walk straight through and out into the cannery. There still seemed a chance that, left alone, Swann might regain control of himself. Pushing back the canvas, however, he saw that his office was empty.

Miss Payne confronted him, her face blanched. "Mr. Swann went out, Mr. Lord. Is he ill? He looked just awful."

"Yes, I think he decided to go home," he said tightly, the first thing that came into his head.

Joel was at his desk now, standing as he approached, his deep concern unmistakable. "Anything I can do, sir?"

"No, I don't think so," he said, and kept walking, stopping after he got through the swinging door to the cannery, reassuring himself that asking for Kennan's advice was the right thing to do.

Kennan saw him at once, almost as if he had been waiting for him, and walked quickly toward him, seeming to sense what had happened. "Alf?"

He nodded and, looking around for some place of privacy, saw the door of the cutting room. Kennan followed him inside, closing the door behind him, nodding silent understanding as he listened to a description of what had happened, finally saying, "I was afraid of something like this. I almost called you last night — after that session Joel and I had with him."

"I wish you had," he said half critically.

"So do I," Kennan said regretfully.

"What is it, Frank? Be perfectly honest with me. I want to know. Is it just jealousy of Joel? Or is it me — the way I've handled him?"

"No, you can't blame yourself," Kennan said heavily. "I should have told you what's been going on. I kept hoping —" There was a long pause. "Do you remember that day when you talked to me about making Joel sales manager? It was the day he made his presentation on a new line."

"Yes, of course."

484

"You remember how rough Alf was on him?"

"Yes." He blinked in the memory. "But how could Alf have felt badly that day? We bought his plan, not Joel's."

"I know, it doesn't make sense," Kennan said. "There's not much of this that does. Alf came over to my place that night. He was there until — oh, I don't know when I finally got rid of him but it was pretty damn late. What it amounted to was — well, to get it right out in the open, Alf was so keyed up about having shown up Joel in front of you that he thought he had him all ready for the final stab in the back. He wanted me to do the dirty work — talk to you and tell you what a mistake it would be to make Joel sales manager. We had a hell of an argument about it. I finally told him to go fly his kite, that I didn't want any part of cutting a good boy's throat just because he happened to be a Jew."

Groggily he asked, "You can't mean that's what it's all about — simply that Joel's a Jew? How could it be? Alf surely isn't prejudiced against Jews. He worshipped Sol Zurich. Or at least that's the impression he's always given me."

"No, it's not just ordinary prejudice," Kennan said. "But still it's because Joel's a Jew."

"Then it is jealousy?"

"No, it's more than that," Kennan said. "Jealousy is too mild a word for it. It's something that — well, I'm no psychologist but you know how they claim that every time something really scares the hell out of you, it leaves sort of a scar on your brain?"

"Yes."

"Well, when Joel was brought in here it gave Alf a scare that he's never gotten over. It's a scar that never healed, and I don't think now that it ever will."

"What happened?"

"It's a little hard to describe — well, you said a minute ago that Alf worshiped Sol Zurich. That isn't quite the way I see it. It was more like —" He cocked his head. "You know how some wives are — they think they're in love with their husbands but what they're really in love with is a chance to manage his life? Well, that's the way it was between Alf and Sol Zurich."

"Do you mean — ?"

Kennan broke in hurriedly. "No, I don't mean that there was ever anything queer about it, hell no, but still that's what it always made me think of — kind of a husband and wife relationship. Alf was always jealous as the devil of anybody who ever threatened to get closer to Sol Zurich than he was."

"That checks," he agreed, remembering that Swann had used almost those same words.

"The first real jar Alf got was when Sol married Kira. That damn near killed him. You see — well, in Alf's mind, Kira was a bitch who came in and wrecked his whole life by stealing his man away from him. I'll never forget what I went through for a couple of months. I was more or less new here then, I didn't really know Alf well at all, but for some reason he'd taken a shine to me — I guess because he didn't have anyone else to talk to. Anyway, he started coming over to our house at night. He'd get one drink and — well, there was more than once when he'd just go completely wild —" He paused, obviously embarrassed. "This is what I meant when I said that you can't blame yourself. This goes back a long way."

"You mean that he's gone off the deep end before?"

Kennan nodded. "It was bad enough when Sol married Kira but when he hired Joel that was even worse." He paused. "I'm sure you must have noticed this when you first came down here — Joel's the only Jew around the place."

"Yes."

"That was Alf's doing. He was always dead set against Mr. Zurich ever hiring another Jew, and until Joel came along he'd always gotten away with it."

"But why?"

"He was afraid that a Jew would have a bond with Mr. Zurich that he didn't have. You know, the idea that the Jews always stick together?"

"Which, of course, they don't."

"And particularly a man like Sol Zurich," Kennan agreed. "But you couldn't argue with Alf. When Joel came in — well, that was the end of the world as far as he was concerned. Somehow he got the idea that Mr. Zurich was going to adopt Joel as his son — he was going to be his heir, he was going to take over the company, god knows what else. That was a hell of a week, trying to get Alf back on the rails again. He was really flying. If it hadn't been for —" His voice cut off, and the dull red of a deep flush rose above his collar. "I'm not very proud of the way I finally got him settled down. I've been ashamed of it ever since. It was a lousy thing to do and I was absolutely wrong

— but Joel was new and I didn't know then how much he had on the ball. And Mr. Zurich needed Alf pretty damned badly, somebody to keep a finger on the purse strings —" His voice ran out with the exhaustion of self-justification. "It was my fault that Joel was put under Alf as his assistant. I suggested it. That satisfied Alf, having Joel under his thumb so that he could control him, but it was damned unfair to Joel — and it just can't go on, that's all. Joel's too good a man. There's too much danger that we might lose him. I wish I'd said this before —"

"So do I," he said, almost sharply.

"But that was three years ago — there'd been no real trouble since and —"

"I know," he said. "No one wants to blackmark a man, but I do recall that first day I was here, how strangely Swann acted —"

"And I said he was solid as a brick, didn't I?" Kennan said, at least partly absolving himself by acknowledgment. "I thought you knew — that someone must have told you about him — and what I was trying to say was that it wasn't anything to worry about any more. And I didn't think then that it was. I honestly didn't, Linc."

"Well, I'm afraid it is now."

"So am I," Kennan said. "It can't go on this way."

"What's the answer?"

"Well, that's up to you. But something has to be done."

He silently considered several possible approaches, finally deciding on the most direct. "How old is he — how far from retirement age?"

"Three years," Kennan said instantly. "He's sixty-two. I suppose you know that Mr. Zurich left him a paid-up annuity? It doesn't start paying off until he's sixty-five but it wouldn't be too much of a load on the company to make up those three years."

"Of course he may shake out of it —"

"If you want my opinion — ?"

"I wouldn't be talking to you if I didn't."

"He won't," Kennan said solidly. "Oh, he'll get himself under control, or at least I hope he will, but as far as his staying on here is concerned —" He shook his head. "The more responsibility you give Joel, the worse it's going to be — salt in an old wound that's never going to heal — and you can't hold Joel down any longer. It's going to be no kindness to Alf to keep him on. Another blow-up like this and he'll crack for good."

"Well, that would leave a hole — losing Alf."

"It wouldn't be too hard to plug, would it?" Kennan asked. "I know you want Joel on the sales side, but after things settle down and get into the groove — and with the G & G organization — couldn't Joel handle the office operation, too?"

"Oh yes, I'm sure he could. That isn't what I had in mind." He hesitated again, thinking his way through. "Frank, you told me once that all you wanted was production — that you had no interest in general management. Do you still feel that way? Or would you be willing now to step out and take in a little more territory?"

Alarm etched itself on Kennan's face, misinterpreted and then explained as he said, "This puts me in a hell of a spot, Linc — makes it sound like I'd been talking about retiring Alf in order to feather my own nest."

"I have too much confidence in you to believe that," he said. "If I didn't, I surely wouldn't be talking to you like this."

Kennan was looking down, his face hidden. "I honestly don't know what to say, Linc. Yes, I'd pretty much made up my mind that the only way I could be happy would be to stick to a job that I knew I could handle — and handle right. It's always seemed to me that the unhappiest guy in the world is the poor bastard who's running a bluff and trying to get by without having enough on the ball to really cut it."

"I'll agree to that," he said, pleased by Kennan's reaction. "But on the other hand, Frank, a man can miss a lot of happiness by not really making use of the ability he has."

"I suppose that's true."

"And you've been underrating yourself, Frank. You're a bigger man than you've given yourself credit for being. I've seen that too many times to have any doubt about it. Your attitude toward Joel — your honesty — the way you've faced up to this problem of Alf —"

"It's torn my guts out, worrying about it, I can tell you that."

"If it hadn't, you wouldn't be the man I want sitting next to me." Kennan's head came up. "Can I ask you a question?"

"Of course."

"Would this mean that if anything happened to you — if for any reason you were to leave here — I'd be expected to step in and take over?"

His mind jarred to a stop, suddenly struck by the realization that, incredible as it seemed that he could have overlooked it, he had not related any of the events of the morning to the possibility of his accepting the presidency of Chesapeake College . . . if the company lost Swann . . . only Frank and Joel left . . .

Alarm faded . . . he hadn't been seriously considering it, anyway. It had been impossible from the beginning . . . he couldn't leave . . . Frank had probably seen that newspaper squib about the ICA job, the same one that had gotten Kip so upset . . . Maggie . . .

Memory supplied both words and a smile. "Well, if I were going to make a change, Frank, it wouldn't be Washington."

"That's what I meant," Kennan admitted with an embarrassed little smile. "I guess you know, I saw that business in the paper —"

"Newspaper reporters have fertile imaginations."

"Well, I'm glad there isn't anything to it," Kennan said. "That would worry me a little, ever trying to fill your shoes — more than a little, a hell of a lot!"

"No, it wouldn't, Frank," he began, meaning to go on, but suddenly realizing the need for caution. "Of course, that's nothing that I could promise, anyway — that you'd ever take over. That decision would have to be Mrs. Zurich's."

"Oh sure, I understand that. I didn't mean — well, it was just the idea of your leaving, that's all that was worrying me." He looked at his watch. "It's twenty to eleven, Linc. If we're going to get together with Joel —"

It took a moment for the suggestion to register. "Golly, I'd forgotten that. We do have to make a decision on the Gellman business, don't we."

"Maybe Joel could stall them for another hour."

"No, there's no need for that."

"I don't think there is either."

"You're for doing it?"

"Unless you see some reason why we shouldn't."

He shook his head. "All right, let's do it."

"I'll get Joel," Kennan said, rising.

"Just tell him to go ahead," he said. "And then come back here."

Kennan hesitated. "You want *me* to tell him?"

"Why not?"

Kennan's curt nod was crisply decisive, a willing acceptance of responsibility, and as he went out of the door Lincoln Lord was more certain than ever that he was making the right move in elevating Kennan, a feeling heightened by the assurance that it was not something done merely to meet an emergency situation . . . this was what he had been planning to do, anyway . . . now he could do it without all the slow and awkward maneuvering that would otherwise have been involved . . . really a lucky break . . .

He cringed inwardly, shrinking from the realization that he had been guilty of a cruel lack of human compassion in thinking, even for an instant, of Swann's mental breakdown as something fortunate. In subconscious retribution, he began to consider what might be done to help him, a start no more than made when Frank Kennan threw open the door, his face ashen as he said, "We've got trouble, Linc. Alf didn't go home."

"But he's hardly had time —"

"Gus was working out front when he left. He saw him make a right turn at the high school."

"A right turn?"

"That's the road to Haven Home."

"You don't suppose — ?"

"God only knows what he'll do. He's always hated Kira. As crazy as he is — Linc, I think I'd better get over there right away."

"I'll go with you," he said, an instant decision. "Come on! My car's in the warehouse."

They ran out through the cannery.

For once there seemed some point to the Pantheon's roaring getaway and, as they shot out of the big warehouse door, some purpose to the power that sent them hurtling down the road. He drove in silence, not asking for Kennan's anticipation of what they might find, his own imagination more than enough to fill his mind with horror. It was entirely believable that the insane man who had taken that wild plunge down the stairs and out of the office was capable of physical violence.

The farther he drove, the faster he drove. Coming down the straightaway before the turn into Haven Home, the throttle was flat on the floor. Driving demanded total concentration. He braked hard and skidded into the turn but the car kept its footing and straightened away, slowed then by the gravel lane.

"Look for a gray Buick," Kennan said, directing him. "Kira's place — no, it's not there. The lab."

He spun the wheel, whipping the car around, heading for the research center.

"Well, I'll be damned," Kennan said, exhaling sharply, the collapse

490

of tension as the car stopped. "His car isn't here. He must have turned off. Unless —"

He threw the car door open and ran into the building, unmindful of the light rain that was still falling.

Lincoln Lord waited, finding himself strangely out of breath, his heart pounding, his mind seemingly too exhausted for coherent thought. Even with the long wait before Kennan came out again, he still felt his mental faculties dulled as Kennan said crisply, "He just left. Don't know why we didn't pass him. He must have taken the other road back to town."

"But he was here?"

"Your boy saw him."

"Kip?"

Kennan nodded, catching his breath. "Alf ran into Kira's office, stayed about five minutes, ran out again."

"She's all right?"

"Kip says she just went over to her house. I think you'd better go over and talk to her."

"Yes, I probably should," he acknowledged, seeing now that Kip was watching him through the glass door. He beckoned to him and got out of the car. "I'll see what I can find out."

The rain had almost stopped and Kip met him on the sidewalk, waiting silently for his question.

"What happened, Kip?"

"You mean about Mr. Swann? Gosh, I don't know — nothing, I guess."

"Did you see him come in?"

"Sure."

"Well, what did he do? How did he act? Did he seem nervous — excited? Tell me anything you can."

"Gosh, I don't know, Dad. It was more like he was just mad or something. He went in Mrs. Zurich's office, and he was there a little while, and then came out again. That's all."

"You didn't hear him say anything?"

Kip looked down, kicking at the concrete. "Only something about Mr. Morris — and being a Jew, that's all. And I guess I wasn't supposed to hear that."

"That's all you heard?"

Kip nodded.

"And after he left, Mrs. Zurich went over to her place?"

"Yes sir. Right away." He made another scuffing pass with his shoe. "He must have made her feel bad or something. Anyway, that's how she looked."

"Thanks, Kip. This is a help." He started for the car, stopped by a thought, calling back and asking Kip to wait. "You're right, Frank, I'll have to talk to her. My guess is that it's going to be a long session and I think I should handle it alone. Do you want Kip to run you back to the plant?"

"Yes, I ought to get back," Kennan agreed.

As always, Kip was delighted to be asked to use his car, dashing off to bring it around. While they waited for him, Kennan said, "I think I'd better try to run down Alf and find out what's happened to him. If there's anything we can do, I guess we ought to do it."

"By all means," he agreed instantly. "Do you know who his doctor is?"

"Doc Waldron," Kennan said. "Over on Tern Beach."

"You'd better get hold of him."

"The first job's going to be to get hold of Alf."

Kip drove up then and Kennan changed automobiles. Lincoln Lord watched them go off down the drive, waiting to start his own car until he had attempted, not too effectually, to plan what he would say to Kira Zurich. The main thing, he decided, would be to tell her of his plan to retire Swann, assuring her that she would be subjected to no more such unpleasantness as she had just experienced.

The rain had started again and, as he pulled up in front of her cottage, he wished that he had not dashed off hatless and coatless. The front door was unprotected and, standing there ringing the door-bell, he was becoming rapidly soaked. When there was no response to his third ring, he decided to give up and turned back to the car, stopped suddenly as the door finally opened. Driven by the impulse to get out of the rain, he quickly pushed his way inside, only then aware that there had been no invitation to enter. There was no warmth of greeting on Kira's face, only a blankness that he took to be the aftermath of fear.

"I'm awfully sorry about Swann bothering you this way," he said. "I hope it wasn't too bad."

Her voice was as cold as the rain. "You'll have to do something about this, Mr. Lord. It can't go on this way."

"I know that," he said quickly. "I didn't realize until this morning how serious it really was. Unfortunately, I'd not been told that there'd

492

been trouble before. If I'd known, I might have been able to prevent it."

"You can do something about it now," she said, still not inviting him into the living room, standing directly in front of him, keeping his back pinned against the door. "Surely you must know how terribly disturbed he is?"

"I wouldn't have followed him out here if I didn't know, Mrs. Zurich," he said uneasily, puzzled by the rigidity of her grimly fixed expression.

"A man doesn't get into that state of mind without provocation."

"I think I understand now —"

"Then you know what has to be done."

"If you mean — ?"

"I mean that you've got to get rid of Joel Morris." She turned on her heel and left him.

Unbidden, he followed her into the living room, so stunned that he would not have been able to speak had it not been for the urgent necessity of stopping her before she went out through the door to the dining room. "That's impossible."

"Impossible?" She wheeled to face him. "Why?"

For a moment it seemed that the madness he was seeing was in his own mind . . . first Alf . . . now Kira . . . what had happened to everyone this morning?

He took a deep breath and half expelled it, steadying himself. "That would not only be a serious loss to the Coastal Foods Company, Mrs. Zurich, but also brutally unfair to Joel."

"If he's as good as you seem to think he is, he should have no trouble getting another job."

"He won't."

"All right then."

"But the Coastal Foods Company would have a great deal of trouble finding another Joel Morris. Surely you can see — our new line — the whole Wonderfood promotion —"

"Don't try to give him credit for that," she said with a sardonic little laugh. "You read his report, didn't you? He was against it from the beginning."

He could hear the echo of Swann's words. Incredible as it seemed, Kira had apparently bought Swann's whole story with no discount for his obvious lack of sanity.

"I think we'd better talk this over, Mrs. Zurich," he said, adopting

493

the same purposefully calming tone that he had tried to use in dealing with Swann.

"There's nothing to talk over," she said, her distraught manner again reminiscent of Swann. "You'll have to get rid of Joel. There's no other way."

He sensed that she was bent on escaping and, with no time for gentle argument, he said bluntly, "That would be getting rid of the wrong man. Swann is sixty-two, Mrs. Zurich. He could be retired —"

"No!" It was a defiant bark, sustained in the expression that had frozen on her face.

Quietly, he said, "I'm sure it's unnecessary to remind you, Mrs. Zurich, but when I came here you agreed to give me full responsibility for the management of the Coastal Foods Company."

"Yes," she snapped back. "But there was a condition on that agreement. I told you very plainly that nothing was to be done that would affect Mr. Swann. I meant that. I still mean it."

"This affects far more than Alf Swann."

"You agreed to that condition, didn't you?" she demanded.

"Not in those terms —"

"Then you're breaking your agreement!"

Her darting eyes seemed almost a mimicry of that moment before Swann had made the wild dash out of his office. Snatching at what seemed the only way to stop her, he shot out, "Are you asking me to resign, Mrs. Zurich — is that what you want?"

For an instant it seemed that he had won. She stared at him with unblinking eyes, her expression vague, unfocused. Then suddenly she said, "If that's what you want to do —" the words seemingly whipped out by centrifugal force as she spun around, cut off then by the sharp slap of the door into the dining room.

4

Something made Maggie Lord look toward the window and when she saw her husband getting out of the car it seemed the proof of premonition, a fulfillment of fear so complete that even his appearance, startling as it was, struck her without shock, barely with surprise. He wore neither the hat nor the raincoat that he'd had on when he left the house, his suit jacket sodden, wrinkled into a shapelessness that gave his shoulders the slumped set of total defeat, seemingly proof that she had been right all along in suspecting that something had gone wrong at the company.

And then her conscious mind took over, propelling her toward the door, and she ran to meet him, surprised and shocked, gripped by a fear that was in no way lessened by expectation.

"Linc, what's happened?" she cried out.

"What hasn't," he said in a hoarse whisper, using what seemed the last breath of air in his lungs.

"Oh, Linc, you're sopping! You've got to get out of these clothes."

He muttered agreement, shrugging his shoulders to help her remove his coat, and she pulled it from his back, struggling against the drag of wet fabric against wet fabric. He was soaked through, his shirt translucently clinging.

"I've got to change," he said, a long-delayed response. "That's why I came home."

He pulled away from her, walking toward the bedroom and she ran after him, passing him just before he reached the door, throwing it open for him, hurrying then to find him a wool robe. He stripped and put it on and she said, "You'd better get a hot shower, dear," knowing that it would delay his telling her what had happened, yet knowing too that it really made no difference . . . he'd talk only when he was ready to talk . . . this was the way it had always been, this long wait for the truth. He must have been walking in the rain . . . afraid to come home and tell her . . . only three months this time . . . two months and a half . . .

"Swann went off the deep end this morning," he said suddenly, surprising her. "Cracked up completely — absolutely wild — crazy as a loon."

As always happened when there was any reference to mental illness her mind choked with the memory of her mother. "You don't really mean — ?"

He shivered, cinching the belt of the robe, and she knew that she ought to again tell him to get into the shower, but her lips were clamped by the hope that he would now explain that no one but Swann was involved.

"I knew something was wrong," he said, dropping to the edge of the bed. "He's been getting jumpier and jumpier, harder and harder to handle — particularly when anything's come up that involved Joel. But I had no idea that he'd crack up like this. I might have guessed it if someone had only told me that it had happened before."

"Then it's — ?" She stopped, mentally fumbling through the awkward synonyms for insanity. "What is it, Linc — a nervous breakdown?"

"Worse than that." His voice gained strength. "The man's completely mad."

"Oh, Linc, that's awful," she said, an exclamation that leaped to her lips over the sudden rise of exultation ... if Swann was out of the company, then Linc couldn't possibly leave! He'd said last night that they could get along without him, but that was when there were three of them, Swann and Kennan and Joel ... if Swann was out, only Kennan and Joel left ... and Linc *knew* that he couldn't leave now ... yes, he had been planning on it, no matter what he'd said ... if he hadn't been he wouldn't be so torn up now ... walking in the rain ...

"Hadn't you better get in the shower?" she suggested, a response to compassion ... Linc would get over it ... Chesapeake College had been a silly dream, anyway ...

"You might as well know the rest of it," he said abruptly, tugging the robe over his knees. "After this blow-up at the office, Alf made a wild dash out to Haven Home. Frank and I went after him. Crazy as he was, we had no idea what he might do."

He was suddenly silent and, waiting, she asked, "What *did* he do?"

"I don't know," he said abstractedly, staring. "By the time we got there, he'd already talked to Kira and left. She'd gone over to her cottage. I followed her. At first she wouldn't even let me in."

"Wouldn't let you in?"

"That's how I got so wet," he muttered, and for a moment it seemed as if that were his point. But he took a deep breath and went on. "I thought Alf was crazy — and god knows he is — but Kira's even worse. She ordered me to fire Joel."

"Fire him? But what does Joel have to do with —"

"Because Alf hates him, because — oh, there's no use trying to explain it. It doesn't make sense, none of it does. Frank claims he hates Kira, too — we were even afraid that he might attack her — but instead of that, she falls for his crazy story." He caught a quick breath, angrily expelled. "All right, she bought it — she can pay for it!"

"Linc, what are you going to do?"

"What can I do? It's either fire Joel or else."

"Or else what?"

496

He stood up. "Thank god I've got this Chesapeake College offer."

Her lips barely trapped the cry that leaped in her throat, a pointless restraint because Linc would not have heard it, anyway. He had gone into the bathroom and she heard the burst of the needle spray as the hiss of fire, the mind sound of his anger, and she reacted to it as if it were a challenge to her understanding, unfair because he had told her so little about what had really happened . . . but she did know Linc . . . the same old story . . . afraid of losing Joel . . . imagining that he *had* to have him . . . yes, just as he'd always been dependent on Brick. Why? What was he afraid of? Why couldn't he see that Joel wasn't important to him? The publicity campaign hadn't been Joel's idea . . . nor going ahead with Wonderfood . . . nor using Haven Home for a brand name . . .

That was probably the trouble at the office, giving Joel so much more credit than he deserved . . . and there had been trouble . . . yes, Linc had admitted it . . . "I knew something was wrong" . . . oh, why hadn't he told her! But this was the way it had always been, never knowing until it was too late . . . *crazy* . . . *insane* . . . that's what he'd always said about all the others, too . . . blaming someone else . . . running away to another job, pretending that it was something he wanted . . .

The telephone rang . . . Kira? Maybe it wasn't too late . . .

For an instant, she debated running out and taking the call on the hall telephone . . . no, Linc might come out of the shower before she got there.

She lifted the receiver. "Yes?"

"Mrs. Lord? This is Frank Kennan. Is Linc there?"

"Yes, he's here, Mr. Kennan, but —" She recoiled from the high-pitched strangeness of her own voice. "He's in the shower. Can I have him call you back?"

"Well, I'm over at the hospital and it would be hard to reach me. Just give him a message, will you?"

"Of course."

"Just tell him — well, I guess Kip's told you about what we found?"

"Kip?"

"Isn't he there yet?"

"No."

"Oh. Well, then I guess you don't know — about Alf?"

"I know about his going out to Haven Home."

"Oh, good," Kennan said. "Well, Kip ought to be there before long

497

— he can give you the details — but, anyway, I was worried about what had happened to Alf, where he'd gone, so on a hunch I had Kip cut over to the highway and we came in that way. You know where that poultry auction is, just before you get to that Howard Johnson? There was a big crowd around, a lot of cars stacked up, so we stopped. It was Alf. He'd driven right off the road and smashed into a couple of parked trucks. When the ambulance came, I hopped in and went along to the hospital. What I wanted to tell Linc — well, I thought he'd want to know — Alf's all right. As far as they can tell out here, there's no serious physical injury. They've got him knocked out with dope now — he was pretty wild — Linc will know what I mean —"

Linc stood before her, his robe clutched to his dripping body. "What is it?"

"Just a minute, Mr. Kennan. Here's Linc." She handed him the receiver, watching his face then as he listened, learning no more from his monosyllabic responses than she had already been told, but that was enough to prove that Linc had not used the word *insane* as loosely as she had imagined.

"There's no point in my coming over to the hospital?" she heard Linc ask. Again there was only his solemn nodding, his muttered acknowledgments. Finally he said, "All right, Frank, I'll meet you at the office as soon as I can get dressed."

He hung up, abstractedly shaking his head. "I shouldn't have let Alf get away — ought to have stopped him. He could have killed himself. Wonder he didn't." He snapped out of it, moving quickly back into the bathroom. "I've got to get dressed."

"I'll have Viola hurry lunch," she said.

"No, don't bother," he called back. "I'll pick up something at the plant."

His anxiety to get to the office encouraged hope. "Oh, Linc, this will change everything."

"Change what?" he demanded, snapping the folds out of a pair of shorts.

"I mean Kira — when she finds out what's happened. She'll realize now that she shouldn't have listened to Alf Swann."

Her words seemed to bounce back from the stony mask of his face, rebounding without impression. He turned away without answering her, silent until he said, still without looking at her. "There's Kip. Call him, will you?"

She ran out, meeting Kip as he came in the front door. "Come back and talk to your father," she said, telling him about the call from Kennan.

Kip was obviously deflated by learning that the news had gotten there ahead of him, disappointment fading only with his father's encouragement to recount all the details. They talked as Linc dressed and she stood apart from them, listening but taking no part in the conversation, most of which dealt with a reconstruction of how Swann, apparently on an open road and neither meeting nor passing another car, had simply turned off and driven into a line-up of trucks parked at the poultry auction. Nothing that was said, neither Linc's hurriedly prompting questions nor Kip's detailed responses, seemed to have any pertinency until she heard Kip ask, "You remember what you asked me before, out at Haven Home, about whether Mr. Swann was acting — well, you know — funny or something?"

"Yes?"

"I guess maybe — well, anyway, he sure was crazy out there when we were waiting for the ambulance to come. There was a couple of guys — you know, trying to hold him down and make him lie still because they didn't know whether he was hurt or not? Man, he was really wild."

Linc said offhandedly, searching for a necktie. "Out of his mind, probably, didn't know what he was saying."

"No sir," Kip said, disagreement so formal that it surprised her.

Linc, too, seemed taken aback, his hurried dressing suspended as he looked sharply at his son.

Kip squirmed but gave no ground. "It wasn't just because he got smacked. He was yelling the same things he did out at Haven Home."

"What things?"

"You know — what I told you?"

"You didn't tell me anything he said."

"Sure I did," Kip said anxiously. "You know — about Mr. Morris?"

"Oh," Linc acknowledged, released, starting to knot his tie, then suddenly frozen again as Kip added, "And about Mrs. Zurich being a Jew, too, and how —"

"What!" Linc exclaimed. "A Jew?"

"Yes, sir."

"Kip, you didn't tell me that."

"Yes, I did. Don't you remember? Anyway, that's what I meant."

Linc stared at him. "If you did, I missed it." His head turned in her direction, but he looked past her, asking himself, "Do you suppose she is?"

"Sure she is," Kip said forcefully. "But, gosh, if it's something that she doesn't want anybody talking about —"

"Wait a minute," Linc reached out to touch Kip's arm. "Are you sure of that?"

Kip swallowed hard, his eyes down. "Yes sir."

"How do you know?"

Embarrassment loaded Kip's shoulders. "Dr. Perrill told me. I wasn't supposed to say anything, but with old Swann yelling it out to everybody —" His eyes raised. "I guess I did kind of a dumb thing — you know, when we had the open house? That's why he told me. Some of those newspaper fellows were acting kind of smart and — well, I said something about their being Jews. I don't mean to them, they didn't hear me, but Dr. Perrill did and he laid into me about ever saying anything about anybody being a Jew, especially around Haven Home where Mrs. Zurich might hear it."

"Because she was a Jew?"

"Sure. He used to know her a long time ago. He said she was a Jew then. If you're a Jew once, you always are, aren't you?"

"Yes, I suppose you are," Linc said heavily.

"Gosh, I don't know what difference it makes —" Kip began, but seeing that he was getting no attention from Linc, he turned to her and concluded, "Anyway, what business is it of old Swann's? Gosh, all the things he was saying — if I'd known he wasn't hurt, I'd have socked him."

"Now, Kip —"

"Well, I would have!" he said belligerently. "I don't care if Mrs. Zurich is a Jew —"

"Kip —" Linc interrupted. "Did Mr. Kennan hear him say these things?"

"Sure, everybody heard it — you know, all about Jews sticking together, and how she wasn't going to get away with it — all that kind of crazy stuff."

"All right, all right," Linc said, putting an end to it. "Kip, listen — I don't think we ought to say anything about this to anyone. Do you understand?"

"Sure."

"And don't blame Mr. Swann too much. He's a sick man."

"I guess so," Kip granted, shifting uneasily.

"Okay, boy," Linc said, giving him a light clap on the shoulder, a signal of release to which Kip instantly responded, out of the door even before the forced smile faded from Linc's face.

"I'm glad you said what you did about Alf Swann," she said.

He made putting on his suit coat an excuse for not hearing what she said, crossing to her dressing table to comb his hair, and when he spoke he was talking to himself in the mirror. "I've had a crazy hunch about this all along, ever since Frank told me that there couldn't possibly be any question about Sol Zurich's being a Jew."

"You mean that story about the orphanage?"

"Of course. Kira invented that."

"Do you really think she did?" she asked, pretending doubt that she no longer felt, reminded of the artificiality in which Kira Zurich had always seemed cloaked. "Why would she?"

Linc put down the comb. "Why do so many of them change their names? Why do they bob their noses? There's no mystery about it. They're trying to pass, that's all. And it's a one-way street. Once they get away from being a Jew, they'll do anything to keep from being put back again."

"Oh, Linc, how can you blame them, all the awful prejudice they have to face?"

"We weren't talking about blaming anyone. You asked me *why*."

"I know," she acknowledged. "I suppose she thought that if she married a Jew, and let him stay a Jew — but it was so silly if he looked so Jewish that no one ever believed her."

"Worse than silly," he said, dead serious. "Remember the Starrs — blackballing every honest Jew that ever tried to get into the country club?"

Her shiver of apprehension came not from the direct recollection of Jack Starr but rather from the memory of that terrifying night when Linc had cut him down at Walsh's party, slashing out with an attack so vicious that it had been almost unbelievable. It was the first time that she had ever seen Linc so angry that he lost his self-control — and almost the last. But if that was the way he felt about Kira Zurich . . .

"Linc, don't you think that Swann must have done something to frighten her terribly? He probably threatened to expose her, tell everyone that she was a Jew. Oh, Linc, I don't think she really meant what she said about firing Joel."

He turned slowly, facing her with an expression so penetrating she

501

had to fight to keep from averting her eyes. "Why are you defending her?"

"Because —"

Volition was no longer necessary to keep her eyes fixed upon his face. They were held now by the illusion that words were being spoken by his silent lips, the same words he had hurled at her that day on the Parkway, accusing her of never having been honest with him, of never saying what she really thought, of holding him accountable for decisions that she had refused to share.

And now, no less clearly, she heard herself answering him, not the evasive words that she had used then but in words that had never been spoken aloud before, soundless words drawn not from memory but from the never vocalized thoughts of a hundred nights . . . no, I don't want you to run away again . . . I'm tired of running away . . . tired of being afraid . . . tired of being married to a man too weak to face up to . . .

"Because of what?" Linc demanded.

The super-reality of his voice convinced her that her own had been unheard and, desperately grateful, she said without thought, "I'm not defending her, Linc."

He looked at her as if she weren't making sense . . . maybe he *had* heard . . .

But no, he couldn't have heard because now he was saying, "Everything depended on her promise to let me run the company my own way. I wouldn't have come here otherwise, you know that."

"You don't think there's a chance — even when she comes to her senses?"

He was shaking his head. "It happened once, it could happen again. I'd always have that hanging over my head."

"You're going to resign?"

His lips parted and then closed again, an instant of indecision that was her only hope. But it was a hope much too tenuous to count upon, all but lost as Linc went out of the door without answering her.

Viola met her in the hall. "You decided yet, ma'am, 'bout having them folks to dinner next Saturday?" Viola asked. "If we're going to be needing Lizzie Pearl —"

"No, we'll be away next week end, Viola," she said without hesitation. "We've been invited down to Maryland."

XII

Lincoln Lord had lived through the seven days of this new week in a strange state of mental equilibrium. There had been a suspension of decision so effective that he had not consciously considered either his resignation from the Coastal Foods Company nor his acceptance of the presidency of Chesapeake College. Early in the week, when Maggie had asked him what he intended to do, he had told her with complete honesty that he did not know, an admission that had not made him feel either weak-willed or indecisive — Swann was still in the hospital and, until he was released and attempted to come back to work, there was simply nothing to decide. If any move was to be made before then, Kira Zurich was the one who had to make it. There had not been a word from her since she had slammed the door in his face a week ago today at Haven Home.

After what had happened, she could hardly avoid knowing that she had been completely wrong in opposing Swann's retirement. But whether she would admit her mistake and withdraw her demand that Joel Morris be dismissed remained an unanswered question. There was, however, still a chance that she might call to apologize. Experience counseled against impatience. His life had taught him the wisdom of delay. There had been too many times when he had erred by not waiting for the last development, too many times when he had been saved from error by some new fact that had come to light only under the pressure of a final demand for decision.

Although he had been expecting Kira Zurich's apology ever since the moment when he had first heard of Swann's madness-proving crash, he had — until today — successfully counteracted the tension of waiting by completely filling his mind with the affairs of the Coastal Foods Company. At least in the beginning, this escape had not been knowingly made, excused as it was by the evident necessity for a quick take-over of Swann's work, a need made all the more evident by the fear that his handling of the company's financial affairs in recent weeks might turn out to reflect his mental derangement, and he had felt himself almost forced to plunge in to help Joel make a checking audit over the week end.

Although it was many years since Lincoln Lord had done any office detail work himself, once he discovered how pleasantly impossible it was to think of anything else while adding a column of figures or calculating a string of percentages, he had kept on and on, digging into bills and vouchers, working out cost figures, making product-by-product profit projections, re-examining budgets and performance records. He had made no disturbing discoveries, learning little that he had not known before, yet this intimate involvement in the operation of the company had made him understand, in a way that had never before been possible, something of the attraction that the Coastal Foods Company must have held for Sol Zurich. It was a feeling that would have argued against his resignation if the subconscious demand for mental equilibrium had not awakened a balancing realization of how blind he had been in his vague hope that the Coastal Foods Company might somehow be rapidly built into a much larger company. It was only too plain that, even with an optimistic estimate of how much extra volume might be obtained from Wonderfood and the new Haven Home line, it would be a long time before there would be any worthwhile increase in the company's net earnings.

Disturbingly, it seemed now that much of the new volume would no more than offset a drop-off in the Gellman business. Sales of the Mother Gellman products had never regained their old high level. Once the stores had been restocked, orders had been sharply reduced. A special promotion staged the past week had produced disappointing results. Joel had told him of the Gellman management's fear that they might not be able to stem the strong trend toward frozen instead of canned pre-cooked foods, but it had not seemed a serious threat until he began to study figures that he himself had developed. Now he could see that Haven Home Foods, instead of giving them bonus volume, might no more than balance the loss of anticipated business from Gellman Stores.

This realization had started him off on an intensive re-examination of every detail of their new merchandising plan. Again he had learned little that was new, found nothing that required change, and there was the positive gain of a renewed conviction of Joel's value to the company. The Wonderfood promotion that he had worked up with Gellman Stores looked better and better — even Art Gerhart had agreed that giving Gellman the bulk of the immediately available supply was the right thing to do — and Joel's idea of having the Gellman market research staff make a fast consumer survey might prove even more valuable. It was to be started today in two stores whose selling areas had been saturated yesterday with a sample distribution of Wonderfood. If the results were favorable, everything was set to go ahead with Frank Kennan's plan to expand production. All of the new equipment that would be needed had been located and Kennan was now waiting only for a final decision before he ordered it shipped in. The needed capital had been found. On Wednesday it had taken no more than a telephone call to New York to arrange the loan that Anderson Phelps had offered that day at Haven Home. Swann, for all his mad behavior, had been alarmingly right in his concern over depletion of the company's working capital. Cash was being rapidly drained away by the step-up in production, mounting inventories of raw materials and the rising accounts receivable — plus, of course, the cost of the new offices on the second floor. As he had just noted from the top voucher in the pile that Miss Payne had given him to approve, the final payment to the contractor would be due on Monday.

"Miss Payne," he asked as she went out of the door. "Will you see if you can find Mr. Morris and ask him to come in."

"He's right back here," she said. "I'll call him."

Joel came to the door of his office and he asked him, "When will we be getting some word on this Gellman market test?"

"The survey crews are on the job in both stores now," Joel said. "I talked to Sam a few minutes ago. Everything was all set to start checking customers at noon. I don't suppose they'll have anything tabulated until the first of the week, but I've been thinking — well, I'd like to see the thing in operation, anyway, so I thought I'd leave here at five o'clock and drive over to Roman Hills."

"Why wait until five?" he asked, unguardedly impatient. "If you left right now, they'd have a couple of hours of results piled up by the time you got there. Probably wouldn't be conclusive but it might give us at least some indication of what way the wind's blowing."

"I would like to get over there as soon as I can," Joel said eagerly.

"My desk's pretty well cleared up — and if you're going to be here, anyway — ?"

"Yes, I'll be here," he said. "Go ahead."

Left alone in the deserted office, Lincoln Lord became slowly aware of the nervous tension that, until now, he had been able to hold below the level of acute consciousness. The signing of the pile of vouchers that Miss Payne had left on his desk was finished all too quickly. He tried to interest himself in a trucking loss claim, but it was strangely difficult to concentrate. Loose-ended, he found himself edged toward an admission of the possibility that Kira Zurich might never call him . . . this was Friday . . . a week today . . . if she were ever going to call, wouldn't she have done it by now? Frank Kennan had said last night that Dr. Waldron had told him that Swann would probably be released from the hospital sometime this week end. If he came back to work on Monday . . .

Impulsively, he picked up the telephone and called Dr. Waldron's office in Tern Beach, expecting to ask only for a report on Swann's condition. The doctor himself answered the telephone, quickly saying, "I've been hoping that you'd call, Mr. Lord. I'm rather worried about Swann and I'd like a chance to talk to you for a few minutes. I'd prefer not to discuss it over the telephone —"

"I'd be glad to come over to see you if you're free."

"I'm free," Dr. Waldron said, clearing the way, and Lincoln Lord left immediately, welcoming this chance to talk to someone. Many problems could be solved simply by talking them out and, up to now, there had been no one to whom he could talk. A frank discussion with Frank Kennan had been barred by the need to keep him from knowing about Kira Zurich's demand for Joel's dismissal — it was a president's responsibility to protect his men from gut-tearing worries — and, as had been demonstrated earlier in the week, trying to talk to Maggie had put him in the impossible situation of being asked to decide what he was going to do before he had the facts upon which a decision could be made.

Crossing the causeway to Tern Beach, his hope for a frank discussion rose higher and higher. His initial impression of Dr. Waldron, gained last Saturday morning, had been highly favorable — he was a Johns Hopkins man, several cuts above the average small-town physician — and there had not been then, nor would there be today, any need for embarrassing explanations. Swann was a long-time patient and Dr. Waldron was, from the hints he had dropped, thoroughly familiar with the nature of Swann's obsessions. Furthermore, Dr. Waldron was not a man to beat about the bush. He would, he guessed, get to the point in a hurry.

He did. After a short pipe-puffing preliminary, the old doctor said abruptly, "I'm about at the end of my rope, Mr. Lord. I can't hold Swann any longer. To be quite frank about it, the few scratches he got in that automobile smash-up hardly justified hospitalization in the first place. I put him in for observation — justified under the circumstances —"

"Of course."

"— but the justification was far more mental than physical."

"I understand."

Dr. Waldron knocked out his pipe. "Would it be possible, Mr. Lord, to retire him immediately?"

He felt a burst of elation, choked back as he asked, "You don't think that he should return to the office at all?"

"That's my opinion," the doctor said positively, silent then until he had refilled his pipe and put a flaming match to it. "Unless we can get him away from the atmosphere in which these obsessions of his have generated, I'd say the prognosis was highly unfavorable. These attacks have been getting progressively worse, more and more severe. This one was bad enough. The next one might —" He blew out his match.

"Have you discussed this with Swann — the possibility of his retiring?"

"Yes," Dr. Waldron said. "At some length."

"What's his attitude?"

Dr. Waldron watched a puff of blue smoke rise toward the ceiling. "Rationalizing the irrational — and that's always a risky undertaking — I'll stick my neck out far enough to say that once it was over and done with he'd welcome it."

"But he'd not retire of his own free will?"

"In his present state of mind, I'd say that was most unlikely. He's counting on going back to the office on Monday morning."

"You're releasing him from the hospital?"

"I'll have to. There's no basis on which I can hold him any longer."

"Let me ask you this, Doctor," he said, intent upon plugging the one last loophole. "If the source of Swann's irritation was centered in one person — and if that person were to leave the company — ?"

"You're referring to young Morris — Joel?"

"Yes," he agreed, sharply reminded that this was a small town where there was no such thing as anonymity. "But putting all other considerations aside, thinking only of what would be best for Alf —"

Dr. Waldron was shaking his head. "You're starting with a false premise, Mr. Lord. Yes, at the moment Joel's his mental whipping boy —"

"If it weren't him it would be someone else?"

"Exactly." The doctor tamped his pipe. "The trouble started long before young Morris came on the scene — he didn't cause it and his leaving won't cure it. I'm not certain that anything will — you never can be sure in these cases — but the one best bet, it seems to me, is a complete change of scene, a total break with the past. He does have a brother in Florida, you know — he's mentioned that often enough so I know it's on his mind — and in my judgment the kindest thing you could do would be to arrange things so that Swann could pack up and leave Goodhaven without ever going near the Coastal Foods Company. I realize that retirement may be a difficult thing to manage on short notice, but I'm quite convinced that it would be the best thing for everyone concerned."

"I agree," he said quickly, suddenly seeing how the situation might be handled. "But I'm afraid that my own hands are tied."

"In what way? Or aren't you free to discuss it?"

"I will ask you to treat this as a confidence."

"I'm a doctor, Mr. Lord," Waldron smiled.

"Under the terms of my agreement to manage the Coastal Foods Company," he said precisely, "Mrs. Zurich retained full authority over any move that would affect Swann's status with the company. Last Friday, after he'd been out there, I suggested exactly what you're proposing — that we retire him."

Dr. Waldron cocked his head. "She wouldn't agree?"

"No."

"That surprises me. In view of his attitude toward her — and she must be aware of that? Or isn't she?"

"I really don't know. I suspect not." He paused. "I also suspect that she had no idea that Swann's mental condition is anywhere near as serious as it is."

"When did you last talk to her?"

"Not since last Friday," he said, the admission grating yet necessary to his purpose.

Dr. Waldron regarded him for a moment, silence extended as he puffed his pipe. "Am I to assume, Mr. Lord, that you'd like to have *me* talk to Mrs. Zurich?"

He was momentarily taken aback by the doctor's quick perception, pleasantly surprised that he had to go no farther to gain his end. "I don't like to put you to any extra trouble, Doctor, but it is a rather abnormal situation —"

"That's a doctor's life," Dr. Waldron said with a twinkle. "Just one damned abnormal situation after another. All right, I'll give her a ring." His eyes narrowed, compressing a small smile. "I suppose you'll be interested in knowing what happens?"

"Naturally."

"Well, if you don't mind waiting outside for a minute or two, I'll call her right now."

"Thank you, Doctor, thank you very much," he said, yet vaguely disturbed as he went out into the waiting room, closing the door behind him, struck then with the full implication of what he had done . . . why had he gone out of his way to get Dr. Waldron to call Kira Zurich? Why did he want her to agree to Swann's retirement . . . so that he could stay on himself . . . not have to resign? Could that be true? Didn't he want the presidency of Chesapeake College?

Denial rushed into the vacuum of his suddenly blank mind, a torrent too turbulent to bring under quick control, sweeping him on to the brink of decision . . . Kira would agree to Swann's retirement . . . of course . . . how could she maintain her position against Dr. Waldron's recommendation? She couldn't. But did that mean that his own future was automatically sealed? No, he still had the right of decision . . . Frank and Joel could carry on without him . . . wouldn't have to leave until September . . . everything could be set up by then . . .

The door of the office opened. Dr. Waldron stood facing him. All that Lincoln Lord needed to see was his eyes. They were the eyes of that surgeon who, in the climactic tragedy of his childhood, had silently told him that his father was dead.

The bleak walls of that hospital corridor faded out and the knotty-pine paneling again became visible as Dr. Waldron said, "I'm afraid I wasn't very successful. She says that it's all up to Swann — that if he wants to come back to the office, she won't interfere. I tried to reason with her but she was absolutely adamant." A humorless smile crinkled his eyes. "I rather suspect, Mr. Lord, that Swann isn't the only neurotic that you have on your hands."

He nodded agreement, abruptly denied by the realization that now he no longer had either of them on his hands . . . his decision had been made . . . Kira Zurich had made it for him.

2

After lunch, Maggie Lord had wandered into the bedroom and sat down on the edge of her bed, hopelessly wishing that she could manage a short nap, telling herself that she was still much too tense to drop off in the middle of the day. Two minutes later she was sleeping soundly.

This had been a week of hope slowly regained, her spirit crawling upward from the black depth to which it had plummeted last Friday when Linc had come back from Haven Home and, for a few minutes, given her the impression that nothing could possibly stop him from resigning the presidency of the Coastal Foods Company. The rise from that low point had been tentative, never without apprehension, always aware that she was relying too much upon intuition, knowing that what little solid evidence she had was negative rather than positive. Nevertheless, justified or not, she had reached the point where she intuitively felt that the crisis had been safely passed.

Her first lift of spirit, almost immediately effective, had come with the news of Swann's hospitalization. Then, starting that very afternoon, Linc had plunged into a day and night concentration upon the affairs of the company. Although this was memory-matched to the fact that he had never resigned from any company without a similar burst of intense activity — in order, so it had always seemed, to clear his conscience by leaving everything in the best possible shape — she had nevertheless sensed something that had never been there before. True, it was intangible. And, pointedly, Linc had done nothing to give substance to her hope. Only once, last Monday night, had she tried to prod him into talking. Unsuccessful, she had made no further attempt. There had been few opportunities, except at breakfast and dinner when Kip was present, and late at night after he had gotten home from the office so obviously worn and weary that his reluctance to talk had been too obviously justified to combat. Furthermore, she had decided that it would be a mistake to press him, partly because she feared that any question might irritate him into making a wrong decision, more because she sensed that time was working in her favor. Every prior resignation had come as a violent outburst, an explosion of tension touched off by some one event, with Linc suddenly throwing all caution to the winds, abandoning everything and blindly running away. The situation last Friday had been hair-triggered to just that result — that was what had so terrified her — yet as the hours had crept by, the clock moving faster and faster, she had felt the danger grow less and less.

What had most encouraged her today was that Linc had obviously turned down Jay Quincy's invitation to come to Brighton for this week end. That had worried her considerably during the first days of the week when it had seemed almost a certainty that, if Linc went to Brighton and was again exposed to the peculiar charm that Chesapeake College had always exerted upon him, he would be incapable of resisting acceptance of the presidency. Her last thought before she had fallen asleep had been a self-comforting assertion that now, having reached Friday noon, she was safely past even a remote chance that Linc might make a last-minute decision to go to Brighton.

Her first realization upon being suddenly awakened was that Linc had just tossed an open traveling bag on the other twin bed. For an instant she felt herself still in the grip of a nightmare, her struggle against belief an attempt to save herself by awakening.

"Linc, what's happened?" she demanded, her voice sounding unreal and sleep-fogged. "Where are you going?"

"Brighton," he said, a single-word exclamation that exploded in her mind, a skyrocket bursting into the suddenly illuminated memory of the way he had left her in Bermuda and flown back to New York to resign from Luxor Pharmacal . . . running away to Florida when trouble had started at Frazer Glass . . .

She leaped up from the bed, clutching her dressing robe as if it were a protection against terror. "I didn't know that you'd told Jay we were coming. If I had —"

"I'm not going down to see Jay," he said, turning away from her, slamming open a dresser drawer. "I want some dope from Dean Whittaker, that's all."

He made it too obvious to be questioned that he didn't want her, yet she could not keep herself from asking, "Don't you want me to go with you?"

"No need of that," he said curtly. "I'm just going to drive down and back."

But he had tossed two clean shirts into his bag . . . *two* shirts . . . "Linc, what's gone wrong?"

"There are some things I have to find out."

Two pairs of socks . . . "What's happened?"

"Nothing new."

A little packet of handkerchiefs fell with a thunderous crash . . . "Linc, have you talked to Kira again?"

"I didn't have to," he said. "Doc Waldron did. He told her that Swann had to be retired. She wouldn't listen to him." He went into the dressing room. "She's not going to give in. I know that now."

"But Linc, if you didn't talk to her yourself —"

He confronted her in the open doorway. "What do you want me to do — crawl on my belly — beg her to keep from wrecking the company? Why should I?"

Every word hit like the blow of a doubled fist and she felt herself reeling. Never, not once in all of the twenty years of their married life, had he ever struck out at her like this. There was an instant of groggy disbelief, suddenly ended as if he had battered down a never-opened door, releasing her voice to shout, "Linc, you can't run away again — you don't dare!" The door, once opened, could not be closed against the flood that poured through it. "You can't go on like this — running away every time something goes against you. You've got to stand up and fight back. If you keep running away and running away, before long there won't be any place to run."

"So you're on Kira's side." He wheeled away from her. "I thought so."

She had been close to the exhaustion of instinctive defense but his coldly lashing words whipped her into retorting, "You know that isn't true. I want you to stand up to her — fight her!"

"Why?" The demand boomed at her with the hard reverberance of the bathroom's tiled walls. "Because you don't want to give up this house?"

She felt herself crumble as the blow struck home, hit again as he said, "Because you don't want to move Kip to another school? Don't blame me for that. It wasn't my idea to take him out of Forgehill."

Blindly, the ground sinking under her, she grasped at the last handhold. "Linc, that's not true. You're not fair. You never have been. You accused me once of not taking my share of the responsibility — that first day we came down here — but you've never given me a chance. You said that coming here was something that we'd decide together, but when it came to making a decision you didn't even bother to ask me what I thought. All you did —"

"You said I could trust Kira Zurich," he accused her, snatching up his toilet kit and starting back to the bedroom.

She tried to raise her hand to stop him as he brushed past her but it was suddenly too heavy to lift. He was around the corner now, out of sight, and she tried desperately to regain some semblance of balance, horrified by how far she had let herself go, yet still unable to humble herself to an apology for truth.

"I don't know what I'm going to do," she heard him say, and for an instant she thought he was weakening. Then she heard his bag slam shut, the dull thud of a blow, the click of the lock. "I'll be back sometime tomorrow."

Unavoidably, she let him go without a word. She had lost the strength that would have been needed to follow him down the hall. She stood at the bedroom window, trembling, watching the black Pantheon disappear through the cut in the trees, as that day in Bermuda she had watched his plane lose itself through a break in the black clouds of a storm front. She threw herself on the bed, burrowing her face into the pillow, hoping for the relief of tears that somehow refused to come.

How long she lay there she had no idea. She had not fallen asleep, but any measure of time was as surely lost as if she had, and there was no less a dark-of-the-night quality about the directionless flow of thought, finally broken by a dreamlike awareness of a knock on the door and then Viola's voice saying something that could only have been said in a nightmare.

She sat bolt upright, shattering illusion, demanding, "Who did you say?"

Viola looked startled into uncertainty. "Maybe I ain't right, ma'am, but I's just sure it's that same gentleman that was here before. You 'member about a month ago — Mr. Lord took him into his office to talk to him? Ain't that his name — Mr. Brick?"

"Yes" . . . but it couldn't be true . . . Linc throwing them together again, the same thing he'd done when he'd run away from Luxor Pharmacal . . . the Bermuda boat . . . "Did he ask to see me?"

"Yes'm," Viola said positively. "First he asks if Mr. Lord is here, and then when I told him that Mr. Lord he'd just gone away, he asks please if he could talk to you. I told him you was lying down just now and maybe you couldn't see him — "

"No, I'll come out," she said. "I'll have to dress but I'll be there as soon as I can. Tell him to wait."

513

She found a dress, changed her mind and selected another, putting it on slowly and methodically, assuring herself that the steady hand that held her lipstick meant a recovery of self-control. In the dozen steps that it took her to reach the living room, however, what she had thought to be poise came to seem no more than a rigid suppression of unaccountable inner stress.

Brick rose to greet her and his fumbling of a thickly stuffed manila envelope gave her the momentary illusion of having the upper hand, less ill at ease than he was.

"Hello, Brick," she greeted him, her tone made brittle by preoccupation with the resolution that she would not let Brick know what had happened, giving him no chance for I-told-you-so gloating. "I'm sorry that I had to keep you waiting."

"At least you're here," he said, his weak grin too obviously forced. "Drove down here to see Kira — ten minutes before I got there, she leaves for New York. Came over to see Linc — they told me at the office that he'd just left. I was beginning to think I was getting a run-around everywhere."

"You wanted to see Linc?" she asked emptily.

His odd hesitation seemed suspicious but, in quick recovery, he said, "I just wanted to give him some of this stuff. Thought he'd like to have it." He dumped the envelope, exposing a thick packet of clippings, then the carbon copy of a manuscript and a sheaf of mixed galley proofs. "Everything's marked so that he'll know what it is. The stuff's really starting to roll in now. I figured we'd do all right with the magazines, but I never thought we'd get this much newspaper space."

His tone was a bid for compliment, but she side-stepped it by keeping herself in the safe role of an intermediary, saying only that she would turn everything over to Linc and that she was sure he would be grateful, thanking Brick as if she were Lincoln Lord's private secretary. Still he made no move to leave, starting now to identify everything in the pile in a way that he had already admitted was unnecessary, then dredging up bits of news — the possibility that Dr. Perrill might be on the Garroway program, the telephone call that seemed to indicate that a *Life* story might appear next week, something about Wonderfood being given a big plug in someone's syndicated baby-care column — all a little vague and unpointed, the impression growing stronger and stronger that he was holding something back, the true reason of his visit still unrevealed. Nor did he seem any closer to his purpose when he mentioned the featuring of Wonderfood in the Gellman Stores ad-

514

vertisement that had appeared in this morning's newspapers, asking a question then about how orders were coming in without really seeming to care how she answered.

Then, suddenly, he looked at her, dead serious in what was obviously the end of evasion. "There's something else I wish you'd tell Linc — how sorry I am that I can't be down there this week end. If it were any other week —"

In the instant before she caught herself, an expression of surprise had slipped through. Brick saw it and asked, "Didn't you know that Jay had invited me?"

She shook her head, confused into wondering if even that was too much of an admission.

Brick said, "I guess Jay wanted it to be sort of a reunion — all of us together again."

Something close to panic made her say, "I don't think Linc's going down to see Jay either.

"I hope that doesn't mean —" Brick's narrowing eyes twisted his face into a scowl. "Maybe I'm not supposed to know this — but I do. Jay told me."

"Told you what?"

"That they've offered him the presidency of Chesapeake College," he said. "He's taking it, isn't he?"

"I don't know," she said, only as an evasion, yet almost instantly realizing that Brick might hear it as an admission that she didn't dare to make . . . but what else could she say?

"It would be a tragedy if he didn't."

Unreasoned anger flashed, for an instant seemingly centered upon Brick's unjustified interference in her life, then more solidly buttressed by the duplicity of his pretense that he was honestly concerned about Linc.

Her silence should have stopped him but he went on, "I mean that, Maggie — it would be a tragedy — for him, for the college, for everyone. He'd do a terrific job down there. He couldn't help it. And he'd be happier than he's ever been in his life. He's had enough bad breaks — he deserves a good one for a change."

Anger was challenged by credulity and the result was confusion . . . could Brick be fool enough to think that she'd forgotten what he'd said about Linc? But why was he doing it? What reason could he possibly have . . . was he imagining that she . . . ?

"I guess that sounds a little funny coming from me, doesn't it?" he

asked, words forced out against evident embarrassment. "I know what you're thinking — the things I said about him once. More than once, I guess. Or at least I thought them more than once. I've tried to forget all that — put it out of my mind. I can't. When you've been as much of a heel as I was — it isn't something that you can just toss off and forget. But it isn't something that you can live with either. Maybe this is just selfish, trying to get back my own sense of decency — and the hell of it is that I can't really apologize to Linc. He wouldn't know what I was talking about."

"I'm afraid I don't either," she heard herself say, knowing that Brick wouldn't believe it because she didn't believe it herself.

"Yes, you do," he said, more an appeal than an argument. "You know how wrong I was —"

"There's no reason to tell me all of this."

"Yes, there is. I was wrong about you, too. You know what I thought — that you were crazy to stick by him the way you did — that he didn't deserve you. But I was the one who was wrong. You're right, Maggie — he's a wonderful guy, he really is."

What had been anger and then confusion had now become something that could only be satisfied by escape, yet enough of that first feeling remained to make her say sardonically, "This *is* a change, Brick."

She expected nothing, certainly not a smile, even less an expression of oddly boyish embarrassment. "Remember once — you told me that I didn't understand anything about what it meant to be in love?"

She did remember. But she shook her head.

"Well, you did. And you were right. I didn't. But I do now." He waited until he caught her eye and then there was the cautious release of exultation in the sound of his voice, low as he said, "Tommy and I are being married today. That's where I'm headed now — down to her old home — Dover."

There was no feeling of shock, only a numbness, an absence of sensation that lasted so long that it began to seem something expected. Then, with electric suddenness every cell of her brain burst forth in a simultaneous outpouring of disordered sight and sound and memory, all sense of origin so completely lost that when she heard Brick say, "We haven't told anyone else," she seemed to be hearing, not Brick's voice but her own, on that night when she'd told him that she was going to marry Linc. And then there was the wild feeling that she was being victimized by his retaliation. But it was a threat withdrawn before it ever achieved the substance of thought, caught up and swirled away in a whirlwind spinning so fast that it blurred all perception. Suddenly everything stopped, not as an ending of something that had been but as a shocking proof that it had never existed, everything an hallucination, the only reality a disembodied voice that was saying, "Brick, I can't tell you how happy this makes me," finally the realization that the voice was her own and that, willed or not, she was committed to believing what she had said.

"I want Linc to know," Brick said earnestly. "I wouldn't want him to think that I'd turned down Jay's invitation because I didn't want to be there."

He seemed a stranger now, yet as she watched his face the strangeness was as transient as a fleeting smile. He was the old Brick now, old enough to be young again, as they had all been so very young those first years at Kingdom Come. "He's always been a friend of yours, Brick," she said quietly.

"I know," he said. "He's done so damned much for me, so much more than I'd ever let myself believe. I guess that's always been my trouble, never being able to admit that I needed someone else. I used to think that Linc was — well, you know, getting by because of me. I was the smart guy, the idea man, the big brain that he couldn't get along without. The truth is — I know it now — it's always been the other way around. Linc wasn't getting by because of me — I was getting by because of him. When I look back and pick out the things I've done that meant something, the jobs that I can still feel a little proud of — none of them would ever have come off without Linc. I guess I just didn't realize that it takes more than ideas to make the world go round. I don't know what it is — maybe it's like these enzymes of Doc Perrill's — but whatever it is, Linc's got it. He's always had it. Remember old Cornelia down at Rabson? My idea about going into frozen foods? How far would that have gotten without Linc? And where would Rabson Foods be today if she hadn't finally gone ahead with it? Rabson would have been on the scrapheap. Instead of that — well, where are they? Six or seventh in the whole industry — anyway, somewhere in the top ten."

"I didn't know that," she said, honestly bewildered. "You mean they went ahead with a frozen food line after you and Linc left?"

"Sure. And it was the same way at Union Packing. Frazer Glass —" He shook his head groggily. "When I think of how unfair I was to Linc, accusing him of running away — you were always right about him, Maggie. I ran into Dewey Franklin one day a couple of months ago, just before you came down here. You remember him, don't you — the way he battled Linc on that new plant? You ought to hear him now. He gives Linc most of the credit for what's happened to them — says it was Linc that got them out of the rut, that Frazer Glass couldn't possibly be the company that it is today if it hadn't been for all that Linc did for them. He sees it — a lot of people see it. I don't know why it took me so long."

She flinched, an involuntary movement outwardly controlled yet sending a wracking tremor through her mind, a shifting of surfaces that momentarily exposed the suspicion that Brick knew that he was talking about her as much as he was about himself . . . but, no, he wouldn't dare!

"This Japanese business," Brick went on. "All those men on his committee, all the work they did — what would it have added up to if it hadn't been for Linc? What *did* it mean until he got up before that committee himself? Nothing but a report that nobody had ever read. And now — well, at least they've got Congress stirred up enough to take a square look at what's happening."

"Yes, that's meant a lot to him," she said hurriedly, oddly grateful for the chance to speak.

"That's the hell of it, Maggie, there've been so many things that haven't. He'd done so much for so many people, and so little of it's ever really paid off for him. Take this place — flat on its back. Linc comes in and — well, how long's it been — three months?"

She nodded.

"Who else could have done what he's done — three months and they're back on their feet again, running full. Take Doc Perrill's baby food — kicking around for years and what had happened? Nothing. In comes Linc — it's on the market. And look at me — beating my brains out, trying to get by on my own — I guess even trying to prove to myself that I didn't need Linc. Then in comes the Haven Home account and I'm finally over the hump. I know it was your idea to toss it my way —"

Strangely desperate, she felt forced to break in. "It wasn't my idea, Brick. It was just one of those times when —" An errant thought slipped into her mind, making her pause as she thought of that afternoon when Linc had too generously given her credit for the idea of using Haven Home as a trademark. "It really was Linc's idea."

"Well, anyway, it's meant a lot to me," he said. "We've had two new accounts come in this week. That's not the important thing but still —"

"Oh, Brick, of course it's important. At least it means —" She caught herself. "I know it's not as important as what's happening today —"

"No, that's what really matters." A bemused smile spread over his face. "Funny how things work out, isn't it? I spend all my life trying to sell myself the idea that I don't need anyone else — and then all of a sudden there's somebody who slaps me into realizing what a dope I've been."

She was surprised by how easily a smile came to her face. "That's not a very romantic way of describing how you fell in love — but at least it's different."

"And at least it's true," he grinned, then suddenly sobering. "It's like starting life all over again. Or at least that's the way I want it to be — a clean slate without any marks on it."

Her smile held but it changed its quality now. "Yes, I believe you, Brick — you *are* in love."

His grin came back. "Well, there wasn't really any doubt in my mind about it — but thanks just the same." He stood up. "Tell Linc, won't you?"

"Of course. And he'll be delighted."

"And say hello to Jay for me."

Thought moved with the speed of light, faster than the flight of words, leaping ahead to stop her before she could say she wouldn't be seeing Jay. He reached for her hands.

"Thank you for coming, Brick," she said, not caring now that there was a tremor in her voice. "I can't begin to tell you how happy all of this makes me."

It was only after he was gone, the cool imprint of his lips on her cheek, that she became fully aware that what she had just said was wonderfully and gloriously true. But it could only remain true if Linc forgave her . . . she had to tell him how wrong she had been! If she didn't . . .

Her eyes darted to the telephone and then the clock . . . ten minutes after three. There was no use trying to call him now . . . he wouldn't be there yet. She had to wait . . . how long? How many hours would it take him to drive to Brighton . . . three? No, longer than that . . .

Kip's car was stopping in front of the house. She hurried to the door to meet him. "Kip, can I have your car?"

He blinked at her. "I guess so."

She ran back to the bedroom, trying to think what she would need,

519

but the demand for orderly thought carried the threat that if she stopped to think she would be afraid to do what had to be done, and she snatched up only what came to hand, tumbling it into a hatbox that was the first piece of luggage she saw when she opened the hall closet.

Kip had followed her. "Where you going?"

"Brighton," she said, and the name struck her ear with the same tone that Linc had used, jarring her into an awareness of Kip's troubled bewilderment. "Your father's on his way down. I have to meet him there."

Kip's mumble was unintelligible.

"I'm sorry about having to take your car, Kip. Were you planning to use it?"

"Just going over to Haven Home," he said.

"I could drop you off there."

He shook his head. "Maybe I wouldn't have gone, anyway. I haven't been over there much lately — not this week. Things have been kind of funny — you know, the way Mrs. Zurich has been acting."

She had turned to her closet, remembering that she hadn't even put in a robe, but Kip's voice stopped her.

"I guess something's wrong," he had said, an enigmatic half question, and she saw now that his eyes were not looking down at his shoes, as she had expected them to be. Instead, they met hers, solidly fixed as he asked, "Dad's going to leave, is that it?"

There was no choice but the truth. "He's been offered the presidency of Chesapeake College, Kip. That's why he's gone down to Brighton."

"Is he going to take it?"

"I don't know."

"But I guess you hope he does, huh?"

Never had there been a moment when her son's understanding was more important to her, yet her throat was choked and all she could do was nod.

Kip stared at her until, finally, he ended an eternity of waiting, his tone heavy with concern as he said, "You better stop and get some gas — the needle's bumping. But you don't have to waste any time having 'em check the oil. That's okay. So's everything else. There's nothing you have to worry about" — amazingly, he grinned "— except cops, I guess."

3

In conformity with the life-governing traditions of Weeks, Phelps & Harrison, Anderson Phelps answered his own telephone, protected from annoyance only by the care that he exercised in releasing his private number. He had, of course, given it to Sol Zurich, and now upon hearing Kira's voice he felt again the oppression of an obligation that seemed to have no end. He had, at her insistence, attended that affair at Haven Home ... and, confound it, been so taken in that he'd made a fool of himself by actually offering Lord a loan! When a man got to be sixty, he ought to stop exposing himself to emotional situations ...

"Mr. Phelps, I called to ask you about Mr. Lord's contract," Kira Zurich said. "I've just been reading it over and I can't find—"

Without listening, he knew what she was about to say ... he'd written in no limitation on the size of Lincoln Lord's bonus ... and with the way things were going, Lord would make a ridiculous amount of money this year, far more than a little company like Coastal Foods could reasonably afford to pay its president ... yes, it had turned out to be a bad bargain, she didn't have to tell him that ... and, of course, she'd never see the other side of it, the protection that she would have had if Lord hadn't worked out ... only twenty-five thousand dollars a year and the right to get out from under any time she wanted to ...

Kira was saying, "I've read all through it and I can't find anything about —"

"Yes, yes, I know," he interrupted her. "As the situation has developed, it might be well to consider negotiating an employment contract with Mr. Lord. I had that in mind the day I was down there, but the atmosphere hardly seemed right to bring the matter up. It would have been difficult —"

"What do you mean by saying that we should negotiate an employment contract? Isn't this letter a contract?"

"No, not in the legal sense," he admitted. "It's only —"

"Then he *can* resign?"

"Resign?" He cleared his throat, a reflexive act as instinctive as the counter-move of a tightrope walker. "Not without being fool enough to throw away a great deal of money. I'm sure no one would pay him as much as —"

"But he can resign?"

He flinched from the metallic rasp in his ear, lifting the receiver, wondering if he'd been wrong in what he'd told Judge Crockett that morning when he had called him, canvassing the Chesapeake College regents by telephone to get a vote on offering the presidency to Lincoln Lord. He'd told Crockett that Lord would make an excellent president ...of course ... why wouldn't he? But had he been wrong in thinking that there was absolutely no possibility of Lord even considering it ... twenty-five thousand dollars a year when he'd be collecting at least three times that much at Coastal Foods? Possibly ... yes, they were a strange crew, these fellows like Lord ... very impressive when you met them ... but unstable ... no solid sense of value ...

"Mr. Phelps, didn't you have an understanding with Mr. Lord that he had to stay here for at least —"

"Has he actually resigned, Mrs. Zurich?" he demanded.

"No," she said, "but I'm afraid he's going to."

He had heard a break in her voice, a warning that if he asked for details he would never get her off the line. "I don't think I'd worry if I were you, Mrs. Zurich. There's still a good chance that nothing will come of it."

"But what if he does resign?" she asked, now clearly evidencing the feminine emotionalism that forty-two years of marriage had taught him to be one of life's most harrowing burdens.

"Your company is in very good shape now, Mrs. Zurich," he said firmly. "I've just made Coastal Foods a substantial loan, and I'm sure you know me well enough to realize that I wouldn't have done that if I had any doubts whatsoever about its future. As for Mr. Lord — yes, his resignation might prove inconvenient, but if worse comes to worse and he does leave you, I'm sure you'll have no great difficulty in finding someone who'll be capable of carrying on from here on out — and at a substantially lower level of compensation than you'll be obligated to pay Mr. Lord under the present arrangement. As a matter of fact you may well have such a man all ready and waiting to step in."

"Who do you mean?" she asked, her voice hardly louder than the humming buzz of the empty line.

"Young Morris," he said. "From what I understand, he's proving himself a very capable young man."

There was a discourteous click in his ear, the connection broken, and he wondered again how a man as sharp as Sol Zurich could ever have entrusted his financial affairs to such a foolish and bad-mannered woman.

4

Joel Morris had reached the outskirts of Roman Hills shortly after three o'clock, but his cross-town passage to the shopping center where the Gellman supermarket was located had been slowed to a crawl by the traffic that glutted the winding streets. Even with an allowance for the fact that the day shift was just leaving the enormous electronic plant that had brought the town into existence, Roman Hills hardly seemed the perfectly planned town that its publicity had credited it with being.

Roman Hills was not the result of man's normal instinct for gregarious habitation. Instead, it had been created by decree, ordered into being by the board of directors of the Roman Instruments Corporation. Imbued with the enlightened spirit of the post-war industrial world, the directors had decided to rescue their employees from the blighted slums of three big cities and transfer all production activities to one model rural community where all would live in scientifically designed machines-for-living, tastefully incorporated into a restful panorama of green hills, safely isolated from the machinations of unscrupulous union organizers.

In the year of its creation, Roman Hills had been widely hailed as a laudable accomplishment, not only by architects interested in obtaining similar town-planning commissions but also by sociologists, industrial psychologists, public relations experts, aging New Dealers with a nostalgic concern for the common man, and a great many industrialists anxious to impress local politicians that there *was* an alternative to submitting to constantly mounting taxes.

Joel Morris had read very little about Roman Hills during the last few years, however, and as he drove through its streets he could understand why. As he looked about him it seemed that the beautiful four-color centerspread of the prospectus had been faded by carbon monoxide, scrawled upon by a thousand do-it-yourself addicts, trampled underfoot by the crowds that thronged the shopping center. The only evidence that Roman Hills had turned out to be a successful sociological experiment rested upon acceptance of the premise that active procreation was a valid index of the better life. The Maternity Annex of the Roman Hills Community Hospital was the second largest building in town, exceeded in size only by the factory itself. There were children everywhere. It was evident why the Gellman research group had chosen this area for a test of Wonderfood, thoroughly understandable why this particular supermarket had the highest ratio of baby-food sales of any store in the chain.

By the time he found a parking place and got inside, it was well after three-thirty, almost four before he could introduce himself to the leader of the survey crew. Waiting, he could see what was happening. There was a small red light fixed to the off side of each check-out station, flashed by the cashier every time a customer went through with a can of Wonderfood. The light alerted an interviewer who stepped up and, after first making certain that the customer had actually tried the free can that had been given to her yesterday, asked five simple questions about reactions of herself and her children to the contents of that sample can. The red flashes were coming so rapidly now that the interviewers could no longer keep up, slowed as they were by the many mothers who were not content with answering the five questions.

When he finally got to talk to Paul Dagan, the manager of the survey crew, Joel found that there had been, since noon, thirty-four authenticated purchases of Wonderfood by mothers who had tried it yesterday. A few said that they had thought the sample tasted strange but, reassured by the label's warning that such would be the case, and impressed by what they had read and heard, had decided to buy more. Although the actual number of customers at first struck Joel as being disappointingly small — almost two thousand samples had been distributed — Dagan had pointed out that it was really amazingly high in view of the short lapse of time since the sampling, and the further fact that the Haven Home publicity was only now starting to impress casual readers. Even the current buying ratio, when projected over no more than the Eastern market, predicted a sales total more than large enough to justify an immediate call to Lincoln Lord.

Searching out the harried manager of the store, he was given permission to use his office telephone and put in a call for Goodhaven. To his astonishment, he learned that Lincoln Lord had left the office shortly after he had, saying that he would be away for the entire week end. Switching the call to Frank Kennan, Joel discovered that he knew no more than Miss Payne about where Mr. Lord had gone. Incredible as it seemed, he had apparently disappeared without telling anyone where he could be reached.

"All I know is that he said he wouldn't be back until Monday morning," Kennan said. "How are things going?"

"Good," he said, enthusiasm tempered now by example, realizing that the aplomb with which Lincoln Lord had been able to walk out of the office was the hallmark of a seasoned executive, his own lack of poise evidenced again by the gush of boyish exultation that he had been ready to pour out. Settling down, he gave Kennan a factual report, concluded by warning him that the first consumer reactions seemed to indicate that it might be wise to consider packing Wonderfood in glass jars instead of cans.

When he hung up and stepped out of the office he was confronted by a man who, under his dark jacket, was wearing a high-collared white coat. "I understand that you're with the company that's making this Wonderfood product?"

"Yes, Coastal Foods," he said extending his hand. "Joel Morris."

"Dr. Simmons — chief pathologist at the hospital," the man introduced himself. "This is probably a wild goose chase, Mr. Morris, but I'm trying to run down the source of what appears to be food poisoning of some sort. Could you tell me what's in this stuff? I've read the label, of course, but that really doesn't give us too much to go on."

Joel Morris felt the breath suck out of his lungs, the propellant of speech lost until he finally managed to say, "It couldn't be Wonderfood."

"I know the odds are all against it," Dr. Simmons agreed. "I've never yet traced a case of food poisoning to any commercially canned product — but we do have to run down every possible lead. That's our big bugaboo here at Roman Hills — letting any sort of an epidemic get a start."

"Epidemic?" he choked out. "You don't mean — ?"

"We've had three cases turn up since noon," Dr. Simmons said. "It may be only coincidence, but the first mother told us that she'd given her baby some of this stuff of yours, so naturally we checked the other two cases."

"And they — ?"

"Yes, they'd eaten it too."

"But it can't be Wonderfood," he said, the strength for protest finally mustered.

"It is a new product, isn't it?"

"No, no, we've been making it for years. Shipping it all over the country. Dozens of children have been eating it every day. There's never been any trouble of any kind. I've even fed it to my own children — they've been raised on it —"

"Please don't be alarmed, Mr. Morris. We're not jumping to any conclusions or making any unwarranted accusations. All we want —"

525

"I know," he said, reminded of the need for poise, struck then by the realization that it was impossible to get hold of Lincoln Lord. Hesitant for an instant, he decided that the thing to do was get in touch with Dr. Perrill. "I'll put in a call for Dr. Perrill at the Haven Home Research Center. I'll get him on the line and you can talk to him. He can give you the information you want a lot better than I can."

"Fine," Dr. Simmons agreed. "I'm sure that would be helpful."

The doctor followed him into the manager's little office. "By the way, Mr. Morris, how many samples of Wonderfood were distributed?"

"Two thousand," he said as calmly as he could manage, but it demanded the full power of his will to keep his hand from trembling as he lifted the telephone instrument.

He placed the call, looking at his watch to make certain that the Haven Home operator would still be on duty. It was five minutes to five.

5

Maggie Lord was driving with a superconsciousness of the relationship between time and distance, her watch pitted against the mileage counter on the speedometer. It was five o'clock. Linc should be arriving in Brighton. She still had two hours to drive, perhaps longer — the highway ahead was bumper-to-bumper with Friday night's five o'clock traffic.

Again, as she had done countless times since she had left Goodhaven, she fought off the urge to give up and turn back . . . she couldn't even be sure of finding Linc when she got there . . . by the time she arrived he might have talked to Dean Whittaker and started back . . .

Or he might have gone out to Kingdom Come to see Jay . . .

Or to any one of a dozen other places . . . there were so many old friends of his still in Brighton . . .

Or he might have changed his mind and not gone to Brighton at all . . . that time when he started home from Florida and wound up at the Coates plantation in South Carolina . . .

Or something might have happened to him . . . the way he'd be driving, as keyed up as he was . . . that wreck she'd seen on the Turnpike . . .

There were too many possibilities against her, only one long chance

526

that she might succeed. But she drove on. Somehow she had to find Linc and apologize, erase those awful words from his mind. If she let them stay there all night, festering into hatred — what might happen then was too frightening to contemplate.

Her fear was all the greater because she could not remember what she had actually said in that horrible hour-long minute, startled and not fully awake, when she had struck out in what had then seemed self-defense but now could be recalled only as madness. She could vaguely remember having hurled one awful accusation after another, yet it was a memory too uncertain to be trusted — there had been too many times before when she imagined the sound of unspoken words — and it was incredible that she could have burst out with what, for so many years, she had successfully kept bottled up in the tight container of her secret mind. But she must have hurt him ... and terribly! If she hadn't he would never have said ...

This was no trick of memory, those words of his that kept pounding at her eardrums, again and again and again with the relentless beating of a storm surf ... *"Because you don't want to give up this house?"*

No, this was no hallucination ... it couldn't be. Linc had said it. She couldn't be imagining something that had never occurred to her ... and yet it was true ... terribly, horribly, awfully, selfishly true! She could see it now ... so foolishly afraid and the house had seemed to mean so much ... Kira had been clever enough to guess the kind of woman she really was ... a stupid wife all primed and ready to snatch at the bait of a silly symbol of security ... oh, damn Kira Zurich!

But it was her own fault ... she couldn't excuse herself by claiming that Linc hadn't given her a chance to share his decision ... yes, she had accused him of that, too. Or had she? Anyway, it didn't matter. Nothing would have changed if he had asked her. He'd probably known ... of course he had. How could he have helped knowing, as plain as she must have made it? Maybe that was why he had taken the job ... no, no, no ... he'd made his decision before he'd come back to the house. He'd wanted it, too ... imagining that Goodhaven was going to be such a wonderful place to live ...

She was lost again in a maze of contradiction and conflict, resolved only by accepting the realization that had come to her as she had driven down the New Jersey Turnpike, admitting that their life in Goodhaven had not been all that she had visualized, nor was there any real hope now that it would ever be ... at least not the kind of life that Linc ought to have. He needed the constant stimulation of bright-minded friends ... and there was little chance for anything of that sort in Goodhaven. They'd met almost everyone in town ... good people, nice people, but dull. At the college, Linc would be surrounded with good minds, dozens of them ... some of them would be offbeat but still they'd give him what he needed ... not someone to do his thinking for him ... no, he had the discrimination to know what was sound and what wasn't ... the judgment to make his own decisions ...

There was a signpost ahead and she searched it for some clue to the road that would cut across to Maryland. A town name leaped out at her ... DOVER ... that's where Brick was being married ... maybe right now, this very minute ...

For an instant there was the exciting of old brain centers, the anticipation of some expected response. Then, with no more than the faintly rustling mind-sound of thoughts slipping off down a new but already well-worn path, she let her subconscious mind take over, admitting what could never have been admitted before. She knew, and now seemed always to have known, that she had never been in love with Brick, yet she had always been able to believe that he had been in love with her, and the sensing of that continuing affection had, in its very hopelessness, been a sustaining force in her life. Now that was gone, lost forever, yet it had been replaced by something else, the restoration of a friendship that was once again warm and honest and good. It was something that Linc needed ... but she had needed it, too. No matter what Brick had done to help Linc in the past, nor what he might do to help in the future, she would always be the one who owed him the greatest of debts.

She had ceased wondering how much of what Brick had said to her today had been calculated for its effect upon her — it was possible to believe now that he'd had no other purpose than, as he had said, to clean the slate — yet, whatever his reason, it had taken a humbling of pride that made him a bigger man than she had ever imagined him to be, exhibiting a kind of courage that hung before her now as an example.

Her recollection of Brick's words was no more trustworthy than the memory of her own, yet she knew that what he had said had been true ... Linc should never have taken this Coastal Foods job ... it was too much like what he'd done before, too obviously a come-down ... but if he went to Chesapeake it would be like starting over again ... *a clean slate* ... yes, that's what Brick had said ...

She saw the route marker and turned left.

6

Dr. Lee Perrill had often protected his sensibilities by telling himself that nothing that could happen to him in the future could possibly be worse than what had already happened to him in the past. He thought he had suffered through and survived every adversity, both personal and professional, that life could inflict upon him. And then he had gotten the call from Roman Hills.

Fortunately, Kira Zurich had been in his office when the call came, fortunate because her neurotic exhibition of terror had been the only thing that had saved him, that and a lifetime of rigid training in the necessity of never lifting the mask of professionalism. Behind that mask, however, there was a terrifyingly vivid resurrection of the dream that he'd had that night in India after the Tokali gruel had been fed to all those babies, and he felt again the bone-rattling cold of that predawn moment when he had lain there listening in the awful stillness, unable to hear the crying of even one baby. All that sustained him now was the hopeful memory that his fear had been unjustified.

He had wanted desperately to get away from Kira Zurich, but she had insisted upon driving him to Roman Hills and with no alternative — the ownership of an automobile had always seemed an unnecessary temptation to fritter away time — he had agreed to let her drive him. While she was getting her car — and for some unaccountable reason, wasting the time needed to change her clothes — he gathered together a kit of instruments and drugs, searched out several references on food poisoning and took the volumes with him to read in the car. Then he called Frank Kennan. Luckily, Kennan was still at the cannery. The two thousand samples for Roman Hills had been shipped as a separate lot and Kennan remembered that they had been taken from Monday's production. He insisted that nothing could possibly have gone wrong, all the more strongly after he had checked the foreman's log and the charts from the recording thermometers.

But it was new production, made after the change in processing procedure.

By the time Kira Zurich had come to pick him up, Dr. Perrill was already aware of the little lightning-flash darts of pectoral pain that he recognized as his own most reliable symptom of psychosomatic reaction to stress. He found some slight relief when it again proved necessary to quiet Kira's concern because she had been unable to find any way to get in touch with Lincoln Lord. Even Mrs. Lord had disappeared.

Kip was home alone, but all that he had been able to tell her was that his parents had gone to Brighton, Maryland.

7

Flashing red lights and a harshly clanging bell stopped Maggie Lord as she approached the bridge to Brighton. The draw was up for a fisherman's skipjack sliding downriver toward Chesapeake Bay, silently except for that moment when the pung-pung exhaust of its engine echoed hollowly upward from the black water. The warm wind was southerly, heavy with the spice smell of the marshes and the memory of her father... *"Promise me one thing, Maggie ... when you pick out someone to marry, be sure that he's the man you want to spend your life with, not someone that you imagine you can make over into something that he was never intended to be ..."*

Brighton lay across the river, the wharf sheds along the shore rising darkly from the water, the white houses on Hill Street bronzed by the last light of a lingering sunset, the sky over the stores along Front Street faintly reddened by the glow of neon.

Her eyes were drawn to the left, away from the lights of the town, searching out the old Quincy cannery, seeing it not as she saw it now, lifeless and two-dimensional in the gathering darkness, but alive with steam-jetted bustle as it had been on that morning twenty-three years ago when she had come to Brighton to go to work for the Quincy Canning Company. Beyond sight but clearly seen, there was the road to Kingdom Come plantation, across the marsh and through the pines, the long driveway to the mansion house, old Adam Quincy waiting for her in the library... *"So you think you'd like to put your roots down here?"*

And she had put roots down there, deeper than they had ever gone down anywhere else. That was where she had fallen in love, and married the man who loved her, and borne his son.

Apprehension erased memory... where would she find Linc? And if she didn't find him ... ?

The drawbridge was coming down. The lights changed from red to green and she drove ahead, searching out landmarks as she came to the far end of the bridge. It had been thirteen years since she had seen Brighton, thirteen years since that morning when Linc had come to tell her that he wasn't coming back to the Quincy Canning Company, thirteen years since that last backward glance as they had crossed this same bridge. Everything seemed the same ... Proctor's Store on the corner, the Sugar Bowl, the angle-parked cars of the Friday night shoppers ...

And then she turned right on Seminary Avenue and nothing was the same. Where she had expected picket-fenced white houses, there was the red brick wall of a large building and, beyond, another and another. Unnecessarily, she slowed to read names chiseled into limestone, knowing that they must be the new Chesapeake College dormitories yet hardly able to believe that the campus now spread all the way from Widgeon Cove to the bridge. Katie Rafferty's millinery shop was gone, and Mrs. Thompson's, where she had roomed until she moved to Kingdom Come — and, worst of all, the scroll-worked old house where the dean of the college had always lived, where tonight she had hoped to find Linc's car parked.

She pulled to the curb, interrupting a pair of wandering arm-in-arm lovers to ask where Dean Whittaker lived. The boy told her in a nasal drawl that made her remember Hooper Island, a memory almost instantly pushed aside as she followed the directions he gave her, swinging in through the stone gateposts, quickly finding the second of the new houses on Faculty Row. But there was no black Pantheon parked either in front or in the drive.

Her next best bet was the College Inn — that was where Linc had stayed the last time he had come back for Homecoming — and she followed the curving campus drive back to Seminary Avenue, everything so strange that she thought for a moment that the Inn, too, had been torn down. But then she saw it farther down the street, smaller than she had remembered it to be, dwarfed now by the bigger buildings of the college. She stopped the car, scanning the parking lot. It was full — but no Pantheon.

She checked off the order of search that she had set up in her mind ... Kingdom Come was next ... should she call Jay? If Linc wasn't there ... and if he didn't want Jay to know that he was in town ...

There was still the possibility that Linc might be staying at the Inn, that he might have gone out somewhere for dinner but would be back later. She parked the car and went into the lobby. Here nothing had changed — the same sailing canoe pictures on the walls, the same ship model precariously perched on the rickety mantel, the same long wait for someone to come to the desk. And when the room clerk came he was still the same college boy, crew-cut now and wearing a brass-buttoned blue blazer instead of the "C" sweater, but not a day older than he had been twenty-three years ago.

"Is Mr. Lord staying here?" she asked. "Mr. Lincoln Lord?

"He with the conference?"

"No," she said. "He would have checked in late this afternoon, two or three hours ago."

"Could'nt've," the boy said, yawning. "We been full up with this conference crowd for two days."

"Is there anywhere else — ?"

"Ma'am?" a soft voice said behind her, and she turned to face the Negro bellboy. "This gentleman you're looking for, ma'am, was he driving one of them foreign cars?"

"Yes — a Pantheon."

"Don't know if that's the name," he said doubtfully. "But is he kind of a big-looking man, like maybe he was somebody from New York — ?"

"Yes, yes," she broke in. "Do you have any idea where he might have gone, any idea at all?"

"Yes, ma'am. I told him about the new motel and that's where he went. It's right down to the end of this street, ma'am, right where the new road comes in."

She thanked him fervently and hurried from the lobby, seeing the motel sign as soon as she stepped outside.

And there was the Pantheon!

She parked beside it, seeing Linc's hat on the front seat. There was no answer when she pounded on the nearest door . . . but he couldn't be far away!

An old man came limping out of the office, regarding her suspiciously when she said that she was looking for her husband, maddeningly slow to respond when she asked him if he had noticed which way Linc had gone when he left. But he finally said cryptically, "Yeah, I seen him leave. Maybe an hour ago. Crossing over to the college. Didn't look like he was going no place special, though. Just walking."

She ran across the street, ducking one car and then another, stopping for a moment to catch her breath as she stood looking out over the campus, trying to decide which way to go, wondering if it might not be better to go back and get her car and drive the campus roads. But the pull of intuition was strong and she hurried on, rounding the corner of one building and then walking the length of another, in and out of the pools of light under the lampposts, suddenly looking up to see against the night sky the unmistakably turreted façade of Chapel

Hall. It stood apart from the new buildings, seemingly preserved out of sentiment, marked now with a bronze plaque that traced the history of Chesapeake College back to the founding of Chesapeake Seminary by the Reverend Ephraim Tuttle in 1757. The lights were on in the chapel, the double doors open to the night, and it was against that bright-glowing rectangle that she saw a silhouetted figure . . . *Linc!*

A silent shout must have somehow reached her lips because she saw him turn, his face featureless because of the strong light behind him, but she saw the fingers of his clenched fists fall open and she ran into his arms. "Oh, Linc, Linc, Linc, I was so afraid I wouldn't find you!"

Surprise accomplished what she might not have been able to do with words alone, and his arms went around her, his voice meaningless because all he was asking was how she had gotten there and that didn't matter now. "Oh, Linc, I was so wrong, so terribly, terribly wrong!"

"Maybe you weren't," he muttered, and she felt the grip of his arms go slack, a weakening of the force that held them together, and she tried to restore it with her own strength, clinging to him. But that first moment was over, her initial advantage lost, and she saw now that there were people inside the chapel watching them. She gave direction to her strength, pulling him away from the door, and that was enough impetus to start them walking, off into the darkness and a silence that she knew had to be broken.

"Linc, I know all of the horrible things that you must be thinking about me. And I'm not trying to deny them. I can't. They're true."

A groan of denial broke from his lips and he stopped her, crushing her to him but looking away from her. "I don't know what got into me, Mag. I don't know why I said those things."

Stunned, she realized that he was apologizing to her, and for an instant there was the temptation to accept this easy way out . . . but if she did . . .

"No, Linc, no. I was the one who was wrong. And I've been so wrong for so many years — so selfish —"

"You've never been that," he denied. "You've always stood by me, no matter how much of a fool I've been — all these years. I never realized what I was doing, how wrong I was."

"You weren't wrong, Linc," she said, her words hard-driven. "And you aren't wrong now. This is where you should be — here."

He looked away from her. "I can't leave Coastal Foods."

"Why not?" she demanded. "You've done what you came there to do.

What more could you do if you stayed? There's nothing to be done there now that someone else can't do. But here — oh, there's so much to be done and you're the one to do it. No one else could possibly do it even half as well as you could. This is so much bigger, so much more important — oh, Linc, this is what you've been building up to all your life. Everything else has just been a preparation for this. Can't you see that?"

"I don't know," he said, looking past her. "It would be different if I were an educator, if I'd been in college work —"

"But if you had been, you wouldn't be what they need. And they do need you. They know that. That's why they want you so badly. Linc, listen to me —"

"It would just be running another business," he said, but almost as a question, almost in anticipation of her denial.

"In some ways — yes, it might be," she said. "But the product is so much more important. Look at them, Linc —" She paused, watching his face as his eyes followed three boys, locked in animated discussion as they walked down a cross path ahead of them. "Isn't turning those boys into good men more important than — well, packing beef stew?"

His abrupt chuckle was the key to joy and she said, "Oh, Linc, I'm right, I know I am."

"It would cost us a lot of money," he said, an abrupt change of tone. "There'll be no bonus if I leave —"

"We've always been broke, anyway," she laughed, surprising herself. "We'll get along. We always have, we always will. Just so you don't stop loving me."

"Don't ever worry about that," he said, a throaty whisper as he reached out, gripping her shoulders. "Not after this. If you hadn't come —" He closed his eyes. "I don't know what I'd have done. That's what I was trying to decide."

"You do want it, don't you, Linc?"

"Not as much as I want you."

"That isn't a choice you'll ever have to make," she whispered. "Whatever you do, wherever you go —"

He kissed her. And this was Kingdom Come in the spring again, a dream surely restored when she opened her eyes and saw a halo of new-green leaves around the lights that marked the path ahead. "I thought you might have gone out to see Jay."

"No, I haven't seen anyone," he said, his arm still around her shoulder as they walked ahead, retracing the way she had come, back toward the motel.

"How in the world did you get here?" he asked, not as he had done before but now as if he were bewildered by a miracle.

"I took Kip's car."

"Did you tell him —" His arm dropped. "— why I came down?"

"Yes."

They walked in silence until he said, "I suppose he'll miss Haven Home."

"He hasn't been there all week."

"He hasn't? I didn't know that."

"I didn't either until he told me." There was a corner to be turned. "He frightens me sometimes, Linc, it's so hard to get close to him, so hard to know what he's really thinking."

"I know," he said. "But I never realized that you felt that way, too. I always thought it was only me."

She was surprised by an admission that she had never imagined he'd be able to make, yet intent now on picking up the thread he had broken. "He's a lot like you, Linc." His stabbing side glance was more felt than seen. "There's so much in his mind that he never lets anyone else know about."

"It isn't because I've wanted it to be that way," he said, making the translation of reference from Kip to himself. "It's just that — I guess it's something we all do, building things up inside of ourselves. And then when they come busting out, you realize how foolish you've been — how wrong."

"You weren't as wrong as I was. I've given you so little and you deserve so much. Oh, Linc, you've done so many wonderful things —"

She felt his arm stiffen under the hand that she had reached out, his attention suddenly lost. They had come to the curb of the street and he was looking across at the motel.

"What do you suppose that's all about?" he asked.

Following his eyes, she saw a sweeping beam of light, and then that it came from a flashlight in the hands of a state trooper who was now walking toward the office.

"He was looking at my car," Linc said anxiously, uncertainly hesitant. "Probably going to hang a speeding ticket on me."

"But why wouldn't he have stopped you on the road?"

"I don't know," he said. "But there's no use trying to duck it. Come on."

535

He guided her across the street, coming up behind the trooper who was standing now with his back to them, talking to the manager who stood in the open door of the office.

"That's him now," the manager said.

The trooper did a smart about-face. "Mr. Lord?"

"Yes. I saw you looking at my car."

"That's the only way I had of running you down," the trooper said. "They said you'd be driving a Pantheon. Didn't know for sure what I was looking for — first one I've ever seen — so I had to check."

"No, there aren't many of them around."

The trooper took a notebook from his jacket pocket and slipped a folded note from under the heavy rubber band. "You're to call the Roman Hills Community Hospital as soon as you can — Roman Hills, New Jersey — and ask for Dr. Simmons's office."

"Joel!" Linc exclaimed. "He went over there to check the Gellman survey. He must have been in an accident —"

"I don't know about that, Mr. Lord," the trooper said. "All I know is that it must be something pretty important or headquarters wouldn't have put an emergency pick-up on it."

"Thank you, officer," Linc said calmly, but as he stepped hurriedly inside the office, it was almost as if she could hear the pounding of his heart.

Her own seemed to have stopped . . . first Swann and now Joel . . . both of them gone . . . Linc would feel that he couldn't leave Coastal Foods . . . no, no, no! He couldn't stay, not now . . . no matter who, no matter what . . .

8

Joel Morris paced the corridor that separated the pathological laboratory from the sunroom that had been pressed into emergency service as a headquarters for all the town officials who had been drawn to the hospital as a result of the epidemic — and that, beyond any doubt or quibbling, was what it had now become. Eleven children were already in the hospital, the ambulance had just pulled up at the receiving door again, and no one knew how many more cases were represented by the calls that were stacked up ahead of the town's physicians.

Pacing, Joel was attempting to keep his eyes off the wall clock that was already accusing him of being on borrowed time. He had stalled off any decision until an eight o'clock deadline, hoping that by then Lincoln Lord would have called and lifted from his shoulders the terrible responsibility of agreeing to broadcast a general warning against Wonderfood. Now it was five minutes after eight with hope all but gone that his emergency call to the Maryland State Police, made after he had talked long-distance to Kip Lord, would produce results. Any moment now, someone would come out through the open door of the sunroom and say that they had waited long enough. It would probably be Zimmer, who, as public relations director of Roman Instruments Corporation, was spokesman for the town. Zimmer had been insisting for the last half-hour that a warning be broadcast over the local radio station. If that happened, there would be no way to stop it from spreading. Other news agencies would pick it up and, before morning, the whole country would accept as a certainty what was still only a strong suspicion — that Haven Home Wonderfood was dangerously toxic. The scare headlines would be all the blacker because of the widespread publicity that Haven Home had been given.

Joel had found it difficult to fight back against Zimmer's demand that something be done at once — he himself had been badly torn by the emotional impact of imagining helpless babies being poisoned — yet there had been the justification that Dr. Perrill had given him as soon as he had arrived and talked to the hospital officials, the argument that there was as yet absolutely no proof that Wonderfood was at fault. The suspicion that it might be the cause of the epidemic was supported only by the circumstantial evidence that it had been fed to the first three babies to be brought to the hospital.

As repugnant as it was to weigh the prospect of sickened children against other considerations, Joel Morris could not escape consciousness of the widespread havoc that would be wrought by spreading a nation-wide alarm, a consciousness momentarily centered in Kira Zurich's face as he saw her watching him through the door of the sunroom. Everything that she had been working for at Haven Home would be lost, the research center's new-found reputation as quickly destroyed as it had been created. Dr. Perrill would be discredited, the work of a lifetime lost. The Gellman Stores Corporation would be dealt a serious blow, having so closely identified itself with Wonderfood through yesterday's full-page advertisements. But it was the Coastal Foods Company that would be hit the hardest of all. Not only

537

would Wonderfood be killed off but the use of the Haven Home trademark would be the kiss of death to the whole new line, making it impossible to sell — Gerhart & Gerhart would be hurt, too — but for Coastal Foods it might well be a calamity of disastrous proportions. The company's financial resources, even the loan from Anderson Phelps, had all been gambled on promotional expense and the building up of stocks. Issuing a public warning would light the fuse of a chain-reacting explosion . . . and if it turned out to be unjustified, not the fault of Wonderfood . . .

Joel Morris shuddered, overwhelmed again by a terrifying visualization. This afternoon, the 3,200 cases of Wonderfood that had been shipped from the cannery seemed pitifully inadequate. Now, he saw it as 76,800 individual cans . . . 76,800 babies . . . *Yes, Doctor, all of the typical clinical manifestations . . . salivation and then nausea . . . retching . . . abdominal cramps . . . vomiting . . . a little blood in the vomitus . . .*

He closed his eyes, pounding his fists against his temples . . . if he couldn't reach Mr. Lord and had to make the decision himself . . . oh god, it was too much responsibility to ask any man to take!

He caught his breath. The telephone in the laboratory was ringing again. Another false hope? He shifted his position so that he could look through the glass panel in the laboratory door, watching Dr. Simmons as he lifted the telephone instrument. He could not hear what was being said but a combination of subconscious lip-reading and the pathologist's glance toward the hall made him leap for the door.

"There's an extension in my office," Dr. Simmons suggested and, jumping at the chance for privacy, Joel stumbled over a chair in his haste to take the call there, out of breath as he pushed the door shut with his foot, lifting the receiver and asking, "Mr. Lord?" dizzied then by confusion over what he heard, finally realizing that Lincoln Lord had apparently imagined that something had happened to him.

"No, I'm all right — it's Wonderfood," he said, going on then to cover the situation up to the moment, talking into the dead silence that seemed to have blanked out the other end of the line.

Suddenly, he heard Lincoln Lord's voice and, almost with the first syllable, he felt his heart slow its racing pace, his whole being instantly strengthened by transmitted poise.

"Eleven cases in the hospital," Joel said, answering the question that had been asked. "But there are a lot of calls for doctors — how many I don't know."

"And you say that they've traced it to Wonderfood?"

"All I know for sure is what Dr. Simmons told me — that it had been fed to the first three that were brought in. That was about five o'clock. There weren't any more cases until after six. Then a whole bunch of them hit all at once. That's when I came over here. Since then everybody's been so busy that it's been pretty hard to find out what's really happening. That's what Dr. Perrill is doing now, running down case histories with one of the interns. They're checking —"

"Doc Perrill's there?"

"Yes, I called him right away. I thought it was the thing to do."

"Of course. What's he think?"

"He can't believe that it could be Wonderfood. But he really hasn't had time enough to find out what's going on. He's only been here for about a half-hour, maybe three-quarters. Mrs. Zurich drove him down and they didn't get here until almost seven-thirty."

"But it could be Wonderfood?"

"Yes, sir, the doctors here at the hospital think it is. But they can't be absolutely sure until they get their tests through the lab."

"How long will that take?"

"Tomorrow afternoon at the earliest. Maybe longer."

"There's no way that can be speeded up?"

"No, I don't think so. They say they've got everyone going full tilt, all the people they can possibly use — that's where I'm calling from, the lab office — and it sure looks like they're doing all they can. Doc Perrill checked the kind of tests they're running and he didn't have any suggestions. There are a couple of things that they can't do here — they've sent samples to the state lab — but they won't know for at least twenty-four hours —"

"What's been done as far as the public is concerned?" Lincoln Lord asked, and for the first time a tone of tense anxiety slipped through, making it plain that there was no need to alert him to the decision that had to be made. "Has there been any announcement — any warning?"

"No sir, not yet. I've been stalling them off until I could talk to you."

"Stalling who off?"

"Well, there's been a lot of push to put it on the radio and warn

539

people — this is pretty much of a company town, you know, so it isn't just the medical people, it's all the company officials, too. Zimmer — he's their p.r. chief — has been the hardest one to hold down. He's got a couple of kids himself —"

"What about the state health department?" Lincoln Lord asked, quickly answering himself. "Yes, you said they'd sent samples there, didn't you? What about Washington? Have they been notified?"

"Yes, Dr. Simmons called them right away, when he was first trying to get some dope on Wonderfood. Their district inspector is here — he's out in the lab now."

"What's he say?"

"Well, he's darned worried, naturally. We all are — everyone is."

"Does he think there should be a public warning?"

"No, he agrees with Doc Perrill that there's still a chance that it might be something else, and that we shouldn't take a chance on panicking the public until we're more certain that it's really Wonderfood. He's been talking to Washington and they're getting some other men on the job. He came out a while ago and asked me where else we'd made sample distributions."

"I've just been thinking about that," Lincoln Lord said. "Are they having any trouble there? Have you checked?"

"Yes, and as far as we can find out, everything's all right. But the point is —" He caught his breath, swallowing hard. "They started sampling here the first thing Thursday morning. Out on Long Island, they didn't start until noon. There's a six-hour lag. They didn't get the first case here until about three o'clock. That would mean — well, if it hits there, too, it would be about nine o'clock tonight. The Gellman manager has talked to the health officials out there —"

"Then the Gellman people know what's happening?"

"Dr. Simmons came over to the store here — that's how I found out about it — so, of course, the store manager got the word, too. He called New York right away."

"What have they done?"

"Sam told me they'd started calling all their stores, telling the managers to pull what they had left off the shelves and say they were out of stock. In most cases that was true, anyway. It's been selling fast all day so almost every can is out in the hands of —"

"You haven't talked to Sid Arnauth?"

"No, but I think he's at his office. They're all there waiting. I promised to call Sam as soon as there was anything definite here. I think — well, I know they're pretty darned jumpy."

"Do you think I should call Arnauth?"

"Yes sir, I — well, I don't think it would hurt — and it might help."

"All right," Lincoln Lord said. "I'll try to get him to come down and meet me there."

"You're coming up here?"

"Of course. I'll leave here the minute I talk to Arnauth. You can keep stalling until I get there, can't you?"

From somewhere he found the courage to say, "Yes, sir, I'm sure I can."

"Just in case there's some new development, I'll call you every half-hour on the road. Almost eight-thirty now — or will be by the time I can get away. Stay near the telephone at nine — nine-thirty — ten — ten-thirty. I should be there by eleven."

9

Maggie Lord felt as if she had been holding her breath for two hours, clinging to something jet-propelled through the night, blasted from one roadside telephone booth to another, hurtling down the highway in a mad rush toward disaster. Now, finally, they were in Roman Hills, the car slowed by the winding streets, but there was no relaxation of tension. She could see the hospital ahead, lights blazing on every floor, and the siren on the ambulance that cut in front of them as they approached the drive screamed in perfect pitch with her stressed nerves.

Back at the motel, listening to Linc's hurried explanation after he had talked to Joel, there had been a moment — but only a moment — when she had felt herself struck down by disaster, her mind blanked by terror. Then, almost instantly, she had been caught up by the driving urge for self-preservation, every fiber of her being charged with the urgency of fighting back. And it was then, with a peaking of the courage of desperation, that she had begun to sense, by contrast, the weakness of Linc's reaction. He seemed completely unable to throw off his initial terror, incapable of summoning the strength that the situation demanded. Even the way he had driven had frightened

541

her, because he had made it seem a blind rush toward an already sealed fate instead of a courageous response to emergency.

Some of that feeling had been lost as they roared through the night, reasoned away with a growing sympathy for the awful responsibility that had been so suddenly thrust upon him, yet there was alarming evidence that he had no intention of facing up to it himself. Before they had left the motel, he had called not only Sidney Arnauth but also Art Gerhart, asking both of them to meet him in Roman Hills. Kira Zurich and Dr. Perrill were already there. So was Joel. Frank Kennan was on his way. There would be a meeting and Linc, as always, would be the chairman, counting the votes, making the decision that other people wanted him to make, so anxious to please everyone else that he would surely submerge the courage of his own conviction. What made it even worse tonight was his apparent conviction that the decision to put Wonderfood on the market had been his and his alone. Even that was not completely true — surely the pressure from Kira Zurich had been a factor — yet his feeling that the disaster had been the result of the one time that he had gone ahead on his own would surely mitigate against any show of real strength tonight.

Although Maggie Lord sensed that most, if not all, of her anticipation was based upon supposition, it was supported by everything that Linc had said on the way up. No matter what she had tried to tell him, no matter what question she had asked, he had always responded in terms of what this was going to mean to someone else, the damage that would be done to them by a public warning that Wonderfood was toxic. Despite the fact that he had told her after every telephone stop that there was still no certain proof that Wonderfood was at fault, he had said as they had driven into Roman Hills that he hoped Kira Zurich had gotten Brick on the job to handle whatever statement would have to be made to the press. It was then that she had told him, the first chance that there had been, that Brick had been married today, admitting with wracking regret that she hadn't asked him where they were going afterwards, almost hoping that Linc would criticize her for her foolish neglect. Instead, he had started talking about what it would mean to Brick and the future of his public relations agency if the whole Haven Home story blew up in his face, black-marking him with all the magazines that already had gone to press, or were about to, with a story on whose soundness Brick had staked his professional standing and reputation.

None of her attempts to arouse Linc's spirit had been effective, yet now as he parked in front of the hospital entrance she tried again, no more successful than she had been before.

"Would you rather I waited?" she asked as he got out of the car, pleased when he shook his head, yet strangely fear-filled as she followed him to the entrance, suddenly aware that her demand for courage was less soundly based than she had thought . . . what was it that she really wanted Linc to do . . . ?

Joel was waiting at the front door and Linc asked, "Anything new?"

"Not much," Joel said. "Except for the Mancini baby."

She flinched from a dagger thrust as she heard Linc ask, "Dead?"

"No, but the doctors are pretty worried," Joel said. "It's been sick ever since it was born — one thing after another, no resistance — that makes it all the rougher."

There was a strange hush in the entrance lobby, broken only by the voice of the telephone operator placing a long-distance call to Washington and, as they approached the stairway, the low murmur of a man attempting to comfort a weeping woman.

"Downstairs," Joel directed. "That's where they're all waiting."

Linc stopped on the first step. "Arnauth get here?"

"Yes sir, Mr. Arnauth and Sam Mandel. Frank's here now. Mr. Phelps just came."

"Phelps?"

"I think Mrs. Zurich called him."

"Art Gerhart?"

Joel nodded. "And Canning's with him. The Washington crowd's all in the lab office talking to Dr. Perrill. I imagine that's where you'll want to go first."

She followed as they turned into the wide corridor, only conscious enough of the groups of men scattered along its walls to be aware that Linc's appearance cut off all conversation, everyone's eyes on him as he strode toward the door that Joel pointed out. She hung back as she saw the crowd of men inside, but Joel held the door for her and she slipped through, shrinking back into the corner. As a path opened for Linc, she saw Dr. Perrill with his back to the far wall, facing everyone else in the room, breathing deeply in this moment of respite from torture.

Joel introduced Linc to someone and he, whoever he was, said to the room, "Gentlemen, this is Mr. Lord, the president of the Coastal Foods Company."

543

They crowded around him then and she could hear little or nothing of what was being said, encouraged that the general tone seemed free of any air of panicked emergency, yet warning herself that it might be no more than the professional composure of doctors and medical scientists. Finally, Dr. Perrill's voice lifted above the crowd murmur and, judging from his first words, she gathered that he was now picking up where he had left off when he had been interrupted by their arrival.

"With all due respect to contrary opinions," Dr. Perrill was saying, "I do think I may claim some special qualification in the diagnosis of these bacillary infections. I spent a number of years of my life in India where the incidence is very high. Even before that I'd worked on strain classification of the mannite-fermenting paradysenteriae —"

She was quickly lost in a flood of medical terms, yet able to grasp the essence of Perrill's argument that isolation of the specific organism that was responsible for the outbreak could not be accomplished short of some twenty-four tests, and that the blame could not be positively fixed until the presence of that same organism could be demonstrated in samples of Wonderfood taken from the same can from which an afflicted child had been fed.

"And you won't find it there!" Dr. Perrill concluded, fiercely positive, yet with a tremor in his voice that raised the suspicion that his judgment might be warped by pride if not self-interest.

But he was not without support. A white-coated man immediately in front of her said, "In view of the clinical evidence, I'd say that the odds were in favor of Dr. Perrill's position. At that sterilizing temperature and with the pH as low as it is —"

"But the long shots do come in once in a while," someone else's voice broke in, shockingly light in tone. "Remember that bet I collected from you in Pittsburgh — the dried egg case?"

Across the room an old man's pompous voice said, "If I may express an opinion — yes, the law of probability does still apply and, as a matter of principle, I'm opposed to drastic action on the basis of purely empirical evidence. However, when you have a situation where in every case the child has been fed —"

"Not true!" Dr. Perrill backfired. "We have a case where the mother swears that the child was not given a bit of it."

"But didn't Dr. Nelson tell us that she admitted opening the sample can?"

"Yes, she says she opened it," Dr. Perrill said grudgingly. "But what

544

else could you expect — all this publicity? You give a mother a free can — of course, she'd open it. Curiosity if nothing else. But that doesn't mean she fed it to her child."

"But as I recall this boy was almost two — and a two-year-old child, with the temptation of an open can standing around —"

"Gentlemen!" She saw the gray-haired man to whom Linc had first been introduced rise. "I'm afraid that we're not going to resolve anything by going on in this fashion. Even though we did know for sure — which we don't — that every child was fed this product, that still can't be taken as an unassailable indictment. As Dr. Perrill pointed out a moment ago, every child also ingested both water and milk."

Maggie Lord's heart leaped with hope, lost when someone asked, "But if it's either water or milk, Doctor, why aren't we getting some older children, even adults?"

Dr. Perrill snapped him up. "Obvious — we're dealing with an organism where susceptibility is limited to infants."

"Yes, that's possible," the gray-haired man agreed. "The point is, gentlemen, that we're in the same position we're so often in when we're up against an epidemic of this sort. No matter what our suspicions are, we simply do not *know* — and we can't know until sometime tomorrow. There's nothing to do but wait. In the meantime, I surely agree with Dr. Perrill's suggestion that we should start an investigation of the dairy plants and the water works."

"We're on it," someone said over the clatter of chairs as the meeting broke up.

Dr. Perrill and some of the men moved quickly through the connecting door into the laboratory, the others drifting out into the hall. She started to follow, stopped when she saw that Linc, with Joel beside him, was talking to the gray-haired man, who by now was obviously established as being in charge of the investigation.

Linc was asking, "Then you don't feel, Dr. Craggin, that we should put out a warning?"

"I wish I could advise you, Mr. Lord," Dr. Craggin said. "Unfortunately I can't. I do understand from Mr. Morris here that the Gellman people have taken it off their shelves until the situation is clarified. Under the circumstances, I'm sure that was a wise move. But it's still a case of locking the door after the horse was stolen. They've been selling it for several days — quite actively, I understand — thousands of cans are already in the hands of mothers —"

"That's what I can't understand," she heard Linc break in. "If it's

545

Wonderfood, why haven't we heard of anything wrong anywhere else?"

"There's been no concentrated distribution in one area, has there, Mr. Lord?" Dr. Craggin asked. "A can at a time — in an individual case, the cause of infection might easily have gone unrecognized. Please don't misunderstand me — I'm not implying that there have been such cases —"

"I understand."

"That's the usual situation, Mr. Lord — we're only alerted when we get an incidence of epidemic proportions. By then, distribution of the product is already so widespread that withdrawal from sale is only a partial solution. We still have to think of those thousands of cans that have already been bought. They're untraceable, beyond reclaiming. The only way those people can possibly be reached is to release a public warning through all channels of communications."

"You do that from Washington?" Linc asked.

"Yes, if the manufacturer hasn't already taken the initiative," Dr. Craggin said. "But we can't take government action until we have substantial proof that we're justified in doing so. If we were to move too soon — please believe me, Mr. Lord, we're sensitive to the damage that such an action can cause. We know that it's quite possible to ruin a company financially with the issuing of a recall order. We're not unaware of that. And touching off a public panic is not something to be done lightly either. On the other hand we do have a function to perform —"

"Of course you do," Linc said.

"And whenever it's a product that affects babies, the decision is all the harder to make. I don't suppose it should be — hardly rational — but nevertheless there is an emotional factor that can't be overlooked. I was involved some years ago with a baby-food case — a salmonella infection that we traced to a dried egg product. There, I've always felt I waited too long to act — we had five deaths and that's not an easy price to pay. On the other hand, there've been other cases where we would have done great damage to some innocent companies if we'd gone ahead on the basis of a first suspicion."

Linc faced him, eyes narrowed. "Doctor, if you were in my position, what would you do?"

The gray head dropped, finally lifted with a tight-lipped sigh. "I can only say this, Mr. Lord — thank god, I'm not. My own position is bad enough, yours is worse." He averted his eyes. "As far as your corporate liability is concerned, I don't believe anyone could fairly accuse you of not having acted promptly enough if you wait until we have the laboratory reports."

"But if we don't warn people — and it does turn out to be toxic — ?"

"No, it's not a pleasant prospect. I sympathize with you, Mr. Lord. You have a hard decision to make."

As closely as she was watching her husband's face, Maggie Lord saw not a tremor, not the slightest hint of relaxation in the hard muscles of his set jaw. But then she saw him turn to Joel. "Is there somewhere we can get our people together?"

"I'm sure we can use this office," Joel said as Dr. Craggin left. "Who do you want in — Mr. Arnauth, Mr. Gerhart?"

"Yes," Linc said. "And get Frank, of course."

"He's here already," Joel said, glancing past her. Looking back over her shoulder she saw that Frank Kennan had been standing in the doorway behind her.

Linc had added Dr. Perrill's name to those he wanted in the meeting and Joel asked, "What about Mrs. Zurich?"

There was only an instant of hesitation before Linc said, "Yes, of course — and she probably want Anderson Phelps with her."

"I'll get them," Kennan offered and he and Joel went out together.

For a moment they were alone, long enough for Linc to say, "You stay, too."

"Oh, Linc, I —"

"I want you," he said, surprising her with the strength of his voice.

Sidney Arnauth came in the door, his thin face even more drawn than she remembered it, foreboding and darkly tragic. The others followed him and she pressed back into the corner, moving to avoid the swing of the door. She was separated from Linc by the full length of the office, everyone between them, but she could see that he was holding a whispered consultation with Joel, continued for a suspenseful moment after a hush had fallen over the rest of the room. Joel nodded and moved away. Linc stood alone. Never in her life had she felt herself so strongly drawn to his side, so urged by compassion to share what he faced, yet never had she felt less certain that she really had within herself the strength and courage that she so desperately wanted him to display.

The click of a latch shattered dead silence and Kennan slipped in through the side door to the laboratory, stage whispering, "Doc Perrill will be here in just a moment."

She saw Linc give him an acknowledging nod and, thinking he would wait for Dr. Perrill, she took the chance to glance around her, wondering if there was anyone who could possibly appreciate what this meant to Linc . . . his whole world crashing down . . . no, they were all worrying about their own little worlds . . . Sidney Arnauth and Gellman Stores . . . Art Gerhart and G & G . . . Kira Zurich and Haven Home . . . Anderson Phelps . . .

A voice spoke, familiar yet for an instant unidentifiable, too clear to be that of the man who had been beside her in the Pantheon a few minutes ago, too strong to be the vacillating man on the Chesapeake campus, too composed to be the Linc who had stormed in their bedroom this noon . . . but this *was* Lincoln Lord . . . this was the man she loved . . . oh, why hadn't she had more faith in him!

"I have a very important decision to make," he had said. And now he repeated it. "I must decide whether or not a warning will be issued that some or all of the Wonderfood that is now in the hands of the trade and public may be dangerously toxic. I am not asking that you share that responsibility. It's mine and I accept it. But I am asking for your advice and counsel. All of you will be affected as I will be, not only ourselves, but our organizations, all of the hundreds of people who depend upon us for their future livelihood and financial security. Your people are less endangered, perhaps, than my people at Coastal Foods, yet they will all be hurt if I release a general warning. Millions of dollars in business will be lost, even more perhaps through the indirect loss of public confidence and good will than through the products that are directly affected. And once the damage is done it will be irreparable. I know that. Even if it turns out that Wonderfood is in no way at fault, no retraction or explanation can ever erase the fear and distrust that will have been created."

He shifted his position, eyes lifted for a thoughtful moment before he continued. "The Coastal Foods Company is under no compulsion to issue a warning. Dr. Craggin assures me of that. Wonderfood may be the cause; it may not be. We don't know; they don't know. No one can know until the tests are completed late tomorrow afternoon. Legally, we have every right to wait, and the damage that would be done by an unnecessary and unjustified warning surely argues for exercising that right." He paused. "That's one side — the legal side, the material side."

Maggie Lord caught a deep breath and it seemed something simultaneously done by everyone in the room, a mass sigh before another silence.

"The moral side is less clear," Lincoln Lord continued. "If we issue a warning in the next few minutes, it will be on the radio before midnight and it will be in the newspapers tomorrow morning. If we wait for the tests, twenty-four hours will be lost. During those twenty-four hours, Wonderfood is going to be fed to thousands of children. If there's nothing wrong with it, if the trouble here has come from some other source — water or milk, for example — then we avoid the tremendous damage that would be done by a premature warning. On the other hand, if Wonderfood is at fault, we will be morally responsible for having made a great many children ill, perhaps some of them seriously so." He paused. "I don't know that there's much more that I can say — there isn't much more that I know; there isn't much more than can be known. This is one of those cases where a decision can't wait for the facts. But it does have to be made. If any of you have opinions, points of view — Art?"

Maggie Lord had seen, as he had, the nervous shifting of Gerhart's shoulders as an indication that he had something to say, and he did speak up at once; yet the first sound of his own voice seemed to convince him that whatever position he had been about to take was untenable. His fumbling resolved itself into no more than a muttered, "It's a shame that something like this had to happen, just a damn shame."

Sidney Arnauth gave no evidence of wishing to speak out, yet neither did he shrink from it. As he lifted his head, she saw his Semitic face in profile, and in the instant before he spoke it was the face of the timeless merchant, the eternal trader, the man to whom gold was the stuff of life. But the image softened immediately, vanishing as he said, "You've given me an easy way out, Mr. Lord — accepting the responsibility yourself — and I wish I could take it with a clear conscience. But I can't. All this is on my head, too. If it hadn't been for my decision to —" He broke off. "But it is true, of course, that Coastal Foods will be affected more seriously than anyone else, at least more seriously than Gellman Stores, and so we're quite willing to leave the decision in your hands, Mr. Lord. At this moment, I'm sure they're steadier hands than mine. If I had to make the decision myself —" He paused and it seemed that he was about to choose one course over another. But then he shook his head and a bitter smile came to his face as he said, almost to himself, "I'm afraid I'm temperamentally too emotional to be objective."

She saw Joel Morris shoot him a peculiar glance, expressing both shock and approval, a mixing of attitudes too enigmatic to be deciphered during the short lapse before her husband's voice made her shift her eyes to Kira Zurich. It was the first time she had looked directly at her and seeing her tortured face, she felt a sympathy that, for a moment, almost made her forget how cruelly unfair she had been to Linc.

Kira Zurich's first words were hoarsely whispered, only the phrase, "— same temperament —" plainly heard. Then, as if that admission had cleared her throat and released her full voice, she looked at Linc and said firmly, "I'm quite ready to accept any decision you make, Mr. Lord — you and Mr. Kennan — and Mr. Morris."

It took Maggie Lord a moment to translate those few words into the abject surrender that it so plainly represented, yet the quick sensing of victory was lost because it no longer had any real meaning — except that Kira, too, like everyone else, had abdicated her responsibility and left Linc standing alone to take the full brunt of both decision and consequence.

She searched for his eyes, trying to offer him whatever small strength there might be in her understanding and sympathy, but he was looking toward the connecting door to the laboratory. In her preoccupation she had not noticed that it had opened. Dr. Perrill stood in the doorway. His face had the look of the death mask, bone-white under the cold fluorescent lights. His lower lip trembled, stiffened, and then he said in a hoarse whisper, "The Mancini baby just died."

10

Brick Mitchell watched anxiously as Tommy stepped across the harlequin-patterned floor of the foyer and into the gold-satin shimmer of the suite's living room. But her face was radiant as she turned back to him. "Why were you so worried that I wouldn't like it?"

"Just thought maybe you wouldn't."

"Why?" Her eyes were dancing with the rainbow spatter of the crystal chandelier over her head.

"Well, it's kind of — you know, a little plushy plush —"

She whipped her head around for another quick inspection, swirling hair that suddenly made the satin seem dull. "I can't see why. Unless you mean —" Her mock seriousness was gayer than laughter. "Are you trying to say that this isn't the kind of a place where a married man would bring his wife?"

He was grinning like a fool and knew it . . . god, she was wonderful . . . that damn bellboy . . . why didn't he have sense enough to get out!

But no, he had to give them the full suite treatment . . . coats in the closet, bathroom light, check the water carafes, test the telephone, switch on the radio, a routine that couldn't be stopped until he came finally to, "Will that be all, sir?"

He nodded, hurrying him with a quick thrust of a folded bill . . . get out . . . get out . . . get out . . .

"Thank you, Mr. Mitchell. Good night, sir — good night, Mrs. Mitchell — and I hope you have a very pleasant stay with us."

Brick muttered something, turning his back, waiting for the sound of the closing door.

Tommy cocked her head. "You know, you are beginning to look a little like a married man, Mr. Mitchell."

He cupped her cheeks in the palms of his hands. "Do you want me to tell you what you look like, Mrs. Mitchell?"

"I hope you're going to say a very happily married woman who's very much in love with —"

The raucous blare of a brassy fanfare crashed in and he flailed out with a searching hand, trying to find the radio switch.

An echo-chambered voice intoned, *"This is John Paul Scott with your midnight news from near and far — from Washington, Hollywood, Geneva and Berlin — but first from the famous industrial community of Roman Hills, New Jersey, where —"*

He found the switch.

11

"— late this afternoon an epidemic of food poisoning struck with fearsome force. One baby is dead and more than twenty children are hospitalized. Doctors and health officials are still unable to positively identify the source of the infection. However, there is a possibility that it may be traced to a new product called Haven Home Wonder-

food. Minutes ago, just before we went on the air, a statement was issued by Lincoln Lord, president of the company that is putting out this product, warning all mothers —"

Maggie Lord switched off the car radio as she saw her husband finally break away from Kira Zurich and Joel Morris and push out through the glass door of the hospital entrance, anxious to protect him from a cruel reiteration of the self-destroying words that he himself had written, insisting that the warning be issued in his name.

He walked toward her, a black figure against the light, silhouetted as he had been endless hours ago when she had caught sight of him in the doorway of Chapel Hall . . . would he go back to Brighton?

She opened the car door for him. "Don't you want me to drive, Linc?"

"No, I'm all right," he said, getting in behind the wheel. "Let's go home."

12

There was a faint loom of light in the eastern sky as they approached Goodhaven, abruptly demanding Maggie Lord's recognition that a new day lay before her. Habit forced an attempt to anticipate the demands that it would make upon her, but she was quickly aware that the night had changed the landscape of her mind. It was no longer possible to think ahead as if she were walking a familiar path in the dark, vision supplied by memory. This was a new Lincoln Lord — either that or she had lived with him for twenty-two years without ever really knowing the inner man. In either case, the danger was the same. Unwittingly, she might again respond to some false clue to character, as wrong as she had so often been before in imagining that she understood him. Strangely, it seemed now that her fault had been less a failure of understanding than a too great effort to achieve it.

But no thought was clear, no conclusion certain. She was dead-tired, exhausted both physically and mentally, sustained only by compassion for the man she loved and the fear that she might somehow fail him. She had been most afraid when, stopping for coffee at a Turnpike restaurant, he had talked on and on, reviewing every detail of everything that had happened. Time after time, she had wanted to respond in some way that would comfort him, but she had said almost nothing, sensing that what she was hearing was not something intended for her ears. Even listening had seemed almost an invasion of privacy. To have spoken would have been an unwarranted breaching of his secret mind, and with that feeling she had approached an awareness, vague and ill-defined though it was, that a too hard-driven quest for understanding could defeat its own end, that love was not a product of the rational mind but a mystery of the unthinking heart.

And this had been a night of love.

But the day lay ahead. Color was beginning to show in the sky as Linc made the left turn and drove down Main Street toward the dead-end blackness of the warehouse wall. As he turned the corner and circled the building, unthinkingly she expected to emerge into the night-blasting blaze of light poured out by the Coastal Foods cannery. Instead, there was only an extension of the blackness. The plant lay prostrate in the night, dead and lifeless, and then she remembered having heard Linc approve Frank Kennan's suggestion that the night shift be called off . . . "No, we won't need it now."

She anticipated that Linc would glance right as they passed and she stared straight ahead, offering him the privacy that she knew he wanted, filling her own mind with a visualization of the darkly shadowed house. But again she was wrong. As they came through the wall of trees, the house was a glowing island in the night, every window bright with light. There was even more of a surprise when the head-lights picked up Kip waiting for them at the bottom of the steps.

Kip opened the car door, not for her but for his father, and she heard him say, "Dr. Perrill called you from Roman Hills and he wants you to call him back. But he was afraid maybe he wouldn't be there when you did, so he said I was to tell you that they've found something that might mean it isn't Wonderfood."

For an instant, Linc's head dropped to the rim of the steering wheel, the instinctive posture of a prayer of gratitude, and then he was out of the car, running into the house.

Something kept her from hurrying after him and, almost as a knowing reward, Kip waited for her, silent for a moment, then saying, "I guess it's been kind of tough for him, huh?"

"Yes, very," she said. "And thank you for waiting up, Kip."

"That's nothing," he said. "When Mr. Morris called about their having to find him so they'd know what to do — and then hearing it on the radio — well, holy creeps, if it's a fellow's own dad, staying up and waiting's nothing."

"Yes it is, Kip," she said, choked.

Linc was on the telephone and had apparently gotten through without the expected difficulty because he was already nodding to what someone was saying on the other end of the line. With his first response, however, she realized that he was not talking to Dr. Perrill but to Joel. What Kip had already said gave enough meaning to Linc's short comments and brief questions so that there was no longer any doubt that Wonderfood was, if not completely absolved, at least partly cleared of suspicion.

Although Linc was obviously relieved, she saw no reflection of her own burst of rising spirit. His expression was still one of deep concern, and when she heard him say, "It's too bad we didn't know this a few hours ago," she remembered his having said in the meeting at Roman Hills that once a public warning was issued the damage could never be undone ... *but at least Linc wouldn't go on blaming himself for having put Wonderfood on the market* ...

She saw him hang up, lost in thought for a moment, finally saying, "It looks now as if it might be some kind of a milk-borne infection. One of the Washington men just came back from the milk plant. He discovered that one of their pasteurizers has been out of commission for the last three days."

Kip said, "Gosh, Dad, you've got to get that on the radio — you've got to tell that to the people."

"We can't, Kip," Linc explained quietly. "They're almost certain that it's the milk — but a few hours ago they were almost certain that it was Wonderfood. Almost isn't enough. They can only be sure after the tests come through. That won't be until this afternoon."

"But it's such a darned tough break for you, Dad. I mean — well, holy creeps, it just is, that's all."

She saw their eyes meet, cling for a moment, and then Linc said, "I'm sorry about your car, Kip. We had to leave it in Brighton. I needed your mother with me."

"That's okay," Kip said. "I guess we'll be going down there pretty soon, anyway. And if we aren't — well, I can pick it up pretty easy — you know, one of the guys, just have him drive me down."

"Yes, that's what you'd better do," Linc said, turning then and starting slowly back toward the bedroom.

"Thank you, Kip," she whispered huskily.

"He's kind of a terrific guy, isn't he?" Kip said. "I mean —"

She gripped his hand through a steadying moment and then hurried down the hall, wondering if Linc really meant what he had implied to Kip, that he had decided against Chesapeake College.

He was waiting for her as she came in the bedroom door. "I'm sorry, Mag, but this is the way it has to be. I can't leave here now."

"You can if you want to," she said quietly. "Yesterday you were ready to leave."

"That was yesterday."

"Nothing's really changed. If it isn't Wonderfood — and you don't think now that it is, do you?"

"No. Perrill's positive that it's the milk. But as far as Wonderfood is concerned — it's just too late. The damage has been done. It'll be in all the papers this morning. And nothing will ever erase those headlines, Mag. No matter how we try to make people forget, the minute they taste it they'll remember. That's always been a hurdle, the way the stuff tastes. We might have gotten away with it if it hadn't been for this. But now —" He shook his head. "Of course it means a lot to Doc Perrill — justifying himself."

"It means something to you, too, doesn't it?"

"What?"

"That you weren't wrong in putting it on the market?"

He looked away from her. "That isn't what's bothering me."

"Do you mean releasing the warning? Oh, Linc, after that baby died, there was nothing else you could do. Everyone felt the same way."

He was shaking his head, a strangely puzzled expression on his face, and his eyes were the eyes of a man confronted by some mysterious revelation. "Something happened last night, Mag. I don't know what, or why, or when. All I know is that when I stood up there and started to talk — Mag, I knew what I was going to do. It didn't have anything to do with that baby dying. I'd have done it, anyway. And it wouldn't have made any difference what anyone said. I'd still have done it. And I knew what it meant — all the damage that would be done if I was wrong — and I *was* wrong —"

"It was something you had to do, Linc. It wasn't your fault. No one could blame you for —"

"Listen to me, Mag — that's what I mean, that's what I'm trying to tell you — I wasn't worrying about it being my fault and I wasn't worrying about anyone blaming me. That didn't matter. That's what was so different last night. Always before, it's been someone else's company — Mr. Quincy's company, Cornelia Rabson's company, old man

555

Kassleman's company — all I ever did was what I thought they wanted me to do. But it wasn't that way last night. Coastal Foods wasn't Kira Zurich's company. It was *my* company. I've never felt that way before. I suppose that's why I've always been running away, trying to —"

A cry broke from her throat. "Oh, Linc, Linc — please! I didn't mean all those awful things I said. They weren't true. Oh, Linc, please forget that I ever —"

His fingers slipped over her lips, stopping the onrush of words. "No, Mag, I'll never forget that. Or at least I hope I won't. It's true. That's what I was doing — running away."

"No, Linc, no — not running away."

"But always running," he said with a faintly rueful smile. "I don't know why unless — yes, I suppose that's it — I've always wanted something and I've never really known what it was."

"Until last night," she whispered.

He nodded. "Frank said something once — that there was so much difference between being part of a company and having a company be a part of you. I thought I understood what he meant. I didn't. But I do now. That's why I can't leave. I'd be running away from myself."

"Linc, just tell me one thing — are you staying because of me, because you think it's what I want you to do?"

He stared at her for a moment as if the question had shocked him, then as if his answer had to be something pushed forward by honesty against the resistance of judgment. Finally he said, "No, I'm not doing it for your sake, Mag. This is completely selfish. I'm doing it for my own sake. I'm not even doing it because I think the company needs me — maybe it doesn't, not with Frank and Joel to carry on, and no more business than we'll have now. It's the other way round — I need the company. Maybe you don't understand, maybe you can't —"

"I don't even want to," she cried out, finding his lips as he crushed her in his arms, oblivious to thought yet somehow aware that something had happened to her last night, too. For the first time, she realized that love was a mystery beyond the need of understanding. Love was faith. And now as she felt its full strength, so strong and unyielding that it could never again be challenged, there was almost the feeling that this was the first moment of true love.